THE EVA SERIES

LEAVING EVA
LOSING EVA
SAVING EVA

BY

JENNIFER SIVEC

SOUL SISTER PRESS, LLC

Cover Design by Brenda Gonet
Edited by Rogena Mitchell-Jones; JC Wing

This is a work of fiction. Names, characters, places, brands, media, and incidents are either the product of the author's imagination or are used fictitiously. Any resemblance to similarly named places or to persons living or deceased is unintentional.

ISBN-13: 978-0-9981932-9-8-| ISBN-10: 0-9981932-9-1

The Eva Series

ACKNOWLEDGMENTS

This was a gut-wrenching, heart-breaking series to read and write, and when I released Leaving Eva for the first time, I wasn't sure if I could go through with it.

Each book has it's own soul and life, which I love about these stories so much. At it's heart, is Brynn; always Brynn. I love her strength, her heart, and her pain, because it reminds me so much of my own. No matter how many books I write, in my lifetime, I will always be reminded that this journey began with *her*. She awakened my heart and stirred my soul and because of her, I followed my dream and her story became alive, and so did I.

I'm grateful for the love, support, and nearly daily reminders that this story has made a difference in people's lives. It reminds us to be grateful, appreciative, and kind, while remembering that some of us suffer greatly, and struggle far more than anyone could ever imagine.

Above all, this series is about love.

Imperfect, ugly, awkward, fierce, and beautiful love.

I'm so thankful for everyone who has been with me on this journey through this series. I have learned, grown, cried, and loved throughout every step, and Eva's story will always hold an incredibly special place in my hear

To everyone who has ever believed in me, my heart is eternally grateful.

VOLUME ONE

LEAVING EVA

CHAPTER ONE

Stupid Girl

Daddy. No!
Daddy, please stop!
Daddy, you're hurting me!

She never saw it coming. She didn't even know he had hit her until her right cheek and eye were exploding. With so much rage on his face, his anger emanated toward her, dangerous and hot.

She'd never seen Daddy so angry before, not even with Mommy.

She was stunned, her feet frozen in one spot. She wanted desperately to run but was unable to move. It was almost as though she was trapped in a bad dream and couldn't wake up. Her heart was pounding hard in her chest, and her mind was racing. Daddy's massive body was blocking the way, and she thought wildly that maybe if she didn't move, he wouldn't hit her again.

She was wrong.

He smacked her again, hard across the mouth, and she could feel blood pouring from her bottom lip. The saltiness of it made her want to gag. He reached out, grabbing her small thin arms, squeezing them so hard they felt as though they may break in two. He picked her up until her feet were dangling off the ground and threw her down, hard. Her head snapped back and hit the wood cabinets. The cracking sound resounded in her ears, and there was an instant blinding pain.

She knew she was crying, but couldn't feel any tears. She was afraid, and it was a strange familiar, haunting feeling that she knew she had felt sometime before in her seven and a half years. Daddy was never overly affectionate or kind, but he had never hurt her. She had been with them for three years, and during that time, he had barely ever touched her, good or bad. But now, he was intent on hurting her for reasons that didn't make sense.

She begged him to stop, trying to come up with the right words as they tumbled out in between the sobs. "Daddy, please! I–I–I–I'm sorry. I'll be careful. I'm s–s–s–sorry."

"You should be sorry! You need to be more careful, damn you. You ruin everything you touch with your filthy little hands!" He growled, grabbing hard at her long dark hair, pulling some of it out sharply at the roots. He yanked on the ponytail as she reached out blindly trying to get him to ease his grip.

Daddy's blue eyes were dark and full of something that she didn't recognize at all. His face was distorted, almost trance-like, looking through her as if he weren't seeing her at all. She struggled away, but his grasp on her hair wouldn't let her escape. She felt trapped and helpless, like a mouse in a cage. Without any effort, he grabbed her again and threw her back down to the ground.

The girl was crying so hard, her small body trembling in fear of what would happen to her next. "No, no, no, no," she cried over and over. "I'm sorry! I didn't mean it."

She crouched down tight against the cabinets, and she pulled her body in, hoping to shrink. *Maybe if I'm small, I'll be hard to get, and he will stop. Maybe Daddy will stop!*

He kicked clumsily at her sides with hard steel-toed work boots. "Damn stupid kid! Why do you have to be so clumsy? Jesus Christ, you're ALWAYS spilling and dropping things." His voice was so loud, and he was spitting as he hovered over her.

The girl was trying to remember why he was so mad and then she remembered the spilled iced tea all over the floor, soaking into the beige carpet like a sponge.

"I'll be more careful. I'll be more careful! PLEASE DADDY, you're hurting me!" She was screaming, but he didn't hear.

"I work my ass off to provide for you and your mother, and this is how you repay me! I should never have let your mother convince me to buy you, you stupid Bitch!" Daddy's voice was ugly and full of hatred. The girl didn't know if the pain was from the blows or if the mean words were what hurt the most.

She raised her hands over her head futilely as a shield. *I'm sorry, I'm sorry. I'm so clumsy and bad! Please, Daddy, please.* Her head was pounding, and there was pain everywhere.

One, two, and then three more times Daddy hit her. There had been so many that she had actually lost count. His hands were open one second and closed the next. There were blows coming from every direction, first hitting her on the head, then the arms, both sides, and occasionally the face.

The smell of whiskey was hanging above the tiny girl in a large cloud, curling her nose with its sweet insipid smell. She was gagging and crying at the same time, and it was hard to breathe. She was choking on her own stupidity and carelessness. *Mommy keeps telling me to be more careful. I'm a bad girl. I'm too loud and stupid, and I always spill things. Mommy will hate me now, too. I'm a bad girl!*

She dared a glance upward and could see that Daddy was starting to pant, his face red, while sweat poured down his forehead. *Please God, make him stop. Please help me be more careful! Why can't I just be a better girl?*

"Please stop, please," she cried desperately, in a small, frightened voice that she hadn't heard before. *Daddy doesn't love me because I'm stupid. Daddy hates me. I hate me, too. I'm so stupid.*

He looked at her, his gaze slicing through her. "You're the reason your mother hates me! It's all your fault, you stupid useless brat!"

It was true. *Mommy has me so she can't love Daddy. She told me. It is my fault!*

It felt as if he had been hitting her for so long, but after only a few minutes, he was spent.

He finally staggered backwards clumsily, not looking her way at all. Daddy didn't look well, his skin pale and wet with sweat, the rage replaced with confusion and shame.

"Go to your room, right now, Brynn!" His voice was barely audible as he looked away.

Brynn stood feeling unsteady for a moment, her body shaking uncontrollably as she willed her legs to move. *I'm going, Daddy. I'm going.*

Daddy turned and staggered out to the porch and lit up a cigarette. The cool night air came in with a welcome gust soothing her burning face, and she forgot about the pain momentarily. The danger was still palpable in the air, and Brynn realized that she needed to get to her room.

The journey up the stairs was difficult, but she finally made it, falling onto the bed with relief. Brynn buried her face into the pillow smearing bright red blood and tears on the crisp white pillowcase.

He hates me! He hates me, and I'm so stupid. It's my fault. I'm so clumsy and stupid. If I run away, maybe Mommy will love him and then he will love me. I ruined everything! I wish I had never ever been born!

After what felt like hours, she stood up, carefully walked into the bathroom, and locked the door. Brynn looked in the mirror and searched all over for bruises. The right cheek and eye were swelling and turning purple. The split in her lip was also swelling at an alarming rate as the blood was starting to crust and dry up. Her eyelids were swollen from crying so hard, and there was nothing but pain in her ribs, back, arms, and legs from all of the kicking they endured.

Brynn wished Mommy would hurry home. *Mommy, where are you? Mommy, I need you!*

Daddy had never been this mean before. He was to Mommy, but not to Brynn. He yelled occasionally, but had never kicked, hit, or swore at her. Daddy never kissed or hugged her, but Brynn always thought he loved her. After all, he bought her things from time to time, like big lollipops and candy from the store. He gave her presents for birthdays and on Christmases. *My Daddy hates me! He wishes I were never adopted. He hates me more than anything in the world.*

What if Daddy hits me all the time? The thought struck suddenly. *I should run away.*

Brynn knew Mommy couldn't protect her. Mommy couldn't even protect herself. While Daddy had never hit Brynn before, he hit Mommy. He even shook Mommy hard making her flop all over the place like Brynn's favorite doll, Betsy. Mommy said it wasn't

Daddy's fault. She said it was only because of the alcohol. Today, Daddy was drinking a lot of alcohol, and Brynn noticed that it was a lot more than usual.

The "special" glass was filled up five times, full to the top. Usually, Daddy only had Brynn fill it two or three times, and then Mommy did the rest after bedtime. Daddy never filled his own glass because he said it was their responsibility. "I put a roof over your heads, and give you food to eat, and clothes to wear. I buy everything!" He reminded them of this often.

Even though Daddy was mean to Mommy, Brynn still loved him. *You're supposed to love your Daddy. That's what happy families do. They love each other.* She wanted to have a happy family more than anything. Even though her only friend, Stacy, had a sad family, families were supposed to be happy. Mommy didn't like Brynn to have a lot of friends because she didn't want her away from the house much. Mommy always made her come home so she could spend time with her. Mommy said that she missed Brynn too much when she was gone.

Brynn was sad because Mommy didn't love Daddy. Mommy told her repeatedly, even if Daddy was in the room, that she didn't love him. She always whispered it loudly, pretending that it was their little secret. Brynn knew that Daddy could still hear. But Daddy was quiet like he didn't care, even though he had a funny look on his face. Mommy and Brynn were best friends, and Mommy told her everything.

"We only stay with him because he takes care of us, Brynn. I only love *you*," Mommy always told her. Brynn thought that maybe Daddy loved Mommy. Why else would he take care of them? *Maybe Daddy will stop taking care of us now that he is hitting me, too.* Brynn was afraid of what would happen to them.

There must have been something wrong with her or Brynn's real Mommy would have wanted her. Brynn picked up the picture of her and Mommy Rose that sat next to her bed. It was a picture of them right after her "Gotcha Day." Brynn looked very different then, so skinny and scraggly with a permanently sad expression on her face. She thought about her real Mommy, and again wondered where she was and why she left her. Brynn wondered if her real Mommy ever thought of her and what she looked like. *Would my real Mommy care that Daddy was hitting me? Would she save me?*

Brynn reached up carefully touching her cheek. It felt big and was throbbing and stinging. She felt hot. She lifted up her shirt and saw the skin on her sides turning red and purple. Her arms were tender and painful to the touch and there were handprints bruising her skin.

She moved slowly to her bed and waited for Mommy Rose to come home. Every part of her face was burning, and her lip kept bleeding. As hard as she tried, she couldn't stop crying, salty tears burning the open wound on her lip. *How could Daddy be so mean?*

Mommy! When she finally heard the car in the driveway, her heart leapt for joy. Brynn dared not leave the bedroom for fear Daddy would see her.

Mommy will come kiss me good night. Brynn waited for Mommy to come up. When Mommy saw her face, she would know what Daddy had done. Brynn was ashamed that Daddy had to punish her.

Maybe Mommy won't love me anymore either, she thought suddenly. *She'll think I'm too clumsy, too. She hates when I spill things because he always yells at me. Maybe she will hit me, too.* Brynn was suddenly afraid. She hadn't thought of that before.

She waited anxiously. When Mommy's light footsteps echoed in the hall, Brynn held her breath, waiting for the door to open. *Did Daddy tell her what I did? What if she hates me, too?*

The door opened slowly and Mommy walked in looking like an angel. Mommy's brown eyes were very serious as she looked at Brynn. She didn't say anything but instead, walked over to the bed slowly, and hugged Brynn. Brynn held her tight and sobbed into her chest.

"Oh, Brynn," Mommy said in a soothing voice. "What did you do? Why were you so clumsy? Why can't you just be more careful? It will be okay."

Brynn couldn't speak. She couldn't say anything between the sobs.

Mommy gently touched Brynn's swollen cheek, tears forming in her own eyes. She started to reach toward Brynn's cracked lip and stopped before touching it.

"Brynn, you have to be more careful. Daddy doesn't like messes. You can't spill because he gets really mad." Mommy scolded gently. Mommy didn't look angry like he had. Instead, she had a different look on her face. It was a look that Brynn didn't understand. Brynn breathed a sigh of relief. Mommy didn't hate her like Daddy did.

She held Brynn close. *Mommy smells like flowers.* Sweet.

For the first time that night, Brynn felt safe. Mommy went to the bathroom, got a washcloth, ran cool water over it, and washed Brynn's tearstained face. She wiped Brynn's swollen cheek and gently swabbed her bloody lip. She was careful as she tried to clean up the crusted blood. Mommy spoke gently, soothing, as she did when Brynn was much smaller. Then she tucked Brynn into bed and kissed her first on the forehead and then on the cheek. Brynn winced in pain and then smiled weakly, relieved that Mommy was home.

"There will be no school until your lip and face looks better, sweet girl," Mommy said attempting a smile. "We'll stay home and do puzzles together all day and drink hot cocoa. We'll have a 'girl's day'." Mommy stroked Brynn's hair lightly, "But you can't tell anyone about Daddy hitting you. If you do, they will take you away from me."

Brynn didn't want to be away from Mommy. She loved Mommy.

"I promise, Mommy, I won't tell," Brynn said, her voice small and serious.

"You're a good girl, darling," Mommy said looking at Brynn with adoring eyes.

"No, I'm not, Mommy, I'm a bad girl. I took your love away from Daddy. It's my fault you don't love him," Brynn cried. She wanted to confess because she didn't want to keep a secret from Mommy.

Mommy's face got angry and then she suddenly smiled, showing her pretty white teeth. "Oh, Brynn. It's not your fault I don't love Daddy. I never loved Daddy. I only married Daddy so that I could find you one day. Even if you weren't here, I still wouldn't love Daddy."

Brynn was relieved. It wasn't her fault after all, but then she was sad. *Poor Daddy.* Not to be loved was so sad.

"Is Daddy going to hurt me again? It really hurt, Mommy," she said sadly, trying not to whimper.

"No, Brynn! Mommy won't let Daddy hurt you like that again!" Mommy said. But Brynn was still afraid because Daddy hit Mommy, and nothing could stop him.

Mommy answered without Brynn asking, "I know Daddy hits me, but we can't leave because he takes care of us. We need him. I'll talk to Daddy and I won't leave you alone with him again."

Brynn was relieved. She wasn't alone with him much, but if it were never, then he couldn't hurt her again.

"Thank you, Mommy!" She loved Mommy so much. Mommy was pretty and nice, and Brynn loved her with all of her heart—to the moon and back, "I love you so much, Mommy!"

Mommy gave her baby girl a sad smile. She bent over and tucked Brynn in, leaving the night light on.

"Go to sleep, sweet girl. I love you, too," she whispered softly.

Brynn closed her eyes and got as comfortable as she could. She moved around trying to get more comfortable despite the pain. All of her muscles hurt and her lip were stinging. She didn't realize how tired she was, and she quickly started to drift off.

Mommy went downstairs, and just as Brynn fell asleep, she was jolted awake by the sound of Daddy yelling. Daddy was yelling at Mommy!

She covered her ears tight trying in vain to block out the voices. Mommy was screaming, and then there was a slapping sound. Something made a loud cracking sound, like the sound of wood splintering and breaking, which made her jump. Mommy cried out loudly.

Brynn huddled up tight in her bed and squeezed her eyes closed as she felt tears running down her face. *Daddy, please don't hurt Mommy.* She wanted to run downstairs, but she was afraid. *What if he hits me again? Mommy, Mommy!* Brynn grabbed her dolly, Betsy, and hugged her until the screaming stopped. Then there was an eerie silence in the house. She tried to stay awake, because she was terrified that her door would open, and then he would come in and try to hurt her again. She strained to hear Mommy's voice, but there was nothing but quiet. She listened hard for Mommy to make a sound, but she didn't hear anything in the house. Her eyelids started to get heavy and she finally fell into a restless, painful sleep.

Chapter Two

Ellie

Ellie had been in labor for eighteen hours, and she was exhausted.

When the pain began, the real fear had set in. *He* was supposed to take her to the doctor, but she had left him, and now she was on her own. She had no money, and nobody to take care of her, and she didn't know what to expect.

She had started to feel pain early in the morning but did her best to ignore it. She had waited as long as she could, but when the water ran down her leg and into a puddle on the floor, she knew the time had come to do something.

"Honey, are you okay?" It was Martha, the kind gray-haired lady who volunteered at the shelter. Martha had been watching the pretty dark haired girl sit in the corner by herself for some time, in obvious pain. Ellie was quiet and kept to herself, so the older woman had tried to leave her alone, but she realized that she couldn't any longer. As far as she knew, the girl had no family, no money, and no friends.

"I... think... I need to go to the hospital now," Ellie said reluctantly, her sweet voice low but obviously in distress.

"Let me get my coat, then we'll go," Martha said moving faster than usual.

Ellie was shy and they had never talked much, but Martha was happy to be able to help because Ellie clearly needed it. Martha pulled the rusted old gray station wagon in front of the shelter and helped the girl into it. The twenty-minute ride to the hospital was quiet except for Ellie's heavy breathing and occasional moaning. Ellie tried to focus on the scenery trying to forget the pain as they drove past the town's library, the worn down elementary school, and the Piggly Wiggly.

Martha was driving as fast as she could drive, barely going five miles over the speed limit. She wasn't used to going anywhere in a hurry, and now as Ellie started moaning louder, holding her heaving belly in pain, Martha wished that she had called 911, instead.

"Please... hurry," Ellie pleaded. The pressure in her belly was mounting as they drove. She wanted to cry out but held it in. *Momma, why can't you be here with me? I need you. Oh Momma!* Ellie had thought about going home many times in the past few months, but it had been so ugly the last time she was there. *I can't face them after everything I've done. They probably hate me.*

Ellie didn't know what to expect at the hospital. She was used to stares and whispers in town, but she was terrified to face it from the people who were going to help deliver the baby.

The old station wagon chugged into the Emergency Room driveway. Martha got out of the car wincing as the arthritis reminded her that she was nearing seventy years old now. She told Ellie to wait, and then disappeared through the automatic doors. A few moments later, Martha came out accompanied by a young man dressed in all white and pushing a wheelchair. When they got to the car, he immediately felt sympathy for the young, small girl in the front seat. She looked fearful of him, her swollen belly speaking for her.

"Don't worry, Miss, we'll take good care of you," he said gently, trying to reassure her.

They quickly got Ellie settled into a room with Martha by her side, assigning their most experienced nurse to her.

Ellie tried to relax, but the pain kept building inside, threatening to rip her in half.

Martha offered to stay, but Ellie knew that it was only out of kindness. Everyone at the shelter knew that Martha babysat every night for her granddaughter who was the light of her life.

"Thank you, but go to your granddaughter. I'll be all right," Ellie panted gratefully, squeezing Martha's hand.

"Are you sure? If you're sure...you're welcome, honey. I wish you the best of luck," the older woman said kindly, wishing she could have done more. Martha was anxious to get to little Lucy, but felt bad for leaving Ellie all alone.

Ellie smiled faintly. It was the first time that Martha had ever seen her smile and she was struck with how beautiful she was. Martha hesitated for a moment, and then turned around and walked away. She couldn't wait to tell sweet little Lucy how Grandma had helped someone today.

After Martha had left, Ellie lay on the hospital bed gripping the cold rails firmly. As each wave of pain overtook her, each one more intense than the other, Ellie wanted to cry out but did her best not to. It felt as if her insides were pulling apart, ripping from the inside out, with one horrible cramp after another radiating through her. She was certain that something inside of her was being torn apart.

The nurses had poked her with needle after needle, taking blood, putting medicine in her back, putting bags of liquid up on a metal rod and into an IV, and hooking her to all sorts of monitors. The drugs they gave helped, but for some reason they didn't alleviate all of the pain. Ellie tried imagining childbirth. She could never have foreseen this feeling of being split in two, her insides wrenched.

They tried to distract her with television, but it didn't work. It had been so long since Ellie had watched her favorite sitcoms, but even her favorite show couldn't make her forget her misery. She had always wished the family on it were her own. The parents understood the kids and everything always ended up happy. Ellie had been close to her mom and dad, but when she started seeing *him,* they had disapproved. They wouldn't allow her out of the house, even after much begging and pleading.

"He loves me!" she had pleaded with them, trying to make them understand. Her parents obviously didn't love her because if they did, they would have wanted her to be happy. They said he wasn't right for her, and they wouldn't listen when she disagreed. The last time they fought about him, Daddy told Ellie that she was grounded forever and not allowed out of the house without permission again. Daddy was yelling, and Ellie and Momma were crying, but Momma was still on his side.

How can they keep me from the man I love? She just couldn't understand it.

Ellie knew they would never understand!

"It's like we're Romeo and Juliet," she had whispered to him late at night on the phone, after her parents had gone to sleep. "I need to be with you. I just can't live without you. I love you so much."

"I need you, too," he said his voice full of wanting for his little schoolgirl. Ellie loved how just the sound of his voice could stir her up so much inside. She had never met anyone like him before. Nobody ever made her feel the way he did, especially not the immature little boys at school.

"You'll have to rescue me. Pick me up from school tomorrow and then we can always be together." Ellie had given it a lot of thought since the fight with her parents. She packed as much as possible in her biggest Luis Vuitton bag, and hid it in the back of her closet. If he picked her up from school as soon as Daddy dropped her off, then they could swing by the house, pick up the bag, and run away together.

"Are you serious?" he seemed hesitant. He was definitely into her, but wasn't sure that Ellie was worth risking another stint in jail. The parents would definitely call the cops.

"Don't you want to be with me?" Ellie said in her best pouty voice, obviously hurt.

"Of course I do, Princess. I just don't want your parents to call the cops on me. I know they will!" he said watching his words. She was young but feisty, which is what he liked about her the most.

They talked out their plan, and the next day after Daddy dropped her off at school, she watched for *him* to pull up. As soon as

Ellie saw him, she ran out of the building, jumped in the car, and they raced to the house. The drive home was glorious and freeing, and she felt something inside of her come alive. The sun was out and Ellie lifted her head to the sky grabbing the warmth on her face for as long as possible. This was going to be the first day of the rest of her life and Ellie was finally going live it as her own. She wanted to savor it, taste every bit of it with her beautiful man by her side.

Getting the bag was easy as she dodged the service help, but then again Ellie was used to sneaking in and out of the house. When she retrieved her prize and ran out of the house, she threw the bag into the car, drunk with anticipation and excitement.

They managed to duck the cops for months by moving from one spot to another until they began to feel safer. Ellie couldn't imagine that her parents would continue searching for her for too much longer, and they settled into a scant one-room apartment in the worst part of town. Ellie didn't care where she lived as long as she could be with him.

They were so happy together in the beginning. Ellie loved that he knew so much more than she did and that he was just a little dangerous. He was the best-looking guy she had ever seen, and he made her feel beautiful and special. Ellie didn't care about his bad reputation for using and selling drugs because she knew that he only did it for fun. His mother was a free spirit, and she taught him how to be one, too. Now he was teaching Ellie to be one, and she enjoyed the freedom.

He introduced her to marijuana and wine coolers, and Ellie loved how relaxed they made her. They smoked and drank and made love all day long. Ellie forgot how much she missed her parents and home, at least for a little while.

But seven months later, she missed her period.

One after another and then another and Ellie realized that as her pants grew tighter and the morning sickness took over, she was pregnant. But he didn't want her to stop smoking and drinking even though Ellie knew that would hurt "it" inside of her. She didn't know what to do with "it" yet, but she knew that she didn't want to kill it or harm it in any way. He didn't care about hurting "it" and told Ellie that she wasn't any fun anymore.

As Ellie got rounder he refused to touch her. "You're getting fat!" he said, his disgust clear, in his eyes. "I don't have sex with fat girls. Maybe you should stop eating so much, so you don't get so large."

She was in disbelief. At four months, her belly protruded only slightly from her thin frame and the pregnancy was barely visible. "You're so mean!" she said, trying not to cry again. Everything he said seemed to make Ellie cry.

The second she started to show, everything between them instantly changed.

"Maybe you should have thought about that before you got yourself pregnant," he said cruelly. "I'm going to need to find someone else until you're back to your old self. You don't turn me on looking like that, and I didn't bring you here to play 'family'! I can't believe you did this! You've ruined everything!" He took a big drag off his cigarette and blew smoke in her face, making her cough. The next day, he came home with a girl that looked suspiciously like her, only not pregnant. "This is Tricia," he said barely looking at Ellie. "She's here to take care of my needs while you're out of commission. I'd have you join us, but I don't think I could stomach it."

Then he dragged the girl into the back bedroom, and Ellie could hear them. The apartment was small, and the unmistaken sound of the bed creaking was horrifying. She ran to the bathroom and crouched on the floor with her hands over her ears, but she could still hear the moaning and the screaming, the good kind.

She realized that he didn't care about "it," or about her and she felt betrayed. She had left her family for his love, only to find out that he didn't love her at all. She had never wanted to have a baby, and now she was pregnant with *his* child, and he didn't even care!

A week later, Ellie waited until he passed out, and she left him in the middle of the night. She hated him now and couldn't wait to get away.

She remembered that her church had donated clothes to a woman's shelter a town over. As Ellie walked down the road, a nice woman stopped her car and asked if she needed a ride. She didn't usually take rides from strangers, but Ellie made an exception this time. The woman dropped her off at the shelter and wished her well.

As Ellie's belly got bigger, she became more and more frightened. *I don't know the first thing about having a baby,* she thought. *What kind of mother will I be? I have no idea what I'm doing.*

Now as the labor pains came, the panic started to grow uncontrollably. And she was scared and alone, except for the nice nurse that never seemed to leave her side. The nurse had introduced herself but Ellie forgot her name. All she knew now was that she was gripping the nurse's hand with all of her might as the pain grew inside. An older man appeared in the room wearing a mask. All she could see were his wire-rimmed glasses, his kind brown eyes, and a shock of white hair under his blue hospital cap. It was obvious he was in charge. "Oh, she's a young one," he said to no one in particular as he looked at Ellie's sweaty, exhausted face.

The pain had been going on for hours, and Ellie's body was close to ready but she was exhausted and needed sleep.

"You can't sleep now, young lady. I'm going to need you to push for me. You're ready and your baby needs to come out," the doctor said in a firm, but kind voice.

But as the pain came hot and fast, Ellie was terrified and she thought for sure she would pass out.

CHAPTER THREE

Birthday

Push?!

Ellie started to cry uncontrollably. The needle in her hand was pinching, and the sharpness in her belly was unbearable. Her skin felt dirty and the inside of her mouth, slimy. Ellie didn't know how she was going to push.

"I can't!" she cried, her voice breaking. "I can't do it! I'm so tired and I need to sleep. I just can't, please don't make me." Ellie's youth was apparent, and the nurse was filled with pity.

The nurse squeezed her hand speaking in short, clear sentences so that the girl would understand her through the pain. "You need to push. Now. Or you and the baby will be in danger. I am here for you. You can do this!"

"I can't, I can't!" Ellie cried. Her belly was exploding but she didn't have the strength to push. "Please no, please! I can't do it!"

The nurse took her face in her hands and looked her in the eyes. Then Ellie's tears suddenly stopped. She thought she had never seen eyes like the nurse's before. They were a deep well of blue gray, and were staring deep into Ellie, calming her. Ellie didn't understand why, but she felt better, stronger.

"I am with you!" the nurse said in a strong lovely voice, never taking her eyes off her for a minute. "You. Can. Do. This! You. Will. Do. This."

The room was silent for a moment.

"Okay!" the doctor said breaking through the stillness, "Let's do this, young lady. Push!"

Ellie pushed down as hard as she could while gritting her teeth.

She held tightly to the nurse's hand, absorbing her strength. "Puuuuuuuuush," the nurse said in Ellie's ear, holding it out as long as she could. Over and over, they did this, allowing Ellie to catch her breath for a moment until they made her do it again.

Ellie was sweating and panting and she could feel that her armpits were moist and warm. She was tearing apart from the inside and she screamed, loud and long. Just when she thought she couldn't do it any longer, she heard a cry.

Thank God! It was finally out!

The other nurses quickly whisked the baby away while Ellie's nurse squeezed her hand and hugged her hard. Through the haze of exhaustion, Ellie could hear the other nurses in the room whispering in hushed voices. The nurse looked at Ellie, wearing an expression that the girl couldn't read. "You did a wonderful job," she said to Ellie smiling under her mask, her beautiful blue-gray eyes glistening. Ellie looked up and smiled weakly. The nurse hurried over to the other nurses with the baby.

"I'm going to push on your belly, and you will feel pressure while we get the placenta out," the doctor said. Ellie was so tired that she didn't care. She just wanted to sleep. Her eyes were closing uncontrollably and she was drifting. *Momma, I miss you. I wish you were here to tell me that everything was going to be okay.*

Ellie felt as if she were dreaming about the last time that she saw Momma. She could see them standing in the foyer of their big house and Daddy was yelling. Momma was standing behind him sobbing loudly, but nodding in agreement. Ellie felt tears on her cheeks. *I miss you both so much.*

Ellie heard a tiny cry. She quickly opened her eyes, feeling her heartbeat quicken. *My baby!* "How is my baby?" She said weakly.

"She's doing pretty well. Her Apgar is a little lower than we like, but we will just keep an eye on her," one of the nurses she had not met said brightly. "She is five lbs., two ounces, and nineteen inches long!"

Apgar? What is that? "Is that good?" Ellie didn't understand.

"Your baby is a little on the smaller side, but we will just have to teach you how to fatten her up. Do you want to see her?" Ellie heard her nurse's voice, and she felt better. She felt lost without her and was relieved that her nurse was still there. The shift had already changed over once, but her nurse stayed with her.

Ellie's nurse knew her shift had been over hours ago, but she couldn't leave. She was drawn to Ellie's helplessness in a way that didn't happen with all of her patients. She had two daughters to go home to, and she would never want them to be as alone as Ellie. She had been a nurse for a long time and was typically a favorite amongst the patients because of her compassion and sincerity and this time was no different. Something inside of her told her that Ellie would need her, and she wasn't ready to leave just yet.

"Yes! Yes! Please, let me see my baby!" Ellie suddenly felt eager and excited for the first time since she found out she was pregnant.

It was a girl! Her heart was full of pride and happiness at the thought of having a daughter. Ellie hadn't even allowed herself to think of the baby as a person referring only to as *it* in her mind. And now she felt a flutter in her chest, suddenly realizing that her baby was real and she could actually hold her.

My baby! Ellie was no longer tired and suddenly nothing else mattered than to see and hold her baby.

Her nurse brought the tiny bundle to Ellie and laid it in her arms. She arranged Ellie's arms around her daughter, holding her own hands over hers for a moment as if to seal them there. "Here's your sweet girl," her nurse said smiling. The nurse never grew tired of this moment, and wrote it in her heart every time she introduced the parents to their children.

Ellie took a deep breath and looked into the blanket. *Oh my! She's so small!*

The baby's face was dark and wrinkled with tiny lips that were slightly purple and puckered. Ellie tentatively pulled the blanket back and reached for her tiny fingers. One by one she touched them staring at each one for long moments. "So perfect!" she sighed, her voice barely audible.

Each tiny fingernail amazed her, and Ellie was in awe. The

baby's skin was so soft, like rose petals, and when she pulled her close and nuzzled those round cheeks, she could smell her sweet fresh innocence. Ellie prayed she would always be that way. She breathed the baby in, enjoying her daughter's newness and reveling in the beauty that was somehow created in her own body.

Ellie was in love.

She shyly pulled off the little hat and tentatively touched the soft dark billowy hair. "Wow!" she whispered. There was so much of it! She ran her fingers through each curl, and she smiled as the entire world fell away.

"It will probably fall out," Ellie's nurse said, startling her. She forgot that she was still in the room. Her world had shrunk to the tiny being in her arms.

Ellie's eyes got big. "Fall out?"

"It's supposed to," her nurse said quickly, trying to reassure her. "It happens with most babies. It will grow back." *She has so much to learn, and no one to teach her.* Ellie was completely alone in the world now, no longer speaking to her parents and no father of the baby anymore. There was nobody to take care of her now, she had confided to her nurse in between contractions.

Her nurse had no idea how Ellie would take care of her baby, and she feared for both her and the child.

Instead, she pushed those thoughts aside and decided to think positive. Ellie seemed smart and if a social worker from the hospital could point her in the right direction, maybe she would have a chance.

"Do you have a name for her?" She forced a smile as she asked Ellie.

Ellie thought hard, her pretty dark brows furrowed in thought. Even after eighteen hours of hard labor, her beauty was evident. She had the smooth untarnished face of a young girl, but her eyes told a different story. Big, dark and brown, the color of rich coffee, they had a depth that girls at her age didn't usually have. Most girls at her age were going to sleepovers and hanging out at the mall with their girlfriends but the nurse could tell this girl had chosen a different path.

As the girl thought hard for a name, she looked exactly as the child that she was

"What is your name?" Ellie asked her almost shyly, her voice pretty, and almost musical.

"Eva," the nurse said quickly surprised at the question.

"Then I will name her Eva. Eva Elizabeth. You have been so nice to me and..." Ellie's voice trailed off as though she couldn't finish the sentence.

Nurse Eva blinked back tears, overwhelmed by the gesture. She was saddened that Ellie had nobody else in her life to name her precious baby after.

"Well, naming your baby is a big decision, and you should give that some thought dear. I would be honored, but you'll want to be sure. She will have that name for the rest of her life."

"I'm sure," Ellie said without hesitation. "Eva Elizabeth."

She smiled for the first time, and she was beautiful.

Nurse Eva nodded at Ellie, and left the room before the girl could see her tears. Eva walked down the quiet sanitary hall to the supply room. She knew that Ellie's life was about to become a great deal more difficult and that there was nothing that she could do. *Take care of her while she is here, steer her in the right direction. That is all you can do.* Eva busied herself organizing the supplies, filling out charts and checking on the rest of the babies.

It was time for her to go back and check on Ellie and as she got closer, she heard yelling from inside the room. Ellie had barely spoken above a whisper since entering the hospital, but Eva knew that it was her voice. Then Eva heard a man's voice coming from the room yelling just as loudly. Eva rushed into the room and was surprised to see a young man standing over Ellie's bed. As she got closer, she realized that he wasn't all that young, at least not as young as he should be.

He looked to be about twenty-seven, and this girl was barely fifteen.

"I'm Eva. I'm the nurse. Is everything okay in here?" She said to the man realizing that her voice sounded brittle, nervous.

"Yep," he muttered, his green eyes darting away so that they would not meet hers. He was standing close, too close to the hospital bed. He could tell that he was making the nurse anxious, and he sneered, "I came to see my baby."

"She's beautiful." Nurse Eva set her steely eyes on him without wavering. She felt like a rabbit in the presence of a hungry lion. He was handsome but in a way that unsettled her. She didn't like him, and he could tell and she could tell that he didn't really care.

Ellie was quiet, eyes downcast. She didn't look happy to have him there, but she would not allow her dark eyes to look up. She looked only at her baby, and Nurse Eva saw that she was holding her tightly.

The room fell silent, and time passed slowly as the man and Nurse Eva sized each other up. He was big, much bigger than she was. His frame was lean and muscular and he had a strong jawline and dark green eyes that glittered at her dangerously. Nurse Eva was petite, but she knew that she was deceptively strong. She had taken some self-defense classes at the Y, and worked out regularly in order to stay fit.

He sat down on the hospital bed. He had put his arm around Ellie, and she looked as though she didn't welcome it much by the way she leaned away from him as far as she could, without falling off the other side of the bed. The closer he pulled Ellie, the more anxious Nurse Eva felt.

"Well, visiting hours are just about over, so I'm afraid that you'll have to leave. You can come back tomorrow at ten a.m. after rounds, if you would like," Nurse Eva said glancing quickly at the clock on the other side of the room. She shifted her eyes back to him and allowed them to remain on him, even though her heart was pounding in her chest. He had done nothing, had not moved, had barely spoken, but she knew there was clear danger.

"I'm not leaving," he said, his voice rising as he stood up. He towered over her.

Ellie quickly spoke up, her voice trembling. "Please, don't!"

"I. Said. I'm. Not. Leaving." He repeated as he emphasized each word. Then he looked back at Ellie, his gaze softening for a brief moment. "You left me, and I'm not leaving. I'm not letting you out of my sight again." His gaze sharpened, and the softness was gone.

"Sir, if you don't leave then I will be forced to call security," Eva said trying to sound as authoritative as she could. "She and the baby need to rest."

The baby started crying as if on cue. Softly at first, and then in short, staccato cries that sounded more and more desperate with each one. Everyone stopped and looked at her with surprise. For a brief few minutes, they had forgotten about her completely.

"She's hungry. That's her hungry cry and she needs to be fed," Nurse Eva said trying not to sound as anxious as she felt. "I have to show Ellie how to feed her, which means that you need to leave. She needs to be able to relax so she can learn." She felt relieved for the distraction and prayed that this could get him out of the room so she could call security. Nurse Eva hadn't spoken to Ellie about him, but she knew that Ellie didn't want him there. It was reflected in her wide fearful eyes. Nurse Eva *needed* to try to get him to leave.

Eva's daughters popped into her mind. She knew that they wouldn't want her to put herself in danger. And although he had not done anything yet, she felt as though he were simply biding his time until he pounced. She loved her girls so much and suddenly couldn't wait to be with them. Her husband had died so young, and she was all they had now.

The baby continued to cry, louder and louder until there was nothing but the sound of her cries filling the room.

He took a step toward Nurse Eva as she held her breath, knees buckling, and palms sweating. She had never needed to defend herself before and didn't even know if she would be able to react if she had to.

Unexpectedly, the menacing look on his face fell away. He looked only like a handsome young man in extreme pain. He slumped, and it seemed as if all of the air came out of him like a balloon.

"Fine!" He cried, "I'll leave. But I'll be back tomorrow."

He turned around and looked directly at Ellie. He took a step toward her, and she shrank away. He immediately looked defeated and hurt. He ran his hands through his sandy hair that *desperately needed a cut*, Nurse Eva thought. He was frustrated.

Nurse Eva was surprised to see his pain.

She could feel his sincere disappointment. *Maybe he really loves her*, she thought. She quickly dismissed the thought. She could not sympathize with him now. He was still a threat, and she couldn't wait for him to leave.

He walked slowly to the door and turned around right before he walked through it. "I'll be back tomorrow, El. I'll take you home when it's time, and you are going to be with me. You don't have anyone else. You need me, and we belong together."

Nurse Eva watched him walk out and when he was finally gone, she glanced at Ellie who was still clutching her crying baby. She nodded quickly at her and then rushed out of the room to call security. She wanted to get to them quickly so they could catch him and escort him out of the building. She contacted her supervisor and briefed him on the incident.

In the meantime, she had one of the other nurses check in on Ellie and instruct her on how to feed the baby. She hoped that it would go well since Ellie seemed so timid with everyone but her. Nurse Eva felt as if she had been away from the room for hours, but it had only been one.

When she returned to the room, she was confused. She checked the bathroom, under the bed, and in the closet. She walked every inch of the small room and then sank into the chair facing the bed.

Ellie was gone, and so was Baby Eva!

CHAPTER FOUR

Saving Ellie

Ellie had to escape from the hospital.

She always ran. She ran from Momma and Daddy then she ran from *him*. Now she was running from the hospital, and from Nurse Eva who had taken such good care of her.

Ellie had no idea where to go. She knew that she should stay at the hospital, and let Nurse Eva teach her more about taking care of the baby. But she had to get out of there. If *he* came back, nobody was going to be able to help her and she didn't want her wonderful nurse to get hurt. He looked like he wanted to harm Nurse Eva, and was certainly capable of it. She felt threatened and knew he could hurt someone, even her, which is why she had to leave. She loved him, but she wasn't going to let him hurt her again.

She didn't want him to touch the baby even though she knew that Eva was his baby, too. But he hadn't wanted a child and now here she was, beautiful, soft, and perfect. Suddenly, Ellie wanted to take care of her and protect her always.

Ellie waited until well after he was gone to escape from the hospital, though she disappeared from her room as soon as the nurse left. She couldn't bear to face Nurse Eva. Ellie looked carefully out the main hospital doors, but she didn't see him. It was evening, and people walking into the hospital looked at her funny, but she didn't care. *Haven't they ever seen someone with a baby before?* She was annoyed. *God, I need a smoke!*

Where would she go?

I don't want to go back to the shelter. I don't want my baby raised in that place!

She walked down the street from the hospital holding Baby Eva, desperate for an answer. Ellie's body felt tired, and bruised like she had been hit by a car, but she had to find a place to go. She was wearing only a hospital gown and slippers, and was starting to get cold. She hadn't even thought to change, and she left her clothes in the hospital room. Thankfully, it was a warm autumn night with only a slight chill in the air.

She walked for a few blocks and finally spotted a pay phone. She was careful to walk slowly because Baby Eva was sleeping. She still felt awkward holding her, afraid to jostle her too much or hold her too tight. She held her close feeling her warmth and she still couldn't believe she actually had a baby to take care of now.

Ellie picked up the receiver and made a collect call, and then sat on a bench and waited.

Eva was still sleeping, and Ellie was happy for the quiet. She was exhausted and felt as if she could sleep for days. But she was anxious, too. *What kind of life will I be able to give Eva? What am I going to do with my life?* Ellie could go back to school if she wanted to, and she really wanted to finish. She didn't want to end up a burnout or stoner and she decided that she didn't want to continue drinking or doing drugs, either.

Ellie was intelligent. But she had been captivated by his good looks, his charm, and by the fact that he was so much older. Ellie had felt stifled by her parent's love and protectiveness, an unwilling prisoner in her privileged life.

She didn't expect that things would end up like this.

She isolated herself from the only two people who cared for her, punishing them for loving her. But now Ellie was a mother who needed to take care of her child. She made the call, and then she waited for what seemed like hours, shivering in the cold, fearing that they may not come.

She knew that it would take a while, but the anticipation was difficult to bear.

Finally, she saw a big black Cadillac approaching and felt her heart leap in her chest.

The car barely stopped when the passenger side door flew open, and a petite, beautiful blonde woman in her mid-thirties, got out of the car. She and Ellie could have been mistaken for sisters only Ellie had the dark features of her father. She started running toward her, "Ellie, my Ellie!"

"Momma!" Ellie cried, tears running down her cheeks. She had no one in the world now but them and her heart felt heavy with remorse and sadness for what she had done.

The driver's side door opened, and a tall handsome man with a goatee and dark brown eyes identical to Ellie's, gracefully stepped out. He didn't run toward her, but walked with long strides until he was hugging them both tightly. The tiny bundle in her arms squeaked and gurgled, and for a long moment, they were all one.

"Daddy! I've missed you so much. I am so sorry for what I've done! Please forgive me, please." Ellie cried and cried.

James Harper held onto his little girl fighting back tears. He was shocked at how gaunt and small his daughter looked. Her still swollen belly was so awkward on her tiny frame. He blamed himself for all of their pain. He had almost lost his daughter and his wife, and now they were finally back together!

It terrified Ellie to see her Daddy cry. She had never seen him cry before now. He was strong, and she had made him cry, and it made her feel like her heart was breaking. She had done this to him, she had hurt Daddy, and suddenly she felt as if she were six years old.

"Oh, Elizabeth, don't cry. We are here now. We've been looking for you for months and months, and now we have you. Don't worry anymore," Momma gushed as she smoothed Ellie's dark hair and kissed her cheeks over and over. She missed how silky Ellie's hair used to be. She couldn't wait to help wash and brush it as she used to do. Ellie was a mess, and Amy wasn't used to seeing her baby girl like this.

She took the baby gently out of Ellie's arms, holding her close. She looked just like Ellie had as a newborn. She smelled so fresh. Amy was disappointed that Ellie would have to lose her childhood so young, but in a split second, she was already in love with this beautiful infant. *Oh my God, I'm a grandmother.* The thought nauseated her and pleased her at the same time.

"Amy, let's get her back to the hospital," Daddy said, straightening himself. He was back to his usual composed, practical self. "We need to make sure that she and the baby are healthy before we take them home." He looked down at Ellie and took her chin in his hands, "Peanut, you are going to have to make better decisions now that you are a mother. Leaving the hospital before you have been discharged is irresponsible."

Ellie nodded in agreement. She needed to be a good girl in every way now, and she knew that she could do it.

After another night's stay in the hospital, and hired security looking over her, Ellie and Baby Eva were ready to leave. Nurse Eva was so relieved to see her return, and this time with parents. Momma hugged Nurse Eva so tight and thanked her repeatedly for being there for Ellie.

Eva could tell that Ellie was much loved and it made her very happy.

She couldn't wait to go home to see her own daughters who had been calling nonstop asking when she was coming home. Eva couldn't leave the hospital when she found Ellie's room empty. She had to stay hoping that she would return. She knew that she wouldn't be able to stop worrying about her and the baby. She was so worried about their safety and prayed that *he* wouldn't find her.

James called in his own security. *He* returned the next morning as promised, but the security team caught him at the hospital main entrance and forced him out. James gave them orders to "make sure that he didn't *ever* return."

Amy was thankful and looked at James with so much love, "Thank you for keeping Ellie safe and for bringing us here." He peered down at her with gratitude and love. He didn't know what he would have done if he'd lost her, too. She was his muse and everything in his life was done for her.

After James and Ellie fought and Ellie left, Amy was angry. He had never seen her so angry. "If we don't find our baby, I will leave you for good!"

James was mortified, "I can't lose you Amy! You and Ellie mean everything to me. I'll do anything in my power to find our little girl. I won't give up, please don't give up on me. Please!" He begged, and she relented. Amy loved him, and didn't want to give up, but she couldn't live without Ellie.

When Ellie called to come home, James fell to the floor and cried in relief. Amy had given him an ultimatum, and was planning to leave him that very week. As hard as she had tried, she couldn't take the pain and anguish of losing Ellie any longer, and she blamed her beloved husband for forcing her out.

"This is your fault, James!" she yelled at him while standing in the middle of Ellie's empty bedroom. She slept there every night, crying herself to sleep and wishing her daughter home. She ran her hand over Ellie's pillow, remembering her brown-eyed sweet little girl. "I will never forgive you if she doesn't come back to us. I love you, but she left because of you! I hate you for making her leave us!"

But now all was well, and finally they were at peace.

That night, Ellie slept like she hadn't slept in ages. Her hospital room had around the clock security, and nobody could get to her. She knew that Momma and Daddy were sleeping on the couches in her hospital room, keeping a close eye on her and Eva. Daddy offered to take Momma to a nearby hotel, but Momma wouldn't hear of it. She couldn't bear to be away from Ellie for one more night.

When they woke up the next day, Ellie was discharged and they said their goodbyes. Nurse Eva had gone home to her own family, but the rest of the hospital staff had been kind to her, as well. Ellie didn't hear the details, but she knew that Momma and Daddy were sending an expensive gift to Nurse Eva's house for taking care of their precious girl. Momma and Daddy were generous with their money. She figured it would be something like a car or an all-expense paid vacation. And Ellie hoped that Eva would be pleased.

They made the long drive from the hospital to their own home, and Ellie couldn't wait to get there. Daddy must have driven fast to pick her up at the hospital. The drive home seemed so much longer than the time she had sat waiting for them. She thought that it might be that she was just so anxious to be back home. It felt like a lifetime since she had stepped foot in her house, or slept in her own bed and she didn't realize just how much she missed it.

James had built his own company from the bottom up years ago, and they reaped the benefits of it every day. But there was nothing that he loved more than Amy and Elizabeth. He was so angry with Elizabeth for getting involved with that disgusting drug dealer. She was young and didn't know exactly what he was or what she was getting herself into, but James knew.

James hired men to track him down so that he could make sure that he always stayed away from his daughter but they were unsuccessful, and he was frustrated. He was used to getting what he wanted, and was finding that he couldn't control the universe where his spirited Ellie was concerned. She scared him. *Of anything in life, she terrifies me.*

He glanced at her in the rearview mirror, and she looked like the sweet young girl he remembered. But he was plagued with fears that he didn't want to share with Amy because he didn't know if she would understand. Ellie had already experienced and seen so much. *How am I going to help her get her innocence back? Is she really going to be happy as a mother?* James knew that nothing was certain, and he prayed that her venture into the world taught her something about the importance of family.

When they finally got home, Ellie walked around the house with Baby Eva sleeping in her arms, as though she were seeing it for the first time. It looked so much bigger than when she left over a year ago. *How I missed you*, she thought adoringly as she marveled at the spaciousness and beauty of her home.

"We have a surprise for you," Amy said with a big smile, showing pretty white teeth.

"What, Momma?" It had been a long time since anyone had surprised Ellie with anything.

"You'll have to wait and see," James said slyly.

Ellie was excited because she always loved surprises. She handed Eva to James, who held the baby awkwardly.

"Close your eyes, Peanut," Amy said excitedly holding her hand and leading her up the long flight of stairs. When she was finally able to open her eyes, her breath caught in her throat. They turned her room into a beautiful nursery. "How did you do this?" she was amazed.

"I had it done as soon as you called me. I knew that you would love it!" James said proudly. "I had her name painted on the wall today, so be careful because it may still be wet," he added.

She did love it. It was perfect! Her parents still knew her so well. The room had always been pale pink, her favorite color. Now it was decorated even more frilly and girly. They had chosen the perfect fabric and finishing for the crib, the bassinet, and the changing table. It was as though Ellie had chosen it herself. She walked around in wonder.

Her bedroom was her favorite place in the world, her sanctuary. It was huge, the size of the entire second floor. She had her own bathroom, her own dressing room, and a huge walk in closet. She opened the closet door, and it was full of baby clothes, as were the drawers to the dressers. Now everything in the room was not just hers, it belonged to both her and Eva. She was happy and excited! She sat on her bed, sighing with both happiness and relief.

Ellie was so grateful to be home.

CHAPTER FIVE

Unhappy Ellie

She looked around the massive nursery at all of the things that still needed packed up, and threw her hands up in the air. There were still piles of frilly little clothes, diapers, blankets, and shoes that needed to be put into boxes. Where was her help? She sat on the bed exasperated, her deep brown eyes full of tears.

Ellie was done!

She endured the crying and the sleepless nights, when Eva was a baby. She changed all of the diapers, wiped the baby spit-up, and had taken Eva to every checkup. Momma wouldn't even let her have a nanny! She had done everything.

Now Ellie was being left on her own. Momma and Daddy told her that it was time to be an adult, and they were abandoning her.

"But I finished high school like I promised, and I've stayed far away from *him*! I can't believe that you are kicking me out. I don't want to live on my own!" Ellie was angry and whining because Daddy was being unreasonable!

"Elizabeth, enough!" he said angrily. He was sick of her selfishness and how spoiled she was. His Momma had raised him, and his two brothers on her own and Ellie couldn't take care of one child without complaining. "You've been given a great deal of help! We've given you a roof over your head, and you've wanted for absolutely nothing!"

"I'm your daughter! You're supposed to take care of me always, you're my Father!" Ellie felt betrayed. She couldn't believe what she was hearing. *How can he just cut me off, and expect me to live in an apartment half the size of my bedroom? Why can't he just buy us a little house and get me a nanny?* She deserved it, after all she had sacrificed for the baby, for them.

She stayed away from Eva's father, even after he said he was still in love with her. It had already been three years, and she hadn't been out with any boys since she was with his because nobody in their town wanted to date a girl with a baby.

She always turned him away but now Ellie was tired of saying "no" and tired of being alone and she couldn't do this on her own. Momma always expected her to have Eva and she could never get away from the little imp! Ellie hated that she couldn't even go shopping or out with her friends, without Eva tagging along.

Sometimes Ellie just wanted to be alone!

The only time she could get away from her was at school but that just wasn't enough.

Then Momma and Daddy announced they were going on a long trip to Europe, and Ellie hadn't been invited! They wanted Ellie to live by herself and take care of her own life.

James and Amy agreed that they sheltered her too much. They thought that leaving for a couple of months would help teach Ellie how to grow up. But instead, Ellie felt they were abandoning her, and she was angry. She thought they would take care of her and Eva for as long as she needed them to, and she still needed them.

"You need to grow up, Ellie. You're too much of a child, and you need to learn to take care of yourself! College is right around the corner, and you haven't even picked one yet!" James couldn't believe what they had done. They thought they were helping her, but now Ellie was helpless and lazy, and she didn't want to do anything without their help, and their money.

Ellie had just turned eighteen, but she didn't want to be an adult yet. She wasn't ready, and she wanted to go to Europe! She deserved to go to Europe and see the world.

Momma agreed with Daddy, as always, even though Ellie could tell that she really wanted her to go. Momma was no help.

Momma had come into Ellie's room the week before they left for the trip. She knew that Ellie was angry with them, but she was helpless to change it. Ellie's room was packed with all of their belongings, and the movers were coming the next day. Momma was planning to help Ellie settle in, but she wanted to spend some time with her before she left.

"I know you're mad, Peanut," Momma said as she sat down on

her soft bed. Momma hadn't called her that for a while, and it made Ellie soften, until she remembered that she was angry.

"Mad? Mad doesn't even begin to say it! Momma, I just don't understand. Why can't you take me with you?" Ellie was beside herself, and was on the verge of tears.

"Gamma, Gamma," Eva walked over to her and put up her arms. Amy pulled her into her lap and nuzzled her against her, "Eva looove Gamma."

"Grandma loves Eva," Amy said smiling down at her sweet face. She worried for her. She had argued with James that Ellie wasn't ready to be a mother on her own but James insisted. He reminded Amy that when they were young, they didn't have what they had now. He said that Ellie was too spoiled and that she needed to learn to stand on her own two feet. He knew who Ellie was and didn't like the kind of woman she was becoming.

Amy sadly agreed with him. She had gone to college, but hadn't finished because James had swept her off her feet. He had been young, handsome, and brilliant, and she had fallen head over heels. James had blinded her with his strength and enthusiasm, and Amy knew that she would always follow him to the ends of the earth and beyond. She usually agreed with him simply because she loved him so much. But this time she agreed with him because she also didn't like how useless and selfish Ellie had become and deep down inside she blamed herself.

They had even asked Ruth, their cook, to give Ellie cooking lessons six months ago. Ellie had been resistant, and had grudgingly gone along with it, but she wasn't happy. Six months later, she could cook a roast and grilled chicken, and that was it. Ruth, who had been with the family ever since Ellie was a baby, had thrown up her hands in frustration, and told them that she was "impossible to teach!"

Amy was worried for Eva more than anything. She knew well, how immature and rebellious her daughter could be when she didn't get her way.

Leaving Eva terrified Amy.

"I don't know if Ellie can take care of Eva on her own," she had argued with James. When Ellie ran away, she finally found her voice with her husband and she used it. "You know what happened the last time she was on her own, and now she has Eva. What if she can't do it?"

"We have to try to teach her some responsibility, Amy! She believes that the world owes her everything, and that's our fault. We need to practice some tough love and hope it isn't too late." James felt guilty. He never wanted to raise his child to be so purposeless in the world. He thought that when he rescued her from the hospital that she would have stopped living her life in such a selfish fog but he was wrong. She was even worse now as she left Eva with Amy every chance she got. Ellie thought that James didn't know, but he did.

"I'm going to be all alone, and you don't even care!" Ellie sounded like a child, her pretty lips puffed out into a pout.

"I *do* care," Amy said, feeling helpless. Where was James when she needed him? He was always so good at this sort of thing. Amy was never good at fighting or arguing, and she hated it. "I do love you, sweetheart. But Daddy thinks it best if you learn to live on your own! Daddy thinks that you will be able to take care of yourself better!"

"Oh, like *you* take care of yourself?" Ellie sneered at her.

Eva toddled up. "Mommy, no fight! No yell at Gamma!"

"I'm NOT yelling!" Ellie said, not taking her eyes off her mother. She felt powerful for a moment. She knew she was right. If it weren't for Daddy, Amy wouldn't be able to take care of herself. Ellie hated the hypocrisy!

Maybe it was better that they left so she could do what she wanted.

He was calling her a lot lately. Maybe she would see him and see how he had been doing. She could finally introduce Eva to her Daddy. She could even see him tomorrow if she wanted to!

"You're pathetic," she said to Amy. Ellie enjoyed watching Momma flinch as she inflicted her with the painful words she always wanted to say. "I'm glad you're leaving. Eva and I don't need you. We will be just fine on our own."

"Ellie, please," Amy begged. "Don't say things like that. We are only going to be gone for a couple of months, but it will go fast. I don't want to leave things like this!"

"Like what, Mother? You are leaving me here, alone! You haven't let me have a nanny, or a driver! You expect me to do it 'on my own', and for what purpose? You don't think that I am capable of finding a rich handsome husband like you did? Well, that's not what *I* want, even though I could get one if I tried! I just wanted to have some help. I'm your daughter! I'm not a stranger begging for money!" Ellie let her have it. She poured out her anger and her resentment with every syllable. She showered Amy with every mean thought and word that had ever crossed her mind. She didn't care that Mother was leaving.

"I don't need you!" Ellie spit out the words through clenched teeth.

Amy was crying. She didn't understand her hatred. "Let me take Eva with us. I'll take care of her from now on, Ellie. It's okay if you don't want to be a mother. You don't have to do it anymore," Amy cried.

"No way!" Ellie was enraged, "You aren't going to raise my child only to turn her out and let her go like you're doing now to me! I will raise her on my own."

Eva was tugging at Ellie and crying. She didn't like that Mommy was yelling at Gamma. She loved Gamma. Gamma was crying so hard, and it made Eva sad. Eva loved Mommy, but Mommy was being mean.

Amy looked down at Eva with sad, beautiful eyes. "It's okay, Peanut," she said trying to smile. She picked Eva up and held her tight. "I love you and I will see you soon. Grandpa loves you, too. We will see you as soon as we get back from our trip!"

Eva planted a soft wet kiss on both of her cheeks, "I love you, Gamma Peanut."

Amy looked at Ellie, and smiled a sad smile, "I don't care what you think. This is for the best. We love you and want you to be an independent adult. We are not withholding anything from you. We are giving you a gift."

Ellie glared back with eyes of steel, and Amy was unnerved. She had never seen this side of her daughter before and it frightened her. "I love you, Ellie, ever since you were *my* little Peanut. Please take good care of our Eva."

Ellie was silent. Amy paused before she walked out the door, waiting for some kind of response. She wanted to hear Ellie say she loved her, like on the night they rescued her from the hospital. But it was clear that Ellie was not going to give in. She stared at Amy, and for a split second, Amy saw her when she was four, tiny and chubby, with eyes that were too big for her face.

Little Eva ran after Amy breaking her reverie and put her arms up for one last hug. Amy picked her up and held her tight, breathing her in. She wanted to pick Eva up and run out the door with her, but she knew she couldn't. As much as Amy loved her, she couldn't steal away Eva's chance to be with her mother. Amy smoothed Eva's soft hair and looked into her big brown eyes, so much like her mother's, so much like her own.

"I love you, Peanut Eva," Amy said, dreading letting her go.

"I wuv you, Gamma Peanut," Eva said in her soft sweet voice, her little soft arms squeezing her as hard as they could.

Amy gave Eva one last kiss. She stepped toward Ellie, but Ellie gave her a hard look, and then turned around. Amy knew that it would take her daughter time to forgive, it always did. She hoped that when they came back from Europe, things would be different.

She walked out the door feeling a pit in her stomach. She couldn't ignore the feeling that it would be the last time she saw either of them ever again. Amy chastised herself for being so paranoid and forced herself to keep going.

She urged her feet to continue moving as she tried desperately to quiet her own fears, ignoring the growing crack in her heart.

CHAPTER SIX

Leaving Eva

Eva was hungry.

"Mommy, hungry!" Eva cried. She looked down at her tummy. It was making a lot of loud sounds, and it was grumbling.

"Mommy, eat, NOW!"

Eva shook Mommy. Mommy didn't move. She was tired. She put the sharp thing in her arm, and now she was tired. She had been awake, but now she was sleeping. Eva couldn't wake her up. Eva was hungry. No food. No juice.

And Eva was cold. Too cold. The room was dark and cold. The Mean Man was there, but he had been sleeping for a long time, too. His arm was lying over Mommy, and they were both sleeping. He was snoring so loud. It must be nighttime because when Eva looked outside, it was dark. She was afraid of the dark. She didn't want the monsters to come and get her. She felt like anything could come out and grab her at any moment.

She missed her Gamma and Gampa. If they were here, they would feed her! They loved her. They never ignored her.

No light, no food, no juice, no TV, no toys. She only had her favorite doll, Betsy to keep her company.

Eva was mad. "Mommy, wake up! Wake up! WAKE UP! HUNGRY!"

Eva's tummy kept making those loud growly sounds. Her

tummy hurt. The Mean Man brought her a cheeseburger and French fries, but that was a long time ago, when he was trying to be nice to her. Then he started drinking the stuff that smelled like medicine out of the big bottle, and he started pulling her hair and pinching her for no reason. He kept saying, "Eva, come sit on Daddy's lap," and Eva kept shaking her head "no." She didn't want to sit on his lap. She just wanted to go home.

Eva needed to go to the potty. Mommy needed to help her. The potty was so tall, and there were no steps in this bathroom like there was in their bathroom. She still had her icky pull-ups on. They were wet and heavy. Mommy said they were out, and Mommy needed to get more but then she fell asleep. Eva wanted the icky nasty pull-ups off. She wanted new ones, dry ones. She wanted her potty at home. She wanted her bed. She hadn't been to sleep in her bed in a very long time, and she missed it. She wanted to see her kitty. They had been in the Mean Man's dirty apartment for a long time. He wanted her to call him daddy but she didn't call him daddy. It made him very mad, and he called her ugly names. She didn't like him. He yelled at Mommy, and then Mommy cried and ignored her.

And now she was hungry. *HUNGRY!*

She wandered around the dirty room. It smelled bad, like puke and pee. She looked on the shelves and in the cabinets, and she saw lots of black little bugs scurrying away. They frightened her. There was no food, no cookies, no fruit snacks, and no cereal. There were no juice boxes in the refrigerator. There was nothing.

Her tummy wouldn't stop growling, and she was hungry and cold. She hated it here. She was getting really mad.

HUN-G-RY! "WAKE UP!"

She found some crackers in a cabinet far in the back. They were not good. But she ate all of them. She shoved them into her mouth all at one time, her cheeks full as she savored the stale salty flavor. Now she was thirsty. She didn't know why her Mommy brought her here. With nothing for her to do, she was bored.

She begged Mommy to take her home. The Mean Man told her to stop whining and then pinched her, leaving a mark on her arm. Mommy got mad at him and slapped him on the face as Eva hid behind her.

"Don't you ever slap me, you bitch," he said grabbing Mommy's arm hard. "You need to calm down. I know what you need." Then he pulled the sharp thing out of a drawer and put it in his arm, then in Mommy's arm. They forgot about Eva, and they didn't care that she was hungry, and dirty, and cold.

Mommy, wake up. Wake up. I'm cold.

She huddled under a scant little blanket that she found in a cabinet. She tried to lie close to Mommy on the bed, but there was no room. The Man was taking up all of the room. She had no place to lie down. She didn't want to go into the other room. She didn't want to be alone. She still had to go to the potty.

She lay down on the floor. It was hard and cold. She could hear breathing from Mommy and the Man on the bed. She tried to get comfortable, but the floor was hard. She hated it.

She heard the mattress creak as someone shifted. Then she finally drifted off to sleep.

She awoke to the sound of screaming. She realized that she was wet. She had to go potty for so long, and when she was sleeping, she couldn't hold it.

She followed the sound of the screaming. She found herself in a hallway. It was so dark and then her eyes adjusted to the light. She looked up and saw Mommy at the top of a long set of stairs. Mommy and the Man were screaming at each other. Mommy looked sick like she was going to throw up. She was crying. He was trying to push her down the stairs. He was pushing her, and Mommy was crying. He was saying lots of bad words. The Mean Man and Mommy saw her and stopped fighting.

Mommy I'm wet, and I'm hungry!

Mommy ran down the stairs to Eva and picked her up. She hugged her and then pushed her away. "Eva, you smell like pee."

"I had to potty, Mommy. I couldn't hold it," Eva was ashamed. She looked down at her ruined dress. It was her favorite, and now she couldn't wear it anymore.

Mommy, don't cry.

"I know, baby. It's not your fault. I'm so sorry." Mommy was stroking her hair and kissing her head. She liked when Mommy did that. She didn't like when Mommy fell asleep after being poked with the sharp thing. She didn't like when Mommy wouldn't wake up. It scared her.

Mommy was so pretty. She had pretty dark hair and pretty dark eyes. She loved Mommy so much.

But ever since they came to the Mean Man's house, Mommy looked sick. She didn't look like Mommy. She looked slimy, and sweaty, and she had ugly circles under her eyes. She smelled dirty, too.

The Mean Man had stayed at the top of the steps staring at them. He walked down slowly giving Eva mean eyes as if he hated her. His eyes looked like monster eyes.

"You gotta do something about the kid, El!" He was mad. He was standing close to Mommy, and Eva didn't like it. Eva kicked at him, and he laughed. Then he kicked her, and she yelped.

"Don't do that!" Mommy yelled at him.

"Ditch the kid, El. Nobody wanted a kid. I didn't want a kid. I told you that in the hospital. I told you to ditch her there, and they would have found her a good home. But you had to run from me. And then I found you. I told you that I would always find you. I need you!" he was holding Mommy close now. Mommy was hugging him. She was kissing him. He looked like he was going to swallow her face. It made Eva mad, and she stomped back into the room with the dirty bed.

"Fine. What do I do? I don't want her to go. She's gotta be safe," Mommy loved her, Eva knew.

"Just let her go in the next town, or over the state line. She'll be fine, someone will find her."

Mommy was going crazy. She cried. She screamed. She slapped him again. "I can't let her go like a dog. I can't dump her out of the car like that. She won't understand. What if nobody finds her? I can't let her go if she's not going to be safe. What if we just wait until my parents come back? We could take her to their home! Pleeeaase!"

"Your parents aren't coming back for a long time! They left you, baby! We need a clean break. If you leave the kid with them, they'll just come looking for you. If you ditch the kid, they'll figure you ran off with her." He was annoyed with her. He hated her parents, but he didn't have to worry about them now, he just didn't need Ellie to know that. Her dad had his thugs rough him up, and he had paid them back. They were gone for good, and now Jonas was going to have their little Princess, too. His guys had dumped their bodies so deep in the lagoon that nobody would ever find them.

One day, he would have Ellie cash in on the inheritance, and they would be set for life. But not yet. He had a plan, and he needed to be patient. They had to lay low for a while and get rid of the kid, or Ellie would have to split the money with her. He wasn't sharing his money with a snotty ass kid.

"They'll look for me, anyway," she said.

"They won't find you. They won't find the kid, either! We're leaving her."

Eva was scared. What were they saying? Was Mommy going to leave her? *No, Mommy!*

Eva was crying now.

"If we let her go over the state line, which is about four towns over, close to dawn when people are going to work, someone will find her. We can't keep her, El. If we keep her, we'll end up partying too much, and she'll be neglected. Then she will really get hurt," he was stroking Mommy's side. He could tell that she liked it. "It'll be okay, baby. She will end up with a nice family. You're just not the mothering kind. You like to party too much. Look at her, El. She's a mess."

Mommy ran to Eva and looked at her big sad eyes. Mommy shook her head back and forth. She was mumbling to herself and wiping her eyes hard, over and over. She was walking in circles around the room pulling at her hair.

"No, No, No," she said over and over. She kept shaking her head, looking at Eva, and shaking her head. "No, No, No."

Her parents were going to be so mad at her. They were going to be so upset! They should never have left her! How could they leave her to take care of herself and the baby? They should know by now that she couldn't do it. They should know her by now.

After a very long time, she looked at the Mean Man and nodded. She thought Eva didn't understand. Eva did understand.

Mommy was going to let her go.

It wasn't long before the Mean Man made Mommy put Eva in

the car. "We're going for a little drive," he said.

He told Mommy that she didn't have to go, but Mommy insisted. She said that she needed to make sure that Eva was safe. Mommy made him give Eva a big heavy shirt, and she put it on her. It was too big, and the sleeves kept falling down over her hands. "It will keep you warm," she whispered in her ear, her voice sounding as if it were broken.

Eva was afraid. She didn't know where Mommy and the Mean Man were taking her. She didn't like his car. It smelled bad like his apartment. It was bumpy, and he was going fast. Really fast. Eva couldn't stop crying which was making the Mean Man even meaner. "Shut her up, El!"

Mommy was holding her in the front seat. She was never allowed in the front seat before, but she was glad that Mommy was holding her tight. Mommy kept saying "Shh, Shh" in her hush voice, but Eva couldn't stop crying. She knew something bad was going to happen. She could tell. And Mommy was crying, too.

They drove, and they drove, and they drove. It was dark the whole time. Eva was still hungry. The crackers hadn't been enough. But she had been hungry since they had been staying with the Mean Man, so she was getting used to it.

Eva fell asleep, even though she tried hard not to. She didn't want to, but she was so tired. She didn't feel it when they started to slow down.

She woke up, and the Mean Man was holding Mommy's ponytail hard in his fist. "We've talked about this a hundred times before, El. When I found you after you tried to duck me after the hospital, I told you that you weren't the Mom type!"

"But I can't leave her! I can't." Mommy was crying hard. She grabbed Eva, and held her so tight she couldn't even breathe.

They were stopped on the side of the road. It was a dark quiet road, and Eva was confused. Mommy was talking really fast, and Eva was trying to figure out what she was saying.

"You need to party. You need the rush. You need it, I need it, and I need you. You need me, too. But you don't need a kid. A kid gets in the way. And look at her! She's dirty, she smells, and she cries all the fucking time. Jeez, El, why can't you just think for once in your life?" The Mean Man's face was close to Mommy's face, and his face looked like it was going to explode.

"It's either the kid or me. You decide." The Mean Man looked at Mommy with hard eyes.

Eva was getting colder. It was cold outside, and the Mean Man's shirt wasn't keeping her that warm. It was wet and dark, and there was a lot of water and leaves on the ground. There was nothing around them but trees.

"You decide. If you want me, then make her get out now!" he said to Eva. He never said please or thank you, and Eva thought that his Mommy hadn't taught him very good manners. Eva was afraid of him, and she didn't like him at all.

"Get out!" He said again looking right at Eva. This time he sounded even meaner. Mommy started to pick her up, and get out of the car with her.

"NO!" he yelled at her. "YOU STAY IN THE CAR!" Mommy jerked Eva back and held her tight.

Eva was begging and crying. "Mommy, No, No, No! Don't leave me. I promise I'll be good. Don't leave me here pleeeeaaaaase! Mommy, No!"

Just then, it got really bright. He got really quiet as the lights came toward them, and just as quickly went away.

"See, El! There are cars on this road. She will be fine. Someone will find her."

Mommy was crying. "My baby! My baby! I'm so sorry. Please forgive me," she cried over and over. Tears were running down Mommy's face, and Eva could see that her nose was running, too. She was hugging her tighter and tighter. Eva could hardly breathe.

"Let her go, El. She'll be fine. Don't cry." The Mean Man was trying to pull Eva away from Mommy.

"Mommy, NOOOOO!" Eva was screaming.

Mommy, don't make me get out of the car. I don't know where I am. Don't leave me!

"GET OUT!" the Mean Man was pulling her arm hard.

She was out. He threw Betsy at her, and she fell to the ground.

She felt Mommy let go of her. She kept reaching her arms out, reaching for her but grabbing only air.

"Mommeeeeeeeeeeee!" Eva's big brown eyes were full of tears, and she had a hard time catching her breath. She could see Mommy looking at her through the window, her hand on the glass as though she was trying to touch her. "Mommy, Mommy. Don't leave me! I'll be good, I promise. Don't leave me, please!"

The Man pushed her hard, and Eva fell back and landed on the cold hard ground. When she got up, he was already in the car and the car was pulling out fast. She ran after it screaming, but all she could see were the bright red taillights getting farther and farther away. She hadn't even gotten to look at her Mommy one last time.

It was starting to rain.

She ran and ran until she couldn't run anymore. Her legs gave out. Her heart was beating out of her chest, and she was cold, so cold. She fell to the ground and could feel the cold wetness soaking through her body, but she didn't care. Her Mommy didn't love her, didn't want her anymore. What would she do without her Mommy? Who would take care of her, feed her, kiss her, and hug her? Who would put her to bed?

She laid on the ground, and she felt so cold, so tired.

She was afraid. It was black outside, and there were no lights. Only trees and road. She told herself her Mommy would come back. She lay there for what felt like hours. She could barely feel her feet or her fingers, and she was sleepy.

Mommy didn't come back. She was never coming back.

She didn't see the headlights pull up, or the woman get out.

She didn't care. Her Mommy was gone.

CHAPTER SEVEN

Finding Mommy

Eva lay on the ground feeling the water soak through her dress.

Her dress was dirty and disgusting. At least it didn't smell like pee anymore.

"Mommmeeeee," she croaked her voice hoarse from screaming and crying, "Mommmmeeeee."

She didn't see the headlights coming toward her, or hear the car door open.

"Hello? Hello?" A woman's voice was calling out. Eva could barely hear her in the rain.

"Oh my God!" The woman said as she got closer and saw the girl. She couldn't have been more than three or four years old. She was tiny! The woman looked around for someone, anyone. She couldn't believe that this child was out in this weather alone. There wasn't a house for miles, and they were at least six or seven miles from the next town. It wasn't more than forty degrees outside and this child had no coat. She couldn't understand it.

She walked closer to the girl, her high heels clicking on the wet ground.

"Hello? Little girl?"

The little girl looked up at her. All she could see were huge brown eyes staring up at her from her soaked, bedraggled hair. She was small and afraid, like a scared little rabbit.

"Please come with me, I'll help you. It's freezing out here!" She reached for her, her big diamond on her fingers glittering in the headlights of her car. She had a giant umbrella, and Eva could hear the pitter-patter of the rain as it bounced off it.

Eva started to get up. She grabbed Betsy and held her tight even though she was soaking wet. She looked at the woman. The woman looked nice. She had kind blue eyes, and a nice pretty smile like Gamma had. Eva didn't think that the woman would hurt her. Maybe she could help her find Mommy.

She let the nice woman help her get into her car. Her car was so big, and it was warm. Eva hadn't been warm all night. She shivered with cold, her lips were numb, and her hands and feet felt like pins and needles.

"What are you doing out in the cold? Where are your Mommy and Daddy?" the nice woman asked her. She had buckled Eva into the back seat and had the heat on full blast. Eva started to feel warmer, the pins and needles were fading away.

"Do you know Mommy?" Eva asked the nice woman.

"I don't know. What is her name?" the woman asked her.

Eva thought hard. "Mommy, her name is Mommy."

"I know, but what is her first name?" the woman smiled.

Eva was getting upset, "Mommy! I said her name is Mommy!"

The woman asked her another question, "Do grownups call her anything else? Sometimes grownups will call someone by a different name."

"Lizbet," said Eva proudly. She was getting all of the answers right.

"Elizabeth?" The lady asked.

"Lizbet!" Eva repeated. She didn't know what the lady said when she asked her if she knew her last name. "My name's Eva Lizbet," she said. That must be her last name.

The lady was getting frustrated.

"Do you know where you live?" she asked.

"We drove far. I don't know," Eva said sadly. She didn't know where she lived. Mommy moved them a lot. She liked their last apartment. It was nice. But they hadn't been there long, and then Mommy took them to be with the Mean Man.

They drove for a little while in silence. Eva wondered where they were going. Was the nice woman taking her to Mommy?

"Where we going?" Eva asked shyly.

"We need to get you some food and some warm clothes. It's late though. I don't have a daughter, so we are going to stop at my friend's house. She has a daughter whose clothes should fit you and we will call the police from there. My cell phone battery is dead. " The nice lady said.

"Are we going to see Mommy then?" Eva missed Mommy. She wanted to see her so badly.

"We are going to try and find your Mommy," the nice woman said.

Eva was happy now. She closed her eyes and dozed off. She woke up with a start. The car stopped.

She didn't know where they were, but wherever they were, they were far away from Mommy. She needed Mommy! *Mommy!* Eva was getting upset. The nice lady wasn't taking her to Mommy, after all. Suddenly, the door opened.

Eva jumped out of the car and ran as fast as she could run. She heard the lady calling after her, but she kept on running until she no longer could hear her voice.

She *needed* to find her Mommy.

CHAPTER EIGHT

Going Away

Amy had left Eva and Ellie, and walked to her room, lost in guilty thoughts that consumed her. She felt uneasy, but decided that it was simply due to the impending stress of leaving her daughter and granddaughter behind.

She went to her spacious bedroom and checked her packed bags once more to make sure that she had everything they needed for their trip. They had never been away for two months before, but James insisted that it was the right thing to do.

They had discussed it the night before while they were packing as Amy made a last ditch effort to dissuade him.

"What about the company, James? You've never been away for so long," she asked innocently. The company was his baby, and she knew that he would never risk its well-being.

"The company will be fine, Peanut. You know that I've been grooming John for some time to be able to manage things for me. He wouldn't be Vice President if I didn't feel that he could handle it. Besides, this will be a good test for him." James tweaked Amy's nose. He knew just what his precious wife was doing, and he wasn't about to let her. "Elizabeth will be fine on her own. Don't worry so much, my darling."

Amy sat down petulantly on the bed, her blonde bob bouncing as she did so. "I just don't feel right about this. I don't feel right about leaving Eva alone with Ellie."

James was losing his patience. He loved Amy, but this was the type of attitude that crippled Ellie, and they were both guilty. He needed to put a stop to it, for all of their sakes. "Amy, enough! Elizabeth is Eva's mother. You need to... we need to, let her be a mother, an adult. We are going to go to Europe to enjoy the things that we have worked hard to earn. End of discussion." Amy recognized James' tone well, and realized that there was no point arguing with him. His mind was made up.

Amy tried to convince herself that she would be all right with it, and she was. But the uneasiness returned after her argument with Ellie. Amy could hear the sound of the moving truck backing up into the turnaround, and she stood at her bedroom window for three hours and watched them pack up Ellie's things. She forced herself to let Ellie manage the movers, instead of stepping in as she always did where Ellie was concerned. She hoped that Ellie would come to her room to say good-bye, but when they were packed up, Ellie got into her sleek black Lexus that James bought for her, and drove off.

Amy cried for the rest of the day until James returned. He held her close and whispered over and over that everything was going to be all right. He loved Amy, and he hated seeing her so upset. He was able to coax a little food into her, and then put her to bed that evening. He sat next to her on the soft mattress, gently stroking her soft silky hair in his strong fingers.

"It's going to be okay, Peanut. Eva and Ellie will be fine. You'll see, darling," he said in a low quiet voice.

She looked at her handsome husband with big brown eyes, the same eyes he had passed on to Elizabeth and Eva. "I hope so. I have a knot in my stomach that just won't go away. I hope you're right." Then she drifted off to sleep.

The next morning they said goodbye to the help and gave each of them bonus money for their extended vacations. While they were still responsible for the house, James had booked them each a vacation of their own to go on. He appreciated their loyalty, and their hard work, and he treated them well. In turn, they cared for the house and family as though they were their own.

Lou, their driver, wanted to take them, but James insisted on driving himself. He liked to do as much on his own as he could. The drive to the private airport took a little over an hour taking the back dirt roads, and James wanted to enjoy the sunshine with the top down on the shiny silver Aston Martin convertible. James closed Amy's door for her and gave her a rare bright smile. He sprinted over to the driver's side, excited like a little boy on Christmas morning.

Amy and James chatted pleasantly for the first half hour of the trip. Amy seemed in much better spirits, her blue eyes clearer, and her beautiful smile readily on hand. She seemed to have taken James' words to heart, and she was looking forward to going away. They were so caught up in their growing excitement that they didn't see the disabled car nearly blocking the entire road in front of them.

"Jaaaaaaaaaaamessss!" Amy shrieked pointing to the road in front of them. James pumped the brakes, careful not to slam on them for fear of flipping the car over. They came to a stop right before hitting the other car, a brown run-down wreck of a Ford that didn't look like it was even road worthy any longer.

James' heart was nearly pounding out of his chest. He looked at Amy, making sure she was all right. He put the car in park and got out. He thought it odd that the driver's side door was wide open. He looked into the driver's seat and saw a man slumped over. He motioned to Amy to stay in the car and walked over to the Ford cautiously.

"Hello?" he said tentatively at first, then louder. "Hello?"

The man in the car didn't move. James got closer to the car. *This car doesn't make sense out here. Who would even stop like that?* James heard a small, almost imperceptible squeak. He turned around and looked at Amy. To his horror, he saw a tall man pulling her out of the car with a knife to her throat.

James quickly tried to turn his attention back to the driver's seat. Suddenly James felt pain, deep, sharp, slicing pain ripping into his stomach. He looked down and saw a large handle sticking out of his gut. The driver who had been passed out was standing up, close to him, blood on his hands. James was confused. He saw a large stain in his neatly pressed Polo shirt starting to expand and grow. For a moment, he wondered what it was. *Where is that stain coming from?* Then he realized that it was his own blood. He touched it, and it was red, sticky. He was lost in his fascination, and then he realized, *Amy!*

He looked up and saw the other large man holding Amy close to his massive body. He was standing a few feet away, but James felt as if it were a mile, the distance growing between them. The man who had stabbed James was gone now, but the knife still remained. James needed to get to Amy. She was crying for him. He couldn't hear her, but he could see her face. The only thing he could hear was the sound of his own blood pumping through his body — thump, thump, thump. The sound of the thumping was slowing, and James realized that he was falling to the ground. He could see Amy struggling, screaming, her delicate silk top torn as she struggled with the bigger man trying, in vain, to get to James. James could see how rough the man was with her and how he clawed at her and held her close to his body, and James screamed in agony, but then he could see nothing.

Suddenly James felt his cheeks stinging and he opened his eyes quickly.

The man in the driver's seat was standing above him with his face an inch from his, and James could smell the tobacco and beer on his breath. "Jonas Miles said to say 'hello'. He wanted you to know that he will take good care of your little girl from now on. This is payback."

James closed his eyes. He couldn't hear Amy screaming anymore. He couldn't hear his blood pumping. He didn't even feel the pain anymore. He felt nothing.

There was nothing.

CHAPTER NINE

Vanishing Harpers

John Palmer thought it was strange that James hadn't checked in on him yet. He had been the Vice President for six months, but James kept a pretty tight leash on him. Even though John knew that James trusted him, he didn't anticipate such freedom just because he was going out of the country. It had been three days since he heard anything from him, which was out of the ordinary.

John had been working for James since he was eighteen years old. He was the classic story of a man who "worked his way up." He owed everything to James, who had seen his potential and taken a chance on him early and often. There was much that John didn't know yet, and he was feeling increasingly unsettled without any word from his mentor.

On the fourth day, he sent him yet another email and texted him once more. Then he left James another voicemail, and then another until James' voicemails were full.

John called the airport to see if his plane had ever taken off, and the response was that they never arrived at the airport. John drove like a bat out of hell calling every law enforcement authority he could think of in order to report James and Amy missing. He tried calling Elizabeth with the number that James had given him, but she wasn't picking up her phone either. John was worried. He called his wife, Tricia, who told him to slow down. She was pregnant with their third child, and he kicked himself for calling to worry her.

The police met him at the Harper House where the help were frantic. They had left days ago for their trip, and thought they were well on their way. *Where is Elizabeth? Where is Eva?*

John and the police drove the road between the Harper House and the airport and saw nothing. John made them drive it two more times. It was as though they had vanished.

They drove to Ellie's apartment and found it empty. There were no signs of her or Eva there.

There was nothing that could be done, and John felt helpless. He was in charge of the company until James could be found, and he thought he was going to vomit. He was ready to be Vice President with James at the helm for many long years, but this... this was too much. John was only thirty-years-old, and not ready for so much responsibility. He prayed that he wouldn't run it into the ground.

Tricia was devastated and worried for the Harper family, and her sweet husband. "Where are Amy, and Ellie, and Eva? What could have happened to them?" Amy had been so kind to them, and she adored Eva, though she could have done without Ellie. Tricia was a smart girl with motherhood coursing through her veins, and when she saw Ellie with Eva, she cringed. She wondered if she was being too judgmental, but Ellie had an emptiness that Tricia couldn't understand. Eva was so sweet and such a beautiful child, and it was unfathomable how Ellie could be so cold to her own child.

"I don't know, honey," John said, feeling lost. "It's as though they have disappeared without a trace. They have vanished into thin air."

"What will happen to the company? What will happen to Ellie and Eva?" Tricia cried when John returned home after their search, her blue eyes full of concern. She knew that John was tired, but she couldn't imagine what would happen now.

John was tired. His face was already showing wear from the worry of the past few days.

"I don't know. I guess that the company will be left for me to run. It's private, so I can manage it until... until, James returns." John's confidence in James' return was wavering.

"What happens if..." Tricia's voice trailed off. She wasn't able to verbalize her fears, even to John, her best friend.

John didn't answer right away. "If they don't return... If they don't... then eventually we would have to have them declared deceased. James was a smart man and took measures to ensure that his company and his family were taken care of if... if something ever happened to him. Strangely, he even accounted for this type of situation. He left me in charge of everything. Everything." John spoke slowly, as if in disbelief. He felt too young, too inexperienced to deal with this type of situation.

Tricia looked at her husband with sympathy and love. John was a good man, cute, boyish. She looked at his beautiful hazel eyes and sandy hair and thought for the thousandth time how lucky she was that she had found him.

"I've got someone already searching for Ellie and Eva. We will find them." John said trying to sound confident.

Tricia rubbed her belly and thought of sweet little Eva, and her other two children. She thought that Ellie wasn't the most responsible person, and about how helpless Eva would be in her care.

John walked slowly into the bathroom and looked in the mirror at his tired face. *What happens if we don't find any of them? What happens to James' fortune? I'm not ready to be the executor of his estate as he asked me to be. It's just too much.*

John was sick with worry. But above all, he missed his mentor and his friend.

Chapter Ten

Wedding Rose

care that she didn't love him. "It's okay Rose," he said Rose never imagined that her wedding day would come. She didn't even know if she wanted to get married, but as the day approached, she realized there was no choice. It was happening, and she couldn't stop it.

When Rose and Thomas started dating, everyone was surprised.

Rose was excited for the first time, running into the house to find Momma. "Thomas asked me out," she panted, pushing her hair carelessly out of her sweaty face. Rose had run all the way home from the market, and in her excitement she had forgot the groceries. Nobody had ever asked her out on a date before, not even in high school. She was the wallflower, invisible to everyone, especially the boys. While Rose wasn't unattractive, she had never been called beautiful.

Rose decided early on that she was as far from extraordinary as one could get.

When Thomas asked her out in the middle of the frozen foods aisle, she thought it was a joke. She'd known him all of her life, and knew that he only dated the pretty, popular girls. He had a good job and was considered a "catch." It was unfathomable that Thomas would want to go out with her.

She certainly didn't look like any of those pretty girls with their long flowing hair, long lean legs, and tight youthful bodies. Instead, she was tall, "lanky," and much to her Momma's dismay, was almost masculine with her long limbs, and absence of feminine softness.

"She's all arms and legs," she once overheard Momma Clara say to Aunt Jeannie. Momma hadn't meant to be critical, but she always wished her daughter were more like Aunt Jeannie's pretty girls.

Momma would have been happy if she had turned out like her. Daddy would often say that Momma was an "exotic flower" with her long dark hair and her deep brown eyes, though Rose never heard him say anything like that about her. With Rose's wiry brown hair, straight white teeth, thin lips and unassuming brown eyes, she looked far from a beautiful flower. She looked more like a useless weed.

Momma loved Rose in her own way but never expected much for her. She hoped only that someone might take pity, and marry her so that Rose could be taken care of, but she wasn't optimistic that anyone would settle for Rose. Thomas wasn't the most attractive boy in town, but he was certainly much better looking than anyone Clara thought would ever choose her daughter.

Within two months of dating, to everyone's astonishment, Thomas and Rose were engaged. At first, everyone thought that she was pregnant. Rose could hear the whispers, and girls like Natalie and Cindy had outright asked her what she had over him to force the marriage.

Rose was stunned herself that he asked. Thomas didn't even quietly in his usual steady voice. "You will learn to love me, and I will learn to love you." And though she should have, she didn't wonder why a man like him would ever want to be with her without love. She didn't care. She only cared that now she wouldn't ever be alone.

The day that Rose married Thomas was the prettiest she ever was or ever would be again. Her wedding gown belonged to Grandmother Johnson and was all lace. It was beautiful with its intricate design and exotic feel. Grandmother Johnson had truly loved Rose, from the moment she was born. Rose was her namesake, and she reserved a special place in her heart for her sweet granddaughter who wasn't loved as deeply as she should have been.

Grandmother Johnson never understood her Clara's coldness toward Rose, but she tried to make up for it as much as she could until the day she died. Giving Rose her wedding dress was a small gesture, but one she knew that she would love.

The long, lace dress was beautifully preserved, though Clara never believed that Rose would get to wear it.

On her wedding day, Rose found that she felt beautiful.

In spite herself, she felt some happiness and hope. Daddy captured her happiness in a black and white photo, which Rose had kept, displayed every day for the rest of her life. Despite the ugliness of their marriage, Rose could never put the photo away. It reminded her that for one brief moment in her life, she had hope. Often, as she pondered the sadness of her life, she would pick up the picture and stare at herself glowing in the dingy photo. And when she did so, she momentarily forgot reality, lost in a fog of one happy moment.

At seventeen, Rose married young, but she did not marry for love. She married the first and only man who ever asked her, though she worried that he drank a lot. Her father drank a lot too, and she never thought about what kind of effect it would have on her life.

After all, Rose and Thomas knew each other since they were small children, attending the same little church, and she decided that she knew enough about him. He was three years older, but they had never really been friends. She admired how tall and sturdy he was. That served him well at the plant, which required physical stamina and strength.

They married the weekend after he asked her because there was no reason to wait.

"I want to have a child," Rose said to Thomas shyly, "More than anything, I wanta daughter."

"If that's what you want," he said in his usual quiet way. He never gave many of his thoughts away, so there was nothing to ever talk about.

Having a child would assure Rose would never be alone. A child would fulfill her and complete her, and she envisioned a daughter who would be her best friend. Rose saw her as a constant companion, the keeper of her secrets and her soul, unlike her own mother. She knew that if she had a daughter, she would never need anything else.

But she knew, in order to have a child, she would need a husband to care for her financially. Rose didn't come from money. She barely graduated high school, and she didn't have any marketable skills. Marrying Thomas was Rose's only chance at a halfway decent life, and she needed to take it. Her mother reminded her of this every chance she got.

"Rose, a girl like you can't afford to be picky," Momma said to her in her twinkly voice that she reserved for when she was being critical, which was always. As she helped Rose get ready for the wedding, she gave her the best advice she could give. "Just be happy someone is marrying you."

After two months of courting, Rose still didn't know Thomas that well, and she was glad to get the ceremony part of out of the way. Rose figured they would get to know each other better after the wedding.

After their wedding, he still rarely touched her. On their wedding night, they didn't consummate their marriage, and Rose was relieved. He didn't try to touch her, and their marriage wasn't much different from when they dated. Neither of them talked much, and the closest they ever came to intimacy was holding hands.

They didn't consummate for a couple of weeks into their marriage. And when they finally did, it was painful and awkward, and both were relieved to finally get it out of the way.

When he did touch her, it made her uncomfortable. His touch was too stiff and awkward to stir up anything within her. Their lovemaking was infrequent, but when he did make the attempt, he often passed out or lost interest before he was done. She was far too shy to try to seduce him herself, and she wouldn't even know where to begin. He was the only man she had ever been with. If it weren't for the hopes of having a child, she would have only wished for him to pass out every night and forget she was in his bed, altogether.

She wanted to be filled with a child even if it was *his* child, but his thrusts were awkward. His eyes never looked at her, his face screwed up as though the task at hand took much concentration. In the end, it was always anticlimactic, and she was always glad when it was over.

Year after year went by, and she failed to get pregnant.

"Why can't we have a child? It's been two years?" she asked Thomas who had little response.

"It's been three years."

"It's been four years."

"It's been five years. I want to have a child! If we can't have one on our own, then we need to adopt. It's the only thing I want, Thomas, the only thing that I will ever ask you for." Rose was tired of watching the years pass her by, alone. They lived in silence, in a forced routine, that made Rose question if this were truly a better life. She missed living in her parent's house, where Father ignored her and Momma backhandedly criticized her. At least there was some life in their home.

When their brief and occasional trysts failed to make her pregnant, she knew she had to convince him to let her adopt, or she would always be alone.

"Fine, Rose," he said, after the fifth year. "If you want to adopt, then we can adopt. But the child is your responsibility. I don't want one, but if that's what you want, then maybe you can finally be happy." His voice remained even as it always was, and Rose spontaneously kissed him on the cheek, which made Thomas smile slightly.

The paperwork and process were easy. On paper, they were a solid couple. He had a steady job at the plant as a supervisor, they went to church every Sunday, and they had been married for many years. The reference from their pastor, his boss, and their fellow church members were appropriate if not glowing, and they sailed through the process with virtually no issues.

Rose was excited about choosing her child, and she knew the moment she saw the file that this would be her daughter.

The girl was found abandoned and alone, wandering the streets of a nearby town, for an indeterminate amount of time. They guessed that someone passing through dropped her off. They tried to find parents, but nobody surfaced to claim her. It was a miracle that she was alive as her clothes and condition told an untold story.

When they found her, she was malnourished and had a severely broken leg that required surgery. She was in the hospital healing for a couple of months and then placed with a foster family for eight months after that. The girl was difficult, and the foster family couldn't deal with her anymore because the comments from the social worker were "she needed undivided attention if she were ever going to thrive."

Rose knew that she could give that to her and chose her without hesitation.

CHAPTER ELEVEN

Rose's Perfect Fit

The social workers assumed that Brynn's fate would be to bounce from foster home to foster home until she was old enough to grow out of the system. They guessed that she was at least four or thereabouts. Most people only wanted to adopt babies, tiny people without anyone else's imprint, with a fresh slate to be molded as their own. People weren't looking for kids Brynn's age to raise as their own.

While Brynn was sweet with her long dark hair and her big eyes, she barely talked, and she had many issues. When they flipped through her file, they read between the lines, and they always moved onto the file with the infant or the youngest child that had not yet been scarred by life.

She was already struggling in one foster home and ready to move to the next. All she did was cry, and she needed constant attention.

The moment that Rose saw Brynn's file and saw her history, she knew that this was the child for her. This child was already old enough to walk and talk, and Rose had never wanted any of the messiness of an infant. She knew that this child would cling to her with needing and wanting, and she knew that she would be able to do the same to her. This child had been thrown out like yesterday's garbage, and Rose anticipated that she would be forever grateful to be rescued.

Rose was anxious for the adoption process to be over. She just wanted to have her daughter in her own home. The sooner she got her home, the faster her life could truly begin.

Finally, when the day arrived, Rose found that she was nervous. Thomas went to work as usual, but Rose busied herself straightening and cleaning and straightening again. She had the entire house clean from top to bottom, and then she went over it again. She had waited for this day for as long as she could remember and now that it was here, she was fearful. *What if she doesn't love me? What if she doesn't want me?*

When the kind social worker with the stutter came over to drop her off, the house was spotless, and Rose was a nervous wreck. The Social Worker walked into the house, her hand holding a small child who looked up at Rose with scared eyes.

"Do you want me to stay home tomorrow?" Thomas asked her.

Rose was surprised that he offered. Her stomach was already doing flip-flops, but she knew that having him there would make it worse. "No, thank you," she said giving him a small smile. "It's better if you just go to work. I'll be fine on my own."

She offered the social worker and the girl some cookies and tea. The social worker declined. She said that she needed to leave but that she would check back with them in a few days to make sure that they were acclimating well. Rose smiled at her and thanked her for bringing her daughter home. When the door closed, Rose turned around and looked at the girl.

"Hi," she said quietly as though she were talking to a scared kitten.

The girl didn't talk. She just looked at her, suspiciously.

"I'm your new Mommy now. I'm Rose." Rose said squatting down and getting to eye level with her. She kept a distance between them. The girl stood on the other side of the couch eyeing her with big brown eyes, but not moving. Rose didn't move either, suddenly wishing she had thought to leave the TV on. The plain little house, too quiet, Rose thought she could hear her heart beating through her chest. Even though this was what she always wanted, she didn't feel prepared.

She stared at the girl for a while, smiling until her face felt frozen and her cheeks hurt.

"I'm your new Mommy. I'm Rose." Rose repeated. The girl looked at her.

"Mommy, I want MY Mommy," the girl said, turning her head and looking around.

"I'm your Mommy now," Rose said.

"No, you're not Mommy. I want MY Mommy!" The girl said anxiously.

"I'm Mommy."

"No, No, No, No!" the girl was getting agitated. The social worker warned her about this, but Rose ignored her advice. She shouldn't have mentioned 'Mommy.'

"I'm Rose," she said, hoping the girl would forget 'Mommy.'

"Rose," the girl said more calmly, accepting it. "Rose."

"Would you like a cookie?" Rose held out a brown and white cookie to the girl. The girl took a small step forward with her tiny feet, and then hastily retreated.

"I won't hurt you, sweetheart," Rose said gently.

"Cookie." The girl said, in a small quiet voice, taking another step forward. She eyed Rose suspiciously and hesitated. Then she took another step, her eyes never leaving Rose's eyes.

It took a half an hour for her to accept the cookie. She was clearly afraid, and Rose knew that she was going to have to take it slow. Thomas called from the plant, and said that they needed him to work a double shift, and Rose was relieved. She didn't know how the girl was going to respond to Thomas. She wanted her daughter to be more comfortable before she introduced them. She continued to keep her distance, hiding under tables and behind the couch. Rose decided to ignore her, and go about her day, hoping she would eventually come out.

Rose started cooking dinner. She was making a roast, and after a while, the house started to smell of meat and vegetables. Rose made meatloaf and roast, and that was all she knew how to cook well. Everything else turned out bland or overcooked. She planned roast for tonight because it was a special night.

The house smelled good, warm, and comfortable.

After a couple of hours, Rose saw the girl come out from under the coffee table quietly.

Rose went back to busying herself, and tried not to look at the girl too much. She didn't want to make her any more scared than she already was.

When dinner was ready, Rose set two plates on the table and wordlessly sat down. She took small bites and waited. After a half hour, the girl came to the table and climbed on the chair opposite of Rose. Rose warmed up her food, cut it up into bite size pieces, set it down in front of her, and continued to eat. The girl poked at the food with her fork cautiously. Rose could tell that she was hungry, but she fought the urge to tell her to eat.

Finally, the girl took a bite. "Mmmm," she said quietly and then stopped suddenly.

Rose smiled at her. "That's okay," she said gently. "I'm happy you like it."

They ate the rest of the meal in silence, glancing at one another shyly from time to time.

When her plate was clean, Rose thought she still looked hungry. She had given her a lot, and had been surprised at how quickly she devoured it. She couldn't imagine that someone so tiny could consume so much. "Would you like more?"

The girl nodded, and her eyes got huge when Rose piled her plate completely full.

She started to eat the food from her second plate as quickly as she ate her first. "Slow down," Rose urged. "There will always be plenty of food for you to eat." The girl didn't listen, and she piled the food into her mouth until her plate was empty.

Rose sat and watched her in amazement.

When they were done eating, Rose asked her if she wanted a bath and the girl shook her head "no." Rose led the girl upstairs to her new bedroom where she had eagerly laid out pajamas earlier that morning. She wasn't sure what size she would be, so she bought three of the same nightgown, all in different sizes in anticipation that one of them would fit.

Rose was happy that dinner had gone so well, but there was still so much more ahead, and Rose continued to be nervous. She put the smallest nightgown on the girl, and was surprised that it was still so big on her. *She is so small for her age,* Rose thought in awe. The girl was about five, but she was the size of a three year old. After Rose had tucked her into her bed, Betsy her worn doll tucked in right next to her, she decided that it was time to try something.

"Brynn." Rose said, looking at the girl intently.

"No, I'm Eva." The girl said understanding what Rose was doing.

"No. You're Brynn now." Rose said carefully.

"No, I'm Eva." The girl repeated stubbornly.

"Brynn."

"Eva."

Rose was not going to call her Eva, but she decided not to push it with her for now. She didn't want to be reminded that she had been someone else's daughter. She knew that it was a big adjustment and that even though she was young, she had been through a lot. She expected from going through her file that she would be a weak, needy little thing. But after looking at her, she realized how strong and tenacious she must have been to survive on her own so young. After being abandoned so carelessly, she could have easily frozen or starved to death. Rose hated to think of all of the horrible things that could have happened to her.

The next couple of months were a blur. Rose got her daughter into a new routine and introduced her to their church and the neighbors. The girl clung to her now and wouldn't leave her side. She seemed to understand that Rose was her mother and that she wasn't going to leave her. Rose even took to sleeping in her room to keep her company and comfort her, although Thomas didn't like it at all. Rose didn't care. Her daughter was there now, and that was all that mattered.

It took months for the girl to answer to the name Brynn, but finally Rose's persistence paid off. Slowly, she seemed to forget all about her life as Eva.

Brynn learned to love her new Mommy, but she still cried out in the night for her other Mommy. Sometimes she just cried out for no reason, and Rose had to cradle her through the night. Eventually, she slept more peacefully through the night, much to Rose's relief.

Rose was finally happy.

Thomas realized that she no longer needed him. Rose refused to share his bed more and more often, preferring to sleep in Brynn's room instead.

His frustration started to get the better of him, and he started to drink more and more. He loved the smell and taste and the warmth of the whiskey. The whiskey was all that gave him peace. "I thought that adopting that little brat would help me and Rose to become closer. I thought she would be thankful, but now she wants nothin' to do with me." He mumbled into his glass while she was upstairs one night bathing the kid. "She hates me."

The kid was afraid of him, he could tell. *Stop looking at me like you're scared of me, you little shit*, he thought angrily. *Rose will know I don't like you, and I must like you for her sake. She doesn't know that I don't want you around. But now you're in the way, and she doesn't even smile at me anymore. She just smiles at you!*

Thomas felt foolish in his jealousy, but he wished that he had never agreed to let Rose buy her. It wasn't even his kid, and as much as he tried, he didn't like her. He knew that she had it tough early on, but he couldn't bring himself to feel bad for her.

She stood in the way of him and Rose, which is all he ever wanted.

But now it was too late.

Chapter Twelve

Brynn's Good Pain

Brynn liked watching the blood bubble up slowly from her skin as she drew the blade slowly across it. *It didn't hurt! It didn't hurt at all!* Brynn anticipated terrible pain, but there was none.

She always took her time, savoring it. It was a different pain than the harshness of his fists, his belt, and his hands. It was Brynn's pain, and she controlled it. She could make it hurt as much or as little as she wanted it to, depending on how deep she pushed the blade in. Sometimes it didn't even hurt at all, until after. Then she could feel it hurting all day, and it focused her. It kept her from thinking of how he chased her and dragged her on the floor to get a better hold of her. She didn't think about how his boots somehow found the same place in her ribs every time. The pain made her think of anything but how his big calloused hands clutched hard at her hair to make sure that she couldn't get away. It made her forget his hot whiskey breath on her face, curling her nostrils, making her gag.

Pop, pop, pop. She visualized the bead of blood popping up on her skin. She wiggled in her chair in her geometry class, feeling her skin, tight around her cut. *I bet there's a good scab growing over the cut by now. It's red, and fresh, and tight. If I pick at it, it will bleed. I wonder if I can make another cut right next to it.* She was obsessed, and it was the only thing that kept her from jumping out of her own skin all day.

The first time she hurt herself was an accident. She didn't even realize that she was doing it. She opened a can of pop and carelessly cut her finger on the inside of the can. She was fascinated for a minute with how it felt. Just that tiny thin slice in her finger consumed her, the blood only oozing for a moment, but the pain lasting for hours.

She realized that it distracted her. When she thought about the pain, she didn't think about him. For a few moments, she felt different—she felt better, she felt relief. She thought she should try to cut somewhere else on her body to see how it felt. Just once, she thought.

She found a razor blade in the medicine cabinet of Thomas and Rose's bathroom, and snuck it into her bathroom. She felt her heartbeat quicken. *What if it hurts too much? What if I like it? What if I cut too deep?* She was afraid, but she knew she would do it. She was too excited not to do it.

She didn't want anyone to know what she was doing. She thought her stomach might be her best choice since nobody would ever see her stomach. At thirteen, she thought who would ever see her stomach?

She stood in front of the full-length mirror and took a deep breath staring at her thin body. The girl looking back at her barely looked like her. She was small and thin, almost too thin. The eyes were too big for her face. *Just do it! Do it! Don't be afraid. It'll be fine. You liked when the can cut you. It was sweet.* It was a different pain from the sting of the belt and the ripping of hair.

Brynn took the razor out and her hands were trembling. She held it up to her side and held the cool metal against her skin for a brief moment. *Ouch! So sharp!* She saw a tiny bubble of blood rise up, and she stared at it for a long moment. She slowly drew the blade across her side making a long line from the middle of her stomach to around her side as far as she could. She didn't feel the pain at first as she just watched the blood pop up in a perfect thin line, fascinated. She thought about making another line, but she hesitated. She wanted to enjoy this one first. She wanted to think about this one for the rest of the day.

I can't believe how brave I am! I can do it! She was proud of herself.

She blotted up the blood with a tissue until it stopped bleeding. She was careful not to go too deep, even though she knew that she could go deeper. She didn't want to keep bleeding all day and give away her secret.

She didn't want anyone to know, not even Stacy. She just wanted to keep it to herself.

She got dressed after she bandaged her cut and she went to school. All day, she could feel it stinging as she moved, as she sat in class, as she ate lunch with Stacy in the cafeteria. She thought about the scar that must be forming by now and felt strangely happy.

Stacy never saw Brynn happy. It was something they had in common. She thought that she even saw Brynn smiling to herself, and she was curious.

At the end of the day, Brynn realized that she hadn't thought about Thomas once. She was so obsessed with her secret scar that she didn't feel choked up as she usually did. She almost felt free as her mind was distracted with her secret.

She didn't know how she survived up to this point without something else to occupy her mind. *How have I lived this long without doing this?*

She couldn't wait to do it again.

The next day she found herself with the razor blade in hand staring at the girl in the mirror again. *Do it again! Cut somewhere new!* She stared at herself naked, focusing only on the smooth skin of her stomach, and her cut from the day before. She cut a perfect straight line above the other one. She took her time, savoring the feel of the blade against her skin. She hoped that this could be her salvation.

At thirteen, she already knew that without this, she would have nothing, and that she would be nothing. Without this pain, that she could control and find her peace in, the other pain would overcome her, overtaking her. The pain of her birth mother leaving her, and her father hating her, would consume her, and she knew that she would die.

She knew that this tiny sharp blade would save her.

CHAPTER THIRTEEN

Thomas

Thomas was sick.

He hadn't felt well for days, for years. In fact, he couldn't remember the last time that he had felt well. But this was different. He was nauseous and his stomach hurt. It didn't stop him from drinking his Wild Turkey every day after work, but he cut back by a drink or two hoping that would help.

He rarely ate lately, and he knew he was losing weight.

"I made meatloaf," Rose said when he came home from the plant on Monday night. Brynn was staying over at her friend Stacy's house. She was glad that Brynn had her friend. She knew that their secret was safe because she knew that Stacy's dad hit her, too. Everyone knew.

Rose was a terrible cook, but for some reason she could cook meatloaf well, and roast. Thomas blamed her mother, Clara, who always thought she was above cooking so she never gave it much effort. She refused to cook with any seasoning and everything she made was dry and bland. Rose cooked the same way. But her meatloaf was a mystery. It was actually quite good, and she made it at least once a week. Brynn hated meatloaf, so on meatloaf night she would stay at Stacy's house.

She had his drink waiting for him when he walked in.

"Thank you," he mumbled sneaking a look at her when she

turned away. He knew she was plain, but to him she was pretty. He always thought she was pretty.

He had never been able to talk to girls very well, and when he got older, he couldn't talk to women. Women always made him so uncomfortable but he never felt uncomfortable around Rose. Maybe it was because of her plainness, but even when they were kids in church, he liked to be around her.

His daddy hadn't loved his momma, and he had only talked mean to her. He had never really heard a man talk to a woman in a normal way. Try as he might, his tongue always got twisted up, and he could never get his words out the right way. So he stopped trying. Except with Rose.

But Rose never really liked him much. In fact, she had never cared for any man much. She hadn't even wanted to marry, but she knew that she would have to get married in order to have a child.

He knew that he would need to get married because he wanted someone to cook and clean for him. He wanted someone to watch TV with who would keep him company. He also wanted someone that he could take his sexual tension out on when he needed to. He really never pictured himself with anyone but Rose. He had gone out with other girls as his friends had. He had even done *it* with other girls like all boys were supposed to. But he always felt awkward doing it with the other girls because the only person he wanted to do it with was Rose. He could tell that she didn't like it, only tolerated it with the hope they would create a baby. He didn't want a baby. He never wanted a baby. He didn't know what he would do with a baby. The only thing he wanted was Rose, and he was able to get her, but she made it clear that she didn't love him and never would. He knew that he was her only chance to marry, and he was happy about that. It made it simple for him, and easy. But he wanted her to like him at least and not cringe when he touched her to let her know he wanted her.

It frustrated him to have her there knowing how much she disliked him. He felt like exploding sometimes when he felt his feelings were going to boil over. But she never saw it in him. She only saw him as someone to pay the bills and give her a roof over her head, and even then, she didn't appreciate him. She only tolerated him.

He thought in the beginning that if he could get her to marry him, she would eventually grow to love him. He had liked her since the first time he had seen her in Sunday school. She hadn't remembered, but he had picked her a flower at their Sunday school picnic. She had looked at him so sweetly, and from then on, he had been smitten. But he had always been too shy to ask her on a proper date. He had gone out with other girls, prettier girls, but they never really wanted to talk or date the right way. They just wanted to fool around in the hopes that they could get him to marry them. He was happy to fool around with them, but his thoughts always went to Rose. He could never understand why he liked her so much.

After all, she was tall and gangly, and plain. He didn't figure she was very smart because her Momma always said she was lucky to barely finish high school. But by then, he already had a job lined up at the plant where his daddy had worked, and he had already planned to marry her.

It all worked out exactly as he had planned, except for her falling in love with him. He had become his father, and she was becoming his mother, with that worn sad look about her.

He wanted to be different with Rose, but most of his friends were the same way with their wives when they wouldn't cooperate or listen. He hated it, and he knew that it made her hate him all the more, but there was nothing he could do about it now. The dice had already been rolled.

When he finally gave in, and let her adopt that little shit kid, he knew that it was all over for him. He would never have a chance to win her over. At first, he thought it would help her to see how much he really cared for her. He had truly tried everything he could to win her over, but when he offered to buy her things, she refused. She didn't need fancy clothes and the house was fine the way it was she had told him over and over. She just wanted a child, and he was clearly disappointing her by not giving her one. So he gave in. And now she loved the kid more than he would ever love her.

Why can't she see how I look at her? She's so wrapped up in that snot nosed brat that she can't even see me. She barely even lets me touch her now.

He knew that hitting the kid was bad for his cause, but when he drank the whiskey, he couldn't stop himself. He knew the kid liked him because she looked at him, always waiting for him to talk to her, but he never liked kids. They were loud, snotty, needy, and they always broke shit. He never wanted one.

He tried, for Rose's sake, to be nice to her. He even bought her stuff as Daddy's were supposed to do, and that seemed to make Rose happy. But when it was clear that he was always going to be at the bottom of the barrel in Rose's eyes, he figured it didn't matter anymore what he did. Maybe if he just drank his whiskey, and did what came natural, she would at least pay attention to him more. And she did.

When I'm hitting her, at least I get to touch her. I can make her look at me, and I can punish her for not loving me, for taunting me. I can at least put my face close to hers, breathing her in. It's the only time I can get close to her, push myself against her, and wrap my hands around her neck. I can feel her heart pounding through her chest. I can hurt her the way that she is hurting me. I must be the only crazy man to love such a plain looking bitch like her. How dare she not love me? She doesn't even try!

He knew that he wasn't an ugly man. He was rough and rugged. His hands were permanently stained with dirt and grease in the cracks of his skin, but he earned an honest living. Despite being a little thin from drinking too much, he knew that his body had held up pretty well for his age. He was strong and looked decent in his Sunday suit. He even got some looks now and then from the ladies in town. But Rose never looked at him.

He knew that after he started hitting the kid, he would never have a chance with Rose. But he hated that needy kid. The kid stood between Rose and him. Thomas knew that she was the only person in the world that Rose loved.

He was surprised when Rose started cooking for him. She could only cook two decent meals, but now she made one at least once a week for him. On that night, she always sent the kid away. *Is it because she is starting to love?*

"How was your day?" Rose asked tentatively.

"Fine," he said in his usual low, gravelly tone. He was surprised she was talking to him, because she never initiated conversation, "Yours?"

"It was fine. I went to the store and got some things. I got that chocolate cream pie you like." Rose said quietly.

Thomas grunted in acknowledgement, "Thanks."

He liked the quiet. The kid talked too much. He liked when she wasn't there. When she was, she and Rose chattered like a couple of magpies. He always took his dinner into the TV room, and shut the door so he didn't have to listen to their constant chitchat. When he came home, he didn't want to hear all the noise. He just wanted quiet. He liked when the kid was gone, and it was just him and Rose. He could sneak looks at her over his glass, and she would sit and ignore him in silence. It was unusual for her to talk to him, and he liked it. He liked the sound of her voice.

"Maybe after dinner, we can watch that police show you like so much," she said looking at him directly in the eyes, her brown eyes meeting his blue ones. She rarely looked at him directly.

"Uh, that would be good." She made him nervous when she looked at him.

He took a big drink of his whiskey. His first sip had an odd taste, sweet. He took another big swallow and decided it was fine. It was a strange night. He wasn't used to interacting with Rose this much. He liked it, but it unnerved him. He wasn't feeling anxious tonight like he usually felt. He felt anxious in a different way. He didn't think that he would hit Rose tonight no matter how much whiskey he drank.

He found himself hoping they would have another meatloaf night again soon.

Chapter Fourteen

Brynn's Great Escape

Adam had been watching her since the eighth grade, but she never knew it. She wasn't like the other girls in their town who hung out at the McDonald's with their friends, or went to the mall in the next big town, or giggled whenever he walked by. She wasn't like anyone he had ever met, and he was intrigued.

He finally got up the courage to talk to her in the ninth grade. They sat next to each other in English class, and she pretended not to notice him. She also pretended not to notice how he raced to sit next to her in class, practically shoving poor little Kenny Miner out of the way. Kenny didn't even know what hit him.

She pretended not to notice him for as long as she possibly could, but she found herself thinking about him, in spite of herself. After not noticing boys her entire life, she somehow felt as if she had developed a sixth sense. She always knew when he was nearby, and she could see him out of the corner of her eye. She didn't want to like him, and even though they hadn't ever talked, for some inexplicable reason, she felt drawn to him by an invisible thread.

She didn't know what she was doing. At an early age, she made the choice that she was never going to get married or fall in love. She didn't believe in happy families and happy endings. She knew too much of real life with her family, and with Stacy's family, to know how it really was.

She also knew, when people loved each other, they saw each other naked, and she didn't want anyone to see. She thought about her blade, and how she did it for herself. Sharing it with someone else seemed impossible. She didn't want anyone to know, especially not a boy.

Brynn's only goal in life was to get out of town, and she knew that going to college far away was the only way to do that, so she worked hard and was an excellent student.

Rose always bragged to people about her smart daughter. Whether they were on the subject or not, she found a way to say, "My daughter, Brynn, has a perfect GPA! She is one of the smartest girls in her class." Complete strangers smiled politely, and walked away as quickly as they could. But Rose was proud of Brynn, even though she knew that she would leave her one day.

She talked Momma and Thomas into letting her get a job as soon as she was the legal age to start working. She was lucky enough to get a job at the busiest little family restaurant in town. Much to Brynn's surprise, Momma let her, and Thomas only agreed because she could start paying rent.

Even though she was young, she interviewed well, and the older couple that owned the restaurant took to her right away.

"I promise, I'll be a good employee, and I'll work hard! I'm a quick study, and I'll do everything you ask me to do," she pleaded to the sweet old man asking her all the questions. "You won't ever have to worry about me."

He believed her, and he started Brynn as a hostess, greeting people and cleaning tables. When she begged him to teach her everything he could, he did. They came to depend on Brynn, and she became as family to them.

They figured they could make her a manager for them one day, and possibly retire. They were disappointed when she told them that she had other plans, but they decided to teach her anyway, so that when she moved, she could get a job in any restaurant doing anything. It was as though this was what she was meant to do. She insisted that, although she loved it, it wasn't for her for the rest of her life. She wanted to make a lot of money so that she would never have to rely on a man to take care of her, like Rose relied on Thomas.

Brynn was happy that the older couple taught her so much. She was making decent money, and she happily stashed all of the cash that she made in a shoebox in her closet buried under a pile of shoes and clothes. It was her escape money. The rest she put in the bank after Thomas took out his cut. She had long since stopped calling him Daddy and referred to him now only as Thomas which he didn't seem to mind.

Brynn couldn't wait to leave town. And she never thought about any of the boys in her school until Adam Michael sat next to her in English. She was starting to fill her bras out more, and her acne was clearing up. But she didn't hang out with the popular kids or dress for any other purpose than to be practical.

When Adam sat next to her, she knew who he was. He was the only boy who didn't tease and make fun of the girls, or pick on the smaller boys. She thought well of him because he was scrappy, and because he didn't care what anyone thought about him. He wanted to be everyone's friend, and it didn't matter if they were smaller, smarter, weaker, or less popular than he was. She decided that she liked that about him.

He was smart, too, and even better at math than she was. He was talking about college already when most boys in their small town only cared about the Friday night Football game.

The first note he ever passed to her simply said "Hi." When she read it, she couldn't help but smile. She looked over at him and he had smiled back, a nice shy smile, his deep dark blue eyes twinkled with mischief. She noticed that sometimes his eyes were as blue as the ocean, and other times they glittered like beautiful sapphires. They were bold and beautiful, not like the watered down blue in Thomas' eyes.

The second note he passed her said "there."

Brynn giggled without realizing it, and was surprised. She never giggled, and she wondered what was happening to her. She put the note in her worn copy of Jane Eyre, and she kept her eyes straight ahead for the rest of the class, even though she could see him stealing glances at her out of the corner of her eye.

"You liked my note?" He caught her after class. Adam was smiling as he did in class, and Brynn felt like mush inside. She had never really talked to a boy before, especially not someone as cute as Adam, and she had no idea what to say.

"Yes. I got your note." Her voice was barely audible and she fidgeted uncomfortably. *He is so cute, oh my goodness.* He was standing much closer to her than any boy had ever stood before. She felt her palms start to sweat, and her shirt suddenly felt too tight. She was warm.

"You didn't pass back." He was baiting her, and she could feel it.

"I don't pass notes in class," she said straightening up a little. "I don't like to get in trouble." *His voice is driving me crazy. Is it really that deep?*

"Why would you get in trouble? It's just a note." He was laughing at her, she could tell.

She didn't like when people laughed at her. "I don't break the rules."

He could tell by Brynn's tone that she was frustrated with him. That's why he liked her. She was different. Sometimes when he looked at her, she looked so sad, and other times she looked indignant. She always looked like she knew what she was doing, especially in class when she was smart and confident, and he liked that about her, too. But he never really saw her happy, and when she giggled in class he felt happy. He knew that, for some reason, he needed this girl in his life. He needed to be able to make her happy.

He was going to say something else when he realized that she had walked away.

Adam spent the entire rest of the year trying to get Brynn's attention. She ignored him. She decided that no matter how cute he was that she didn't like him. She knew that he would just end up hurting her in the end. His note was funny, but he was making fun of her, and she didn't like that. It confused her how he could be funny and cute one moment, but was mean the next, and it scared her. She was mistaken about him. She wondered how she could think that he was nice and good to everyone, when she was certain he was just like the other boys.

"I don't have time for boys," she said to Stacy about a week after the note-passing incident while sitting at her special place, the dock. She had found it by accident one day on her way home from school and knew instantly that the rippling of the water and the sound of the lake could give her some much-needed peace. It was the only place she could go and hide completely, and Stacy was the one person on earth she trusted it with.

It was their special place, where they escaped to talk and dream, and sort out the ugliness in their life that nobody else could understand but them.

"I have to work and save money to get out of here. I can't take being here much longer. Thomas doesn't hit me anymore, but he drinks so much now that he is always getting sick. And Momma, she just won't leave him."

"I know how you feel," Stacy said quietly, although she didn't know what it was like to have a boy who liked her. She was much quieter than her best friend was, and not quite as good in school. Her only salvation was Brynn and the chocolate cupcakes her mom baked for her every day. She figured it was her mom's way of apologizing for her father, so she felt obliged to eat them.

Brynn looked at her only friend.

Too many chocolate cupcakes.

Brynn wondered if their lives hadn't been so similar, if they would've ever been friends. They met in Kindergarten and gravitated toward each other like the pull of the earth to the sun. And they circled one another throughout their school years, even if they weren't in the same classes. She loved her friend, and Brynn understood her, but she felt that they were growing up and growing apart. She was worried.

Brynn wanted to have other friends. But she didn't look like them, or dress like them, and she found that she didn't share the same interests as most girls in her class. She always kept a low profile whenever possible immersing herself in her studies, or going to work, just as Rose had taught her.

"What are you going to do when you get out of high school?" Brynn asked Stacy.

"I don't know," Stacy shrugged. It was a small gesture, and hard to tell as her shoulders had been getting broader, along with the rest of her, throughout the school year, "I guess I'll go to college, get a job."

Brynn gave Stacy a lecture on her grades. *You have to try.* Stacy refused to try. She ate cupcakes all night in her room with the door locked and the TV on, so she wouldn't have to hear her parents fight. She never studied and her grades reflected it. Stacy had been smart throughout elementary and junior high, but when she got to high school, she gave up. Brynn was afraid for her.

"You know that I'll be going away," Brynn said looking her in the eye. Stacy looked down.

"I know, then you'll leave me, and I'll be alone."

"You could get your grades up. Come with," Brynn said earnestly.

"I don't have money to go to college. You know that. I don't have a job like you do. I'm not going with you," Stacy's voice was low, defeated.

"The only reason I'm getting out is because I set up a PO Box and have college applications coming to me. You could have some sent to you! Why wouldn't you?" Brynn didn't understand it.

Stacy looked at her pretty friend with the dark brown hair, beautiful skin, and big luminous brown eyes that seemed to stare right through you. Brynn was completely oblivious to just how beautiful she was, and part of Stacy was jealous, and the other part was in awe at how naïve her friend really was. She had always known that Brynn would get out of their town. She never belonged there to begin with. Stacy always knew that Brynn would leave, just as Stacy knew that she wouldn't. Stacy's mother, and her mother before her, never left. The kids who grew up in her town just stayed, married their high school sweethearts, had babies, and then repeated the cycle all over again. But Brynn was different from the rest of them. Never once in her mind did she accept that fate, although Stacy had a long time ago.

"You know that I'm not like you. I'll never get more than a high school education! I'll end up marrying some boy like my Daddy, if I even get married at all." Stacy said trying not to sound angry. It wasn't Brynn's fault that Brynn was exceptional. When she looked at Brynn, she was surprised that they were friends. Brynn was even prettier than most of those stuck up cheerleaders, the ones who made fun of her and called her "Stacy Pastry."

Brynn should have been friends with one of them, but instead she was friends with Stacy Pastry. Stacy was always waiting for the day that Brynn realized that she was friends with the ugly fat girl. "You're always lecturing me on my grades, but I'm not going anywhere! The only reason you're going somewhere is that you weren't born in this shit hole like everyone else. You'll get out because Rose isn't you're real Momma."

Stacy knew that eating all those cupcakes would make her fatter. But she already knew how fat and ugly she was, because Daddy told her all the time. He didn't know how he could have such a fat pig for a daughter. Stacy's other sisters were thin and pretty, and Daddy was nice to them, too nice if you asked Stacy.

She wanted to be fat so that her Daddy would hate her. Getting a beating every now and again was much better than the other thing. The thing her sister's got.

She knew that Brynn would get out. She never belonged there to begin with, and Stacy dreaded that day. She knew that when Brynn left, she would be alone, completely. Stacy didn't know how she could make it without her best and only friend.

Chapter Fifteen

Brynn Discovers Eva

If I hide, he won't find me. I can run and find Mommy! Brynn was running in a dark place. But she was so confused. In her dream, she was a different person. She was someone else, someone much smaller, and her name was Eva.

She was running, running, running. Someone was calling after her to stop. *I just want to help you little girl, please stop! I won't hurt you, I promise!* She could hear fast clicking, like boots on pavement. Running, panting. He kept running after her. It was dark and cold. She was cold, hungry, and tired. She was so tired, she just wanted to sleep, but she couldn't find anywhere she felt safe enough to sleep. Her clothes were wet and she couldn't feel her fingers or her toes.

She hadn't eaten in so long! It felt like days, or was it longer? She was so hungry that her tummy was growly. The last thing she ate was *crackers?* She was in pain but couldn't stop running. She had to find Mommy!

She was trying to find something to eat in a garbage can, but the man started calling after her. He wanted to grab her and stop her, and she couldn't let him! She had to keep looking. She was looking everywhere, walking everywhere. Her feet hurt.

She was running, and the man was chasing her. He said he wanted to help her, but she couldn't stop until she found Mommy.

She was falling! *Mommy! I want to find my Mommy!* Falling, head over feet, many hard things poking, falling, and not stopping. Pain!

Lots of pain.

I'm bleeding! She felt her head and there was blood, lots of blood. She tried to stand up but couldn't. She could hear the man still calling after her. She was far away. Maybe if she were quiet, the man couldn't find her. *My leg hurts! Mommy! Mommy! Come and get me! Mommy!*

Brynn woke up screaming. Adam had already gone to work and she was alone.

She reached up and touched the mystery scar right above her eyebrow. *Is that how I got my scar or was it just a dream? Did I break my leg? Who's Eva?*

Brynn was upset. This felt different from a dream. *Was it a memory?*

It upset her that she had virtually no memories from her childhood. She only had the bad ones and she spent years trying to block those out. But she had been almost five when Rose adopted her, so why didn't she remember anything? It never made sense to her.

I wonder if my life would have been better with them. She used to think about her birth parents all the time, but now it seemed less and less. Her dream felt so real, and it made her heart ache as if she were missing someone, her mother. Brynn wondered for the thousandth time what she looked like, what she had been like. She often wondered, *'what parts of me look like my mother? My face? My eyes? Whose lips do I have... my mother, or my father? Am I anything at all like them?'*

Brynn wondered who she would have become if she had been loved by her birth mother and birth father. Even though she didn't have her own children, she couldn't imagine leaving her own child. She assumed she was abandoned. There was no other explanation.

She didn't know much about what happened to her, but she knew she was found by someone and then taken to the police after she was discovered. Brynn knew that when she was found she was hungry and that she not in the best condition physically.

Adam always laughed at her because she agonized over throwing away something simple like a pair of shoes but she couldn't imagine throwing away an entire person.

Where would I be without my sadness, my angst? Who would I be? If it weren't for Adam, I don't know what I would do. He is the only one who brings me happiness.

Her birth parents were a mystery that she would never know. She tried putting her name in with the adoption agency to reconnect with her birth family, but she didn't hear anything, and didn't really expect to. Brynn gave up hope long ago that she would ever find them, and didn't feel that the effort was worth the disappointment. After all, she reminded herself, they didn't want her. They didn't even try to make sure that she was safe or taken care of... they simply left her.

As a child, Brynn imagined that they died in a horrific car accident and that she was the only survivor. She reasoned that they didn't leave her at all, but by some sad twist of fate, their leaving her was beyond their control, and that they loved her very much. But nothing that Brynn knew supported that theory.

All that Brynn wanted was a connection to someone. She thought that if she could find it, life would somehow make sense. How could she have been abandoned, only to end up in a home where her father hated her and hurt her? It didn't make reasonable sense that the universe could turn out to be so cruel.

The only thing that Brynn and Rose had in common was that they both had brown hair and brown eyes. But that is where any other physical similarity ended. They were nearly opposite in every other way, especially in their personalities. Rose was awkward and tentative, while Brynn was confident and strong. Strangers who didn't know that Brynn was adopted were always baffled that they were mother and daughter, because they were as different as night and day.

Brynn thought that Rose may know who "Eva" was, or if that had been her name as a baby. She had asked Rose repeatedly about her past for as long as she could remember. Rose refused to tell her anything, although Brynn could always tell she was hiding something. Rose simply wanted to pretend that Brynn's only past was with her.

Brynn drove over to Rose's apartment not sure of what she would find. It was a quick ten-minute drive, but it felt longer.

When Brynn walked up to her apartment door, she knocked. She had a key, but she knocked anyway.

As always, Rose was overly happy to see her.

She greeted Brynn at the door with a lit cigarette, a dirty housecoat with snaps up the front, and no teeth. She was clearly not expecting company.

"Hold on honey, I'll be right back" she said quickly and scurried off to the bathroom. When she reappeared, she had her false teeth in, and she had combed her hair. But she remained in the dirty housecoat, and still had the lit cigarette.

Brynn hated smoking. She made it clear to Rose when she took up the habit that she couldn't stand it. Just the smell of it made her flashback to Thomas, and his horrible breath. Rose took a long drag, and stubbed it out in an overfull ashtray sitting on the kitchen counter.

Her apartment was large, but very dirty. It looked like she hadn't cleaned in weeks or longer. It reeked of cigarette smoke and dirty clothes. Brynn gagged.

"I haven't cleaned in a while," Rose said unapologetically.

"A while? Mom, it doesn't look like you've cleaned, ever!"

"Well, hello to you, too. You haven't come by to check on me as much as you should. Now you do, and you're going to criticize? That's rude." Rose was agitated. Rose knew that Brynn and Adam were fighting. Brynn had even asked her what to do, but Rose ignored her. She didn't know what to tell her, and she wasn't going to pretend to, either. It still didn't give Brynn an excuse for not coming to the apartment for a couple of weeks.

"I'm sorry, Mom. I just haven't been up for anything," Brynn said apologetically. *God, I need to get a cleaning lady in here as soon as possible.* "Do you want a drink? I have pop," Rose said as she tried to sound gracious.

Brynn looked around the apartment trying to find a place to sit. There were clothes everywhere. Opened cans of chips and pop littered the entire apartment. There was an ashtray every five feet, and they were all overflowing with butts. Brynn was thankful that the apartment building didn't allow pets. She couldn't imagine if she had an animal in there, too. *When was the last time I came in here?*

Wasn't it just a couple of weeks ago? God, it smells.

"No, Mom, I'm good." Brynn said not looking at her. She didn't want Rose to see the disgust in her eyes. When she had been younger, Rose had been a pristine housekeeper. Brynn didn't understand the change. How long had it looked like this? Brynn had been picking her up for their outings and dropping her off, and she hadn't seen the inside of the apartment for a while.

"Well, sit, sit." Rose said reaching for her cigarettes in the pocket of her housecoat. She hesitated as she looked at Brynn.

"Oh, Mom, do you have to smoke?" Brynn asked not attempting to hide her disgust now.

"I suppose I can wait, even though this *is* my apartment." Rose said sarcastically.

Brynn thought she was not acting like herself. Rose rarely used sarcasm. And wherever Brynn was concerned, she was usually gentler and kinder.

"Sorry, Mom, but it's so bad for you. And secondhand smoke is horrible for... anyway. I have a question to ask you." Brynn took a deep breath and paused, "Did you name me Brynn, or was that always my name?"

Rose froze and avoided her eyes, pretending to look in the pockets of her housecoat for something. "Why do you want to know?"

"I had a dream last night, and I was a little girl named 'Eva'. Does that sound familiar to you at all?" Brynn asked slowly.

Rose didn't respond. She didn't say anything, and Brynn was frustrated. She had faced Rose's refusal to answer any of the questions about her short life before she was her daughter for as long as she could remember. Brynn anticipated this response from her. She *never* had a memory in the form of a dream before, and if that's what it was, then she *needed to know*.

"Mother, please!" Brynn pleaded.

Rose ignored her. She reached into her pocket again and pulled out a cigarette. She looked evenly at Brynn and lit it, taking a big long drag.

"Are you going to answer me at all?" Brynn asked, her voice taking on a sharp edge to it. "Was I a little girl named Eva?"

Rose reached for her hand. Brynn couldn't allow herself to be touched lately. She didn't know why, but it felt like an intrusion into her soul when someone touched her. She usually maintained a distinct barrier. She typically recoiled anytime anyone tried to be affectionate with her in any way. But this time, Brynn allowed her to take her hand.

"You were named something with an 'E'. Eva, Evie, Edie. It was hard to tell." Rose said quietly.

"How do you know?" Brynn asked thirsty for any truth to her past.

"Because that is what you called yourself when you came to me." Rose said, almost shamefully.

"Why didn't you keep my name?" Brynn asked.

"I didn't want you to be someone else's child anymore. I wanted you to be my Brynn. I wanted to start out clean. I didn't want you to be someone else's anymore." Rose said irritated with the question. "I wanted a baby more than anything. I would have loved it if you had come out of my body, but you didn't. I didn't want to be reminded that someone else carried you for nine months."

"Did I break my leg or hurt myself in any way?"

"Yes, you broke your leg. That's why there was such a gap between when they found you, your first foster home, and when you were adopted. Your leg had to heal"

"So what happened to me, Mother? Why didn't you tell me any of this?" Brynn was angry. *Rose knew this all along! What else does she know?*

"I didn't like to think about it. You were so little, and to think of you running and hiding, and trying to find food to eat," Rose paused, clearly affected. "They said you were always looking for your Mommy. You were running when they were trying to help you. They only caught you because you fell and broke your leg. They didn't know how long you were alone. Months? A year? You were always looking for your Mommy. Even in your dreams, you were looking for her. But I wanted to be your Mommy. I *was* your Mommy."

Rose was smoking fast and furious. "The first foster home you were in didn't work out because you were so difficult to deal with.

You kept trying to run away to find her. They couldn't keep up with you and you refused to stay with them."

"But why didn't you tell me? I've asked you a thousand times to tell me what you know, and you never did! Do you know what happened to my parents?" Brynn pressed Rose determined to get an answer.

"They searched for your parents and nobody reported you missing, so nobody knew where you were missing from. You were even on the news. After a year of finding you and nobody claiming you, they were able to put you up for adoption. And that is when I found you. And then I gave you a home."

"You gave me a home, mother. But it wasn't a happy home! You made us stay with that bastard instead of saving us from him. You never protected me, and you just let him hurt me over and over!"

"I did the best I could. I couldn't leave him! He took care of us. I couldn't have done that on my own," Rose's words were ignored. Brynn had heard it all before.

"You could have left! Other women have left in that situation. But not you! You were too weak! What kind of mother allows someone to treat her child so cruelly and doesn't protect them?" Brynn was exasperated with Rose. Rose never gave her a clear answer, and she felt her frustration mounting. She was angry with Rose for being so evasive and so nee

Brynn couldn't understand how Rose wanted a child for so long, but then allowed Thomas to break her.

"I did protect you." Rose looked like she was going to throw up. She was feeling nauseous. She stubbed her cigarette out, nearly missing the ashtray. "If you only knew what I did to protect you."

"You made it seem like it was normal what he did. You made it seem like he wasn't horrible for what he did. You told me that they would take me away from you. You knew how afraid I was of being left alone, and you used it to keep me in that house while he hurt us!" Brynn never said these things to Rose. She didn't want to hurt her, but it was as though her words had no choice as they started tumbling out of her. "You were a weak, cowardly woman. And you were a horrible mother. I wish... I wish... you weren't my mother."

And for the first time, it was true.

CHAPTER SIXTEEN

Rose's Diagnosis

Rose couldn't find her keys.

She lost her keys all of the time lately. She was never someone who lost things. Instead, she knew where she kept everything. But lately she couldn't seem to keep track of anything. Her reading glasses were constantly missing, her keys, her purse, her checkbook. She couldn't find anything, and it was so frustrating.

Shortly after Thomas died, she realized that she started forgetting little things. She started forgetting items that she was shopping for at the store. Then she started forgetting doctor's appointments, and when to pay her bills. She found that if she didn't write it down, she couldn't remember anything.

It was becoming more and more frustrating for Brynn, although she just thought it was more carelessness than anything else. Brynn had finally gotten the cleaning lady into Rose's apartment, and told herself that she would need to check in on Rose and the apartment more often.

"Brynn, my lights won't work," Rose called her from her cell phone, sitting in the living room in the dark.

"Mom, did you forget to pay your electric bill again?" Brynn sighed.

"I don't remember."

"I'll call the electric company, Mother."

"Brynn, I don't have water coming out of the faucet," Rose called a month later.

"Mom, did you pay the water bill?" Brynn sighed.

"I don't remember."

"I'll call." It was a regular thing for Brynn to call a utility company until she was forced to take over Rose's finances.

Now it was daily that Rose lost her keys, or forgot to put on shoes, and she was even starting to forget the names of people she had always known.

Then Rose forgot Brynn's birthday. She never forgot Brynn's birthday. When Brynn didn't receive a call from her at six in the morning with her singing both verses of "Happy Birthday", she knew something was very wrong. Brynn thought it was strange, but Rose refused to let her go to the doctor with her. Rose knew what he was going to say which was why she put off going for so long.

The doctor told Rose that Alzheimer's was difficult to diagnose, but that was the direction he was leaning based on her history. He said that they would perform tests, and continue to track her condition. Clara, Rose's Momma died from Alzheimer's, although they called it dementia at the time. When the final diagnosis came in, early onset Alzheimer's, Rose wasn't surprised one bit. She asked the doctor how much time she had, and he responded soberly that he had no way of knowing.

"You seem to be in the second stage, Rose," he said slowly. She had been his patient for years, and he found that if he talked slowly to her, she wouldn't ask him to repeat it another three or four times. Rose liked to have all of the facts because she said Brynn would want to know. "It could be months, it could be years. But I do know that the smoking is bad for you, Rose. You have to stop. It will create other issues and expedite the Alzheimer's."

She scoffed stubbornly. "I'm not giving up smoking now, Doc. I just started, and this is one thing in my life I really like!"

"I would recommend that you start thinking about an Alzheimer's facility where they can take care of you properly." Her Doctor told her already knowing what her response would be.

"My Brynn will take care of me," she said indignantly. Rose knew what her diagnosis meant. She knew that it meant that she would forget who she was, how to go to the bathroom, and walk. She would forget how to dress herself, how to eat and to swallow. But worst of all, she knew that she would inevitably forget her Brynn. Rose knew she would forget how she had protected and loved her. But in the meantime, Rose knew that Brynn would take care of her.

Rose also knew that it would not be a pretty or graceful exit. Clara refused to allow her to stay with her when she was dying. She was a prideful woman, and didn't want anyone to watch her suffer while she was in her worst state. Father told her that Clara didn't remember a soul when she died. Father died shortly after from a broken heart, so Rose had no one to talk to about Clara now.

Rose hadn't thought of her mother for over a decade now. Now she wished that she had been able to ask Clara how it felt to lose her mind, forgetting every single thing or person that she had ever known and loved. But she knew that Clara never would have told her. Conversations between Rose and Clara always involved Clara talking 'at' Rose, and voicing how much of a disappointment that Rose was. Rose sadly knew that Clara wouldn't have opened up to her about something so personal.

Rose didn't want Brynn to know about the diagnosis. She didn't want to be even more of a disappointment to her. Brynn would still be there for her, even though she had felt a strange distance from her recently. Rose thought that hiding this from Brynn could be something that she could do for her as a way of taking care of her. It would be one of two very important gifts that Rose could ever give to Brynn, even though she wouldn't realize it right away.

Rose went out, and she bought ten packets of sticky notes, two packets of pens, and she started to leave herself notes for everything.

When Brynn asked how her doctor's appointment went, she simply told her she just had low blood sugar.

CHAPTER SEVENTEEN

Leaving Brynn

"Shit!" he was screaming at her, his handsome face was distorted with anger and bright red. "Why does everything have to be such a fight with you, Brynn? Why can't it just ever be about us? Why is it always about every other damned person in the world?"

Brynn was angry, too. Her big dark eyes were almost black, her eyebrows furrowed. Her mouth was pulled into a thin line. She dared not speak for fear that ugly words would come flying out. He never understood how much Rose needed her, and how tired she was. Her restaurant was a popular destination and busy, which she could not complain about. She had worked hard for six years and hired a great manager, Jane. Now the restaurant was on autopilot with the usual hiccups arising from time to time. But at least she had people she could trust, when she would let them. When she was there, she was lost to the rest of the world, including him. It was her sanctuary and the one place where she didn't have to think too much about life.

Adam never understood that about her. He couldn't understand how she couldn't turn things off, and just enjoy herself. Even when they were in high school, she was like that, but he thought she would just grow out of it. He was realizing that she wasn't growing out of it, and it frustrated him.

Brynn's phone rang. It was that distinctive ring, Rose's ring. She fumbled as she silenced it. This just wasn't the time. *She always knows just when to call!*

Adam turned away. It was becoming a familiar scene between them, angry and repetitive. The frustration was ongoing and palpable in every encounter, to the point that they were beginning to avoid one another. They were watching TV in separate rooms, reading the newspaper in silence, and finding reasons to not spend time together. They started slipping farther and farther apart without realizing it, more out of apathy than anger.

Now he was angry, and he had every right to be this time. But she fought him as she always did. Even when he was right, she still fought. It drove him crazy that she wouldn't just admit when she was wrong. It was as though she had something to prove all of the time, and it was becoming harder and harder to be married to her. He was tired of the constant battles. *Is everyone's marriage this difficult all of the time? Dammit!*

She was late again, an hour this time. She didn't call him because she knew he would yell at her, so she did nothing. They both knew that her chronic lateness was a sore point for him, and Brynn always had an excuse, which was even more frustrating.

Brynn thought for sure she would get out on time, this one time.

Then one of the waitresses came to her after her shift and asked if she could confide in her. It was bad timing and Brynn had been rushing all day to get out of work early so that she could get home and get ready. Brynn was conflicted as usual about leaving early, but she knew it was important and that she needed to.

"Please, Mrs. Michael, it won't take long, I promise."

Brynn couldn't say no. She had taken a gamble on hiring Lucia, and she had won big. She loved how hard the girl worked and Brynn was unable to refuse her in anything from the first moment she met her.

Brynn fell in love with restaurants when she worked for the older couple, and she realized early on that it was in her destiny to have one of her own. She graduated with a Business Degree in college, and saved as much money as she could while working at a popular local restaurant. Before she graduated, she started to scout

out places of her own. She found one in the city where she and Adam were planning to move. It was once a popular place, but service and quality declined over the years, and so did business. The present owners were selling it for a song.

Adam's parents fell in love with her years before, and loved her passion. She never asked them, but they offered to invest in her. They figured that it was an investment into their future grandchild's future. They gave her free reign because she was smart and determined. Brynn hired every employee personally knowing that she was entrusting her reputation and her livelihood to each one of them. She finally built a tight knit, committed crew who were happy in their work, and in their roles. They took care of her, and she took care of them.

Brynn's was a popular spot, and Lucia would have to come to work at five a.m. for the six a.m. breakfast open when she worked Monday through Friday. Then she still had to make it to school by eight-thirty a.m. Brynn wasn't sure if she could make it to work so early, and still be able to work efficiently enough to get to school by eight-thirty.

"Please, Mrs. Michael." Lucia's mocha eyes were large and imploring. "Give me a chance. I promise I won't let you down."

They were sitting across the table from each other in a booth in the dining room. The room was painted a cool blue with airy curtains on the big picture windows with fresh floral arrangements set on every table. Brynn insisted that the dining room reminded her guests of walking into their mother's kitchen, not that she knew what that was like. But she read it somewhere when she was a young girl, and somehow it stuck with her. Even though fresh flowers were more expensive, she had worked out a deal with the florist, and he kindly charged her a little less in exchange for the occasional free food delivery throughout the week.

Brynn was proud and protective of her creation, and while she took a chance with many things, she was hesitant to hire those without experience.

But Lucia tugged at her for reasons that she couldn't explain. Brynn had originally breezed over her application, and had put it in the eighty-six pile. But Lucia was persistent, and Brynn felt obligated to bring her in for an interview based on that alone.

When Lucia had sat down at the table across from her, Brynn found that she was pleasantly surprised. Lucia was young, sixteen, or seventeen at the most, and had obviously dressed up in anticipation for their meeting. She had letters of recommendation from her English teacher, her math teacher, and her pastor. And she had a resume with nothing on it but extracurricular activities and church programs.

Brynn was ready to give her fifteen minutes of her time, and no more. But she felt herself drawn in. Lucia was young, but ambitious and passionate about everything. She reminded her of someone she had once wanted to be.

"I can talk to anyone. And I know that waitressing is hard work, but I promise that I will work hard, and that you will be able to count on me! I really need a job. My Papi got laid off and my Mama doesn't make enough money cleaning houses to support us." Lucia talked a mile a minute, but her energy was infectious and Brynn was mesmerized. She loved the lilt of her Spanish accent and the beautiful huskiness of her voice. She could listen to her talk all day.

But Brynn was a businesswoman, and she didn't make decisions based on feelings. She gave her many reasons why it would be difficult for her to hire her, but Lucia countered every one.

"I know I would have to leave by eight to get to school, but I can come back after and finish any work that I had to leave! I'll work dinner shifts if you need me, and I'll do extra work to make up for anything that I can't do because of school. The other employees won't care because I'll make sure that they like working with me."

Brynn was skeptical. Bertie and Stella were crusty experienced waitresses who had been serving for forty plus years, each. They were sweet to the guests, but extremely impatient with anyone else, and they never hesitated to let Brynn know if they thought she was making the wrong decision or screwing something up. At times, they could even be a little "politically incorrect" referring to all Spanish-speaking people as "Mexicans" and blacks as "colored." That had been the language of their time, and even though Brynn had tried correcting them, they always reverted to their ignorant way of speaking. It made Brynn cringe waiting for the day someone would sue her, but the other employees told her to let it go. They knew that Bertie and Stella never meant to hurt anyone. Brynn figured that if Lucia could win them over, she could probably run for president one day.

Brynn relented, and against her better judgment, took a chance and hired Lucia. A year later, she had no regrets. Lucia had become one of the most popular breakfast servers. She was fast, efficient, and Bertie and Stella had adopted her like the granddaughters that they had who never came to visit. She had done everything she said she would do, even working through the dinner shift and helping Jane close down the restaurant. Since they closed down at eight p.m. and didn't have any alcohol service, Lucia was still able to close a couple of times throughout the week and get home to do her homework.

She was, by far, Brynn's best hire in the six years since she had opened her little restaurant.

Brynn had come to be like an older sister to he, and she trusted her with everything. Lucia was an only child, and since she had been hired, her parents separated with the stress from her father being laid off. Now they were losing their house. But Lucia didn't let that affect her at work. Brynn had taken a chance on her, and she wasn't going to let her down. But now, she was in trouble and she didn't know what to do.

"I'm pregnant."

"Oh, Lucia!" Brynn was visibly upset. She kept looking at her phone and then looking at Lucia. She knew she should text or call Adam. It was their anniversary. Surely, she could be on time just this once.

This was not going to be a quick conversation. She needed to be on time, and she couldn't forgo a shower. She had been cooking all morning, prepping the dinner specials from scratch. She had an excellent and reliable cook to do this for her, but Bob had called off for the first time in four years because he was sick, so Brynn had gone in. It was therapeutic for her to work in the kitchen and every time she did it, she chided herself for not doing it more often. *Maybe I could save money on the shrink if I just did this every day.* Brynn was covered in dough and sauce and she had worn a hat all day. She *needed* a shower.

Lucia and Brynn talked for two and a half hours. Brynn could not pull away.

And now she was going to be at least an hour late. An hour late for the anniversary dinner that Adam had been planning for weeks was unacceptable! *He is going to be so angry.*

She knew that Adam would be furious if she texted him to say she would be late. They were already on shaky ground. She felt it every time she looked at him and he didn't look back.

After eight years of marriage and seven years of dating, he felt that his life with her was drifting away. She was no longer the fifteen-year-old girl he fell in love with, and he just didn't know the woman that she had become. For some reason, she had shut him out and he didn't know why.

He tried connecting with her so many times, but she was always distracted. If there wasn't a natural disaster, or a call off, a product shortage, or some type of crisis at the restaurant, Rose had an issue or crisis of some kind. Rose couldn't make the simplest of decision without Brynn. She called for anything and everything.

Adam tried helping her with Rose, but both Brynn and Rose refused, she only wanted Brynn.

When they met, he knew that Brynn was different from the other girls. It was the reason he fell in love with her in the first place.

But he was realizing that the reasons that he loved her were also the reasons that he was beginning to feel so separate from her. Her independence and inability to open up and trust him, even after all of this time, were creating an even larger chasm between them.

He blamed Thomas, and Adam was glad he had died a slow painful death in Brynn's last year of high school. But then there was Rose. There was always Rose. Even when they were in high school, he knew how much she depended on Brynn and needed her. He thought that as they grew older it would stop.

Brynn always answered her calls, her texts, or her emails. She never hit ignore. Adam was naïve when he thought it was cute, and that she was just devoted to her mother. Now, he just felt neglected.

"I'm not a priority to you!" he would tell her even though she wasn't really hearing him. "Your mother sucks up all of your time and energy." It was the same old fight.

"Yes, you are. She just needs me more than you do!" Brynn would argue. Adam exhausted her, and she couldn't get him to understand no matter how many times they had the same conversation.

"When are we going to start a family? When are we going try to have a child? Are you ever going to not be too busy for me, for us? Brynn, we don't even go out anymore!" The louder he talked, the less she heard him. They were on separate schedules, with separate agendas, and priorities, and she didn't even care that they weren't on the same page. He missed his Brynn, but Adam had exhausted all possibilities. Brynn didn't even seem to care anymore.

He decided that their anniversary would be his last attempt to wake her up, to reel her in, and try to make Brynn his wife again. After all, he loved her, and he had forgotten how it was to *not* love her.

He had fallen for her when he had raced to get the seat next to her in their high school English class. To him, she was always special. But there had always been an unexplained darkness to her, and now he felt that it was beginning to overcome her.

The dinner was at Brynn's favorite restaurant where they had not gone in years. He even stopped to pick up her favorite flowers. He hadn't gotten her flowers in so long, he realized with a pang of guilt. It struck him that at some point he had stopped trying, too. Adam sat at the restaurant for over an hour, waiting for her. He had three scotches, while he waited, and finally asked for the check.

Just then, she flew in through the door looking lovely but disheveled.

Adam hadn't seen her dressed up in so long. His breathe caught and he thought how beautiful she looked. He used to love looking at her when she didn't know it. He knew it was cliché but he truly thought she was the most beautiful girl, especially when she smiled. Prior to meeting him, she hadn't had much to smile about in her life. He vowed years ago that he would make her smile and laugh as much as he could, even when he didn't know her darkest secrets.

Adam just knew that he needed to make her happy. He surprised even himself at times, with what he was capable of doing just for that smile. It was as though he could reach into himself and pull out something completely unexpected, just to make her laugh.

Adam was as inventive and creative as he needed to be, and his reward was when she smiled at him, her big brown eyes sparkling, her beautiful white teeth shining. He swore at one point that was all he needed in life. He could never explain why, he just knew that's how it was for him.

But making her smile and laugh became increasing more difficult, and she stopped appreciating his efforts. So he stopped trying. She was still so beautiful to him, but he was angry with her.

"Where have you been?" he said stiffly when she got to the table.

"I'm sorry. I had a problem to deal with." She was afraid to meet his glance so she looked down as she always did. *I should have texted him or called.*

There is always a problem! He thought bitterly. "Let's just order. I'm starving."

She eyed his scotch in disapproval, but he didn't care. He knew how much she hated alcohol, but he needed it. He took a big swig of it, making his enjoyment obvious as he did so.

After they ordered, they sat in an uncomfortable silence, neither of them willing or able to break the ice.

This isn't how it's supposed to be. He thought angrily. *It's supposed to be easier than this. Better than this. She doesn't even care about me. Happy Fucking Anniversary.*

The waiter was uncomfortable. Adam told him at the beginning that they were celebrating their anniversary, but he was confused. This didn't seem like an anniversary dinner and he dreaded having to approach the table. The tension was so thick he could choke on it. He was so happy when they asked for the check and declined dessert. He thought he was home free, but the manager made him take out the complimentary special occasion dessert.

He didn't want to.

He didn't want to hurt his tip, but he was required to take it to every table with a special occasion. When he set it on the table, they were horrified. They wanted dinner to be over more than he did.

"Thanks," they both muttered.

He had never been so uncomfortable in all of his twenty years of serving. He had seen many unhappy couples over the years, but this beautiful couple oozed nothing but misery. He was relieved when they finally got up and left, not speaking, not touching, and not even looking at one another.

And he was relieved when he saw that they left him a twenty-five percent tip.

Brynn was thankful that they drove separately to the restaurant. The ride home was quick, and she dreaded the inevitable.

"I sat and waited for you Brynn! You never called, you never texted. I was humiliated. It's so typical of you to be so rude!" His beautiful blue eyes, usually so bright and sparkling, were downcast and sad, reflecting the storm that was passing over them.

He would not look at her, all of the rage gone now, and replaced by something more terrifying. Silence.

Brynn stared at him helplessly. *How did this happen to us?* He felt so distant from her though he stood two feet from where she was standing. He towered above her at over six feet and she stared up at him trying to gauge where he was now. His strong jawline was set stubbornly, and she realized that he was a different man than the one she had married so long ago.

She felt afraid, as she always did from her childhood. She felt herself bracing, her body rigid, anticipating the slap to come. Adam tried to reassure her time and time again that he would never lay a hand on her.

She still expects me to hit her! He realized that was part of the growing distance between them that he couldn't bridge. No matter how many times he told her that he would never hurt her, she always separated herself from him, just in case.

She realized as they argued about the dinner that she had not truly looked at him for a long time. Even in his anger, he was so classically handsome. She was not immune to him, and she saw how women looked at him. *How that little slut Annie from his office looks at him.* She knew that Adam was a catch and that women swooned when they saw him. She had done the same. His face was still boyish and handsome, his cheekbones high, his hair a dark chestnut brown. He was physically beautiful, but he was more than that. *He still makes me breathless.* She stopped looking at him for some reason.

Brynn loved his hair so wavy and thick, and thought about how she loved to take her hands and just bury them in it. She used to do it every chance she got whether absently while they lounged, or intensely when they made love. She loved the thickness of it between her fingers and it gave her comfort. Brynn melted when he moaned, almost purred while she played with his hair, which made her want to do it all the more. But that almost seemed like a lifetime ago.

They were so disconnected from each other now. Had it been two months, three months, six? She was so caught up in her work and with Rose. *When did we stop looking at one another?* She could feel him slipping away from her slowly like the tide, gone a little at a time until he was gone completely. She felt helpless.

Being late for dinner was her fault, completely her fault. She had no excuse, but a small part of her thought he might understand if she explained it. Perhaps he might even respect it, and appreciate that he had a wife who others sought out when they were in trouble. But she knew in her heart that he wouldn't.

She hadn't even bothered to call. This was a recurring issue in their lives, and she always chose those in need over him. He wasn't helpless, and he didn't need her.

Brynn didn't know what to say. So she didn't say anything.

He interpreted her silence as indifference.

He took a long sad look at her and finally turned around toward the door. In disbelief, she watched him walk out without as much as a backwards glance.

She waited for hours but he didn't come back. She realized that what she always knew would happen, finally had.

He was gone for good and she was abandoned once more.

CHAPTER EIGHTEEN

Alone

Brynn was incredibly lonely and once again found herself at the one place she could think. It was an old dock that reminded her so much of her childhood refuge, with the creaky wood and sound and smell of the water. It reminded her of the one place that had given her comfort at the home she had no desire to ever return to.

She had found the lake when they had first moved to their new home, and she often escaped there when she needed to quiet the chaos in her mind. When the memories of Thomas came crashing down on her, threatening to overtake her, she would sit on the dock and dip her toes into the cool water. Brynn knew that when she closed her eyes and listened to the sound of the tiny waves lapping at the wood, she could forget, even if just for one moment. But Brynn was disappointed to find that nothing could comfort her in the wake of Adam's absence. Without him there was a large gaping hole right in the middle of her and nothing could close it.

For the first time in a long time, she was truly alone. After Adam left, he didn't call or text or email. He just disappeared. She didn't even know where he went.

After Adam left, she thought that if she just went back to life as usual, that she would come home and find him sitting there waiting for her. Instead, she came home one night after working at *Brynn's* to find all of his things gone. The same week, she stopped getting his mail.

After that, Brynn rarely left the house in case he returned for something. She couldn't bear the thought that he would come back and that she would miss him.

She wanted desperately to hear from him, but Adam remained silent. She didn't try to contact him. If he was walking away then it was a clear sign that Adam no longer loved her and that he no longer wanted to be with her. Deep down Brynn couldn't help but hold onto the hope that he would come home, profess his love, and say it was all a mistake.

After fifteen years of her life, she didn't know how to be without him.

Brynn missed the sound and feel of another person in the house. The subtle click the light switches made turning on and off, the sound of the shower, the movement of the bed as he shifted through the night. She was alone in the stillness and she hated it.

She found herself in the bathroom staring at her face in the mirror several times throughout the morning and in the evenings. Brynn didn't know why she was so drawn to her own reflection. Ever since she was a little girl, after the first time Thomas hit her, she had been pulled to the mirror where she would sometimes sit for an hour staring. It was as though she thought the mirror would tell her how she had become the person that was staring back at her. How had she become the woman that she no longer recognized?

She stared until nothing she was looking at made sense. She knew every pore and every line of her face, yet she had no answers.

Brynn took off her clothes.

Brynn felt free in her nakedness. Free to look at her scars. She did it all the time as a child, especially after a hard day when the shiny blade was her best friend. But Adam saved her from it all, and made her normal. And now, he was gone and she stood in front of the mirror staring like she had so many times years ago. Some were faded and only tiny unperceivable lines that Brynn could barely see. They were surrounded by countless others—some longer, some lighter, some more pronounced. She tried to count them once but gave up. There were so many.

Brynn remembered all of them. There was the one after she dropped and broke a plate from the dishwasher, the one when she was one minute late. There was the one when he thought she was meeting a boy from school, and the one she gave herself when she spilled his Wild Turkey as she carried it across the room. He had beaten her black and blue for spilling and being so "god damned clumsy." That was a deep one, scarred by red because she kept picking at it to renew the blood.

Her scars defined her, and Brynn often stood admiring them for hours, concentrating hard to remember each one of them. She was a smart girl, and she kept them isolated to her stomach and her sides, so she wouldn't have to hide them so much when she grew older.

Brynn knew that the mirror was her best friend, and her worst enemy. On some mornings Brynn's face was so puffy from crying all night, she just couldn't even see the girl who she had once been. The girl who had fallen in love with Adam, who laughed only with him, was now unrecognizable. He pulled something out of her that she didn't know existed before she met him. *Joy? Happiness? Freedom?* She never laughed or smiled so much before he came into her life. Adam taught her to recognize when things were funny, and gave her permission to breathe and enjoy life. And now he was gone, and she didn't know how to do that without him.

Before him, Brynn's blade kept her sane.

Brynn no longer answered her phone, or left the house, or went to the restaurant. She ignored all of Rose's phone calls, text messages, and emails. She could not deal with her neediness.

Unless she was crying, Brynn didn't feel anything. She was dead inside and she remembered how her beloved razor had always made her feel something. She craved it. She needed it. She thought that the pain was getting to be too much, and that she just couldn't take it anymore.

They worried about her at the restaurant. But Jane, the single mom she hired as the manager, was taking care of everything. She briefed Brynn via email and text, and assured her that everything was going to be okay, even though Brynn could barely bring herself to respond. Bertie and Stella kept the place clean and organized, and everyone worked hard to keep it together. They never realized before how much they relied on her. They missed her and couldn't wait for her return.

They missed her energy and her smile, and how she always cared about them and how they were doing. They missed her generosity, and they missed how she pulled them together in their personal lives, as well as in anticipation for a busy shift. Jane was doing a good job, but it just wasn't the same and they missed Brynn.

She was more than just their boss. She had become their friend.

When her visits into the restaurant became less frequent, Lucia came by and checked on her every couple of days. Her tiny baby bump was starting to show. She finally told her parents and they were standing by her, though she hadn't decided what she was going to do. She desperately needed Brynn to snap out of it, so she could help her. Lucia needed her. But every time she saw her, she looked worse and worse, and she was worried, which she shared only with Jane. She didn't want Bertie and Stella to be worked up about it. They were getting older, and she worried about them, too.

Brynn didn't eat or sleep anymore. She lay awake in bed at night, her mind racing and replaying every moment of her life with Adam. She was taking mental snapshots and highlighting all of the things that went wrong that were her fault. She tortured herself to where she couldn't lay in their bed any longer.

When she did, she laid on his side of the bed to see if she could still smell him in the sheets and she tried to remember what it was like to have him laying next to her. Brynn often laid pillows out on the bed, the length of her body and held them, pretending they were him just so she could sleep. Other nights she just wandered around the house from room to room, picturing him in them, and crying.

On the really bad nights, she would lay on the bathroom floor feeling the cool tile on her cheek. She would lie there for hours doing nothing until the sun came up. Some days Brynn made it out of the house, other days she made it to her car. Some days she just continued to lie on the floor. Try as she might, on those days she could not come up with one viable reason to get up.

Adam was no longer in her life, and she didn't know how to function without him. He had provided her levity and laughter. Without him, there was no chance for anything other than misery.

Maybe I should get a dog. Adam wanted children. I wanted a dog.

Brynn was afraid to have children.

She was terrified to bring a child into the world. *How can I be a mother? There is no one to teach me how to be a good mother. There's no way I'll be one on my own.* She couldn't see how that would work out for her or for the child.

Brynn knew that Rose wouldn't be any help. She couldn't even help her with her marriage. Rose didn't have any romantic experience of her own, and Brynn knew that she shouldn't have expected her to give her any worthwhile advice. But she needed Rose to be her mother just for one moment. She needed the roles to be reversed. Brynn realized, in many ways, she didn't have the mother that she needed and it broke her heart.

Brynn didn't even know if she had it in her to be a good mother. *I've never even held a baby before, what would I even do with one? Who would ever teach me?*

Brynn knew that Adam would be a good father. *He's good at everything he does.* But Brynn couldn't even be a decent wife. Every time Adam brought up having a baby, Brynn shut down, and refused to discuss it, which frustrated him. She knew that she would have to eventually make a choice.

Now she sadly realized that it was no longer going to be an option.

In her solitude and mourning, Brynn cried for the children she would never have with Adam. She cried because she slept alone every night. She cried because he walked out the door on their anniversary. She had not heard from him for weeks, which turned into months.

She knew how stubborn and hurt he was. Adam had been angry with her before, but this was different. This was the last straw and Brynn knew it. He warned her in so many ways, she had just missed the signs.

Brynn needed to be completely alone to consort with her misery, and mourn her marriage. As a girl, she never imagined there would ever be a man like Adam in her life. Then Brynn met him and he made himself a necessity in her life. But then he left her, just as he promised he would never do. He abandoned her like her birth parents did, and Brynn knew that it had to be her fault.

She was alone now, and realized that she didn't even know how to exist without Adam.

CHAPTER NINETEEN

Rose's Mind Maze

The sticky notes weren't working.

Rose couldn't ever find where she put the notes to remind her where her keys were, or where she needed to go or what she needed to do. She was more confused lately, and she found that the only place she knew where to go was the restaurant. Otherwise, she was lost in the maze of her mind.

Jane was always so nice to her. She made sure she ate, even though Rose couldn't always remember if she had eaten. She often chastised her for the clothes she was wearing. "Sweetheart, its spring, and you are wearing your winter coat!" Jane was nice, and so were the other girls. And Rose adored the little pregnant Spanish girl.

They all knew how much she missed Brynn. They missed her, too.

While it was true that Rose once amused them, now she just reminded them of how lost Brynn was to them, and how much they missed her. They were a family at the restaurant, and now they sympathized with Rose's loss because it was their loss, too.

Even Jane hadn't seen Brynn since the memorial for her friend. After Stacy's memorial, the girls all told Rose that something bad had happened. Rose had known Stacy, but Brynn didn't want her to go to the memorial. She said it would be hard enough without having to worry about her, too. When they came home and Rose asked Jane how Brynn was, she said that she was okay, but Rose knew that she wasn't telling her the whole story. She asked the other girls, but they wouldn't tell her what happened. She heard the whispers but she would forget what they said. She just knew it was bad.

After a while, Jane wouldn't let her drive to the restaurant anymore. She insisted on calling her a cab, or having one of the girls pick her up. Rose would stay at the restaurant for hours. She had nowhere else to go and nothing else to do, so she would sit in a corner booth sipping on tea and staring out of the window watching the cars go by.

Jane had taken her car keys and had hired a girl to help her with her grocery shopping once a week. Rose was thankful. Those were the things that Brynn would take care of for her. She didn't know how to do it on her own anymore.

Jane emailed Brynn updates on Rose. She even tried to call her, but Brynn ignored the calls and the emails. Jane didn't even know if she was checking them. She was frustrated but there was nothing she could do but wait it out. She hated that Brynn was absent, but she reminded herself that it was because of Brynn that Jane and her girls had such a good life now. Helping her with Rose was the least that she could do.

Jane had even made Rose sticky note with Jane's phone number, and taped it to the phone. She knew that when Rose found the phone she would be able to find her number. But she was becoming increasingly worried. Rose was starting to call at odd times now to ask her who was picking her up.

"Hello?" Jane woke up out of a dead sleep, her heart pounding and grabbed the phone. It was one a.m.

"Hello? Yes dear, when is someone coming for me?" said the thin voice on the other end.

"What? Who is this? What time...? Rose?"

"When is someone coming for me? I'm hungry now!"

"Rose, it's the middle of the night!" Jane was wide-awake now.

"It's lunch time!" Rose insisted.

Jane tried to convince her that it was nighttime, but it was futile. "Rose, go back to sleep. We will pick you up for breakfast."

Rose hung up. She looked at the receiver in her hand. Who was she calling? Was it Thomas? Where was Brynn, she wondered. Did she stay overnight at Stacy's?

She got up and walked around the apartment looking for Brynn. She couldn't find her anywhere. She forgot why she was out of bed and what she was looking for, and she lay on the couch and went to sleep.

Jane noticed that Rose appeared more and more confused and disengaged. She was having trouble walking, and she was slower than usual.

One of the newest regulars flagged Jane over one day. "I think it's awfully nice, dear, that you let the homeless come in and you give them tea," the older woman said warmly. She pointed to the table where Rose sat, and Jane smiled kindly. "Oh sweetie, that's not a homeless woman, that's our good friend, Rose."

"Oh," the woman said confused. The cacophony of colors that Rose had chosen to wear that day was a strange departure from her usual neutrals, and difficult on the eyes. Rose's appearance had changed drastically in the past few months, as did her hygiene. Her usual tidy appearance had become uncharacteristically messy.

Jane's mother died a decade before, but even then, she lived a state away, and Jane didn't need to do anything to take care of her. Now she was feeling the stress of taking care of the girls, the restaurant, and Rose. Taking care of Rose was sometimes a full time job and Jane wondered how Brynn had done it for so long.

Jane was worried about Rose and begged her to go to the doctor. She offered to take her, and she even tried tricking her and driving her there, but Rose sat in the front seat of the Focus and refused to get out of the car. Jane thought she could convince her, but Rose was becoming more and more unpredictable and difficult.

Rose flat out refused to go to the doctor. She hadn't shared her diagnosis with anyone and she wasn't going to, either. She didn't want them to put her in a nursing home on a locked ward. Rose wanted to be able to breathe the fresh air for as long as she could. The doctor said that there were different medicines she could try but Rose knew that it would just postpone the inevitable. She didn't want to simply postpone the inevitable. She knew where she was headed and how she was going to get there. Prolonging the journey seemed silly to her.

Rose thought sadly, *Brynn was right. I've burdened her long enough. I don't want her to hate me.* Rose substituted Jane in some ways for her daughter, but Jane wasn't her daughter. There was enough for Jane to worry about as a single mother, and taking care of the restaurant. Rose knew that. And while she liked Jane, Jane wasn't Brynn and she missed her Brynn.

Even when she was little, Brynn would comfort her. She would hug her and tell her, "Mommy, its okay."

After Thomas hit her, Brynn would cuddle up next to her, grab her hand, kiss it, and tell her that she loved her. Rose found comfort in her child, and Brynn was such a perceptive little girl. She knew when Rose needed her, and she was always there. As an adult, Brynn was the same. She took care of Rose, letting her stay near her, keeping her safe. The past few months were hard on Rose. She felt alone and abandoned, and even though she knew that Brynn needed to be away from her, she was still hurt.

Rose had certainly not been herself for a while. She even stopped going to the restaurant as often. On the way home from the restaurant the last time, Jane had asked her if Thomas was the name of her husband.

"How do you know that?" Rose asked her. She made it a point to never talk about Thomas.

"You told me. You told me he died." Jane said.

"Yes, of course he died. Everyone knows my husband died." Rose was annoyed.

"Yes, but you said he died because of you and Brynn." Jane said lightly, keeping her eyes on the road.

Rose felt like Jane was testing her. *What did I say? What did I tell her?*

Jane's curiosity was peaked. Rose talked to Jane often as if she were Brynn. She had said to her in a very motherly voice Jane had never heard before, "I'm sorry my, little Brynn, for what I made you do to him, but he had to die." Jane knew that Rose was no longer in her right mind, but she wondered what she had done to him. *What did she make Brynn do?*

After Jane asked her about Thomas, Rose stopped going to the restaurant. She was afraid she would say too much. She even stopped going out altogether. She had the girl Jane hired bring her groceries and cigarettes, but that was it.

The diagnosis of early onset Alzheimer's was years ago, and Rose held on longer than she thought. When the cleaning lady came over, Rose tried to remember to hide in her room. She didn't want to see or talk to anyone. She found that her moments of lucidity were becoming less and less. Rose felt that she was in jeopardy, but she didn't know why. She just had a feeling of impending doom.

She woke up one day and found that her head had that fuzzy feeling that she had been getting lately, and the weakness was back in her arm. She tried to pick up the phone, but she couldn't make her hand do what she wanted it to do no matter how hard she tried.

Rose knew something was wrong, but she didn't know what to do. She called for Momma but there was no answer. Daddy didn't answer either. Rose opened the bedroom door to try to find her. There she was! She was cleaning the bathroom. "Momma! Momma!"

"Rose?" Lea said. The older woman had been cleaning for Rose for many months now. Rose stayed out of her way, and she liked Rose, despite her strangeness. *What is she saying? She isn't making any sense. Why is she calling Momma?*

"Momma, help me. Help me," Rose's tongue felt very thick and she couldn't see very well.

"Rose, you're not making any sense. I can't understand a word you are saying."

The last thing that Rose heard was Momma calling her.

Then there was blackness.

CHAPTER TWENTY

Annie

She was quickly approaching thirty, and unmarried.

Her friends were all getting married and constantly asking her to be a bridesmaid. It was humiliating. She saw them whispering about her at the weddings. But she held her head high and fulfilled her duties, knowing that when it was her turn, she would show them all.

She was the oldest of her sisters, and she was tired of the questions about when it would be her turn. They were all getting engaged or married, and she wasn't even close right now. At least her youngest sister was in high school so she wouldn't be the very last to marry. She would never hear the end of it from her mother.

Although she was close to getting married once, her mother still didn't approve of her choices in men. At least that one had given her a ring that she got to wear around for a year. The engagement had been more for convenience, and less for love. The sex had been seldom, and mediocre at best, so when he broke it off, she was relieved. She said yes because as shallow as it seemed, he was a lawyer and she always dreamed of being the wife of a lawyer or a doctor. She knew she would need to marry someone worthy of her, who could afford to give her the life that she deserved.

But now the clock was ticking and she was beginning to wonder if she should have let him break it off so easily. *Maybe our life together would have been fine,* she lamented. *He would have gotten the better end of the deal.*

So now, she would have to keep looking. She was anxious to find "the one." She thought the guy she was dating now might be him, but she was still skeptical. He had broken up his engagement to be with her, but after being engaged to the lawyer, she had decided she wanted a little more excitement in her life. Her guy was nice, but she wanted something more. She wasn't sure if he was going to live up to his potential, and she didn't want to be stuck with a dud for the rest of her life. After all, she was tiny, smart, blondish, and pretty. *Men look at me all the time. But not Adam!*

But lately, she had found that as she got ready for work, she looked forward to her day more and more. Her face was pretty enough but she worked out constantly, doing lunges and squats to accent her best feature. She made sure that her skirts and pants were always tight enough to show it off.

Every guy she ever dated eventually told her that it was the first thing they had noticed about her. She didn't mind. She was proud of how she looked and felt that she should be.

She knew that Adam noticed her, but he didn't act like the other men, and she supposed that is what intrigued her about him. It was almost a challenge to get him to notice her, so she made sure that she really turned it on anytime he was nearby.

She flirted with him innocently enough, but he was the devoted married type, and it was always just friendly.

"Hey, how's your Day? A," she emailed him daily.

"Going to get coffee. Go with? A."

"Getting lunch. You? A." She made sure she kept in close contact with him emailing and texting him, innocently dropping hints about how much she thought of him so that they could be "friends".

"Hey, boy problems, talk? A." They worked together for a couple of years, and she talked to him about her engagement when it ended as well as about the new guy in her life. She often went to him for advice, sounding as though she sincerely needed someone to steer her in the right direction.

"Brynn wouldn't mind me talking to you about my 'guy' problems, would she?" Annie asked Adam innocently.

Adam laughed. "Brynn won't mind. She doesn't care about

things like that."

Annie knew she was walking the line of inappropriate talking to a "married man" but she figured she could be friends with anyone she wanted.

Recently, she caught Adam looking at her more and more, and she was pleasantly surprised. Trouble in paradise, she presumed. He never even really looked at her before, at least not the way he was looking at her now. And she found herself looking forward to seeing him more and more.

Annie never minded when men looked at her, even the married ones. But she really enjoyed when Adam looked at her. She started making more excuses to talk to him as often as she could. She started substituting texts messages for emails and found herself "dropping by" his office sometimes "just to say hi."

She always liked men like him. Tall, dark, handsome. Adam was smart and funny, and when he walked into a room, he took command of it without realizing it. Adam had charisma and was unlike anyone Annie had ever met. When Annie first met him, she remembered how disappointed she was to find out that was married.

Annie also admired how committed he was to Brynn and found herself imagining what it would be like to be "Mrs. Michael." She knew it was silly, but she even resented his wife for finding him first. But as she caught his eye more frequently throughout the day, Annie decided that she had no loyalty to his wife. Hers and Adams' friendship was their own, and she could do with it what she wanted.

Adam came into work one Monday looking as frustrated and forlorn as she had ever seen him. When she was able to corner him alone that morning, she did the best she could to hide her delight when he said he had left Brynn.

CHAPTER TWENTY-ONE

Adam's Heart

Adam couldn't believe that he had walked out on Brynn.

And he couldn't believe that he walked out on their anniversary. He hadn't intended to leave right at that moment, but he just couldn't take it anymore.

He had looked at an apartment several weeks before, but reasoned that he was just exploring his options. Adam needed to have a backup plan if he ever decided to leave Brynn. When he walked out on their anniversary, he got a hotel room and the next day rented the apartment. It was a years' lease, which was a big commitment to make. But he and Brynn had been on the outs for a long time and he couldn't imagine that Brynn wanted their marriage anymore. Not after she just let him go, let him leave, and didn't even say anything as he walked out the door.

Adam had nowhere else to go.

His parents still lived in their hometown, which was too far away. His best friend, Sam and his wife, Alyssa, just had their first child, and he wouldn't dream of trying to intrude. Alyssa would never allow it, and he had no desire to upset either of them.

In fact, he was jealous of them. They had a baby and although they weren't sleeping, they were happy. He was ecstatic for them, but he was sad for himself. Their life was the life that he was supposed to be living with Brynn. He always dreamed of having a baby with her.

"Don't you want a baby with your beautiful eyes, my awesome hair, my sense of humor, and your brain?" he asked her trying to wake her up. They were lounging on the bed on a rare Sunday afternoon, reading and relaxing.

"Adam! Can't we just rest? Do we have to talk about having a baby? That's all you ever want to do." Brynn became agitated quickly. She sat up and glared at him with dark eyes.

Adam looked at his wife. Her cuteness always disarmed him, and today was no different as she lounged in his old t-shirt and her favorite pink boy shorts. "All we ever do is 'talk' about it, but we never get anywhere."

"I'm not ready, Adam. Period." Brynn tried to end the conversation.

"I've wanted to have a family with you since we were fifteen. You're just afraid! You'll be a wonderful mother because you are a wonderful beautiful woman. Please believe me, Brynn. I know you better than anyone." Adam pleaded with her, trying to keep her attention. Brynn turned away and left the room without a word.

At one point, Adam even had his mom talk to her to try to reassure her that motherhood was just a normal part of life, but Brynn was still irrationally afraid.

Adam loved Brynn, but he had been thinking of leaving for a long time. He was unhappy, and he was too young to be so unhappy. He wanted a family. He wanted a child.

But more than that, he wanted his wife to love him. It had been a long time since he felt loved. Adam was her first love, and Brynn was his. But instead of growing in love, they were stalled. It was as though Brynn had a limit to what her heart could feel and, she closed it off. They stopped growing, or at least she did.

And now he came home, and she was rarely there. When she was, she acted as though he didn't exist. Brynn couldn't see how much he needed her because she was too busy being needed by everyone else. Most of the time, Adam was alone and he missed her. She was so close, but he missed her every day. Adam even tried telling her that he needed her, but she never heard him.

Adam missed kissing and hugging her. He missed seeing her

light up when he got home from work, and he missed sending her cute little text messages throughout the day. He missed her smell and how soft her skin felt on the flat of his hand. He missed the hollow of her neck and the curve of her back. He missed everything about her.

Adam taught her how to laugh and Brynn had given him purpose in life. He enjoyed introducing her to a normal family life with his family. He knew that her own family was screwed up, but she never confided in him until after Thomas had died. He had met and spent time with Rose, and that was all that he needed to see to know that her family was atypical of most.

Soon after they began dating, Adam introduced Brynn to his family, and she was in awe of them. Their house was light, clean, well furnished, and yet comfortable. Even though Adam hadn't known her entire story, he knew that he had to be delicate with her, and he told his parents so.

"Why do I have to be 'gentle' with her, Darling? What does that mean?" his mother has asked. She wasn't used to being told how to act by her own son, and she was a little offended.

"Mom, trust me, you'll see once you meet her." Adam didn't know how to explain Brynn to them. He just didn't want them to scare her off. They were fun loving people with big personalities, and Brynn was not used to people like them.

But then they met her and understood how lovely, yet cautious and broken she was. They could see it in her eyes. They knew that it would take time for her to trust them. They were desperate to know her story but didn't pry for fear that they would ruin it for their son, who was clearly in love with her.

The Michael's home was unlike anything Brynn had ever seen before. Adam's father was nice to his mother. He even flirted with her and made her laugh, and Brynn watched them both uncomfortably, yet amazed at how they genuinely like one another. Adam was just like his dad. He was quick with a smile and easy going, and he tried to make her feel comfortable even when he could tell she wasn't.

Adam's mom was funny and youthful, but Brynn could tell that she was also strong and Brynn liked her immediately, though she didn't usually like most people right away. Adam's mom spoke to her gently and protectively as if she were a lost puppy, which made Brynn more comfortable with her. Brynn's exposure to "normal people" had been minimal and she could tell that they were easing her in, and for that, she was grateful. She was also grateful that they didn't ask her very many questions about herself. The more she spent time with them the more comfortable she became, but she was always careful not to reveal too much.

After a year and a half of dating, Brynn was finally beginning to relax.

But sometimes Adam would catch her frowning for no reason and he didn't understand it. Brynn didn't even realize she was doing it, but even during the lightest of moments, her face would grow dark, and he would see a storm brewing behind her big dark eyes. He couldn't understand what was happening in her head and when he asked, she smiled quickly and changed the subject. It took two years of dating for him to finally get her to share her thoughts with him, but he still felt as though she didn't trust him. She was still holding back.

He didn't truly understand her pain until the first time that he saw her naked.

He was willing to wait for her for as long as it took. He knew the first time that he kissed her that she was a virgin. He was too, and he wasn't ashamed to admit that to her. But she was different from the other girls he kissed who hadn't done it yet. The other girls were stiff, robotic, and tentative when they kissed him. But when he kissed Brynn, he felt her warmth, her wanting. She became vibrant and alive, and it excited him just to be near her. He knew that she was the one, but Brynn made it clear that he would have to wait for her to be ready, and she didn't budge.

The first time that he saw her naked, he knew that it was only by her choice. His parents weren't home, and they lay together on the couch watching TV. They were at the point where she was letting him feeling on top of her clothes, but never let him go under, no matter how many times he tried. She seemed to keep him away from her side and her stomach, always moving his hands to her back or shoulders. She did it so much that it became a game, and they laughed and kissed, but they both knew he would try again.

With his parents gone for a guaranteed long period, Adam knew that this time was different. She was different. Sometimes when he kissed her, he felt that she was somewhere else completely, but this time she was there with him with every touch.

He tried to take off her shirt as they kissed, but she held tight to it. He was so distracted with her mouth on his, and how she was breathing faster, that he didn't realize when he was completely naked and she wasn't. He looked down at her dismayed to see her top remaining, while everything else was gone.

"Take it off," Adam said hungrily between kissing her ears, her neck, and her throat. "Take your shirt off."

Each deep wet kiss felt like electricity zapping her in all of the right places, but she knew she couldn't let him see her. He didn't know about the blade, and she knew that he wouldn't approve. Brynn didn't want him to judge her. She could lose him if he realized how screwed up she really was. "I can't," she whispered. She was hoping to distract him as she pulled his muscular body down on top of her, almost pulling him inside of her completely. They were so close that they could both feel it.

He groaned with excitement and anticipation, and she could feel his nakedness against her. They were never this close before. She hadn't allowed it. He wanted to have all of her, to see all of her. He kissed a trail down her neck, on top of her shirt pausing as he buried his face in between her breasts and pulled her as tight to him as he could. Adam loved how she pulled gently and twisted at his hair, and he loved how she smelled. He couldn't get enough of her sweet, clean smell. He paused and before she could stop him, he pulled up her shirt and started to kiss her belly.

He froze.

"What the hell?" He stared at her perfect taut belly in disbelief. It was marred with long thin scars all over her sides and her stomach. Some of the lines were perfectly patterned, and some were long and haphazard with no rhyme or reason. He had never seen anything like it ever. Yet somehow, he knew what it was.

"What are you doing to yourself?" He sat up, the moment shifting from passion to shock. He looked at her, his dark blue eyes almost black, with angry tears welling up, quickly threatening to overflow. "Brynn, what are you doing to yourself? Explain this!"

Brynn refused to look at him, pulling her shirt down to cover herself. She pushed him off her and looked around desperately for her panties. She found them as quickly as she could, sliding them on, careful not to look at him. She was angry. He ruined The Night, because he had to see her stomach. *Why did he do that?* She was so angry. *Why couldn't he have just taken me without needing to see everything? Couldn't he have just been happy with the part of me that I was willing to give? Why did he need all of me?* She didn't understand it. She was humiliated and embarrassed. Now he knew her secret and he would think that she was pathetic and disgusting and sick. *He will leave me now!*

"Brynn, answer me! What are you doing to yourself?"

She never had to answer to anyone before for her razor blade. Brynn she didn't know what to say, she hadn't even imagined this moment before. She put her head in her hands and told him the best way that she could in between sobs. "Cutting... it... makes me think of anything... but the present."

Adam sat next to her rubbing her back, trying to understand that hurting herself was the only thing that kept her sane.

"The blade... makes me focus... and forget... It... transports me outside... of my mind... my body. I need the pain..." she paused, she wasn't sure if she should tell him the rest. "I... like the pain. It... helps me."

He could tell that some of her cuts were fresh while others were older. He couldn't understand why she would need to cut herself now; after all, she was abandoned so long ago. He knew that she needed help but he didn't know what to do. He just knew that he needed to protect her always. Adam held tight to her stomach, and cried as though her cuts were his own. And then he made love to her as she begged him to. She was ready and didn't want the ugliness of her scars to ruin it.

She wanted him to love her, in spite of her scars, and when he was deep inside of her, she knew that he did.

But she kept some of her pain to herself. She wasn't ready to tell him everything.

She didn't tell him about Thomas. Not until much later when he was dead. After all, they were in high school, and she could still end up in a foster home, and she didn't want that. She was so close to graduating and having the choice at a different life that she didn't want to be ripped from Rose's grasp in the twenty-third hour. She wanted to leave on her terms.

And she wanted to take pity on her beautiful Adam. She knew he had discovered enough for one night, and he was still there, and he still loved her somehow.

CHAPTER TWENTY-TWO

Brynn Letting Go

Adam reluctantly agreed not to tell his parents about Brynn's scars.

But now she was his and he made her promise that the cutting would stop for him. Somehow, only for him she thought that maybe she could. He eased her pain and she let him. He became her safety and her sanctity, and she didn't think about her blade as much anymore.

She knew that she cared about him deeply when finally, she trusted him enough to take him to her safe place. She had shyly led him to the long-forgotten dock that had become worn over the years. Brynn seemed to be the only one who remembered that it existed. She still spent many hours alone there, but now, she wanted to share it with Adam.

It was at the dock, after Thomas died, that Brynn decided it was time to tell Adam about her tortured childhood.

"I didn't want to tell you this before," she said avoiding his gaze as she looked down at her hands, an expression that Adam couldn't read spreading all over her fragile face. She had wanted to tell him for so long, but she wasn't ready. "He was ... horrible to me. He... hit and kicked me... a lot. Mostly when he drank... he said I wasn't going to ever be much of anything in life." She could tell that Adam was getting angry as his breath was getting faster and she saw him clenching his fists tightly.

"Why didn't you tell me?" he said trying to control his anger. "I would have killed him. I would have protected you! Why didn't you let me protect you?"

"Nobody could protect me from him. Not even my mother, she couldn't stop him." Brynn was ashamed, and Adam could tell. "He hurt me because he said he could. He said he bought and paid for me so that he could do whatever he wanted. He hated me because Rose never loved him, and he said it was because of me."

He sat quietly by her side holding her hand. He knew that he couldn't talk because he knew that if he talked he would cry, and he didn't want to cry. He wanted to be strong for her. He sat silently in disbelief trying to take her words in and understand how Thomas could possibly hurt someone as sweet as Brynn. Adam thought about what he would have done to him if he had known.

He realized that, as close to her as he was, he still wasn't close enough. He knew that she kept space between them and he was determined to bridge it, even if it took all of his life to do it.

"I'll never hurt you, Brynn." He was stroking her hair as he held her.

"I'm afraid all of the time," she said into his chest. "I'm afraid that I will trust you, and that you will end up hurting me. I'm afraid that I'm not good enough for you. I'm afraid to laugh and to just enjoy my life. I don't know how to." Adam was the only one she could talk to, the only one she could tell her secrets and her thoughts to, and he understood how she felt. Brynn was the only one that really listened to Adam and loved him for who he was. Adam felt that Brynn understood him. She drew out his best, and she inspired him to reach his fullest potential when they were together.

"I will always protect you, Brynn. Your bastard father is gone now, and he can't hurt you anymore."

"What if I turn out like her. Like Rose? I love her Adam, but I don't want to be her." Brynn was ashamed to say it out loud.

"You could never be her. You are you, and only you." He smiled that beautiful smile. "And I love you. I will never *not* love you. You are mine, and I am yours, always."

Just as he had followed her to the dock, he then followed her to college, then to the city they chose to call home. He made sure that he never forgot the night when she finally trusted him with her truth or his promise to protect her. Anywhere Brynn went, Adam wanted to go. He couldn't imagine not being with her. He wanted to buy a house and settle down as soon as they could. He was eager and excited to begin a life with her, and he wanted her to be excited, too. His parents cautioned him to wait on the house until they were more established, so he told him that he was just looking.

But when Adam found their house, a beautiful four-bedroom buttery yellow Victorian with large windows and a lot of open space, he fell in love. He knew it was the perfect home to raise their children in. When he showed it to her, she thought it was too big. But he disagreed. He knew that it was perfect for them the first time he walked through it, because he could see Brynn and his baby in every room.

Now he was living in an apartment.

Adam still couldn't believe that he had left her. He did exactly the opposite of what he had promised her he would do. He couldn't protect her when he wasn't with her. He knew that he couldn't help her battle her demons now.

The memories were flooding through him, ripping him apart.

"To have and to hold, to love, honor and cherish, for better or worse, through sickness and health, until death do us part." She was so beautiful in her great grandmother's wedding gown. It hugged her in all of the right places, and the beautiful lace veil framed her lovely face. He loved her so much and he could tell by the look in her beautiful brown eyes that she loved him.

Adam couldn't remember the last time she had looked at him like that.

Was it on their anniversary two years ago? Was it during their trip to Mexico? Was it the last time they made love?

Adam was sick. He could hear Brynn's voice in his head. She was so serious, but he loved playing with her and making her laugh.

"You're not funny," she would giggle.

"You think I'm hilarious," he said as he nuzzled her neck.

"You're ugly and you smell," she teased holding him tight.

"You're ugly and YOU smell," he said kissing her with those

sweet little kisses that he liked to give her.

He loved her for sure.

Now he didn't know what he was going to do. He left her, but if she had only said something, given him any indication that she still loved him, he would have stayed. He would have fought. Instead, she let him walk out, and she hadn't contacted him since.

It couldn't always be up to him. She had to give, too. He knew that she was afraid to give because of Thomas, but he had done everything that he could to show her that he wasn't her father. She had a lot to work out for herself. If only he had realized she was so damaged, would he have fallen for her?

Of course, I would have.

Adam knew the answer. There was no choice in the matter. Once his heart found Brynn so young, he knew that it would not let her go.

But now Adam had made a different choice, the choice to leave.

He just didn't know if he could live without her for the rest of his life.

CHAPTER TWENTY-THREE

Brynn's Homecoming

Brynn's phone rang, and rang, and rang. Since Adam left, she rarely answered it anymore. She simply let it go to voicemail.

"Hi, you've reached Brynn and Adam, please leave a message."

"Hi, you've reached Brynn and Adam, please leave a message."

"Hi, you've reached Brynn and Adam, please leave a message."

"Brynn! Please pick up, or call me back as soon as you get this message. This is Samantha, Stacy's Momma. I got some real bad news for you about Stacy, Darlin'. Call me back at soon as you get this. You know the number." Brynn hadn't heard that familiar drawl in a long time, and her heart fell to the pit of her stomach when she heard it. Brynn worked hard to rid herself of that drawl. People in the town she grew up in talked like they moved. Really slow, and it drove her nuts.

When Brynn called Samantha back, she was afraid. She knew that something awful had happened to her friend. She knew that something terrible must have happened to her friend, and immediately felt guilty. Brynn hadn't called or talked to Stacy in so long. The last time she saw her was at her wedding a few years back. And even then, they had drifted apart.

Brynn missed her friend. Stacy had been the only one she could ever talk to about Thomas. Stacy's daddy had been even worse to her and to her sister's because he could, he was the law, and nobody was going to question him.

Brynn always loved Stacy's honesty and sweetness, and Brynn had begged her to come to the city with her and start over. She begged her to go to college and get away from that life, but Stacy refused. Her grades were bad and she was going to have to repeat her senior year. She couldn't go away with her.

Two years after high school and Stacy was getting ready to marry daddy's new officer.

Brynn and Adam had gone back for the wedding, and they were going to stay with Adam's Momma and Daddy. They had so much fun on the drive down, laughing the whole way.

"You know what I love about you?" he said suddenly very serious.

"That I'm stunningly beautiful, and so much smarter than you are?" she said striking a cross-eyed pose from the passenger seat. He taught her how to be silly and there were times when she was even good at it.

"I love that I can completely be myself with you. Good, bad, stupid. I love that you accept me for who I am." He was sincere and she felt herself go limp inside. She felt the same, but she wasn't so good at always saying things from her heart. She wanted to be, but it didn't feel natural letting it go.

Adam was looking at her, waiting. His eyes were not on the road and he was making her nervous. He was imploring, pausing, waiting.

Brynn said nothing.

"Um, eyes on the road there, handsome," she finally said feeling awkward. She knew that the moment had passed. Her opportunity to tell him how wonderful he made her feel, and how he made her life worthwhile was gone. Brynn always hesitated and missed the moment. The words didn't slide off her tongue directly from her heart as his did. It was a constant problem for her and she wondered once again how she got so lucky to have someone like him love her so much.

His face fell, and he gave her an awkward smile, and looked back to the road. They drove in silence for a bit and she turned the radio on.

"I love you," she said a few minutes later.

"I love you," he responded flatly.

When she relived their downfall years later, she realized that was the end for them. It was *the moment* that began their demise. Brynn's inability to express her love for Adam was the root of their undoing.

They spent the rest of the drive in silence. She liked the quiet, but she saw the road starting to change, and she started to feel nervous.

About an hour into the trip, the scenery went quickly from clusters of towns and cities to rolling hills and trees. She could see towns dispersed sparsely at a distance one here, and one there. But it was far from the life they had chosen even if it was only a few hours away. She hated going back.

But Stacy begged her. She wasn't having a big fancy wedding, but she wanted Brynn there to stand up for her. She wanted her best friend.

Brynn and Adam's own wedding had been done at the Justice of the Peace, without any family or friends there to stand up for them. They told themselves at the time that it was ideal, no muss, and no fuss. But Brynn uncharacteristically, yet secretly, had wished for the big fluffy gown. Adam secretly wished for the big ceremony to celebrate his love for his bride. They didn't realize at the time how much they needed the public declaration of their love. They even wondered years later, when it was too late, if it contributed to the growing distance between them that they had not celebrated the beginning of life together with their family and friends.

Adam asked Brynn if she wanted to drive past her old house. After Thomas died and Brynn graduated from high school, Rose moved wherever Brynn moved. She sold that old "house of horrors" and followed her daughter everywhere she went. Everyone but Brynn thought it was strange that her mother picked up and moved wherever she was. Brynn knew that Rose would not be okay on her own and that she needed her.

Brynn didn't want to drive past, but she felt compelled to see it and asked him to, anyway.

It was so much smaller than she remembered. When Brynn was little, she remembered how massive it seemed with their two bedrooms and one bathroom. But looking at it now, even with the second floor it still looked small. It was much smaller than their own two-story Victorian. They had made their home bright and airy, like she had done with the restaurant. Her childhood home had been anything but, and she didn't want anything that reminded her of Thomas.

Brynn smiled a sad smile as she remembered riding her bicycle down the cracked old sidewalk. She fell on it when she was ten and skinned her knee really bad. And when she was twelve, she broke her arm roller-skating down that same stupid sidewalk.

She looked up at the windows and tried to suppress the flood of memories that threatened to overcome her. Brynn wondered if anyone had ever seen her looking through her bedroom windows as a child wishing she could just jump out, or escape and never look back. She hated that house and remembering how she used to walk up the steps to the front porch after school not knowing what the evening would bring. Brynn hated how the house smelled of him, whiskey and cigarettes. Even as an adult whenever she smelled either, it would make her think of him, and she hated it.

The house was still the same faded blue color it was when she was a girl. Only now, the paint was peeling and it desperately needed to be repainted. It was clear that the current owners weren't much on upkeep. Looking at the house made Brynn want to weep. It reminded her of all of the horrible memories that she had long since buried deep with within. She spent much of her life trying to forget Thomas, but looking at the house now, she half expected him to walk out the front door, and she suddenly felt terror in her heart.

Adam saw the look in her eyes and knew immediately that she didn't want to be there any longer. He quickly drove away allowing her one final look.

That was the last time she had been home.

The wedding had been fun. It was a loud, rambunctious party until the wee hours of the night. Stacy's new husband, Toby, seemed nice and not like Brynn expected at all. He wasn't like the other roughneck boys from town. He was quiet and reserved, and Stacy seemed genuinely happy. Brynn could tell that she had cut back on the cupcakes in recent years, and was trying to take care of herself. She was happy for her friend.

Even though she didn't drink alcohol, she still had a good time dancing and laughing with Stacy and Adam. Adam was always so nice to Stacy, and Brynn loved that about him.

That had been the last time they had seen her, or had even talked to her. Stacy called a few times and left messages for Brynn, but she was too busy to return her calls.

Brynn dreaded calling Samantha back. Her message had the sound of sadness and finality, and she felt that she didn't even need to call her back to know what she was going to say.

"Oh Darlin', sweet girl," Samantha blubbered. She was always a bit too dramatic for Brynn. The days of hitting and cheating, and whatever else he did when he was drinking, were long over for Stacy's dad because he was the Chief of Police now. He had beaten his demons and found God. For Samantha's sake, Brynn was glad. But she still had never liked him. She would never forget what he had done to her friend, or to her sisters.

"Samantha," Brynn said almost curtly. "Is everything okay? What is going on?"

"It's Stacy, honey girl. She's gone." Samantha was crying so hard that Brynn could barely understand her.

"Gone? Gone where?" Brynn was dreading the answer. She had a feeling that her friend had not gone anywhere. She had a horrible feeling in the pit of her stomach that her friend was.

"Dead! She's dead!" Samantha was howling now.

Brynn held the phone away from her ear. She knew in her heart that Samantha was telling the truth, but she didn't want to believe her. *How can she be gone? How could this have happened?*

"Toby's girlfriend done shot her, and killed her, and the baby inside of her. It's all Toby's fault. HE KILLED MY BABIES!"

Brynn wondered where this horror and sadness had been when Stacy and her sisters were children, and their Daddy was hurting them. Suddenly, Brynn was disgusted with Samantha and sick to her stomach. Bile was gathering in the back of her throat. She was going to vomit.

"How could this have happened? How?" Brynn choked out. Toby had seemed so nice when she met him at their wedding. He really seemed to love Stacy and it hadn't even been all that long ago. *His girlfriend shot her? His GIRLFRIEND? And Stacy was pregnant?*

After she hung up the phone with Samantha, she Googled it on her phone. There it was in black and white. Toby had a girlfriend. He was getting ready to leave her and go back to his pregnant wife. His girlfriend went into a rage and went to their house and killed Stacy and her unborn child that was due two months later, after Toby went to work the next day.

Brynn was sick.

She never even knew that Stacy was pregnant. With all of the phone calls Stacy had made to Brynn, and she hadn't returned any of them. And now, her sweet friend was gone, and she would never talk to her again. She would never get to hold her baby. She was barely thirty, and she was dead.

Brynn wanted to die.

CHAPTER TWENTY-FOUR

The Hospital

Brynn was grateful that she was adopted, and that she didn't share her mother's genes.

It was an awful thought that she repeated to herself often, but she was sure to never speak it aloud knowing it would make her sound like a terrible person. While she didn't often care about what others thought of her, she loved her mother and would never want to hurt her. So she kept it to herself as she did with many things.

It was Alzheimer's, and due to a stroke, Rose was now in a coma.

The fluorescent light of the hospital room was hurting her eyes. Her contacts were so dry.

Her head was starting to pound. The blip, blip, blip of the heart monitor was keeping time with the pound, pound, pound in her head. She rubbed her face and was disgusted with the grease and oil that had built up over the past thirty-six hours. But there was nothing that could be done until she had a proper shower. There was no point in just washing her face when she could feel the dead skin collecting on the rest of her body. Her teeth felt filmy and sugary from the numerous cups of sugary mocha vending machine coffee, two packages of M & M's, and a pack of Starburst. She needed a shower and she needed to feel clean.

Please live! She didn't know why she needed her mother so much, but she did. Her heart felt twisted and heavy as though her own life were dependent upon the blip, blip, blip of the machine.

They did not have the typical nuances of any mother daughter relationship. Her mother had always needed mothering, and as she got older, her eccentricities made it worse. Initially, she undertook her responsibility out of love and devotion, but now she found that she did it more out of necessity and obligation. After all, Rose had no one else. It took a great deal of patience and energy to deal with her mother on a daily basis, and even in her slumbering state, this time was no exception. Brynn felt the ever-present guilt that went hand in hand with her frustration, and she futilely tried to suppress both with no success. She had learned to accept that the frustration, guilt, irritation, and inexplicable anger were simply part of what defined their relationship.

Up and down, up and down the cursor goes, Brynn thought, exhausted. The heartbeat of the woman who raised her as her own, loved her as though she had grown in her womb, continued in its same uneven rhythm. Brynn had studied it for hours. The jagged lines on the screen told her that the heart was still beating, and that was all she cared about. She loved Rose.

She looks at peace as though she doesn't have a care in the world, Brynn marveled, despite the tubes jutting out of Rose's throat and nose. Brynn stroked her hand. Rose's eyes were closed and her skin was pale, but her face was relaxed and serene. She looked as though she were content to sleep and not wake up again. She looked younger somehow in her coma-induced slumber than she did when she was alert and awake.

At fifty-seven, Rose looked aged beyond her years. Her husband and life had not treated her well.

She had endured enough, and Brynn thought that this might be her way of escaping a hard life that she no longer wanted to live. And Brynn could relate. She felt the same.

Brynn stretched, and she tried to curl herself up as best as she could to try to rest.

She drifted into a restless sleep. Her mind falling back into a time when she was a child and there was a lot of yelling, a lot of screaming. She felt desperate and fearful and wanted to hide. But Brynn found that she was moving closer to the sounds, instead of further away. There was a man in her dream and his voice was angry, and had a dangerous edge to it. She could hear him swearing, using words that scared her with such a mad voice. She could hear him yelling words like "hit" or "hurt" though she wasn't sure which one. And she could hear the stifled cries of a woman—*Stop. Don't. She will hear you.*

She awoke with a start.

Her head felt fuzzy and it still hurt.

A nurse was in the room. She was quiet, efficient. "Go back to sleep, honey. I'm only checking her vitals. So far, so good."

Brynn knew the nurse was trying to be encouraging, but there was a look of pity in her kind green eyes as she regarded her. She was a short, plump, pretty blonde woman with puppies all over her purple scrubs. She even had a bejeweled little puppy pin that held her pen to her pocket with a matching pink chord. Brynn guessed she liked puppies. *Adam and I were going to get a puppy.* There were so many things that they didn't get around to doing, yet. And now they never would.

She felt the sadness that cut through her when she thought of him, and tried to shake it off. There was enough to be sad about right now and she couldn't think of him and their lost life now, or she would lose it completely.

She turned her attention back to the canine loving nurse. She guessed that the nurse's name was Cindy from the board where her name was written with smudged blue dry erase marker. Cindy was checking the lines of her Rose's IV and checking her over in a very business-like manner. She lifted the bag to check urine, she felt her pulse, and she noted oxygen levels.

"Any changes?" Brynn croaked out.

"No, honey. She's still the same." Cindy tried to sound somewhat cheerful, but did not succeed. "Sometimes it takes a couple days for them to come out of it."

Brynn was immediately annoyed. If Cindy were doing her job, she would know it had already been a couple of days. If Cindy had read her chart, she would know that she was on her third night. She scowled to herself, her dark eyes blurry. She tried not to make eye contact with Cindy. She knew that her eyes would tell Cindy that she was full of it. Thankfully, Cindy left the room before Brynn's eyes could tell her she thought she was incompetent. Brynn's eyes always told the truth whether she meant them to or not. It was both a blessing and a curse.

If Cindy were a good nurse, Rose would have woken up when she was touching her tubes and checking her vitals. She would have opened her eyes. Brynn knew she was being ridiculous. Cindy had been one of several nurses, none better or worse than the other. They had all been equally efficient and genuinely concerned. But Rose never woke. It didn't matter who was in the room.

It didn't even matter that Brynn was in the room.

She still lay there quiet and unable to breathe on her own in her stubborn half death.

Brynn couldn't take it anymore. She couldn't sit in that sterile tiny room anymore with all of the beeping and blipping machines. She had to pee and she had to escape, so she decided to take a walk and look for a bathroom. She had to get out of the morbid silence of the ICU.

I'm free, she thought briefly as she stepped through the swooshing automatic doors.

She walked through the quiet, sterile halls of the hospital and marveled at the quiet. *It's three a.m. and all's well,* she thought happy to be out of the ICU.

After a little bit of walking, she found a bathroom not that far away. She was pleased to see how clean it was. The floors were clean and the lights were bright, even the toilet was sparkling. *Thank God,* dirty bathrooms always grossed Brynn out.

She clumsily pulled off the seat protector and sank down on the toilet seat in exhaustion. She knew that she could fall asleep there. She tried to keep herself awake. She wanted pajamas, a soft pillow, and a nice warm bed. She wanted to sleep, like Rose, completely unaware of the world around her. She just wanted to be comfortable. She didn't want to have to think anymore. She actually felt that her mother was being a little selfish in her slumber, and for a moment, she was jealous.

She grimaced at herself for being so irrational, but as she became more exhausted, she found her thoughts heading more in that direction. *Mad, as in crazy*, that's what I am. She splashed water on her face after she washed her hands for what seemed like five minutes. She tried to avoid looking at her face, but couldn't.

She was more tired than she ever remembered being in her entire life. Her dark hair was starting to look and feel greasy and she wished she had a rubber band or something to pull it back with. It was limp and lifeless. She readjusted her bobby pin hoping to give it a little lift. She readjusted repeatedly until she gave up. There was no point, and she laughed at herself for even caring about her appearance.

Whom am I trying to impress anyway? I'm certainly no prize! Sadly, she thought about how lonely and desperate someone would have to be to want to take her home.

She allowed her eyes to wander to the empty space on her left hand where her wedding band had been. She hesitated for a moment, but then rubbed it absently. She was missing the hardness of the metal, and the reassurance it had once given her. Brynn looked at her reflection in the mirror as she often did when she was rubbing her finger. She missed him, her Adam.

It had been nearly six months since he left her but it felt like so much longer. She was beginning to feel as though life was somehow playing a cruel joke on her.

Thomas must be laughing now, from Hell. He always enjoyed my misery, she thought wryly.

Thomas died when she was in high school, and the only good thing that came out of his death was the insurance money for Momma. For some strange reason, he was ridiculously generous in his death, and she was well taken care of for the rest of her life. Brynn thought that so strange considering how much he must have hated her to hurt her the way that he did. But Brynn never understood and had long since stopped trying. Her only goal in life was to stay far away from him and his memory, in every way possible.

She had detested nothing more than sitting at the funeral with everyone going through and saying how sorry they were for their loss. Brynn hadn't even cried, not one tear. Her mother told her time and time again how much she despised him, yet she sat at his funeral and cried. Brynn thought Rose was such a hypocrite after how abusive he had been to them. She hadn't thought of him as her father for a long time, he was only Thomas to her, now and forever.

Brynn bit her lip and winced. Her lips were dry and she had forgotten to bring her lip balm with her. Her mouth was a little wider than she liked, and her lips were considered "pouty," even though she thought they were her best facial feature. She rubbed her eyes as she saw the mascara rub off on her hands. She sighed.

Tears began to form in the corners of her eyes and the familiar tightness in her throat started to squeeze her neck slowly cutting off her air. She stared hard at herself. *Stop!* You *can't do this now. You can't lose it now! Don't freak out! Rose is dying.*

Rose is dying!

Brynn's heart jumped for the wrong reasons and suddenly she realized that this was her excuse. Her face gave away a hint of excitement.

Now she could call him because she had an excuse. Surely, Adam would care. She could call him and tell him about Rose. Wouldn't he want to know?

Oh my God, I should be so ashamed of myself for even thinking to use Rose as an excuse! She felt flush with anticipation and she couldn't contain herself with the thought of hearing his voice. She loved his deep strong voice, and she missed it. His voice had always been able to reach inside of her like a powerful song, and she missed how it made her feel.

He *had* been trying to get in touch with her a lot lately, but she avoided him. He never left a message, and she figured that after what she saw at Stacy's memorial, he was just calling to tell her that he wanted a divorce. She couldn't bear hearing it, and she wasn't ready. She had only just taken the ring off because she figured he was never coming back.

She rolled it around her brain for a while trying to figure out what to do with the thought of calling him.

No! No! No, you idiot! He left you. He doesn't care about Rose, and he doesn't care about you.

"Stop trying to find reasons to bring him back into your life!" She chastised herself loudly, her voice echoing against the tile and the porcelain.

"He walked out on you and he doesn't want you anymore! You made him leave because you're pathetic, and now you want to call him? Now you want to pull him back into your life? You're disgusting!"

Brynn knew that she must look so sad because once she started crying she couldn't stop. Her eyelids were already getting puffy and her cheeks were getting red. She hated how distorted her face looked when she cried. Her wide mouth and generous lips were pulled tight as the tears fell rapidly down her smooth cheeks. The first signs of crows' feet were starting to appear which was more evident as her eyes squeezed tight as she tried to stop crying.

She felt bad for being so angry with the woman she had become, the one who had let her husband go. At times she even loathed her, hated her even.

But she was angry with him, too. *How can I miss him so much when he left me?* She wondered how repulsive and sad she would be to him now. Where was her pride? Where was her self-esteem?

If he ever loved me so much, he never would have walked out on me. If he ever loved me, he would have called to try to make amends. He would have fought for us. How could she care about him now when he made it so clear that he no longer loved her or wanted anything to do with her?

She was so devastated by the loss of his love that she barely even recognized herself anymore.

Her shrink called him "her first big love." In truth, he was her only love. She didn't see how she could *ever* love anyone else. She didn't want to love anyone else. She only wanted to love him but now he was gone.

"He does not love you. He left you. Let him go." she hissed at herself, hating her weakness, and her neediness for someone who clearly did not want her any longer.

Brynn took deep breaths. That is what her shrink told her to do. She had been practicing that in her yoga class, while she was driving, when she was in the shower, while she was eating dinner, or even emptying the dishwasher. When Brynn felt she was drowning, she would try to breathe. It felt ridiculous. But she was desperate to breathe, so she sucked as much air into her lungs as she could and blew it out slowly. She repeated this over and over, until she almost felt lightheaded. She could feel the sensation that she was coming up above the water, and she didn't feel as though she were drowning any longer. This worked for her, at least for the moment, most of the time.

She was glad she was alone in the bathroom. She knew the hospitals locked psych ward was only two levels up, and while the drugs may be welcome and needed, she had too much to contend with to have a breakdown now.

Finally, she felt calmer, and she dared a peek at herself in the mirror. Her eyelids and face were puffy from tears, and she took a cold paper towel and tried to repair the damage. *It's hopeless*, she conceded. She readjusted her bobby pin once more, and walked out the door and headed toward the ICU

When she re-entered the room, Rose was still sleeping. The tube in her mouth was making the breathing sound for her, her chest rising and falling with each swoosh and click of the machine. Nothing had changed. She didn't even know Brynn had gone, and she didn't care that she had returned.

Brynn squeezed her hand. It was still cold like it had been for days. "I'm back, Mom," she said, her low husky voice wavering. She was trying to sound strong. She didn't want Rose to know how tired and scared she was. Rose would have liked the attention but Brynn's appearance would've alarmed and hurt her.

Brynn held tight to her hand. She closed her eyes as she tried to forget where she was.

CHAPTER TWENTY-FIVE

A Thorn for Rose

Don't you see, Darling Girl? I chose you. Rose was speaking to Brynn. She knew Brynn was in the chair next to her, but Rose was oddly aware that her lips had not moved and that she hadn't actually spoken.

Brynn. Brynn. Brynn. Rose was testing her voice. There was nothing. Rose didn't understand what was going on. *Am I actually talking?*

Brynn couldn't hear her.

Where am I? Oh, the hospital. I'm in the hospital.

It was coming back to her now. She had been home, waiting for Brynn to come over, but lately Brynn didn't come. Rose was mostly alone, and not aging well. She wasn't that old but at fifty-seven, she appeared older than most people she knew in their sixties, and some even in their seventies.

Rose could hear the machines with their beeping and their blipping. When Cindy the nurse came in to take care of her, she knew that the prognosis must not be good. Cindy wasn't telling Brynn the truth.

I'm thinking now. I'm hearing everything that everyone is saying so my brain must be working just fine. And I feel no pain. So strange to not feel any pain at all. It's so strange to feel so peaceful. I haven't felt at peace my entire life, and now I feel peace and no sadness, no pain. I feel nothing but warmth and peace. But, Brynn, I have to tell you what I've done. I have to tell you all of the things that I am supposed to tell you before I go.

Rose was contemplating how she could talk to Brynn. She tried moving her hand. It didn't move. She tried wiggling her toes. It was the same. She tried to open her mouth and realized that the breathing tube was taped down tight and that even if she wanted to talk, she couldn't. *Damn breathing tube!*

She concentrated on waking herself up.

Nothing!

She knew Brynn loved her even though they had not been as close over the past year. Brynn had created a chasm between them that Rose couldn't understand.

With Adam gone, it was as though Brynn had become someone else, someone who Rose did not know and it scared her. The more that Brynn edged away from her, the closer Rose tried to get. If Brynn ignored her phone calls, she continued to call. If Brynn ignored her emails, she just continued to send more emails. If Brynn didn't text her back, she continued to text until Brynn texted her back.

Brynn needed to be away from Rose. For the first time she didn't want to be the center of her world. She resented that Rose needed her and wanted her so much. She needed to be alone to revel in her own abandonment, in her own pain. She needed to protect her pain, even from Rose, and she held onto it desperate to keep it close to her. It was the only way that Brynn knew that she was alive.

Rose wasn't used to a life without Brynn. Brynn had been her whole life, her entire reason for living. Rose could not function without her. She was used to calling her for everything, whether it was day or night.

When Adam and Brynn were together, Rose regularly called Brynn when she got up at six a.m. Even though she knew that Brynn often worked late at the restaurant, she still called.

"I'm out of bananas," Rose said brightly, during one of her calls. She sounded very alert and awake.

"Mom, its six a.m.," Brynn said grouchily. She knew she should have turned off the ringer. The early morning phone calls from Rose weren't unusual. Rose didn't understand that the rest of the world wasn't on her schedule.

"I know. I've been up since four," Rose said ignoring Brynn's tone. "And I need bananas. I'm out. I also need bagels, milk, cream cheese..." Rose continued to tick down her list as Brynn lay there sleepily fading in and out of sleep, the phone lying in the bed by her ear.

"Is that Rose?" Adam said, annoyed. He would recognize that nasally voice anywhere. When Rose needed something, she sounded like a needy, petulant child, and listening to her grated on his nerves in a way that nothing else did.

"Yep, go back to sleep honey," Brynn said patting his back, trying to soothe him, and loving the feel of his muscles through the sheets.

"Brynn! Brynn!" Roses voice as getting louder.

"Mom, what do you want?" Brynn was irritated. She was more and more demanding. Rose seemed to need her now for everything. And it seemed that there was never an option.

She always wanted Brynn to accompany her on her errands, even when Brynn was a young girl. But now Rose just assumed she would join her, as though she had nothing else to do. She called her to take her grocery shopping, to get her haircut, to go to the doctor, to the dentist. Brynn found that she couldn't say no, to anything. After all, she had always been Rose's entire life. And even though Brynn had a fledgling restaurant to run, a new husband, and a house to take care of, Rose wanted her undivided attention.

Brynn was frustrated with Rose. She found herself canceling dates with Adam, or changing her schedule around at the last minute because Rose needed something. If Rose's cat got sick, Brynn was affected. If Rose forgot her wallet or needed to make an appointment or go somewhere, Brynn was affected.

Adam didn't understand why Brynn refused to say "no" to her.

"Brynn, she's a grown woman. She can take care of herself." He raged at her the fourth time she had changed their dinner plans because Rose's doctor appointment ran late. They had made the reservation months in advance for a restaurant that was difficult to get into. But now they had to cancel and Adam was furious.

"She can't! She's never been able to be alone and take care of herself," Brynn said helplessly.

"She can! You just don't let her."

"Adam, you don't understand. She needs me!"

"Let someone else take her, for God's sake!" It was an ongoing conversation between the two of them.

"There is NO one else! There's just *me!*" Brynn was completely alone in Rose's neediness. There was no one to understand or help her, and she was frustrated that he couldn't see it.

It seemed that Brynn was more often on the go from sun up to sun down. She would spend the days with Rose, and then she would go to the restaurant, not getting home until late at night. It crossed her mind repeatedly that if she weren't so fearful to have a child, it wouldn't happen this way. She never had time for her husband, and with Rose's demands on her schedule, she would never have time to care for a child, anyway.

There was a time when Brynn appreciated her time with Rose. But the new assumption that her time was always at Rose's expense was creating a distance between them. They were drifting further and further apart, as Brynn was manipulated by Rose's weakness.

Their outings consisted only of Rose's needs, never of the usual mother/daughter pleasantries that Brynn knew happened between some. There were no shopping trips, or luncheons, or outings that didn't involve something that Rose needed. Brynn found that their conversations had begun to shift as well. She couldn't remember a time that they talked about anything other than what Rose needed. And when Brynn did try to carry on normal conversation, Rose drifted. It was almost as though she had forgotten how to focus on anyone but herself.

Adam saw himself slowly losing Brynn. It was either work or Rose. He knew he was last in the lineup, and he pretended to be okay with it. But in his heart, he knew that he wasn't.

"I miss cuddling with you!" he would complain to her. But she would dismiss him, or try to placate him with a distracted "I'm sorry." He missed making dinner with her, or going to the movies on a mindless date. Squeezing in dinner was becoming increasingly more difficult and Brynn was becoming so crabby with her overextended schedule, and even when they did find time together, she wasn't pleasant.

Now that Adam was gone, Rose thought it would be so much

easier to have her undivided attention. But now Brynn was ignoring her.

Rose couldn't take it anymore, and showed up at her door after weeks of being ignored. She rang the bell non-stop until Brynn finally answered the door. She was furious. It was an emotion that Rose had never seen from Brynn. "Stop calling me!" Brynn had raged at her, looking more like a crazed stranger than her beautiful daughter. "Stop calling me, emailing me, and texting me. I need some space, Mother!"

"Oh Brynn, stop being so mad at me." Rose tried to pacify her. She hated when Brynn was mad at her. She tried to rub her arm, but Brynn jerked away. She wouldn't let Rose touch her anymore. Rose couldn't hug her, or pat her, or even get too close to her. Brynn always seemed to radiate in anger and it was usually directed toward Rose. They were so close all of Brynn's life, but now it was as though she couldn't stand to be near her.

"You are a selfish woman. If I gave you an inch, you took a mile. You never let me just live my life. So now, Adam is gone, and I have no one. You stole my life, and you don't even care! All you have ever cared about was you!"

Brynn's eyes were blazing. Rose had never seen her like this before. There was something in Brynn's eyes that she had never seen. *Hatred? Resentment? It can't be!*

"You left us there, in that house, with *HIM*!" Brynn was ranting now. "And you left me with him even when you said you wouldn't, and you let him hurt me time and time again. You didn't protect me like you said you would. You promised that you would protect me and you didn't! You did nothing!" Brynn cried out like a wounded animal, pulling at her hair as though she needed to be reminded of her pain. She thought about her razor, and she missed it. She thought about her scars and touched her side reminding herself that they were still there. She missed the control, and she felt dangerously out of control yelling at Rose.

Rose was in disbelief. It broke her heart that this girl, who she had rescued from an uncertain life in a foster home, now saw her as someone who ruined her life. This was her little girl! She wanted nothing in life other than to have a child. Brynn was her child, her only child, and the only real love of her life. Rose thought for a second of how Brynn had clung to her when she was little. She thought about how she needed her, and now those days were gone.

There was nothing that Rose could say to Brynn to convince her that she had done everything that she could to protect her and to watch over her. There was nothing that she could say to convince her that she hadn't meant to hurt her life with Adam. She knew that Brynn wouldn't be able to hear her. She was lost in the depths of her pain where Rose's voice could not reach her. Rose recognized that look in Brynn's eyes. She had seen it in her own eyes years before she ever found her Brynn. Rose knew that she would have stayed lost without her. She decided to absorb Brynn's anger, if it meant Brynn could heal.

And now, in the hospital, Brynn's anger was forgotten. She was Rose's sweet girl once again.

Brynn is holding my hand! Rose was so happy. She wished she could stroke Brynn's head as she did when she was a little girl. She soothed her so many times when she was young, whether it was after Thomas had beaten her, or when she was just sad for no reason. Rose was always able to make her feel better, but there was nothing that she could do now.

I'm stuck lying here in this damn hospital bed, and I can't even move. I'm dying, and I can't make her feel better now. Don't worry, beautiful girl. Rose was thinking hard trying to make Brynn hear her thoughts. She had so much more to tell her.

CHAPTER TWENTY-SIX

Difficult Decisions

The doctor was coming in. He was an older guy, Indian. Rose couldn't understand a word he was saying although Brynn didn't seem to have a problem. *Smart kid*, Rose thought. Brynn had always been smart. That's how she had gotten out of their little town, moved to the big city far away, and opened her successful little restaurant in a nice part of town.

Brynn was always smarter than Rose, always smarter than Thomas. Rose knew that she was destined to do more.

That's why Rose protected Brynn, and she needed to tell her. *I always protected you. When I knew Thomas was angry and drunk, I made sure he couldn't come after you. I looked after you every chance I got. I swear my dear, I did.* Rose knew that Brynn thought she didn't. But then again, Rose never told her how she punished Thomas, and how she made him pay for what he did.

The doctor was talking, but Brynn could only pick out certain words. "Unresponsive." "Deteriorating rapidly." "Odds she will not survive on her own."

Brynn couldn't say anything. Rose didn't have any written directives. Rose left it up to her as she did with everything else.

Don't let me go yet, Brynn. I need to wake up and tell you that I did protect you. Don't let me go.

Brynn couldn't think. She looked at Rose and battled with love and resentment. Rose had sucked the life right out of Brynn day after day until Brynn was forced to keep her distance just to be able to breathe. Brynn hated that she was afraid to have a child because she didn't want to be the type of mother that Rose had been. She was terrified that after having a mother that abandoned her, and a mother who was basically a child, that she too was destined to fail as a mother. Because of her crippling fear of love and motherhood, Brynn lost the only man she ever loved.

Wake me up! Wake me up! Rose pleaded.

"Miss? Miss?" the Doctor was speaking to Brynn interrupting her thoughts. "Do you know what your mother would want?"

"I don't know. I don't know." Brynn felt helpless. She didn't know what to do and there was no one in the world to help her now. The one person she would have turned to had abandoned her, and she was lost.

"You don't have to know right now, but you don't have much time. If something happens to her, then we will need to know what to do. It's been less than a week, but things are not looking very promising." The doctor was sympathetic but impatient. It was clear that he wanted Brynn to make a decision.

He walked out of the room, and Brynn was left alone with the beeping machines and the lifeless, comatose body, whose existence was now completely in her hands. A small part of her just wanted to pull the plug and be done with it, but she couldn't bring herself to think it, let alone make it happen.

Brynn fell into the chair, burying her head in her hands as she started to cry. Her small body shook as she sobbed, muffling her cries in the arm of her shirt. *What do I do? Oh Mom, what do I do?* They had never talked about what to do in this type of situation, and Brynn didn't know what she would've wanted. Brynn was conflicted with love for her mother who had saved her, and this woman who had ruined her.

Yet Brynn held Rose's hand, and prayed hard for her to live.

CHAPTER TWENTY-SEVEN

Rose's Clarity

Rose lay motionless in the hospital bed, tubes going down her throat, through her nose, in her veins. She was forced to be still, and she was frustrated.

How did I get here? How will I get out of here? How do I get to talk to Brynn again?

It was maddening not being able to move her arms and legs. Rose felt trapped in her body even though she couldn't feel any of the tubes or needles. Thank God she couldn't feel the catheter. It was unnerving Rose that she could think, but couldn't move. Her mind was wandering. It was almost as though she were on some kind of fabulous drug, watching a play with actors that she knew, and she was the star. Rose could see everything so clearly, and she felt a sense of clarity.

She was remembering her life. Her life with Brynn. Her life hadn't begun until Brynn showed up.

Every Halloween they dressed in matching costumes, even as Brynn got older. *Our costumes have to match Brynn! That's what makes us so special.* Rose loved sewing their costumes. She was good at sewing, and she had started making all of her own clothes. She tried to make clothes for Brynn, but she refused to wear them once she got into high school. So Halloween was the one time of the year that she could go all out for her Brynn. She remembered the poodle skirts, and the butterfly costumes, and the princesses. Rose loved every costume she made for her, and she kept them all. It was another way of connecting the two of them together. Rose needed to connect with Brynn as often as possible.

You can't leave me to go to college; she had said to her when she was a child, and showing promise in school. *If you go, I will go. I'll have to follow you. I can't live without you.* Rose was true to her word, and when Brynn went to college, Rose went with her, renting an apartment close by.

When Brynn was in high school and wanted to go to parties or to the mall with Stacy, Rose insisted on going, too. She reluctantly let Brynn have a job only because they needed the money, and she knew that Brynn would be happy making her own money. It was the one unselfish thing that Rose let her do. She knew that it meant a great deal to her and that she couldn't stop her from doing it. So at least three or four times a week, she would go up to the restaurant and have coffee just so they could chat, even though Brynn was busy working. She just loved watching her work and telling all of the customers, "There's my girl!"

Brynn's co-workers and the restaurant owners always remarked how interesting it was that Brynn and Rose were so close. Rose could tell by their faces that they thought it was a little odd, but she didn't care. Brynn didn't seem to mind, so she didn't mind.

Even when Adam came along, Brynn was still Rose's best friend. She made sure that Brynn knew how special she was and how much she needed her. She could tell that Brynn would get frustrated with her at times. Brynn even began telling her that she was becoming eccentric, but Rose knew that Brynn still loved her.

Rose didn't care what anyone else thought. Brynn's was the only opinion that mattered. She wasn't completely oblivious and could tell that sometimes people thought it was a little strange that Rose was too fixated on her grown child.

She knew that it annoyed Brynn sometimes that she would text her whenever she left the house and then again upon return. But what if something happened? How else would Brynn know to come looking? If Rose made multiple stops, she would text when she left and arrived at each one.

And if something funny happened at the store, she would text

Brynn to tell her all about it. If it were too long of a story, she would call. Brynn always answered. And if she didn't, Rose would just keep trying until she did because Brynn really liked Rose's stories.

Rose's mind uncontrollably went back to the darker days. *Damned coma!* When Rose was awake, she could control her thoughts, and she tried never to think about Thomas. But now, her mind was just drifting.

She had already visited her childhood. She was glad to stop thinking about that because it made her sad, too. Daddy was unhappy that she hadn't been a boy. But she adored Daddy anyway, and it made Rose sad that he never loved or wanted her, despite her deep affection for him. Momma Clara just never accepted Rose for who she was. Brynn knew that she would never treat her own daughter as Clara treated Rose. Rose was happy to get away from her childhood. It hadn't been a happy place to go.

I don't want to think about Thomas. I don't want to think about Thomas.

But it was too late. Rose's mind had already gone to Thomas. When she saw him in her mind, he wasn't the demon she remembered. He was just a man, and a fairly good-looking man. *Why hadn't I ever noticed that before?*

Rose was surprised to see the way that he looked at her, how his eyes followed her across the room and then darted away whenever she looked at him. *Why didn't I ever see that when he was alive?*

He was shy with her. But when they sat in silence, she could tell that he relaxed and was comfortable with her. When he did try to talk, she rebuffed him, which was often in their younger days of being married. It got to the point that rebuffing him was her only way of communicating with him, or just outright ignoring him.

I never realized it before how hard he tried to talk to me or just how much he loved me. He told me but I thought he was just punishing me to be cruel.

I hated that man so much for how he hurt my Brynn, and how he hurt me. She watched him in her mind, as he got drunker and drunker on his whiskey and how his face changed over time.

The whiskey distorted him into an angry man filled with demons that he couldn't begin to face. It was during those times when he would grab her and hold her so tight to him as though he wanted to crush her. She never understood it and thought he was merely trying to suffocate her. But when she saw it from her mind, it almost looked as though he were hugging her, holding her, cherishing her. She could see his face for the first time and it was almost as though he was breathing her in.

She would tell Brynn that she didn't love him loudly enough that he could hear her. She thought that he loved her as men love their hunting dogs; they took care of them and needed them but still treated them like bitches. She knew it made him mad and that it hurt him to hear that she had no use for him, but she didn't realize that it was for a different reason. This man was *in love* with her and she had never quite seen it before.

She wondered if she had ever been nice to him if he would have not had a reason to hit her. *Did he hit me to be close to me? Or was it for control or power?* If he was in love with her, he shouldn't have hit her, but he did it to punish her. He always felt she was mocking, and sometimes she was. The only control Rose ever had over her life was to withhold any love or affection. After all, in the beginning, he was nice to her.

She saw him as a younger man trying to talk to her, and he was just shy. She was oblivious to his stumbling because she didn't realize what he was doing. But he was just terrified, of her. *HE WAS TERRIFIED OF HER!* She couldn't believe it. How had he turned into this hideous monster, beating his wife and his child?

He really did resent Brynn for coming between them. The one thing that Rose ever wanted from him, he gave her. Then he hated Brynn. He hated Brynn, and he hated himself for giving her to Rose.

If I knew he loved me, would I have cared? Would it have mattered? Would it have been any different? She was so caught up in having a baby that she didn't realize that Thomas married her because he was in love with her. She thought that he married her because he wanted a wife, and not because he wanted *her* as his wife.

In her mind, she saw them as children. She saw him watching her when he was a young boy and she could tell that he was smitten. *So it went back that far? I had no idea. Did he ever say he loved me? Did he ever tell me or was he just always mean? I don't know if it would've mattered.*

The first time he slapped her, she was stunned.

Brynn was turning six and Rose was busy planning her birthday party. The slap came unexpectedly. He had started drinking early, and he was angry because he said she had spent too much money on the party. "I don't know who you are tryin' to impress," he had slurred angrily. She hadn't purchased anything more than the year before, so she was confused by his anger. Rose's cheek was stinging where he had slapped her hard. Nobody had ever slapped her in the face before, and she couldn't believe how much it hurt. Thomas didn't even apologize.

She looked over at Brynn who watched him slap her, and she could tell that it frightened her. So she smiled at her to make her think that she was all right, and Brynn smiled back showing her pretty little teeth.

"What the hell are you smiling for?" he said frustrated. Rose could tell that he wanted to slap her again, and she braced for it. "Oh, Jesus, relax. I'm not going to hurt you. You're such a paranoid idiot." He had started to become meaner and Rose didn't understand it. She didn't know how to stop it. There was nobody she could talk to, and she knew that she couldn't talk to him.

There were so many times after that when the slapping turned to hitting, and the hitting turned to punching. Eventually, the punching turned to kicking, and Thomas managed to throw shaking and shoving and pushing in, too. Rose didn't understand the anger and the violence in him, and she was afraid. He would bubble up out of nowhere at times and there was nowhere that she could go.

When he got to be too drunk to hit, he was mean. He said vile, horrible things. Rose knew that he said mean things to Brynn, too, spitting out words that made them both feel stupid and small. He could turn any word into a curse just by the tone in which he said it.

Rose wanted to leave him more than anything. *If I leave him, Brynn will starve.* She stayed year after year. There was nothing else that she could do. But she made sure that he knew that she didn't love him, it was the only way she knew how to fight back. If she had loved him, would it have been different for them? Would he have been nicer?

Rose wished she could shut off her mind. She wished that she really was asleep and couldn't see her life from so many different perspectives. If only Rose could just allow her mind to go blank. She shouldn't have to see her life like this, especially now when it was too late to change anything. What was the purpose of having clarity and perspective now when nothing could be done?

Now Rose almost felt bad for what she had done to him. What *they* did to him. But how could she have known?

CHAPTER TWENTY-EIGHT

Adam's New Friend

He didn't plan to date someone so soon.

Adam hadn't talked to Brynn in months and felt so lost. Even though they were living separate lives while they were under the same roof, he still missed her presence. Adam missed her voice and her smell. He missed looking at her when she didn't know that he was looking, and seeing Brynn's dark hair fall all over, and how she impatiently pushed it to the side. Adam had already spent half of his life with her, and didn't know if he was going to be able to survive without her.

Adam worried that she was cutting herself again. It had been so long, but he didn't know if she would still want to. He hoped that she wouldn't, but he knew that he couldn't stay with her for that reason alone. She had never cut herself deep enough for any medical treatment. Most of the time, she just made superficial cuts, even though she still felt the pain, and the scars were evident.

He kept telling himself that he was going to call her. Every day he woke up and said, "This is the day." But then the day would go by and he would find that he hadn't called her, and he didn't know why. He felt like such an asshole for not calling.

Adam felt like such an asshole for walking out and for giving up so quickly.

He had driven by the house numerous times thinking *if I just went in. If I just walked up to the porch and rang the bell, we could talk and everything would be all right.*

But he was afraid. It had been so long and with each passing day, more and more time went by. More time that he didn't talk to her, didn't call her, and didn't see her. He knew she was pissed at him, and disappointed, and so hurt. He felt like such a coward but he couldn't face her. Sometimes he would just sit outside the house in his car and dare her to see him. *If she sees me, shouldn't I go in? If she sees me, maybe I could apologize to her, and we can start all over. After all, I still love her, don't I? I think I still want to be her husband.* He thought the answers would come if he sat outside of the house that he once walked into every day, happily married to his beautiful Brynn.

It scared Adam that he didn't know the answers. One moment he wanted nothing but Brynn, and the next he didn't know at all. He thought maybe the wood and the beams would just speak to him and tell him what he should do.

But the house was silent.

He just didn't know anymore. The more time that went by, the more confused he was. He began to forget the sound of her voice. The pictures in his phone reminded him of what she looked like, but he hadn't taken one of her in a long time. Brynn used to smile at him, but at some point she stopped and when she stopped, he didn't take any more pictures. He didn't want to see the scowl on her face or the darkness in her eyes. He wanted to see the girl that he could make laugh, and she had disappeared without any warning.

He just wanted to turn back the clock and go back to a time when they were happy. *Was it when we were fifteen, or when we were in college? Or was it in our first apartment, or when we moved into our house? Maybe it was never, maybe we were never really happy, and I just imagined it all.*

Adam seemed to remember that he was so happy to be with her, but had she ever been happy? Or had she always been so tired and miserable. Was she always this complacent in their love?

One morning he woke up, and Brynn was a distant stranger to him. He had heard of this happening to couples, but he never thought that it would happen to them. They were Adam and Brynn, Brynn and Adam.

He waited a couple of weeks before he called his parents to tell them that he had left Brynn. Even though they told him he should come home for some perspective, he declined. He couldn't face them. He couldn't deal with the guilt and the lectures.

He didn't want to deal with it, at all.

His parents loved Brynn almost as much as he did. After all, they had believed in her enough to invest in her restaurant. They felt that somebody had to.

"What happened to you and Brynn?" his Mother asked, trying not to pry but needing to know. In the beginning, Lillian was admittedly hesitant to give Adam over to this fragile girl. But when she saw how much he loved her, she relented. She was afraid that he wouldn't enjoy his youth and his life. But she knew that Adam followed his heart, just like his Daddy, and she let herself fall in love with Brynn, too. She couldn't bear the thought of losing her now, not when Adam and Brynn had been through so much. Adam's Mom knew that Brynn was more reluctant in her love, but it was there as clear as day.

The Michaels had met Rose once early on and knew immediately that her relationship with Brynn was strange, to say the least. It was almost as though she were completely dependent upon Brynn for everything, which was a lot to bear for a girl so young.

Lillian loved her son with all of her heart, but she could never imagine depending on Adam for so much. After all, she was the mother. He was a young man and it wasn't his responsibility to take care of her. It was up to her to take care of him. Lillian felt that her gift to him was his childhood, his adolescence, and the freedom to live his life protected and free.

Lillian knew that it must have gotten bad for him to just give up on his love for her. "Honey, you know you can just come home. You know that you don't have to stay there all alone!"

"I'm okay Mom. I'll come home when I'm ready." He dreaded the call, but knew that he needed to make it. He kept it short without much detail and hung up as quickly as he could. Adam was keeping to himself. He had only been out with Sam once since he left, but being with Sam only made it worse. There was a day when hanging out in a crowded bar was fun for both of them, but it was clear that neither of them really wanted to be there.

"I'm sorry, man," Sam had said after they had gotten their third beer and were settled in to what was once their favorite table, optimal for harmless girl watching. They were men, and liked to look, but they never ever touched. Sam had been his best friend for a long time now. They were similar in many ways and cut from the same cloth. They were both handsome and youthful, Sam with the boyish good looks, Adam more mature. But both in committed relationships and both devoted to their wives.

"I really thought you loved her, man." Sam said, trying to mask his disappointment. He really liked Brynn, and thought she and Adam were good for one another.

"I do!" Adam had said his frustration evident. "That's just it. I do love her. But I can't talk to her. We've been separate from each other for so long."

Sam's phone vibrated for the tenth time that night. He jumped and read the text from his wife, smiling as he did it.

"Sorry about that." He said trying to hide his boyish smile. "The baby just smiled. The wife sent me a pic." He held up his phone to show Adam his pink head banded daughter's mushy little smiling face. Sam couldn't contain his excitement in his sparking blue eyes.

Adam had tried to smile. "Listen, man, why don't you go home? Spend time with your family. I'm okay, really. At least I will be."

Adam could tell that Sam had mixed feelings. "I'm good, really. I can stay." Sam said, his voice wavering just a little.

Adam convinced him to leave when he finished his beer. He knew that there was no point having his friend there when he clearly wanted to be somewhere else. He was jealous. He wanted what Sam had. He wanted to be the guy getting the pictures of the squishy-faced baby. He wanted to have a family of his own and he wanted to have it with Brynn. But now he couldn't.

Sam finished his beer, man-hugged his friend, and left the crowded bar, happily.

Adam stayed and hung out by himself until he felt sufficiently drunk, and then grabbed a cab back to his apartment feeling more depressed than ever.

He found that the only thing that distracted him was work.

He liked going in and knowing what he needed to do every day. A bright spot in his day had turned into Annie, his co-worker who he had confided in after he first left Brynn. Adam always liked her sunny disposition and it didn't hurt that she was easy on the eyes. She was the queen of strange relationships, which he could never figure out, but he never really tried to analyze her love life before. He thought she was engaged at one point, but she no longer wore the ring.

He could never keep up with his co-workers and their love lives, and he intentionally never tried.

But he appreciated that Annie had seemed to make it her mission to brighten up his day every time she saw him. She brought him coffee every morning and occasionally one of those blueberry muffins he loved. She always asked how he was doing and made it a point to email him funny stories or cartoons to make him laugh. She seemed genuinely concerned about him, which caught him off-guard.

He hadn't had anyone dote on him for quite a long time, and he was flattered. He had forgotten what it was like to have someone care about him, and want to make him smile. But then again, when he thought really hard about it, he couldn't remember if Brynn had ever made as much of an effort for him as Annie seemed to be making.

After all, Brynn had her mother and the restaurant and a million other things occupying her mind. Annie was his friend and more and more he found that she tried to make sure that things were going well for him as she checked in throughout the day. He liked that she lit up whenever she saw him, and he found that more and more often he looked for her emails and texts.

I'm still married. He said to himself. Even though he hadn't done anything, he felt guilty.

He knew she had a boyfriend, so he reasoned with himself that they were just friends. *So why do I feel awkward mentioning Brynn's name? Why do I feel guilty when she smiles at me?*

He tried not to look at her as all the other guys did. But he found that more and more he was noticing how tight her skirts were and how pretty her face was. He had never noticed that before. He had always felt pretty comfortable around her, but he was starting to find that he felt awkward, almost shy when she talked to him.

What in the Hell am I doing?

He was confused. He knew that involving himself in any way with Annie would confuse the outcome with Brynn. But Brynn didn't care about him. If she did, she would have called. He hadn't spoken to her in nearly three months now, and still there had been no word. *How has it been three months already? How can I have abandoned my wife for three months?*

He knew that he was a good guy. He had always been a good guy, defender of the weak and taking care of others. He was the guy that did the right thing. But now he felt that he was on a slippery slope. He hadn't done anything wrong, but he knew that he was on the verge. He reasoned that he was separated. That he was no longer in the same committed relationship that he had been in once. He reasoned that he was on the verge of divorce and that one drink or one dinner wouldn't hurt. She had been asking him, but he always found an excuse.

He knew that he wasn't going to be able to make excuses for much longer, and he was coming to the realization that he didn't want to.

"Okay, Mister" she said sitting on his desk, just enough so that he got a good view of her ass, but also so that he could see how toned her legs were.

He noticed that her skirt was exceptionally short and tight today. *Oh Good God. What is she trying to do to me?*

"You keep dodging me. You can go out with me for a drink, you know? We are just *friends,* after all." She was staring up at him with that cute little smile she reserved only for him these days. She made sure Adam knew that she was ignoring her boyfriend when he called her at work these days. The boyfriend was getting frustrated, but she didn't care, which she let him know that, as well.

Now that she knew that Adam wasn't talking to his wife at all, she figured that it was the time to solidify their *friendship.*

"I know Annie," he stammered a little. *What the...I never stammer. God, she's making me nervous.* "It's just that...I..."

She was enjoying his discomfort. He always walked around with such confidence, but she was actually making him nervous. *This is good. Very, very good.*

"I'm still married to Brynn," he said finally trying to make his voice strong. *What would Brynn say if she knew that I was about to agree to go out for a drink with Annie?* Brynn already disliked her. She met her once at an office Christmas party and she hated the way that Annie fawned all over him. "You better watch out for her," she had warned him. He told her that she had nothing to worry about, and that Annie was harmless, which was very true at the time. He was beginning to wonder about that now.

He hadn't had sex for a long time. He couldn't even remember the last time that he and Brynn had been together. He tried but every time he tried, he got lost in thoughts of Annie and her nice tight ass. *I'm going to Hell, I'm going to Hell, I'm definitely going to Hell.*

"I know, silly!" Annie said giggling innocently. "We're just friends, remember? It's okay to have one drink." She hoped that she wasn't coming across as desperate. But she was desperate. After all, the clock was ticking and she wasn't getting any younger. *This* could be the guy.

She wanted Adam more than she had ever wanted anything. She knew that he was married, but he wasn't talking to his wife. It was a minor detail, and Annie knew that once she reeled him in, it would only be a matter of time. He would forget about his wife, and she could end up being his new wife. She had already thought about how beautiful their babies would be. After all, Brynn didn't deserve him. All she needed to do was to get Brynn out of the way and make him forget her. It was already becoming more of a reality with each passing day.

"Okay, one drink," Adam relented. He knew that he would. "Just one."

Annie felt glorious.

They worked out the details and Annie left his office with that little smile on her face. As soon as she crossed the threshold into her own office and closed the door, she allowed her smile to spread across her face as she threw her arms up in the air and celebrated with a happy dance.

Finally! Tomorrow is the night, and then it will be the weekend and... I guess we will just have to wait and see. She imagined them spending the weekend together in bed twisted in her eight hundred count sheets.

Adam has no idea what he is in for!

Chapter Twenty-Nine

Lost Brynn

Brynn was spiraling downward. With Stacy and Adam gone, she no longer had anyone.

Rose kept calling, but she didn't answer. Her voicemail filled up, but she didn't care. The only two people that she wanted to talk to were gone. She didn't even read the daily emails from Jane about the restaurant.

She couldn't care about anything.

Adam's mom tried to call her several times, but Brynn knew she wouldn't be able to talk to her without crying the entire time. How disappointed his mom must be in her. Brynn always knew that they had taken a chance on her twice, first with their son and then again with the restaurant. When she was able to pay back their loan, she felt so good. They believed in her, and she had lived up to their expectation. But she hadn't with Adam, who was more important, and she couldn't bear the thought of answering to them for that.

Brynn cried for days and days. She couldn't believe that she could keep crying the way that she did. How could she produce so many tears? Her lips and her skin were dry, and her throat was parched. She was becoming dehydrated, and she stopped being able to breathe normally. She thought that if she got a paper bag like the people did on TV when they couldn't breathe that it would help her. But it didn't.

Brynn thought about her blade. How sharp and beautiful and shiny it was, and how it could make her feel better. How if she cut a little deeper, in a different place, how it could make it all go away.

She couldn't breathe.

Every day she told herself she had to breathe. It was no longer a natural normal function. Sometimes no matter how hard she tried to take air into her lungs, she just couldn't.

Brynn felt her chest get tight as though someone were sitting on her and would not get up. Her breath caught in her throat, and it wouldn't move through her lungs. She thought if she could will herself to breathe, she could get some relief as she could feel the oxygen flow through her lungs. But she couldn't. She felt as if she were suffocating.

She felt as though someone was strangling her, but there was no one there. It was just her and she was terrified.

She didn't know what to do. She couldn't even remember to eat. She had no appetite, and when she did eat, she just felt nauseous. She was amazed at how little food she really needed to survive and she didn't see herself eating much ever again.

Brynn knew she was spiraling. Adam was gone for three months now, and it was evident he was never coming back.

Stacy's memorial was coming up. *Next week, the week after?* Brynn had lost track of time. She knew she needed to go, and say goodbye to her friend. They had waited so long to say goodbye, because the police had to do their work.

According to Samantha, "that bitch shot my baby in the head. And just to make sure, she shot her in the belly to make sure her baby died, too." They couldn't even have a proper burial so they decided to cremate her. It devastated Brynn that she couldn't even see her friend's lovely face one more time.

Brynn was in pain. This pain was punishment. Brynn deserved it for being such a terrible friend to Stacy. She let it run through her like a million knives over and over, sharp, stabbing, beautiful, and constant. Without it, she felt as though she would just be dead. And she needed to feel the pain. She wanted to feel it to punish herself for failing the two people who meant the most to her.

Brynn could hear him saying that they needed to spend more

time together and that he missed their dates. She could see how disappointed he was when she would read in another room, and for the first time, she was beginning to understand how much he missed her. She saw how disconnected they had become, and she was ashamed of how she stopped trying. She allowed Rose, her ambition for the restaurant, and so many other things, to pull her from him. And she did the same with Stacy.

She understood why he left. Brynn had been absent from him for a long time. She was so wrapped up in her own head most of the time that she even forgot that he existed. They abandoned one another. She hadn't done it physically as he had, but she knew that she left him emotionally.

She didn't blame him for leaving now. She would have left her, too.

But why wouldn't he at least have called? Why couldn't he try to come back and give her the chance to love him again? They were married. Didn't that mean something?

When she could leave the house, she did. But more often than not, she stayed home. She didn't shower. She didn't wash her hair or change her clothes. If she could get out of bed or off the bathroom floor, she felt like she had accomplished a great deal for the day. Brynn was getting weaker, and she needed to find her razor blade. She couldn't hold off any longer. She just needed to hold it in her hands, and put the cool blade against her face. She needed to find it.

She couldn't wait.

CHAPTER THIRTY

Jane

Jane kept calling, but Brynn didn't answer.

Even when there was a knock on the door and the doorbell kept ringing over and over and over, she thought she would just ignore it. For a half an hour, it went on and on, knocking and ringing, until Brynn drug herself to the door and peeked outside.

It was Jane.

Brynn opened the door reluctantly and squinted into the bright sunlight.

Jane stood in the doorway staring at her, trying not to look surprised at her appearance. Brynn knew that she looked bad, gaunt, scraggly, and ugly. She had stopped looking in the mirror a while ago. She knew what she looked like.

Jane looked at her silently. Brynn opened the door and Jane walked in.

They sat down in the living room and didn't speak for a long time. Brynn curled up on the couch and pulled a blanket up over her as far she could, as if she could hide from Jane. "How is the restaurant?" she finally said without emotion.

Jane could tell that she didn't really care what the answer was.

She was so worried for Brynn. Brynn was her mentor. She was the only woman that Jane had ever worked for, and Brynn had believed in her far more than Jane ever believed in herself. She was a single mom to two beautiful girls. When Jane first met Brynn, she couldn't believe that this young girl was the owner of the restaurant. She barely looked old enough to even have a job. But the more she talked to her, she saw how sharp she was. She was so thankful that Brynn hired her as the manager.

Jane's husband died young of stomach cancer, and she needed to be able to work but still be there for her daughters who were six and nine at the time. She was at the end of her rope, older than her years and worn out from the stress. She had been a pretty twenty-something, but when Brynn hired her she was thirty pounds overweight, and she looked ten years older than her thirty-five years.

Now, six years later, the girls were doing well, and Jane was grateful to Brynn for giving her such a good job. She had shed most of the weight, and had been able to take care of herself so she looked her age again. With Brynn's encouragement, she had begun dating. She never thought she would after Todd's death. She was so heartbroken and couldn't bear the thought of moving on. But Brynn had encouraged her to go to grief counseling, take better care of herself, and readily lent a sympathetic ear whenever she needed one.

Jane knew that she had to try to get through to her.

Brynn trained her well and the restaurant was maintaining. The employees loved working there and they knew that they had to take care of it while Brynn was gone. They were like a little family, and each one took care of their share and then some. The business was consistent and the regulars were loyal, some even coming in five days a week. Jane wasn't worried about the restaurant at all.

But her friend and boss appeared to be lost. This Brynn slouching on the couch in front of her unwashed, and wearing dirty clothes was someone that Jane didn't recognize. She tried to disguise her horror at the door, but she knew that she'd done a poor job. The pain in Brynn's pretty face was evident, and her eyes were so puffy they didn't even look like they were open.

Jane didn't know what she would need to say to her, but she knew she needed to do something. This was Brynn.

She started with idle chatter about the restaurant. Business was good, prices on meat were stabilizing a bit, the health department had come in, and they had gotten another perfect score, the regular old men, Bob and Dave, were doing well, and always asked how Brynn was doing, and so on and so on. Jane talked on and on pausing so that Brynn could chime in if she wanted to. Brynn stared out the window the entire time not even trying to tune in. Jane didn't even know if she were listening.

"Rose keeps coming in," Jane said. Brynn looked at her and blinked for a moment. "She keeps asking if we've heard from you. She's her usual self." Jane smiled.

Brynn loved Momma. But she knew what everyone else saw. She wanted to smile back, but her lips wouldn't move.

"I make sure she eats every day. I feed her healthy food sometimes when she lets me. But I make sure that she eats something other than her usual peanut butter and jellybeans. She knows that I won't take her crap like the girls do." Jane saw Brynn's lips twitch when she started talking about Rose, so she knew that she was listening.

"Brynn, you need to come back to us. We need you. Rose needs you. I think she's collecting stuff again. She always stops by with bags of stuff that she refuses to leave in her car. She calls them her valuables." Jane paused, her blue eyes searching Brynn's for some sign of life.

"Talk to me. I'm your friend and I'm here for you," Jane pleaded with her. "Brynn!"

She stood up suddenly with her brown hair bouncing as she did.

"Brynn!" she said louder, taking a step closer to her as she said her name. "Brynn! BRYNN!"

Brynn was looking at her now. She had gotten her attention.

"Have you seen Adam? Has he been in?" Brynn asked quietly. Even though she didn't involve him, she knew that he cared about the place. He had done a lot of the painting himself, and the girls adored him.

"No. He hasn't," Jane said afraid that her answer would cause Brynn to withdraw further, but Jane saw relief on her face instead.

"Brynn, you need help. You need to go talk to someone," Jane said quickly, while Brynn was still listening. "Remember what you told me when you hired me and I was still reeling from Todd's death? You told me that I needed to move on, that I needed to find my light. You told me that you could tell that I was a beautiful person, and that I had a lot of life in front of me. You told me not to give up."

She talked quickly replaying Brynn's words back to her. She remembered everything that Brynn told her six years ago. It had made all of the difference to her. It mattered when nothing else did, and she had listened. Brynn gave her strength, and she needed to be able to do that for her now.

Tears were glistening in Brynn's eyes, and falling down her cheeks.

"I'm so tired, Jane. There are things that you don't know about. There are things in my life that have been hard, and now this. I just can't take anymore. I can't. And I'm alone. I'm so alone." Brynn was crying so hard now that Jane could hardly understand her, but she felt what her friend was feeling. She felt it too, at one time.

"You're not alone. I'm here, and the girls at the restaurant. Even Rose is there for you. You're not alone. I will be there for you as you were there for me. I can give you the name of the therapist that I went to. He was great and helped me a lot. I'm here because of you."

Jane could tell that she was getting through. She sat on the couch next to her friend and hugged her. If she could get her to come back into the light, she would have accomplished much. After three months of not leaving the house, not eating, and not taking care of herself, Brynn had a long journey back.

"I don't know what you've been through but you are strong, Brynn. Look at all you've accomplished. Adam will come back, and if he doesn't, then you are strong enough to make it through." Jane saw how Adam and Brynn looked at each other, and she saw real love flowing between them. Brynn didn't realize how she peppered Adam's name into every conversation she was having. Jane had hope for them, even if Brynn didn't. She knew that Brynn could be stubborn and aloof, but she also knew what a beautiful heart she had. And she knew that they loved each other. Jane was determined to make sure that Brynn knew that she was there for her. Brynn needed a friend, someone to take care of her as she had done for others, especially now.

She even volunteered to take Brynn to her therapist, as Brynn had once done for her.

But her first challenge was to get her to change her clothes and eat. She knew that she would have to take it one step at a time

CHAPTER THIRTY-ONE

Adam's Date

Adam and Annie's first date didn't turn out exactly how Annie had planned.

They met at the bar and had a couple of drinks. Adam was nervous, so he drank his especially fast. Brynn didn't like drinking, and Adam respected that, so he rarely drank around her and they never kept alcohol in the house. He knew that drinking reminded her of Thomas, and he never wanted to remind her of Thomas.

He felt the third drink going right to his head.

Annie looked hot and she knew it. As she walked into the bar alone, she could see that guys were gawking at her out of the corner of their eye. She had worn the tightest, shortest skirt she could legally wear. Her black stilettos complimented her lean legs, and she wore a nice tight shirt with her Victoria Secret pushup bra that made her look like she was bigger than her A cup.

Adam's sapphire eyes, that looked darker in the bar light, nearly popped out of his head when he saw her. She was making him uncomfortable again, and she loved it. She couldn't believe that he had even agreed to meet her, but she was going to take full advantage of it.

They got appropriately tipsy. She even got him to dance with her a little, even though she could tell that he felt awkward. She assured him that no one cared about them and that everyone else was dancing. She purposely chose this bar because there were no TVs, and no other distractions, only music, liquor, and dancing. She wanted him all to herself.

When it was time to go, she lingered. He hadn't even so much as kissed her yet, and she was disappointed. She thought by now that they would be making out on the dance floor, but he hadn't even tried to grab her yet. She was bumping and grinding him all night, and he didn't respond at all as she had hoped or anticipated. She even tried grabbing his hand, but he continued to pull it away, gently but firmly. He was the perfect gentleman and she was getting frustrated.

Ok, slow down. He's not ready yet. She chastised herself trying her best to hide her disappointed.

He yelled in her ear over the thumping of the music, "Are you ready to go?"

"Sure! Where do you want to go?" she yelled back.

"I'm beat. I need to go home!" he grinned at her halfheartedly. He really did look tired.

"I can do that," she said flirtatiously.

He looked at her without saying anything and walked outside. She followed him, once again disappointed. She hoped that he would yell something back in her ear. She loved hearing his deep voice that close to her, and feeling his hot breath.

It wasn't as late as she had hoped it would be. He started to walk, and she walked next to him in silence.

"Listen, Annie. I like you and I'm glad we are *friends*. But I'm not ready for anything more than what we have right now," He said apologetically, his voice a little off kilter. He was trying to make his voice sound completely sober, but was having a hard time. "I hope you unnerstand that."

"Of course I do." she said trying to disguise her frustration. "I know you are going through a hard time right now." She had been more careful than he was to pace herself. She didn't like to lose control, so she limited herself to drinking just enough to feel good, but not enough to feel fuzzy.

"Ok, good. I was worried you wouldn't. But hey, you look beautiful!" He was weaving a little.

"Why don't I drive you home? You probably shouldn't be

behind the wheel right now." She said grabbing hold of his arm. She was struggling with her stilettos. *If he goes down, I'm in trouble*, she thought.

Maybe I'll land on top of him. She smiled.

"That's a good idea," he said looking a little sheepish. He didn't usually drink as much, but he had been nervous and the gin was going down faster than usual. "If you don't mind."

She didn't mind. It bought her a little more time to work her magic.

She guided him toward her car and tried to help him in. This time she did fall on top of him as he fell back into the seat. He grabbed her around the waist as he went down, and she felt her body flying against his. For a moment, she was in his arms, as tight up against him as she could be.

Oh God, he smells so good! She didn't move. Maybe if she didn't move, he would kiss her. They locked eyes. *This is it!*

She could tell that he wanted to kiss her. She could see it in his eyes and feel it as his arms tightened around her. She could feel it as his legs started to wrap around hers, and she felt him warming up around her. This is what she had been waiting for. He was what she wanted.

Forget your wife. Kiss me! Kiss me! She demanded hoping that she could will him to kiss her.

He sat up abruptly looking embarrassed, his arms letting go of her pushing her gently off him.

Damn!

The moment was gone, and the mood between them was broken.

She got up and smoothed down her skirt.

"Sorry," he slurred, not looking at her.

This time she couldn't disguise her irritation. "It's okay." He knew that it wasn't okay, but he had too many drinks to figure out how to fix it, at the moment.

She drove him the short distance to his apartment in silence. She was wondering if this was just a big waste of time. After all, she hadn't completely broken it off with her boyfriend yet. She could still salvage that relationship if she wanted to. Adam was hot, and the kind of man she could see herself marrying and having babies with, but this was a lot of work. This wife thing was annoying. She didn't want to keep trying if he wasn't going to reciprocate in any way.

When they drove up to his building, he didn't get out right away.

He turned to her, steadying his beautiful eyes on her. "I like you, Annie. You've been a good friend, but I swear I don't know what I want right now. I don't want to lead you on. If I weren't married..."

"But you're separated," She argued. "You're separated and you don't even talk to her anymore. What harm can it do to have some fun?" She moved a little closer to him.

"I don't want to have fun. I mean, I want to have fun, but it doesn't feel right. You've never been married so you don't understand." He could tell that he wounded her.

She sat up straight so that she was no longer leaning in toward him. "You're right, I've never been married. I don't understand how you can stay married to someone you don't want to be with anymore." She was angry.

"I don't know that I don't want to be with her. I just don't want to be with her *right now*. What I did was wrong. I was wrong to just walk out and now it's hard to go back. Every day it gets harder and I need to resolve it. If you can just be content to be my friend for now, then we can do that." He was confused and sad, and she felt herself soften toward him.

We've been friends for so long, how can that be a bad thing? She reasoned with herself. She knew that she wanted more. But if she wanted to have any chance with him at all then she was just going to need to be content with friendship.

"Okay." She said brightly giving him her best smile. "Friends, it is."

She leaned in to hug him and suddenly his lips found hers, searching, aching.

Finally! She sighed as she leaned in and let herself go.

CHAPTER THIRTY-TWO

Remembering Stacy

He was coming for her.

She was hiding under the bed praying that he wouldn't find her. She could barely see his feet in the doorway. The only light was coming from the hall illuminating his feet. Her bedroom was completely dark. She thought that if it were dark enough that he wouldn't be able to find her. He was coming closer. She could feel her mouth getting dry and her heart pounding in her chest. If he found her, he would hurt her. She knew it.

He was in a really bad mood and he started drinking early.

He was yelling her name in that mean thick voice that he always got about four drinks in. She was trying to stop herself from shaking. She didn't want him to hurt her again. She hadn't recovered from the last time he had beaten her. The feet were getting closer and closer. They were right at the edge of the bed.

She held her breath.

The feet stopped. She couldn't breathe. She was still frozen in fear. Maybe he wouldn't know she was there. Maybe. Oh God, I think he knows!

She saw his big hands quickly reaching for her, and she couldn't get away fast enough. He was grabbing her hair and pulling her out from under the bed. She started screaming.

She sat up in bed covered in sweat, her heart racing. "I'm okay, I'm okay," she repeated over and over. Her shrink had told her to tell herself that she was okay anytime she woke up from a bad dream. He said it would help. "I'm okay, I'm okay."

She couldn't move. She was still too afraid. Frozen. She had to remind herself that he was dead, and that he couldn't hurt her anymore.

Adam used to comfort her and hold her tight when she had bad dreams, which was often. He knew how to soothe her and to make her feel safe. She didn't know what to do when the bad dreams came and Adam was gone. Sometimes she found herself lying under her bed, and sometimes she found herself curled up in a corner of the closet, paralyzed until the feeling of terror passed. Sometimes it would take minutes, and sometimes it would take much longer.

Jane was right about getting help. She had only been to him twice so far, but it had just felt good to talk. The first time she went, she cried though her entire session. She cried so much she could barely talk. She was surprised, but she actually liked her shrink a lot. He was the only person on earth she had to talk to now. He was an older man with kind eyes. There was a genuineness about him that made her trust him almost immediately, which was very rare for her. She found herself telling him things that she never told another living soul, not even Stacy or Adam.

Once the words started tumbling out, it was as though they wouldn't stop. She never talked so much to one person in all of her life, and she felt a little selfish and indulgent, but he didn't seem to mind. He just sat and listened, scribbling occasionally on his yellow legal pad.

After he heard her entire story, he simply said, "You've had so much loss in your life."

She cried. Someone finally understood her.

Brynn's only friend was dead. So now, she only had her kind shrink. He wasn't surprised when she told him about the cutting. She liked that about him. She told him how she wanted to do it every day, and that some days she thought about just letting herself bleed, but that she couldn't bring herself to. He looked worried for her with that, but she told him that he didn't need to worry. That she had only thought about it, but she would never kill herself. She didn't really want to die she just wanted the pain to stop, and giving herself more pain dulled what was buried deep within her, threatening to eat her alive.

And as much as she wanted to just roll over and stay in bed, on this day she couldn't. She was too upset to go back to sleep and she didn't want to get up. But she knew that she had to. The sun was just starting to come through the curtains and she knew that she was going to need to get moving soon.

Today was the day.

This was the day that she would say good-bye to Stacy.

It was four weeks after Jane came to her house. Jane reluctantly agreed to go with her. She knew that Brynn wouldn't be able to do it on her own. She didn't know if Adam was going to be there, and she wasn't strong enough to go by herself. They were only going for the day. It was a three-hour drive there and then a three-hour drive home but Brynn didn't want to stay in town. She didn't say why, but she wanted to leave there as soon as possible. Jane was dreading today, but she promised her friend she would go with her. She knew it was going to be sad and awkward. Brynn had done so much for her when she needed a friend, but she still dreaded it.

Jane pulled her Focus up to the charming Victorian, and sat outside in her car. She didn't want to go in just yet. She was a little early, just as she always was.

She looked around the street and saw a familiar car parked halfway down. *Adam?*

The driver of the car looked at her and they made eye contact. *It is Adam!*

He looked surprised and quickly backed his car up and sped away. *Should I tell Brynn?* She struggled internally. She didn't know if it would help to tell her. She didn't even know if Adam would be at the funeral today. Telling Brynn may make the day more difficult, especially if Adam wasn't there. But if she didn't tell her, then Brynn wouldn't know that he still cared about her. After all, he wouldn't be there if he didn't, *right?*

Jane's phone beeped. Brynn was texting her. "Where are u?"

Jane texted back. "Outside."

"B out in five. Thought u were late."

"LOL. U know I am NEVER late."

Jane closed her eyes in battle with herself.

A few minutes later Brynn got into the car. She looked better than she had in weeks. Her dark brown hair was pulled back and the circles were almost gone from under her eyes, although they were still fairly puffy. She had lost a lot of weight and her clothes hung on her, looking as droopy as her expression. She looked as good as she could look, which was much better than she had looked in months. Jane was just happy that she started leaving the house again and joining the world. She'd even made it into the restaurant a few times, although she still refused to see Rose. She just wasn't up for that yet.

She wore a black skirt and a pretty pale pink silk blouse. Pink had been Stacy's favorite color, and she wanted to wear it even though she knew her friend would never see it.

Jane plugged their destination into the GPS, and they were on their way. The ride was mostly silent. They didn't even play the radio. Jane knew that small talk wouldn't help Brynn. Brynn needed to concentrate on what was ahead of her.

She mostly looked out the window, her eyes blank. Occasionally she would look as though she was going to stay something, but then changed her mind and went back to staring out the window. Jane could tell that she was reminiscing in her mind, and didn't want to intrude on her friend's memories. She decided to keep the Adam sighting to herself. She just didn't want to add to her friend's sadness today.

Jane could tell that they were getting closer as the scenery got greener, and as any sign of city life started to disappear behind them. The towns started getting farther and farther apart. Jane had always grown up in the city, and these little towns always amazed her. She couldn't imagine not being fifteen minutes from a mall, chain restaurants, and five different gas stations. She knew that Adam and Brynn had been from a small town, but she had no idea what to expect. She had never even been this way before. The roads were getting longer and flatter and the scenery became much less interesting. There was a farmhouse here, and a ratty broken down barn there, and then field after field after field.

After driving for what felt like forever, The GPS told them that they were five minutes away.

Jane could tell that Brynn was getting nervous. Her knee started to jump and she started biting her nails, a habit she had stopped a long time ago.

They pulled into the church parking lot and Jane turned off the car.

"Are you okay?" she asked Brynn quietly. She could tell that Brynn wasn't. She was breathing in and out, making a concentrated effort to do so. Jane sat quietly and waited.

Finally, Brynn looked at her, her eyes threatening to spill over with tears. "I'm ready," she said resolutely, trying to sound strong.

Jane nodded and opened her door and waited for Brynn to walk around the car.

They walked in together in silence. The parking lot was already three-quarters of the way full, and Jane could see more and more cars coming in. The parking lot attendant was directing the cars to start double parking. It looked like they were expecting a big crowd. Jane looked at the building. It was an old Methodist church that looked like it had been there for many years, and was in desperate need of repair. The white paint was peeling and wood was rotting off the windowpanes. The landscaping looked like it hadn't been touched in a decade, and the concrete steps had large cracks.

Brynn walked up the stairs as though she was on autopilot. Jane could tell that she knew where she was going.

When they got to the top of the stairs, one of the ushers handed them a bulletin. The front cover had a pretty brunette's face on it. She had round plump cheeks and a big smile. *Stacy!* Jane had no idea what she looked like before. She could tell from the picture on the bulletin that she would have liked this girl. She looked like a sweet, normal girl, and she was suddenly struck by how sad it was that she was gone so young.

Brynn ignored the usher and walked straight in. She was clearly looking for someone and Jane hoped that it wasn't Adam. She hoped Adam wouldn't show up today. She only wanted her friend to have to deal with the tragedy at hand, and not have to face her own heartache.

"Brynn! Brynn, its Brynn everyone! Brynn is here!" a loud high-pitched woman's voice with a slight southern drawl came soaring across the room. It was followed by a plumper, more made up version of the girl in the picture. Only this version was dressed all in black, complete with a small dramatic black hat with netting falling over her face.

"Samantha," Brynn looked relieved.

Oh, the crazy mother. Jane smiled politely.

"Oh, Brynn, I'm so glad you're here. Stacy would have loved to see you one more time, darling girl. She loved you so much! I can't believe you didn't come visit us more often. Oh darling, what a tragedy! My poor, poor, baby girl," Samantha started wailing as people came running over to hold her up. *She clearly loves the attention,* Jane thought feeling guilty for having such negative thoughts about this mother who just lost her child.

Brynn's jaw was set and tight, and her eyes kept welling up with tears that she wouldn't allow to fall, and her face was a mask of nothing but pain. Jane could tell that she was trying to keep it together and she put her arm around Brynn for support. Brynn stiffened and Jane immediately let go. Jane could tell that she needed to be on her own. She had felt the same way when her husband died. Being at the church brought back so many sad memories. She tried to push them away so that she could concentrate on her friend.

Brynn walked up to the front of the old church.

There were poster boards placed all over the front with hundreds of pictures. Brynn slowly looked over every one of them. There were numerous pictures of young Brynn and young Stacy arm in arm, arms around each other, both looking so innocent and so fresh. Nobody could have ever guessed the horror that they were facing every night in their own homes. The front of the church was crowded with people who were going through, like Brynn, one by one with sad expressions. Some were crying and some were simply looking. Some were looking at Brynn and whispering amongst themselves. They recognized her from the pictures and they looked at her with sympathy. She was the only friend in Stacy's life, even as an adult. They all knew how close they were.

Brynn didn't look at, or talk to, anyone.

It was a small town and everyone knew everyone else, but she wasn't there to socialize. She was only there for one purpose. She was there only to honor her friend who she had neglected and ignored in the last years of her life. The pain and guilt were eating her alive.

Brynn was oblivious to anyone else's presence. She was lost in memories, sinking deeper and deeper into her own mind. She was angry.

How do none of these people know what Stacy's father did to her? How does she survive that only to be killed by some thieving whore?

These people staring at the posters were all oblivious, naïve sheep. Some of them worked for Stacy's father or worked next to him for many years. Many even looked up to him. She hated him. She always did.

She could see Stacy's father out of the corner of her eye. He was looking at her with a strange sad expression on his face. He was much older now and didn't look as big, or strong, or powerful as he once did. Now he just looked like an old man, like someone's grandfather. Still tall but with a little hunch, gray, weaker. Not as weak as he would be one day, yet unable to beat a teenage girl with a belt until her entire back was black and blue.

Brynn never really pretended to like him, even as a child. She took out her anger for Thomas on him. With Thomas, she had to play nice but with Stacy's daddy, she didn't. She had always tried to, for Stacy's sake. But now that Stacy was gone, she didn't have to.

He started to walk up to her, but stopped when he saw the rage on her face. Her dark eyes were blazing at him, and he could feel the anger radiating toward him. Even though they were ten feet away from each other, it was as though everyone around them could sense that they should not walk between them. The path remained clear as they stood and stared at each other. Brynn stared at him with such an expression of hatred, while his was an expression of sadness and remorse. His dark green eyes were begging her. *Begging to forgive? To not make a scene? To not punch him in the face?* Brynn thought he looked so old now. He was still tall, but not imposing like he had been when they were children. Now he just looked old, and sad, and afraid.

The rage disappeared as quickly as it came.

She wanted to yell at him. She wanted to scream so that everyone could hear about how he had beaten Stacy, almost daily at times. She wanted everyone to know how he told her day after day that she was fat, and that no one would ever love her. She wanted to tell all of his sheep that he had taken his other girls into the woods, behind the shed, and done things to them that they never talked about. And she wanted them to know that Stacy had only been spared because he told her she was too ugly and fat, like her mother.

Brynn looked away from him. She would not speak to him, not today, not ever. She knew that his caricature of a wife, Samantha, would protect him now that she was the wife of the Chief of Police, and that Brynn had no proof of anything he'd done. His other daughters had fled town, and she knew that they never came back. They hadn't even come back for their sister's funeral.

Brynn continued to walk through and stare blindly at the pictures.

A voice came over the room.

"Please, have a seat everyone. Please sit down. We are going to begin." The old pastor was bent over, his white head of hair hardly visible above the pulpit. His weakened voice could hardly be heard above the din of the crowd. Everyone kept milling about, and ignoring him until he banged on the pulpit repeatedly, with a little gavel, to get everyone's attention. Slowly, people started taking their seats. He was there when Brynn was a child and her parents made her sit quietly in her pew, and she thought that he looked old then.

Brynn and Jane moved slowly to the back of the room weaving through the crowd. Brynn wanted to leave as soon as possible, and knew that she had to sit in the back in order to do so.

The service lasted about an hour. There were songs and prayers that Brynn hadn't heard in years. She only half heard them as she stared straight ahead, her eyes fixed on the giant picture of Stacy that was displayed front and center, right next to the pulpit.

Brynn's eyes scanned the room briefly for Adam and then again for her rat of a husband, Toby. She didn't expect she would see Toby. He was disgraced and there were whispers around the room that nobody had seen him since the story was on the national news.

They said he was hiding out until the trial. She wondered where since his little girlfriend was in jail, and his Momma wouldn't even talk to him now, humiliated and hysterical about the loss of her first and only grandchild.

Brynn was relieved not to see Adam. She only half expected him to come. He had only been Stacy's friend because she was. After walking out on her, she didn't know what to expect from him anymore. It was as though the Adam that she knew was gone. After all, her Adam would not have left the way that he did, so abruptly and cruelly.

She pushed those thoughts as far into the recesses of her mind as she could. She could only deal with one thing and one thing only.

Brynn closed her eyes and prayed silently. She hadn't prayed in so long that she wasn't sure if she remembered how. Her prayers as a child to deliver her from Thomas' hand went unheard, so she decided that God wasn't listening to her and didn't love her. She figured that the Sunday school teachers were wrong. After all, if there were a God, how could He let her stay in a home like hers without saving her? It was the only thing she prayed for all of her life. She couldn't see how a good and gracious God would want her to suffer so much.

She gave up on God a long time ago just as she thought He gave up on her. *Adam is gone and Stacy is gone. What good can prayer possibly do me now?* All of Brynn's reasons for praying were gone and there was nothing left.

But Brynn closed her eyes and bowed her head as she did as a child, and thought that if there were a chance that God would hear her now, it would have to be here, in her childhood church. After all, what did she have to lose?

Despite her fractured relationship with the Almighty, it still made her feel good to pray.

Dear God, I know it's been a while. Please be with Stacy and take care of her soul. Maybe she came to you as I came to you asking for deliverance from our demons. But I know that her heart was purer and that she deserved to be protected more than anyone. Please take care of her unborn baby and let them be together in heaven. She never thought she would have a child, so I'm sure she was so happy to be pregnant. Thank you for a good friend like Jane. Did you send her to me? Please be with Adam, my Adam, who I love and adore. Take care of him. Watch over him. Please. Brynn repeated the same prayers over and over.

She was praying so hard that she only heard bits and pieces of the service. She tried to tune out completely when Samantha went up and blubbered and wailed about how much she loved "her baby." Brynn knew it was all for show. Samantha hadn't loved her daughter. If she had, she would have saved her. She would have saved all of them.

Brynn felt herself struggling to breathe. She needed to get out of there. She motioned to Jane that she was ready to leave. She had done what she came here to do. She came here to say good-bye to her friend, and she had done that.

They stood up to go.

She turned around, and her eyes locked with his. *Adam!*

And next to him was Annie.

CHAPTER THIRTY-THREE

Stupid Adam

Adam was so stupid.

He couldn't believe how stupid he had become. Taking Annie to the memorial service for Stacy, knowing that Brynn would be there had to be the single most stupid act of his life.

He didn't know what he was thinking or why he would have done such a thing.

The look on Brynn's face had broken his heart when she turned around and saw Adam sitting next to Annie. *Was it disappointment, anger, hatred, sadness?* For once, he couldn't read her. He always prided himself on being able to read her thoughts, but since they had been apart for so long, he felt rusty. He thought that it was probably a combination of all of them, and more. He had never seen her with that expression before, but he knew that whatever it meant, it wasn't good.

Brynn always disliked Annie. She knew the moment she met her, at the company Christmas party that she was an "opportunistic bitch," she had called her. Adam didn't believe her. He thought she was just a nice co-worker. But now he could see that Annie always favored him, always flirted with him. And it was too late.

His life was upside down and he couldn't believe that he had been so stupid.

He knew that Brynn was hurt. He tried to go after her when the service was over, but she was nowhere in sight. She walked out of the service early, and instead of chasing her right then, he waited. He didn't want to create a scene.

He tried to call her for days after the memorial service but she ignored his calls. She ignored his texts and his emails. And when he tried to stop by the restaurant, she ducked out the back door and took off in her car. She clearly didn't want anything to do with him.

Four months apart turned into five, and now it was six. He kept waiting for her to call and tell him that she was filing divorce papers. He knew that she wouldn't know where to send them because he had never even given her his address. But Adam knew that it was a small detail. If Brynn filed the papers, he knew that they would find them.

Filing for divorce was the last thing on his mind, but he had a pit in his stomach every day waiting for her to finally do it. After all, he left her, so why shouldn't she?

He continued to sit outside of her house and watch for her. He no longer cared if she saw him. He hoped that she saw him. He wanted her to know that he was out there. But she never even looked his way, and he could never find the courage to let her know that he was there. He was afraid she would just ignore him. Ignoring his calls, texts, and emails hurt. But he just didn't know how he would be able to deal with her ignoring him face to face.

He realized on the day of the memorial that he still loved her. Maybe it was being in their hometown or the pictures of her with Stacy when she was a kid. He didn't know why he had forgotten about his love for her.

When he fell for her at fifteen, the only thing that mattered in his life was being able to make her smile or make her laugh. He knew from the beginning what he was getting into with her. He knew then that there was sadness within her that even she could not explain. But all of his life he had never been able to love anyone else, except for her.

He forgot that.

And now, he didn't know how he could get her back if she wouldn't even talk to him. He couldn't blame her. After all, she gave him her trust, and he completely destroyed it in one thoughtless moment.

He twisted his wedding band over and over in frustration. He knew that it had been too long, but he also knew that she had not yet moved on. He caught a glimpse of her the last time he tried to catch her in the restaurant, and saw that she was no longer wearing her ring. He refused to take his off. He believed that she would come around, if she would just talk to him.

He knew that Brynn assumed that he and Annie were couple by the look on her face. Annie had made it a point to put her hand on his arm when she saw that Brynn was looking. But Brynn didn't see him take her hand off his arm.

She was already gone by then.

He liked Annie, and was attracted to her, but he knew that being friends with her would only cloud his judgment. He didn't want her to distract him anymore. When he explained it to her on the long car ride from the memorial service, Annie had not understood.

"Why can't we just hang out as 'friends'?" she had pouted.

"Because Annie, you want more. And I can't," he said gravely. "I like you. You're fun and sexy. If I met you in another life, we may have been something. But I'm married, and I love her."

"But you left her! There is a reason you left her. She was mean to you, and she didn't appreciate you. You could have so much more with me!" she countered. She was upset. She had put the past few months into him, and now he wasn't even going to let her be his friend.

"She's been through a lot in her life, which I don't need to explain to you. I just can't do this with you anymore. It's crossing the line!" Adam was getting angry with her.

"But what about our date and our chemistry? You know we could be great together!" Annie said angrily, her thin voice going up an octave.

She kept replaying their kiss over and over in her mind. She had never kissed anyone like that before and she couldn't stop thinking about it, how passionate he was and how she could feel how excited he was getting. Their kiss was mind blowing, and she didn't want to let that go. She wanted more, and it was all she could think about.

She knew that it was just a prelude to something even more

fantastic.

She couldn't believe it, but midway through the kiss he suddenly pulled away from her. He looked at her as though he didn't recognize her, his eyes wide. Before she knew what was happening, he backed away from her and got out of the car, his belt flapping around where she was trying to open it.

He looked guilty, his eyes turning dark when he looked at her. "You're right. I shouldn't have kissed you and I'm sorry. I won't make excuses for what I did."

He had been refusing to spend time alone with her, no matter how hard she tried. He said that he wasn't ready, but he seemed ready that night.

"So that's it? That's all you have to say?" she was livid.

"What do you want from me? You know that I am married. I can't give you more! I don't want to give you more." Adam felt defeated but there was nothing else he could say to her. He felt guilty but there was nothing that he could do about his moment of weakness. He had been drunk and lonely, and he knew that he was on a slippery slope but he backed away just in time. He knew that she would be angry with him, but there was nothing that he could do to change it. She was spending time with him under the guise of friendship, hoping that his wedding band would one day disappear.

He didn't want to tell her, but in the moment he had kissed her a life with her flashed before his eyes. He liked her, but he knew that he could never love her enough to endure. He knew that nothing he could ever feel for her could make him forget his love for his Brynn.

They drove the rest of the way in silence and she refused to speak to him since. She was icy to him in the office and everyone noticed. There had been talk about them spending so much time together, and now that she went out of her way to ignore him everyone assumed that their relationship just went sour. He was embarrassed, but there was nothing that could be done now. He knew that he should have stayed away from her in the first place, but he couldn't waste any more time now thinking about her. He knew what he wanted and what he needed.

He loved Brynn and he needed to be able to make it right with her.

CHAPTER THIRTY-FOUR

Falling Back

After the memorial for Stacy, Brynn went back to crying every day. When she could breathe, it hurt. Any emotion scraped against her like an open wound that refused to heal. She tried to summon her strength but any effort felt futile.

She couldn't gather herself no matter how hard she tried to pull it together. Every time she thought of Adam and Annie together, her stomach hurt, her eyes watered, and she wanted to die. She thought that if she just lay still enough on the floor that her body would just give out and stop working.

Even the air she struggled to breathe felt like poison, as she thought about them together. She saw them sitting close at the memorial Service. Their arms and legs were touching. She saw how Annie drew closer to him while she stared Brynn down, as if to let her know that he was hers now.

She thought about what they were doing, where they were going. She thought about him touching her, kissing her, caressing her, looking into her eyes, and stroking her hair. She thought about their naked bodies entwined on satin sheets and about his skin touching her skin. She thought about them making love with every single detail, and it made her want to vomit. She knew that it was demented and sick to torture herself, but she couldn't stop.

She watched herself wasting away. She watched Mirror Brynn

turning into skin and bones, and she didn't care. She wanted her to fade away. She was tired. She had done all that she could to endure. She was abandoned, abused, and abandoned again. She just didn't want to do it anymore.

Adam was in love with someone else and nothing in her life mattered.

She had been with him since she was fifteen and he was the only real love in her life. She had a hard enough time living without him. But she couldn't even find it conceivable that he was already with someone else.

She hated Annie in a way that she didn't even know was possible.

From the first time she met her she knew that she was after Adam. Brynn warned him but he obviously didn't listen. Women knew how to read other women, but he thought she was just being silly and jealous. Brynn realized from the sight of them touching and Annie's possessiveness over him, that Adam was completely lost to her, now.

Brynn had been waiting for Adam to come back but the realization hit her like a brick. *Annie must be why he left in the first place.*

When Jane saw the look on Brynn's face, she felt her stomach flip. She worked so hard just to get Brynn out of the house and now this! She didn't know how she was ever going to save her now. As expected, Brynn cocooned herself again, and this time when Jane went to visit she refused to answer the door altogether, even though Jane rang the doorbell for over an hour.

Brynn thought about Annie and Adam, nonstop. She knew it was unhealthy, but even in her broken sleep she dreamt about them. She slept with her razor blade next to the bed, but as much as she wanted to, she refused to use it. She didn't want to escape just yet. She wanted to feel everything. She wanted to keep thinking of them, as sick as it was.

She never imagined her Adam with anyone else because he had always only ever been with her. He had only ever kissed her and touched her, but that felt like so long ago. She realized when he first left that she may never get to touch his face or his smooth skin ever again. But that didn't make it easier to know that he was already with someone else.

Brynn wondered what Annie's skin felt like and if it was as soft as hers. She touched her fingers to her own lips and wondered if Annie kissed better than she did. She ran her fingers through her hair and wondered if Annie's hair was softer than her hair. She pulled it and imagined Adam pulling Annie's hair. Did she like it? Did he?

Adam always said that they fit together like a puzzle, perfectly. They would often lie as close together as they could, their bodies tight. She missed how safe and small and protected she felt when he held her so close. She wondered if he held Annie so close, and if she felt the same way that Brynn did when tucked in his arms.

She wondered what she smelled like. She wondered if she smelled fresh, or sweet, or spicy. She imagined that she would smell spicy. She imagined that her scent would be overpowering and she imagined herself gagging on it. She wondered if Adam buried himself in Annie's neck like he did to her, and she pictured it.

She thought about the two of them together, and she felt a rage growing within her that she had never felt before. Brynn hated her. And the thought of her with her husband made her sick.

Brynn thought about hurting her, she wanted to hurt her, and she wanted to hurt herself.

CHAPTER THIRTY-FIVE

Perspective

Brynn sat silently staring at the machines, waiting.

It was over a week and Rose was not improving. Instead, she was steadily declining, until the only thing keeping her alive were machines.

She bowed her head, ashamed of herself. *I abandoned my Mother when she needed me the most.*

Brynn knew that Rose couldn't have loved her more if she had have given birth to her.

Brynn was so thankful for Lea, the housekeeper. She called 911, and though Brynn would probably never see Rose awake again, she could at least sit with her as she went. Jane's call from the hospital finally got through to Brynn, and Brynn rushed to the hospital without hesitation. It was the first time she had left the house in days. But she knew that Rose needed her.

She didn't know about the Alzheimer's. She was so wrapped up in her brokenness that she hadn't really seen Rose for a long time. Brynn was living her life half-alive, and had stopped paying attention to anything else that mattered.

Brynn knew what she had done wrong with Adam. She had never opened her heart completely to him. She always kept him at arm's length so that he couldn't hurt her as Thomas had hurt her. She could see it as clear as day. She knew that she didn't listen to him, or hear him when he said how much he needed her. She ignored him when he looked into her eyes pleading with her to look back. But now it was too late. She would never have the chance again, and she had to join the world of the living again.

Brynn realized that she let a lot of people down, and she wasn't sure how she would make it up to them. It was too late for Stacy, but she knew that she needed to make amends. She would have to think about that later, after she said good-bye to Rose.

Brynn was finally awake, but it was too late. *I'll never get to speak to Momma again. I'll never hear her tell me she loves me ever again.* Rose was with her as far back as she could remember up until the last few months. She didn't know what it had been like the last few months of Rose's life. The guilt and shame hung heavily over her. Brynn knew that she would never forgive herself for abandoning her.

She held Rose's lifeless hand that seemed to get colder and colder. She had been alone with her in the room for days. Jane and the girls, Stella and Bertie, Lea, and Lucia, had all stopped in to see Rose.

Brynn was so happy to see Lucia who came to the hospital to visit with Jane. She was nice and plump with baby, and so beautiful. She decided to give the baby up for adoption so that she could finish school. Lucia and the baby's father were still together, but she was too young to start a family. They agreed that it would be the right thing to do. Brynn was relieved that Lucia would be able to finish high school and still go on with her life. She had been right about her from the beginning. She knew that she was a smart girl and she was proud of her for making such a good decision.

Brynn was most afraid to face Jane. They hadn't spoken since Jane had dropped her off after Stacy's memorial. Jane tried, but she only got frustrated with Brynn for ignoring her. She was more upset with her for ignoring her about Rose. She understood that Brynn's heart was broken, but she wanted to shake her friend. She knew first hand that nothing could come from wallowing in her pain. Brynn taught her that many years ago.

"I'm sure you want to slap me," she said to Jane when Jane walked into Rose's hospital room. Jane did want to slap her, but she had spent an ample amount of time, working through her anger.

Jane looked long into Brynn's eyes and saw that she no longer needed to be angry with her friend. Rose's impending demise was enough to bring Brynn out of her own self-induced coma and she could see that Brynn was finally back.

She grabbed Brynn and hugged her tightly. "It's good to see you," she whispered in her ear. They held each other for a long while, and when they finally came apart, both had tears in their eyes that they had held back for so long. Brynn knew that Jane was the best of friends, and she promised herself that she wouldn't let her go as she had Stacy.

After they dried their tears, Jane asked her if she called Adam to tell him. Brynn shook her head and sadly gestured that she hadn't. Ever since Adam left, she promised Brynn that she wouldn't interfere, but Jane couldn't wait anymore. She didn't care if Adam was with someone else. She felt that he deserved to know what was going on with Brynn and with Rose, after all, Rose had been his mother-in-law for years. She didn't tell Brynn that she called Adam for her, unsure of how she might react.

Adam was so thankful for Jane's phone call.

He was terrified to talk to Brynn. He was at a loss for how to get her to talk to him since she had been ignoring him since the memorial. But Jane's call was just what he needed. Suddenly being there for her now was the most important thing to him.

When all of the visitors were gone, and the room was quiet once again, Brynn sat with Rose, holding her hand relishing the peacefulness. Brynn was tired but she refused to leave the room.

"I'm so sorry for leaving you, Momma. If you can hear me, I want you to know how much I loved you. I'm sorry for leaving you when you needed me the most." Brynn said, knowing that Rose would not respond. She looked at Rose's still, quiet face, distorted by the breathing tube, and tried to envision what she looked like without it.

She laid her head on her arms on the hospital bed next to Rose, and wept. She had cried so much in the past few months that she couldn't believe that she had any tears left. Yet they flowed easily. She wished that Adam were here with her. She still missed him. He was the only one who made her feel normal, who made her feel better. And even though she knew that he was with Annie, she still missed him.

Adam walked into the hospital with butterflies in his stomach and palms sweating. He had only been face to face with Brynn once in the past six months. He couldn't get the horrified, disappointed, angry look on her face out of his mind. When she saw him sitting with Annie, she looked at him as if he were the devil. He dreamt about it almost every night. Adam couldn't imagine how Brynn would forgive him, but he knew that she had to, and he just needed to explain. To tell her that it wasn't how it looked, and that his worst sin was stupidity.

Adam didn't know how Brynn would forgive him for walking out. He was trying to forgive himself, and he knew that he couldn't give up. Not on Brynn, and not on himself.

He loved her, he needed her, and he wasn't going to accept a life without her. Now that he had been without her, Adam never wanted to be without her again.

But Adam also knew that he needed things from Brynn, too. She always kept her emotions reigned in, and he needed her to trust him enough to be free. Adam was exhausted trying to free her from herself, and he needed Brynn to work at it, as well. He didn't know if she could. She had survived by protecting herself, and Adam had to convince her that she was safe. But now, he was going to have to start over.

There were so many questions and so many unknowns. When he left her, he didn't want to deal with the unknowns anymore. Now all that he wanted to do and all that he was willing to do was to deal with the unknowns.

Adam stood quietly outside of Rose's hospital room, staring at Brynn. He was alarmed at how dangerously thin and gaunt she was. Jane warned him, but he wasn't prepared for the sight of her. She looked so unhealthy and frail. *Did I do this to her? When was the last time she ate?* He was angry with himself all over again.

He looked at Rose, still in the bed. Adam had never seen her so still, so quiet. Rose had frustrated him with her neediness and her overbearing love for his Brynn. He never knew how to take her, so he hadn't taken to her at all. He tolerated her for many years, and now she was nearly gone. Adam failed to be there for her, and he didn't even know if she realized it. The Alzheimer's was eating away at the woman she once was. He grieved for Brynn.

Jane told him how inaccessible Brynn had become and how changed she was now because of her brokenness. Adam didn't believe it until seeing her now. They needed to heal and they needed to do it together.

He took a step toward her tentatively. He was ready.

Brynn turned toward him and her big brown eyes that he adored so much, widened in recognition. "Adam!" she said in disbelief.

CHAPTER THIRTY-SIX

Good-bye Rose

Adam stepped toward her and before he could think, she was in his arms. He couldn't believe how light she was. She felt like nothing as he picked her up and held her as tightly to him as he could, his nose enveloped in her soft dark hair.

He wasn't sure what to expect, but he didn't quite expect this. "Adam," she moaned like a wounded animal. He could feel her pain radiating through him, and he felt the tears spring into his eyes. He missed her, too.

What if this wasn't real? What if he set her down, and she turned on him like rabid dog?

He anticipated it and expected it. She couldn't forgive him that easily after what he had done to her.

"Adam, Mom is dying." Brynn cried in his ear. "And I left her alone. I was so selfish, and I left her alone." He could hear the heartache and the shame in her voice.

"I know she's dying. But it's not your fault, honey. It's nobody's fault. You didn't leave her. You've always been there for her." Adam was in hell. He couldn't bear the pain in her voice. It had been his selfish fear that caused her this pain, and he didn't know if he would ever forgive himself.

"I'm just like my birth mother, the one who left me. I'm just like her." Brynn was desolate.

Adam held her close breathing her in. He had been afraid that he would never be this close to her again. He felt the weight of the world lifting off his shoulders little by little, the longer he held onto her. He grabbed her hand and pushed her away from him, looking her over from top to bottom. Brynn knew that he was looking to see if she looked different to him, if she had any scars that were obvious.

"I'll never leave you again," He said crushing her to him. "I'm so sorry for what I have done." He pulled away from her, his dark blue eyes searching her brown ones. He looked to see if she saw the truth in his eyes.

"What about...?" Brynn looked away from him.

"There's no Annie. There never was. We were friends. That's it. I was so stupid to bring her to the memorial, but I thought I would get to explain it to you, and I just never realized how stupid it looked. I promise on my life that she was nothing, never anything to me." Adam rambled trying to explain it all as quickly as he could in case she got up and walked away. He was desperate to tell her the truth.

"Did you sleep with her?" Brynn paused.

She didn't want the answer, but she needed it. She needed to hear it in case the answer was yes. She needed the reason to walk away. She couldn't accept his comfort if he had slept with her.

"No! I swear." Adam knew she would ask him if he kissed her and he dreaded answering.

"Did you kiss her or... touch her?" Brynn was standing in front of him now, her eyes still wet with tears. She was staring up at him, still braced for the worst.

There was a long pause. Brynn took a step away from him. Adam reached his hand out and snagged her wrist.

"I kissed her. Once! I swear to God it was only one time, and I was drunk. But it was nothing more than that, ever." Adam tried to stop rambling. He didn't want to seem like he was lying.

She studied him, and he looked at her evenly.

The air between them was thick. He didn't know if kissing Annie was a deal breaker. He knew that sleeping with her was. He knew that Brynn would never speak to him again. But one kiss? He didn't know, but Adam knew that he needed to tell the truth. There had never been lies between them, and he didn't want to begin now.

Brynn was quiet. She didn't know how she felt about it. She

didn't want details, or timeframes, or back-story. She knew what she needed to know.

One kiss.

He was clearly distraught over it. She thought it best to let it go, to sit on it, and see where they were going. They had been through so much that one kiss seemed almost insignificant. She knew that once she thought about it, it would be more difficult to swallow. But right now, she couldn't. Nothing else seemed to matter to her now but Rose.

"Mom has Alzheimer's. Apparently, she's had it for a long time. She was diagnosed a while ago, but she never said anything," she said breaking her stare.

He was surprised. He didn't expect her to veer away from the topic at hand. He expected resolution, but not this. Not subterfuge. *What is she doing?* He was nervous. Brynn didn't let anything go. She always saw it through until the end.

"I heard that," he said nervously. "What is the doctor saying will happen to her? How long does she have?"

"She has nothing left. She's out of time," Brynn said sadly, as she looked at Rose's still body.

It was silent. The only noise was the swoosh of the machine breathing for her. It was an oddly comforting sound as it eased the awkward silence between them.

Nurse Cindy came into the room to check the vitals. She nodded at Brynn. She and Brynn had come to an understanding that there was only to be truth between them, no fluff. Cindy took out her puppy pen and wrote a few things on the chart and left the room.

Adam sat down in a chair next the bed. Brynn sat in the chair at the end of the bed. She was studying him, he knew. He grabbed Rose's hand. It was small and cold in his. *Rose wouldn't like this.* Adam knew that Rose didn't like physical contact, which was hard for him. He came from a very affectionate family, and much to Rose's dismay, he had always tried to kiss or hug her. She ignored Adam, and saw him as a necessary annoyance in her life. They tolerated one another for the sake of Brynn's sanity.

But now Rose was dying, and he truly felt at a loss.

While Adam felt distant, he had a strange affection toward her that he couldn't explain. He didn't know if it was pity or love, or both. He had tried to help her, but Rose wouldn't allow it. She didn't like men, and Adam couldn't blame her, but he tried anyway. He knew that Rose needed Brynn, even though he needed her, too. And he knew that Rose was like a child, selfish and needy, unable to handle most things for herself. She was emotionally unbalanced, and she gave Brynn purpose. As much as Adam hated to admit it, Brynn needed her, too.

But he also resented Rose for taking Brynn away from him, and for making Brynn afraid to have children of her own. He resented Rose for never including him and stealing away his wife without apology.

Adam hoped that if Brynn took him back, they could revisit the part of their lives that Rose had incessantly interrupted, the part where most people had babies and created families. He wanted a child more than anything. If it were up to him, they would have a lot of children, but with Brynn, he would be happy with one.

Adam planned for it and envisioned it for so long. He knew that Brynn would be a good mother. He saw how she gave of herself to others and how much love she had in her heart. He wished that she could see herself through his eyes, because then she would know that she could do it.

Brynn turned to Adam. She held his arm, feeling the muscles beneath his soft cotton button down shirt. She loved the look and the feel of him, and she couldn't believe he was really there. "I... I just want to tell you how much I love you, Adam," Brynn said slowly, cautiously. "I'm so happy you are here. I missed you so much... I..."

Adam stopped her. "We are going to have plenty of time to make it up to one another. I realize how much I love you, how I will always ever love only you. You give me a purpose that I don't have without you. I hated being without you, and I'll never do it again."

Brynn's breath caught, and she was speechless. She leaned into him and he kissed her, his mouth open and wet, and wanting. Brynn missed his mouth and how his lips connected to her core and made her want things she never imagined existed, until there was him.

Adam pulled away. "I love you."

"I love you," Brynn said without hesitation. She leaned in close to him, not minding the hardness of the hospital chairs now. They sat for a long time in silence.

Nurse Cindy came in again. This time she was with a doctor. They spoke directly to Brynn. Adam was confused.

They are turning off the ventilator, already?

Brynn just kept nodding and crying, crying and nodding. They had her sign paperwork, and then she grabbed tight to Adam's hand. The doctor went over and flipped a switch on one of the pieces of equipment. The ventilator that had been making the *swooshing* sound started to slow down, and then the room was silent.

Brynn held tight to Adam, and he put his arm around her and held her as close to him as he could. He tried to shield her with his body, knowing what was coming.

The doctor left the room and said he would be back. The nurse who liked the puppies did the same. They knew that Brynn needed her privacy. They had watched her over the past week and knew that they were unusually close.

It was just Adam and Brynn now. Rose was in there, but barely. They could see the vitals dropping on the machine, the rising and falling of the lines on the heart monitor were moving slower and slower.

Rose also knew that it was almost time to go.

She could tell. She couldn't explain it, but she knew.

She wanted to tell Brynn, but she couldn't tell anyone. She couldn't say anything. She was trapped in her body and she was desperate to get out. She could tell that her time was coming. She had lived long enough.

Rose didn't want anything. She just wanted to go. She was tired of this life. It hadn't turned out anything like she had expected and she was done with it. Rose didn't know how long she had been in the hospital. *Days? Weeks?* It didn't matter how long. Rose knew that Brynn looked tired. She hadn't slept or left her Roses' side since she came to the hospital.

Rose couldn't have picked a better child if she had given birth to one. In fact, she thought that if she had given birth to a child it could have been worse.

Rose knew that she was never going to be able to tell Brynn how she really did take care of her. How she gave her the gift of protecting herself. She planned to tell her when she was lying on her deathbed, but now Rose would never have the chance. She knew that Brynn would understand the dramatics behind waiting to tell her until then. Rose regretted that she would never know, even though she thought that she needed to know.

Rose hoped she wouldn't run into Thomas wherever she was going, although she doubted that they would end up in the same place. She couldn't imagine that they could after everything that he had done to her and to Brynn. She knew that if she saw Thomas that she would be in trouble. She had tried to live a good life and do the right things.

But there was that one thing.

Surely, God would understand about that thing. It had been necessary.

Rose reasoned with herself for a while. She had no sense of time, she just knew that she had been like this for long enough, and she was ready to go.

She knew that she had loved Brynn enough. She had done everything that she could do.

Rose felt herself fading. It was as though she could feel herself disappearing. There was no light, no tunnel, no floating above her body. There was just the sense that she was going away. She was disappointed at how anticlimactic it all was. Where were all of the special effects? Rose wanted to know where she was going. She felt less and less.

And then there was nothing.

The room felt very still. Adam was afraid to move. He kept looking down at Brynn.

She was holding tight to Rose's hand. She hadn't held Rose's hand in so long, and she felt so guilty. They told her it could be minutes or hours.

"It's okay, Mom, you can go now," Brynn cried.

Rose didn't move.

"I have loved you my whole life. Thank you for loving me." Brynn was sobbing as tears racked her tiny body.

Adam looked up and there was a long straight line on the heart monitor.

It only took an hour, and Rose was gone.

CHAPTER THIRTY-SEVEN

New Beginning

Adam moved his things home.

They knew that it was going to take a long time to work through their problems. But their time apart gave them a fresh perspective and both discovered a new appreciation for the other.

With Rose gone, Brynn she could give Adam the time and energy that he needed. But she was still afraid. Besides Adam's parents, she had never really seen a healthy relationship and didn't know what one looked like. She didn't trust her own instincts anymore, and Brynn wasn't sure that she would know how to be a good wife on her own. Starting over terrified her beyond anything she had ever known. *What if I screw it up? What if I have no idea what I am doing?* She was afraid of disappointing Adam, again.

But Brynn was also afraid to trust him. She was afraid that he would just give up and run from her again, with no warning.

"I promise I will never leave you again! Don't be afraid," Adam said to her over and over. He knew that it would take time. They were trying to settle into a new routine and not sink back into the old one. They had to remind themselves that they were given a new beginning for a reason. It was a work in progress every day and they were learning forgiveness and love all over again.

One early morning, the phone rang unexpectedly.

Brynn was half-asleep. *Rose? Why is she calling so early?* Then she remembered that Rose was gone and that she would never call

Brynn again. Just the thought took her breath away.

It was Michael, Lucia's boyfriend. "It's time!" he said sounding panicked and excited at the same time. Even though they agreed to give the baby up for adoption, they were still excited for the baby's birth. They knew in their hearts that they were doing the right thing.

The couple they chose was exceptional and loving. They couldn't have children of their own and they wanted to be parents more than anything. When Lucia met them and chose them to adopt her baby, they wept and thanked her over and over. Lucia knew that they would take good care of her baby, and it made their decision feel right. Lucia knew that she couldn't take care of her baby the way that her baby deserved at this point in her life. This couple was young, successful, and clearly in love.

She was happy with their choice.

Brynn and Adam quickly dressed, and rushed to the hospital as excited as they would be if it were their own child. Lucia was family. They loved her like the little sister that neither of them had. She was compassionate, smart, and funny and she had been there for them when they needed her most. Brynn wanted more than anything to be there to support Lucia when she met her child, even if it were for a brief moment. They told her that they would sit in the waiting room and for her to call them when they needed her. She knew that Lucia would feel better just knowing they were there.

When they arrived in the quiet waiting area, Lucia was already in the birthing room, and they found her father pacing. The only one with her was Michael. They sent word with a nurse that they were there and thinking about her, and a few moments later the nurse came out and gestured for Brynn.

"She would like you to come back," the nurse said putting her hand on her back.

Brynn was caught off guard. She wasn't expecting to be with Lucia during the actual birth and she was hesitant.

Adam looked at her, silently encouraging her. Brynn was amazed at how he could make her feel better by simply giving her a look. It was as though Adam could see into her soul and knew exactly what she needed. She stood up straight and took a deep breath. She was ready.

She followed the nurse back into the birthing room. Brynn had never been in one before and was surprised at how nice it was. She was surprised to see a nice couch, cherry armoire, and a nightstand, and thought it looked more like a hotel room than a birthing room. The colors were soothing pastels and there was even a floral print on the wall that looked like it belonged in a nursery. She thought that it was such a pretty room.

Lucia was so happy to see Brynn. She grabbed Brynn's hand as soon as she was close enough. Already in hard labor, Lucia was panting and sweating, her beautiful dark hair matted against her head. The epidural was helping to take the pain away but there was still a lot of pressure. The nurses said that it was almost time, and that Lucia was going to need to push very soon. Brynn felt dizzy from the flurry of activity in the room. She didn't know what to expect but it was nothing like she saw on TV. Lucia wasn't screaming or crying, but Brynn could tell that she was uncomfortable. Every time there was a contraction, Lucia squeezed Brynn's hand really hard. Michael was on the other side of her and every time Lucia squeezed, they both grimaced in pain, and then smiled at each other reassuringly.

A doctor entered the room without either of them noticing. All they could see were the doctor's bright green eyes above the mask and they both startled a little when she spoke. "Okay Lucia, I'm going to need you start giving me some really good pushes, but only when I say."

Lucia nodded, her face twisted up with the contraction that was squeezing her insides. She waited.

"Puuush," the doctor said looking up in anticipation.

Brynn could see Lucia gathering herself from the inside and then pushing with all of her strength. She wondered how she felt, and for a moment, she envisioned herself in Lucia's place. Brynn pictured herself pushing and tried to imagine how it would feel. She thought she would be so terrified, not of the pain or the pressure, but of the tiny person that would come out. She couldn't imagine how she could ever take care of such a tiny thing. She shook her head, trying to get rid of the vision. She needed to be present for Lucia who needed her right now.

"Come on, honey, you can do it!" Brynn said trying to sound confident in her encouragement.

Lucia let out a loud grunt as she pushed as hard as she could, a large vein popping out of her forehead.

"Good, Lucia! Good!" the doctor said, obviously pleased with her effort. "I can see your baby's head. It's crowned."

Lucia looked at Michael. Her pretty brown eyes were a mixture of happiness with a deep undertone of something else that Brynn couldn't quite read. It looked like sadness, but she wasn't quite sure. Lucia was a smart girl who knew her own mind, and Brynn knew that she was confident in her decision to give the baby up for adoption. Lucia talked with her about it at length, knowing that as an adopted child Brynn may have some insight for her. Brynn knew that her life was a result of Thomas and Rose, and nothing else, and didn't share her horror with Lucia.

Brynn just told her that she needed to make a decision based on what her heart and her head told her that she should do. She told her that she needed to be willing to live with her decision for the rest of her life. And Brynn told Lucia that she was a good person.

Lucia and Michael were confident that the couple they chose was the right decision for them, and for their baby. They loved their baby enough to give him or her more than what they could give a child right now. Brynn was proud of Lucia for knowing herself well enough to know that she wasn't ready to be a mother, and to have the heart to give that gift to someone else.

"Puuush," the doctor repeated, this time a little more forcefully.

Lucia's face contorted again, and she summoned every bit of strength that she could. She felt herself pushing from somewhere deep inside of her with a strength that she didn't know existed. This time when pushed, she let out a sound that resembled a warrior exploding into a battle. She was battling within, fighting her fatigue and her weariness. She knew she had to push, as many times as it took, but she was getting tired.

"Good Job, Lucia! She's almost here! One more good push should do it." the doctor said sounding like a coach.

Lucia fell back onto the bed. She was gathering herself more time for the final push. Brynn stared at her amazed. She had never experienced anything so intense, and she felt herself choking up with emotion. She couldn't wait to see the baby. She tried to peer over Lucia's legs, feeling a little embarrassed, but all she could see was a dark shock of hair poking out from the top of the baby's head.

"Okay, Lucia. Get ready!" the doctor said, her voice full of energy and anticipation. "One more good push and your baby will be out. Let's do this!"

Brynn looked into Lucia's eyes. *You can do this,* Brynn said to her silently. She squeezed her hand as tight as she could. *Take my strength. You can do this!*

Lucia closed her eyes and took a deep breath. And then she pushed as long and hard and deep as she could, the warrior within gathering herself one more time.

"You did it! It's a beautiful baby girl" the doctor exclaimed excitedly. "Good work! You did very well. Now lay back, and we'll finish things up."

She handed the baby to the nurses who whisked her away. Lucia's eyes filled with tears of joy and relief. She was overcome, and she clung to Michael and Brynn as she allowed all of her emotion to spill out. She had been keeping it in and drawing strength from it, but now she didn't need it anymore. Lucia knew that if she let it out too early that she wouldn't have the strength to push the baby out, or to do what needed to come next.

Brynn was alarmed. Lucia was sobbing now, and Brynn could feel the sadness flowing out of her all at once.

"It's okay, it's okay," Michael repeated over and over through his tears. Brynn's heart ached for them, as she couldn't imagine the pain of what they were about to do. She clung to them trying to give them her strength, but soon they were all crying holding each other as tight as they could.

Brynn wondered, for a brief moment, if her own mother felt this sadness when she was letting her go. She wondered if she had cried, or if she just simply tossed her aside and not looked back. Brynn felt her heart hurting for them, but also for herself.

The room was quiet, and then they heard the tiny cry of the baby.

"Please, please, may I see her?" Lucia asked the closest nurse, after they had cleaned Lucia up.

"Of course, you may," the nurse said looking at her sympathetically. They all knew that the beautiful young couple was giving their baby away to the anxious couple in the waiting room. They admired how they talked about their baby with such love, even though they weren't going to raise her.

The nurse brought the tiny bundle in the white blanket with the pink and blue stripes, over to them with a big smile. "She's perfect and beautiful," she said as she presented her to them proudly. She wanted the first moment that they saw her to be perfect.

Lucia held out her arms and the nurse placed them where she would fit perfectly. Lucia let out a loud sigh as her eyes filled once again with tears that she couldn't wipe away.

The baby looked at her with tiny squinting eyes, awake and alert to the world. She was beautiful with light caramel colored skin and dark brown hair and eyes. The hair on the top of her head was thick and long. Brynn was amazed at how long it was. She tentatively touched it and loved how soft it felt. She looked at Lucia and Michael who were fixated on their baby. Brynn felt such love coming from them, and she hoped that their baby felt it, too.

"I'm your momma and this is your daddy," Lucia said softly with that beautiful Spanish lilt in her voice. Lucia spoke through tears, holding her baby's soft hands and caressing the soft little face. The baby stared up at her silently, fixated on Lucia's pretty face as though she knew that she had just come from her. "You are going to have a new momma and a new daddy and they are going to love you very much."

Michael and Brynn were crying as she spoke. Brynn didn't know how Lucia could be so strong. The baby seemed to be captivated by Lucia's every word, staring steadily into her eyes.

"We want you to have a happy life. And right now, we can't give that to you. You deserve so much more than what we can give you. The only thing that we can give you is love, and that's just not enough. Your new mommy and daddy will give you so much love too, but they will give you much more. They will give you everything. They've been waiting to meet you, praying for you every day. We want you to have what you deserve. But we will never forget you. We will never stop thinking about you, and you will always be a part of us."

The baby looked at Lucia, her dark eyes seeming to understand what Lucia was saying, loving her soft voice as she spoke. "They love you very much already. Your new mommy and daddy have always wanted to have a baby, so you are a precious gift to them, my Nena. *Te quiero con todo mi alma.*"

Lucia held her close for a long moment, and kissed her forehead. Michael kissed her forehead and without speaking, they handed her back to the nurse.

The nurse took her out of the room and Lucia and Michael broke down in tears. Brynn looked at the nurses who were left in the room, and saw that they were wiping their eyes as well. The entire room felt full of heartbreak and sadness, and nobody said a word.

After a while, when Lucia had fallen asleep with Michael curled up in the bed next to her holding her tightly, Brynn left the room and went out to find Adam.

Adam had been in the waiting room with Lucia's father for hours. They didn't realize that they were sitting next to the new parents of Lucia's baby.

They didn't notice the anxious young couple in the corner who were terrified that after the birth that the birth parents would change their minds. They talked back and forth about how they didn't know if they could take it again, and they cried in their fear and anticipation.

They didn't notice when the nurse came out and summoned them and the happiness on their faces when the nurse said, "Yes, she's yours." And they didn't notice the tears of joy as they followed her into the room to meet their new daughter.

Brynn was spent. She wanted to go home. She was full of so many different emotions that she needed to be able to sort them out. They hugged Lucia's father and walked him to the door of Lucia's room.

Lucia's Papi knew that he couldn't see the baby because he didn't agree with the adoption, but Lucia didn't give him a choice. She was giving her baby away out of love, and she needed him to support her. Her Papi could never say no to his Lucia so he waited outside and promised to be there for her. They felt bad leaving him, but he insisted that they go. He saw how tired Brynn was, and he was thankful that Lucia had such a good friend.

The drive home was silent. The air felt heavy with so many unspoken words between them.

There was one moment in the birthing room that Brynn couldn't get out of her mind. While Lucia held her, the baby locked eyes with Brynn, and Brynn found herself lost in her. And for one brief moment, all of her fear and sadness disappeared. Brynn ached with longing to hold her, but she knew that she wasn't hers to hold. Brynn had never felt that way before and it scared her, but she knew that it was a natural longing. She had always denied that feeling before out of simple fear.

Adam knew that Brynn was deep in her own mind. He didn't know what happened in the room, but based on the look on Brynn's face, he knew that she wasn't ready to talk about it just yet. He waited for her to come to him and tell him about it.

When they got home, she settled in on the couch and Adam made her tea.

He sat down close, next to her and waited to see if she would talk. For a while, they sat in silence until she finally spoke. She told him about what happened in the room and how beautiful and heartbreaking it was all at the same time. Brynn spoke in jumbled sentences and he had to pick through her words to understand what happened. She didn't make complete sense, but Adam didn't want to stop her from talking. He loved listening to the sound of her voice when she talked to him from her heart. It felt like forever since they talked like this.

When she finally stopped speaking and he was formulating her words, she paused and looked at him, her big brown eyes seemingly bigger, almost pleading.

"I'm ready now, Adam. I'm ready. I want to have a baby."

CHAPTER THIRTY-EIGHT

Truth in the Box

Brynn dreaded going through Rose's apartment after she died.

But she knew that she had to, and she put it off until the last minute. It seemed wasteful to continue paying rent on an apartment that they no longer needed. Lea, the housekeeper that Jane hired, did a nice job cleaning the place up. She volunteered to help Brynn clean it out and much to her surprise, Brynn agreed. It was a Herculean task that Brynn wasn't looking forward to, and she was willing to accept all of the help that she could get.

The apartment was spacious, and Lea warned her that there was one bedroom that Rose refused to let her touch. Brynn decided that they would tackle that room last. She was impressed with how efficiently Lea worked and decided that if she were available that Brynn would ask her if she wanted to work for her. She figured that with the restaurant and her newfound focus on her marriage, that it would be one less thing that she would need to worry about.

She didn't want anything to stand in the way of rediscovering Adam. They were getting along very well, and Brynn was finally making time for him. She found that giving herself permission to enjoy her life with him was easier than Brynn thought it would be. Adam seemed happier too, although, they both had dark days when they still couldn't seem to connect the way that they wanted to. On those days, they would talk, and they decided that they would just need to continue working through them.

He still needed her to open up more, and she still needed to learn to trust. They knew that it was a work in progress, and while they both had many feelings of frustration and resentment to work through, they also had great love.

Brynn took a few days off from the restaurant to tackle the job at hand. She and Lea sorted through the apartment, avoiding the one bedroom that she knew was going to be the worst room to tackle. They tagged everything for trash, donation, or sale throwing the little things out as they went and putting everything in the appropriate piles.

Brynn stopped on the second day and stood in front of the bedroom where they kept the door closed. She didn't want to go in.

Adam told her to call him when she got to that room. He said that he would help because he knew how much she was dreading it. Adam had two more meetings, and then he said that he would be there as fast as he could.

She went on in and she and Lea got to work. Rose shoved as much as she could in that room, piling boxes upon boxes upon boxes. The boxes were full to the top, with no rhyme or reason as to what she had in them. Rose collected various items over the years that made no sense. There were bookmarks, fans, teacups, candleholders, shot glasses, and all sorts of knick-knacks. There were about a hundred pairs of reading glasses, coasters from various restaurants and bars, and lots and lots of matchbooks. Brynn couldn't believe how much Rose kept, and she wondered why she never realized that she kept so much. She was with her all the time. She couldn't believe she never saw her collecting everything. There were random boxes of tools, old DVDs, magazines, books, pictures, and many miscellaneous items that made no sense.

Adam got there when they were halfway through. He couldn't believe how much was left. They laughed when they got to the box with the mismatched socks, until they realized that they weren't washed.

There wasn't much of significance in Rose's apartment. They decided that they would donate the clothes to Goodwill, as well as the dishes, glassware, and kitchen items. In fact, they planned to donate most of her things, and throw out the rest. The furniture smelled like cigarette smoke and they didn't plan to sell any of it, the items that smelled really bad were going on the tree lawn. It was a shame because most of the furniture was still in good shape, but just reeked of cigarette smoke.

The last box on the very bottom of the pile was marked "Brynn." Brynn was exhausted but curious. The box was very light and when she opened it up, there was nothing in it but an envelope. She opened the envelope intrigued, and inside she found only the name of the local bank and a safety deposit box number.

Brynn was frustrated. Leave it up to Rose to make it difficult. *Why couldn't she just leave whatever it was in the box?*

She grabbed her purse, and she and Adam drove to the bank, tired, cranky, and hungry. It was getting to be dinnertime and they were ready to be done. Brynn wanted a cheeseburger and a glass of wine. Adam introduced her to wine, and she realized that it wasn't the alcohol that was bad. Instead, it was Thomas that was bad. She was still reluctant to admit it, but the wine was pretty good, and she enjoyed the newfound freedom to enjoy a glass of wine occasionally. Now she found that she *really* wanted one. It had been a long couple of days, and she wanted to just relax a little and unwind.

They decided that after the bank, they were going to a local watering hole to have a big greasy burger and a couple of drinks. Adam was enjoying this new side of Brynn, and liked that she was learning to relax a little bit. They were both feeling a little tense about the contents of the safety deposit box. Brynn thought that she knew everything about Rose, but then again, she didn't know about the Alzheimer's. Adam was just as curious about the safety deposit box. *What could possibly be so important that Rose needed to lock it up?*

They barely got to the bank before closing time. The bank manager led her and Adam to the safety deposit boxes and pulled hers out after scrutinizing her ID. She and Rose were the only ones authorized to open the box.

He pulled it out, gave it to her, and then left the room.

Brynn's hands were trembling. She wasn't sure if it was from fear or anticipation, but she was anxious to see what was in it. When she opened it, she found a simple white envelope with her name scrawled on it in Rose's rounded, almost childlike cursive writing.

It was dated two years earlier.

My Dearest Brynn,

If you are reading this, then you've gone through my things and I am probably dead.

I hope you know how much I have loved you and how much I needed you in my life. I hope that as you are reading this that you don't hate me. I hope that I wasn't too much of a burden on you. You were my only reason for living my entire life. And even though I didn't have any children of my own, I couldn't possibly have loved you more than I did.

I hope that I get to tell you in person how I protected you. But in case I didn't, then I hope this won't come as too much of a surprise to you.

I know that you were always mad at me because you thought I didn't protect you. But I did! I did protect you, and I even had you protect yourself from time to time.

Think about what Thomas drank.

"Whiskey," Brynn whispered, frowning at the memory.

He drank Whiskey. Wild Turkey. Think about how he drank it.

"With ice," Brynn said aloud. Adam was looking at her, bursting with curiosity but he stayed silent and waited.

Think about how you made his ice cubes sometimes.

Brynn thought, *how silly Mother.* Brynn made them with water. She took out the ice cube tray and she poured water from the tap in them. The ice cube tray she used was *blue,* and it was always the *blue one.* Why? Why the blue one? Why not the white ones? She was never allowed to use the blue ones for her own drinks, only the blue ones for Thomas' drinks. Why?

What did you put in them besides water?

Brynn thought hard. Oh, yes. Momma always had a special dropper of sweetener that she had her put in the ice cubes. *"Just one itty-bitty little drop, sweetheart,"* Momma said to her, showing her how careful she needed to be. "Like this?" Brynn asked, dropping a tiny bit of the dropper into the ice cube tray, showing her how careful she could be. *"Just like that,"* Momma smiled at her, kissing her on the forehead. *"Just like that."*

What was in the dropper? Brynn froze. *What was in the dropper?*

I told you that it was his sweetener. And we used it for a long time. And then I started to send you away when we started to have meatloaf nights. Usually you spent the evening at Stacy's house. Do you remember?

Brynn was horrified. *What in the hell was in the dropper? What did you do, Rose? What did we do?* Brynn was starting to remember. Right about the time that they started adding the sweetener to his ice cubes, he started getting sick. He was hitting her less and less. He was still awful and mean, but he didn't hit as much. He started going to bed earlier, and on the nights he drank less, he was still able to get to her. But on the nights he drank more, he didn't seem to have the strength to hurt her. Why didn't she remember that before? How did that escape her?

You see, I did protect you. I don't know how long it took, or how much it took, but I do know that I protected you.

I got the idea from Whiskers.

Mrs. Snyder was her neighbor growing up and she had a grey and white tabby cat. She loved that cat, but one day Whiskers knocked over a bottle of antifreeze in their garage and she lapped it up and died. Mrs. Snyder was devastated.

Antifreeze? She poisoned Thomas with Antifreeze? How was she not caught? Brynn felt sick to her stomach.

I thought that it would take time, but I just didn't know how long. I still don't know how long. But I knew that it would work. I read a little bit about it and figured that he would never know. I thought he would just think he was getting sick from the drinking. That's what his doctor thought, too. They thought he was just getting sick from drinking too much, and they told him to stop. But he never did.

I just wanted you to know that I did protect you. I always looked out for you. I'm sorry that I let him hurt you, but I protected you the best way I knew how.

Brynn was stunned.

Rose poisoned him. She remembered those nights that Rose sent her away for meatloaf night. She never minded because she didn't like meatloaf, but Thomas looked forward to them. It was the only time she ever really saw him happy for anything. And then the next day, he would get sick. Brynn remembered him getting sicker and sicker slowly over time. She never minded because he had gotten too weak to hit her until finally he stopped altogether. He stopped around the time she got into high school. He tried, but he just couldn't do it anymore.

She knew that Adam was staring at her, burning to know. She handed him the letter, and then realized that she didn't read the rest of it and grabbed it back to finish reading the rest.

I let you do it too so that you would know that you protected yourself, too. I know that it was wrong which is why I told you like this. I hope I get to tell you in person, but if I don't I just wanted you to know.

You weren't a victim. You defended yourself even though you didn't know that you were at the time.

Brynn stopped reading. *She had me poison him! I poisoned my own father!* Brynn was horrified and suddenly felt nauseous. She knew that she should feel ashamed, but she didn't. She knew that she should feel regret, but she didn't. She felt nothing. Then she paused and felt, elated.

She hated Thomas.

Brynn thought back to all of the bruises on her face, her arms, and her ribs where he had kicked her and how she had to cover them up so that no one would see. She thought about the black eyes, the swollen cheeks, and the sprained wrist that Rose just splinted herself. She remembered how afraid she was that someone would find out and take her from Rose. She remembered the snap of his belt and how it stung on her bare skin. She thought about how he pulled her hair yanking it until she yelped in pain and about how he growled profanities in her ear, and told her how ugly and worthless and stupid she was. She remembered how she learned to lean her chair against the doorknob every night because she was petrified that he would come into her room while she was sleeping and kill her in her sleep.

And Brynn remembered with horror, watching him beat Rose almost daily, often slapping her and shaking her until she cried out.

And she thought about how many times she wished she could kill him, how she prayed for him to disappear, and to die a painful horrible death. She thought about taking her razor blade and slitting his throat with it, but she knew that she wasn't capable. She was too weak.

I hope that you won't hate me for what I did, and what I made you do. I want you to know that I was a good mother to you and that I took care of you in every way. You were the love of my life, and I am so thankful that you were my daughter.

Always yours,

Momma

Brynn handed the letter back to Adam. She felt numb.

Adam read the letter, and then reread the letter. He swore, and then he swore some more. And then he hugged Brynn and waited for her to react.

She didn't know what to say.

The bank manager came quietly into the room. It was forty-five minutes past closing time and he desperately wanted to leave. He paused when he saw the expression on their faces and started to back out of the room.

"I'm sorry," Brynn said, emotionless. "We'll leave."

She took the letter from Adam and put it carefully into her purse and zipped it up.

They walked out of the bank hand in hand, separating only to get into the car, and driving in silence to the local restaurant that they planned to go. Adam kept looking at Brynn on the drive there, searching for a change in her. She sat staring straight ahead with a strange look on her face. Adam had never seen that expression before and couldn't read it. She exuded a strange emotion that he couldn't identify.

They got to the restaurant, and sat in a booth as far away from everyone else as they could.

When the server arrived, Brynn ordered two shots of Wild Turkey, and didn't seem to notice the look of shock on Adam's face as he stared at her mystified.

When she finally spoke, her voice was low and without expression, her dark brown eyes staring at Adam earnestly. "She freed me, Adam. I'm free now, from Thomas, and from her."

Adam was silent. He had read the letter. He knew what she had done.

He understood that because of Rose, now Brynn was no longer a victim to her past. As dark and ugly as it was, Brynn was a sweet innocent child who had somehow been given control of her destiny without realizing it.

When the shots of Wild Turkey arrived, they simply stared at them for a moment. Brynn always detested the smell because it made her think of Thomas. But with her newfound knowledge of his demise, the smell no longer made her fearful. She held the shot up in front of her and Adam did the same.

"Here's to Thomas, that bastard. He can never hurt me again," she said, looking deeply into Adam's dark blue eyes. "If it weren't for him, I wouldn't be here, and then maybe I wouldn't be with you. Every moment of my life, both good and bad, has led me here to be with you."

Adam paused. What she said was true and he knew it. He just never thought of it like that before. He raised his glass to clink with hers, and then downed it, never taking his eyes off hers. Faced with the realization that she unknowingly helped kill her abusive father, she sat with him doing a shot. She was strengthened instead of weakened, and he was never more in love with her than he was at this moment. She was as raw and transparent to him as she could ever be, and he felt himself drawn in to her in a way that he never imagined.

He wasn't sure what he expected, but he didn't expect this.

Adam didn't realize when he met her how strong she was. He just knew that she was damaged for reasons that he couldn't begin to understand. And even though he didn't understand her, his heart recognized her immediately. She was her own person, and now she was his.

Brynn felt relief. For the first time, she understood Rose and she wanted to thank her for loving her the way she did.

Rose finally felt that she had the strength to go on and build a life and have a family of her own. She knew that she was strong enough and she was glad that Rose didn't let her secret die with her. Rose somehow knew that she needed to know that she had stood up for her, and that she had allowed Brynn to protect herself. Brynn didn't feel guilt or sadness for what Rose had her do. Instead, she felt vindicated and strong. She knew that she could be a mother, and that she could be a good wife now.

Brynn looked at Adam in wonder and marveled at how this man could possibly love her, but at least now she felt somewhat worthy and deserving. She knew that she could go on and live the life that she had only dreamed about because she finally had hope.

She never had hope before. She yearned for it and craved it, but there was never really the promise of it, other than the gift of having Adam in her life.

And to her, having both hope and Adam were the only things she could ask for.

EPILOGUE

It was an exciting day.

Jane was getting married and she asked Brynn to be the Matron of Honor. Brynn was excited. She had spent the last year dealing with her ghosts and putting away the past.

Her shrink helped her come to terms with Rose, and Brynn now felt at peace with how much she needed her as a child. She was beginning to feel more at peace with having been abandoned, but was still plagued with nightmares about running and hiding, and being terrified in the woods.

Adam still comforted her through the dreams every night when they happened, but it seemed that she was suddenly having them more and more often. The feelings of abandonment were strong, and they weren't going away. Brynn was trying desperately to push them aside. There was so much to look forward to now.

"Brynn, we have to go soon, sweetheart," Adam's voice called up from the bottom of the stairs. He was always the early riser, and Brynn knew that he was already up, dressed, and had breakfast waiting for her. She showered the night before and got up slowly. She was so tired and could use another hour or so of sleep, but she knew that Jane would kill her.

Jane's husband-to-be was a good man, and Jane credited Brynn with giving her the courage to date again. She wanted Brynn to stand up with them at the altar, and Brynn knew that she couldn't be late.

As Brynn brushed her long dark hair, she looked at herself in the mirror. She finally looked happy and peaceful. Brynn was no longer searching for answers to questions that plagued her and kept her up through the night, and she couldn't remember ever being this happy.

She brushed her hair in long strokes, finally able to let it grow out. She knew that there was nobody in her life anymore who would grab it and yank it. Brynn felt the fear diminishing with every passing day.

She sighed contentedly, and smiled at herself in the mirror. Her cheeks were rounder now that she had put back on some of the weight she had lost. She looked so much healthier, and she almost glowed.

The doorbell rang, startling Brynn. She waited to hear Adam answer it, and then it rang again.

Brynn padded down the stairs, moving a little slower than usual, her long cotton nightgown flowing out behind her. When she reached the front door, she hesitated for a moment and felt a shiver run down her spine.

Don't be silly, she told herself. *There's nothing to be afraid of...*

When she opened the door, she froze, her big brown eyes opening wide in disbelief.

On the other side of the screen stood an almost exact replica of herself, aged about fifteen years. Her hand instinctively went to her belly.

They stared at each other silently.

"Brynn, honey, who is it?" Adam called coming up behind her.

When he got close behind her, he put his hand on her shoulder, and stared. Nobody moved.

The woman on the other side stared down at Brynn's swollen belly and smiled.

She spoke first, her voice sounding eerily like Brynn's voice. "Eva? Eva? It's me. Do you recognize me, sweetheart?" She was petite like Brynn, with the same dark hair and coffee brown eyes. But as much as she resembled Brynn, Adam could tell that there was something missing.

Adam thought that she looked worn down, her skin thin and dull, and her hair unkempt. But there was more that unsettled him. While Brynn's eyes were bright and beautiful, this woman's eyes reflected darkness and duplicity, and Adam automatically felt as though he didn't trust her. He instinctively moved a step closer to Brynn.

Brynn was quiet, and the moment stretched out in front of her in slow motion. She felt a chill run down her spine, and she shivered.

Ellie stared at Brynn with a mixture of curiosity and jealously.

"Eva. Are you okay? You don't look so good, honey. I'm you're Momma. Can you let me in? I'd love to talk to you."

Brynn didn't want to let her in. She knew that she should want to, but she didn't. Against her better judgment, she reached out toward the door to unlock the screen. Brynn suddenly felt dizzy, the woman in front of her was making a strange face.

Brynn could hear Adam's voice calling her name and she wondered why he was yelling so loudly when she was standing right front of him. The last thing that Brynn saw was the distraught look on Adam's face as she fell to the floor.

VOLUME ONE

LOSING EVA

PROLOGUE

It was a beautiful day.

Brynn couldn't ask for anything more perfect. The sun was shining and bright. The leaves on the trees and blades of grass were the greenest green, almost as if the ideal shade was painted on just for her. The weather had been dismal lately, but the beauty of the day was unsurpassed by any so far.

Brynn sat back in her lounge chair with a book, looking forward to getting lost in it for a few hours. She hadn't been able to enjoy the simplicity and beauty of their large backyard for a long time.

These days she needed it. Her doctor wanted her to take it easy, and as difficult as it was, she was trying.

She sat back and nestled deep into the Adirondack chair made comfortable with soft cushions and closed her eyes.

Suddenly, she felt the hairs on the back of her neck stand on end. Someone was there in the backyard watching her. Somehow, she knew that it was him. She looked around frantically trying to find him. How did he find me? How did he know where I was? She felt completely naked and exposed in the spaciousness of the grass and the trees.

Maxie, their 80-pound pet Lab lifted his head and looked around. He seemed to sense something, too—almost as though he could smell him in the air. He let out a few loud barks as a warning while being sure to stay close to Brynn.

Thomas was close, and he was watching her. Brynn knew it. She felt the saliva building in the back of her throat, nearly choking her. It was a familiar feeling, one that she hadn't felt for a long time. *How can this be? How can he be here? He's dead, gone for almost two decades. How can he be here now?*

Brynn frantically gathered her things and turned to go into the house. Suddenly he was there, standing in front of her, towering as he did when she was young.

He glared at her, ice blue eyes piercing through her soul, hatred, and resentment radiating dangerously. Brynn was in danger, and she felt it in every fiber of her being.

"W-w-what do you want?" she croaked, barely able to utter the words. Maxie stood next to her, alarmed. He was more of a lover than anything else, and Brynn knew that she couldn't count on him to protect her, despite his size.

Thomas didn't speak. He just stared at her. Brynn wanted to cry.

"You're supposed to be dead! Dead!" Brynn yelled, backing away from him cautiously, slowly. It felt like the house was a mile away from her as she tried to move her feet faster, yet keep her eyes on him. Thomas seemed to be getting closer and closer to her. "Oh my God, you're supposed to be dead."

Suddenly Brynn felt his hands around her throat, and before she knew it, she had fallen backwards onto the ground, and he was above her. He was squeezing slowly, tightening his grip, and Brynn felt her air supply cutting off.

"Please stop! P-p-please!" she cried, unable to raise her voice above barely a whisper.

She felt him release his grip on her, and she was grateful for a split second as she gasped for breath. Horrified, she watched him roll up his sleeve. *What is he doing?* It was an odd gesture, and she couldn't imagine why he would do that.

He opened his mouth to speak. His voice was different from the low, gravelly voice that haunted Brynn's dreams from her childhood. His voice now was loud, booming, and clear like a bell. "You killed me. You were my daughter, and you killed me. How could you?"

Brynn was stunned. He knows. How does he know?

"I know, because I know everything. And now, since you took something from me, I am going to take something from you."

Brynn was confused. What else can he take from me? He took my childhood, my ability to love openly and completely. He caused me to scar myself. What else can he do to me?

"This is what I am going to do to you." With one sudden movement, Thomas took his fist and shoved it violently into her belly. Brynn couldn't believe her eyes. *Oh my God, what is he doing?*

"I'm killing your baby, just like you killed me," Thomas sneered, his yellow teeth staring down at her as he grinned.

Brynn screamed. The pain was incredible as she watched him pulling his bloody arm in and out of her stomach, his fists squeezing the tiny life inside of her. She could feel that she was in pain, her little baby. She screamed, desperately, trapped beneath Thomas' massive body as he straddled her legs.

Suddenly she felt a sharp slap, then another. "Brynn! Brynn!"

Thomas was calling her name, but it wasn't his strange voice. It was someone else's. "Brynn! Brynn!"

Adam. She heard Adam's voice coming out of Thomas' mouth.

Brynn sat straight up, no longer trapped. "Where did Thomas go?" she screamed in horror.

"Brynn, it's me! It's Adam!" Adam held her with his strong hands, trying desperately to get her to see him. Her eyes were wide and frantic, her pupils huge and black. He knew that she was lost in her dream, as she was so many nights. "Brynn, sweetheart, it's me, honey. It's Adam. Wake up. It's just a bad dream."

Brynn stared straight ahead, her thick dark hair a tangled mess, tears running down her face. Maxie was sitting at her side, his big head lying next to her as he whimpered.

Slowly, her face started to relax a little, her hands flying to her belly, rubbing desperately. She shifted her gaze down to Maxie and then over to Adam, and then back to Maxie.

"Adam!" she cried. "Adam!" She was back, and Adam felt relief flood through him. This was a bad one, maybe even the worst one. He was afraid he wasn't going to get her back.

"It's okay Brynn. You're safe. It was just a bad dream."

"It was Thomas."

"I know it was Thomas. You screamed his name. It's always Thomas. But he's dead. He can't hurt you anymore." Adam took her hand and pulled her into his arms so that he could hold her close.

Brynn kept rubbing her stomach. She could feel the scars through her cotton nightshirt. Several of the deeper ones were pretty bumpy. She was sure those would never go away. Thomas was her father, and he was supposed to protect her. But instead, she had to protect herself. The cutting always allowed her to cocoon away into her own world for a bit so that she didn't have to feel the pain and the fear. If she didn't have the cutting, and then Adam, she knew that she never would have survived.

"Do you want to talk about it?" Adam asked gently. Sometimes she did, and sometimes she didn't. The shrink had told them that it was up to Brynn, so Adam always asked. He didn't want to pressure her.

"No. Yes...no." Brynn wasn't sure. She was trying to shut the dream out of her mind, but the sobs kept coming, and it was still difficult to breathe.

Adam looked at her cautiously. He had made the mistake once of leaving her behind. He was never going to do that again, but he wondered if they would ever be able to have a normal life. He wanted one, he needed one. He loved Brynn and he couldn't live without her.

"Let's go to sleep then, sweetheart. We need to rest. You need to rest." Adam turned off the bedside lamp, and they settled into the soft, comfortable sheets. They felt Maxie jump on to the end of the bed, which jostled as if an earthquake struck until they were all comfortable. Adam could tell that Brynn was smiling, and he smiled, too. Maxie had been good for both of them.

"I'm sorry, Adam," Brynn said in the dark, still sniffling.

"Don't be sorry. You can't help it," Adam said sleepily. "It'll be okay."

As they drifted off to sleep, Adam heard Brynn's voice.

"Adam, he was killing our baby."

CHAPTER ONE

Jane's Wedding Day

Brynn was excited for the day.

Jane was finally getting married to a wonderful man, Andrew, and she had asked Brynn to be the Matron of Honor. Brynn had spent the last year dealing with ghosts and trying to put away the past, and Jane's wedding was the first time she had felt hopeful about anything for awhile.

Brynn's therapist helped her come to terms with her past. Most recently, they were working out her relationship with Rose, and the resentment she continued to feel toward her, even though she was dead. Theirs had been far from the ideal mother/daughter relationship. Brynn was finally beginning to understand, and to feel more at peace with just how much Rose had needed her, even when Brynn was just a child. Brynn missed Rose and had loved her, but the memory of how dependent Rose had been on her continued to plague her. It took a year for her to stop expecting the early morning phone calls or the constant text messaging, but Brynn felt herself finally able to relax rather than feel "on call" at all times.

The shrink also helped her come to terms with being abandoned, but the nightmares about running, hiding, and being terrified in the woods still tormented her. The nightmares were violent, intense, and brutally real, often leaving their imprint on Brynn for days.

Adam did his best to comfort her through the dreams when they happened, and he was glad when they began to occur less often. For awhile, it had stayed that way, but recently, they seemed to occur more often, almost nightly. The feelings of abandonment were strong, and they weren't going away, even though Brynn tried desperately to push them aside.

But with Jane's wedding and so many new things on the horizon, there was so much to look forward to now.

"Brynn, we have to go soon, sweetheart," Adam's voice called up from the bottom of the stairs. He was always the early riser, and Brynn knew that he was already up, dressed, and had breakfast waiting for her. She showered the night before and got up slowly. She was so tired and could use another hour or so of sleep, but she knew that Jane would kill her.

Jane's husband-to-be was a good man, and Jane credited Brynn with giving her the courage to date again. She wanted Brynn to stand up with them at the altar, and Brynn knew that she couldn't be late.

As Brynn applied her makeup, she took a long look at herself in the mirror. The woman looking back at her was finally happier and more at peace than she had been her entire life. Brynn was no longer obsessed with finding answers to the questions that had plagued her all of her life.

Why was I abandoned? Why did Thomas hurt me? Why didn't Rose stop him?

Brynn's shrink told her that there was nothing she could do about her past; she actually began to believe him. Brynn couldn't remember ever being happy, and it was a strange feeling.

She slowly brushed her thick dark hair in long strokes. It had taken her entire life, but Brynn was finally letting it grow. She knew that there was nobody in her life anymore, who would grab it and yank it or use it to hold her captive while he hit her as Thomas had. The fear slowly diminished with every passing day. As far as adopted fathers went, Thomas was the worst, but he was dead now, and she didn't have to be afraid any longer.

She sighed contentedly, and smiled into the mirror. Her cheeks were rounder now that she had gained some weight. She looked healthier, almost glowing.

The doorbell rang, startling Brynn. She waited to hear Adam answer it, but then it rang again.

Brynn padded down the stairs, moving a little slower than usual, her long, cotton nightgown flowing behind her. When she reached the front door, she hesitated for a moment and felt a shiver run down her spine.

Don't be silly, she told herself. *There's nothing to be afraid of...*

When she opened the door, she froze—her big coffee colored eyes opening wide in disbelief.

On the other side of the screen stood an almost exact replica of herself, aged about 15 years. Her hand instinctively went to her belly.

They stared at each other silently.

"Brynn, honey, who is it?" Adam called coming up behind her.

When he got close behind her, he put his hand on her shoulder and stared. Nobody moved.

The woman on the other side stared down at Brynn's swollen belly and smiled.

She spoke first, her voice husky, sounding eerily like Brynn's. "Eva? Eva? It's me. Do you recognize me, sweetheart?" She was petite like Brynn, with the same dark hair and beautiful brown eyes. But as much as she resembled Brynn, Adam could tell there was something different, almost absent, in this other woman.

She looked worn down, her skin thin and dull, and her hair unkempt. But there was more that unsettled him. While Brynn's eyes were bright and beautiful, this woman's eyes reflected something different, something darker, and Adam automatically felt anxious. He instinctively moved a step closer to Brynn.

Brynn was quiet. The moment stretched out in front of her in slow motion. She felt a chill run down her spine, and she shivered.

Ellie stared at Brynn with a mixture of curiosity and jealously.

"Eva. Are you okay? You don't look so good, honey. I'm your Momma. Can you let me in? I'd love to talk to you."

Brynn didn't want to let her in. She knew that she should want to, but she didn't. Against her better judgment, she reached out toward the door to unlock the screen. Brynn suddenly felt dizzy, the woman in front of her was making a strange face.

Brynn could hear Adam's voice call her name, and she wondered why he was yelling so loudly when she was standing right in front of him. The last thing Brynn saw was the distraught look on Adam's face as she fell to the floor.

CHAPTER TWO

Brynn's Mother

Brynn woke up, her head aching and heavy. She was in a curtained area. She could hear beeping and the quiet scuffle of feet and voices, but she was alone. Squinting, her eyes tried to adjust to the harsh impersonal lighting fixtures. Brynn looked around and realized she was in the hospital and wearing a gown that was two sizes too big. *Where are my clothes?*

The last thing that she remembered was opening the screen door and seeing...what? *What did I see? What made me faint?* Brynn's head felt fuzzy, and it hurt. A lot. Her tongue felt dry and thick, and too big for her mouth. She desperately wanted water. She reached up and pulled at her long thick hair, trying to make the headache stop.

She instinctively put her hand over her belly. Oh my God, the baby. *Is the baby okay?* Brynn's heart was starting to race. *How long have I been here? Is the baby alright? Adam, where are you? Why is this happening now that everything has been going so well? Why?*

Brynn still couldn't believe that she was pregnant. After all this time, she was finally ready to be a mother. Adam was ready to be a parent much sooner than she was, but now she was at peace with her past. And with everything they had been through together — they had endured a separation, but now they were repairing their marriage and their lives. With Rose gone for over a year, Brynn now had faith that she was capable of being a good mother.

She was done being afraid.

Adam said he was never going to leave again, and Brynn somehow believed that it was true. She was finally learning to open up and embrace life with him, and there was a connection between them that was stronger than ever before. She knew that he felt it every time she looked at him, and she could tell that he was happy. They were finally on common ground, and for the first time, she felt as if she were contributing to their relationship as much as he had since they were fifteen years old.

But now, her whole world felt as if it were crashing in, and there was no way to stop it. The baby isn't moving, oh God! The baby isn't moving!

She looked around and saw a plastic box by her side.

She pushed the red nurses call button frantically, terrified to be alone, and desperate for answers. I need Adam! I need someone!

"Yes, may I help you?" a distant voice came from nowhere, a subtle clicking sound accompanying it.

"Yes, I need my husband. Where is he? How is my baby?" Brynn said in one breath, talking to the air. She was lost. She needed Adam.

"We'll be right there," the voice said.

"Okay," she said weakly, to no one. She hated to be alone. What happened?

The moment came flooding back to her, almost overtaking her. Brynn remembered, and then her heart started to race. The woman! That woman who was at my front door... the woman who called me Eva!

The woman looked so much like Brynn—small, petite, with dark, pretty features, and big brown eyes that seemed too big for her face. She could have been Brynn's sister, only she wasn't. The woman said she was Brynn's Momma.

Brynn hadn't even gotten her name.

Could it really be my Mother? Why would she come into my life now, when I'm finally happy, when I have finally found some peace? Why would she bother to show up now when my life with Adam is starting to be really nice? Brynn's head was swimming with questions. How did my Mother even find me?

It didn't make sense. And then Brynn realized that the woman must have found her because years earlier, Brynn had put her name in with the adoption agency. She always thought that she wanted to connect with her parents someday, but now that the day had come, she wasn't as sure.

But why wouldn't someone have called her to give her some warning? How did this woman just show up at her door? It was the moment that Brynn had always dreamt about, her Mother coming to find her.

She thought back to when she was a little girl, kneeling beside her bed, earnestly folding her hands to pray. *Dear God, please help my real Mommy to find me and take me and my Momma away from Daddy so he can't hurt me anymore."* Brynn thought that her real Mommy would rescue her from Thomas' fist and feet, and protect her from his rage. Tiny brown-eyed Brynn, with her long hair and high-pitched little girl voice, prayed night after night to be saved.

Thomas blamed her for stealing all of Rose's love so that there was nothing left for him. Young Brynn would pray desperately that her birth Mommy would take her away. But she never came. So why now? Why did she show up now? It didn't make sense.

Brynn thought about the woman's face, even though she had only seen it for a fraction of a second. Brynn could tell that she had been beautiful at one time, but the beauty looked like it had slowly been erased. The woman looked like the shadow of someone else, someone that Brynn didn't know.

The nurse was taking so long, and Brynn worried about the baby. She saw that she had a strap, with what looked like a monitor of some sort, around her belly. The machine that the strap was connected to displayed a steady, green line that ran across the screen at a consistent pace, making the same up and down lines every time it went across. Brynn watched the monitor for a while feeling better. It was the same type of monitor she use to stare at as she sat by Rose's bedside for hours.

Brynn heard a noise, and turned from the monitor to see Adam racing into the room. His thick, brown hair was disheveled, and his beautiful blue eyes the color of the sea, wide with distress. "Brynn, you're awake!" he said, his voice full of concern. Brynn never tired of hearing him talk. She loved his voice and everything about him. To think that she nearly lost him forever still gravely chilled her. Living life without him in it for those long months was the worst time of her life. Even thinking about it made her want to cry, so she pushed the memory from her mind. She knew that if she thought about it, she would remain in a dark mood for the rest of the day. And there were too many other things to contend with right now.

Brynn couldn't blame Adam for leaving those months back. She had inexplicably withdrawn her love, leaving him alone even after he had always taken care of her. She knew he left without much of a choice.

"You've abandoned me, Brynn!" Adam would say to her time and again in total frustration. "You won't even discuss having a family with me! You just wallow! If I had known this is who you would become when I married you..." Adam never finished the sentence, but Brynn knew that he would never have married her in the first place.

They fell in love at fifteen and Adam was the only person to teach Brynn how to live, to laugh, and to smile. Even though Adam knew she had endured more than any one person should have ever had to, he wanted Brynn to want to be happy, with him. And as much as he loved her, he needed her to love him, too.

Adam needed her to let him love her, but Brynn refused, and so he left.

Those months without him were hell.

Now Brynn knew what life was without him, and she vowed to never lose him again. Adam returned with love, finally winning out over her anger and confusion.

Brynn sometimes wondered whether he would have come back if Rose hadn't died. She knew it didn't matter, because her adopted mother did die, and Adam did come back, and she chastised herself for trying to over think it.

But it wasn't an easy road for either of them, and they had worked through much in the past year and a half since he moved home.

"I'm never leaving you again Brynn," Adam would say to her repeatedly. "I'll never hurt you again."

"I want to believe you, Adam." Brynn was stubborn and her heart had a hard time letting go of the fear. "I want to, but I just don't." Adam would try to hold her, and Brynn would stiffen up, pushing him away with her fear.

"Stop pushing me away. You don't have to push me away anymore." Adam won out, and he held her close, feeling her heart beating in her chest from the anxiety. "I'll never abandon you."

Brynn always felt herself give into the deep, low tone of his voice that she loved so much. She allowed herself to be enveloped in his strong, sturdy arms, but a tiny part of her still wanted to shrink away. She wondered if she would ever stop fighting the happiness he gave her.

She had experienced so much loss in life that she had come to expect it. First, her birth parents abandoning her. Then Stacy, her childhood friend who had been killed by her husband's lover. Then Rose. And now Adam. Brynn finally decided that she would give herself permission to accept Adam's love, no matter how long she was able to have it.

When she gave in, there was finally peace.

And now they were having a baby together. Brynn was five months along, and her belly was nice and round. When Brynn looked at her belly, naked in the mirror, she saw the scars from years of cutting stretched out wide. Some were still painfully visible while others were beginning to fade, but they all still served as a horrific reminder of her painful childhood. The first time she went to have her ultrasound done, Brynn was embarrassed. The technician didn't even blink twice, and proceeded with 'business as usual.' Brynn was grateful.

She knew that she needed to accept the pain from her past and move on in order to be a good mother.

Now she was enjoying every moment of her pregnancy. There was no morning sickness, and she loved how the growing baby was giving her an excuse to eat a little more. She finally looked healthy, and was actually glowing and radiant. Brynn looked so different from the sick, bony woman she had become when Adam was gone.

But now Brynn worried for her baby.

Jane! It's Jane's wedding day, and I am supposed to stand up with her. Brynn was horrified. Jane was her closest friend. She was the one who saw her through when Adam was gone, and Rose was dying.

Jane helped pave the way for Adam to come home, and she took care of Brynn when Brynn couldn't take care of herself. And now it was Jane's day, and Brynn failed her... again.

Brynn was indebted to Jane in the same way that she was indebted to Adam. They both had brought her out of the darkness, and she loved her friend with all of her heart.

Before Jane, Brynn only had one friend in all of her life, but now Stacy was gone, murdered by her husband's lover. Now Jane was her very best friend, and only the second real friend she'd ever had.

"Oh, Adam! The baby!" she cried. "...and Jane!"

"Jane is fine sweetheart," Adam said smoothing her hair, which instantly calmed her. He knew just how to touch her to make her feel better. "She understands. She said she could postpone it, but I told her to just go ahead. This isn't our day. It's her day. She said it wouldn't be the same without you."

Brynn cried. She was looking forward to seeing her friend get married and finally find her happiness. Jane had come to work at Brynn's restaurant years before and was broke, overwhelmed, and grieving the loss of her husband from stomach cancer. Brynn helped her get on her feet and find hope again.

Now, Jane and her two girls were finally getting the happiness they deserved. Ryan was a great guy, and he loved them all so much. Brynn was so happy for her friend.

A nurse came into the room and started checking the monitors and wires efficiently. She smiled politely at Brynn and asked her how she was feeling. Brynn said she was fine. Brynn always said she was fine, even when she wasn't.

"How is my baby?" she asked, afraid of the answer. She was trying to live life unafraid for the first time ever, but this was a new kind of terror.

"Oh, the baby is fine. Don't worry, the doctor will talk to you when she gets in," the nurse smiled and patted Brynn's arm softly. Brynn sighed with relief.

When the nurse left, Brynn looked at Adam, her eyes filled with questions.

"She's in the waiting room," Adam said, answering her first, unspoken question. "She felt bad about shocking you the way that she did, but refused to leave."

Brynn was quiet. She didn't know what she would do with this woman in her life after all this time. Brynn didn't know this woman, and didn't know if she even wanted to... After all, this woman hadn't wanted her before, abandoning her as a toddler, leaving Brynn to fend for herself. Brynn broke her leg, and she had nearly starved to death trying to look for her mother.

Now that Brynn was about to have her own baby, she couldn't even imagine leaving a child. She had been terrified to become pregnant, but now that she was, she was terrified that harm would come to her baby. She couldn't even imagine a circumstance in which she would walk away from her child now.

Brynn looked down at her belly and smiled. She loved her baby with something inside of her that she hadn't even known existed. It was as though the moment she knew she was pregnant, a switch turned on. Now she thought it had been so silly to be afraid of motherhood. Protecting her child and caring for it seemed like the most natural thing in the world to do.

"What does she want?" Brynn asked even though she knew that Adam wouldn't know the answer.

"I don't know, sweetheart." Adam was asking himself the same question. While Ellie seemed concerned about Brynn, there was something in her demeanor that appeared detached. It made him uncomfortable.

His first impression of Ellie was unsettling, even though she was making every attempt to be friendly. Adam thought that he should give her a chance, but he couldn't shake the uneasiness. "Don't worry about that right now. I just want you to get some sleep. Please rest. The baby needs it, and so do you."

Suddenly Brynn felt a sharp pain, followed quickly by another.

The nurse was just about to leave the room when she noticed Brynn's face, grimaced in pain. "Are you okay?" She asked looking anxiously at the monitor, its lines jumping erratically. She quickly pushed the red button on Brynn's bed. "I need some assistance in room 210, Stat!"

Brynn felt pain. Sharp, stabbing pain and she yelped as she felt herself getting hot and starting to sweat. Oh God, no! No! You can't have my baby!

"Brynn, Brynn, can you hear me?"

Brynn could hear Adam's voice, but she couldn't answer. She was lost in pain, trying to gather herself, fearing for the tiny life growing inside. She felt pain, and then she felt wetness as a pool of red started to stain the crisp white sheet of the hospital bed. Adam and Brynn stared down in horror, and Brynn started to feel faint.

She felt the room growing dark, and she knew she was going to black out again.

The last thought she had was of the tiny baby inside fighting for life, and all she wanted was for her to live. She knew it was a girl, even though everyone else thought it was a boy. She knew with all of her heart that she was a girl. She even had a name picked out, even though she kept it to herself. She hadn't even told Adam. Not until it was time.

Please baby, fight. You have to live. I need you to live. Mommy needs you, and she wants you more than anything in the world. I have fought to have you, so don't leave me now.

Brynn felt herself getting weaker. She could still feel Adam in the distance holding her hand, calling her name. She knew that there was a flurry of excitement in the room, and that she was being hooked up to more monitors. She even thought that someone might have been pumping her chest, but she wasn't certain. Everything felt like a blur. She thought she saw the woman who claimed to be her mother at the door fighting with a nurse to get in. Her long hair was flying about as she yelled at the nurse, and Brynn could tell she was upset. But Brynn felt strangely calm, peaceful. Even though Adam looked like he was about to explode with fear and concern, and her birth mother fought desperately to get into the room. Still, Brynn felt at peace, so she talked to her baby and prayed.

Baby, fight! Mommy won't leave you. We will be together in this world, I promise. I won't abandon you like my mother abandoned me, and I will never hurt you. You will always be mine…mine and Daddy's. God, please let us live! Please! Amen.

Brynn prayed over and over, while the commotion in the room continued.

And then there was nothing.

CHAPTER THREE

Guilty Ellie

The guilt was crushing Ellie from the inside out. She felt it as they had driven home from abandoning her child; she felt it in the morning when she woke up, and at night before she went to bed. She carried it with her like a sharp dagger not too far from her heart, wounding herself daily.

Jonas didn't understand it. He was a man, and he had never created life inside of his own body the way that she had. Ellie made sure to spend her entire pregnancy detached, but the moment Eva was born, she was in love.

But Jonas hated Eva. From the moment he found out Ellie was pregnant, he didn't want anything to do with her. Ellie couldn't believe how cold he could be, and how mean he was to his little girl. She could understand if Eva was an ugly child, but Ellie knew that she was beautiful, with big brown eyes and that cute little chin. Eva was the spitting image of her momma, and if nothing else, she thought Jonas should appreciate that.

Ellie wanted to leave him, but she loved him. She needed him. He was her drug, and she was addicted to him in a way that terrified her yet satisfied her all at once. But watching her baby lying on the cold ground crying as Jonas sped away was an image that was burned into Ellie's mind.

Ellie almost killed Jonas in his sleep that night.

When they arrived back at Jonas' dirty little apartment, Ellie was almost hysterical.

"Calm down, El. She'll be fine!" Jonas lit a cigarette and handed it to her. She took it, her hand shaking uncontrollably, her eyes unfocused. He was losing patience. She had cried and screamed for the entire two-hour drive back. She screamed for him to turn around. She pulled at her hair. She cursed him and herself. She was hysterical, and Jonas could do nothing to calm her down.

He thought about pushing her out of the car, *but even he wasn't that cruel.* "There were cars all up and down that road. The kid is going to be fine!"

Ellie looked at Jonas in a daze. What will Momma think? Daddy is going to hate me. What have I done? She felt something squeezing her heart, like a giant fist. Squeezing, squeezing. Her heart was going to explode. She knew that if it did, she would deserve it. She deserved a horrible death after what she had done to her baby girl.

Jonas looked at her in disgust. So young! He loved his little sweet Ellie, but she was so young and so dramatic. He didn't usually pick them this young, but Ellie had captivated him with her innocence. The twelve-year age difference didn't bother him, and it wasn't as though he planned to be with her forever. He got bored easily and didn't usually stay with his women very long. She had proven to be different, though. She tried to ditch him when she was pregnant with the kid, but he always made it a point to find her. It was an effort he wasn't used to making for a piece of ass, but for some reason, he couldn't seem to shake Ellie.

"My baby, my baby, my baby," Ellie had rocked back and forth on the floor, sobbing. Jonas had never seen anyone cry so much. And all over a snotty kid. He knew that he should feel bad, but Jonas' dad split when his mother was pregnant with him, and he turned out pretty good. Jonas didn't think that people should even have kids, and he certainly never wanted one. Not now, not ever.

He went to the drawer and pulled out a syringe. If he didn't quiet her down, he was never going to get any sleep, and he needed to sleep. He was tired from all the driving. And he needed to go out and move some product, or they weren't going to be able to eat. He pulled out the syringe and prepared it while she rocked and cried behind him.

"Ellie, shut the hell up. The kid is going to be fine! You'll see. We are going to be so much better off without her." Jonas used his sexy voice, the one that usually made her climb all over him. He knew that she liked it, but this time it didn't do anything to her.

He grabbed Ellie's arm and wrapped the stretchy band around it. She winced when he tightened it, but didn't move. Jonas watched Ellie's face when the needle went in, and her expression didn't change. Good, he thought. She'll be out of it for awhile, and I won't have to listen to her cry anymore. She will see how much better off we are now.

Ellie's body consumed the drug while Jonas watched her go limp. He knew that she needed it to cope, but he figured that after a few days she would forget, and things would be better. He had hoped anyway. For some reason he needed Ellie, and it was getting harder and harder to think about a life without her. He shook his head, trying to clear it. *Don't get all sappy, you idiot. She's just like anyone else, take or leave her.*

Ellie was lying peacefully on the ratty couch, and he laid a blanket over her and smoothed her hair. He sat next to her, careful not to jostle her too much. He thought about how young she looked, how innocent. He let his thumb run down her face and admired her perfect smooth skin and the long eyelashes that skimmed her cheeks. Five years after he met her, she still stopped his heart, even after everything they had been through. She did something to him that no one ever had before. He couldn't explain it.

The first time he saw her walking through town, Jonas was instantly drawn to her.

He had been driving with the windows of his beat up Mustang rolled all the way down. The car was his baby, and he was trying to pull in enough scratch to fix her up, but was far from doing anything yet. He saw Ellie on the other side of the street as he pulled up to the light, and Jonas felt his heart stop. She was young. Too young. But something about her made him forget all about her age. She had looked at Jonas and smiled—a beautiful smile with small perfect teeth, big brown eyes shining bright. He felt instantly blinded, not even realizing when he did a U-turn and pulled up next to her.

She looked unfazed.

"Hi," he said ignoring his heart in his throat. He hoped she wouldn't see his nervousness.

"Hi," she smiled, boldly, making him uneasy.

"I'm Jonas."

"I know who you are," she kept smiling, amused.

"You do?" he was curious. He had never seen this girl before in his life, and he would have remembered. She wasn't the kind of girl who lived on his side of town, or who would know the people that he knew. He could tell by looking at her that she was a little girl with money, and certainly not the kind of girl who usually hung out with the likes of him.

"Of course I do. You're Jonas Miles." She was having fun. He was much older than Ellie, but his reputation was big in town. All of the kids knew that he was the guy you could score dope from, or anything else you wanted. She had attended a few parties where her friends had gotten their "stuff" from him. He was legendary. She thought it was funny that he didn't know it.

"Yes," he looked surprised, his dark green eyes widening. He didn't think that someone like her would have any idea who he was. He looked at her tight cashmere sweater, and her nice expensive shoes and shook his head. She didn't make sense to him. "Where are you going?"

"Why?" she said coyly.

He cleared his throat. He knew she was toying with him. But why? "I thought I could give you a ride."

"Okay." She said matter-of-factly. He expected her to say "No" and was taken aback by how bold she was. Before he knew it, she hopped in the front seat, throwing her book bag in the back. It landed with a thud, and he thought it sounded too heavy for such a small girl like her to carry.

"Where are you going?" he repeated.

"Wherever," she said, smiling that blinding smile at him.

He smiled back, feeling his heart flutter with something he wasn't used to feeling. Excitement? Weird! He was confused. She was just a little rich girl who was way too young for him. But there was just something about her.

They spent the entire rest of the day together. And the following day he picked her up from school, and the day after that.

Jonas knew that Ellie was smitten with him, and he with her. He had been with a lot of girls, but he had never met anyone like her before. He was careful to keep his feelings hidden. He wasn't going to let some little rich girl take advantage of him. Jonas had seen it with his mother and her men, how they only used her for a little while and then left when they were done. All of his life he watched his mother's heart get broken, so much so that she abandoned love entirely and stayed high and loose most of the time. Jonas wasn't going to let anyone do that to him, ever.

But as Ellie lay in a drug-induced sleep, for a moment, Jonas let himself get lost in her. He stroked her cheek and kissed her forehead, and thought about how he would hate to ever lose her. She made him happy, even though she infuriated and frustrated him. He knew that he didn't want to ever be without her.

And now that the kid was gone, it would just be the two of them always.

CHAPTER FOUR

Ellie and Adam

Adam was frantic. He felt as though his head were about to explode. Everybody was ignoring him, and he just wanted to know what was happening to his wife. His purpose—nearly his entire life—had been to take care of Brynn, and not being in control of what was happening to her was unbearable.

"How is Brynn? What is going on? Someone needs to give me some answers, right NOW!" Adam was furious as he stood at the nurse's station, daring someone to make eye contact with him.

The nurses had kicked him out of Brynn's area, and had closed the curtain and the glass door so that he couldn't see in. No one would tell them what was going on. One moment he was holding Brynn's hand, and the next they were practically pushing him out of the room.

"Sir, Sir! Please, quiet down! I don't know anything yet, and as soon as I do, I will let you know. All that I know is that they are assessing her," a mousy little nurse with brown hair was trying not to show her frustration with him. "Please, go sit down. We will call you as soon as we know something!"

Ellie came up and stood behind him. "Adam," she said, startling him. She sounded so much like Brynn that it made him want to practically crawl out of his skin.

"What?" he turned on her angrily. If she had never shown up at the front door, none of this would have happened!

"Let's go sit down," Ellie said gently as she started to reach for his arm. She pulled back when she saw the look on his face.

Adam didn't want to sit with her. He couldn't sit right now. He needed to know what was happening. The last thing he saw before they closed the curtain was Brynn's face. It was as white as a sheet. His first thought was that she was dying. Only fifteen minutes had passed, but it felt like a lifetime.

Just then, the curtain to Brynn's room flew back and he saw the foot of her bed emerge as they quickly pushed it through the doorway.

Adam ran over to the room as the doctor stepped out and was following the bed.

"What's going on?" Adam said blocking his path. "I'm her husband. Tell me what is happening."

"The baby is in distress and your wife is in danger. We have to get the baby out immediately! We are going to do an emergency C-section." The doctor was clearly in a hurry, and Adam stepped quickly out of his way.

He was stunned. After everything that he and Brynn had been through, Adam couldn't bear the thought of losing her and their baby. He put his hands to his face and swallowed back a sob. One of the nurses appeared beside him and put her hand on his arm sympathetically. "I've called for one of our helpers to take you to the waiting room. They will come out and brief you as soon as the surgery is over."

The helper was an older gentleman, Henry, who was much chattier than Adam would have liked. Henry talked to Adam during the entire slow walk to the waiting room, up four floors and halfway across the hospital. Adam tried to tune him out, but the older gentleman kept talking, distracting him from his current mission, which was to get to the waiting room to see how Brynn and the baby were doing.

Ellie walked slowly behind them, careful to keep her distance. She could tell that Adam didn't like her, and she couldn't blame him.

She had shown up at the door, and now Brynn was in the hospital, though by no fault of her own. Ellie knew by the look in

Adam's eyes that he blamed her. Ellie blamed herself, too. Trouble always seemed to gravitate toward her, and had all of her life. Why should this be any different? Ellie was feeling sorry for herself, and was trying to shake it off. She really needed something, anything, to calm her down.

Her hands were shaking and her nerves were a wreck, but Ellie knew that if she could make it through meeting her daughter, that she could make it through anything.

They finally made it to the quiet waiting room, and Ellie and Adam realized that Henry had stopped talking. "Here we are," he said, pleasantly pointing them to the small open room in front of them. "There is a television, some magazines, and there is coffee at the end of the hall."

Ellie couldn't get over the hospitality that he was showing them, and thought with irony that they must charge extra for Henry to show them around. She thought back to that night so long ago when she was just a young girl in the hospital, her belly swollen and awkward as she was about to give birth. There hadn't been anyone like Henry to show her around. She had been all alone and frightened. Ellie shook her head in awe at how much things had changed.

She snuck a peek at Adam, who had taken a seat across from her, and thought how lucky Eva must be to have someone like him. He clearly loved her deeply, his deep blue eyes awash in fear and pain. Ellie felt a twinge of jealousy and tried to shake it off. *How can I be so jealous of my own daughter? But she felt it deep in her bones. If it weren't for me, she wouldn't have him, so I must have done something right.* She must not have needed me as much as I thought she would!

Ellie and Adam were alone in the quiet little room, and she felt the weight of the awkwardness. They hadn't been completely alone yet. Ellie knew from the way he kept his distance that not only did Adam not like her, he didn't trust her. That made Ellie angry.

How dare he judge me? He doesn't know anything about me! Ellie peered at Adam through the corner of her eye. He was wearing a crisp button down shirt and dark gray slacks. They were getting ready to go somewhere nice, but were interrupted. By me? Or would this have happened anyway?

Adam cleared his throat, breaking the silence. Ellie realized that he was staring straight at her, and her heart stopped. She held her breath and waited for him to say something. His eyes were speaking, but she couldn't figure out what they were saying.

"Why are you here?" he said, his deep voice carrying a hard edge.

Ellie's eyes seemed to get bigger. She had been prepared to talk to Eva and explain herself, but she hadn't anticipated this. She was never good answering to men, and it was even more difficult for her now. She shrank down in her chair, looking even smaller than she already was.

"I..I don't think that this is something I can talk to you about," she said, her voice quiet and low. She fought the urge to run. He was bigger than she was, much bigger. Ellie knew that he wasn't like Jonas, but she was feeling the old familiar fear creeping up in her.

"If you can talk to Brynn, you can talk to me. I'm her husband. There is nothing that we don't share." Adam's jaw was set, and he stared hard at Ellie.

Ellie sat as still as possible. *I don't have to answer to him. I don't have to answer to any man! I'm here for my daughter, and that's it.* She fought the terror rising inside of her belly, fighting with the anger inside of her. She was nauseous.

Adam was getting impatient. He knew that he was making her uncomfortable, but he didn't care. This woman needed to answer for what she had done to Brynn!

"I just wanted to explain things to her. To. My. Daughter." Ellie was having a hard time speaking, her voice shaking almost as hard as her hands. She tried to sound confident but her voice gave her away.

Adam was quiet. He wanted to push her, to break her. He wanted her to answer for all of the pain she had caused Brynn. He stared at her, filled with disdain and overwhelming curiosity. She looked like Brynn, and sounded like Brynn, and she had probably even been as beautiful years ago. But Ellie's yellowed teeth and stringy hair painted an unfamiliar picture for Adam, and he could tell that this woman was nothing like his Love.

"You can talk to me," Adam said quietly, changing his tact. He knew that being aggressive with her was going nowhere. "You can...."

A nurse walked silently into the room. She looked at the woman and the man sitting opposite of one another and immediately wished that someone else had been sent to get them.

"Mr. Michael?" she said nervously.

Adam stood up immediately. "Yes, I'm Adam."

"The doctor wants to talk to you," she said, gathering herself.

"Where is he?" Adam asked, looking behind her for the doctor.

"You'll have to come into one of our private rooms, and the doctor will come in and talk to you."

Adam was confused. They couldn't have been in the surgery room for even an hour. How can he be done already?

Adam followed the nurse into the room without so much as a backward glance at Ellie and waited. He wasn't good at waiting, especially now that he and Brynn were back together. He had been waiting for years for her to decide that she trusted him. Adam had been patient with her, but now that Brynn was in jeopardy, the only thing that he cared about was making sure that she and the baby were safe.

He waited for the doctor to enter the private little room that felt more like a prison than a conference area. Five minutes felt like an hour. All that Adam could picture was Brynn's face when she passed out, and he fought back tears every time he let the image come to him.

The door opened and Adam stood up quickly. He was on edge, and every nerve in his body tingling with fear and anticipation.

The doctor was a young woman, tall, almost masculine, wearing clean, colorful hospital scrubs. She had a confident air about her that made Adam feel better.

"Please, sit," she said with a polite smile that didn't seem to reach her eyes.

Adam sat down quickly. He could tell that she had something serious to tell him.

The doctor started talking. Her words came out quickly and automatically, and Adam found himself confused. It seemed as though she were talking for an hour, when in reality it was only for a few minutes. She used words that weren't familiar, and he intentionally squinted his deep blue eyes as he tried to make sense of it all. At the end, he only understood when she said, "I'm sorry to be the one to tell you that you may have to make a choice."

"Choice? What choice?" Adam said, irritated. "I don't understand half of what you just said."

"Oh, I'm sorry." She said, taken aback. "I thought I was explaining it clearly."

"From what you just said, I have to choose what, the life of my wife, or my baby? How am I supposed to do that?" Adam ran his hands through his thick dark hair over and over, hoping to let the message sink in. How can she ask me to choose? How am I supposed to make a decision like that?

"I'm hoping it won't get to that. Dr. Emmett is very good at what she does. I'm hoping you don't have to make a choice. But Brynn has lost a lot of blood, and we want to prepare you for what may come if we can't stabilize her." The doctor looked at Adam sympathetically. Adam realized that he didn't even know her name—and that he didn't even care.

"So what do I do? Do I have to tell you now? What do I do?" Adam said, feeling on the edge of hysteria. Adam couldn't imagine needing to choose. He knew that he couldn't do it now. He knew that he needed help making the choice. He couldn't do it alone. "I need to call my parents."

She hated this part of her job. "If something happens, we won't be able to wait. We need you to make a decision about whose life you want us to save. Think about what your wife would want. We can't wait." She had been sitting across from Adam, and she stood up and rested her hand on his shoulder. "Think about what Brynn would want you to do."

"Save Brynn," Adam blurted out. "If you have to make a choice, save Brynn." Adam hated himself, feeling as though he just put a big X on his daughter's head. He felt like he was going to throw up.

Adam didn't look up as she left the room. She had asked him to do the impossible, and he hoped he would never have to see her again.

CHAPTER FIVE

Difficult Ellie

Jonas Miles was used to compliant, cooperative women. But Ellie was different. She was stubborn and difficult, and even though there were times he hated her, he always had the uncontrollable urge to go back to her. He couldn't help himself.

When Jonas and Ellie got into a fight, he took it out on her as he usually did, by sleeping with another woman in their bed. He often punished her with the other girls, some younger and some older, all with dark hair and brown eyes like hers.

Ellie was tortured, but she loved Jonas, and needed him in ways she couldn't explain.

She hated how he flaunted the other women in front of her. Alcohol made him mean, and he had a venomous tongue that lashed out at her in his drunkenness. She wanted him to let her go, but he wouldn't, and she didn't know how to purge him completely. He was selfish, and she loathed herself for letting him treat her as if she were nothing, until she truly began to believe she really *was* nothing.

But Ellie really hated him for making her get rid of Eva. Ellie was weak and let him throw her baby out of the car. He cared so little about his own daughter that he threw her out as though she were little more than trash. Ellie despised him for it, and she let him know that every chance she got.

"Stop telling me that you hate me!" he said to her, exasperated.

Two years had passed, then three, and five, and Ellie still told him how much she hated him. "The kid is gone. She has new parents and a new life, and I'm sure she's fine by now."

But Ellie couldn't believe him. She yearned for a simpler life. She had even tried to go back home, but her parents were gone. They moved and she had no way of finding them. All she knew was that the big house that she grew up in was empty. And she blamed him for that, too.

They fought viciously.

"You'll never change! You'll never let me go! I need to go home. I need to find my daughter. YOU'VE RUINED ME!" She slapped him and kicked at him. She scratched his beautiful face with her fingernails. She didn't care if he was scarred. She wanted him to be as ugly on the outside as she felt on the inside.

At only nineteen, Ellie had abandoned her daughter, her parents, and herself. She was living in a tiny apartment with a man who kept her drugged all of the time.

"It's the same fight, Ellie. The same damned fight!" He grabbed her and pulled her to him hard. He was crushing her with his arms until his face was only an inch from hers. His green eyes pierced her brown ones until she had to look away.

Ellie knew that as long as Jonas was alive, she would never get away from him. She imagined that he was dead. She daydreamed about it, dreamt about it. She didn't know if she could really ever survive his death, or if she could be the one to end him. But she did know that if she didn't, it would be the end of her.

Ellie considered ending it all for herself, but she dreamt of finding her Eva again. She knew that as long as Eva was out there, she would need to find her baby girl. She didn't care how long it took her. She just knew that she needed to be with her daughter.

There was hopelessness and futility in her life every day. When Ellie looked in the mirror, she hated what she saw—a disgusting reflection of a weak, desperate woman who allowed Jonas to take everything away. She had been too weak and too stoned to fight, but she was finally beginning to find clarity, and she realized that she wasn't happy.

When she met Jonas, she was a young, spoiled little girl flirting with danger. She was showing her parents that she could make her own choices and do what she wanted. She loved Amy and James, but she felt that they owed her. When they left for Europe, and Ellie had to fend for herself and Eva, she felt betrayed.

Looking back, Ellie realized that they were only trying to make her stronger. But it was too late. There was no going back to them now. She had made her choices and lost the only real love she had ever known in them. And there was no way she could return now without Eva.

She hated Jonas so much at times. She imagined the blood oozing out of him, thick and red. She thought of how it would look, and smell, and feel, and she pictured how she would make it flow. *Do I shoot him, or stab him? How do I kill him?*

She loved him, but she also hated him for what he had done to her, and what he had done to their baby. Ellie imagined Jonas' green eyes wide and staring up in disbelief. She knew he could never believe that she was strong enough to hurt him. Jonas thought she was weak. He used both drugs and words to keep her that way.

But life seemingly got better, and she forgot about it for awhile. They lived in a condo, which Jonas promised Ellie could decorate as she pleased.

"I told you that I would take care of you, baby," he said on moving day. "I always keep my word to you." He kissed Ellie full on the lips. It was important to him that he took care of her. He had never seen a man take care of his momma the way he was taking care of Ellie, and he was proud of himself. He had built a good business catering to wealthy kids and their parents, and had a reputation for being discreet.

But Ellie didn't care about the condo, or the beautiful clothes, or about decorating. She still dreamt about that night when she held Eva in her arms for the last time and had let her go.

"Mommeeeee, don't leave me!" Eva's tiny voice still echoed in her ears. She was clutching Betsy, wearing Jonas' oversized shirt for warmth. Ellie had preserved the picture of Eva in her mind, and nothing could steal it from her. When she needed it the most, she closed her eyes and pictured Eva with the pretty pink dress. Only in Ellie's mind, it was still clean and pretty and lacy. It wasn't soiled with urine and dirt like it had been on the night she last saw her.

"Mommeeeee, I need you. Don't leave me!" Eva's voice was small, like tiny tinkling bells, and Ellie couldn't get it out of her mind. She felt like her head would explode with the sound of it. Nothing she did could rid Eva's voice from her mind.

"Mommy, I peed. MOMMMEEEEE..." Ellie could see Eva disappearing as she watched through the back window of the car. Sometimes in her dreams, the car was the beater car that they had driven off in that night, and sometimes it was a limousine. Sometimes the car was a boat, but the dream was always the same. Ellie was leaving Eva behind, and Eva was running after her crying, her little face stained with dirt and tears.

Ellie woke up one day and decided that she had to do something to find some peace. She needed to try to find Eva, and find her parents. But she knew that Jonas would never let her go. She knew that she would need to do something to get away from Jonas before she could ever return to find her family.

CHAPTER SIX

Petey Sullivan

Jonas' employees were like all of his women, except for Ellie. Easy, obedient, and stupid.

Petey Sullivan had always been loyal. Jonas knew that he could count on him for anything, but killing wasn't anything that Petey had bargained for.

"I'll do whatever you want me to, Jonas, but I can't kill nobody. I just can't do it." Petey was beside himself, shuffling his big body back and forth as he shifted his feet and looked down to the floor.

Jonas smiled at him with his girly lips. The guys secretly thought that Jonas looked like a girl with his big full lips and his pretty boy look. But for some strange reason, the girls seemed to dig him. Petey just didn't get it, and he didn't really like Jonas. But Petey's big brother, Mike, had hooked him up with the job, and would kick Petey's ass if he screwed it up. Petey wasn't sure who he was more scared of, Mike or Jonas. At the moment, it was Jonas.

Petey had heard the stories of what happened to people when Jonas got mad. They weren't ever seen again, or they were seen with missing digits, or unexplained scars. For as big as Petey was, he didn't like violence, and he didn't like getting hurt.

"Petey, you'll do whatever it is that I need you to do. And if that involves, um, disposing of someone, then you'll just have to do it." Jonas' voice had a hard edge to it as he stared Petey down.

Petey was uncomfortable. He didn't sign up for this. The money that Jonas paid him over the past year was good, but Petey wasn't into hurting nobody. Usually Jonas just had him take packages from place to place, and pick stuff up for him. Jonas had other people to do the "people thing." Petey had just wanted to handle the packages.

"It's simple really," Jonas said staring at him with his dark green eyes. "You'll stop the car, you'll hold onto the Missus, and Sy will take care of the rest. You think you can handle that?"

Petey could tell that Jonas was getting really frustrated with him. It was best if he just agreed to whatever Jonas wanted him to do. Jonas' reputation preceded itself, and Petey was just a small town kid compared to him.

"I can do that," Petey said, his voice squeaking as he said it. He was twenty-three, big and bulky, a small-time player most of the time, and he was okay with that. He had been that way with football, and in everything else in his life. He knew he wasn't that smart, and he didn't want the responsibility. He just wanted to do what he was told.

But blood made him squeamish, and it made him upset when girls cried. He never knew what to do when they cried. And with what Jonas was asking him to do, he was sure to see a woman cry, and it made him sick to his stomach.

He drove down that old road with Sy, and they cornered the rich couple. It had all gone as planned. But then Petey couldn't take it no more, and something inside of him, for the first time in his life, made him act different from what he was told. He didn't want to do it, but he couldn't watch the pretty lady cry no more. What Sy did to her husband was bad enough, but what Sy was getting ready to do to her next, Petey couldn't take it. He looked at her tiny face, her pretty eyes staring at him, terrified and pleading.

Petey could never hurt a woman, and he couldn't let Sy. So he stopped him, and then he disappeared, leaving Sy dead from the big gash in his head.

Petey knew he had to hide. He couldn't face Jonas and lie to him. Petey wasn't a good liar, and he knew that Jonas would see right through him. He didn't even care if he wasn't paid. He didn't want to be paid for this. So he hid at his cousin, Lily's house. He knew nobody would look for him there. Lily was the old maid of the family, and nobody even talked to her anymore, except Petey. He just didn't tell anyone.

He showed up at her door on foot. He had ditched the car that he and Sy drove in, after hiding the bodies as best as he could, and then he took off on foot. Him and the pretty woman. He didn't know what else to do with her, and he had to carry her every step of the way, keeping to the back roads and hiding in the woods. Sy had started to hurt her, started to tear her clothes off her, started to hit her, but then Petey stopped him. But not before Sy knocked her down, and she hit her head on a rock, blood gushing out freely and staining her pretty blonde hair.

He snuck up to Lily's door, exhausted. Her house was about five miles from the road they were on, isolated and quiet. She lived off money from her dead parents and rarely left the house.

"Petey!" Lily cried, her surprise obvious when she opened the door and saw him standing there. Her gray eyes widened in shock as she realized that he was covered in blood. She hadn't seen her cousin in a few months, but she would've recognized him anywhere. "Are you hurt?"

It was dark outside and when he stumbled in, she realized he was carrying something, someone.

"Petey! Are you hurt? Are you okay?" Lily was suddenly afraid, and she looked outside to see if anyone was out there. She shut the door quickly and locked it behind them.

"No, no. I'm okay. But I think she may be hurt." Petey was tired. The pretty lady didn't weigh much, but after carrying her for five miles at a pretty good clip, he was beat. "I just need some water."

Lily motioned to the couch where he set the woman down as gently as he could. The bleeding on her head had stopped a while ago, but she was still a mess, and needed cleaned up. She was unconscious but was starting to make little sounds, as if she wanted to wake up, but couldn't. Petey didn't want her to wake up. He didn't want her to look at him, remembering how he held onto her while Sy stabbed her husband. He shook his head at the memory of the blood. So much blood.

Lily's voice brought him out of his reverie. "Go get cleaned up, Petey!" she ordered him. "There are some of Daddy's old shirts upstairs. Those should fit you. Go get cleaned up, and I'll take care of her. Bring your clothes down with you and we'll burn them."

Lily looked down at the tiny woman lying on her couch. Her beautiful soft hair was coated in dried blood, but Lily was used to cleaning up blood. She had done it so many times, and had become used to it by now. Daddy used to come home covered in blood, and sometimes he brought home his guys who were covered in blood. Lily learned never to ask questions. She just cleaned them up, sometimes even stitching their wounds. She thought she could get away from it. She decided to go to college, become a veterinarian, get married and have her own babies. But Daddy had called her home when he said he was dying, and she ended up taking care of him and his cancer for a decade, all of her dreams fading away. So now she was alone, but she had the money he left her, which wasn't much comfort when she was all alone.

She took warm cloths and cleaned the woman up, careful not to reopen her wound. It wasn't as bad as it looked once she got the crusted blood off. It could use a stitch or two, but that was it.

She cleaned up the dirt from the pretty woman's face and admired how smooth and perfect her skin was. Lily wished she had been as pretty. All of her life, Lily knew just how plain she was. Not ugly, not hideous, just plain. Plain gray eyes, plain dishwater blonde hair, plain build. Nothing spectacular, nothing special, just plain. When she changed the woman into some of her own more sensible clothes, she saw that everything the woman wore was fine and expensive. Even her underwear.

Lily admired the woman's clothes. She had money to buy clothes like that, but nowhere to wear them, and nobody to wear them for, so she didn't. She just wore sensible clothes to fit her sensible, unremarkable life.

Lily could hear the shower running upstairs for what seemed like an hour. Petey must feel very dirty, she thought to herself. It was strange to hear the shower running when she wasn't in it.

Finally, he came out, and was fresh and clean smelling like the Irish Spring soap in her shower. She liked it. He was surprised when he saw her and the woman. Lily had done a good job cleaning her up, and the woman lay peacefully on her couch.

"How is she?" he asked, his voice in a low whisper.

"She's doing well. She only needed one stitch, and she didn't even flinch when I did it. I used a very small needle." Lily lifted up the woman's hair in the back of her head and showed him. The cut was barely visible now, and Petey breathed a sigh of relief.

"Is she going to be okay?" he was afraid of the answer.

"I don't know. We will have to see when she wakes up. What happened to her?" Lily was full of curiosity. She was disappointed that her beloved cousin had taken this track in life, but intrigued with him, just as she had always been. He had been the only one in the family not to shun her, for reasons that she didn't understand.

They left the woman sleeping on the couch and went into the kitchen.

Petey told her everything. He could always tell her everything. Ever since they were children, they had been close, until the families had divided over reasons that neither of them were completely clear about. But Petey refused to abandon her as the rest of her family had done.

She always admired him and thought how handsome and sweet he was. *I don't understand why nobody has ever snatched him up,* she found herself thinking often, and feeling slightly incestuous in her thoughts.

She listened as she poured him a drink and made him something to eat. She was happy to have some company for once. After he had eaten and was full, she told him to go upstairs to rest.

"What about her?" he said pointing to the couch. The woman was still in a deep sleep, though she cried out every now and then.

"I'll stay up with her. You can rest," Lily said graciously. She was happy to have a mission, to have a task.

Petey looked at Lily with gratitude. "Thank you," He said lumbering up the stairs. He was exhausted and needed to think of his next move. He didn't like thinking. He just wanted to do what he was told. Now he was stuck having to think about what to do. *I never should've taken that woman with me. I shoulda just left her there! Somebody would have found her! Now what the hell am I going to do with her?*

Lily stayed up all night, watching the woman sleep. As the sun came up, the woman slowly opened her eyes and looked around. She looked across the room and saw a weary looking woman in her forties, sitting in an old recliner across from her. Lily's eyes were closed as she leaned her head back, and the woman thought that she had a kind face. She looked up to the ceiling and tried to sit up, but the blinding pain in the back of her head told her to lie back down. The woman could tell that she was in an old house; it smelled old anyway.

She realized suddenly that the woman in the recliner was staring at her. "Hi, I'm Lily."

"Hello. I'm...I'm..." the woman on the couch was at a loss. Her mouth became dry and she felt herself panic. "I'm..." she couldn't remember. Her mind was a blank.

Lily looked at her evenly, and the woman couldn't read her. For a split second, Lily looked... grateful, but then she looked concerned. "It's okay. Don't push yourself. It's common in this type of situation to not remember."

"Situation?" the woman thought hard. "What kind of

situation?"

"I mean, you just had a bad gash on your head. It would be a normal side effect to not remember." Lily's voice was comforting, and the woman felt a little better. Something about Lily made her feel safe.

The woman heard footsteps, and she looked up to see a large man coming toward her. Her big brown eyes grew wide in horror. She didn't know why, but she was suddenly very afraid.

CHAPTER SEVEN

Ellie's Sins

Ellie stared down at Jonas. His green eyes that seduced her time and time again, staring up at her were wide in disbelief. Blood was oozing out of the side of his mouth, and he was clutching his chest where the bullet went in and exploded.

Ellie's hands were shaking, and she was sweating uncontrollably. She wasn't sure if she could kill the man she had once loved so desperately. But right then, she felt nothing as she aimed the gun at him and pulled the trigger.

Even as the bullet ripped into him and she heard his blood-curdling scream, she felt nothing. Nothing, but relief. Only freedom. She had felt like a caged animal for so long that she knew this was her only escape from Jonas' prison. She had been *his* ever since she was a young girl, and now she was twenty-five, and now the only thing she needed was to find the baby she had abandoned so callously.

Jonas was on the ground writhing in pain. His long lean body stretched out, blood running down the marble tile of the beautiful foyer that he had chosen just for her.

"El…El, how could you?" his voice was barely above a whisper, and she leaned in to hear him, no longer afraid like before.

"I hate you. I hate you! You've ruined me, and I don't love you anymore!" Ellie snarled at him, her pupils were huge, turning her eyes nearly black as she glared at him with a complete absence of love. "I've dreamt of this moment, and now that it's here, I don't feel bad for you. This is what you deserve."

Ellie had given shooting him a lot of thought, but she wasn't sure if she could really do it. She had never even shot a gun at a real person before, but she knew that if she aimed it at him she had better be able to do it, or she would never have another chance.

Jonas was in shock.

When he walked in the door, the last thing he expected to see was his Ellie pointing a gun at him. Today was supposed to be a special day. He was going to ask Ellie to be his wife at dinner that night. Business was good and he knew that he needed to change. Ellie had stood by his side for years now, and he was finally ready to make the commitment. He had never wanted to get married before, but it was starting to look like a good idea now. He was done with the other women. Even though he often used them to punish her for misbehaving, he was starting to regret it, something he had never done before.

He figured that must mean something.

"What the…" Jonas hadn't finished his sentence when he heard the crack of the gun and saw the smoke. He felt the bullet tear into his chest, fast and sharp, and he fell to his knees as the blood started pouring out. "Ellie, Ellie."

She had been the only woman he had ever loved, except for his mother. His mother who taught him that he should never stay in one place too long, or love only one person. Jonas had watched a string of men come in and out of her life—some stayed for a month or two, none of them ever paying much attention to him. When he met Ellie, Jonas knew that she was special, and he fell for her right away. He was careful to keep her in line, though.

Now he didn't want to just keep her in line, he just wanted to marry her. He wanted to have a real life with her, a legitimate life with her. He was in disbelief now as he lay on the ground, his lifeblood flowing out of him, his body growing weaker.

Her face was inches from his, and the venom of her words spewed hatred. *I can't believe this is my Ellie. My Ellie who I've loved more than anyone else in my life.*

"You've hit me, you've drugged me, and you stole my innocence and my life. Because of you, my parents left me. But most of all, you stole my baby. How could you ever think that I would ever forgive you for making me abandon my baby?" Ellie was fighting back tears as she spit the words at him. "I loved you, but you betrayed me with your selfishness, and I let you. If you would have just let me go, I wouldn't have to do this."

"Ellie, Ellie," Jonas was getting weaker. His body was turning cold, his mind was racing, and his thoughts were becoming mush. *Do I tell her that I killed her parents? I'm dead already, so what does it matter now? She already hates me. She already....* The pain of her hatred made the physical pain from the gunshot seem insignificant. "Ellie, Ellie, listen to me..."

"You have nothing to say that I want to hear. I am going to be free from you once and for all." Ellie shook her head back and forth trying to block out the sound of his voice. Jonas thought that Ellie was just as pretty now as she was the first time that he saw her.

"You want to hear this..." His voice was barely audible and she leaned in close. "I love you. I've always loved you and I'm sorry."

She shook her head, the hatred starting to dissipate as the adrenaline started to fade. The reality of what she had done was starting to hit her as she saw the life flowing out of Jonas.

"Come closer," he was barely breathing, "I... had... your... parents killed."

Ellie watched his head roll over to the side, his dull green eyes opened, staring into nothingness, and she screamed as she heard the sirens coming for her.

CHAPTER EIGHT

Rose

Brynn couldn't believe that she was seeing Rose. It didn't make any sense. She looked down at her belly and was relieved to see that it was still swollen, full of her growing baby. She was still wearing her nightgown, her long flowing white nightgown that made her feel so pretty and feminine.

And now, out of nowhere, there was Rose coming toward her, almost floating.

Where am I? She thought, confused. She had never been in a place like this before, and it was nothing that she recognized. It was like a place in a dream where there were no ceilings, floors, or walls. There was just space, and Brynn felt like she was dreaming.

You're nowhere. Rose answered her wordlessly, and Brynn was surprised that Rose could read her thoughts. *Don't think about where you are. You are here with me, and that's all you need to know.*

Brynn had a thought. *Am I dead? Are my baby and I both dead?*

No! Rose's voice in Brynn's head seemed to laugh a musical, pretty laugh that Brynn had never heard before. *You aren't dead. I'm just looking out for you for the time being. Your body is going through a great ordeal right now. Don't worry. You'll be fine.*

Brynn felt better, relieved. She put her hand on her belly and rubbed it gently as though to tell her baby that it was going to be okay. *Are you okay, Momma? I'm sorry for abandoning you before you died.*

Oh, baby girl, don't worry about that. I was fine. Jane was wonderful to me. Rose was always forgiving, and Brynn wasn't surprised that she forgave her so easily.

But Momma, I left you when you needed me the most. And I'm so sorry for what I did to you. I didn't know how sick you were. Brynn was so ashamed. She had been living with the guilt for abandoning Rose for over a year. Rose had loved her too much, and Brynn was suffocating under the weight of her neediness. And when Adam left her, Brynn couldn't deal with Rose any longer. She was fighting her own battles, and she couldn't deal with Rose's anymore. *If I had known…*

I know, baby girl. I know. Brynn felt Rose's forgiveness flowing through her, like a tingling feeling from the inside out. Rose was different here. She made sense and was motherly; unlike how she was all of Brynn's life. Brynn wished Rose had been this way while she was alive.

I wish that I had been different, too. I know that I needed you too much. I know that I wasn't much of a mother to you. But I couldn't be that person to you. I didn't know how. And by the time I figured it out, it was far too late.

Brynn was ashamed of herself. How could she let Rose know her thoughts? She had to be more careful. *I know that it wasn't your fault, Momma. I know now that you did protect me from him. You did try to keep him from hurting me.*

I didn't do everything that I could have, Brynn. You know that. I should have left. That was the only sure way to protect you. Brynn felt Rose's sadness, and it made her want to cry.

Oh, Momma, why weren't you like this when you were alive with me? Why now? Why are you so different now? Brynn's heart was filled with longing for a life that she could've lived with this Rose.

I was afraid. But I'm not afraid any longer. I was a coward, and I failed at my most important and only job. And I'm sorry. But you'll be different. You'll be a much better mother than I ever was.

Will I? How will I? Brynn was curious how this Rose could know.

Suddenly it got blindingly bright, and Rose disappeared with a flash. Brynn felt as though she were flying at a high rate of speed, controlled and even.

She realized that she wasn't afraid anymore.
She was finally ready to be a mother.

CHAPTER NINE

Ellie's Long Road Home

The sounds of the sirens were distant, but audible. She knew that the sirens were coming, because someone had heard the gunshot. She knew they would come for her, looking for her.

Ellie did what she always did best. She ran.

Everyone knew that she was Jonas' main girl, and would be looking for her. She was careful to wipe the gun off, and shove it in her purse after she took out the remaining bullets. She was careful to have an alibi.

She was careful not to let anyone see her go into the house, and she was careful to write a "Dear John" letter to Jonas explaining that she was sorry, and that she no longer loved him. She told him that she was going far, far away. And she left it in a place that the cops would easily find it. She planned everything out, hoping to get away. She knew she would run. She had to find Eva. He had so many enemies that it wouldn't be hard to imagine that one of them did it. She knew where she needed to go, and she wasn't going to let anyone stop her from getting there.

Momma, Daddy. Ellie tried hard not to let her grief overcome her as she took off on foot. She wanted to crumble on the ground. She wanted to pummel his newly dead body with her small fists. *How could he do that? How could he take them from me forever? Why? Why?* Ellie pushed the thoughts from her head as she ran as fast as she could. The sirens were getting louder, even as she ran further away. She took the back way and ran the two miles where she hid her car and stashed her bags. She ran as if her life depended on it, her body ragged and worn from the drugs that he had filled her with over the years.

It felt as if she had been running forever, and when she finally got to the car, she let out a sob. She jumped in and started the car, careful not to pull out too fast. She didn't want to get pulled over for something stupid. She just wanted to get away.

I'm going home. Now I'm going home to nothing. NOTHING. They are dead. Who knows how long they've been dead! God Dammit, why didn't he die before he told me what he did? Why? Ellie gripped the wheel as tight as she could, her knuckles white, tears running down her face uncontrollably. Slow down! Slow down! Ellie looked at the speedometer. Fifty-five in a forty-five. Slow down, you idiot!

Ellie tried to get a hold of herself. She knew that anyone looking in at her through the car windows would think that she was a mess. She wanted to look normal. You needed to look normal. Ellie couldn't be caught now. There were too many questions. Too many questions that needed answered. But she knew that she couldn't get those answers alone. She had been gone from home for seven long years. Eva would be ten now. *How long have Momma and Daddy been gone? Oh, Momma!*

Ellie pictured Amy in her mind, petite, pretty. Ellie was the spitting image of her, only with dark hair instead of the pretty blonde hair that Amy wore so well. Ellie had been proud of her beautiful mother, and now Amy was dead. Ellie couldn't stop the picture of Amy's rotting corpse full of worms from entering her mind.

Her chest felt heavy, and Ellie felt as if she were going to drive off the road. She held the wheel tight, praying for control.

She knew that she had to get away from Jonas. He hadn't given her a choice.

"Jonas, do you ever want to have a baby with me?" It wasn't the first time Ellie had ever brought it up. She wanted a child. She wanted someone in her life who loved her unconditionally, who looked up to her and admired her. She wanted to re-create her time with Eva. She wanted to redeem herself for what she had done to Eva. She wanted the nightmares to go away.

"Jesus, Ellie. Do we have to go through this again and again and again? We've been talking about it for seven years. You've been bringing it up since we ditched the first kid. NO! I. Do. Not. Want. A. Child. Ever." Jonas couldn't believe how thick she could be sometimes. He knew that she was still haunted by losing the first one, but he definitely didn't want another one.

Ellie knew that was the last time that she would ever ask him. She was only about six weeks along, but she knew that she couldn't afford to have him shoot her up again, or have her abandon this one, too. She knew he would make her. He would make her leave it as a newborn. He would've made her leave Eva as a newborn if she had been with him then. But she hadn't. She had been smart then, and had left him. But then she went back, because she was blinded by love.

Not this time. He won't take my child away from me again this time! Ellie knew where he kept his gun, and knew where he kept his bullets. He taught her how to shoot it in order to protect herself, because he had a lot of enemies. Little did he know that she would use it on him. *I was protecting myself, and my baby.*

Ellie looked down at her tight small stomach that would soon be swelling with the growth of new life, and she was excited. Jonas hadn't shot her up for at least three weeks, and she knew that if she were strong, she could stay off the drugs and keep her baby strong and safe. Her body hurt, and her back and legs ached. She craved the drug, wanted it bad.

But she knew that she needed to stay away. She had already gone through a lot of the ups and the downs that the withdrawal took her through, but usually she didn't have to go through an entire cycle. Jonas always made sure that he shot her up just before she started to go too crazy. But she didn't let him do it to her every day, just often enough to keep her from crashing too hard. This was the longest she had gone in a long time, but she was doing it for her baby. She didn't want to screw it up this time.

She didn't want to lose the baby as she had lost Eva. And she didn't want to hurt him. Somehow, she knew that it was a boy, though she couldn't explain how. She was going to name him after her daddy, James. But now Daddy was gone, and it didn't feel right to name him after a dead man.

Ellie felt her heart breaking. She hated feeling this way. She missed the euphoria of the drug. She missed being happy.

STOP IT! STOP IT! You need to stay straight for your son! You need to find Eva! You can live without it. You can live without the drugs! Go home! You'll figure it out.

Ellie forgot about the police and recklessly drove about five more miles. She stopped the car in front of a familiar apartment building.

The door to her car opened suddenly, making her jump.

"Shit! Don't do that to me!" she said angrily.

"I'm sorry, babe. I thought you saw me." The young man leaned over and kissed her tenderly on the lips. She felt herself melting into him, her whole body leaning in, inviting him as she had already done so many times before.

"I'm sorry. You just scared me." Ellie smiled. She was so taken with him. He was tall, handsome, with light sandy hair and hazel eyes. He was so different from Jonas, so much kinder to her, so much gentler. When she met him by chance three months ago when he was fixing her car, she knew that he would never treat her the way that Jonas had. She also knew that she wanted him, possibly even needed him.

"Where are we going?" he asked, tossing the duffel bag that he had been holding on his lap in the back seat.

Ellie paused. She needed a solution now that her parents were gone. *John! John will know what to do! John Palmer was Daddy's Vice President, the man that Daddy had been grooming to be his second in command.* John and his wife, Tricia were always so nice to her, though Ellie had not always returned their kindness. *I wonder if he will help me. He has to help me. Daddy would want him to help me!*

Ellie was excited. She knew what she would do.

"We're going home, babe. We're going home." Ellie turned the car toward a familiar road that she hadn't travelled in nearly a decade.

CHAPTER TEN

Petey and Carly

"It's okay," Lily said to the woman. The woman saw Petey coming toward her and fear gripped her for no obvious reason.

"Lily, who is that?" the woman asked, fearful.

"That's my cousin, Petey. He saved you." Lily was studying her carefully. The woman seemed delicate, timid.

"Saved me? Saved me from what?" the woman was surprised. She couldn't imagine that she would ever be in danger. But she couldn't imagine anything at this point. Her head was still pounding and fuzzy, and she couldn't focus well on anything.

Lily didn't want to tell her who she was. It wasn't her place. Petey had detoured into the kitchen, and he was making his way back to the living room, awkwardly carrying three glasses of orange juice.

"Here ya go," he said holding one out for Lily and the other one out for the woman. He saw that she was finally awake and figured that she was probably thirsty. The woman took it from him tentatively, almost as though it were a snake. Her fear wasn't lost on Petey. He had tossed and turned all night trying to figure out what to do. He had brought her back to the house, but had no idea what he was going to do with Amy Harper now.

Lily looked at Petey evenly, her gray eyes cool and steely. "She wants to know who she is Petey, and what you saved her from."

Petey looked surprised. He wasn't sure what Amy was going to remember, but he hadn't expected that her memory would be completely gone. He was comfortable leaving her overnight with Lily, because he knew that his cousin knew how to handle herself. With a father like hers, she was far more capable than she looked.

"Um, uh, she doesn't remember anything?" Petey was talking to his cousin, ignoring the pretty woman sitting on the couch staring up at him.

"I don't," Amy said bewildered that he was talking about her, yet ignoring her at the same time.

"I'm sorry, Ma'am." Petey said, embarrassed by his rudeness. His Momma wouldn't be very happy with him right now.

Petey was confused. How can she have no memory of what happened? How can she not remember watching Sy stab her husband, and watching Sy and I fight? How can she forget me killing Sy, trying to defend her? Petey was out of his league.

"I think we should have breakfast," Lily said breaking the uncomfortable silence that was starting to fill the room. "And then we need to figure out what to call you," she said looking pointedly at Amy.

"Okay," Amy said miserably. "Maybe you should take me to a doctor?" she said hopeful.

"Well, um... Lily is kind of a doctor," Petey said shyly. He had been watching Amy for some time and was taken with her beauty. Those long days staking her out so that they would know when to pounce on them had him watching her for hours, sometimes days. It didn't matter to him that she was in her late thirties. Petey was in his mid-twenties, but he knew a beautiful woman when he saw one. Even after everything she had been through, she was just a natural beauty.

"Kind of a doctor?" Amy said tilting her head at him. "What does that mean?"

"She's an animal doctor, but a doctor nonetheless." Petey was getting frustrated. He felt like Amy was making fun of him.

"Oh," Amy said blankly. She looked at Petey with curiosity. He looked familiar to her, yet she was afraid of him. He stood tall and awkward in front of her, avoiding her eyes. He looked strong and capable but strangely shy, and she was confused by him. "Well, what is my name?"

Lily ducked out of the room, careful to stay close by in case Petey needed her. She wanted to protect him as she always had, but she knew that he would need to face Amy alone.

Petey looked at her blankly, his palms starting to sweat. He knew that this moment was coming, and he still didn't know what to tell her. "Uh, I don't know. Let's call you… uh, let's call you Jessica."

"Is that my name?" Amy said stubbornly.

"I don't know. But I have to call you something!" Petey said nervously.

"Why Jessica? Does my name start with a 'J'?"

"I don't know! I don't know if your name starts with a 'J'. If you don't like it, then you can choose something else." Petey hated facing Amy alone. He looked around desperately for Lily. "What do you want me to call you?"

"Jessica? That doesn't sound like it fits me." Amy said thoughtfully. "What about…Carly? I like the name Carly."

"Fine. We can call you Carly." Petey was ready for the conversation to be over. He never liked talking to women, and this one in particular made him very nervous.

"I want to leave. Do you know where I live? Do you know who I am? I just want to go home," Amy said, her voice low but demanding. She didn't want to be in this house anymore. She wanted to go wherever she belonged, and she knew that she didn't belong here.

"I don't know who you are or where you live." Petey lied, avoiding her gaze. "You just need to stay here for now, and that's final."

Amy stared up at him defiantly. He towered over her, but she glared at him. She was angry. She knew from the way he was refusing to look at her that he knew more than what he was telling. She stood up quickly, determined to make him look at her. Suddenly, the floor gave way beneath her and she felt herself fall to the floor.

Before she knew it, Lily was by her side, grabbing her arm gently, but sturdily.

"It's okay," Lily said in a soothing voice. "You're okay. You just need to take it easy and not be in such a hurry. It's going to take you some time."

Amy nodded very slowly. She was dizzy, and her head was pounding. It felt like someone was hitting her in the back of the head with an axe, and she was starting to feel nauseous.

"She don't look so good, Lily," Petey said concerned.

"Let's take you upstairs to the spare room so that you can have some peace and quiet," Lily said taking her by the arm and leading her toward the stairway.

Amy went with her slowly, dragging her feet. She hated feeling so helpless, but she had no choice and nowhere else to go. She looked at Petey, her eyes turning hard for one second. He refused to look at her, but he could feel her growing resentment bouncing off him. It made him uncomfortable, and he looked down at the ground until she was out of sight.

A few moments later, Lily came silently down the stairs. She sat in the chair across from where Petey had settled on the old couch. They sat and stared at each other, exhausted.

"What are we going to do with her?" Lily finally asked, breaking the silence.

"I don't know," Petey said quietly. "I don't know. Their disappearance is all over the news. We can't let her know. She can't know."

"I'll do whatever you need me to," Lily said looking him directly in the eye.

"You've always been there for me, Lily," Petey said staring at her. *Why is she all alone here? Why hasn't she found a good man yet?* Petey always thought the world of her and couldn't imagine why she lived by herself.

"Yes," Lily said smiling. "I always will be. You are my only family now."

They sat in silence, lost in their own thoughts.

"Can she stay here for a little while?" Petey asked slowly. "I know it's a lot to ask, but..."

"Of course, she can stay," Lily said quickly. She was relieved that he finally asked. She knew that he would. After all, he had no one else and nowhere else to turn.

CHAPTER ELEVEN

Something Terribly Wrong

The lights in the room were blinding.

Brynn felt as if she were still in a dream, only Rose had disappeared, and she could hear the echo of metal and the hurried hushed voices of people in masks surrounding her. Her brain was working in slow motion, and every movement reverberated slowly.

"Brynn, can you hear me?" Brynn knew it was her doctor, but she couldn't remember her name. Her doctor was a small woman who moved and talked quickly. Brynn liked her confidence, but right now, she didn't care who her doctor was. She felt her eyelids fluttering and she was fighting to stay awake.

"Brynn!" The doctor was talking to her, and Brynn could see dark brown eyes above the green hospital mask. "I need you to stay strong and stay with me."

Brynn was trying to nod, but her head felt like it weighed a hundred pounds. *Where is Rose? Momma?*

Brynn squinted and closed her eyes. She just wanted to fall asleep. She felt herself fading as the din of the room became silent.

She awoke in another room. It was quiet and not as bright. She was nauseous. She needed to throw up. She looked around desperately for someone to help her, and then felt her stomach heave violently. She opened her mouth and watched helplessly as she threw up all over the side of the bed, all over the floor. It landed with a loud splat, and she felt the warmth of the liquid on her skin and on her side. She wretched and heaved violently for what seemed like forever, though she knew it must only have been a few minutes.

Every time she heaved, she felt a sharp pain in her stomach. When she was done, she looked around desperately for her call button. She pushed it relentlessly until she heard the familiar click of the speaker.

"Yes, can I help you?" the voice said sounding a little bored.

"I need help, now," Brynn said her voice hoarse and barely audible.

"I'm sorry, can you repeat that?" the voice said, this time irritated.

"Help me, NOW," Brynn was angry. "NOW!'

"Someone will be there right away, Miss." The voice said hurriedly.

Brynn was soaked in her own vomit. She looked around for Adam. *Where is Adam? Why am I alone?* Brynn was still nauseated, gulping and gasping for air. She fought the waves that threatened to overcome her. She didn't want to throw up anymore. Every time she heaved, the sharp pain in her gut returned. She felt dehydrated, and her head was pounding.

Where is my baby? Why am I alone?

Brynn waited for long moments staring at the door.

When the nurse came in, she looked at Brynn and her eyes immediately widened. She pushed the call button and asked for help. Another nurse came in and they both cleaned her up quickly. The nurse kept looking at Brynn apologetically, and Brynn knew that she must be the nurse who had been so short with her.

When Brynn was dry and clean, the first nurse started to walk away, and Brynn grabbed her by the arm. "Where is my baby? Where is my husband?"

The nurse looked startled. "Hasn't anyone spoken to you?"

"No, nobody." Brynn's heart was pounding, and she felt her breath catch in her throat. "Why? What's going on?"

The nurse pulled away. "I can't talk to you. You need to talk to a doctor." She started backing out of the room, trying to maintain her composure.

"Why can't you talk to me?" Brynn was starting to panic. "Why can't you tell me what is happening?"

"I just can't," the nurse said apologetically. "I'm not allowed. I could get fired." The nurse looked like she was barely twenty-five and Brynn felt bad for her for a split second, but then the anger returned.

"I don't care. I want to know!" Brynn was desperate. "Get me a doctor. Where is my husband? Find my husband! I need answers. Oh my God, what is happening? Tell me now! Tell me now!" The nurse raced out of the room and returned quickly with an orderly.

"Miss, Miss. You have to calm down. You have to calm down now!" the orderly said.

Brynn felt desperate. She was alone, and she knew that something must have gone terribly wrong or Adam would be with her. *Adam would be here.* She knew that Adam would never leave her, never abandon her when she needed him the most. Not now. Not after everything they had been through.

She looked at the familiar monitor above her and knew that her heart rate was off the charts as she watched the line spiking one after another after another.

She felt something sharp going into her arm. "What are you... doing?" she said feeling her body starting to relax. "Why? Why?"

The nurse looked at her with a small, sad smile. "It's going to be okay, Brynn. Just try to relax."

Brynn felt her mind start to drift, and she felt her body go limp. Her hands felt numb, and she felt as if she were floating.

Why would they do this? Something must be terribly wrong

CHAPTER TWELVE

Ellie and Dylan

Ellie met Dylan by accident when he was working on her car.

There was an immediate, undeniable attraction, and she felt drawn to him in a way that she had never felt before, not even with Jonas. She knew he felt that same. When they spoke, it was as though there was no one else around, and she couldn't help staring in his eyes when he was around. It was like a moth to a flame, uncontrollable and hot. And she knew that if Jonas found out, something bad would happen. Something horrible.

Ellie knew that Dylan felt the same way about her. Again, those eyes. The way his beautiful, hazel eyes lit up when she was around told her so. She started making excuses to have him look at her car, and eventually, she asked him to go have coffee with her in the next town over. She could tell that Dylan was equally as smitten with her.

He had never met anyone like her before in all of his life, so beautiful and confident. He wasn't used to girls like her.

Dylan had barely graduated from high school, but found that he knew his way around cars. He had taken vocational classes and landed a job in the garage, much to his surprise. He was young, but wanted to get out of his little town. He couldn't wait to grow up so that he could move, and now that he was growing up, it didn't look like he was going anywhere. His story was typical, and he didn't like where it was headed.

"But, you have so much potential!" Ellie said to him, peering over her coffee cup. She had gotten fancy coffee and ordered him just a black coffee since he couldn't decide. He would have just as soon had a beer, but she insisted on going to a fancy coffee place instead. She missed fancy coffee, and he couldn't believe it when their check was almost ten dollars.

"Potential for what?" Dylan asked, his tone as dark as the blackness in his eyes.

Ellie shrugged. "I just think you could do so much more than change oil and work in a little garage."

Dylan was offended. "I work hard, and I make good money. I don't know who you think you are, but I'm doing pretty good on my own considering that nobody handed me anything."

Ellie immediately regretted her words. "I didn't mean it like that." She knew that she had a tendency to speak too quickly at times.

"Well, how did you mean it?" he said, glaring at her, his mood shifting noticeably.

"Uh, I just meant that you could go to college, or do something else. You seem smart," Ellie said staring down at the froth in her cup.

"What if I don't want to do anything else?" he said, lightening his tone to almost teasing.

"Well, then..." her cheeks turned bright red, and Dylan found himself enjoying her discomfort immensely. "I guess you just have to be happy doing what you're doing."

"Well, I'm not," Dylan said, finally letting her off the hook. "I would love to go to college. I would love to get out of this town. I would love to do a million things that don't involve ever seeing this shitty place ever again."

Ellie smiled a big bright smile, and he was hooked.

He didn't know why, but after having coffee with her, he couldn't stop thinking about Ellie. Everyone in town knew that she was hooked up with the drug dealer, but it didn't stop him from thinking and fantasizing about her.

"I just don't know what I want," she said to him one night, months after their coffee date. They had been meeting secretly a few times a week for months when Jonas was "working."

"It's simple," Dylan said sighing, tracing her jawline with his fingers. He didn't want to keep having the same conversation with her. "Either you leave him, or you don't. Do you want to be happy?"

"It's not that easy," Ellie said exasperated. "It seems that easy, but it's not."

Dylan was beside himself. "It really is that simple. You just make it more difficult than it is."

Dylan made choices and never looked back, not even for a moment. When he decided to enroll in college after their first coffee date, he knew that it was the right decision. He knew he would graduate and not look back.

Growing up without a father made him bitter, but realistic. Dylan knew what he needed to do in life. He knew that he was in control of his own destiny and that nobody could do it for him. Not his alcoholic mother, and not even a confused little girl that was involved with the wrong people. Dylan was smitten with Ellie, but he felt like she wasn't quite what she seemed, so he was cautious.

"I don't get you," he said one afternoon a few months later as he was tracing her slender, naked back with his index finger. It was a beautiful summer day, and they had stolen away for a couple of hours.

"What don't you get?" she asked, her eyes closed enjoying the hot sun and the feel of his fingertips on her skin.

"You don't seem like you belong with him. You seem more, I don't know. Independent. Maybe the word is stubborn." He struggled with the words. He had always used his mouth and hands to speak for him with the girls he had been with, but Ellie made him talk to her. She made him want to talk. "I don't know why you would want to be with him."

"I don't know," Ellie said, annoyed. She didn't know why Dylan always wanted to talk about Jonas. She didn't want to talk about Jonas when she was with Dylan. She had only agreed to be with Dylan on the condition that he knew she wasn't leaving her life with Jonas. "Why do you always want to talk about it?"

He shrugged, his handsome face wincing from the sting of her words. She pretended not to notice.

She looked at him out of the corner of her eye. When she looked at him, he astounded her. Ellie loved how she could see his muscles through his t-shirts. She could feel the strength in his back when she hugged him, and it made her heart beat quicker.

She loved the feel of his fingers on her skin. His hands were rough and hard from his years of manual labor, and she loved the feel of them on her body.

She had only ever been with Jonas, and occasionally one of his other girls, but she dared not to tell Dylan. She didn't want him to know the power that he had over her. Once he knew, she figured he would end up treating her just like Jonas treated her, and she couldn't bear it.

She rolled over on her back, reveling in her nakedness. She never felt this free with Jonas. Dylan's eyes got big as he looked down at her, enjoying the view. "I really like you," Ellie said pulling his face close to hers. "I want to spend time with you. But I don't want to talk about Jonas when we are together. I just want to enjoy us, our time. If you can't do that then we can't be together. You are ruining this for me."

He was quiet as he looked into her eyes, searching. He liked that she never looked away. He knew that she was missing something inside, but he had fallen for her, and he didn't want to give her up.

He nodded ever so slightly. He had never been asked to share anyone before, and never imagined that he could even consider it. However, he knew that if he wanted to be with her, that this was his only option.

For now.

I'll do this for her. But not always. I'll make her love me. I'll make her want only me. Dylan knew he would never allow her to stay with Jonas forever. *I have to get her away from him.*

"What are you thinking?" she said, smiling at him.

"I'm thinking about how I can't believe what you do to me." He said nuzzling her neck, tasting her saltiness.

"Mmmm," she sighed, smiling as she felt his hot breath on her neck. "I know. You do the same thing to me. You make me forget my life. You make me…" Ellie paused. *Be careful not to tell him too much!*

Dylan waited for her to finish. He had been waiting for months for her to say how she felt about him.

"…want to have a cheeseburger. Ellie jumped up suddenly and threw her shirt on laughing. "Let's go. I've got to get going!"

Dylan sighed and got up after her. He knew he would have to continue to wait. But he knew he wouldn't wait much longer before he took matters into his own hands.

CHAPTER THIRTEEN

Sophie

Brynn was on the verge of hysteria. She was still nauseated, but the medicine they gave her was starting to kick in and she was feeling better.

"Where is my baby?! Where is my baby?! Is my baby alive? Somebody please, please, help me!" Brynn cried helplessly, burying her face in her hands, trying to block out the fear and pain that grew inside.

"Brynn, Brynn. Calm down." A familiar voice was by her side.

"Dr. Nguyen! Oh my God, where is my baby?" Brynn looked up at the doctor, desperation pouring from her big brown eyes. The doctor was beautiful, middle aged, exotic looking, and typically very poised and calm. But today, she looked different. Today she looked slightly disheveled and messy, and Brynn had never recalled seeing her look quite this way.

"Brynn. I need you to calm down and breathe. Everything is going to be okay, but I need you to calm down and breathe first." Patricia Nguyen had been Brynn's obstetrician during her pregnancy, and though she never asked Brynn about her scars, she knew that they told a horrific story. From Brynn's visits and the scars, Patricia knew that she needed to be careful with Brynn.

Brynn could tell that the doctor was biding time. She tried to take deep breaths and calm herself down. But the anxiety was swelling over her like the tide, and she felt like an elephant was sitting on her chest.

Just then, Adam flew into the room, eyes wet and red. Brynn was alarmed, and immediately felt her heart start to race. He stood next to Brynn and held her hand, gripping it tightly and looking into her eyes.

"Brynn," Dr. Nguyen took a deep breath. "Your baby was premature. When you came in, we found you and the baby in distress. We acted as quickly as we could..."

The room was silent and Brynn felt the roar of quiet resounding in her ears. All she was aware of was that she was not breathing, not thinking. It was as though the moment had stopped, waiting for the doctor's next words to move it forward in whatever direction it was meant to go.

Brynn dared not breathe, waiting for what Dr. Nguyen was going to say next.

"Your baby is in the NICU. Her lungs are still not fully developed, and with the loss of oxygen to her brain..."

Brynn faded out. She could see Dr. Nguyen's lips moving and see the sadness on her face that she was trying to mask with her professionalism, but Brynn could see. She could see Adam out of the corner of her eye, and feel his hand gripping hers tightly.

She could make our words like *ventilator*, *lung function*, *brain damage*, but the rest of the words jumbled together into nothingness. She could tell by her expression that the message wasn't good, but the words ran together into incomprehensible sounds, and Brynn was silent.

Dr. Nguyen finished talking and looked at Brynn expectantly, not realizing that she hadn't been listening the entire time.

Adam looked at Brynn, waiting.

After what felt like a lifetime of silence, Brynn turned to Adam, her eyes overflowing with tears as she smiled. "A girl, Adam. We have a baby girl. We have our baby Sophie."

Adam was dumbfounded. It was as though Brynn hadn't heard a word the doctor had said.

"Brynn, Brynn. Do you understand? Do you understand what

Dr. Nguyen said?" Adam was beside himself. He had expected many different reactions, but this wasn't one of them.

Brynn looked at Dr. Nguyen, her eyes pleading. "Can I see my baby girl? When can I see her? I want to see her now. Now!"

The doctor looked at Brynn, tears welling in her own eyes. "We can go see her now if you would like."

"Yes, I would like to go see her now," Brynn said her voice strong and resolute.

After fifteen minutes, they made their way to the elevator, Brynn secure in a wheelchair with an escort, and Adam, and the beautiful doctor leading the way. Brynn was excited, although Adam had warned her about the incubator and the tubes, but Brynn didn't seem to hear him. She didn't hear anything. As they got closer, she was flush with anticipation, and was oblivious to everyone around her.

They made their way into the NICU, and Adam stayed as close to Brynn as possible. He knew that she was not prepared for what she was about to see. Dr. Nguyen led them to a single room and held her breath as the reached for the handle. "Brynn, are you okay? Are you ready?"

Brynn didn't look at her. She looked around her through the glass of the room. "I'm ready. Just open the door," she said, a hint of frustration in her voice. She was anxious to meet her daughter.

Dr. Nguyen opened the door and they wheeled Brynn into a room full of monitors and a mini bed enclosed in plastic. Brynn was confused. *Where is my baby?*

She looked frantically around the room and couldn't find the crib. *Where is my baby?*

Her big brown eyes settled on the mini bed encased in hard plastic. She peered inside.

Her breath caught as she saw the tiny arms and legs inside. *She's so small, how can she even be alive? Oh my God, how is she alive?*

She looked at Adam helplessly.

"Honey, we've been trying to tell you..." Adam said, his voice trailing off.

The room was silent as Brynn took it all in, looking but not seeing.

"Can I touch her?" Brynn finally said, quietly. "I want to touch her."

Dr. Nguyen started to speak, and then cleared her throat. "You can reach in through here," she said pointing to two holes that were big enough for Brynn's hands to reach through. "But for right now, she needs to be isolated. She can't be exposed to any germs."

Brynn looked at the baby, her eyes wide and her face glowing against the incandescent light of the incubator. She was in awe. The tiny body was full of tubes. Brynn couldn't believe there were so many.

Dr. Nguyen showed her where to put her hands and how to touch the baby, and Brynn put her hands in eagerly. The gloves frustrated her, and she hated not being able to feel her with her own skin. Dr. Nguyen explained that it was to protect the baby.

Brynn needed to touch her baby.

"Sophie," she said in a singsong voice that she had never heard come out of her before. "Sophie, it's Momma."

Adam watched silently as Brynn talked to her. He had listened to every word that Dr. Nguyen said, and he doubted that Sophie would make it past week two. But he loved her in spite of himself. He was worried about Brynn. He knew that Brynn would love her even if they said she wouldn't make it for another day. He knew his Brynn, and he knew how deeply she loved.

Brynn looked at the tiny body in the incubator. Barely four pounds, the tiny body was nothing but skin and bones. She couldn't believe how small the body was. Sophie's arms were so little, and Brynn stared hard at her spindly arms and legs. She had never seen anyone so frail.

"Sophie," Brynn said, putting her face as close to the baby's head as she could. "Sophie, Mommy's here. We love you. I love you so much."

The baby lay still, her tiny chest moving up and down ever so slightly with each labored breath. Brynn watched, fascinated with her tiny body, wanting so desperately to touch her hands, to feel her skin with her fingers. She looked at Adam with an expression that he had never seen before. Brynn had known deep sadness in her life, but this was something more than she had ever felt before. Even in the depths of her misery, after an especially harsh beating from Thomas, she had never felt as desolate as she felt now—separated from her baby by a thick plastic enclosure.

It was torture to be so near her, but not be able to pick her up and hold her. She ached from somewhere deep within a part of her soul that she never knew existed, when she looked at Sophie.

"Oh my God, Adam," she said turning to him, her big brown eyes bigger than he had ever seen them before, "Oh my God."

Adam stood behind her and held her tight. He could feel the frailness of her body, and he got as close to her as he could to try to give her some of his strength. He had been down in the NICU while Brynn was sleeping and had come to terms with the inevitable. He knew that Sophie wouldn't make it, and he was preparing himself. But he didn't know how he could prepare Brynn.

Tragedy seemed to separate them, and he was terrified of what losing Sophie would do to her. He prayed that Dr. Nguyen was wrong and that Sophie would come out of it strong and well.

"What do we do?" Brynn whispered to no one in particular, as she stared down at Sophie's tiny body. She marveled at her dark fluff of hair, much like her own. She imagined what it would be like if Sophie were a little girl, and she could brush and braid her hair.

Dr. Nguyen's voice came from beside them, low and quiet. "She's suffered a lot, Brynn, and she isn't doing well. I don't know how much longer she will have. You have to decide how and when to let her go when the time comes."

Brynn felt her heart stop.

"You can't ask me to do this! You can't ask me to let her go!" she said angrily. "I can't, and I won't."

"I hope you don't have to," Dr. Nguyen said slowly, looking at Brynn sympathetically. "But you and Adam need to talk about what is realistic, and what may happen."

Brynn stared at Sophie. Brynn's heart beat loudly in her chest. She hadn't imagined when she woke up this morning that this would be the conversation she would have with her doctor. She imagined a beautiful day watching her friend get married, not this. *How does it come to this? How can my life become this, after everything I have gone through?*

"We don't have to do anything now, honey," Adam said holding Brynn close to him. Brynn stared over his shoulder at the incubator, her eyes dark. "We can take our time."

The room was silent with only the sound of the machines working to keep Sophie alive, humming and swooshing quietly.

Brynn closed her eyes and tried to clear her mind. She ignored the voices echoing through the room, telling her that everything was going to be all right.

CHAPTER FOURTEEN

Ellie's Return

John Palmer opened the door and stared. He couldn't believe his eyes.

"Ellie!" He yelled, reaching out and engulfing her in a hug before she could step away. He was so excited to see her that he didn't notice when she didn't hug him back. "Where have you been? Where's Eva?"

Ellie looked at him coldly. John realized that he was still holding her, and he let her go abruptly. Caught up in his excitement, he had forgotten how Ellie was. John could just feel James' disapproval in his mind. James would never have approved of John losing his composure the way that he did.

"Where is Eva?" John repeated looking around.

Ellie knew that this would be the first question that he asked her, but she still didn't feel prepared to answer him.

Ellie said the first thing that came to her mind. "Eva's dead."

John stepped back, his deep hazel eyes wide with grief. He had imagined the worst, but now that it was reality, he was saddened beyond expectation. "How? How?" he whispered motionless.

Ellie didn't answer. She put her head down and pretended to cry, loud, wailing sobs that shook her entire body. *Shit! Shit! Shit! Why did I say she was dead? Shit! Now I am going to have to figure out an answer!*

Just then, John realized that there was a young man on the porch behind her. "Who...who is this?" he said to Ellie.

"This is my friend, Dylan." Ellie sniffed loudly, keeping her head down and avoiding John's gaze.

John knew that he should have felt more sympathetic toward her, but he didn't. Something just didn't feel right. Realizing that they were still on the porch, he stepped aside, even though he didn't feel comfortable letting them in.

"John, who is it?" Tricia's voice startled him from behind. She appeared and gasped when she saw Ellie. "Oh my God! Ellie! Where is Eva?"

Ellie was annoyed. *Why is it always about Eva? Why can't she just ask me how I am? Jesus!*

John turned around and looked at Tricia, his eyes big, and Tricia froze. She could read her husband like an open book, and she knew what that look meant.

Tears immediately sprung up in her blue eyes, and she turned away, stifling a sob. She had been hoping and praying for so long that everything was going to turn out well, and that they would find Ellie and Eva safe and sound. *How can God do this?*

"Do you want to come in?" John said slowly, opening the massive oak door just a little wider.

"Um, sure," Dylan said awkwardly, pushing Ellie toward the door, her head still down.

He was beginning to question why he was even there. He had agreed to go to Ellie's hometown with her, but he didn't know what they were doing at this stiff's home. *What the hell is she doing?*

They stepped into the foyer and paused.

"Have you been home?" John asked Ellie, looking only at her and ignoring the young man behind her.

"No," Ellie said quietly.

"Then why are you here?" John was confused.

"I heard. I heard they were missing. I heard they were possibly even dead. I knew you would know," Ellie spoke mechanically, coldly, almost as though she had no feelings whatsoever.

"How did you hear?" John said, trying not to sound annoyed. He wanted to know where she had been. He wanted to know what happened to Eva. She wasn't volunteering any information, and he wanted desperately to know what happened to her over the past decade.

"I just did." Ellie avoided his gaze.

He should have known that Ellie wouldn't offer more than she wanted to. She was straight to the point, and never gave more information than she needed. This infuriated James, but John had never dealt with Ellie before, and now he felt frustrated. How can she go missing for nearly ten years, and then reappear with no explanation?

John turned around and looked for Tricia. She had been his rock, helping him to grow in confidence so that he could run the company that James was no longer there to run. They had their difficulties, but overall, the company was solid, and John knew that his mentor would be proud of him. John felt lost without Tricia. She was his confidante and the person who knew all of the right things to say. Aside from being at work, she was never too far from him, and that is the way he liked it.

She came around the corner and he breathed a sigh of relief. At not even forty, she had barely aged a day as far as he was concerned. He smiled at her and she smiled back. Everything is going to be okay, he could almost hear her telling him.

"Ellie," Tricia said warmly. "Come with me, you look tired, sweetheart. Let's get you some tea, and then you and your friend can stay here for the night if you'd like."

John was struck with how warm and wonderful Tricia was, even though she had never liked Ellie.

"We don't want to impose," Ellie hesitated, and John realized that her eyes were dry, even after all of the crying.

"We can stay," Dylan's deep voice surprised them all. He hadn't spoken at all, and they had forgotten that he was even there.

Ellie gave him a sharp look, but then smiled sheepishly at Tricia. "Sure," she said following her slowly down the long hallway toward the kitchen.

When James and Dylan were alone, John gestured toward the great room, and Dylan walked in, slowly looking around as he went.

Money. Money. Money. Dylan thought, shaking his head.

"Do you want a cigar?" John asked him, pulling one out and cutting it for himself.

"Uh, sure." Dylan said, surprised by the gesture.

John pulled another one out and cut it, giving it to him slowly.

They smoked their cigars in silence, each lost in their own thoughts.

"So, what happened to Eva?" John said finally, breaking the uncomfortable silence.

"I don't know. It was before me, and she won't talk about it." Dylan said hesitantly. Ellie had warned him about what to say. He didn't want to say something he wasn't supposed to.

"I'm sure you know," John was challenging him, and Dylan could tell. *Dammit, Ellie.*

"I don't know. I really don't." Dylan was desperately puffing on his cigar, hoping to escape the conversation.

"How can you not know? Did you just meet Ellie? How can you not know what happened to her daughter? Where has she been? God dammit, give me something!" John was frustrated. He couldn't imagine how this idiot standing in front of him could have no knowledge of Ellie's child whatsoever.

"I don't know. I don't know." Dylan was looking for somewhere to stub out his cigar. "I don't know anything. We've only been together for a few months. She hasn't told me anything!"

"I don't believe you. I can tell you are lying." John was angry.

"What's going on?" Ellie's voice was angry and strong as she entered the room. Dylan looked at her, grateful that she had appeared.

"I want to know what happened to Eva. You don't understand, there is a lot at stake here," John said, directing his attention toward her.

"Like what?" Ellie said, curious.

"I can't tell you that."

"You're grilling Dylan about something that he knows nothing about. So what is at stake?" Ellie glared at John angrily, feeling a strange sensation of power coming over her. Shooting Jonas had awakened something in her that she hadn't realized she possessed. She wasn't about to let John bully her now. "I have a right to know."

"Everything, Ellie! Everything is at stake." John looked at her, searching her face for something honest and real. "Your parents were missing. And when you didn't appear, and then we couldn't find you, we had no choice but declare them dead. Your father left control of the company to me and to the shareholders, but he left everything else to Eva. The house, his fortune, everything!"

The room was silent and nobody moved. Ellie couldn't believe her ears. *How could he have left everything to Eva? What about me? What did he leave for me?*

"He left you as guardian of Eva. You benefit as a result of being her mother and having control over his estate," John said, almost as though he could hear her thoughts. "He wanted it that way on purpose to make sure that you remained her mother. He wanted to make sure that you still took care of her the way that he wanted you to."

Nobody moved. Ellie hadn't realized that she wasn't breathing.

"I'm pregnant."

Tricia gasped. She had been standing behind Ellie, silently watching the conversation.

"What?" John asked, not believing his ears.

"I'm pregnant," Ellie repeated. "So what does that mean?"

She looked at John who had turned white, and then she turned and gave Dylan a small smile.

CHAPTER FIFTEEN

Helpless

The NICU reminded Brynn of a church, quiet and reverent, where healing was happening slowly and silently. She couldn't wait to have Sophie out of the NICU and onto the regular floor so that she could eventually take her home. Brynn hated being in the NICU. She just wanted to have Sophie to herself in their nursery at home, caring for her there.

"Sophie, it's Mommy. I'm here," Brynn said quietly, her hand grasping the tiny hand in the incubator. "I'm here, baby girl."

Brynn looked at Sophie's tiny body covered with tubes and tape, trying to stifle a sob. She had never felt so helpless in all of her life. Even when Thomas was beating her, Brynn knew in her mind that she could escape. She knew that her adopted father would eventually stop, and that she could hide in her room and escape when she would cut herself. *But this — this was torturous and with no apparent end in sight.*

"Oh, baby girl, I'm so sorry that this had to happen to you," Brynn choked back a sob. She didn't want her tiny baby to hear her cry. She stepped out often to cry in the hallway or in the bathroom, but she refused to let her baby girl hear the sound of her crying. *If there is a small possibility that she can feel my sadness, I won't allow her to. I will be strong for her.*

Brynn marveled at how small her daughter was, her tiny chest moving up and down with the ventilator. Her hair was dark like

Brynn's, but the tape obstructed Sophie's face, and Brynn couldn't clearly see the rest of her features. *Does she look like Adam, or does she look like me?*

"Baby Sophie. You have to wake up. You have to be strong. I know that you've been through a lot, but you can make it. You can do this. I know that you can." Brynn felt her voice wavering. *No, no, no. I have to sound strong. She has to know that I believe in her.*

Brynn sent Adam home to sleep. He had been up for three days straight, and he needed to sleep. Brynn knew that he couldn't continue on this way. He fought her, but she won. He was too exhausted and he knew that he needed to sleep.

Sophie was silent. She lay motionless in her plastic enclosure, her tiny chest moving up and down with the ventilator that was taped gently to her mouth. Brynn felt the familiar heaviness on her own chest. The heaviness she felt when Adam left her, when she was completely alone. She tried so hard to forget it, but the familiarity of that feeling now terrified her.

I can't lose you, Sophie. I can't! You have to pull through this. You have to be able to breathe on your own. You have to!

Brynn knew that Sophie couldn't hear her well, but the nurses told her to talk to Sophie as much as she could. They said that Brynn's voice could soothe her. She sat and watched Sophie for hours, marveling at her smallness, at how vulnerable she was.

Jane called on her way to the airport. She and her new husband had delayed their honeymoon until she knew that Brynn's baby was safe and out of the woods. "I'll stay with you until Sophie is in the clear," Jane said to her friend. She had always been there when Brynn needed her most.

"No Jane! No. You deserve your happiness!" Brynn was grateful for Jane, but she couldn't let her put off her honeymoon. Jane left the restaurant prepared for her absence, putting Lucia in charge. Lucia was an Assistant Manager now, making money while she went to school. Both Brynn and Jane were confident having her in charge.

"Are you okay, honey?" Jane asked her voice full of concern. She knew what happened to Brynn when Adam left. She couldn't imagine how she may react if Sophie didn't survive.

Brynn was silent. She couldn't talk. Expressing her sadness was still so difficult for her. The words always wanted to come out, but stopped right before they could come out.

"I... I... don't know. I don't know," was all that Brynn could muster. *I want to tell her that I'm dying inside. I want to tell her that my heart is breaking with every breath. I want to tell her that I don't know how I will go on if Sophie dies.*

Silent tears burned hot down Brynn's face as she sat silently on the phone.

"Don't shut down on me, Brynn. I'm here if you need to talk. I'm here for everything. I'll only be gone for a week, and then I will be back, and you can call me anytime you want. Oh shit, I shouldn't even go. Brynn..." Jane battled with herself. She didn't want to leave her friend. They had been through so much together.

"I'll be okay. Please go. I couldn't live with myself if you didn't enjoy your honeymoon. I don't think that Andrew would ever forgive me if you put your honeymoon off." Brynn tried to smile as she spoke because she knew that she would sound stronger to her friend that way. "I have to go now, but I need you to go on your honeymoon. I need you to have the happiness you deserve."

Jane was quiet. She knew that Andrew would understand, but she couldn't ask him to put their honeymoon off. It was the only time he was going to have off for the remainder of the year, and with their hectic lives, she doubted they could reschedule it.

"I'll go, but if something happens you have to call me, and I will be on the first flight back!"

"I will. You are my best friend, and I love you. I'll call you if I need you." Brynn was just getting comfortable telling Jane how much she cared about her. She had only ever told three people in her life that she loved them, with Jane being the fourth.

Brynn turned her attention back to Sophie. The nurses bustled in and out, checking monitors, hanging bags of fluid. Brynn hardly noticed them.

She stared at Sophie and willed her to move, to breathe, and to do something that would let Brynn know that she was going to survive. She pictured Sophie bigger, older, with Adam's blue eyes, and her own brown hair. She pictured Sophie's small sweet cheeks, and she imagined kissing them, and snuggling her face. She envisioned herself holding her, and singing to her, and doing all of the things that Brynn's own mother had never done for her—or at least imagined that she had never done for her.

After all, how could she have done all of those things to me and then let me go? Brynn's thoughts went to Ellie. She hadn't seen her since she arrived at the front door of Brynn and Adam's house. Adam said that he hadn't seen her since the waiting room, and Brynn wondered briefly where she had gone. What does she want? Why is she even here?

Brynn couldn't help but feel anger when she thought about Ellie. She was curious and excited, but the anger won out. She couldn't imagine what Ellie would want with her.

Brynn looked at Sophie and felt a strange sensation of fullness in her heart that she had never known before. "I will never leave you, baby. I will never let anyone hurt you. I will always protect you."

They sat in silence for a few moments, and then Brynn realized that Sophie's color had changed. Oh my God, she's turning blue. Brynn screamed for help, desperately punching the nurses red call button. Suddenly, two nurses flew into the room, and before Brynn knew it, one of them had her on her feet as they pushed her to the door.

"What's going on?" Brynn demanded, startled. The nurse looked at Brynn, trying to suppress her own panic.

"You're baby isn't breathing," the nurse said, grabbing Brynn's arm and pulling her to the side as three other people entered the room. They pulled the curtain and Brynn couldn't see. She could hear the flurry of activity, and felt her heart pounding loudly in her ears. There was bile coming up in her throat, and suddenly she felt faint.

"I have to call Adam! Someone has to call Adam!" Brynn cried desperately.

"We called him, honey. He's already on the way." The nurse's knew to call him immediately if anything happened.

The nurse led Brynn to a well-lit, comfortable looking lounge where Brynn waited. Moments passed slowly, and every minute felt like an hour. She felt like she was dying inside, waiting to hear something as she paced the lounge like a caged animal.

Brynn was anxious for Adam to get there. She couldn't stand to be alone, not knowing what was going on with her baby. Brynn heard the sound of footsteps running down the hall and saw Adam race into the lounge. He frantically searched the room until he met her gaze, and he rushed toward her, engulfing her in a hug. Only in his arms did she feel safe, as though he could take away all the pain of the world and protect her in his embrace.

"Adam, S-S-S-Sophie..." Brynn couldn't speak. She had only known her tiny daughter for a day, but already she was so in love with her that she could barely breathe with the thought of losing her.

"I know, sweetheart. I know." Adam held her close, smoothing her hair and kissing her over and over. Brynn could tell that he had been crying, his beautiful blue eyes rimmed in red, bloodshot from lack of sleep.

They sat in silence, holding onto one another tightly. Minutes turned into an hour, and they sat waiting, their hearts fragile and worn.

They looked up expectantly when Dr. Nguyen walked into the lounge, her expression sober.

"How is Sophie?" Brynn and Adam said in unison, standing together quickly.

"Please sit," Dr. Nguyen said, motioning them to sit back down. "I'm afraid that the news isn't good."

Brynn listened half-heartedly, and could tell that Adam was absorbing everything. She only heard "...the news isn't good."

Brynn watched Dr. Nguyen hand Adam something to sign, and he scribbled his name without even looking at the paper. Adam's eyes filled with tears, and she could feel the tears filling up her own, even though she hadn't heard a word the doctor had said. She could tell from Adam's face that whatever she was saying was terrible, and Brynn could hear Thomas' awful dream voice in her head saying over and over, "I'm killing your baby like you killed me."

Brynn stared at Dr. Nguyen, but didn't say a word. It was clear that Brynn wasn't listening, as the doctor looked at Adam anxiously. Brynn heard Adam talking and saw Dr. Nguyen nodding and attempting a sad smile. Dr. Nguyen squeezed Brynn's arm and walked out of the room.

Adam looked at Brynn and sat her down on the couch.

"Brynn, are you listening?" Adam said gently, but firmly. "I need you to listen to what I am going to tell you."

Brynn felt like a small child. She nodded, unable to speak.

"Brynn."

Again, Brynn nodded.

"Sophie suffered a stroke and almost died. She's not doing well. Brynn... we have to say good-bye to Sophie. We have to let her go."

Brynn looked at Adam blankly, tears streaming down her face.

"We have to say good-bye to our baby."

CHAPTER SIXTEEN

Mother of the Year

Ellie walked up the steps of the big house she had lived in with her parents. She hadn't been there in over ten years, and everything looked old, worn, cracked. Nothing like it had looked when they all lived in it. She tried to remember what her parents looked like, what they sounded like. It had been so long since she thought of them.

Ellie sniffed. The house smelled. But looking at it made her feel... sad. And now here she was with Dylan and her infant son. She wanted to make it work with Dylan. The infatuation had worn away, but she still really liked him, and he took care of the baby.

Dylan had stood by her, taking care of her, even when she gave birth, even knowing their son might not be his but may have belonged to Jonas. And even now that they knew that the child was... different. Dylan said he would always be there for Ellie, and as they walked into the big house, Ellie tried to believe that he would.

John Palmer had come through and taken care of everything. He had been able to get her back into house, and to get her the money that was rightfully hers. He had done everything she had asked him to do. *He and Tricia had even let them live in their home even though that stupid cow hates me,* Ellie thought bitterly.

Stupid Mother of the Year, Little Miss Know-it-All, Fake Bitch. Ellie hated Tricia and tried not to let it show too much, but Ellie was never good at being fake. She loathed how domesticated and subservient Tricia was to her husband. *She disgusts me.*

John had taken care of it all, which Ellie found extremely appealing. She knew now why Daddy had made him his successor. Ellie owed everything to John, and made it a point to tell him so every chance she got. She even offered to show him how grateful he was, but after that, he made it a point to avoid her like the plague. Ellie pouted, but then got over it. After all, Dylan may not be all that bright, but he was pretty.

Ellie thought that her baby boy was going to be her redemption. "Noah will make everything right—for me, for this family."

But when he wasn't developing the way he should, the tests showed that there was something wrong with his brain.

"This can't be!" Ellie raged at Dylan. "You gave me a retarded son!"

"Hey, I don't even know if he's mine." Dylan said defensively. Dylan didn't know the first thing about kids, but for some reason, this baby tugged at him.

"Maybe it was all of the drugs that you did when you were pregnant," Dylan said angrily. Dylan had fallen hard for Ellie, and he knew that he could make it work with her if she would just let him. If only she would stop pushing at him.

He thought how lucky he was to find her, and the fact that she had all of the money now was just an added bonus.

But the kid was special. Not just mentally special, but special in a way that Dylan didn't understand.

"I didn't grow up with a dad, so I'm not gonna leave this kid ever," Dylan said to Ellie. He didn't understand why Ellie was acting so indifferently to her son. Dylan was thankful for the nannies that Ellie had hired, because when the baby cried, the nannies took care of him. They were even teaching Dylan how to bathe, change, feed, and take care of him. And as Noah got older, they taught Dylan how to adjust to his changing needs.

Ellie was happy to settle into the house, replacing all of the old furniture with new. She had the house repainted and cleaned from top to bottom. She even had her old room made into a suite for Dylan and the baby. "Sometimes I just need to be alone, so we are going to have separate rooms," she explained to him. Dylan didn't care, as long as he got to be near her, and close to Noah.

The nannies adored Dylan. They thought he was such a good daddy, and couldn't understand what he saw in Ellie. Nanny Lisa was tiny, blonde, and pretty. She enjoyed teaching Dylan about his baby. She loved Noah from the moment she set her eyes on him, and knew that he would need special attention. Nanny Lisa was glad that Dylan was so committed to his son, and thought about both of them long after she went home for the evening.

John Palmer stopped by every so often to check on them, but Ellie was over him almost as quickly as she became infatuated with him. She only cared that the money kept coming in. John told her that as long as Noah was with her, she would continue to be taken care of. She knew that it didn't matter if she loved her son, it only mattered that they lived under the same roof. When she saw how much Dylan truly loved him, she knew that she could be free to live as she wanted, keeping Dylan captive under her own roof.

Noah had beautiful green eyes, but his features were growing to be slightly asymmetrical. Ellie was embarrassed when she took him out in public and people stared. She tried to hide him in hats, but people still stared. He made weird noises and didn't respond when she talked to him. He only seemed to respond to Dylan and after a while, Ellie stopped taking him out altogether. "You can take him out from now on," Ellie said to Dylan angrily. "It's embarrassing. Everyone stares, he drools and it's disgusting. I hate it."

Dylan didn't understand Ellie, but he never said anything. But when Noah was three, he couldn't take it anymore.

"Ellie, he's your son! He's beautiful!" Dylan said exasperated. "How can you be such a bitch about your own child?"

Ellie narrowed her dark eyes and glared at him. "I can say whatever I want about him, because he is my son. And you live in my house, so you have no right to judge me."

"What if I didn't live in your house any longer?" Dylan said angrily. He had been thinking about leaving for quite some time. He didn't love Ellie, and she never even let him touch her anymore. He couldn't stand watching how Noah tried to communicate with Ellie, and how Ellie shunned him time after time. He had special needs, but Ellie didn't want to take care of even one of them.

Ellie froze. "What do you mean, Dylan? Do you want to move out?"

Dylan was silent. "I dunno. But I don't want to be with you any longer. I'm not happy."

Ellie smiled. "Fine, then go. But Noah doesn't go with you. Noah stays with me. And you'll never see him again." She watched him flinch. She knew how much he loved Noah.

"You can't do that! I love him!" Dylan knew he shouldn't be surprised by anything she did, but he didn't think she would use Noah to trap him.

"I can, and I will," Ellie said looking deep into his eyes. She tried to remember what she found so appealing about him in the first place. She missed Jonas as she often did, and she wished that she had thought things through more clearly.

Dylan was such a disappointment.

"I'll stay," Dylan said, defeated, looking at the floor. In the old days he would have cut and run. He was always the one in control, and now Ellie clearly had all the power. Ellie was the one who called the shots, and they both knew it. Dylan hated himself for giving in so quickly.

"Good," Ellie said patting him on the chest. She felt his muscles through his shirt, and she found herself remembering what she liked so much about him. She pulled him close and breathed him in like she used to. She closed her eyes and thought about how he tried to take care of her, and how she tried to let him. She paused with her hands splayed out on his chest and felt him catch his breath.

She pulled away from him quickly.

"Okay, good," She said turning away from him.

The next morning she woke up and the house felt unusually quiet.

She went to the suite and found that Dylan and Noah were both gone.

CHAPTER SEVENTEEN

The Long Good-Bye

Adam knew that the moment was coming, and he knew that it would be up to him to convince Brynn.

"I can't! I can't say good-bye! I'm not giving up on Sophie." Brynn said angrily, refusing to look at him.

"Brynn, she's suffering. She's not breathing on her own and her brain has too much damage. We need to do what's right and let her go." Adam's voice was deep and hoarse. He was in pain, more than any pain he had ever experienced before. He knew that he was going to have to talk to Brynn. He knew that she could never let Sophie go on her own. *I wish that just for once Brynn could see things for what they are, and not what she wants them to be! If she could only see this is the right thing to do.*

"I can't leave her to die. I can't just let her go. I can't! How can you ask me to let my child die? How dare you?"

"Your child? How about my child? Brynn, she's ours!" Adam couldn't believe what he was hearing. *She's doing what she always does, making it about her and not about us, or about me.* Adam was trying not to get frustrated. The marriage Counselor had warned them that they had to remain united, and that they couldn't think independently all of the time, or else they wouldn't make it.

"She needs a chance. She needs a chance to live. She can live," Brynn was desperately pleading her case.

"She's already dead, Brynn. She's brain dead. Her brain went too long without oxygen. We have to let her go," Adam's tone was final.

Brynn dropped to her knees. This was worse than anything she had ever experienced, or imagined in her worst nightmares. It was worse than when Adam left her. It was worse than the ferocious beatings, and it was worse than wondering what was so wrong with her that her parents just discarded her like garbage. This... this was far worse.

She thought of Sophie's tiny body growing inside of her own. And then she pictured her struggling, fighting for every breath, ever since she was born. *How can this be? How is this fair? I can't say good-bye to her, I've barely even gotten to meet her. I haven't even held her. How can I let her go?* Brynn felt her throat closing in. Something was squeezing her so tight she was gasping for air.

"Breathe, Brynn. Just breathe. Slowly, in and out. Breathe," Adam said, his voice full of concern, but something else that Brynn couldn't put her finger on. "Please, sweetheart..."

"Adam, I need to hold her," Brynn said looking at him, terrified that he would say "no."

"The doctor said we could hold her. We can spend as much time with her as we need to. But then it's only right to let her go. She can't go on like this. It's just too hard, and it's not right to put her through it." Adam was amazed at how little Brynn heard, almost as though she wasn't even in the room.

Brynn nodded slowly. *I need to call Jane. I can't call Jane! I can't ruin her honeymoon. I have no one else to call. There is only Jane.* For a brief moment, she thought about Ellie. But she knew that she would never confide in Ellie, or go to her for anything. Brynn felt very alone.

Adam wanted desperately to call his parents, but they were overseas on a mission trip with their church, and there was no way to get a hold of them. He watched Brynn carefully trying to gauge her reaction, but as usual, he couldn't read her.

He just didn't know which way she was going to go with the news, and he wanted desperately to be there for her, but he didn't think she would let him. They had made so much progress over the past few months, but Adam felt as though he was instantaneously watching them slide backwards.

Brynn already felt like she was slipping away.

"Sweetheart," he said gently. "What do you want to do? Do you want to go in?"

Brynn was still sitting on the floor, her chin resting on her knees, her arms encircling them. She looked like a child, and Adam felt strangely annoyed with her. He wanted her to make him feel better. He needed her to make him feel better.

Almost as though she read Adam's mind, she suddenly stood up and wrapped her arms around him tightly.

"I'm sorry," Brynn whispered. "I got lost for a moment, and I'm sorry."

Adam kissed the top of her head. "It's okay. Don't worry about it." This is the Brynn I want and need. He paused. "What do we do? Do we want to say 'good-bye' now?"

Brynn's heart sunk. She nodded. She wanted to shake her head and run away, but she nodded instead, her heart feeling as though it were being stabbed with a thousand jagged knives.

They walked slowly, hand in hand, down the long corridor into the locked maternity ward. They stood outside and waited to be let in. As they walked to their room, they knew that the nurses knew, everyone knew, what they were about to do. The nurses all looked at them with sad, teary eyes. Brynn hid her face in Adam's shoulder so that she wouldn't have to look at them.

They paused at the doorway of the room and looked at each other silently. Brynn knew that he was waiting for her to let him know she was ready. She took a deep breath and stepped into the room.

The room was different. Quiet. There was only one machine on, the one keeping Sophie breathing, the one keeping her alive. But all of the other machines were gone. They looked around the room and realized that her plastic enclosure was missing too. The only thing left in the room was a standard hospital bassinet. The nurses had dressed Sophie in a pretty pink onesie, and Brynn stared down at her daughter and sighed.

"She's beautiful," she breathed. Brynn was caught off guard by how beautiful her baby was, how amazingly small and beautiful and perfect. And Brynn was horrified by what she was there to do, her heart caught in her throat, unable to utter another word.

A nurse appeared out of nowhere. "Would you like to hold her?"

Brynn looked at Adam, her eyes frantic with fear, but he was lost in his own grief. She hadn't gotten to hold her yet, and now that she could, she wasn't sure if she would be able to let her go when the time came.

Brynn looked at the nurse and nodded her head, slowly.

The nurse gestured to the nearby chair and picked Sophie up, wrapping her quickly in a blanket. She handed her gently to Brynn who felt like she was being handed a secret prize, an invaluable token. She felt nervous and awkward as she looked up to Adam for reassurance. He smiled at her sadly, and Brynn realized that this was going to be the one and only time she was going to get to hold her baby.

"She's so light!" Brynn said with wonder, amazed at how Sophie felt like air in her arms. She closed her eyes and imagined herself getting to hold her every day, waking her up in the morning, and putting her to bed at night. She felt her heart start to swell almost uncontrollably. It was so full of despair. She held her for what felt like forever, time frozen, the room still.

Brynn felt Adam's hand on her shoulder and it startled her. She looked up and saw tears in his blue eyes. "You hold her, honey," Brynn offered, her voice a small whisper.

"Keep her a little while longer," Adam said, smiling down at her, blinded, barely able to see. He wiped the tears away and looked deep into her eyes. "Keep her as long as you want."

Brynn held Sophie, talking to her, rocking her in her arms. She was careful not to talk about sad things. *I doubt she can understand but I'm not going to take the chance.*

Adam watched her, mesmerized by the sound of Brynn's voice. He loved watching her talk to Sophie. It confirmed what he had always known about her—Brynn was going to be a wonderful mother, even though she had no one to teach her, and no role models of her own. He felt his heart cracking, but he tried to stay strong just a little while longer. He knew that he would need to for Brynn.

She eventually handed Sophie over to Adam, and they took

turns gently passing her back and forth. The nurse watched carefully from a distance, trying not to cry. This part never got any easier, no matter how many times she saw it, and this young couple was no exception.

"I love you, Sophie. I didn't know if I could be a good Mommy, but here you are. And now I know that I can be. And I have you to thank for that," Brynn fought back the sobs that were beginning to engulf her. Her heart felt like a raw open wound. Even Adam's abandonment felt minimal compared to the pain she was feeling trying to let her daughter go.

Adam held her and Sophie tight, enveloping them with his arms. "Oh God, I wish I could just protect you from this, but I can't!"

Brynn wasn't for sure if he was talking to Sophie or if he was talking to her.

"I can't do this. I can't. Let. Her. Go." Brynn was crying hard, her entire body shaking as she tried not to let herself scream. "I can't say good-bye. I just can't. I can't!"

Adam held Brynn and Sophie tight. He didn't want the moment to get past him. He didn't know how he was going to survive. He looked at his small, beautiful daughter in the arms of the only woman he had ever loved, and he wanted to keep them like this, with him always. He couldn't imagine how he was ever going to get Brynn past this, or how he was going to get past this.

Adam held Brynn through her sobs, tortured and raw, wishing that he could ease her pain. Brynn tried desperately to stop crying. She didn't want Sophie to go without her realizing it, and she knew that if she kept crying that she would miss her last moments. She summoned her strength and quieted herself as best as she could.

Brynn held Sophie close, breathing in her sweet scent, and feeling the slight rise and fall of her chest as it moved slower and slower. They had given the doctor permission to stop the machines, knowing that it would mean an end to her suffering. Brynn didn't know what to expect. She didn't know if Sophie would float away, or if she would cry. She just knew that she couldn't let her go. She stared at her face. Will I know when she's gone?

Brynn held her breath, waiting.

The doctor had said that after they stopped 'taking measures,' it wouldn't be long. Brynn wanted it to last forever. She couldn't bear the thought of letting her go.

They sat for an hour, and Brynn felt every minute as though it were a lifetime. She touched every tiny finger and toe, tracing them with her own fingers, enjoying the softness and the newness. She nuzzled Sophie, enjoying her smell, knowing that she would never get to smell her again, and praying that she would always remember what she smelled like.

Finally, Sophie was still, her tiny chest no longer moving and Brynn marveled at how she simply looked as though she were sleeping. Brynn gasped, realizing that Sophie didn't move at all, as she looked at Adam helplessly. Adam blindly fumbled for the nurses call button, not seeing it through the tears that were flowing down his face. He stood up, unable to look at Brynn, unable to look at his daughter.

"Did we do the right thing? Adam? Oh God, did we do the right thing?" Brynn's voice cracked as she begged Adam for an answer.

Adam nodded, his blue eyes dark and somber. "She's not suffering anymore, Brynn. She isn't in pain anymore."

"But she never knew us. She never knew that we loved her." Brynn held Sophie close to her chest, desperately searching her mind for a way she could be with her forever. She refused to believe that she was truly gone.

"She knew us, Brynn. She knew us before she was ever born. She knew we loved her. She loved us, even if only for a brief time. She knew, Brynn." Adam couldn't believe anything different. He knew that if it weren't true, that nothing else in the world could ever make sense again.

Brynn nodded. She couldn't see Adam or Sophie. She could only see the tears that kept coming no matter how hard she tried to make them stop.

Brynn handed the still bundle to Adam, and Adam took her, carefully. Adam held her and rocked her back and forth in his arms, humming quietly. Adam kissed Sophie's cheek, taking in its softness and knowing he would always remember how it felt on his lips.

When he started to hand her back, Brynn shook her head. She didn't want to hold her dead child any longer. She wanted the moment to be over. She wanted to stop looking at the tiny beautiful face that would have been her daughter. She just wanted to go home, and she didn't want to feel the pain anymore.

The nurse had been waiting respectfully, silently. She looked at Brynn who sat with her head in her hands on the bed. She refused to look at the nurse even though she could feel the heaviness of her eyes.

"Do you want to hold her one last time, and say good-bye?" the nurse said gently to Brynn.

Brynn was silent. The nurse waited.

Brynn stood up and walked toward the nurse. She walked as though she was in a daze, and the nurse recognized the glazed look in her eyes. Brynn took Sophie slowly and nuzzled her against her neck, knowing that this would be the last time that she would ever hold her.

"I love you more than you will ever know, and I will never forget you. Never." Brynn kissed her on the cheek and then on the forehead, hating the coldness that was starting to settle into Sophie's skin. She took one last look at Sophie's face and couldn't believe that she was going to have to live her life without her.

The nurse entered the room, quietly. Brynn handed Sophie to the nurse and immediately turned away unable to believe what she had just done The nurse quickly left the room, and the room fell eerily silent.

Neither Brynn nor Adam touched one another or spoke. Each was lost in their own pain oblivious to the other as they sat isolated and surrounded by a deep shroud of impenetrable sorrow. Without speaking, they both knew that absolutely nothing in their lives would ever be the same again.

CHAPTER EIGHTEEN

Carly's Life

Carly smiled at Petey. She had been living with them for several years now, and after the initial first year, found that as time went on, she smiled more and more often. The biggest black spot in her life now were the headaches, the terrible headaches that always came, and then stayed for days.

Other than that, she had learned to be content with her life. The doctor told her that she may never get her memory back, and she was coming to terms with that. She wanted to know who she was and what her life was like before coming to live with Petey and Lily, but with every passing year, she found that it didn't bother her quite as much.

"What are you smiling at, honey?" Petey said smiling back. He remained stunned by Amy's beauty, as he was from the first moment that he saw her. He was careful to call her 'Carly' now, instead of 'Amy'. *Carly, Carly, Carly. Don't ever mess it up, Petey.* He had been calling her Carly for several years, but he was still afraid that he would forget and call her Amy one day. Amy didn't know that he knew who she was. She thought he just found her wandering somewhere, and he had saved her from some terrible men who were trying to hurt her.

"You," she said leaning her chin on her hands. "You're so handsome and serious all of the time." She pretended to pout.

"I just want you to be happy," Petey said trying not to sound nervous. He leaned over and kissed her, feeling that familiar rush as he did so. He had never cared about anyone like he cared about her. For the first time in his life, he felt as though he had a lot to lose.

"I am," Carly sighed happily. She busied herself making breakfast, knowing that Lily would be leaving for work soon at the veterinarian clinic.

"Why are you so happy?" Petey asked, curious.

"I don't know. I woke up this morning and I felt... happy. I can't explain it. I just felt at peace." Carly shook her short blonde hair, mussing it up, and Petey felt his heart thump in his chest. He thought she was beautiful from the moment he saw her, which is why he couldn't let Sy kill her as he had killed her husband. They met with such violence, Petey didn't believe she would ever be able to let that go had she remembered what he did to her. He never believed she could have come to love him. *But she doesn't remember!* Petey reminded himself.

Lily came into the kitchen silently. "Good morning," she said brightly.

"Lily, I made breakfast," Carly said proudly. She loved Lily like a sister and wanted her to be pleased. Lily had taken care of her, taught her how to cook, how to sew, and how to clean. Carly was ashamed of how much she didn't know how to do, but Lily had taught her to be useful around the house.

"It looks wonderful," Lily said, smiling at Carly with approval. Lily was surprised at what a quick learner Carly was. It was evident that Carly hadn't cooked or cleaned in a long time, and Lily needed her to be able to help around the house. She was pleased and surprised at how eager Carly was, and was even more surprised that she wanted to learn how to sew. When Lily was offered a job, she and Petey were hesitant about leaving Carly alone, but she had already been with them for a couple of years, and there was no sign of her memory returning.

"I'm glad you found a job," Carly said, looking at Lily. "You seem so much happier."

"I am. Thank you." Lily didn't realize that it was so evident.

"I just wish that I could do more," Carly said, a trace of sadness in her voice.

"You don't need to work, honey. Not with your headaches. We will take care of you," Petey said quickly. "I don't want you to hurt yourself."

Carly was quiet, busying herself with pouring coffee and juice and buttering the toast. "I haven't had a headache in a month now," she said quietly.

The room was silent, with only the sound of thoughtful chewing.

"You do a lot around here," Lily said breaking the silence. "I honestly don't know what I would do without you."

Carly smiled as she looked around the room. She had sewn the new curtains on the windows and repaired the tablecloth. She would do the laundry, clean the house, and had been cooking more and more of the meals. But she felt like she was missing something. She was happy, but she fought the feeling that she should be doing more.

"Don't worry about it, sweetheart," Petey said, his mouth full of eggs. It pained him to think that Carly could be unhappy. "You do plenty. If you're bored, then I can get you a dog or..."

"I'm not bored," Carly said quickly. "I'm happy. I'm just talking."

Lily and Petey exchanged quick glances, each looking away quickly. Carly knew they were cousins, she knew that they looked out for her, but she didn't really know who they were, or that they lived in fear every day that she would find out. They both loved her. She fulfilled a need in them that neither recognized until Petey inadvertently moved her in with Lily.

"Why don't we do some online shopping when I get home?" Lily said, smiling. She knew how much Carly loved to shop online. She shopped for everything online with a small budget, and she enjoyed it.

"Okay. Or..." Carly paused, "Or... we could go into town and shop there."

Carly didn't miss the look that passed between the two people she loved the most. She had posed this question on numerous occasions, and every time she was denied.

"You know what we've said, Carly. It's just not safe," Lily said slowly. "We don't know who was after you or why. We don't want anything bad to happen to you, or for anyone to know where you are."

"The men who were after you were bad men. We can't protect you if they find out where you are," Petey added.

Carly nodded. She knew what they would say. She knew that it didn't matter how many times she asked, she knew that the answer would still be the same. She wanted to be safe, but she didn't feel like she was in danger. She couldn't imagine who would ever try to hurt her, or why anyone would ever want to, but then again, she couldn't remember. She couldn't remember anything, and she was trying to find happiness in her current state, but sometimes it was just too hard.

"Okay," Carly said with a small smile. "I'm ruining breakfast."

"I know it's hard, but it will be okay. You'll see," Lily said getting up and hugging her tight. "I hate to see you sad. Try to be happy. You are with people who love you."

"I can stay with you for a while," Petey said, wiping his mouth as he finished the last of his breakfast. "If you want."

Carly smiled. "I'd like that."

Lily went to work, and Carly and Petey sat on the couch, sitting close together in silence.

"I wish I knew who I was, and where I came from," Carly said after a little while. "I am happy with you and with Lily, but I feel like I'm missing something."

"I know." Petey never knew what to say when she started talking like this. He didn't want to discourage her, but he had never spent much time talking to girls before. He wasn't much for talking. He was a better listener.

"I wonder if I had a family. I wonder if…if…," Carly hesitated.

"If what?" Petey asked, not sure that he wanted to hear the question.

"I wonder if I had any children. If I have any children," Carly said, her voice barely audible. "I always dream of a beautiful little girl with big brown eyes. She's holding out her arms to me and…"

Petey felt a knot in the pit of his stomach. He knew that he didn't want to hear the rest.

"I just feel like I know her, and I can't get her out of my mind."

Petey held her tight, pushing away his own fear. *When she figures out who she is, she'll hate me. I can't let that happen.*

Carly snuggled up against his big, strong frame losing herself in the only comfort she knew.

CHAPTER NINETEEN

Noah

"Lee-uh," Noah lifted his arms up begging to be picked up.

"No, no, no. Noah sleep. Sleep!" Lisa ordered gently.

"Lee-uh, Pick up!"

"Noah. No. Sleep." Lisa said firmly. "It's nap time. Sleep."

They had driven for hours all through the night, and Lisa was exhausted. She wanted to sleep, and she knew that she couldn't sleep until Dylan did. She didn't want to lose patience with Noah, she knew that would just make it worse. He's just a special little boy. He didn't ask for this. He didn't ask for his mother to be a complete and useless bitch. It's not his fault. *Patience, Lisa, patience.*

The door to the hotel room opened. Dylan walked in—tall, lean, and handsome, breathtakingly so...

"He's not asleep yet?" Dylan asked, his voice tired and aggravated.

"No, not yet," Lisa said trying not to cry.

"Lay him on the bed." Dylan said sharply.

Lisa picked Noah up out of the pack and play she was trying to get him to sleep in. She laid him carefully in the middle of the bed. At three he was getting heavy, almost too heavy for Lisa to pick him up.

Noah looked at her with big brown eyes. His brow was furrowed and he was confused. Lisa looked at his little face, at his eyes that were too close together and his forehead that seemed oddly large for his size, and she thought that he was beautiful.

"Lay next to him." Dylan said gesturing to the bed. "He can't sleep when he's alone."

Lisa lay down next to Noah, covering Noah gently with the blanket. She smoothed his dark brown hair over his brow and watched him close his eyes. He fell asleep instantaneously, and Lisa sighed with relief.

"It's going to be okay," Dylan smiled at Lisa. "We have each other. We are away from that bitch, and we can start over. We can start a family without her."

Lisa smiled sleepily. She loved Noah and wanted him to be happy. She had been dreaming of the three of them being a family for a long time. She just never believed it could happen. Finally, after three years of flirting, and talking, and pretending like they weren't in love, they decided that they couldn't deny it anymore.

And now here she was.

She drifted off to sleep with her arm protectively wrapped around Noah. "Goodnight, Noah bug," she whispered as she did every night.

Dylan watched them sleeping, his whole world wrapped up in them. *I thought that Ellie would make me happy, but she's nothing but a selfish, drug-addicted whore. I can't let Noah know who his mother really is.*

Dylan imagined a world where the three of them could be happy, but he knew they would have to get further away. He knew that as soon as Ellie realized they were gone, she would call John, and that they would call the police.

He drifted off in the chair, watching over them.

The next thing he knew, the world sounded as if it were crashing in, and he jumped up as the door flew open. He then found himself staring down the barrel of several guns in his face, and he was being thrown to the ground.

"Police! Don't move! Don't move!" Dylan felt a boot on the back of his neck and the sound of Lisa's screams.

Noah was moaning, and Dylan felt tears running down his face. "Noah! Noah!" He cried out.

"Don't move, I said!" A strong angry voice was shouting down at him. "You're under arrest for kidnapping."

"He's my son!" Dylan screamed. "He's my son!"

"We'll see what the court says," the voice said hand cuffing him roughly and picking him up. He looked around desperately for Lisa, but she was already gone. All he caught was a glimpse of Noah on the bed.

My poor baby boy. Daddy loves you! Daddy loves you!

CHAPTER TWENTY

Brynn and Adam's Meeting

The table was large. Dark. Cherry.

The room was massive. Cold. A place where hopes were dashed and dreams were destroyed. It was a large room that didn't care about the tears that were shed, or the hearts that were broken. It was created for sadness and misery and devastation.

Brynn stepped into the room first.

She was ushered into the room by the secretary, a young, serious woman with black-rimmed glasses who gestured toward one of the large leather chairs. "Mr. Black will be right with you," she said in a no-nonsense tone. Her tone was very business-like, and lacked any warmth or compassion.

Brynn sat down, the chair swallowing her instantly, making her feel very small. She shifted in the chair trying to get comfortable. Her feet barely touched the floor, and she immediately questioned whether she should be there.

A few moments later, a heavyset man in his late fifties entered the room carrying a heavy leather bag filled with files, and sweating profusely. "I'm sorry, Mrs. Michael, traffic was terrible and…"

Brynn wasn't listening. Her eyes were large and panicked as she looked around the room. She kept smoothing her dark hair behind her ears as she squirmed in her chair.

He could tell that she was nervous, and she looked like she was going to throw up. He had warned her that it wasn't going to be easy. He warned her that this was going to be a difficult day. "You can back out any time you want. This isn't going to be pleasant," he told her at their last meeting. "If you aren't sure you want to go through with it, then maybe you're just not ready. You have to be sure that this is what you want to do. This is permanent."

Brynn had nodded at him. She was sure. She knew that this is what she wanted to do. She knew that there was no other choice.

Mr. Black unloaded his bag. He set the files on the table and poured himself a big glass of water from the crystal pitcher on the table.

"Would you like some?" he asked, gesturing to Brynn.

Brynn shook her head. She was afraid that if she opened her mouth she would vomit all over the beautifully polished table.

"You should have some," Mr. Black said pouring her a glass of water and setting it clumsily in front of her, some of it spilling out onto the table.

Brynn watched the water spilling on the table and looked around for a napkin. She didn't want water all over the table in front of her. She grabbed a tissue from the box in front of her and wiped the table down.

"Are you sure you want to do this? Is this what you really want?" he said, some of the redness from his face disappearing, the sweat still dripping from his double chin.

"Yes." Brynn said, offering nothing else.

Mr. Black busied himself with pulling out his papers and his legal pad, making notes as he thumbed through the pages. Brynn could see her bank statements, papers from the restaurant, and various pages that she had given him over the past few months. It made her sad to see her entire life reduced to pages in a manila folder in the hands of a balding, middle-aged stranger, who she was going to owe a lot of money to when it was all said and done.

The big glass door to the room opened and a masculine looking woman who must have been at least six feet tall entered the room with Adam trailing behind her. Brynn's breath caught in her throat.

She hadn't seen Adam in months, and now here he was walking around the large table avoiding her eyes. It had been so long since she had seen him, even longer since she had touched him. She suddenly fought a strong urge to run up to him and grab him, but after Sophie's death, things between them had steadily declined. He wanted nothing to do with her now.

Oh, God. What are we doing? Brynn suddenly realized that she had been holding her breath.

Adam and his lawyer sat down on the other side of the table, neither of them saying a word.

"Mr. Black," the mannish looking woman said curtly, her voice oddly deep.

"Ms. St. George," Mr. Black said with a trace of contempt.

Brynn sensed that this wasn't their first meeting, and it made her uneasy.

She tried to catch Adam's eye, but he refused to look at her. She finally gave up and looked down at the table, fighting the tears that threatened to spring up.

"Well," Ms. St. George said, her low voice resonating in the large room. "I think we know why we are all here."

"Yes," Brynn and Adam said at the same time. Adam glanced up quickly, his blue eyes flashing toward Brynn and then looking away.

"It would be nice if we could get through this quickly, civilly. If anyone needs a break, please say so. We will try to get through the division of property as quickly as possible." Ms. St. George wasted no time getting to the point. "There will simply be the matter of going to court to stand in front of the judge after this, and then everything will be final."

Adam nodded, and Brynn felt the lump in her throat getting bigger. She had been dreading this meeting all week, and now that it was finally here, she couldn't believe it. She hadn't spoken to Adam in months, and she longed just to hear the sound of his voice. She wondered if he missed her as much as she missed him. It doesn't matter now.

The lawyers started talking, dividing assets as Brynn and Adam nodded in agreement. There was nothing that either of them wanted to fight over. The beautiful Victorian was going to be put on the market, with the profit of the sale being divided equally; the dishes, the cars, even the candle holders they had received for a wedding gift, everything. The only thing left to determine was the fate of the restaurant.

"I want her to have it. She can have it all, " Adam said looking directly at Brynn for the first time.

"Are you sure that you want to do that?" Ms. St. George said skeptically. The profit of the restaurant had quadrupled over the past few years.

"I do. I want her to have it. She's worked for it. It's hers." Adam's tone was firm. He had given it a lot of thought. He didn't feel as though he was owed anything from the restaurant.

"No. No," Brynn said, shaking her head. "He deserves half. He should get half."

Mr. Black and Ms. St. George looked at each other.

Nobody spoke as the lawyers communicated silently with one another.

"If that is what you want, Adam, but I strongly advise against it," Ms. St. George said finally.

"That is what I want," Adam said never taking his eyes off Brynn.

Brynn's eyes filled with tears, and she couldn't stop it. Adam knew how much the restaurant meant to her, but she didn't expect him to leave it to her completely. Not after he had blamed her for everything else. Not after he had blamed her for Sophie. She blamed herself for losing Sophie, so they at least agreed upon that.

His words came back to her. "You never wanted a child! You never even wanted to be a mother! Your selfishness is the reason Sophie is dead. If you had wanted her more, if you had loved her more, maybe she would still be here!" Brynn felt the venom of his words cutting through her like they did the first time that he said them. He blamed her for the loss of their beautiful daughter, and nothing that she could say or do could make him think differently.

She didn't want him to think differently.

But she resented him for forcing her to decide to get pregnant in the first place. Even after he knew how afraid she was to be a mother, he still wanted to have a baby, and she knew that in order to keep him, she would have to concede.

And now Sophie was gone, dead, buried over a year ago. And here they were, dividing their lives together as though it never even existed, as though it never mattered.

Brynn agreed to everything that Ms. St. George proposed after that, and within an hour and a half, they were done.

"Thank you, Ms. Michael. I know how difficult this must be for you." Ms. St. George said smiling sympathetically. It was the first show of emotion that Brynn had seen from her.

Mr. Black stood up, pushing his chair back from the table, and Brynn stood up next to him. Ms. St. George stood up and, even though they were some distance apart, Brynn could tell that she towered over her. Adam stood up slowly, his shoulders slumped, his eyes red from lack of sleep. Brynn knew that he was miserable, but there was nothing she could do for him anymore.

"Mr. Black," Ms. St. George said, nodding to him respectfully and putting her hand on Adam's shoulder.

"Ms. St. George, Mr. Michael." Mr. Black nodded back.

Adam looked slowly at Brynn. He missed her. But he couldn't look at her any longer. She reminded him too much of Sophie, and he knew that if he stayed married to her that she would continue to remind him of his precious daughter that he lost, every day.

They locked eyes for a moment, both of them fighting back tears. The sorrow in the room was evident. The room was use to hatred, anger, and resentment, but sorrow and love in this room were rare. Even the lawyers, who orchestrated these deals daily, squirmed. They could tell that there was still a great deal of love between Brynn and Adam, even if they were completely unaware.

Adam and Ms. St. George walked out of the room slowly. Brynn avoided his eyes. She looked down at the floor and knew that she would only see him once more, in court. She realized that after that, she might never see her beautiful Adam ever again. There were no children to tie them together, and they just divided everything that had ever been between them.

At least they were trying to keep it civil between them. The last night before Brynn left, Adam agreed to let her keep Maxie before the lawyers got involved. He had gotten Maxie for Brynn as a gift, and he wasn't going to take him now. He knew that Brynn would need him for security since Adam was no longer going to be sleeping next to her.

She had protested as he had expected her to. "I can't keep Maxie. He's our dog. Can't we just... I don't know, share custody of him?"

"No. He's yours. He was a gift." Adam said in that strange monotone voice he had been using for months now. Brynn hadn't grown accustomed to his lack of emotion, and it still cut her deeply.

"But you love him, too. He loves you. He needs both of us." Brynn argued.

"He's just a dog, Brynn. He'll be fine," Adam said as a matter of fact. "He'll be fine. And besides..."

Adam stopped.

"Besides what?" Brynn said, prodding gently.

"Besides, if we share custody, I'll have to see you. I don't want to see you anymore."

Brynn felt like she had been punched in the stomach.

"I... I... didn't realize..." Brynn was speechless.

"I've tried to forgive you. I've tried to love you again, but I just can't." Adam said as he turned around and continued to pack his bags. "Part of me knows that it may not really be your fault, but I can't change how I feel. I hate that I just don't love you anymore."

Adam's words cut through her, but the look on his face hurt her more. There was a complete absence of love, almost as though she were looking at someone completely different. Sophie's death had changed him, and the old, sweet, hopeful Adam had been buried with their beautiful baby.

Brynn had no defense.

She knew that Adam was partly right. "I'm sorry," was all Brynn could say.

Adam was leaving her for the second time, and this time she knew he wouldn't be back. She could tell by the look in his eyes. He was a changed man, and there was no trace left of the boy that she had fallen in love with.

But then again, the old Brynn had been dead and buried, too.

CHAPTER TWENTY ONE

Brynn and Ellie

The doorbell rang, startling Brynn.

Maxie took off toward the door, his nails clicking on the hardwood floors as he let out a deep bark and growl. He stood by the door waiting for Brynn to get there.

Shit! She thought looking out. It's her. What does she want?

She hadn't seen Ellie since the first time she saw her, standing at her door. *When I was pregnant... with Sophie.*

Brynn pushed down the sadness as she did hundreds of times a day. She turned around and looked at the house, the hallway littered with boxes.

Ellie stood, waiting patiently for Brynn to open the door.

"It's okay, boy," Brynn said to Maxie, patting him on the head. "Maybe if you're good, I'll let you bite her."

She opened the screen door a few inches. "What do you want?"

"Brynn," Ellie paused. She was shuffling her feet back and forth. "I uh... was hoping, that we could... uh, talk."

"Talk about what?" Brynn's voice had a hard edge to it.

Ellie peered hard at Brynn through the screen door. "I just want to talk to you, if you would let me."

Brynn hesitated. What does she want from me now?

She looked down at Maxie who looked at her blankly. "You're no help," she muttered.

She opened the door and stood to the side. Ellie walked by her and Brynn was surprised at how small she was. She was actually a few inches shorter than Brynn, and about ten pounds lighter. Brynn knew that she looked like Ellie, but not completely. What did my father look like?

Brynn walked in front of Ellie and led her to the living room. Brynn moved boxes off the couch and gestured for Ellie to sit.

"I'd offer you a drink, but I'm kind of busy. So if you could just tell me what you want, I would appreciate it." Brynn got straight to the point.

Ellie was tapping her foot.

"I, uh, am so sorry about your baby," Ellie said slowly.

"Okay. Thanks." Brynn said, impatiently. Brynn didn't think about Sophie, she couldn't think about Sophie. She knew that if she did, she would die. She blocked her out of her mind and refused to talk about her with anyone. "What else? That's not what you came here to say."

"No, but I wanted to say it." Ellie looked around the room. Everything was disheveled as Brynn was starting to pack, and Adam had already taken his belongings. "You're moving?"

"Yes. That's what happens when your husband no longer loves you, because he thinks you killed your baby."

Ellie took a sharp breath. "Oh, Brynn, I'm sorry."

"Don't be. You have nothing to do with it. But really, what do you want?" Brynn's face was hard, her brown eyes as black as coal.

"You're not making this easy, are you?" Ellie said, clearly getting frustrated.

"Why would I make it easy for you? Did you make it easy for me?" Brynn's anger was palpable.

"No. No, I didn't. I'm trying to fix things, though. I'm trying to make it right, now." Ellie's voice was weak, and Brynn felt an awkward surge of strength.

"Why now? I don't understand why you would bother, NOW?"

"Because, there is a lot at stake," Ellie said quietly.

Brynn looked at her suspiciously. Ellie's clothes were nice enough, Designer, Brynn thought. But it didn't fit with her dark teeth and her sallow skin. It didn't make sense. She wants something. But what?

Ellie took a deep breath. "I have a son. You have a brother."

Brynn froze. A brother? Oh my God, I have a brother?!

Brynn was silent. She looked at Ellie, her mouth open. She knew that she looked shocked, but she didn't care. "How... I mean, what happened? Where is he now?"

The mood of the room shifted, and Ellie knew that she had the advantage. Brynn had been playing hard to get, but now Ellie had something that Brynn wanted. Family.

"His name is Noah. And he can't wait to meet his sister," Ellie said, smiling at Brynn. "I know that I wasn't a mother to you, but I've done what I could do for him."

Brynn looked at Ellie and narrowed her eyes.

"Why? Why did you leave me?" Brynn sat next to her on the couch and stared evenly at her. She held her breath. She had always imagined herself asking the questions, but had never been able to imagine the answers.

"Do you really want to know?" Ellie hesitated. She knew that she was going to have to tell her, but she dreaded it. She wanted to cleanse herself of the truth, but she knew that it meant that Brynn might never want to see her again. She had been dreaming of this moment for almost thirty years, but now she wasn't sure that she could go through with it. "You will hate me."

"I already hate you," Brynn said instantly wishing she could take back the words when she saw Ellie's face fall instantly. "I'm sorry, I don't hate you. I hate myself."

Ellie's eyes filled with tears. She wanted to be high. She wanted to fade away and not to have to face Brynn. She realized that this is what she had been running from her entire life.

"I left you on the side of the road." Ellie went on to tell Brynn every detail that she could remember about the horrible night she had abandoned her, and of the years that followed. She talked without stopping for what felt like hours.

Brynn sat quietly, wringing her hands in her lap as she listened. She cried out in pain when Ellie told her about how little Eva ran after the car screaming for Ellie not to leave. But Ellie kept talking, almost as if she were in a trance. Ellie told Brynn about her life, about Noah, and about Dylan.

"What happened to my father?" Brynn asked when Ellie paused.

"He died. He was a bad man, and he died." Ellie said quietly. "I was messed up on every drug he could give me, and he died."

"What about now? Are you on drugs now?" Brynn asked angrily.

"No. I'm clean. I've been clean for five years," Ellie said, wincing from Brynn's anger. "I never meant to hurt you. I never wanted to hurt you. But I know that I did. I was a terrible mother. I know."

"How were you a mother to Noah if you've only been clean for five years? Surely he is older than five!" Brynn was confused.

"He's been in a home, getting the best of care. I've been able to visit him. It was the best place for him. Truly!" Ellie spoke quickly trying to convince Brynn with every breath.

There was silence as Ellie stopped talking. Brynn was taking it all in, replaying the information repeatedly in her mind. It doesn't make sense that she was coming to her now after all of this time. "Why are you here?" Brynn asked, refusing to let go of her suspicion.

"I'm here for you," Ellie said attempting to smile.

"But why now? How long have you known how to find me?"

Ellie stopped talking. "I've known for a long time."

"Then why, NOW?"

Ellie sighed. She knew that this part was going to be the hardest. Brynn will just think that I am using her, and she wouldn't be entirely wrong. "Noah and I are going to lose everything. But now that I've found you, it'll be okay. I can take care of him again, and everything is going to be fine."

"Why? Why are you going to lose everything?" Brynn asked curious.

"There are rules to the estate. Rules to the money. They thought you were dead, and now they know that you are alive, and so you have a right to some of the money." Ellie knew that she wasn't making sense. She was trying to explain it the best way that she could, but she knew that John was going to have to tell her about it.

"Estate? What estate are you talking about?" Brynn was getting frustrated. Ellie isn't what she appears after all! I knew it!

"My parent's estate. They were very wealthy. They've been gone for a very long time, and you are entitled to some of the money. Noah and I need you. Without you, we lose everything." Elli was trying not to sound desperate.

"How much money are we talking about?" Brynn said slowly, her mouth very dry.

Ellie paused. "Millions. Millions."

CHAPTER TWENTY -TWO

Carly's New Home

Petey's heart was broken.

After loving Carly for ten years, one day she woke up and something inside of her brain had changed. The doctor said she must have been experiencing mini strokes for years. Carly had been deteriorating for a long time, but now she was beyond the place where Lily could continue to take care of her.

Carly still looked the same on the outside, beautiful, tiny and fragile, her hair only slightly gray. But her brain was a scrambled mess of scattered memories from a different life, and the inability to retain anything from her current life.

"She needs to be in a home where she can be cared for properly," the doctor, a family friend of Petey's who never asked questions, told Petey and Lily when they called him to look at her. "Whatever happened to her is only going to get worse and not better. I can get her into a place a few towns over where nobody will question where she came from, or whom she is. But it's a couple of hours away."

Petey nodded. He knew that his life with her was never meant to be permanent, but she was the only woman he knew how to love. *I don't know how I'm going to let her go.*

After the doctor left, Lily looked at Petey, her gray eyes full of concern. Petey was closer than a brother, and his pain hurt her. "Are you okay?" she hesitated to ask him, she knew that he wouldn't want to talk about it.

"I'll be fine. I just need her to be taken care of," Petey said sadly. "This home that the doc is talking about is expensive. And she needs to go now. I don't know what to do, Lily. She needs more than what I can do. I ain't got that kind of money."

"I do," Lily said without hesitation.

"No you don't," Petey said. "You can't afford it any more than I can."

Lily's expression was one that he hadn't seen before.

"I can," Lily said her tone firm. "Daddy left me a lot of money. A lot. I've never told anyone, because I didn't want anyone to come after it. But I can afford it, and I'm going to."

Petey's eyes filled with tears. "But why? Why would you?"

"Why would I?" Lily couldn't believe that he didn't see it. "Before you brought her here, I was completely alone. But then she came and suddenly, I had a family. YOU became my brother, and she became my sister, and I haven't been lonely since. So I would do anything for her. And I would do anything for you."

Petey started to cry, and Lily realized that she had never seen this giant man cry before.

"It'll be okay. We will take turns visiting her, but it will be okay." Lily's heart was broken. Somehow, Lily knew that she would never get married, but having Carly with her made her not care anymore. She didn't want to go back to the solitary life she had before Carly and Petey came into her life.

"Its a few hours away, Lil. How often am I going to get to see her? And she may not even know me. So then what?" Petey was beginning to realize what it all meant.

"I don't know, Petey. But maybe this will mean that..." Lily hesitated. She never should have said anything. She knew Petey would be angry, and she wanted to kick herself for opening her mouth.

"What?" Petey asked, curious at Lily's expression.

"Nothing. I shouldn't have said anything."

"Maybe it will mean that I can have a family? I can get married? I can have a wife? Is that what you were going to say?" Petey asked quietly, almost guiltily. As much as he loved Carly, he knew that he could never have those things with her. It wouldn't be right after what he helped do to her husband. He wouldn't have felt right.

"Yes," Lily said. "That is what I was going to say. I'm sorry."

"Don't be sorry, Lil. I thought the same thing lots of times. I always wanted a family, kids to call me Daddy. I knew it wasn't going to be happy with Carly, but I just didn't care. I was trying to make up for what I did to her."

"But you loved her, and you took care of her, and she's been happy. You did make up for it," Lily put her hand on Petey's massive arm. "We need to get her packed."

Carly had been lying in the bed, half-awake, half-asleep. She stretched out her arms and looked at Petey.

"What are you doing?" she asked, yawning.

"I'm packing for you, sweetheart." Petey said trying to smile.

"Why? Where am I going?" Carly asked trying to sit up. Her head hurt, and she winced in pain.

"You're going to a hospital. You're going to live there where they can take care of you better," Lily said gently.

"Oh, James. What is wrong with me?"

Petey looked at Lily, his eyes wide. *Oh God. She thinks I'm James.* "James? Who is James?" Petey asked trying not to reveal the panic in his voice.

"My husband, of course, silly." Carly said smiling. "I don't want to go to the hospital. I want to stay here with my sister. I don't want to leave Lily."

Lily felt the tears welling up in her eyes. "This will be best for all of us, Carly. The hospital will be able to take care of you best. I don't want you to leave, either."

"Carly? Who is Carly? I'm Ellie."

CHAPTER TWENTY-THREE

Adam's Mess

Adam was hung over. Again.

The day in court to finalize the divorce was hard. It was much harder than he thought it would be. He almost didn't go. *If I don't go, maybe it won't be real. If I don't go, I can still change my mind. If I don't go, maybe I will wake up tomorrow and it'll all be a dream and Sophie won't be dead.*

When he finally did arrive in court, he was fifteen minutes late and smelled like gin and beer. The judge shook her head, but the process was short and painless. And then they were divorced.

It was easier than Adam thought it would be. No sobbing, no tearful good-byes. It was simple and short, and when it was over, it was over. It was very anticlimactic. And Adam felt let down, disappointed. He wanted Brynn to cry, he wanted Brynn to throw herself on the ground and beg him to reconsider. He wanted to see her suffer as he was suffering.

When it was done, he glared hard at her and left the courthouse, walking right into the closest bar. He didn't care that it was eleven in the morning. He didn't care that he was wearing the same clothes he had worn the night before.

After six Beefeater and tonics with lime, he felt much better. He felt clearer. The bartender was getting ready to cut him off, but Adam was tipping so well, he thought a few more might be fine.

A pretty young redhead sat down on the bar stool next to Adam, and he pretended not to notice.

"I'll have a Bloody Mary, spicy, top shelf," she said smiling at the bartender.

"Sure," The bartender said, smiling back.

"Bloody Mary? Have sssome gin," Adam slurred, grinning at her.

"No, thank you," she said, wrinkling her nose. He was handsome enough, but he was already drunk, and it was still light outside. Experience told her to stay away from men like him.

"Why? You got something against gin?" Adam said, slightly offended by her expression. "Or me?"

"No, no. You're fine," she said quickly, wishing she had sat down at a different place in the empty bar.

"Sssorry. Bad day," he said hanging his head.

She took pity on him. "It's okay," she said smiling sympathetically. "Let's start all over. I'm Jessie."

"Adam," he said putting out his hand to shake and accidentally hitting her in the head. "Oh God, I'm sorry."

Much to Adam's surprise, Jessie laughed.

"It's okay. You're a mess. Are you always this bad?" she said, resting her pretty face on her hand, gazing at him with sincere interest.

"No." Adam laughed for the first time since he could remember. "I got divorced today."

"Oh, I'm sorry," Jessie said, immediately sorry for dismissing him so fast. "That must be difficult."

"Yeahhhh," Adam said taking a drink of gin & tonic number seven. "It sucked."

They talked for a while, and by five p.m. Adam was drinking water and messily eating a greasy Rueben. Jessie found herself drawn to him. At first, she thought it was because he reminded her of a stray puppy, but then she started to think that it was because she really may like him. She didn't usually drink so early in the day, but she was supposed to be meeting a guy from the night before who was a no show.

"Can I see you again?" Adam said, not sure of what he was

doing. *You just got divorced today. What in the hell are you doing?*

"I don't know," Jessie said, smiling a beautiful toothy smile. "I think you have a lot to work out, with the divorce and all. You may not even want to talk to me when you are sober."

"I haven't been sober for months. So it won't really matter," Adam said, a little embarrassed.

"Oh, great. In that case, we're definitely meant to just be friends." Jessie smiled again, and Adam thought that he hadn't ever met anyone who smiled so much.

The bar was getting crowded with the after work crowd, and their daytime bartender had ended his shift a couple of hours prior. There was a young girl with a short skirt and tight top running the length of the bar, missing half of the people in front of her who needed drinks. Adam only cared that his and Jessie's drinks were full as they talked well into the night.

The next morning, Adam woke up face down on the bathroom floor. The tile was cool on his cheek, but the pounding in his head made him want to kill himself. "Shit!" he said groggily, his voice hoarse.

He looked in the toilet. Fuck. That sucks. Adam hated throwing up.

He washed off his face letting the cool water revive him a little. Thank God, I took a couple of days off work to get my shit together.

He stumbled into the kitchen, his dry throat begging for something wet. But his stomach promised him that it wouldn't keep much down. Adam tried to remember the night before. There was a girl. There wasn't usually a girl. No matter how drunk he was, he didn't usually mess with the girls. The only girl he had ever been with had been Brynn, but since he couldn't love her anymore, he couldn't imagine himself with anyone else.

He chugged a glass of cold water and immediately regretted it as it came up as quickly as it went down. *SHIT!*

Adam was angry. He felt angry often. All of the time, actually. He didn't want to be angry, but there was no other emotion he felt at home in anymore. He wanted a family with Brynn for so long, and when the time finally came, it was taken from him far too quickly. He blamed Brynn. He knew that it wasn't right, but he blamed her anyway, and no matter how hard he tried, he couldn't stop.

He splashed cold water on his face, over and over.

He stumbled around his apartment. He hated it. He missed his big house. He stared at the bare walls. He hated it.

Shit.

Suddenly he heard a sound. A groan?

What the hell? He froze. *Where was I last night? How did I get home?*

He heard it again. A small, almost imperceptible groan. *Shit! Who is that? What did I do?*

He stumbled into the bedroom, trying to focus his eyes. The room was dark. There was nothing in his bedroom except for his bed and a bunch of boxes. He hadn't even bothered to unpack. He had been living there for months, but he couldn't bring himself to take anything out of the boxes. All he had unpacked were his clothes, as he needed them, which were mostly all over the floor.

The room was dark and he squinted trying to find the source of the noise.

There!

He stared at the bed and saw a perfectly naked girl laying there, twisted in the blankets, red hair spilling over her beautiful ivory skin.

Oh, shit. What did I do?

He looked down at himself and realized for the first time that he was naked.

He looked up and saw a big pair of beautiful green eyes staring at him.

"Hi," the pretty red head said bashfully.

"Hi." he said feeling embarrassed.

"How are you feeling?" the pretty girl said, her voice hoarse, sounding concerned.

"Like Shit," he said, smiling wryly.

"Me, too," she said smiling back at him, her pretty teeth perfect and white.

They stared at each other, both unsure of what to say.

"Do you remember anything?" the girl said, pulling the sheet up around her naked chest.

"Not really. You?" Adam said wishing he could disappear, his head feeling as if it were going to explode.

"Some," the girl said, her cheeks turning red.

"Um... what is your name?" Adam hated asking. He didn't know what else to say.

"Jessie."

"I'm Adam."

"I know," Jessie said, knowing that he didn't remember who she was. She looked at Adam's naked body and remembered how he had cried in her arms. They had just lain together in their nakedness; neither of them able to do anything more than just hold tightly onto one another. She loved lying next to him, staring at him.

Adam felt ashamed. He had never done anything like this before and wasn't sure what to do next. She looked like a perfectly nice girl—too young for him, but beautiful.

"I don't remember much from last night. I had a bad day, yesterday."

"I know. It's okay. I've had a lot of bad yesterdays," Jessie said smiling again. "Come, lay with me."

Adam hesitated. He wanted to be alone. But something about her made him want to lie next to her, too.

"Come. I won't bite you," she said pulling the sheet around her, covering her body up. "Besides, you need to sleep and so do I. I promise I won't do anything to you."

I have never been in bed next to anyone but Brynn. But Brynn is gone now, forever. She will never be with me again.

Adam felt the tears welling in his eyes.

He walked slowly to the bed and laid down, his head pounding, his body stiff from lying on the hard bathroom floor. He needed sleep.

He laid down, pulling the sheet over him. Jessie snuggled up next to him, and he could feel her warm flesh against his. Her even breathing made him relax as he felt her warm breasts on his back, her arms wrapped around him. Her body was nestled against him, and he felt immediately at ease.

For the first time in a long time, Adam didn't feel completely alone.

He closed his eyes, and he drifted off to sleep, his mind deliciously blank.

CHAPTER TWENTY-FOUR

Million Dollar Baby

"Millions? Millions?" Brynn was beside herself.

"Yes, millions. Actually, more than millions," Ellie said matter of factly.

"Who are you that you have that kind of money?" Brynn asked, completely stunned.

"The question you should be asking is 'Who am I?'" Ellie said, almost as though she had rehearsed this.

"Okay. Then who am I?" Brynn asked, not sure that she wanted to know the answer.

"You are Eva. Granddaughter of James and Amy Harper. Harper Enterprises? I think you know about Harper Enterprises," Ellie said as Brynn noticed a trace of pride in her voice. "Of course, you'll need a DNA test, but I've assured them that you are the real deal."

Brynn stared at Ellie, her big brown eyes much larger than usual. "How can this be?"

"It's easy," Ellie sighed as she hated explaining the details. "I am their daughter. You are the granddaughter. They went missing years ago, presumed dead. I have a son who is you're half-brother, Noah. Noah needs constant care and can't be on his own. He has the mental capacity of a five year old, though you will clearly see that he is much older than that."

"So why did you even bother to tell me about the money? You

could have pretended like I didn't even exist and kept it all to yourself." Brynn wondered what Ellie wanted from her.

Ellie paused.

"You're right. I could have just pretended that you didn't exist. But I have more money than I need. And when I'm gone, Noah will need someone to look out for him, to visit him, to explain things to him, and help take care of him. I'm the only family he has now, and he needs someone else in his life."

"What do you mean? He needs someone else in his life?" Brynn was confused.

"He needs family. A mother. A sister. People who understand him, who will take care of him. The money provides for his physical needs, but he needs more. God knows I've been a shitty mother, but this is the one thing I can do for him." Ellie was tired of all of the explaining. She just wanted to go home and medicate so that she didn't have to think of anything else.

"You're young so you'll be around for a while. Why now? Why not wait?" Brynn felt like she was being set up. She couldn't figure out what Ellie wanted no matter how hard she tried.

"You never know what will happen in life," Ellie said, her voice low and distant. "Like I said, I haven't done much right in this world. This is the only thing I can think of to do that can possibly buy me some decent karma."

"So you just assumed that I would do it? That I would step in for you after what you did to me? Why would I take care of a brother I have never met when YOU abandoned me?" Brynn's voice was rising, and Ellie took a step backwards.

"I-I-I just thought you would want to know your family," Ellie stuttered.

"Why would I want my family when my family didn't want me? Why in the hell would I want you when you dropped me off on the side of the road like a piece of garbage?" Brynn was furious, her hands clenching uncontrollably.

"It wasn't like that Eva... I mean Brynn. It wasn't like that. I didn't mean to... I was just really messed up at the time. I'm just not a good person. I've made horrible, horrible choices." Ellie was pleading with her.

"You are not a good person! You're not even a person. I don't know how you can even live with yourself. What kind of person leaves their child by the side of the road?" Brynn felt her face getting hot. She had dreamed of this moment her entire life, and now that it was here, she wasn't sure if she would be able to find the words. "You left me! And then you left your son in a home for other people to take care of! You're not even a mother at all! You don't even take care of him. I can't even imagine what happened to my father, or to Noah's father, but neither of them are obviously in the picture anymore."

"You don't want to know, and you're right." Ellie stood up to leave. "I know that it's a lot to take in, Brynn. I know that you hate me, and you have every right to, but I'm just thinking of what's best for Noah now. And that will be you, his sister, one day."

Brynn turned around and refused to look at her birth mother. She had been staring at Ellie in shock and disbelief. But mostly Brynn was stunned by how much she resembled Ellie. She was even more surprised by how secretly pleased she was by the resemblance. Brynn hated that even after everything Ellie had done and how so much time had passed, she still wanted this woman to love and need her. And now, here she was telling her that she needed her, and Brynn needed to fight it. Fight Ellie.

"I'm leaving my number for you. I'll wait for you to call me. I want you to meet Noah." Brynn heard Ellie set something on the end table, and then she heard the sound of her footsteps walking away, and the sound of the door opening and closing behind her. She didn't turn around until she knew that she was gone. She didn't want Ellie to see the tears cascading down her face.

Brynn picked up the card with her name and phone number on it. She took a picture of it with her phone and slowly tore the card up, piece by piece.

A brother! Family!

She thought about Noah. *How old is he? What does he look like? Would he even care that I'm his sister?*

I wish I could tell Adam! Adam would know what to do. Adam would help me.

Brynn felt a pain deep in her chest. It didn't matter how many times a day she thought about Adam, it was never going to change for her. Adam was gone and so was her baby, Sophie.

Brynn had enough for the day. She took a sleeping pill that her doctor had prescribed and laid down in her bed. Maxie was happy for any excuse to be on the bed, and snuggled as close to her as he could. Brynn closed her eyes praying desperately that sleep would overtake her as quickly as possible.

CHAPTER TWENTY-FIVE

Noah's New Friend

"Noah! It's time for lunch!" Kelly the pretty caregiver called out for him.

Noah liked this time of day. Lunch was his favorite time, and they were having his favorite food—hot dogs and macaroni and cheese. He had been looking forward to today's lunch all week.

"Lunch!!" Noah cried out, enthusiastically as he ran to his chair throwing his tall, lean body into it.

"What do we say about running, Noah?" Kelly said chiding him with a smile.

"No running! Sorry," Noah said, hanging his head. His dark brown hair falling into his glittering green eyes.

"It's okay. I just don't want you to get hurt, silly!" Kelly smiled. Noah was her favorite patient, and she loved working with him every day. Noah reminded her of her younger brother whom she missed terribly and who was away at college. *I wish that Noah had a normal life so that he could be away at college now, too.*

"Okay, Kelly!" Noah's smile reappeared instantly as he stared down at his hot dog. "Ketchup, please!"

"Ketchup?" Kelly said giving him a funny look. "You don't like ketchup!"

"I know, I was just teasing!" Noah smiled at her again and then took a big bite of his plain hot dog. "Is my Mommy coming today?" he asked with his mouth full.

"I don't know, Noah. Please don't talk with your mouth full," Kelly said, dreading having to answer the same question every day. "I haven't heard anything, and she usually calls when she is coming. I'm sorry, buddy, but I don't think she will be here today."

Noah's face fell. It had been forty-seven days since he saw his mommy last, and he missed her. He was keeping count on the calendar even though Kelly told him that he shouldn't.

Kelly shook her head, trying to mask her annoyance. *Why wouldn't she come see him? He doesn't even need to be here! She could take care of him at home with help, if she ever wanted to. He's such a joy!* Kelly knew that when she had children of her own one day, she would never abandon them or leave them, as Noah's mother had. She was raised in a close-knit family, and she couldn't imagine not being with her own child when the time came.

"Okay," Noah said, chewing slowly, trying to remember not to talk with his mouth full. He took a sip of his drink and swallowed carefully. "It's been forty-seven days since I've seen Mommy, Kelly. That's a long time."

"I know, buddy." Kelly said smiling warmly at him, her pretty face making him forget his sadness. "Let's finish lunch, and we will go make a new friend."

Noah liked this game. Kelly would take him around and introduce him to people that he didn't know yet. People were always coming and going there. When someone left, someone always took their place. Noah liked where he lived. He always got to make new friends.

When Noah was done eating, he cleaned up his tray like Kelly had taught him and washed his hands carefully. He didn't want to spread germs and make people sick, so he was always careful to wash his hands, and he did so lots of time during the day.

"I'm ready," He said cheerfully. "Where are we going?"

"Let's just go for a walk, and we'll see who we find." Kelly said happily. She loved watching Noah meet new people. He was so friendly and easy to talk to, and the older residents loved meeting him, even the grumpy ones.

They walked down a long walkway for a while past the beautiful green lawn and a large koi pond. There was a woman sitting at the koi pond feeding the fish.

"Hi!" Noah said, walking right up to her and extending his hand. "I'm Noah."

"Hi." The woman said, surprised. She looked at Noah with curiosity. He seemed familiar to her, but she didn't know why. She took his hand slowly and shook it.

Kelly looked at her with curiosity. She doesn't appear to be very old. I wonder what her story is.

"Are you new?" Noah asked standing too close to her wheelchair. The woman was visibly uncomfortable and wheeled herself back slightly.

"Yes, I'm new," the woman said smiling nervously.

"I'm not. I've been here for a long time. Since I was three. I love it here," Noah said happily. "But I live in a different part of the building. This part is for old people."

"Noah!" Kelly scolded. "Don't be rude."

"I'm sorry! I meant..." Noah was embarrassed. He usually had better manners than that.

"It's okay," the woman said graciously. "Why have you been here for so long?"

"My Mommy can't take care of me," Noah said sadly.

"Oh, I'm sorry." The woman said, immediately feeling bad for him.

"That's okay. I like it here," Noah repeated. "Do you have any kids?"

"I don't know. I don't think so," she said squirming in her chair. She wasn't used to such direct questions from a stranger. This one was young, and he wanted to know a lot. The only reason she was talking to him was that he seemed familiar.

Kelly watched Noah and the woman with deep interest. Aside from their eye color, they had a strange strong physical resemblance and a few of the same mannerisms. *Am I crazy? Am I really seeing this? Who is this woman?*

"Why don't you know?" Noah asked the woman, not realizing that he was over stepping the line.

"Why do you ask so many questions?" the woman said, visibly annoyed.

Noah was sad. He didn't mean to make the nice lady mad at him. "I'm sorry. I just like to make new friends."

The woman looked at Noah. He was in his late teens, tall, with dark brown hair and beautiful green eyes. His eyes were a little too close together, but otherwise the woman thought he had a handsome face. She could tell that he was a nice boy, and she felt drawn to him in a strange way. But she was uncomfortable with the questions he asked. *Why does he want to know so much about me?*

"Well, you shouldn't ask people so many questions. It's rude," the woman said scolding him gently.

"I wasn't trying to be rude," he said his voice quiet. "I'm sorry if that I bothered you."

He turned around and started to walk away.

The woman realized that she didn't really want him to go.

"Wait, young man," she said, calling after him. "I don't want you to leave."

Noah turned around slowly. He looked at Kelly and she nodded at him, smiling. She could see why the woman was drawn to him. It was the same reason that everyone was drawn to him. His energy and enthusiasm made Noah hard to let go of.

"Okay!" Noah said brightly. He skipped back to the woman, happy that she changed her mind.

"Wheel me around," she ordered curtly.

Noah grabbed the handles of the wheelchair and pushed her slowly down the walkway.

Noah was careful not to talk. He figured she probably was tired of him asking questions. They walked on for a while in silence, with Kelly trailing behind them.

"Where did you come from, young man?" the woman asked.

"I used to live an hour from here, in a big house. But my Mommy couldn't take care of me," Noah said looking at the woman with serious brown eyes. "So I came to live here when I was three. They've taken care of me ever since I was little."

"So you like living here?" the woman asked, enjoying the sound of his voice.

"Yes. They give me ice cream, and we eat hot dogs. They are nice to me here. Especially Kelly." Noah said happily.

"That's good," the woman said smiling. "I like hot dogs."

"I think we can be friends," the woman said after they had walked on for a little while in silence. "But don't ask me a lot of questions. I don't know anything about myself."

"Nothing?" Noah asked, curious.

"Not much," the woman said, a trace of sadness in her voice.

"Why not?" Noah was hesitant, but he wanted to know why his new friend couldn't remember anything.

"I got hurt a long time ago, somehow. It hurt my brain, I think. And now I get headaches, and I can't sleep, and I can't remember anything."

"How did you get hurt?" Noah remembered the last time he got a boo-boo and he shuddered. He hated getting hurt.

"I don't know. I just know that my head got hurt. I think it shook my brain," the older woman laughed. "At least I know that I have one."

Noah smiled. "I have a brain, but it doesn't work good."

"What do you mean?" the woman asked puzzled.

"I'm not too smart." Noah said sadly. "Not like other boys my age."

"You seem smart to me," the woman said smiling at him for the first time. "You seem very smart."

Noah thought the woman was pretty when she smiled.

"Thank you," Noah said smiling back. Nobody had ever called him smart before. Especially not a new friend. "That's why my Mommy didn't want to take care of me. She didn't want a stupid kid."

"I'm sure that's not true at all," the woman said, patting his hand gently. She was enjoying their walk more than she thought she would.

Noah had a thought.

"What is your name? I know all of my friend's names. Andy, Steven, Kelly, Susan, Bob, Carol, Brian, Joe, Charlie…"

"My name is Carly," the woman said smiling at his long list. "Just call me Carly."

CHAPTER TWENTY-SIX

The Handsome Stranger

Brynn was on a mission to try to work a lot. Jane kept trying to send her home, but Brynn needed to do something.

"I haven't spent much time here, with the pregnancy and all, so it's time that I get caught up," she told Jane stubbornly.

"Yes, but that's why you pay me, and that's why you pay Lucia. We take care of all of these things for you." Jane was beside herself. After running the restaurant by herself for so long, Brynn was interrupting the flow.

"I know. But I have to do something." Brynn said, understanding what Jane was trying to say. "This is different than the first time that Adam left. I know he's not coming back. I know that I can't just lie in bed and lose myself as I did before. I have to work."

Brynn felt like she was going crazy. She couldn't stand to be home, staring at the empty rooms. She had cleaned most of them as the realtor came in and out with perspective buyers. The nursery was the first room to be boxed up with everything put away. The only livable rooms were the bedroom, the kitchen, and the sitting room. Otherwise, everything was in boxes, neatly lining the walls of the garage.

Maxie was beside himself locked in the back sunroom, but Brynn couldn't let him roam like he usually did. Brynn kept telling herself that it was temporary, and that it wouldn't last forever. *I have to get rid of the house. Every corner, every room reminds of him. Smells like him. I have to get out of this house!*

"You've been through a traumatic experience Brynn, both physically and emotionally. You need to make sure that you understand that and don't push it." Jane was concerned for her friend. At least this time, Brynn remained upright and functional every day. Jane was thankful for that.

"I know," Brynn said with a half-hearted smile. "That's why I'm here, to distract myself."

"Well, maybe you should stick to cooking or something else. You're driving Luis a little crazy," Jane said, smiling. Luis was the head prep cook, and he set the specials for the day. He was complaining to Jane about Brynn stepping on his toes, and it had only been a week.

Brynn was annoyed. If it weren't for her, Luis wouldn't even have a job. But part of her understood. She hadn't been hands-on in the kitchen for well over a year now, and Luis had been doing a very good job.

Brynn tried to smile. "I just need to do something."

"I know you do," Jane said hugging her friend. They had seen each other through a lot, and Jane wondered when Brynn was ever going to catch a break. "Why don't you come in tomorrow, get back into some of the book keeping, and work through breakfast?"

Brynn smiled gratefully. The restaurant and Maxie were all that she had now. Brynn had repeatedly tried calling Ellie, but she didn't return her calls. She knew that she shouldn't be disappointed, but she had been looking forward to possibly meeting her brother, after all.

After another sleepless night, Brynn came in the next morning at three a.m., and set to work. She was happy to let Jane have the day off to spend with the girls. The restaurant opened at six for breakfast and Brynn was surprised at how quickly the morning flew by. Lucia still worked a few mornings a week when she wasn't taking morning classes and was happy to see Brynn so early.

"How are you?" Lucia asked her beautiful cocoa brown eyes full of concern. Lucia knew what it was like to lose a child, only she had given hers up for adoption. There wasn't a day that went by that she didn't miss her and say a prayer for her baby.

"I'm okay," Brynn said attempting to put on a brave face. It had been a year since she lost Sophie and she still grieved, but losing Adam was still very fresh in her mind. "I miss them," she whispered.

"I know," Lucia said sympathetically. "I miss my baby, too."

They hugged each other and held each other for a long moment. Brynn pulled back first and wiped her eyes. She didn't want the employees to see her cry.

"I guess we should help the girls clean this mess up, huh?" she said, all business.

Lucia nodded her head, and they set to work getting ready for the lunch crowd.

The restaurant had cleared out after the breakfast rush, but there were still a few people coming and going throughout the morning. Most of the faces Brynn knew, but she was happy to see that there were many new ones.

As the door opened, Brynn looked up and felt her breath catch for a second. She turned away quickly, embarrassed.

It had been a long time since anyone had caught her off guard like that, nobody since Adam. Nobody ever, not since Adam. The man sat down at the small wooden breakfast counter and opened a menu.

Brynn was nervous. She looked around for Lucia or Gertie, but nobody was around. Crap. I'm going to have to go up to him. She paused for a moment, but nobody appeared to rescue her.

You're an idiot. It's just a man. No big deal. You talk to men every day. You can do this, Brynn. Brynn didn't know why this man made her so nervous. He was tall, with chestnut colored hair. And when he walked, Brynn could tell that he was sure of himself.

He probably knows how good looking he is, too. Brynn decided she didn't like him. *He's probably arrogant.*

He was looking around for someone to help him.

Crap, where are Lucia and Gertie?! Dammit!

Brynn walked over to him slowly. "Hi, would you like some

coffee?"

He looked at her, his hazel eyes lighting up as he smiled. "Sure. Thank you."

He's nice. Dammit!

"Would you like to order?" Brynn asked using her most professional tone.

"Sure," he said looking down at the menu.

Brynn stood and waited as he read down through each page. *Why does the menu have to be four pages?*

"Okay. Got it," he said enthusiastically as he looked up at her. "Three eggs, over easy, wheat toast, hash browns, two sides of sausage, two sides of bacon, two buttermilk pancakes, and some corned beef hash."

"Wow!" Brynn said, in spite of herself.

The man laughed. "I know. I just flew in at two a.m., and there was nothing open, so I'm starving!"

"Well, I'll get that in for you right away, then," Brynn said, amused. He was built like he was athletic, but she hadn't expected him to order that much food.

Brynn rang in the order and a few seconds later, Lucia came out of the kitchen. "Is your guest count right on this, Brynn? Is this really for one person?"

Brynn looked over at the man sitting at the counter drinking his coffee.

"Oh my," Lucia whispered, following Brynn's gaze. "He's... he's...."

"I know," Brynn said quietly, trying not to stare.

Lucia smiled. She couldn't remember a time when Brynn ever looked at a man. Even though everyone knew that she loved Adam, Lucia also knew they had their problems. She wanted Brynn to be happy. Brynn was like a sister to her, and she couldn't remember ever seeing her completely happy. It was nice to see her mooning over a stranger.

"You should talk to him," Lucia said casually.

"No way!" Brynn said, her cheeks turning red. She had been working all morning after not getting any sleep, and wasn't feeling very attractive at the moment. "I look horrible."

"You look beautiful, like you always do," Lucia scolded her. "Turn around, he's calling for you."

Brynn turned around, and the handsome man was gesturing for her to come over. She smoothed her hair and tried to compose herself, feeling a strange nervousness in her belly.

"Did you need more coffee?" she asked politely.

"Yes. I mean no. I just wanted to know what there is to do in this city? I'm going to be here for a month or so for business, and I want to get my bearings. I'm assuming that you live here?" he smiled again, and Brynn felt a little out of sorts. "I'm Nicholas... Nick, by the way."

She sat and chatted with him and was surprised at how easy it was to talk to him. She tried to leave when his food came, but he insisted that she keep talking. Brynn forgot her nervousness and chatted away about all of the touristy things in the city that there were to do, until suddenly she realized that the lunch crowd had come in full force, and the restaurant was hopping.

"Oh, I'm sorry. I have to help out," she said jumping up and apologizing. She hadn't ever been that caught up in conversation that she didn't know what was going on around her. The hazel and gold in his eyes kept distracting her, as well as his laugh. She immediately felt guilty.

"I'm sorry," he said looking worried. "Will your boss be mad?"

Brynn laughed. "I'm the boss."

Nick was stunned and then he smiled a teasing smile. "So you mean, this whole time I was sitting here talking to the boss, and I didn't know it? Wow. Your employees must think you're pretty lazy."

"Yes. They hate me." Brynn smiled back. She couldn't remember having this much fun talking to someone in a long time.

"What are you doing tonight?" Nick asked, suddenly serious.

Brynn stood up. "Um, hanging out with my dog, watching Lifetime movies. He's a big fan."

"Why don't you hang out with me? I don't watch Lifetime movies, but I am fun to spend time with."

Brynn hesitated. *Why would he want to hang out with me? Who does he think that I am?*

"Don't say no. I'm going to the restroom, and I expect you to be here when I get back telling me what time to pick you up." As Nick stood up, Brynn realized that he was taller than she originally thought—at least six foot two. Brynn felt her breath catch again. He was casual in jeans and a t-shirt, but she liked the easy way that his body moved. Adam was the only man she had ever been interested in, and Nick definitely unnerved her.

I can't do this. I can't spend time with him. I don't know who he thinks I am, but I'm not someone who just hangs out.

Nick walked into the bathroom and washed his hands. He stared at himself in the mirror and tried to smile. *Damn, I've aged. I look like terrible.*

He thought about Brynn and smiled. She intrigued him. She was the first woman to catch his eye in a long time. She's funny, but so tentative. She can turn it on and off in a blink.

Nick thought about the past couple of years and how he needed to spend some time with someone who could make him laugh. He had spent time with a lot of women, but none he saw more than once. This one, I would come back to see. This Brynn could be worth it.

But when Nick got back from the bathroom, Brynn was nowhere to be found.

CHAPTER TWENTY-SEVEN

Jessie's Love

Jessie was in love with Adam. She knew it would happen even though she fought it. He was a mess, but she found herself in love with him anyway.

She knew he still loved Brynn, but she ignored it and pretended as though he were in love with her instead. Even when he cried Brynn's name out in the middle of the night, or called her "Brynn" when he was so drunk that he couldn't remember the next day, Jessie forgave him. *He's been through a lot.*

When he was sober, he was good to her, but he couldn't remain sober very long.

"Oh baby, I'm sorry," he said his blue eyes filling with tears.

"It's okay," Jessie said kissing his cheek. "I know you didn't mean to forget my birthday. You've been going through a lot."

"It's no excuse. We've been together for seven months, and I shouldn't have forgotten." Adam was angry with himself. He had never forgotten Brynn's birthday, and Jessie was so sweet to him. She was so good, and he had completely forgotten. He had gone to the bar right after work for Friday happy hour, and he didn't even know how he had gotten home.

Jessie was trying hard not to care.

"You shouldn't have forgotten. But you can make it up to me," she smiled that toothy smile at him.

"How? How can I make it up to you?" Adam was miserable. He was failing in every way, and he hated himself.

"You can take me out tonight," Jessie said brightly.

"I would love to. But I can't. My parents are in town." Adam was dreading dinner with his parents. They hadn't been close for a very long time, and he had been avoiding them for as long as he could.

Jessie moved a little closer to him. "Well... I could go with you," she said hesitantly. "That is, if you think it would be a good idea."

Adam stepped away. "Oh no. I don't think that would be a good idea at all. You wouldn't have fun. You would hate it!"

Jessie frowned. "Am I not good enough to meet your parents?"

"Of course, you are," Adam said quickly wishing he had a shot. "It's just them. They loved Brynn, and honestly, I just don't think that anyone will ever measure up for them. I don't think that they're ready."

Jessie was getting angry now. "All you do is talk about Brynn. But you left her, *twice!* And now, you have me, and you don't even care that you have me."

Shit! Adam was frustrated. *I wasn't ready for a relationship, and this is why. What am I doing?* "Baby, it's not about Brynn, or about you. It's about my parents being frustrated with me. Me! Please stop doing this."

"Stop doing what? Expecting, demanding, needing?" Jessie's arms were crossed and Adam thought she looked adorable.

"You look so hot when you're mad," he said grabbing her and kissing her neck. He felt her body loosen up a little, and Adam knew that she wasn't going to stay mad at him for long.

"Stop it," she said half-heartedly pushing him away.

"I can't," Adam mumbled grabbing her and pulling her toward him. "You just make me want you when you look like that."

Jessie tried to fight him off, but she knew that it just made things more exciting. She didn't really want him to go away, but she did want to meet his parents. "You just want me when you want sex."

"That's not true. But I do want you for sex. I want you for other things, too. Just don't push me baby." Adam was too busy with straps and pulling off clothes to continue arguing with her.

Jessie felt her body give into him as it usually did.

She loved him, and there was nothing that either of them could do about it.

CHAPTER TWENTY-EIGHT

Clarity

Brynn knelt at the tiny gravestone. The fall air was cool at dusk and Brynn had forgotten her jacket. But she didn't care.

She tried to make it to visit Sophie as often as she could. She couldn't bear the thought of her being all alone, and Brynn needed to talk to her to help clear her head. She knew it was silly, but the shrink said that if it made her feel better, she should do it.

"I don't know why I just ran, but I couldn't help it." Brynn said, reflecting back on the day's events. "I haven't ever been with anyone since your daddy, and I just didn't know what to do."

She thought about Nick, the guy from the restaurant, who had looked at her in such a way that her insides felt like jelly. She hadn't felt like that since she was fifteen, and Adam was passing her notes in class. Even then, it had been different. Young, innocent. She had never had a stranger make her feel that way before.

"I know that I shouldn't have run away. I should have stayed. I should have made a new friend. The shrink says that I should be open to meeting new people, making new friends, blah, blah, blah." Brynn made a face as she pulled her dark hair back. She liked her shrink, but she was tired of seeing him every other week. *I've been in therapy all my life. When am I going to be normal? When can I stop?*

Brynn sat, caressing the smooth stone with her fingers. "Sophie, Sophie, Sophie. Why did you leave me? Why did you have to go so soon?" Brynn felt the pain welling up in her chest. *Just let it out, let it go. There's no one here to see. You can just cry.*

The tears fell silently down her cheeks, but Brynn refused to make a sound. *If I make a noise, I will scream. I will scream, and I will never stop screaming.*

The tears were so hot that Brynn thought she would see steam coming off her cold cheeks. She cursed herself for forgetting a jacket for the hundredth time. *I really need to start keeping one in my car.*

Brynn sat in silence for what felt like an hour. She didn't want to go back to the restaurant. She didn't want to go to the empty house that wasn't going to be hers anymore. She had nowhere to go and no one to see.

"I should be going home to you and to your Daddy," Brynn said softly. "But all that I have left now is Maxie. How did this become my life? How did I get to be so alone?"

The silence around her resonated, and Brynn felt the temperature dropping rapidly. She wanted to stay, but her fingers were turning numb. She stood up hating to leave. "I'll be back tomorrow, sweet girl. Mommy loves you." Brynn kissed her fingers and touched the smooth stone, imagining for one second that she was kissing Sophie's sweet face.

When she got in the car to warm up, she realized there was a message on her phone.

"Brynn-You left your purse at the restaurant. Again. XO, Jane"

"Damn." Brynn hated how forgetful she was becoming. She sighed and turned her car toward the restaurant.

When she walked in, Jane met her at the door.

"Look who came back," Jane said with a sly smile as she motioned toward one of the booths.

"Oh no," Brynn said, horrified.

Nick was sitting in the booth wearing a hunter green sweater and jeans. Brynn knew without getting close that the sweater would bring out the green in his eyes, and she felt her stomach flip flop without her permission.

"I've been at t-t-the..." Brynn stuttered.

"I know where you've been. You only go to two places and home. Here is your purse. Now go into your office and clean yourself up." Jane ordered.

Brynn looked at Jane helplessly. "I don't know how to do this."

Jane grabbed Brynn and pulled her into Brynn's office. "There is nothing to it. Just talk. Just be yourself. Don't you want to be happy?"

"He lives out of town. There's no point."

"Brynn, honey. You don't have to marry him. You don't have to sleep with him. Just talk to him. Make a new friend." Jane was smiling but Brynn could tell she was getting frustrated with her.

"I don't know if I can be happy. Look at my life. I don't even know if I want to be happy."

Jane pulled out a comb from Brynn's desk drawer, and started combing through Brynn's gnarled hair. "I don't even know what to say to that. If you want to be miserable all of your life, I can't make you do anything else. But Brynn, you have to start making some choices. Adam is gone for good. He is never coming back."

"I know," Brynn said wincing. "Stop combing my hair, I'm not five. I can do it!"

Jane smiled. "You have five minutes. He just ordered, and he's asked about you five times already. You should have seen his face when he came back from the bathroom and you were gone."

Brynn winced again. "I felt bad about that."

"You should have," Jane said as she headed toward the door. "Five minutes and then I'm coming in for you. And don't even think about sneaking out."

Brynn sighed. She went into the tiny bathroom and looked at herself in the mirror. *Bags! From crying, I knew it!*

She frantically pulled out her makeup bag and went to work.

After a couple of minutes, she looked into the mirror and smiled. *Well, better. But not great.* She looked at her long dark hair. It was in desperate need of a cut, and there wasn't much that could be done with it other than comb it and smooth it out a little. *Oh no, five minutes are up.*

Brynn walked into the hallway toward the dining room and took a deep breath. *Deep breaths, deep breaths.* She spotted the back of Nick's head and approached him slowly.

"Hey, there," Brynn said, trying to sound casual.

He looked up just as he was putting a huge bite of mashed potatoes in his mouth, and smiled.

"Oh, hi, Houdini," he said, smirking.

Brynn blushed. "I'm sorry."

Nick stood up, towering over her. Brynn forgot how tall he was. "Please, sit down."

Brynn looked around the dining room. The late dinner crowd was slower than usual, which Brynn was grateful for, because she knew that if it were busy that she wouldn't be able to relax.

She sat down, feeling awkward.

"We don't have to stay here if you don't want to," Nick said, as if he were reading her mind.

"Oh no. It's fine," Brynn said eyeing his plate. "Besides, you've hardly eaten anything."

Nick laughed, and Brynn thought for a second how much she liked his laugh.

"I've been eating here all day. I only left for a few hours, then I came back for lunch, and then I came back for dinner."

"I thought you had to work?" Brynn said, feeling very guilty.

"I had a meeting after lunch," Nick smiled. Brynn felt herself getting lost in his smile, and tried desperately to look away without being too obvious.

"Seriously, I'm stuffed. Let's go somewhere else," Nick said pulling out his wallet.

"Oh, no! I'll have Jane take care of your dinner. It's the least I can do since you are now a part of our frequent diner program," Brynn said putting her hand on his before she could stop herself, and then abruptly pulling it away.

"Thank you. I suppose it's the least you could do since you Houdini'd me earlier," Nick teased making Brynn blush again. "Well, where to?"

Brynn thought for a moment and her mind was blank. She rarely went out, and the first place that came to her mind was the restaurant where she and Adam had their last anniversary dinner, which felt like a century ago. Brynn shook her head trying to erase the memory.

"Are you okay?" Nick asked concerned.

"I'm fine. I just... don't know where to go," Brynn said embarrassed.

Nick stood up and disappeared for a moment. He came back and grabbed Brynn's hand pulling her from the seat. She was pleasantly surprised at the boldness of the gesture, and how it made her heart pound.

"Where are we going?" Brynn asked as he pulled her out of the door.

"That's for me to know and for you to find out," Nick said opening the door of his modest rental car.

The fall air was cool, and Brynn took a moment to breathe it in. This was her favorite time of the year with the crisp leaves and the closing of summer. The smell of the air made her wish for the thousandth time that life could just be simple, not that it ever was. She looked over at her new friend and wondered if it would ever be possible.

Nick caught her eye and gestured for her to get in. As he closed the door, Brynn felt her heart expand for a brief moment at the promise of the evening. She wasn't accustomed to feeling so hopeful, and it terrified her.

Nick got in swiftly beside her and buckled his seatbelt. He squeezed her hand quickly, and gave her a warm smile.

"Are you ready?" he asked sensing her nervousness.

"Yes," Brynn said smiling wide. "I believe that I am."

CHAPTER TWENTY-NINE

Ellie's Demons

Ellie was happy for how the world was evolving.

She no longer had to stick needles in her arms. She could just smoke her drugs, or snort them. It wasn't like the old days when she had to stick herself time and time again making her feel like a human pincushion. But the drugs were a lot of the same with some wonderful new ones thrown in the mix, and she was thankful for that. She needed them, all of them.

She couldn't take the guilt anymore. First, it was Eva, then Jonas, Noah, and Dylan. Dylan who was sent to prison for kidnapping Noah, and then being killed right before his release. *Poor bastard didn't even know that Noah wasn't his.* Ellie thought about all of the people she had hurt in her life.

My Momma and Daddy were killed because of me. Jonas said so.

She knew that she had no proof, but in her heart, she knew that he was telling the truth. On his deathbed, there was no reason for him to lie to her. Not when the truth would hurt her so much. *Jonas loved to hurt me. He lived to hurt me. He showed his love for me by hurting me.*

After abandoning Eva, Ellie prayed for a long time for redemption. But she knew that she was never going to get it. *It's too late. There is no redemption now, no forgiveness. I don't know how I ever thought there would be.*

Ellie lit up.

She inhaled the stench, and she smiled. She didn't want to feel anything else, or think about anything else. She just wanted to be numb.

She took a sip of the vodka she had poured. It burned. Almost like rubbing alcohol. But she loved it. She loved how it felt running down the back of her throat. After a few minutes, she felt the familiar numbness starting to settle in. She smoked, she drank, she swallowed, she sipped, she inhaled, and then she swallowed again.

She slumped back into her big comfy chair, the one she liked to disappear into when she wanted to get lost. It was the one thing she had shipped from home to the apartment she was staying in while she tried to woo Brynn. It was her one comfort.

Ellie thought about Noah, his face swirling around in her hazy thoughts. *My sweet, sweet boy.*

She thought about when he was born, when the doctors realized that he was different. She hated herself for how her first thought was that she deserved better and should give him away. *What kind of awful, terrible person thinks that about their kid? I'm terrible and awful. I've done nothing worthwhile my entire life.*

Ellie thought about how she left him, like she had left Eva. *It was for the best. I would have been a terrible mother. I was a terrible mother. I had two children, and I abandoned them both.*

Ellie tried to get out of the chair, but her legs felt numb beneath her. She struggled and made it up, spilling her vodka all over her pretty lace nightgown. *Shit!*

She stumbled over to the bathroom and looked into the vanity at her reflection.

Old. You got old.

She pulled at her eyes and pinched the skin on her forearms. *Well, you still look pretty Damn good for what you've been through in life.*

Her eyes were bloodshot, and her brown hair was a tangled mess, but Ellie could still see traces of the fifteen-year-old girl she once was buried deep within. Her skin was not as tight and youthful as it once was, and all of the smoking and late nights were starting to show their wear and tear on her face, but men still looked, though not as hard and long as they once did. Ellie reluctantly had to admit that the quality of men that were looking at her now wasn't what it once was, either.

Ellie thought for a moment about her mother. She didn't think of her often, and when Amy's pretty face popped up in her head, she often pushed her away. But today would have been her birthday, and Ellie couldn't make her go away no matter how hard she tried.

Damn you, Momma. Why did you leave me alone? "Why did you leave me when I needed you the most?" Ellie cried out loud, her voice ragged, her words slurring together.

She had never admitted it out loud to anyone, but Ellie's heart broke sometimes from missing her Momma. Her relationship with Momma had always been complicated, but Ellie's heart couldn't deny that she still needed her. It felt like an unbelievable amount of time since she had seen her last.

"Why did you leave me? Momma, why did you abandon me? Oh Daddy, why? Why?" Ellie turned toward her comfy chair and tried to walk toward it, but the tears blinded her. The ground had started moving, and Ellie's stomach didn't feel very good. Ellie reached out to hold on to something to steady herself. She felt nothing but air around her. The ground came up fast and smacked her on the face, and Ellie realized that she was no longer standing. She tried to move to stand up, but realized that it wasn't so bad where she was.

The floor was cool on her cheek. "If I cou jus' ge'my... shit 'tgether, things cou be diffrnt," she mumbled to herself. "I cou do it. I cou take Noah, and we cou be together."

Ellie tried to pick up her head, but realized that it hurt too much to move. Her head felt wet, which didn't make sense. *Vo-ka?* She tried to lift her hand up but it felt like it weighed a thousand pounds. *Shit. Sticky. Sticky? Wha the hell iz so sticky?* Ellie saw a puddle surrounding her head, and Ellie was mesmerized at how pretty it looked on the wood floor. She finally moved her hand and touched it. Red. Ellie felt her eyes closing as she fought to keep them open.

Red. Ellie saw the pool widening around her and felt it reaching her cheek. She couldn't move her head away no matter how hard she tried. *So tired. I'll wake up tomorrow an' have someone clean thissup.* She was tired, and she felt herself starting to fade, she needed sleep.

I'll have someone clean thissup. I promiss. Ellie thought about how

mad whoever found this mess was going to be.
And then she thought nothing.

CHAPTER THIRTY

Brynn's Date

"Jane told me where to take you," Nick said to Brynn as they drove, destination unknown. "That is, after she made me give her my driver's license so she could make a copy and asked me every detail about my life. I believe she may have even Googled me while she was standing right in front of me."

"Oh God!" Brynn said, wishing she could crawl under a rock.

Nick laughed. "You can't be too careful these days. You're lucky you have such good friends. She really cares about you."

Brynn nodded uncomfortably. *What am I doing here? I don't even know him! What was I thinking?* After a few minutes, they pulled into a little local winery, one of Jane's favorite places.

"Oh, I should have known," Brynn said smiling.

"She said they have a wonderful Riesling, and to have you try it," Nick said knowingly.

They walked into the winery, and Brynn was impressed with how cozy it was with the nice leather chairs and the fireplace. It was a perfect night for a fire, and the winery was taking full advantage of it.

Nick chose a comfortable little table away from the crowd where they could sit and talk.

After they ordered a bottle of Riesling, they sat back in their chairs looking at one another. Brynn could feel the chemistry between them. She had felt it the moment she had met him, and it was electrifying, like a constant current was running between them.

With Adam, it had been more sweet and innocent. This felt more daring, more exciting, and completely different.

"What do you think?" Nick said, his warm voice interrupting her thoughts.

"I'm sorry, about what?" Brynn blushed, wondered if she had missed a part of the conversation.

"Of the winery. What do you think of the winery?" Nick asked, amused, his hazel eyes dancing from the light of the fireplace.

"Oh," Brynn was embarrassed. *He must think that I am a complete idiot!* "It's nice, cozy. I can see why Jane likes it so much."

"It's very nice," Nick said looking around appreciatively and then looking directly at Brynn. "So, tell me about yourself. You seem like you've had an interesting life."

Brynn was taken aback by his directness. She had never had anyone look right at her the way that he did, and it unnerved her.

"Um, I don't know about interesting. I, uh, well, I just…"

"Okay, I'll tell you about me first, and then you can talk if you want." Nick laughed in such a way that Brynn could tell that he wasn't laughing at her, and she appreciated his thoughtfulness.

Brynn was thankful for the wine in front of her. She held onto the glass like a security blanket and took big gulps trying to calm herself down as she listened to him talk. She liked the depth of his voice and how warm it made her feel when he spoke. His voice put her in a trance, and she felt as though she could listen to him talk all night. Her mind started drifting, and she realized that she wanted to listen to him talk to her all night, and then listen to him talk to her in the morning. She blushed, embarrassed, and hoped that he wouldn't notice.

"What's wrong?" he said pausing mid-sentence from what he had been saying.

"Why? Nothing is wrong. The um, wine is making me hot." Brynn knew that he didn't believe her and she tried focusing her thoughts on listening to him instead of allowing her mind to wander.

"Okay," he said smiling a different kind of smile than the one she had seen all night. This smile was sexier, more playful, and Brynn thought about how much she liked seeing that smile.

"So, you're divorced then?" Brynn asked trying to participate in the conversation. "Me, too. Just about a year, but he had left me before, and we were never the same after that. Then our baby died and..." Brynn paused. She was never good at talking about it, but for some reason she felt like she could talk to Nick. She could tell that he was really listening to her.

"I'm sorry," Nick said, his eyes looking at her with genuine sadness in them. "That had to have been difficult."

"You have no idea," Brynn said thinking back to the last two years and how everything had fallen apart with Sophie's death.

"I do," Nick said, his voice changing, suddenly very serious. "I lost my son, Teddy. He was three and a half, and he drowned in our pool. My wife... my ex-wife, was supposed to be watching him, but she fell asleep in the sun for just a few moments. And he was gone. She could never forgive herself for what happened, even though I forgave her. We tried therapy, church, retreats, everything that we could think of, but she just couldn't forgive herself for letting Teddy drown. I loved her, but... I couldn't watch her destroy herself any longer, and there was nothing I could do for her."

Brynn was silent, her eyes full of tears that refused to fall.

"Oh, I'm sorry. I'm a horrible date, aren't I?" Nick said his eyes wide as he looked at Brynn, half-expecting her to stand up and walk out.

"No, no," Brynn said quietly. "You're a lovely date. I'm glad you shared with me. I don't know why I feel that I can talk to you, but I just do. I haven't been able to talk to anyone like this in a long time."

"Me, neither," Nick said leaning forward and squeezing her hand.

Brynn felt her hand tingle from the warmth of his touch and was disappointed when he pulled his hand away.

Brynn told him about Sophie and how they lost her and how Adam left her shortly after. "He was unable to forgive me like you forgave your wife. He felt as if I had cursed her somehow, and we were never the same after. He was the only man that I had ever loved."

Brynn barely noticed when the waitress dropped off the second bottle of wine, or when they called last call. Time seemed to stand still as they talked well into the night about every subject they could think of, hungry for the sound of one another's voice.

The winery was closing, and Nick stood up slowly and grabbed Brynn's hand, pulling her up and then refusing to let go. Brynn no longer felt awkward when he touched her. She felt herself leaning in toward him so that he could touch her, and he was happy to oblige.

"Well," he said smiling down at her.

Brynn liked how he made her feel protected, safe. "Well," she said smiling back as they walked toward his car.

"What do we do now?" He said stopping next to his rental car as he pushed her gently against it.

"What do you want to do?" Brynn teased lightly. The wine made her feel a little bit more comfortable, and she found that teasing came easier as well.

"I will tell you what I don't want to do. I don't want to say 'good night,'" Nick said, his eyes serious as they looked right into hers. "I'm not ready to let you go yet."

Brynn sighed. "I'm not ready to let you go yet, either," she said easily. Words had never been easy for her, but with him, she felt them flowing in a way that she had never experienced before.

"I have meetings tomorrow to wrap up and then I can be here for the rest of the week." Nick said looking hopeful, but vulnerable.

"I would love to spend as much time with you as I can," Brynn said feeling her heart opening up to him.

"Good, me too," he smiled pulling her close. He put his face close to hers and closed his eyes. Brynn couldn't explain it, but something hung heavy between them in the air, and she knew that they both felt it.

Brynn buried her head in his chest and held him tight. She could feel his heart beating in his chest, and she loved how his strong arms felt wrapped around her. The night was slowing down just for her, and she wanted to pour herself into it as much as she could.

"Do you want to come home with me?" Brynn said, her voice small, sounding unlike her own.

"I do," Brynn heard Nick's voice above her head. "But not for the reasons you may think."

Brynn pulled away. "What do you mean?"

"I mean, I just want to spend time with you. I've shut myself off from everything since Teddy's death, and I don't want to do that with you. I don't want you to feel like I'm trying to take advantage of you."

Brynn feigned disappointment. "Well, I was hoping that was all you were trying to do is take advantage of me."

Nick's eyes opened wide in shock as he took a step back from her.

"I'm kidding!" she said, pulling him back in close. "I just want to spend time with you, too."

Nick was happy and excited for the first time in a long time. Brynn made him laugh, and he hadn't laughed in a long time. But she was wounded, and he knew that he had to be careful with her. *Don't do what you usually do with women. Don't be an asshole. She's different. She's not a bat-shit crazy drunk like you're used to, so don't take your issues out on her like you usually do.* "Okay, good."

Brynn wanted him to kiss her, but the moment had passed. She couldn't remember ever wanting to kiss anyone as much as she wanted to kiss Nick. She thought about the house, and how it was a mess and that there was only one bed, and for once, she didn't care.

She just wanted be in his arms, listening to the sound of his voice, telling her that for once everything was going to be alright.

CHAPTER THIRTY-ONE

Adam's Disgrace

"So you don't even talk to her anymore?" Adam's mom shrieked, her voice carrying in the quiet restaurant. With a great deal of effort, she lowered her voice while staring at Adam in disbelief. "How do you just walk out on someone you've loved all of your life?"

Hannah Michael realized with dismay that she didn't even recognize her son anymore.

"Hannah, calm down. Let the boy talk," Daniel knew that his wife was beyond upset. Adam was her pride and joy, all of her life wrapped up in his happiness. When they went on their two-year-long mission trip, everything had been going well. Their first grandchild was about to be born, Adam and Brynn had reconciled. But when they returned, everything was destroyed.

Hannah was heartbroken. "I don't understand how you just stopped trying, even after you went home. Don't you love Brynn anymore? She was like a daughter to us. Didn't you think about that?"

Adam couldn't believe his ears. "No, I didn't think about you! I was thinking about me! I was thinking about how I couldn't look at her face anymore without thinking about how she never wanted Sophie to begin with. I was thinking about how I had to convince her to have a family and a life with me. I was thinking about how selfish she's always been and how much I hated her for letting our baby die.

And I was thinking about how I couldn't stand to look at her for the rest of my life!" He grabbed his full glass of bourbon and drank it down in one swallow.

"Who are you?" Hannah said, her blue eyes filling with tears. Adam was the spitting image of her, but his blue eyes had grown dark and empty and it frightened her. For a moment, she flashed back to when he was a boy, and she wanted to reach out and touch his hair, but she knew that he would never allow it. He was only a poor reflection of the man she once knew.

Daniel cleared his throat and pushed his glasses up on his nose. "We wanted to see Brynn. Do you think she would see us?" Daniel asked Adam calmly. "She is still our family, even if you aren't together anymore."

"I don't know, Dad. I just said that I don't talk to her anymore, so why don't you call her? I'm not her husband, so do whatever the hell you want." Adam's tone was angry. He knew that lashing out at his parents was wrong, but he couldn't stop himself. He knew that they would take Brynn's side.

Hannah looked around the restaurant and knew that everyone could hear them. She no longer had an appetite and stood up angrily. "I'm leaving, Daniel. I didn't come here to have my son talk to me this way."

Adam looked up at his mother. He had loved her all of his life, but even for her, he felt nothing right now. "You guys can just go. I'm staying."

Daniel held Hannah's arm. "Sweetheart, sit down. We can talk through this with him. We both know that he doesn't want to push us away like this."

"I do, actually. While you were gone on your 'mission trip', I could have used your help here. I didn't know what to do. So now, I've lost my baby, my wife, my house, and everything else. And you're just now showing up to help me. So, yeah you can go. I don't need you right now." Adam gestured for the server to bring him another drink.

"The drinking isn't going to help, Adam," Daniel said sadly. "It will make it worse."

"It can't get worse, Dad," Adam said leaning back in his chair.

Hannah looked at her son, trying to understand what she was seeing. He had lost at least twenty pounds, and his beautiful blue eyes were streaked with red. He didn't look like he had slept in ages, and his clothes were wrinkled. But what disturbed her most was that he was an empty vessel—this man who had once been so beautiful and giving.

The food arrived and they sat in silence, Hannah and Daniel picking at their food while Adam simply drank.

Hannah spoke up, breaking the awkward silence. "Why didn't you call for us, honey? We would have come home. We didn't know you needed us so badly."

Adam shrugged. "What would you have done, Mom? There was nothing that you could do."

Hannah sighed, trying to hold in her tears. *What will become of my sweet boy now?* She knew that Adam loved Brynn, he always had. She never imagined him with anyone else, even when he separated from her the last time. But this was divorce. This was permanent.

Daniel leaned over. "It'll be okay sweetheart. He's a man, and he will figure it out."

Hannah smiled and kissed him on the cheek. She loved how Daniel always knew what she was thinking. Not a day went by that she didn't thank God for him and his love. She had hoped that Adam would find the same love with Brynn.

"Yes, Parents. I will figure it out." Adam was sufficiently drunk, and Hannah eyed her son distastefully. She wasn't opposed to a glass of wine on occasion, but this was unacceptable.

They asked for the check, and Daniel decided it was best to drive Adam home.

"Home... oh you mean my crappy little apartment, sssssuuuuure, you can drive me there," Adam slurred.

Hannah was happy when he passed out in the back seat.

"He's disgusting and a mess. And he smells," She whispered to Daniel, wrinkling her nose. "What is he thinking?"

"He's thinking that he's in pain, honey. Don't be so hard on him. It's just a phase he has to go through. You went through that once, don't you remember?" Daniel loved Hannah, but her memory could sometimes run short.

Hannah was silent for a while, listening to Adam snore in the back seat. She looked back at her son and smiled thoughtfully. "You're right, Daniel. As always, you are right."

Daniel knew just how to soften her up, which is why she had chosen him over the man she had been engaged to when they met. She had been a mess for a while, but he had gotten her through. He needed her to remember that, for Adam's sake.

They pulled up in front of the apartment and plotted how they were going to get him in.

"Oh my God, this was so much easier when he was five," Hannah grunted as they hoisted his arms around their shoulders and tried to maneuver him in.

"Y-y-ep," Daniel groaned. "At least he's on the first floor."

They half-dragged, half-carried him to Apartment 110.

"Keys, do you know where his keys are?" Hannah asked, feeling the sweat prickling on her forehead.

"Probably in his pocket," Daniel said reaching into his son's pocket to try to find keys.

Just then, the apartment door opened, startling both of them.

"Can I help... Oh, Adam!" the pretty redhead exclaimed, and looked surprised. "Um, you must be Adam's parents."

Hannah looked at the girl in shock. She can't be more than twenty-two years old, and where are her clothes?

Jessie looked down at herself and realized that she was only wearing one of Adam's t-shirts and no shorts. "Oh my God," I'm so sorry. I thought... I mean I didn't realize... I just..." Jessie flew out of the room leaving the door to the apartment wide open.

Daniel looked at Hannah and shrugged. "Okay, well let's get this boy in."

Adam was dead weight, and when they got to the couch, they let him go and he fell in face first.

"Should we go, or should we stay?" Daniel whispered.

"Oh, we are definitely staying," Hannah said smoothing her hair. "We need to get to the bottom of this."

"Bottom of what?" Daniel asked, annoyed. "Hannah, he's a grown man. We don't know everything that has happened. This girl could be..."

"Twenty-one? She's a baby and…"

"Actually, I'm twenty-two."

Daniel and Hannah turned around and realized that the girl had come back into the room, this time fully clothed in yoga pants and a bra under her shirt.

"Well, you look like a baby," Hannah said unapologetically.

Daniel cleared his throat. "Um, so we're Adam's parents, Daniel and Hannah."

"I'm Jessie," Jessie said feeling her cheeks burning. "I'm Adam's… uh, friend."

"Well Adam never mentioned you. Do you know about Brynn?" Hannah was staring Jessie down. Daniel was horrified. He had never seen this side of his sweet wife before.

Jessie seemed to shrink down a little bit. "I did… I mean I do know about Brynn. Not a lot. Just that they were high school sweethearts and now they are divorced."

"Well, they were together half of their lives, so don't rush into anything," Hannah warned.

"Okay, well we should be going now," Daniel said embarrassed. "I'm sorry to be so abrupt. Adam didn't tell us about you, that's all. It caught us off guard. I'm sure you're a very nice young lady."

"It's okay, really," Jessie said her face still red from the earlier embarrassment. "I understand."

Daniel was pushing Hannah out the door before she could say anything else.

Jessie locked the door behind them and stood over Adam, tears burning in her bright green eyes. "How could you do this to me?" she said knowing that he couldn't hear her. "After all I have done for you, how could you humiliate me?"

Adam lay face down on the couch, not moving. She knew that he was out for the count until he woke up with a vicious hangover. *He won't even miss me. He won't even know I'm gone.*

Jessie went into the bedroom and packed her bags. She knew that it would come to this one day, but she hoped that it wouldn't.

That's okay. It's better this way. She thought moving her hand to her belly. It's better if he doesn't even know about the baby. We don't need him in our lives when he doesn't love us.

Jessie found a notepad and left him a note:

Adam,

I met your parents while I was in my underwear. It was humiliating and horrifying. I know now that you don't love me and that you never will. I wish you the best always and wish that it could have been different for us.

I will always love you and remember the time we had together. Don't call me or contact me. I never want to see you again.

J~

CHAPTER THIRTY-TWO

Brynn's Nightmare

Nick awoke to screaming.

"What the…." He jumped out of bed and realized that he wasn't in his own bedroom. He was half-asleep and confused. "Where am I?"

Oh, that's right. Brynn!

"Brynn! Brynn!" Nick looked around the bedroom and realized that it was empty. He followed the sound of the screaming, his heart pounding in his chest.

"No! No! Don't hurt me. Please stop hurting me! I'll be good, I'll be good!" Brynn's voice was sobbing and screaming, getting louder as he got closer to the kitchen.

He opened the door and saw Brynn crouched on the floor, tight up against the cabinets, her arms shielding her face. She was thrashing around desperately trying to cover her body up and protect herself from an unknown threat that seemed to be right above her. Maxie sat a few feet away whimpering.

Nick had never seen anything like it.

"Brynn, Brynn!" he was next to her in a split second, grabbing her tight with his strong arms. "Brynn, you're okay. I'm here. It's Nick."

Brynn kept thrashing, her hair flying as she tried to break out of his grip. "Don't hurt me! Don't hurt me! I'm sorry, I'm sorry!

Pleeeeease stop!"

Nick looked into her eyes, which were wild with fear. Her eyes were even bigger than normal, and they were staring but not seeing. "BRYNN!" Nick screamed grabbing her face with his hands. "BRYNN, WAKE UP. WAKE UP!"

Brynn stopped thrashing immediately, her eyes still wide. Nick saw her trying to focus on his face, and he watched as the realization hit her and her body slumped to the ground.

"Oh my God, I'm so sorry, Nick," Brynn said lying on the floor, her long dark hair covering her face.

Nick got close to her and pulled her hair away, gently caressing her cheek. "It's okay, it's okay," he said trying to soothe her. His heart was starting to beat normally. He felt like his body was on fire from the adrenaline, and he scooped her up in his arms and held her close. "What were you dreaming about?"

Brynn was silent as she curled up as close to him as she could get trying to get control of herself. She wanted to hide from the humiliation of her dream. This is what she had been afraid of when Nick told her that he could push back his return home and stay for the week. She was afraid of the dreams, but somehow being with him, had kept them at bay, until now. "I was dreaming about my father. The one who adopted me, the one who used to hurt me."

She could hear Nick suck in his breath. *This is far more than he ever bargained for*, she thought bitterly. She knew that once he was gone, she wouldn't hear from him again after this.

"I'm sorry. I didn't know," Nick said holding her as tight as he could. He couldn't imagine anyone ever hurting Brynn.

"I know," Brynn said tearfully. "There's no way you would have. I wish you hadn't seen this."

"Why?" Nick asked pulling away and as he made her look him in the eyes.

Brynn looked down. She was mortified that he had seen her nightmares. They got better, and then they got worse. The shrink said she might never get a handle on them. Most nights she took the sleeping pills he gave her to knock herself out, but she didn't take them when Nick was there.

"It's embarassing. I'm sorry," Brynn said, so quietly that Nick could barely hear her.

"I'm sorry you had to go through that. You should never be embarrassed, not ever. Not around me."

Brynn sighed, the emotions still swirling around her. She didn't want to cry in front of him, but she didn't know how she couldn't. She closed her eyes tight and tried to breathe, but she still felt the wave of tears threatening to overcome her.

"Oh baby, you can cry. Don't hold it in," Nick whispered in her ear. Brynn felt the flood coming and for the first time, she let it out, sobbing freely in his arms. Nick held her close, feeling protective. He didn't want anything to hurt her and wanted to look out for her every chance he got. She was healing him from the inside out, and he wanted to do the same for her.

They clung to each other on the kitchen floor for a long time. Nick wanted so badly to protect her. He had gotten to know her so well in their short time together that he couldn't imagine being without her.

Brynn looked up at him, grateful to have him holding her close, sheltering her. She kissed his neck softly, surprising herself. They had been affectionate, but her kiss told him everything that he needed to know. She wanted to be as close to him as she possibly could. She had only given herself to Adam, but she wanted Nick more than she had ever wanted anyone.

"We said we were taking it slow," Nick whispered in her ear as he felt her hands all over him.

"I know, but I changed my mind," Brynn said panting as she pulled him into her. Nick had no choice but to give in. She was more than he ever imagined she would be, and he was drawn to her in such a way that he couldn't deny. He wanted all of her, even if it was only for a brief time. He wanted as much of her as he could have. He needed her.

Brynn made him feel as if everything were right in the world. The feel of her soft skin on his, the curve of her back, and the touch of her fingertips. Nick knew there was nowhere else he wanted to be but with her, close to her, filling his whole world up with only her and letting the rest of it all fall away.

They fell asleep, clothes strewn all over the kitchen floor. Brynn reveled in the deliciousness of lying half-naked on the cool tile of the kitchen floor. She was close to being as free as she could be, yet careful to hide her scars. He had seen enough for one day. She sighed happily, and lay as close to Nick as she could, falling quickly into a deep sleep.

Nick woke with a start.

He hadn't even checked the clock when he ran downstairs, and he was surprised to see the sun coming up through the kitchen windows.

He held onto Brynn, but strained his neck to see what time it was on the microwave clock.

Oh, Shit! I have to leave in thirty minutes to catch my plane! Nick tensed up without realizing it.

"Are you okay?" Brynn said wiping the sleep out of her eyes.

"Yeah," Nick said looking away. She was already good at being able to tell when he wasn't being honest.

"Seriously, what's wrong?" Brynn said grabbing his chin and turning it toward her.

"My plane. It leaves in two hours. I have to leave soon." Nick said apologetically.

"Oh, is it that time, already?" Brynn asked, gathering herself and extracting her body from his grip. She didn't realize that it was so early in the morning.

"It is." Nick hated to leave. He had already extended his trip by a day, but he had to get back home. He had to get back to the office. Then he had to try to figure out when he could get back to Brynn.

Brynn looked at him, her eyes sad. He thought she had sad eyes anyway, but looking into them was heart wrenching even for him.

"Will you be back?" Brynn asked shyly.

"Yes, I will. Definitely. I just don't know when. It's Maryland to Ohio, and I have to try to figure out a schedule so that I can get to you soon and often," Nick said looking straight at her.

Brynn knew that she looked terrible from crying so much, but somehow it didn't seem to matter. When Nick looked at her, she felt beautiful. She knew that she would miss him, even though they just met, the connection between them strong and palpable.. She never imagined she would connect with someone after Adam, but Nick was so much different than Adam and made her feel things she never imagined she could.

Even still Adam had been her first love, and as hard as she tried, she often missed him and found her thoughts drifting to him throughout the day. She wondered if that would ever change for her and hoped that it would. For the first time in her life, she felt truly hopeful.

"Don't look so sad. We'll Skype, and we'll stay in touch. It'll be okay." Nick held her close and breathed in her clean scent. He loved how she smelled and willed it to stay with him for as long as it could.

"I know. I just…" Brynn couldn't continue. She didn't want to define anything yet. *For all I know, he will walk out my door and he won't come back. I may never hear from him again.* "I just want you to have a safe flight."

"It'll be fine," Nick said trying to be cheerful. He got up and took her hand as he walked into the bedroom to pack. Brynn took him in, enjoying watching him move.

He packed quickly, and Brynn sat on the edge of the bed waiting for the inevitable.

"Okay, so this is it," Nick said throwing his arms in the air.

"Okay. Well, have a safe trip and text me when you get back," Brynn said smiling up at him.

"I will. And I'll be back to see you soon. Or you can come see me," Nick said smoothing her hair.

"Okay," Brynn said feeling the awkwardness of the moment approaching.

Nick leaned over and kissed her, and Brynn was lost in time, enjoying the feel of his lips on hers with nothing else to think about.

They pulled away from each other, both of them gasping for air.

"I really need to leave or I'm going to miss my plane," Nick said smiling, his hair tousled from Brynn's hands. She liked how unguarded he looked, and she wished she could take a picture of him at that moment.

"Let me know when you get home safely," Brynn said smiling.

"I will. And I *will* see you soon." Nick said kissing her one last time. He picked up his bag and walked out of the bedroom, looking behind at her as he left.

Brynn flopped down on the bed, her body aching in all of the right places.

She was already replaying the week in her mind. The late night talks, the intimate details about their marriages, their divorces, the deaths of their children. For the first time in a long time, she felt like she could really talk to somebody other than Jane. She tried unsuccessfully to push down the excitement in her chest, even though her head kept telling her not to trust it. She had been so hurt, but Nick was making her feel as though there were possibilities.

She hadn't told him everything about Thomas, or about when she used to cut herself to ease the pain, but she figured those conversations would have to come at a later time.

There's a connection, a real connection. I'm not imagining it; I know that I'm not.

Brynn closed her eyes and let herself get lost in her bliss, thinking about nothing but Nick.

She heard an odd sound, a buzz, and she looked around for the source. She didn't recognize it, and then she realized it was her cell phone, put away in a drawer.

Brynn's heart leapt to see she had a text.

He's texting me already!

She opened it up:

Brynn~ Need to talk ASAP. Adam.

CHAPTER THIRTY-THREE

John's Loose Ends

John Palmer loved his job, but there were parts of it that he didn't like. Specifically, the parts that involved dealing with Ellie Harper.

He knew that he had people to do that for him, but he had made a promise to her deceased father long ago that he would always help take care of the Harper family. He planned to keep that promise no matter what.

And now she was dead.

John was secretly relieved that she was finally gone for good. He had seen the blood soaked body for himself, and was thankful that this time he wouldn't be in store for another surprise return. The coroner said that Ellie overdosed, and then had bashed her head on the floor as she was falling. She had no chance. John knew that it was only a matter of time. On the outside, he played the part of the grieving family friend, but on the inside, he finally felt that he could breathe a little easier.

But there were loose ends to tie up now. Noah. Brynn Michael. He knew that Ellie was going to tell Brynn about Noah, but he wasn't sure if she actually ever did.

He thought that if he took Tricia with him that Brynn might be open to him. He had done his research on her, and he knew that she was a closed book, and that it took a while for her to open up to people. John needed her to be willing to be Noah's guardian, for

Noah's sake. He no longer had anyone to count on, and as his half-sister, John wasn't sure if Brynn would be willing to take on that job. John didn't think that if it were he, that he would do it. But Brynn would have every resource available to her that she could think of, and John wanted her to know that.

He pulled up through the gates of the home where Noah had been staying since he was three. He was dreading telling him about Ellie, and he wasn't sure if Ellie ever told him about Brynn. He needed to see for himself. This was James Harper's family, and he needed to make sure that everything was taken care of as though it were his own. He owed James that much and more.

"Noah Harper," he said to the front desk clerk as he entered the building. John had turned into a very no-nonsense type of person, drastically different from the young man that James had mentored in his earlier years. James straightened his wire-rimmed glasses on his face, and pulled the collar out on his nicely pressed linen shirt. He didn't know how Noah was going to react to the news of his mother and it made him nervous.

He was relieved to see that Kelly, the pretty attendant that Noah liked so much, accompanied Noah to greet John. Kelly's grandparents had founded the home, and Kelly worked there because she wanted to, not because she had to. She was a caregiver by nature, and John trusted her completely with Noah.

"Hi, John," Noah said smiling broadly as he ran up to John and gave him a bear hug. He liked John. John always brought him candy and army men, and today was no different as John handed him a bag full of lots of goodies. "Thanks, John! You're the best!"

"You're welcome, Noah." John said smiling at him. He's gotten big. Really tall. What a sweet kid! He followed Kelly to a common area where John sat down next to Noah and watched him play with his new army men.

"John, do you know where my mommy is? I haven't seen her in a very long time," Noah asked after a few minutes of making shooting and bombing sounds as he pretended his army men were at war with each other.

Kelly looked at John, her face full of concern. John had called and had prepared her for the worst.

"Well, Noah. Your mommy won't be coming to visit you anymore," John said slowly. "She died last week, and she won't be able to come here now."

Noah sat and played with his army men as he had been when they sat down, and John wasn't sure if he heard him. "Noah, did you hear me?"

"Yes, John. Mommy died. She won't be here anymore."

"Do you understand what that means, Sweetie?" Kelly asked Noah putting her hand on his shoulder.

"Yes!" Noah's voice was starting to show signs of irritation. "I'm not stupid! I know what it means when you die."

"Well, um, how do you feel about it?" Kelly asked tentatively.

"I'm fine," Noah said quickly pretending to blow up the plastic tank that sat on the table in front of him, shooting it across the room.

Kelly and John looked at each other carefully.

"If you want to talk about anything, we can do that," Kelly said patiently.

"No. I know what happens when you die. They take your sheets off your bed, and then you don't sleep there anymore. That's what happens here all the time to my friends, and you don't get to see them anymore," *Noah was tired of feeling like they thought he was an idiot, he just wanted to see his mommy.*

"Well, I have a new friend now. I don't need Mommy anymore," Noah announced, busying himself with his toys.

"Oh, do you now?" John asked amused at Noah's independence. He thought back to visits when Noah wouldn't leave Ellie's side, not even to let her use the restroom. It was nice to see him more independent now.

"Yes!" Noah was agitated, and John thought that it was best to let him express himself. He had prepared himself for the worst, and he was still holding his breath and waiting for it to happen. "Do you want to meet her?"

"Uh, sure," John said hesitating. "There's something else I have to tell you, Noah."

"I know. Mommy's dead. She's not coming back. I won't see her again. I know," Noah's voice was rising, and his face was getting red as he concentrated on his army men.

"No, that's not it," John cleared his throat. "Noah, you have a sister."

Noah stopped playing with his army men. *He had always wanted a sister or a brother. He had begged Mommy for one lot of times, but she just ignored him and said she didn't want any more kids. It always made him sad.*

"A sister?" John could tell that Noah was very interested, even though Noah still refused to look at him.

"Yes. Her name is Brynn. She was El- your mommy's daughter before you. She's older," John said trying to keep it simple.

"Is she nice?" Noah asked quietly, keeping his head down.

"Um… yes, she's nice," John said carefully.

They sat in silence for a while, Noah looking at his army men while John and Kelly watched him, waiting for more of a reaction.

Noah jumped up suddenly, "Do you want to meet my friend?"

"Sure," John said standing up. *How am I going to get Brynn here to meet Noah? Or should I bring Noah to Brynn?*

Noah led John and Kelly through the grounds of the home. They walked for a long time. John kept looking at his watch. *It's a long drive back, and I want to be home for dinner.*

Suddenly Noah stopped. "There she is!"

John looked over at the woman sitting in the wheelchair. Something struck him. *God, I know her!*

As they approached, the woman looked up at them, a sweet smile coming across her face as she saw Noah. She reached out her hand for him, and he took it.

John felt his face getting hot as he broke out into a cold sweat. "It can't be…" He whispered to himself as he slowed his gait.

Kelly looked at him, concern written all over her face. "Are you okay?"

John stepped backward, nearly falling over his own feet. The woman looked up at him puzzled.

"W-w-what's your name?" John asked, trying to make his voice sound as normal as possible.

"Carly," the woman answered scowling at him. She didn't like how he was looking at her, and it made her uncomfortable. She tried not to shift in her seat but she couldn't help it, her eyes looking around at everything but the strange man who wouldn't take his eyes off of her.

"Are you sure?" John asked trying not to sound as though he didn't believe her.

"No. But that's what they've been calling me."

"Who?" John asked, curious.

"The people here. My friends, my husband." Carly said, annoyed with all of the questions that the strange man was asking her.

"Your *husband*?" John felt his heart beating wildly in his chest. "Who is your husband?"

"I think he's my husband... I get confused," Carly said rubbing her head. "Petey... his name is Petey. He's my husband."

John was silent for a moment. It was all too much. He looked at Noah and looked at Carly, and the resemblance was uncanny. He looked at Kelly and could tell from the look on her face that she saw it, too.

"Why are you looking at me that way?" Carly asked John, her voice tight and angry.

"Because I know you," John said looking her right in the eyes. "I know you very well."

"How?" Carly asked, her voice slightly quivering. Her expression told John that she didn't want to believe him.

"I know you, and I know your husband. Only your husband's name isn't Petey."

"Who am I then?" Carly asked, quietly. This man looked at her and spoke to her as though he really knew her, and she was intrigued.

"You're Amy. Amy Harper, and your husband is James Harper."

CHAPTER THIRTY-FOUR

Nick's Homecoming

Nick was dreading the plane ride home.

He didn't want to leave Brynn. Spending time with her was the first time that he had felt alive and happy in years. He sat on the plane and thought about what it was like to hold her in his arms. He thought about how she smelled clean, like soap—and how her skin tasted, salty and sweet at the same time.

He sat back in the seat and closed his eyes. *I wish the flight were longer, I need time to regroup.*

The week hadn't been nearly long enough, and he wished he had more time with Brynn. He knew that she was special from the moment he met her. He just hadn't realized how special she was. He had met a lot of women over the years on his trips, trying to forget, trying to ease the pain of his life. But none had affected him like Brynn. None of them had taken away the loneliness and despair like Brynn.

What am I doing? What have I done? What is wrong with me? Nick felt his heart racing in his chest, and he gestured for the flight attendant to bring him some water.

"Are you okay, sir?" she asked leaning over him and putting her hand on his shoulder.

"I'm fine," Nick said, taking a big drink of his water. "I'll be okay."

The flight attendant walked away, giving him a backward

glance. He smiled weakly.

There is a special place in Hell for someone like me. Nick thought wryly.

He hadn't lied, completely. He had merely reshaped the truth a bit, though he knew that Brynn would never see it that way. But he knew that if he told her everything that she would never have agreed to spend time with him. Especially now, after everything that he knew about her.

She can never find out what I've done. She can never know that I didn't tell her everything.

Nick thought back to the last few years of his life and how miserable they had been. He had been a coward though, and hadn't been honest with himself.

I need to be honest with myself. I need to start over clean, for myself. For Brynn. I need to figure out what I'm doing and just do it.

They were safely in the air, and Nick turned his phone back on. It vibrated immediately with a text:

Are you in the air? Are you safe? I can't wait to see you! XO

Nick slammed his head back against the seat. *Shit!*

He spent the rest of the flight with his eyes closed, picturing Brynn in his mind. Her long dark hair flowing down her naked back, her big brown eyes staring up at him, wanting him. Her voice telling him about her sadness and her horror, making him want to hold her forever.

Nick brushed back his dark hair and thought about her hands touching him.

It was clear that he wasn't going to be able to stop thinking about her easily.

Nick felt his chest squeezing tight as the plane started to descend. He didn't know how he was going to get through the next couple of days.

Take deep breaths, it's going to be okay. You're going to be okay.

Nick smoothed out his shirt and ran his hands through his hair again. He was actually nervous!

He grabbed his carry on and pulled it down, letting everyone pass in front of him. He wanted to be the last one off the plane.

He walked off the plane slowly. He didn't have any luggage,

and he walked to the gate, dragging his feet. He was dreading what was going to happen when he got to the other side of the gate.

Oh, shit! He thought, quickly reaching into this duffel bag and rummaging around. There! He pulled out the cool piece of metal that had been buried in the bottom of his bag for the entire week. He slipped it on his finger, immediately squirming. It felt like a noose around his finger, choking the life out of it.

He glanced at his hand one last time and walked slowly to the gate entrance.

"There you are!" he heard a familiar voice say, excitedly.

He felt his stomach flip as he turned around. There she was, standing in front of him, small, blonde, and frail as ever. He couldn't remember the last time that he looked at her and felt any love or passion.

"Hi," Nick said bending down and hugging her stiffly, feeling her bones through her shirt.

"I missed you," she said trying to kiss him, but only getting his cheek.

"It's good to see you," Nick mumbled, kissing her quickly on the forehead.

"Is that all you took with you?" the woman said pointing to his bag.

"Yeah. It wasn't supposed to be a long trip, but it just ended up being that way," Nick said absently as he looked away. "So, did you eat while I was away?"

The woman looked at him, annoyance crossing her face. "You just got back. Why are you asking me if I ate?"

"I just want to know if you ate. It doesn't look like you ate; that's all." Nick said defensively.

"Yes, I ate. I ate every day, at least once. Sometimes twice." The woman said stubbornly.

They walked in silence. "Do you need to stop somewhere before we go home? Did you eat?"

"No. I just want to go home and go to sleep. I'm really tired," Nick said avoiding her eyes. He didn't want her to pick him up from the airport. He had asked her not to pick him up, but he knew that she probably would anyway.

Even though he had told her that he wanted a divorce before he left on his trip, she did what she always did and ignored him.

"Okay. Well that's good. I can drive home then," the woman said grabbing his arm.

Nick pulled away, more violently than he meant to. She looked hurt and he felt terrible.

"Mel, please," he said trying to make his voice gentle as though he were talking to a wounded animal.

"Nicky, you don't want to divorce me. You were just upset when you left. But I'm eating now, and I'm taking my medicine. I'm not drinking much at all. I'll be good, I promise!" Melanie was crying, her tiny frame shaking uncontrollably.

Nick looked around and saw people looking at him in disgust, assuming, as always, that he was the one to blame. "Melanie, please stop. Don't do this here." Nick felt like an animal. He shouldn't have told her like he did. He shouldn't have told her right before his trip. Melanie's doctor had told him to be careful, but Nick didn't listen.

Melanie was drunk when he left. She was drunk more than she was sober, and Nick was disgusted by her.

He told her that he was getting a lawyer, and then he left, just like that. He hoped that she would believe him this time. He had come so close to doing it before, he had warned her before. But she never accepted it. He shouldn't have expected anything different this time.

"Melanie, please. Just sit." Nick walked her over to the black lobby chairs. "We aren't the same. Don't you get that? You're a freaking train wreck. You're an addict and an alcoholic. I just can't do this with you anymore, Mel! You're destroying yourself, and you're taking me with you. "

People were staring at them, giving Nick dirty looks, but Nick didn't care any longer. He had told her the same thing a thousand times, but then she cried and Nick gave in in. He had loved her since they were six years old in the first grade. But he was finally realizing that there was nothing that he could do to help her anymore. She had been teetering on the brink of stability for most of her life, but losing Teddy had put her firmly over the edge.

"Nicky, you can't leave me. I need you," Melanie pouted, her baby blue eyes appearing larger than usual, long lashes holding her tears captive.

"I can't stay and watch you do this to yourself anymore. It's killing me."

"I know. I know. I'll get help. I promise," Melanie's words rang hollow on Nick's ears, and he felt as detached from her as he had been feeling for so long.

"Mel, *I* lost a son, too," Nick said his voice flat. He looked at her long blonde hair, her beautiful small face, and her arms that were nothing but sticks crossed over her small breasts. He closed his eyes for a moment and thought about how beautiful and healthy she had once been, his chest tightening as he did so. *God, I miss her. I miss my wife.*

Without warning, Brynn's face flashed before his eyes. He thought about how she had made him forget about Mel, and about his pain. He thought about how it felt to lie in Brynn's arms and just feel content and happy, even if it was short lived.

"I know," Mel's voice brought him back to her. "Please, just let's go home. Just go home with me, and we can talk about it tomorrow."

Nick sighed. He was tired. He needed to rest. He needed to sleep.

He followed Mel out of the terminal, letting her weave her arm through his this time.

He was too exhausted to fight her tonight and knew that he would need to figure things out once he was rested.

Chapter Thirty-Five

Reunited

Brynn froze as she re-read the text over and over.

Brynn~ Need to talk ASAP. Adam.
Brynn~ Need to talk ASAP. Adam.
Brynn~ Need to talk ASAP. Adam.

Why now? Why does he want to talk to me now?

Brynn felt herself breaking into a cold sweat as she forgot completely about Nick. She stood up and paced. *Oh My God, what do I do? What do I do?*

She started to text him back, but her fingers were shaking too hard for her to be able to type the words in. She threw her phone down on the floor, thankful that it landed on the soft area rug and not the hardwood floor.

She looked around at the empty house and she cursed.

Her phone buzzed again.

Brynn~ Are you there? Adam

Brynn felt infuriated. *How dare he text me now and then expect me to just drop everything and answer him? Who does he think he is?*

Brynn walked out of the room, Maxie trailing behind her, his nails clicking on the floors. "Maxie, sit!" Brynn said, irritated. Maxie put his ears back and looked at her, tilting his big soft head in curiosity. "I know, I know. It's just that... Daddy Adam is texting me. What do I do? Do I answer?"

Brynn sank to the floor next to Maxie and looked at him, wishing he could answer.

Brynn picked up the phone and stared at it.

She typed quickly and paused before hitting send.

What am I doing? Brynn sat on the floor and rocked herself back and forth while absently petting Maxie. His soft fur soothed her. He laid his big head on her legs and gave her a funny look. "I know, I know. I'm freaking out right now," she said looking him in the eyes.

She sat on the floor and time seemed to stop. She had no idea how long she sat there.

The doorbell rang and Brynn jumped. Maxie scuttled up quickly and ran to the door barking. Brynn chased after him and could tell that Maxie was happy to see whoever was on the other side of the door. She felt her heart beating wildly in her chest, and she paused for a moment, trying to catch her breath.

She opened the door slowly and there he was.

"Hi," Adam said shyly looking Brynn up and down, taking her in as he used to so long ago. Brynn felt her body shudder, and she suddenly felt extremely awkward.

"Hi," she said, the word barely coming out.

They stood at the door staring at one another. It had been over a year since they had seen each other last, both stunned with how drawn they felt to each other despite how much time had lapsed. The last time they had been together was in court. Brynn shuddered when she thought of that day.

"Um, do you want to come in?" Brynn asked slowly opening the door a little wider.

"Sure," Adam said looking around as he stepped through. He looked wounded as he took in the empty shelves and the empty rooms. The "For Sale" sign outside now said "Pending," but he wasn't prepared for the hollowness that he felt in his heart.

Brynn watched Adam carefully, her heart going out to him. She had imagined this moment, or a similar one for a long time, but in her mind, it had never been this way. She thought she would be angry, or that he would be angry. She envisioned ugly words, screaming, yelling. She expected the continuation of the war that was going on inside of them to spill out in their hatred, for the loss of Sophie and of their life together. But she hadn't expected this reverence and sadness.

Adam touched the walls that he had painted, and the woodwork that he had sanded, closing his eyes for a brief moment. He looked at each room from top to bottom as Brynn followed him around like a ghost.

When he got to the bedroom, he paused.

He turned to Brynn and looked at her, his eyes sadder than they had ever looked before.

Brynn could smell the whiskey on him. It was an old familiar smell that used to fill her with panic. But Adam had finally convinced her that he would never hurt her, and she wasn't afraid of him now.

"You look terrible," Brynn said, her voice cracking. She didn't like the scraggly beard he was wearing or his unkempt hair. She thought he looked dirty and terrible.

"I know," Adam said wryly. He couldn't remember the last time that he looked in a mirror, but he knew that he looked bad. His pants were falling off him, and his shirt was wrinkled and stained. "I'm sorry."

"Don't be sorry, you just need to clean up. Do you want to clean up here?" Brynn said walking toward the master bathroom.

"No, I mean, I'm sorry. I'm sorry for what I've done to you," Adam's voice was low, but Brynn heard every word. "I left you. I know it wasn't your fault, but I had to blame someone for losing Sophie."

"I know," Brynn said, feeling hot tears stinging her eyes without warning. "We can talk about this later. You need a hot shower right now."

Brynn steered him toward the bathroom. She reached into the closet and grabbed a nice big towel. As she stood closer to Adam, she couldn't believe how bad he smelled. Like whiskey and a combination of odors that she didn't want to recognize. She ran a nice hot bath and started to walk out of the bathroom.

"Wait, stay," Adam said stumbling a little as he turned around.

Brynn grabbed his arm and caught him. "Help me."

Brynn suddenly felt bashful, her cheeks turning red and hot.

Adam chuckled. Brynn's breath caught. She had forgotten how much she loved the easy richness of Adam's voice. He had always gotten to her that way, and she tried desperately to block it out.

"Why are you laughing at me?" she said, her brown eyes angrily at him.

"I'm not laughing at you," Adam said quickly, immediately flashing his best puppy dog look. Brynn smiled in spite of herself. She tried to look away from him, but his deep blue eyes were drawing her in.

She thought for a second about how different Nick's eyes were, and she caught herself. She had never had feelings for more than one man before, and it felt oddly exhilarating.

"Stay, Brynn. You've seen me naked a thousand times. I just want you to stay," Adam struggled with his clothes, finally dropping them in a dirty pile on the floor. Brynn could see the steam rising up from the tub and worried that it may be too hot. But Adam sank right into it, immersing himself for a minute until he came up soggy, but slightly revived.

Brynn sat on the edge of the large tub, careful to sit as far from him as she could.

"What?" Adam asked, looking at her with an amused smile on his face.

"Well… um… Why, I mean why are you here?" Brynn asked trying to avoid his gaze.

"I'm here to redeem myself," Adam said matter-of-factly. "With you, with anyone who will listen."

Brynn stared at him.

"Brynn, in case you didn't know, I was a jerk. I had a wonderful life, a wonderful home, a beautiful wife who I've loved since I was fifteen. And I gave you up. I let you go. Not just once, but twice! Twice! What kind of fucking idiot does that?" Adam's voice was full of torment. "I'm willing to make amends. I'll do whatever it takes for as long as it takes."

Maxie grunted from the corner of the bathroom, making Brynn and Adam both jump. They had forgotten about him.

"I don't know what that means. I don't know what you are saying." Brynn's mind was racing and her legs felt weak.

Adam was running his soapy hands through his dark brown hair and Brynn found herself getting lost in the gesture, remembering running her own hands through his thick hair. She could still remember the feel of it between her fingers.

"Brynn, I've been drunk for a year. For over a year, really. For as long as we have been apart. I don't know how it happened, but I just started drinking and then I didn't stop. The drinking helped me stop thinking about you and what I did to you. And I hated myself for drinking, and I thought a thousand times over how you would hate me, too. Especially, with your bastard father drinking and hurting you…" Adam's voice was low, confessional.

Brynn couldn't stop listening even though she wanted to. She had been through so much with him, and she thought that she was done worrying about him and trying to figure him out.

"What do you want me to say?" Brynn asked searching his face for a clue.

"I don't know," Adam said shaking his head slowly. "I don't know what I expect you to say. If I were you, I would hate me. But I don't want you to hate me. I don't want you to hate me at all. I hate myself enough for both of us. I want you to forgive me, but I don't deserve it. I didn't deserve it the first time, and I don't deserve it now."

Brynn had already been through the period when she hated Adam. While it only lasted for a brief time, she had felt it as true and real as anything she had ever felt before. But now she was done being angry with him, she just couldn't do it anymore. And part of her understood him better than she understood herself, so she couldn't blame him for leaving again.

"I don't hate you," Brynn said carefully. "I wish I could, but I don't."

Adam looked relieved, his face relaxing a little. Brynn couldn't believe how much he had aged in a year. He looked tense and worn, and part of her ached for him and the pain that he was going through.

"Thank you," he said gratefully, grabbing her hand. "Thank you.

You just don't understand how much that means to me. You can't possibly understand."

Brynn felt electricity surging from his touch. She locked eyes with him and felt herself moving toward him.

Before she knew it, his lips were on hers. She barely felt the water drenching her as he pulled her into the tub. She barely felt anything, but his lips and his skin. She vaguely realized that he was taking her clothes off. All she could feel was his hands on her naked body, familiar and exciting, touching her in all of the places he knew that she liked. She felt a groan escape from her throat.

Brynn was lost once again in her Adam, and she didn't want to be anywhere else.

CHAPTER THIRTY-SIX

The Harper House

Tricia Palmer had never known her husband to joke with her. He was earnest and sincere in everything that he did.

When he called to tell her that he found Amy Harper, she thought that he was either joking or that he had lost his mind.

"How? Are you sure?" John could see Tricia's blonde head bobbing back and forth the way that it did when it was animated, even though they were only speaking on the phone. He knew her so well, and wished that she were with him at the home.

"Yes, I'm positive. It looks exactly like her, only older. Trish, she looks exactly the same! It sounds like her. It is her even though she doesn't realize it." John was talking quickly. He didn't want to let Amy out of his sight for very long. "She thinks her name is Carly."

"Where has she been?" Tricia said barely able to speak. "Where has she been all this time? Does she know about Ellie? About Eva?"

"She's been living in a small town called Sullivan. A few hours south of home. Honey, she doesn't even know who she is. She has no idea." John was desperately rubbing his temple in that way that he did when he was baffled by something.

"What are you going to do?" Tricia asked, her voice stunned and shaking.

"I'm already on it with lawyers and with everyone else," John said matter-of-factly.

Tricia's heart warmed. She knew that her husband would have

already gotten the ball rolling. He amazed her with his efficiency.

"Can you bring her home?" Tricia asked. "Is she in good shape?"

"She looks great. But she's older and she can't remember anything. She has no idea who I am, and she doesn't remember what happened to James. She doesn't even remember James." John was trying to disguise the frustration in his voice. He was happy that he found her, but wished more than anything that she could remember what happened to his mentor and his friend.

John hung up the phone and felt better. The sound of Tricia's voice always soothed him. Sometimes she didn't even need to say anything; he just needed her to listen. He turned around, and he walked back to Noah and Amy.

He already had people working on getting her and Noah released from the home. The arrangements were being made to have the Harper House cleaned up and prepared for Noah and Amy to return. And he was working on getting Kelly hired on at the Harper House full time. Three short conversations had gotten the ball rolling, and John felt himself breathing easier.

Now he had to convince Noah and Amy to return with him.

He made the short walk back to Noah and Amy, and sat down on a bench next to Noah. Noah and Amy were engrossed in a competitive game of checkers. John could tell that Noah was concentrating so he waited patiently, pretending to be engrossed in the game.

"Yes!" Noah jumped up, raising both hands in the air in victory.

John high fived him and jumped up and down with him.

Noah was basking in the glory of his win as he sat back down. Amy was smiling, happy for Noah's win. He had been trying to beat her for a week, and it was well deserved.

"Well done, young man!" Amy said pretending to curtsy to him, as she sat in her wheelchair.

"Thank you for teaching me how to play." Noah said happily.

John looked at both them, surprised by their bond. "I have a proposal."

"A proposal?!" Amy said suspiciously.

"What's a proposal?" Noah asked, curious.

Kelly stared at John, fearful. Noah was unpredictable, and with the news about his mother, Kelly wasn't sure how he was going to react.

"A proposal is when I ask you a question and you have to answer 'yes' or 'no'," John said, clearing his throat. *Maybe I should wait. Maybe they aren't ready yet. Maybe I should just hold off on this.*

Noah and Amy looked at John, waiting for him to talk.

"I would like you to come live in the Harper House," John said, getting to the point quickly.

Noah looked at him, waiting for him to say more. "What is the Harper House?" Noah said finally.

"It's a big house where your mommy lived when she was a girl. And…" he said looking at Amy, "You lived there, too."

"I don't remember, and I'm not going anywhere," Amy said stubbornly.

"Don't say 'no' yet," John said quickly. "Maybe you could come see it and then you'll remember."

Amy looked at John angrily, as she backed her wheelchair away from him as quickly as she could, knocking over the checkerboard. "I don't know you. I'm not going anywhere with you!"

Amy started to wheel herself away and stopped suddenly.

"Carly!" John looked past the wheelchair, and he saw a man and a woman coming toward Amy. He immediately noticed how massive the man was—his chest large and shoulders wide with gigantic hands. The kind of hands that could squeeze a man's head in, John thought uneasily.

John, Kelly, and Noah were all frozen where Amy had left them, checkers strewn all over the pavement and the grass. Noah was visibly upset by Amy's sudden departure, and he looked up to Kelly helplessly.

The man and woman froze realizing that they had an audience.

"Carly, don't leave!" Noah said suddenly, jumping up. Amy looked at the man and woman and looked back at Noah, confusion written all over her still-very pretty face.

"Lily, Petey. I want you to meet my friends," she said gesturing to the man and the woman who looked like they wanted to do anything but.

They walked slowly toward her wheelchair and, at her urging, turned her around and pushed her toward the little group.

"I would like you to meet my friends," Amy said, pointedly to Noah. "This is Lily and Petey."

"Hi," Noah mumbled, not hiding his jealousy. He wanted Carly all to himself. He didn't care who these stupid people were.

"...and these," Amy said to Lily and Petey "...are my friends, Noah and Kelly."

John noticed that she intentionally omitted him out of the introductions.

"Hi," he said stepping forward and offering his hand. "I'm John Palmer. I actually am her friend. I've been her friend for a long time."

The big man looked worried, his big feet shuffling back and forth.

"What do you mean, a long time?" the woman asked calmly, staring at John with even gray eyes. John looked at her for a long moment before he spoke. She seemed genuinely concerned about Amy, and her tone even seemed protective.

"I mean, I know her as someone other than Carly. I know her as Amy. Amy Harper," John searched her face for a hint of recognition, as she continued to stare at him evenly. He could see out of the corner of his eye that the big man was backing away slowly.

Suddenly, there was a thunderous sound of feet running on the pavement, and within a second, Lily and the big man were face down on the ground. Men were flashing badges, and there was the audible sound of handcuffs clicking closed. Noah looked on in awe, his big green eyes wide as he clung tight to Kelly.

"Lily! Petey!" Amy was beside herself, wheeling herself as close to them as she could. "Where are you taking them? Petey. Petey! Where are you taking my husband?"

John ran to Petey and grabbed his collar as hard as he could. "What did you do to him? Where is James? What did you do?"

The officer shoved John aside. "Sir, we'll take care of it. We'll find out what happened. Back off!"

John was desperate. Once he realized who Amy was, one of the phone calls he made was to the police. He knew that somehow the people who kidnapped her were bound to show up. They wouldn't have put her in a place like this if they didn't care about her. And if they cared about her, he figured they would come to see her. He just didn't realize it would happen so quickly.

The big man looked down at John, unfazed by John's sudden outburst. John was surprised by the sadness in the big man's eyes as he gestured for him to come closer. John immediately felt foolish, realizing that there was nothing about him that would intimidate this giant. He walked close to him slowly, feeling sheepish.

"Please," the big man said his voice low and gentle. "Please take care of her. I never hurt her. I would never hurt her. Please, make sure that she is happy." The officers jerked him away and they were gone as quickly as they had arrived, leaving the little group to themselves.

John was stunned. It was clear that Petey loved Amy. He looked back at Amy, her eyes following Petey until he disappeared, tears flowing uncontrollably down her cheeks.

"Sir," an older officer stood next to John and tapped him on the shoulder, startling him. John was caught up and didn't realize that there was anyone standing next to him. "We will need to talk to her. When you are settled down, and can make arrangements, I will need her. Sooner rather than later."

John nodded, not taking his eyes off Amy. She looked broken and sad, and it broke his heart. What have they done to her? Did they brainwash her?

John looked over at Noah and Kelly, who were stunned by the sudden turn of events that had just taken place. "Are you okay?"

They nodded without speaking.

"Are you still taking me? To the big house?" Noah asked after a few minutes, breaking the silence.

"Yes," John said, putting his hand on his shoulder. "Yes, I am."

CHAPTER THIRTY-SEVEN

Intruder

Adam woke up, his head splitting, his body aching. It was a familiar feeling, but something was different. The bed he was laying on was comfortable, soft. He closed his eyes and sunk into it. He knew this bed so well. It was his and Brynn's bed. He had missed it.

His head was fuzzy as he tried to remember every detail from the night before. His mind flashed images of Brynn in the bathtub with him, her clothes coming off easily, piece by piece. She was soaked, and she didn't care. He had never seen her so free in her nakedness before. She excited him in a way that he couldn't remember her exciting him before. They couldn't get close enough to one another, both of them clinging desperately, breathlessly, intensely.

He had missed the softness of her skin, and running his fingers up and down the bumpiness of her scars. He loved her scars as much as he loved her; they were a part of her that he couldn't deny.

Where is she? He wondered, realizing that she wasn't lying next to him.

He stood up uneasily, waiting for the throbbing in his head to intensify as the blood started to flow. He took a deep breath and started to walk around the house. He caught his reflection in the mirror, his dark thick hair standing up in messy waves. He grinned, his dark blue eyes lighting up. He was home.

He wandered around the house aimlessly looking for Brynn,

looking in all of the usual spots. He didn't see Maxie anywhere either, but wherever Brynn was he would surely find Maxie. That dog loved Brynn, and rightfully so. She was good to Maxie. She had been good to Adam, too. But Adam had left her twice now. *How will she ever take me back?*

Brynn, Brynn, Brynn. He walked up and down the halls all over the house. *She's gone!*

He sat on the steps, his heart sinking.

Adam decided that he wasn't leaving. He wasn't going anywhere ever again. Living without her wasn't living, and he was tired of being miserable, tired of the constant shifting of his heart. Even Jessie knew that his heart wasn't complete without Brynn, and she had grown tired of it. Adam couldn't blame her. *I tried, Jessie. Honest to God, I tried.*

I'll call the realtor, and I'll call off the sale. I'll tell them that we are keeping the house, and we are going to live here forever. I'll tell them that it was an awful mistake. Adam needed aspirin. He padded around the house getting water, aspirin, looking out the windows. *Where did she go? She didn't even leave a note! I hope she is okay.*

Adam was getting worried. *She probably just went to the restaurant.*

He was hungry. *I'll text her and see where she is.*

B~Where are you?

Adam waited, but Brynn didn't answer. After an hour, he gave up and made a bowl of cereal. *Maybe she's freaked out. Maybe she hates me, and she is waiting for me to leave.*

The house was quiet, too quiet. He hated it. He walked around the house and pictured it the way it used to be. He remembered painting the walls with Brynn, laying the flooring with his own hands. He remembered the first fight they got into about the color of the sitting room, and how she thought the house was too big the first time she saw it. He remembered walking out of it the first time, believing he would never return. And then he remembered coming back and planning to have a baby with her, painting the baby's room, and watching Brynn's belly grow.

The nightmares. The terrible nightmares. He thought about finding Brynn hiding under the bed, in the closet, behind doors, and locked in the bathroom. Night terrors from Thomas and from when she was abandoned. Adam lay awake almost every night, the guilt tearing at him, knowing that Brynn was probably having another night terror and that he wasn't there to help her, to soothe her. He hated himself.

His parents weren't talking to him, and Adam was completely alone. Even Jessie had abandoned him, all because they knew what he had been refusing to acknowledge. Adam loved Brynn. Adam belonged with Brynn.

Adam walked up to the room he had been avoiding. The room with the door closed, that neither of them talked about. Sophie's room.

He opened the door and sucked his breath in. The room was untouched. It looked as it did the day they finished it. The walls were a pale pink, with delicate white butterflies painted whimsically all around the room. The crib sat quiet and isolated, white and pink and pretty. Adam looked around, breathing in the smell of talcum powder. He sat down in the rocking chair and imagined that Brynn often did the same, rocking and remembering the last time they held their tiny baby.

Adam choked back tears.

He remembered standing in this very room drunk and screaming at Brynn who cowered before him. "It's your fault Sophie is gone. You never wanted to be a mother! You never wanted to have children! You're a damaged, broken, useless bitch, and I hate you!"

Adam sunk to the floor from the chair and huddled in the fetal position, the shame, and the guilt washing over him in waves. *How could I? How? I am a disgusting person.* Adam held himself to the floor as tight as he could. He wanted to sink into it, to disappear. The carpet was soft, barely touched, and he never wanted to leave this room.

I need a drink. I need a fucking drink.

Adam hated the thought that crept into his mind a hundred times a day. He never used to drink because he hated what Thomas' drinking did to Brynn. But when they lost Sophie, something inside of him snapped, and he started drinking every day, all day. And now that little voice was telling him he needed a drink, even when he would already be drinking. He wanted to kill that little voice.

I'm not drinking again! I'm not! Not here, not ever. He felt like he had violated Sophie's room just by thinking about it. Her room felt like a sanctuary to him.

How can I ever leave this house again? How can I ever walk away from it? This is Sophie's room, her home, and Brynn's home.

Adam didn't realize that Brynn wasn't in the house. He stopped searching for her, lost in his thoughts as he lay on the floor of Sophie's room.

Brynn had gotten out of the house as quickly as she could in the morning, and drove around searching for clarity. She had never been with another man besides Adam, and despite the night before, all she could think about was Nick. It was strange how spending the night with Adam brought her a sense of closure. Brynn finally felt as though she could move on.

She realized that the only thing she wanted was to talk to Nick. Brynn fumbled for her cell phone and called him. She knew that it was early, but she decided that he would understand once she told him that she needed to hear his voice and to hear his laugh. She couldn't wait to talk to him, couldn't wait to make plans to see him again.

"Hello?" a female voice said sleepily.

"Hello?" Brynn said before she could stop herself. She pulled the phone away from her ear to see if had dialed the right number. His picture danced in front of her face, and she knew that it was no mistake.

"Who is this?" the female voice said, suddenly sounding very awake.

"Um, who is this?" Brynn said suddenly feeling on guard, the hairs on the back of her neck standing up. Who is answering Nick's phone this early in the morning?

"This is his wife!" The voice said swearing at Brynn.

Brynn didn't continue to listen; she simply hung up the phone and sat stunned.

She didn't need Adam. She didn't need anyone. Everyone in Brynn's life who was meant to protect, watch over, love, and listen to her had abandoned her. She couldn't believe that she ever imagined

Nick to be any different.

Brynn looked sadly at Maxie who had been sitting quietly in the back seat. You're the only one who loves me. You're the only who has ever been true, who has loved me unconditionally. Maxie leapt up and licked her face and the tears that were starting to fall.

Brynn was embarrassed, she felt stupid. His wife! Brynn couldn't believe it.

Brynn sped home as quickly as she could with a sudden need to be completely alone. She needed Adam to leave. When she walked in the house, it was quiet, too quiet. Maxie's nails clicked on the floor behind her as Brynn started searching the rooms for Adam. He was nowhere to be found, but she knew that he was still there. She saw his wallet and keys on the side table when she came in.

She walked up to the room where she always kept the door closed and realized that it was wide open. She saw Adam lying in the middle of the floor, a silent trespasser. Brynn never went into that room. She wanted it to remain untainted, untouched. She couldn't bear the thought of anyone disturbing anything.

Adam didn't hear the footsteps walking into the bedroom.

Brynn's voice was low. He could barely hear it. "What are you doing in here?"

Adam jumped, "Brynn!"

"What are you doing in Sophie's room?" Brynn's voice was louder, and Adam realized that she didn't sound happy.

"I-I-I just wanted to see it." Adam suddenly felt as if he were trespassing.

"I don't want you in here. Get out!" Brynn's voice was rising. Her face was contorted in anger as she pointed to the door. "Get out! You have no right to be in here."

"No right? How can I not have a right to be here?" Brynn had touched a nerve with Adam.

"This isn't your home any longer. You didn't want to live here. You don't have a right to be here. Get out!" Adam had never heard Brynn's voice sound like this before. It was high, and shrill, and had a hysterical edge to it. He stared at her in disbelief.

"I'm not leaving. I'm not going anywhere. This is my house. I love you. I want to come back to you. I was a fool to leave. And I know you love me. If you didn't love me, you never would have been with me last night." Adam was pleading. He knew that he was begging, but he didn't care. He would give anything not to leave again.

Brynn stood in the room, her feet planted. She was confused about many things, but she wasn't confused about wanting Adam to leave.

As she stared at Adam in disbelief upon him violating Sophie's room, Brynn felt something break inside of her and she was furious—beyond furious. *Why is he here? What does he want from me?*

"GET OUT!" She screamed at Adam, lunging at him. "I need you to leave RIGHT NOW!"

She grabbed his shirt and started to drag him out of Sophie's room. Adam was taken off guard and was stunned by how strong her tiny body was. The anger was resonating from her, palpable and dark. He had never seen her like this before and he struggled against her, trying to stand his ground.

"BRYNN! Stop! Stop and calm down!" He tried to hold her tightly, tried to soothe her, but she refused to let him. She fought violently against him until Adam put his hands in the air, "I'll leave. God, I'm sorry, I'll leave."

Adam hurried down the stairs with her right behind him.

"You never should have gone into Sophie's room. You never should have come back here. Don't ever come back here again, Adam!" she hissed. "I don't need you, and I don't want you. All you've done is hurt me, and I am done with you. I don't want you in my life anymore!"

Adam was standing outside before he realized it, Maxie staring at him from the other side of the window.

"Brynn, Brynn..." Adam heard the click of the lock and the curtain close on the window.

Adam stared at the front door in disbelief.

It was over. After all of their years together, after he had returned, he would leave again. After last night, Adam finally knew that his life with Brynn was gone for good. And this time Adam knew that it was forever.

CHAPTER THIRTY-EIGHT

Brynn and John

Brynn found out that Ellie died when a man named John Palmer called and asked if he could meet with her. They met face to face at a little coffee shop, and in spite of herself, Brynn liked him immediately. He felt almost like she imagined family should feel. Though she was usually distrustful, John made it easy for her. She liked that he was direct and to the point, and she trusted that about him. He seemed to have no interest other than protecting the family name and assets, and she admired his loyalty to her grandfather and to the family. John talked about James Harper fondly, and Brynn knew that he had meant a great deal to him.

He wasn't sure how Brynn would take Ellie's death, which is why he asked to meet with her in person.

"I hate to be the bearer of bad news, but your birth mother, Elizabeth Harper, overdosed and has died," John said hesitantly.

He wasn't sure how Brynn would react, and was intrigued to find that she barely had a reaction at all. She simply sighed, and said, "Is that all you wanted to tell me?"

Brynn knew that she should feel something about Ellie's death, but she simply felt relief. She never wanted to have a relationship with her. She simply wanted to confront her about why Ellie abandoned her the way she had. Now that Brynn had done that, she realized she didn't need anything from Ellie anymore, or even had any feelings about or for her, good or bad. And now that Ellie was gone, she was shocked to discover that she hadn't thought about Ellie much at all anymore.

Ellie had not been one of John's favorite people, and he was glad to not have to deal with her any longer, even though he struggled with the guilt of feeling that way. He knew that James loved Ellie more than anything, and John felt that he had failed them both by not being able to prevent her death. But he realized there was nothing else he could have done to save her.

He was hoping that Brynn would be very different from her birth mother. He wasn't sure what to expect when he met her, but had done extensive research on her background. He was prepared to hard sell her on being involved with the Harper Family, but he was taken off guard by how much he liked her. He could see a lot of James in her. James had been his mentor, and had taught him everything he knew. John had admired James' focus, his ability to get what he wanted easily. He saw the same focus and strength in Brynn, and he was careful not to underestimate her, but he found that he enjoyed their conversation and felt almost paternal toward her right away.

When he told her about the Harper House and that he wanted her to move in, he could tell right away that she didn't like the idea. She couldn't imagine that she would ever be comfortable in a home so big.

"I can't live in that big house!" she protested, her head still spinning about the inheritance. "That's ridiculous! I'll just buy a little bungalow by the restaurant and call it a day!"

"You can't just go off and live in a bungalow and ignore everything else." John said, and Brynn got the sense that he was a little annoyed. "There's more than the inheritance to consider."

"More?" Brynn's mind was already reeling. He had just told her that Ellie was dead. Then he told Brynn that she was inheriting the Harper fortune, which reached numbers that she had never imagined in her wildest dreams. "How is there possibly more?"

He explained about Noah, and Brynn fought the initial urge to run. Ellie had told her about Noah, but Brynn didn't anticipate that she was ever going to have to be his guardian and take care of him for the rest of his life. She didn't know if she would be able to do what John was asking of her, or even if she wanted to. She wasn't ready to take care of a younger brother she didn't know. Especially not one who needed so much. "Just meet him," John urged. "You'll fall in love with him, I promise."

Reluctantly, Brynn allowed John to set up a meeting between them a week later.

John had started hiring staff for the Harper House, and had the driver, Tony, take them to the home where Noah had spent most of his life. The drive up was pleasant, and John told Brynn a little bit about her family history. He was evasive when she asked about her grandmother, but she was so distracted with the thought of meeting Noah that she hadn't noticed. Brynn was impressed when they drove up. It didn't look like anything she had expected. It looked like an expensive resort, but Brynn was still saddened by the fact that Noah had to live here.

Noah had been waiting for them, and had started jumping up and down when he saw the car pull up. He came bounding up to the car, army men in hand, ready to introduce himself to his new sister. He introduced her to Kelly, telling Brynn that she was his "best girl." Kelly smiled graciously, and Brynn decided that she liked her immediately. Noah was clearly excited as he took her hand and showed her around his home, introducing her to all of his friends, except for his new best friend, Carly, who was in for her morning nap.

"I can't wait for you to meet Carly," he said, talking so quickly she had to concentrate to keep up. "She's great at checkers!"

Despite herself, Brynn did fall in love with Noah—at first sight, actually. He was sweet, vivacious, and energetic, and his adventurous spirit caught her off guard. She knew that she would never be able to leave him behind now, which is what she figured John was banking on. She realized that in Noah, she now had family. When Sophie died and Adam left her, she felt as though her chance at ever having a family were gone forever. Brynn was overwhelmed with the feeling that now she had a brother, and she knew that there would be no going back. She would now have a brother—forever.

A few days after she met Noah, John asked to meet with her again at the coffee shop where she met him the first time. Brynn was suspicious that he was inviting her to have coffee for the second time in a week.

"What do you mean, I have a grandmother?" Brynn was shocked and almost spit coffee out all over him. The look in her eyes told him that she wasn't up for any more surprises, and he almost felt guilty for keeping Amy from her. But he couldn't take the chance that Brynn would reject her. He wanted her to be hooked on Noah first. He knew that if she were, there would be no problem with introducing her to Amy. He also didn't want to overwhelm Brynn with too much at once.

When she got over her initial surprise, and John assured her that there wasn't anything else he was keeping from her, Brynn responded exactly how he hoped she would.

"I want to meet her as soon as possible!" she exclaimed, her eyes glistening with excitement. "I just don't understand how she could be alive this long, and how nobody knew about her."

John explained what he had gotten from Petey and Lily, before they had gone to prison. He knew the whole story now, and went through it with Brynn. Brynn cried as she imagined her grandmother alone, losing her memory, her past, her husband, and her life. She wanted to meet the woman who had adored her so much as a child. John showed her pictures of the two of them together, and the love in Amy's eyes was obvious.

But Brynn agreed to wait until John could bring her home, and the months felt like years.

John finally convinced her that moving into the Harper Home was the best thing for everyone. Brynn was in awe of the beauty of the old house, and she busied herself by setting up rooms and suites and updating the big house so that it didn't feel so empty and lonely.

She planned each room carefully and meticulously based on their needs and the feedback that John gave her. She called Kelly for advice on Noah's room, and since she was also coming to live with them, she talked to her about how she would like her room set up, as well.

The hardest room for Brynn to set up was the nursery. She had set it up with Adam in the Victorian, but she never wanted to do it alone. Sadly, now she realized that she had no choice. She was going to have to do it by herself, whether she wanted to or not.

CHAPTER THIRTY-NINE

Brynn's Discovery

The memory of that day, and discovering that she was pregnant was hard for Brynn to revisit. It had been a hard day for her, and a hard moment for her to make it through. Brynn had sat in the yellow bathroom of the Victorian with Maxie lying loyally by her side on the cool tile. Brynn prayed.

She stared at the stick that sat on the edge of the bathroom sink as though it were a snake, and then stared at her watch. *One minute.*

She couldn't understand why time moved so slowly during the most painful or crucial moments of her life, yet the good ones flew by.

Two minutes.

She took a deep breath and looked at the stick. There was a plus. *Plus? Plus? What is a plus? Pregnant? Not pregnant? Pregnant? Oh no! Pregnant!*

Brynn sat down on the toilet, nearly falling in. She swore and flipped the cover down, and then sank to the floor hugging Maxie tight. *I can't be pregnant! This can't be!*

After Sophie's death, she realized that she wanted to be a mother. But she had never thought that she would do it alone. She thought about Adam, and she thought about Nick, and she realized that either of them could be the father. But neither of them were father material now. Adam, with his drinking and constant abandonment of her, and Nick with his wife. Brynn was disgusted with herself and disgusted with both of them. It had been a few months since she had last spoken to either of them, and she had no desire to have them in her life.

She desperately wanted to cry, but couldn't find the tears.

But now that she had come to terms with it, she was nervous and excited at the same time. She had lived through a lot of horrible things in her life, but bringing life into the world was beautiful, and Brynn felt thankful that she would have another chance to be a mother. Even if it meant she wouldn't get to share it with the man she loved.

Brynn enjoyed watching her belly grow little by little. She looked at herself in the mirror every day, dismayed that the scars from her early years of cutting to escape Thomas' abuse were still visible. She wished that they would fade away so that she never had to see them again, but they remained like the scars that resurfaced in her dreams. She decided that she was happy about being pregnant, and she pushed aside the feelings that Nick or Adam wouldn't be so happy.

Setting up the nursery in the Harper House was turning out to be fun. Jane was helping her, and had convinced Brynn to indulge a little since she now had the resources to do so. Brynn wasn't used to having an unlimited amount of money, and it made her uncomfortable. But Jane kept telling her that it was okay, and that spending money on the baby was a wonderful thing.

Brynn was thankful she had Jane, even though Jane asked her the hard questions that she sometimes didn't want to answer.

"So you are definitely going to do this alone? No Nick, No Adam?" Jane asked while they shopped.

"No, I'm not alone," Brynn smiled weakly, "I have you."

Jane shook her head and hugged her friend. She wondered when Brynn was ever going to allow herself to be happy, to let go and allow someone to love her. Even if she didn't know who the father of her baby was, Jane had hoped she would figure it out so that everyone would be happy. From what Brynn had told her, she knew that both Adam and Nick would be thrilled with the prospect of being a father again. But Brynn was stubborn, and she knew that it would be difficult to change her mind. She just wanted her friend to be happy. Right now, Brynn's happiness was wrapped up in finishing the house and having it ready for her new family.

The nursery was the last room to be renovated, and then the Harper House was complete.

Moving day for Amy and Noah had finally come. John Palmer had wished for it to happen much sooner, but there were many details to wrap up. Finally, he could breathe a sigh of relief knowing that his plans were coming to fruition.

Noah was sad to leave his friends, and the only home he had ever really known. He was happy that Kelly was going to be coming with him. It was the only consolation that he had. Noah had met Brynn a few times. She seemed nice enough, but they weren't quite friends yet. She was pretty, but Noah saw her make sad faces a lot and that made him sad, too. *Brynn reminded him of Mommy, and that made him really sad.*

Noah did like Maxie a lot. He always wanted a dog, but Mommy wouldn't let him have one. Brynn told him that Maxie could be his dog, too, and that made Noah very happy. *He liked throwing Maxie the ball because he liked to fetch, and Maxie liked to give kisses, which made Noah laugh.*

He didn't have a lot to take with him from the home. Just some army men, some clothes, and a few pictures. One of the pictures was of him and Ellie. *He could hardly remember her now, but he missed her and it made him upset to think of her. So he didn't.*

He was happy that his friend Carly was moving with him, too. But he didn't understand that John kept calling her 'Amy'. Noah tried calling her by the 'Amy' name, but he kept forgetting and it came out as 'C-amy'. Carly said he could call her whatever he wanted to. Everyone seemed happy that Noah and Amy were such good friends. *Noah didn't understand why everyone cared so much, he just wanted to keep seeing his friend and playing checkers with her.*

But Carly seemed sad, too. Carly and Brynn were sad women, and it made Noah sad sometimes to look at them. He tried to do funny things to make them laugh, and it did. But then they would look sad again. It didn't make sense to Noah.

Kelly was the only woman in his life who seemed really happy. Noah thought she was so pretty, and he thought he might want to marry her one day. But Kelly said, even though she was flattered, that she had a boyfriend. Noah said that he would keep asking, but Kelly said that he should find a nice girl his own age. He knew he wouldn't. *He thought Kelly was the prettiest woman he had ever met, with her silky blonde hair and bright blue eyes.*

Noah was excited about going to the "Big House," like everyone was calling it. John said he was going to have a big room where he could fit all of his army guys. John said that he would get him a lot more army guys to play with. John said that he could have anything he wanted, but he didn't want much. He just wanted his army guys and a soft bed. He didn't really like his bed at the home, but John said he would love his bed at the new house.

Kelly helped him pack his stuff, and then they went over to Carly's room to see how she was doing.

"C-Amy, are you ready yet?" Noah asked, bouncing on her bed.

"Not yet," Amy said shaking her head. "I don't know where I put my suitcase."

"I packed it for you already," Kelly said putting her hand on Amy's shoulder. "You're all ready to go now."

Amy looked around the room sadly. "I don't know where I'm going."

"You're going to the house you lived in a long time ago," Kelly said gently. "Your old house. The 'Harper House'. Do you remember?"

"No. I don't remember. I only remember living with Lily and Petey. I miss Lily and Petey. They loved me. They were my friends." Amy looked at Kelly, tears brimming in her beautiful brown eyes. "I don't know where I'm going."

Kelly smiled patiently. She had been having this conversation with Amy for weeks, and she hoped that when Amy got to the house it would be different and that she would remember. Kelly hoped that she would at least feel at home there.

"It'll be okay, Amy. Don't worry." Kelly gave her a quick hug. "I'll be there with you. Don't worry."

Amy nodded, trying to smile.

"Do you know what happened to Petey? Do you know what happened to my husband?" Amy was wringing her hands together faster and faster, her voice worried. "Nobody will tell me where my husband is. When he comes back to get me, I won't be here. How will he find me? How will he know where I am?"

Kelly frowned. She hated lying to Amy, but knew that she couldn't tell her the truth. She would never understand that Petey and Lily were gone, to prison, for a long time. She knew that it would only break Amy's fragile heart to know the truth. She grabbed Amy's hands to stop her from wringing them together, and she held onto them tight. "Amy, Petey has gone away, and he's not coming for back for a long time. He said to leave, and he will find you. He said not to worry, and that he wants you to go to the Big House. He said that you would be safe and happy there. Now, we have to get ready to go. The car is coming to get us very soon."

Amy looked around the room sadly. She didn't want to leave. She thought of her big husband, and how sweet he was to her, and it made her miss him even more. *How will he find me when he comes back? How can he think that I will be happy without him?*

"Come on C-Amy! Let's go see our new big house!" Noah was excited, and he couldn't wait to see his new house and his new room. Brynn had been getting the house ready for them and he couldn't wait to see his room.

Kelly's phone buzzed, and she checked it quickly. "Okay, folks," she said a little too brightly. "It's time to hit the road to the Harper House."

Noah jumped up and down in excitement. Amy looked at him, annoyed with Noah for the first time. She wasn't ready to go yet, but before she could protest, Kelly was wheeling her chair out of the room toward the elevator.

Amy watched her room disappear when the elevator doors closed, her stomach feeling sick suddenly. She hoped the feeling would go away, but the nauseousness was coming more and more lately, and it seemed like she never went too long without it.

All three stopped when they got out the front door. The big, sleek truck in front of them was mesmerizing. A sharply dressed middle-aged man in a black suit appeared out of nowhere. "Hi, I'm Tony. I'll be your driver today. Please, get in," he said gesturing to the open door. Noah and Kelly got in promptly, but Amy sat there waiting for Tony to help her, which he quickly obliged.

He expertly folded the wheelchair up and put it in the back of the truck. "When we get to the Big House, Miss, you'll have an electric cart to take you around in. You'll be able to go all over the grounds." He smiled at Amy and tipped his hat.

Kelly wondered briefly if Tony had been at the Harper House when Amy lived there, but that would have been over thirty years ago. Unless Tony was five or ten when he lived there, Kelly doubted it. She was trying to make a connection between the house and Amy. She knew that it would make Amy feel better about the move.

The drive to the House was quiet and seemed to take a long time. Kelly could feel the nervous energy in the car, and she tried to steady her nerves. She didn't know why she was so nervous; after all, this was a short stay for her. Kelly was getting married next year, and declined the servant quarters for a quiet home a few miles away. She wanted to be close, but still have a life of her own.

The car suddenly slowed and turned into a long driveway lined by magnificent pine trees that were hundreds of feet tall. They all peered out the window in awe, Noah's face pressed tight up against the glass, smearing it with breath and spit.

The driveway was long and pulled into a large roundabout. All three stared at the house in amazement. It definitely lived up to the name "The Big House."

Amy looked at the front entrance and felt a strange familiarity tickling at her. She knew that she had been here before, many times. She was eager to get out of the car.

They pulled to a stop before the front steps. Amy noticed that there was a wheelchair ramp that looked new, to the left of the stairs. A petite, dark haired woman was standing in front of the house. Amy thought that she was beautiful and hauntingly familiar.

Tony opened the door, and Noah exploded out of the car like a bullet. Kelly got out and held her hand out to Amy who grabbed it tightly. Tony and Kelly got Amy situated in the wheelchair and Amy took a breath and inhaled deeply through her nose. *I know the smell of this place! I've been here before!* Amy suddenly got a picture of a handsome dark haired man smiling at her. *James!*

Tears pricked at her eyes. *Where have I been? Where did I go?*

The woman standing at the steps looked at Amy, concerned. After she had hugged Noah and Kelly, Amy noticed that the woman didn't move. She just stared at Amy, with curiosity. The woman looked familiar to Amy, but she didn't know who she was. Amy never knew who anyone was anymore.

But this woman was different.

Suddenly the woman started walking toward Amy. She walked as Ellie used to walk and she reminded her of Ellie.

The woman opened her mouth to speak, and Amy thought it was Ellie speaking. The woman's voice had the same earthy tone to it, and Amy closed her eyes for just a second. She opened them quickly, her eyes wide in recognition.

She grabbed the younger woman and pulled her as close as she could, with a strength that she thought disappeared a long time ago.

Chapter Forty

Home at Last

Everyone held their breath as they watched Amy grab Brynn and hold her tight.

"Eva! Eva! Oh my Eva! I thought that I would never see you again!" Amy cried.

Brynn stared into Amy's big brown eyes, the same brown eyes as her own.

She searched Amy's face, a face so much like the one she stared at in the mirror every day, only older. And if possible, sadder. She knew Amy's face, she felt as though she somehow remembered her face. Brynn saw glimpses of a younger face smiling at her with perfect white teeth, almost like an angel.

In all of her life, Brynn couldn't remember ever letting anyone hold her so closely and so soon, without wanting to pull away. Not even Adam. But Amy felt familiar in a way that Brynn couldn't explain.

Amy felt like home.

Brynn saw tears falling down Amy's cheeks and felt warm tears on her own cheeks. The two women hadn't even had a conversation, but Brynn knew that they didn't need words. There had always been something special between them. This had been the bond that Brynn had been missing; not Ellie, not Adam, not even Nick. All along, she had been waiting for Amy. Amy and Noah. They were her family now, and Brynn knew it just as certain as she had ever known anything. With the growing child inside of her, Brynn was struck with the realization that she was finally going to have the life that she had longed for, prayed for, even as a child. She was going to have a home with people who loved her.

Brynn had a family.

There was something about Amy and Noah that felt as familiar to her as anything had ever felt. She had always felt out of place in the world, but now she not only had a physical home, but people who felt like home to her.

Time stood still as Amy and Brynn held onto each other. Brynn closed her eyes, and she felt like a little girl, and imagined Amy holding her as a child. When they pulled away from one another, they smiled the same smile.

Brynn had wanted to meet Amy before. She had begged John. But Amy hadn't been doing well, and John felt it was best to wait.

Kelly watched from a distance and was amazed at how much they looked alike, the resemblance uncanny. She could see the resemblance in Noah, and she was happy that they had found one another. Something felt complete, and Kelly was happy to be a part of it. It had been hard for her to leave the home that her grandparents had built. But Kelly was drawn to Noah and Amy, and when John asked her to take care of them, she didn't hesitate. She didn't need the money that he offered her, but she did it so she could remain a part of them. They were special and she couldn't part with them as she had done with so many of the other residents.

Brynn ushered everyone into the house and had the help show them around. The house was full with the entire staff. Brynn wanted them there for the homecoming so they could all meet and work out their schedules. She was managing the house as she managed the restaurant, quickly and efficiently, giving everyone a role and sending them off to do it.

Noah had noticed her growing belly on his last visit before moving into the Big House.

"Brynn, you're getting fat." He said pointing to her stomach. "Are you eating too much food?"

"No," Brynn smiled, ruffling his hair. "There's a baby growing in there."

"There is?" Noah smiled. "I like babies!"

Brynn smiled back at him. "You're going to be an uncle!"

Noah jumped up and down in excitement. "I'm going to be an uncle! I'm going to be an uncle!"

He stopped suddenly, a worried look coming across his face. "What's an uncle? I don't know how to be an uncle!"

"You will be a wonderful uncle!" Brynn smiled at him, ruffling his hair. She tried to hide her fear from him and from everyone else.

"Who is the baby's daddy? My daddy is dead." Noah asked and stated all at once.

Brynn wasn't sure how to answer him, so she didn't. She didn't want to tell him that she wasn't sure who the father was. Adam, who was no longer in her life, or Nick who she was trying desperately to ignore.

The last time Brynn talked to Nick was before she knew that she was pregnant. She had refused to answer the phone, but he kept calling and texting.

She finally picked up the phone one last time to tell him to stop calling her. "I don't want to talk to you," Brynn yelled at him on the phone.

"Brynn! Brynn! Please, hear me out!" Nick was begging, and Brynn admitted to herself that she loved the sound of his voice. "I'm done, I've moved out. The divorce is almost final. Please, let me visit you. Let me explain it to you. I've been a horrible person, but I never meant to hurt you. I was trying to protect her, take care of things so that she would be okay. I'm so sorry for hurting you."

"I can't!" Brynn said gripping the phone in her hand. "I can't trust you anymore." She wanted to trust him. She wanted to give him a chance. But she couldn't. She couldn't stop thinking about Nick. She couldn't stop lying awake in bed at night remembering his lips on hers, or the sound of his voice in her ears. But she couldn't allow him to hurt her again.

"I can't talk to you anymore, Nick. Please." Brynn was crying, her sobs crushing him. He never wanted to hurt her. After he caught Mel answering his phone, he finally found the courage to leave her. He knew at that moment that he only wanted Brynn. He hadn't loved Mel for a long time, her boozy anger and mismanaged mental illness had slowly destroyed him, wearing him down.

Nick realized that in a few short days, Brynn had begun to heal him, connecting with him in their mutual pain, and that all he wanted was a chance to be with her. He just wanted to be able to show her that even though he lied, his feelings for her were real.

"Please don't call me again." Brynn said, her voice barely audible, and then she hung up, refusing to pick up the phone again when he called.

CHAPTER FORTY-ONE

Family

Brynn's life was so different than it had been a year ago. Jane managed the restaurant solely now, and Brynn had given her full partnership. Brynn was barely involved and trusted Jane completely. Her days were full with Noah and Amy, and as her pregnancy progressed, she found herself more fatigued.

Brynn found that she loved the house and rarely found excuses to leave. She was proud of the work she had done and how it had been beautifully restored under her supervision, years of neglect stripped away. She tried to imagine what it looked like when she was a baby, being carried into the house for the first time. But that had been so long ago and nothing that happened after was happy. Brynn wanted her baby to come into a happy home, and she wanted the home to be filled with love and laughter. With Amy, Noah, Kelly, and the staff, she was finding that there was plenty of love and laughter to go around.

Even though she hadn't had the ultrasound yet, Brynn knew that her baby was a girl. She talked to her baby girl every day, apologizing for her own shortcomings, explaining her decisions when she talked to her baby, she didn't feel so alone.

Walking into the home for the first time with her grandmother, Brynn had been a little afraid. John had assured her that she had done a beautiful job and that the house was beautiful. But she was afraid that she had changed it too much, and that Amy wouldn't recognize it. John warned her that Amy might not recognize it anyway.

Amy looked around in awe as Brynn wheeled her through the gigantic foyer in front of the winding double staircase. "I lived here?"

"Yes," Brynn said softly. "You lived here, for a long time."

"It's beautiful," Amy breathed. "Did it look like this when I lived here?"

"It looked a lot like this, but I made some changes." Brynn said smiling.

Amy patted her hand. "Good girl. It's gorgeous." Brynn couldn't help but beam. Her heart was bursting with pride that Amy liked it. The hard part was over now, and she could get everyone settled in.

John smiled as he watched them move through the home. He had spent his entire life trying to restore the Harper legacy, and now it was finally coming together. He breathed a sigh of relief, happy to see the Big House restored and lived in again. He knew that James, his good friend and mentor, would be proud of him.

The next few months were a blur as everyone settled into normal life. Brynn's belly got rounder, and she and Amy were inseparable. In a lot of ways, Amy was the mother that Brynn longed for all of her life.

Amy's memory came back in flashes, but it didn't matter anymore. She felt at home with Brynn, and she didn't miss Petey, or his sister, Lily, as much, when she was with her granddaughter. She didn't remember baby Eva, but something about Brynn's big brown eyes gave her comfort. She knew Brynn by her eyes. She was the only person she was completely comfortable with...

Brynn and Kelly became close, almost as close as sisters.

Besides Jane, Brynn never had another female friend as an adult. She had never allowed herself to get close to anyone before, but Kelly was different, and for some reason, Brynn trusted her right away. She was helpful with Noah, but it was more than that. She seemed to understand Brynn, and she was a true caregiver. Kelly was smart, organized, and thoughtful. Brynn liked having her around. Kelly noticed that Noah was happier and calmer. The house had a soothing effect on him, and he spent hours pretending that he was an explorer as he discovered every nook and cranny of his new home. Much to everyone's surprise, he was even cooperative with his new tutor, Trina. Kelly took care of more than just Noah and Amy. Even though Brynn didn't realize it, Kelly was taking care of her, too.

"How are you feeling?" Kelly asked Brynn, as she neared her seventh month.

"Tired!" Brynn exclaimed smiling weakly. Brynn rubbed her belly absently. "This little girl is wearing me out."

"I hear it only gets worse," Kelly said smiling wryly.

"Yeah, thanks!" Brynn said sticking out her tongue.

"Oh, wait," Kelly disappeared from the kitchen. She arrived carrying a large bouquet. "These are for you."

Brynn frowned, her face growing dark. Kelly pulled out the card. "Shall I?"

Brynn was quiet.

Kelly pulled the card out slowly waiting for Brynn to protest. "Brynn…" she read slowly.

Brynn was still.

"I miss you."

There was no reaction.

"I need you in my life. You've restored me. Please."

Brynn's eyes filled with tears.

Kelly hesitated, and read on.

"Please," she repeated. "Talk to me. Give me a chance. Let me show you. Love, Nick"

Brynn stared at the beautiful assembly of mixed flowers and smiled. She'd heard it all before. He had been emailing, texting, and instant messaging her for months, but she had ignored him. He didn't know that she was pregnant, and she had no intention of telling him. He didn't know anything. Brynn wondered what he would say if he knew. She imagined that he would be happy. But they barely knew each other. How could they start a relationship with a child?

And then there was Adam. Adam who had just spent a month in rehab. Adam, who wouldn't take "no" for an answer. Adam who kept calling, texting, stopping by unannounced. She had managed to avoid him, until a couple of months ago when he arrived unexpectedly on the porch of the Harper House.

"You're pregnant?!" He was stunned. "You're pregnant, and you didn't tell me? How could you not tell me?"

Brynn tried to ignore the hurt in his voice. She avoided looking into his blue eyes because she was afraid that they would still turn her inside out.

"I didn't tell you because it's none of your business anymore," she said, her tone sharper than she meant it to be.

"My child is my business!" he said bitterly, pacing back and forth in front of her.

"Who said it was yours?" Brynn said angrily.

The tension between them was thick. Adam looked at Brynn in disbelief, trying to find his Brynn in the woman she had become. His Brynn would never sleep with someone else. His Brynn loved him and would never glare at him with those dark angry eyes—eyes that belonged to a stranger. His Brynn would never keep her pregnancy from him.

"Leave!" Brynn said, opening the front door.

"So we're not going to talk about this? How do I know if that is my baby?" Adam couldn't believe she was walking away.

"You don't. And it's not." Brynn walked through the front door and closed it behind her, locking it. Adam always had a way of showing up in her life, but she had spent a lot of time over the years locking him out. Nobody had hurt her the way that Adam had, deep and to the core. She convinced herself that she hated him, and this baby wasn't going to give him a reason to hurt her again. The fifteen-year-old kids that fell in love, so very long ago, were gone forever.

Brynn's phone buzzed.

"Did you get the flowers? I'm in town. I want to see you. Please meet me at the winery. 5 p.m. Don't say NO!"

Brynn shook her head and laughed. *The winery! What will he say when he sees me, and he realizes that I can't drink wine?*

She showed Kelly the text, and Kelly's eyes grew big. "What are you going to do?"

"I don't know. I don't know. I think..." Brynn was hesitant. "I think... that I should go see him and talk in person. I think that I should just do it."

Brynn had spent months convincing herself that she didn't love him. She thought that it was insane to love someone that she had only spent a week with, but she couldn't stop thinking about him no matter how hard she tried. Even if it didn't work out, Brynn knew that she had to at least talk to him. She couldn't go the rest of her life not knowing what it would have been like to at least give him a chance. Brynn had spent her entire life afraid of something or someone. She was tired of being afraid, and of living in fear.

She had given a lot of thought to what she would do if Nick ever came to see her. And now, he was here, and he wanted to see her. She didn't want to live her life regretting her chance, to see what he would say about the baby. At least then, she would know whether her feelings for Nick were true or fleeting.

"Are you going to respond?" Kelly asked, curious to see if Brynn was serious.

"No, I think I'll just show up. That way, if I change my mind, he will never know."

"Brynn!" Kelly scolded.

"I'm going! I know I'll go. He came all this way to see me. I have to," Brynn sighed, already second guessing herself.

Kelly smiled. *It's about time!*

Chapter Forty-Two

Brynn's Happiness

Kelly wanted Brynn to be happy. She had grown to love Brynn and to admire her strength. She could tell that Brynn had scars that she desperately tried to hide, but they surfaced when Brynn's guard was down. Kelly watched her with Amy and with Noah, and even though they were still working through the ebb and flow of their relationships, they were a solid family now. Amy was doing better than Kelly had ever imagined and Noah was thriving every day.

But Brynn's pain was far beyond the simple sadness of most people. It was desolate, devastating sadness, the heartbreaking kind. Brynn didn't talk about it, but Kelly recognized it from her years working at the home and seeing it in the faces of the residents. It was deep, true, pain—the kind that is masked, but never goes away.

"You need to figure out what you are wearing." Kelly said affectionately.

"I don't think it will matter," Brynn said rubbing her stomach. "Once he sees this, I could be wearing a prom dress, and I don't think it would matter!"

She had been so angry with Nick, for lying, and for not being truthful in the first place. She just wasn't sure. And she realized how hypocritical it seemed, considering the fact that she wasn't being honest with him. He didn't know she was pregnant. And he didn't know that it might be his. She had never been with anyone other than Adam. To be with two men during the same time period threw her. She didn't know what to do.

She went upstairs and went through her closet, dreading her meeting with Nick, but looking forward to it at the same time.

She had thought about him so much, imagined what it would be like to see him again. She tried to forget about their week together, but no matter what she did, she couldn't get him out of her mind. She couldn't make herself forget. It was the way he looked at her, the way he touched her. But most of all, it was the connection that she couldn't forget.

She paced her room.

Amy's voice startled her. She hadn't heard her wheel herself in. "Are you okay?"

"Yes!" Brynn said jumping a little. "I'm fine."

"Why are you pacing then?"

Brynn looked at Amy. She was looking frailer by the day. The doctor assured Brynn that she was well, but Brynn was constantly worried. She had just found her and didn't want to lose her so quickly.

"I'm fine, Grandma," Brynn smiled and leaned over to give her a hug. "Don't worry."

"I just want you to be happy," Amy said looking at her evenly. "I don't know that you have ever been happy. You deserve to be."

Brynn felt tears springing up in her eyes without her permission. She hadn't ever been happy. But when she was with Amy, she was happy because she knew that she was truly loved. It was the only time she had ever felt that way.

"I will be, Grandma. I'm always happy when I'm with you." Brynn hugged her gently again.

"Peanut!" Amy said suddenly.

Brynn looked at her, puzzled. "Peanut?"

"I used to call you Peanut when you were little. I had forgotten all about that." Amy said, her eyes looking past Brynn.

Brynn was used to these moments, as Amy seemed to have them more often with some memories resurfacing. Brynn smiled. "Peanut. I love it," she rubbed her stomach. "That's what we can call your great granddaughter."

"Yes," Amy said rubbing Brynn's stomach, affectionately. She was the only one Brynn would allow to touch her like that. "Well, I'll leave you to whatever you were doing."

"I'm trying to figure out what to wear to meet an old, um, friend." Brynn said glancing at her closet in dread.

"Whatever you choose won't matter," Amy said cupping Brynn's face. "You will be beautiful no matter what."

Brynn closed her eyes, cherishing the feel of Amy's soft hand on her cheek. She wished for the thousandth time that she had been with Amy all of her life. "Thanks, Grandma," she whispered.

"You're welcome, Peanut." Amy wheeled herself out of the room, and Brynn was left alone to face her closet.

After an hour, she finally picked out a maternity dress that was both fashionable and functional. Her baby belly was obvious, but it also accented her pretty legs. *It doesn't matter what I wear. The first thing that he is going to see is my stomach. There is no getting around it. Literally!*

She checked the clock. *It was already four-fifteen! Where did the time go?*

She grabbed her purse and moved as fast as she could. She didn't want to be late! She was afraid that he would think she wasn't coming and leave, and the winery was at least forty minutes away!

"Whoa! Where are you going so fast?" Nina, the housekeeper said flustered, as Brynn flew by her.

"I'm late!" Brynn said, trying not to sound panicked.

"You should have Tony drive you." Nina said, concerned about how nervous Brynn looked.

"No! I don't have time for that. I'm ready to go now and I can't wait for him." Brynn said, blindly digging around in her purse for keys.

She finally located them, feeling victorious, and got to her car as quickly as she could. She set her GPS just in case she couldn't remember how to get there, after all she had only been there once, and it had been from the restaurant. She wasn't sure that she would know how to get there from the Harper Home.

As she drove, she felt herself calming down.

What will I say to him? How will he look? What if he leaves the second he sees that I am pregnant?

She felt a little nauseous and fought the urge to turn around and go back home. *It'll be okay. It'll be okay. It'll be okay.*

She tried to take a deep breath and clear her mind. She wanted to be calm when she saw him. She wanted to tell him that she couldn't stop thinking about him, and that she wanted to give him a chance. She wanted him to know that she could see herself with him for a long time, and that he was the only one she had ever felt like she could be completely herself.

She was wrapped up in her thoughts, the pleasant voice on the GPS steering her way.

Brynn didn't see the F150 in the oncoming lane swerving in front of her. She didn't see the intoxicated driver with his eyes closed as he sped toward her, completely overtaking her lane. She didn't see anything until she heard the horrible sound of metal crunching, glass breaking, and then felt her body fly forward forcibly through the windshield. She suddenly felt the pain of a thousand knives slicing through her face and through her body.

And then, Brynn didn't feel anything.

EPILOGUE

The young woman sat at her vanity slowly brushing her long, dark hair. She stared at her reflection in the mirror, seeing a mixture of excitement and sadness on her pretty face.

She tried to hold the tears back, but she couldn't, no matter how hard she tried. This is a happy day!

She kept reminding herself that it was a joyous day. Sadness didn't belong in the day; although, she knew that it would be there no matter how hard she tried to fight it off. It had been there all of her life. It was there on her first day of school, when she got her first bra, when she left for her first date, at her senior prom, at both of her graduations, and it was here now. The sadness was a part of her no matter where she went or what she did. She knew that it would be here today of all days, alive and as palpable as ever.

Will it ever go away? She sighed.

She had asked to be alone right now. Too many people were milling about, in and out of her room, trying to be too helpful. There was too much noise, and no time to think. She needed to think. She needed to reflect. She needed to feel her, here.

She knew that she couldn't do that through all of the noise.

She walked to her window and looked out into the garden. There were a lot of people there, some his and some hers. She held her breath. She knew that there would be. So many people! *I just want to get through this without crying, without ruining my makeup.*

There was a gentle knock on the door.

"Eva, Are you ready?"

"Almost," she said straightening up. She reached up and felt her floral headband to make sure that it was still firmly in place. She took a deep breath and opened the door.

It was Aunt Jane. Jane's eyes immediately filled. "Oh sweetheart, you look so…so…."

"It's okay, Aunt Jane," Eva smiled. She knew what she was going to say, she was thinking it, too. "I look like my mother."

Jane nodded, choking back the tears. "Yes."

"Shall we?" Eva said motioning toward the staircase.

"Oh, yes," Jane said trying to compose herself. "I told myself that I wouldn't cry, but I just couldn't help myself."

"It's okay," Eva hugged the older woman who had been so much like a mother to her. Eva had begged her father from the time she could remember, to let go and find another wife. She desperately wanted to have a mother, but he refused. Now he just said that he was too old, even though he wasn't. She just wanted to see him happy once in her life.

They started down the long winding staircase. Daddy was standing at the bottom of the stairs waiting for her.

"Oh, Eva," he whispered. He was seeing what she had seen in the mirror. Except for the color of her eyes, she was nearly the spitting image of her Mom. "You're a vision, you know that, right?"

Eva nodded. *I wish she were here with me!*

Eva had never known her mother, but she longed for her every day. She had been taken from her in a violent car accident, with a drunk driver. It had been a horrific accident, and her mother had been kept alive for a couple of months after the accident in order to preserve Eva's life that still needed time to grow inside of her. Eva had heard the story a thousand times of how she easily could have died, too. There were days when she wished she had known her. Nobody understood the emptiness she felt without her.

"It was a miracle they were able to save you," Daddy had told her for as long as she could remember. He wanted her to understand how lucky she was. He wanted her to live her life to the fullest and appreciate every moment. The mangled picture of her mom's car was burned into her brain. The twisted blue metal, the shattered windshield, the bloodstains. They stayed with her like a vision, reminding her that she got to live.

Nobody understood the emptiness she felt without her mother. She loved her daddy, but living with him was like living with a ghost. She grew up in the big empty house virtually alone, with Daddy, and for a short time, Uncle Noah.

She loved Uncle Noah, but they said that he died so that he could be with Grandma Amy, who had died of a broken heart. She hadn't known Grandma Amy, but Eva hoped wherever they were that they were there together. She hoped that they weren't lonely like she used to be.

But now that she had Chris, she wasn't as lonely anymore.

"Are you ready to do this?" Eva said looking at her dad.

"I'm ready," he said smiling at her. He had aged. Eva had seen pictures of him from his younger years, and he had been so handsome. But he was a sad shadow of that young man now, his hair white and his eyes permanently sad. She thought of him as Eeyore from her Winnie the Pooh stories, perpetually sad and mopey. She had inherited his beautiful blue eyes, but she tried hard to not let them betray her.

The walk down the aisle was breathtaking. The backyard of the Harper House had been transformed into a beautiful scene for their wedding. She felt beautiful, like a princess, with her handsome prince waiting for her at the end. Chris was wonderful to her, and she knew that her mother would approve. She often talked to her, telling her all about him. Eva didn't know if she could hear her, but she told her anyway.

The moment that Eva had met Chris, she felt her loneliness start to disappear. He was larger than life, and filled her days and nights with laughter and happiness. She couldn't believe how lucky she was to meet him. She hoped that their child growing inside of her would have her blue eyes and his beautiful blonde hair. She envisioned a house full of tow-headed children running around creating chaos and joy, finally bringing the Harper House to life.

The ceremony was beautiful. Their kiss was full of affection and passion, and everyone in attendance stood up and cheered as they walked down the aisle Mr. & Mrs.

Before they prepared for the reception, Eva held Chris' hand and told him that she needed to make a stop.

"I'll be quick," she said kissing him sweetly on the cheek.

He nodded at his beautiful bride knowingly. "Do you want me to come?"

"No, later," she said kissing him, once more.

Eva walked down the quiet hallway to the room at the end.

She opened the door and peered in. Kelly looked up at her and smiled. "Are you married now?"

Eva nodded and Kelly hugged her tight. "Congratulations! I would have felt guilty leaving her all alone."

"I know." Eva smiled. Kelly had been there nearly every day of her life. She had her own family now, but she was still devoted to theirs. Kelly had loved her mom. "How is she today?"

Kelly looked down at the bed. She shrugged.

"She's the same as every day," she said sadly.

Eva sat on the side of the bed. She kissed Brynn's scarred cheek as she held her lifeless hand. "I did it, Mom. Chris and I are married now. The ceremony was beautiful. I wish you could have been there and seen it."

Brynn's body was still, except for the up and down of her chest rising from the breathing machine. Eva hated that she had to live like this, but Daddy refused to let her go. Brynn had never changed him from being her Power of Attorney when they divorced, and he always had the final say. Eva couldn't imagine that she would want to live this way, or that anyone would want to live this way. She had never known her, but she knew enough about her to know that she would hate this! Aunt Kelly and Aunt Jane had told her that she would have rather died, but neither of them could convince Daddy to let her go.

"She's a shell, Daddy! She shouldn't have to live like this. Why can't you just let her go?" Eva had begged him time and time again.

"I can't let her go! I need her. I can't let her go!" Adam argued with her and anyone else who fought him. "She could come back, it happens! There's activity on the brain monitor from time to time. I've abandoned her before, and I'm not going to do it again!"

They had nearly lost her on countless occasions, but Adam

always made them bring her back, hoping she would fully return to him, but she never did.

Brynn's body lay small and motionless on the bed, her muscles deteriorated, and her scarred face sunken in and barely recognizable. She was full of tubes for feeding and monitoring, the big machine next to the bed taking every breath for her.

Eva had been coming to her room, talking to her, nearly every day of her life. But she knew that it wasn't really her mom lying there. Brynn's body was simply an empty shell, a faded vision of the beauty that she once was. Eva was ashamed to admit that all of her life, part of her wished that Brynn had just been taken away permanently when the truck hit her car. Watching Brynn lying in the bed, wasting away and helpless was sometimes more than she could bear. It was torture to have her mother there beside her, but not with her.

"I wish that he would have just let her go," she muttered to herself sadly.

"I know. I do, too," Kelly said a trace of anger in her voice.

The monitor hooked to Brynn's brain blipped, and they both looked at the same time.

"That's why," Kelly said shaking her head. "He thinks she is still in there somewhere."

"What do you think?" Eva asked, even though she knew the answer.

"She's been gone since the moment that truck hit her."

They sat in silence, the world outside of the doorway moving rapidly without them, preparing for the large reception.

"Don't you have to get to your celebration?" Kelly asked finally.

"Yes," Eva said slowly getting up. It made her feel morbid, but she liked sitting here. She liked hiding with her mom. She sighed, hating to leave. "I suppose that I should."

"Bye, Mom. I'm going to my reception now. I'll stop back and visit before we leave for Europe. We'll be gone for two weeks," Eva said, bending over to kiss Brynn's forehead. She smoothed her brown hair across her forehead.

She hesitated. She hated leaving her like this, but she knew that she had to. She had been leaving Brynn all of her life, but this time when she left, she knew that it would be for good.

She walked slowly toward the door and opened it.

"I love you, Mom," Eva said trying to make her voice sound happy. If there is a chance she can hear me, I want her to know that I am happy.

She closed the door behind her and leaned against it for a moment.

She heard the music playing down the hall, and knew that her guests would be waiting for her. She didn't want to keep them waiting. She felt guilty walking away from the room, as she always did. But she forced herself to do it anyway.

She had always longed for her mom, and hated that she was right in front of her but wasn't really there. She had lost her a long time ago. She turned back toward the door and stared at it, wishing that Brynn would walk right out.

But she didn't and she never would.

Eva turned around and walked toward her new groom, her own life, and her own happiness. She knew that was what Brynn would have wanted.

Kelly watched the door close behind her and sighed. She loved Eva, almost as much as she loved her own children. It was sad watching her grow up without her mother, but she had tried to help as much as she could. She could have left a long time ago, but she couldn't leave Brynn. She spent hours with Brynn, talking to her, reading to her, watching the lines on the monitor, and praying for a miracle. But she had given up on miracles a long time ago.

She stood up and cracked her back. The room was too dark and she walked over to the curtain to let some light in. "Well, Brynn, your baby is married. You should be very proud," she said staring out the window wishing her friend understood what she was saying.

Suddenly, Kelly froze.

Someone was in the room with them, she could tell. She could feel it.

The hairs went up on the back of her neck, and she turned around slowly. She scanned the room, feeling as though someone were watching her. She stood stock still, not daring to move. Time passed slowly, and the sensation eventually disappeared.

She chuckled at herself for her foolishness and sat back down in the chair next to Brynn's bed. This house is getting old. I'm getting old.

"Brynn. We're getting old, girl," she said glancing over at the lifeless body of her friend, knowing that she wasn't going to answer. She looked at Brynn not believing what she was seeing.

"Oh my God, it can't be!" she whispered, jumping up out of her chair, her heart beating wildly in her chest.

When Kelly looked at Brynn, all she could see were her huge brown eyes staring right back at her.

VOLUME THREE

SAVING EVA

CHAPTER ONE

Saving Eva

Brynn

I wasn't dead.

I knew that after all I'd been through, I should be, but I wasn't. I'd wished for death, but I was alive in some strange existence I didn't understand. Living had taken on a dream-like state, presumably from the medication they had me on that dripped through the tubes that were connected to me and into my veins, a result of the accident that nearly took my life. But even though I yearned for the peacefulness of death, a small part of me was grateful that I survived at all.

The scene plays before me repeatedly.

The big F150 headed toward me with no time or space to move. My reaction time slowed by my swollen, pregnant belly, and disbelief as to what was taking place before me. I was so excited for the trip I was taking and on my way … somewhere important. I was headed somewhere life-changing …

But I didn't make it.

Instead I ended up in the hospital for months, or years, I'm not even sure. I know the time I lost would never be regained, but I was grateful to be alive because it all simply could've ended at impact. From the appearance of my car, a mangled and twisted mess of blue metal, it should have.

But being alive after the accident was lonely, and the existence I thought I should have has eluded me completely. Time passes like a movie that's set on slow motion and only the time I'm able to spend with my daughter, Eva, makes sense. When I'm with her, it's as though the world is bright with every single color of the rainbow. The world is alive with beautiful music. With Eva, I am awake and alive and my life unfolds before me, exactly the way it should.

I remember the day she was born as though it was yesterday, with Adam by my side, begging me to push. After the accident, he was terrified that I would die, but I knew that I needed to live for Eva. I knew that I had to hold on so she could breathe her first breath and take her first steps. She needed my body for her own life, and I didn't have a choice but to keep breathing. I knew that I wouldn't let her go, even though the pain was sharp and endless, and the effort was excruciating. I held on tight long enough to hear her cry for the first time. When I heard the sound of her tiny cries, like the mewing of a small kitten, I let myself go into the bright light that absorbed me with warm comfort.

For the first time I could remember, I was at peace.

I knew that I had to be dead and I accepted it, but when I opened my eyes again, I was alone in Eva's nursery and somehow I had been spared. The pain from the accident was gone and as I picked her up, gently and carefully, she fixed her large blue eyes on me. She knew that I was her momma and I held her close, breathing in the smell of her fresh, soft skin. This was the moment I had waited for my entire life. This was the brief moment I had with my first-born, Sophie, before she died. With Eva, I knew there would be so many more moments like this and I reveled in the thought of living a life where nothing mattered except absorbing her sweetness and watching her grow.

The years have passed by quickly with no sign of Adam or

anyone else that had been important in my life. I don't know where they've all gone. The accident took them away and I wish I had gotten a chance to say good-bye. They have abandoned me, and my heart aches for a day when they might return. Nothing makes sense other than Eva, not even this house that I put so much of my heart and soul into. When I look through the rooms there are no windows or doors and no way in or out of this place that I loved so much. Even my sweet half-brother, Noah, who I was entrusted to care for, has gone, and so has my beloved grandmother. I'm sure Adam has moved on and so have my best friends, Kelly and Jane. The only person I get to see is Eva, but there is no one in the world I would rather be with than her.

Though it's lonely when she is gone, I'm thankful I get to live in this strange and disjointed existence. The world is a different place than I imagined it would be, but I can't complain because I should have been killed.

Every day, I realize that I'm exactly what I've always wanted to be. I'm awake and alive and able to be what I've always wanted more than anything.

Eva's mother.

Saving Eva

CHAPTER TWO

The Bride

Eva

I awaken slowly to see Eva standing at the end of my bed, dressed in white and beautiful, even in the haziness of sleep. She is small and breath-taking, her long, dark hair soft against the whiteness of her dress. Her blue eyes are bright and she instantly brightens when she sees that I'm wake.

I rub my eyes, waiting for the drowsiness to fade as I take in her floor-length gown and long veil. Her outfit doesn't make sense to me and I strain to remember what I must have forgotten.

At age ten, the thought of Eva getting married is ridiculous, yet the dress seems to fit her perfectly with its long train and fitted bodice. It seems that her age never matters because her personality is always the same, her mind mature, as though she is the adult and I'm the child.

"What are you doing, Love?" I ask, sitting up slowly so I won't get dizzy.

"I'm practicing, Momma," Eva says, smiling with her beautiful, full lips and perfect, white teeth.

"What are you practicing for?" I ask, confused.

"I'm practicing for when I get married. I want to make sure

that I look good in all white and that my dress fits me well." Eva looks at me as though this makes perfect sense as she stands up slowly and makes a few twirls around the room.

I sit up completely, my back screaming, and swing my legs over the side of the bed. I rub my neck trying to ease the painful tightness that never goes away. The accident has left me broken and suffering in ways I never imagined, but I'm determined to get up every day for Eva.

"Well, Love ... by the time you get married you're going to need a larger dress because you'll be much older and this one will be too small," I say, aching to reach out and touch her long dark hair.

Eva stares at me, her cheeks turning red with embarrassment. "Oh ... well, I thought I would practice. I mean ... I've never worn a long dress before and ... I just thought I would practice so I wouldn't look silly."

I look at her small. dainty feet in her clean, white shoes. "I don't think you'll have to worry about that, Love. You're beautiful and will always look good in anything."

Eva smiles at me, a strange expression on her face that is a mixture of sadness and something else that I can't decipher. Unexpectedly, I watch as tears well up in her beautiful eyes.

"What's the matter, Love? Why are you crying?" I grab her and pull her in as close as I can, enjoying the soft fragrance of flowers that seems to emanate from her silky hair.

"I miss you, Momma. I just ... want you to be here when I get married."

"I will always be here for you, Love. Don't miss me. I'm here for you now." I take in her sadness and am confused by her words.

Eva is quiet as she continues to cry, wiping the tears from her face., She never takes her big blue eyes from mine.

"Momma ... but ... you aren't always here," Eva looks at me earnestly as she says the words gently.

"I know that the medicine makes me confused and tired, Love, but I'm doing the best I can. I can't help it sometimes, but I promise that I will be here for you when it matters the most."

Eva sniffles and looks as though she wants to continue crying, but she pushes back her tears for my benefit. "I know,

Momma. I know that you could've died and left me. I know that. Sometimes, I just want to be selfish and be like the other kids ... and ..."

Eva is quiet as she looks at me shyly.

"And what ... Eva?" I ask, unsure of where she is going.

"Never mind, Momma. It's okay." Eva sniffles again as she wipes the tears from her eyes. "I'm happy you are with me now."

I reach for her and she falls into my arms and I know that no

thing in the world will ever stop me from being there for her every day of her life. Nothing will stop me from being at her wedding. Absolutely nothing.

CHAPTER THREE

The Wedding

July 15ᵗʰ, 2016

The young woman sat at her vanity slowly brushing her long, dark hair. She stared into the mirror for a long moment, her pretty face a mixture of excitement and sadness.

She tried to hold the tears back, but she couldn't no matter how hard she tried. *This is a happy day!*

She reminded herself that it was supposed to be a joyous day; the happiest day of her life. Sadness didn't belong, although, she knew that it would be there no matter how hard she tried to fight it. It had been there her entire life. It was there on her first day of school, when she got her first bra, when she left for her first date, at her senior prom, at both of her graduations, and it was here now. The sadness was a part of her no matter where she went or what she did. And she knew that it would be there on her wedding day, alive, and as palpable as ever.

Will it ever go away? She sighed.

She had asked to be alone. Too many people were milling about, in and out of her room, trying to be too helpful. There was too much noise and no time to think. She needed to think. She needed to reflect. She needed to feel *her* here.

She knew that she couldn't do that through all the noise.

She walked to her window and looked out into the garden.

There were a lot of people, mostly her family, friends and those who were obligated to be there because of her name, but there were none of his. This was part of their bond ... their loneliness. She held her breath. *So many people!*

I just want to get through this without crying, without ruining my makeup.

There was a gentle knock on the door.

"Eva, Are you ready?"

"Almost," she said straightening up. She reached up and felt her floral headband to make sure it was still firmly in place. She took a deep breath and opened the door.

It was Aunt Jane who had come back for the big day. Eva was happy that she was there, but sad that she would have to leave immediately after the wedding. Eva missed her so much, but knew that Jane had her own family to take care of now.

Jane's eyes immediately filled. "Oh sweetheart, you look so ... so ..."

"It's okay, Aunt Jane," Eva smiled. She knew what she was going to say because Eva had been thinking the same thing, too. Except for the color of her eyes, she was nearly the spitting image of her Brynn. "I look like my mother."

Jane nodded, choking back the tears. "Yes."

"Shall we?" Eva said motioning toward the door where she knew the staircase was waiting to take her to her groom.

"Oh, yes," Jane said trying to compose herself. "I told myself that I wouldn't cry, but I just couldn't help myself. I'm so sorry."

"It's okay." Eva hugged the older woman who had been so much like a mother to her. Eva had begged her father from the time she could remember to let go of her mom and find another wife. She desperately wanted a mother, but he refused. Even now he just said that he was too old, even though he wasn't. She just wanted to see him happy once in her life.

They started down the long, winding staircase. Daddy was standing at the bottom of the stairs waiting for her.

"I'm going to sit down, Sweetie. I'm sorry that I can't stay after the ceremony, but I have to get back home. Call me after you settle in." Jane hugged Eva firmly but gently, planting a soft kiss on her forehead like she used to when she was a little girl. "I miss you and I love you."

Eva blinked back tears and whispered, "I love you." She had promised herself that she would do her best to only cry happy tears today.

"Oh, Eva," Adam whispered, his deep, blue eyes sparkling and wide. He was seeing what she had seen in the mirror. "You're a vision, you know that, right?"

Eva nodded. *I wish she were here with me!*

Eva had never known Brynn, but yearned for her with an endless ache. Even though she visited her every day, she had never heard her voice or looked her in the eyes. Her mother had been taken from her in a violent car accident with a drunk driver. It had been a horrific accident, and Brynn had been kept alive for a couple of months afterward solely for the purpose of allowing Eva to continue growing in Brynn's womb. Eva had been told many times that she was lucky and easily could have been killed in the accident. But being without a mother was so lonely that there were days she wished she had.

Nobody understood the emptiness she felt without her mother.

Nobody. Until she met Chris.

"It was a miracle that you lived and were healthy after all that you went through," Daddy had been telling her for as long as she could remember. He wanted her to understand how lucky she was and to live her life to the fullest. The mangled picture of Brynn's car was burned into her brain. The twisted blue metal, the shattered windshield, and the bloodstains that nobody thought she could recognize. They stayed with her like a bad memory, haunting her when she closed her eyes, reminding her that she should feel lucky even though she didn't.

Nobody understood the echo that resounded deep within her without her mother there to guide and love her. She loved Adam, but living with him was like living with a ghost. She grew up in the big, empty house virtually alone with Daddy, and for a short time, Uncle Noah.

She knew that she had loved Uncle Noah even though she

could barely remember him. Adam told her that he died so that he could be with Grandma Amy, who had died of a broken heart after Brynn's accident. Eva hadn't known Grandma Amy, but she hoped wherever they were now that they were together and no longer lonely without the ones they loved.

Now that she had Chris in her life, she wasn't lonely anymore. He had come into her life out of nowhere and pulled her out of the depths of darkness, truly sweeping her off her feet. He hadn't even pushed her into sleeping with him and was always a gentleman, keeping a respectful distance. He knew she was an inexperienced lover. The first time they had given into their longing for one another, he had seemed almost embarrassed about it afterwards. They had fallen in love quickly, and Eva was a mess of emotions when she realized she was pregnant. The baby bonded their rapidly growing relationship and, within a couple of months, they became engaged, with an entire life planned out for them. Eva was relieved not to be alone any longer and she seemed truly happy for the first time in her life.

"Are you ready to do this?" Eva said looking at her dad who looked handsome in his tuxedo. For a moment, she could see him as he had been as a younger man and sadness crept into her heart. The gaunt, aged man who stood in front of her reminded her that she hadn't been the only one who had lost. She took a deep breath and gave him the biggest smile she could.

"I'm ready," Adam said, smiling back at her. It was a rare, but genuine smile that made her want to cry with happiness. He had suffered so much and it hurt her heart to see the permanent sadness etched into his face. His smile was like seeing the sun for the first time, and she felt herself instantly lighter as she gripped his arm tightly.

Normally, she thought he resembled Eeyore from her *Winnie the Pooh* stories, his hair more white than the dark hair of his youth, his blue eyes lost and unfocused, and his words slow and often dismal. But today, she saw a little bit of the man he must've been, the one who had captured Brynn's heart as he stood in front of her, combed and polished in a tuxedo that fit his slender build, his blue eyes bright with excitement. As they stood, prepared to make the walk down the aisle, she took a deep breath, trying to exude enough joy and happiness for the both of them.

The walk down the aisle was breathtaking. The backyard of The Harper House had been transformed into a beautiful scene for their wedding, the sweet smell of orchids in the air. Many of the elite had come to wish her well, even though she had never met most of them. It was the cost of being a descendant of James Harper, founder of Harper Enterprises, and heiress to a very large fortune. She felt beautiful, like a princess with her handsome prince waiting for her. Chris was wonderful and she tried to imagine that her mother would approve of him. Eva often talked to Brynn, telling her about Chris just as she had spent her entire life, telling her mother every detail and secret, even though she didn't know if her words were ever heard. It made Eva feel better to tell Brynn anyway because nothing seemed real until the words had come out of her mouth and fallen into Brynn's ears.

The moment that Eva met Chris, her loneliness began to disappear. He was larger than life and filled her days and nights with laughter and happiness. She couldn't believe how lucky she was to have met him and she hoped that the child growing inside of her would have her blue eyes and his beautiful blonde hair. She envisioned a house full of tow-headed children running around creating chaos and joy, finally bringing The Harper House to life the way it deserved; the way James Harper had hoped it would one day be. As she walked down the aisle she thought about those things, happy to have met someone to spend the rest of her life with, promising her that she would never be alone again.

The ceremony was as beautiful as Eva hoped it would be. Their kiss was full of affection and passion, and everyone in attendance stood up and cheered as they walked down the aisle Mr. & Mrs. There had been whispers about how quickly Eva had fallen for her handsome, young gentleman, but when anyone saw the love between them, there was no question that they were meant to be. Chris was clearly smitten with Eva, holding her, touching her, and taking care of her every chance he got. He was the perfect, doting young husband, and it was clear that they were deeply in love.

As they walked up the long staircase preparing to dress for

the reception, Eva held Chris' hand and told him that she needed to make a stop.

"I'll be quick," she said kissing him sweetly on the cheek.

He nodded at his beautiful bride knowingly. "Do you want me to come? I don't mind at all."

"No, later," she said kissing him gently once more, her lips lingering on his as she allowed herself to bask in the love that passed between them.

He smiled at her, his beautiful hazel eyes sparkling as he gazed at her, his lovely bride. She felt special and cherished in his eyes and she hated being apart from him even for a few moments.

Eva walked down the quiet hallway to the room at the end.

She opened the door and peered in. Kelly looked up at her and smiled. "Are you official now?"

Eva nodded and Kelly hugged her tight, a guilty look passing over her pretty face as she pulled the bride to her. "Congratulations! I'm sorry, Honey. I wanted to come down, but I would have felt guilty leaving her all alone."

"I know." Eva smiled. Kelly had been there nearly every day of her life for as long as she could remember. She had taken care of Uncle Noah, and then after Brynn's accident, she had stayed to take care of her. Even though Kelly was married, she was devoted to the Michaels family as though it was her own. With a husband she rarely talked about and children who were grown, Kelly had become more family than she was an employee. Before the accident, Brynn and Kelly had become close, and Kelly was as devastated as everyone else. Eva couldn't remember a day without Kelly in it, and loved her almost as much as the mother she missed every day. "How is Mom today?"

Kelly looked down at the bed. She shrugged and gave Eva a small smile.

"She's the same ... as every day," she said sadly.

Eva sat on the side of the bed, careful with her long gown. She kissed Brynn's scarred cheek as she held her lifeless hand. "I did it, Mom. Chris and I are married now. The ceremony was beautiful and you would've loved it. I wish you could have been there and seen it."

Brynn's body was still except for the up and down of her chest rising from the breathing machine. Eva hated that she had to live like this, but Daddy refused to let her go. Brynn had never changed him from being her Power of Attorney when they divorced, and he always had the final say. Eva hated watching her lie so still and helpless like this. She had never known her mother, but she knew enough about her to know that she would hate this existence! Aunt Kelly and Aunt Jane had told her that she would rather have just died, but neither of them could convince Daddy to let her go.

"She's a shell, Daddy! She shouldn't have to live like this. Why can't you just let her go?" Eva had begged him time and again, the frequency of her pleas increasing as Eva grew older.

"I can't let her go! I need her and what if there's a small chance that she'll wake up one day? I can't let her go, Eva. It's not that easy! You just don't understand what we've been through!" Adam argued with her and anyone else who fought him. "She could come back. It happens! There's activity on the brain monitor from time to time, which means she's in there somewhere. I've abandoned her before, and I'm not going to do it again!"

They had nearly lost her on several occasions, her body and organs atrophying with lack of use, but every time Adam made them bring her back, hoping she would fully return to him, though it was clear to everyone but him that she never would.

Brynn's body lie small and motionless on the bed. Her muscles had deteriorated in her arms and legs with lack of use, even though Adam insisted that Kelly massage and exercise her limbs daily. Although the scars on Brynn's face had faded over the years, her cheeks were sunken in and she was barely recognizable against the pictures that Eva had seen of her. Eva was proud that her mom had been breathtakingly beautiful and was thankful that she resembled her.

Brynn was full of tubes for feeding and monitoring, the big machine next to the bed taking every breath for her, but Eva had learned to tune the noise out. She had been coming to talk to her nearly every day of her life, even though there was a part of her that knew it wasn't really her mom lying there. Brynn's body was simply an empty shell, a faded vision of the beauty that she once was in a lifetime Eva had never known. Eva was ashamed to admit that all her life, part of her wished that Brynn had just been taken away permanently when the truck hit her car. Watching Brynn lying in the bed, wasting away and helpless, was sometimes more than she could bear. It was torture to have her mother there beside her, but not with her.

"I wish that he would just have let her go," Eva said quietly, more to herself than anyone, as she had so many times. Kelly thought about how beautiful Eva looked in her wedding dress and how Brynn would've been so proud of her. She tried to ignore the pain in her own heart as she gazed at Eva, her big, blue eyes overwhelming the face that reminded Kelly so much of Brynn's beauty.

"I know. I do, too," Kelly said, trying to disguise the anger from her voice as she always did when Eva brought it up.

The monitor hooked to Brynn's brain waves blipped and both women looked at the same time.

"That's why," Kelly said shaking her short blonde bob. "He thinks she is still in there, waiting to come out at any moment."

"What do you think?" Eva asked again, a question she often asked Kelly, even though she already knew the answer.

"She's been gone since the moment that truck hit her," Kelly said soberly. "You know that, Eva. We've talked about that many times before. You've got to let go, too, Honey."

They sat in silence, the world outside of the doorway moving rapidly without them, preparing for the large reception.

"Don't you have to get to your celebration?" Kelly asked finally shaking herself out of her reverie, and shuddering deeply as though trying to dismiss a sad memory.

"Yes," Eva sighed, slowly getting up but wishing that she could stay. It made her feel morbid, but she liked sitting here. She liked hiding with her mom. She hated it every time she had to leave and this time was no different. "I suppose that I should go now and get ready for the reception.

"Bye, Mom. I'm going to my reception now. I'll stop back and visit before we leave for Europe. I know that I've said this before, but we'll be gone for two weeks," Eva said, bending over to kiss Brynn's forehead. She smoothed Brynn's faded brown hair across her forehead gently, allowing her fingers to graze her skin.

She hesitated for brief moment and then leaned over and whispered something in her ear so that Kelly couldn't hear. Kelly thought it was strange that Eva would feel the need to whisper when she knew that Brynn couldn't hear her. Eva usually told Kelly everything and she felt the slightest pang of jealousy. She shook it off, reminding herself that Brynn was Eva's mother and not her. Kelly had children of her own that she adored, but she smiled softly, thinking not for the first time, that she would've loved having Eva as a daughter.

Eva stood holding Brynn's hand, unaware of Kelly's admiration for her in that moment. She hated leaving Brynn like this, but she knew that she had to ... she had been leaving Brynn all her life, but this time when she left, she knew that it would be for good. She was a married woman and would have a life of her own waiting for her when she got back. She knew she should be happy, but something about it seemed empty without her mother.

Eva walked slowly toward the door and opened it.

"I love you, Mom," Eva said trying to make her voice sound happy. *If there is a chance she can hear me, I want her to know that I am happy.*

She closed the door behind her and leaned against it for a long moment as she took a deep breath.

She heard the music playing down the hall and knew that her guests would be waiting patiently and wondering where she was. Eva didn't want to keep them waiting, but she felt guilty walking away from the room. With a heavy heart she forced herself to do it.

Eva turned around and walked toward her new groom, her new life, and her new happiness. She knew that is what Brynn would have wanted.

Kelly watched the door close behind her and sighed. Her heart hurt for Eva every day. It was sad watching her grow up without Brynn. She had tried to help as much as she could, but she knew that she could never fill the void in Eva's heart. Kelly could've left a long time ago, but she couldn't leave Brynn. She spent hours with Brynn, talking to her, reading to her, watching the lines on the monitor and praying for a miracle. But she had given up on miracles a long time ago.

She stood up and cracked her back feeling every bit her age. The room was too dark and she walked over to the curtain to let some light in. "Well, Brynn, your baby is married. You should be very proud," she said staring out the window wishing her friend understood what she was saying.

Suddenly, Kelly froze.

She could tell that someone was in the room with them. She could feel it.

The hairs went up on the back of her neck and she turned around slowly. She scanned the room, feeling as though someone was watching her. She stood stock still, not daring to move. Time passed slowly and the sensation eventually disappeared.

She chuckled at herself for her foolishness and sat back down in the chair next to Brynn's bed. *This house is getting old and I'm getting old.*

"Brynn, we're getting old, girl," she said glancing over at the lifeless body of her friend, knowing that she wasn't going to answer. She looked at Brynn not believing what she was seeing.

"Oh my God, it can't be!" she whispered, jumping up out of her chair, her heart racing wildly in her chest.

When Kelly looked at Brynn, all she could see were her huge, brown eyes staring right into hers.

CHAPTER FOUR

The Flashback

April, Ten Years Earlier

Nick had never been able to get Brynn out of his mind completely no matter how hard he tried. Even his therapist couldn't explain it or help him, and he had all but given up on the idea that he would ever be able to forget her.

The night he was supposed to meet with Brynn ten years prior continued to haunt him, even in his dreams. Even years after he had moved on past that tragic night, divorced his first wife, Melanie, and then remarried once again he was never able to purge Brynn from his mind. He couldn't forget how he had waited for hours at the winery where they had their first date, anxiously watching for her to arrive. When she never did, he called her phone repeatedly, getting nothing but her voicemail. And when he finally drove to The Harper House at eleven thirty that night, knowing in his gut that something was wrong, he was alarmed to see that most of the lights in the main house were on. He rang the doorbell, a knot in the pit of his stomach, and was greeted by a sweet housekeeper who introduced herself as Beth. He noticed immediately when the older lady opened the door that her eyes were puffy and rimmed with red, which filled him with immediate dread.

"Yes? Can I help you?" she had asked politely, seemingly

unfazed that it was 11:30 at night.

"I-I-I was hoping to see Brynn," Nick said, barely able to get the words past the huge lump in his throat.

"And you are ..."

"Nick. I'm Nick. I'm a friend ... of Brynn's."

At the mention of Brynn's name, Beth let out a quiet sob and backed away from the door, putting a well-used tissue up to her face as she let Nick in.

He walked in the door and immediately felt sick to his stomach.

"Please, sit," Beth said, leading him into the kitchen and pouring him some tea without bothering to ask if he wanted any.

"Where is Brynn?" Nick asked, anxiously waiting for Beth to talk. He thought about the last time he had been with Brynn, both of them holding one another, healing each other, and barely able to let the other go.

"I'm s-s-sorry," Beth said, sniffling and wiping the tears from beneath her glasses, reminding him of his favorite aunt. "It's just that ... I'm not good at this, and I don't even know if I'm supposed to be telling you anything ..."

"Please, tell me. She was meeting me tonight and she never showed up and I've been calling her cell phone all night, so please ..."

"Oh, *you're* Nick!" Beth said as though seeing him for the first time. "Oh, goodness. I'm so sorry."

Beth tried unsuccessfully to stop herself from crying.

"Please," Nick grabbed the older woman's hands. "Please tell me, where can I find Brynn?"

"Brynn is in the hospital. It was a horrible car accident ... and she m-m-may die, her and the baby ..." Beth continued to cry. She didn't notice when Nick released her hands.

"The baby?! What baby?" Nick said, his voice barely audible as the words sunk in.

"Oh. You didn't know about the baby?" Beth said, her gray eyes wide with alarm. "Oh, I'm so sorry. I didn't realize you didn't know that she was pregnant ..."

"Should I know? I mean ... do you know if I should know?

Is the baby mine? Did Brynn say anything about the baby being mine?"

"Please, you have to talk to Kelly, or to John Palmer. I shouldn't have said anything about the baby." Beth was even more upset now than she had been when Nick rang the doorbell. He worried that she might pass out.

Nick sat down in a chair at the kitchen counter with a thud, his head spinning with a thousand thoughts that he couldn't put into words.

Beth's voice was suddenly close in his ear as she leaned toward him, concerned about the expression on his face. "Are you okay?"

"Yes ... I just ... I ... need to get to the hospital. I need to see Brynn."

"Oh ... Okay, but ... I don't know if that's a good idea. I mean, you're welcome to go if you'd like but ..."

"But what?" Nick was running his hands through his hair in frustration.

"Well ... it's just that ... Adam ... her hus ... ex-husband will probably be there," Beth said, her face red.

Nick had never met Adam. All he knew was that Adam had broken Brynn because, before him, Adam had been her only love. Nick wanted to pummel Adam for hurting Brynn the way that he did, but he knew that confronting him in the hospital wouldn't help anything. He wasn't even sure if Adam would know who he was and what he meant to Brynn. Telling him in the face of such tragedy would be cruel.

Nick debated about whether or not he should go to the hospital, and while he did that, he realized he felt more lost than he had ever been, even in his own disastrous marriage. Ever since he had met Brynn, she'd changed him and he found himself thinking about doing things that he never would've imagined doing before.

He looked at Beth for a moment, unsure of what to do and hoping that the kind, older woman would be able to give him some kind of answer. Her face was full of only sadness and no wisdom. Nick hugged Beth quickly and walked out the door. He sat in his car for a long moment. He was unsure about which direction he should go and tried to decide if he was brave enough to go to the hospital and make his claim over Brynn, even during the worst moment of her life.

Determined, he drove toward the hospital, remembering how he had passed it on his way to The Harper House. He knew that if he didn't go to her now that he may never. As he drove he imagined facing Adam and an uncertain future with Brynn, and he felt his resolve waver as he tightened his grip on the steering wheel. As the exit for the hospital began to appear he suddenly switched lanes, his car careening dangerously off the opposite side of road, his heart pounding in his ears. As he sped toward the airport, he picked up his phone and booked a flight home, his voice shaking as he felt a strong sense of self-loathing and disgust for his cowardice.

A week later, unable to think of anything else, he called The Harper House and asked for Beth who eagerly told him about Brynn's coma. Even though she knew she was giving him far more information than she should, the older woman had seen how heartbroken Nick had been. He made it a monthly habit to call and talk to Beth who was always willing to tell him as much as she could until one day, there was nothing new to tell. The story became the same month after month, and he finally stopped calling altogether.

His decision to walk away from Brynn haunted him day after day.

After his disastrous divorce from Melanie, and then losing Brynn, Nick met and married a sweet woman who loved him more than life itself. Despite the fact that he was never able to return her affection at quite the same level, his sweet wife, Fiona, loved him with all of her heart, even giving him a beautiful daughter, Amanda. Nick gave it every effort to completely love his wife and daughter, but he couldn't escape the coward that stared back at him from the mirror.

He could never truly forgive himself for abandoning Brynn and hiding inside a life and a love that he never felt he deserved.

CHAPTER FIVE

Waiting

July 15ᵗʰ, 2016

The years passed slowly and painfully for Adam Michaels. There were moments when he ached for the courage to end it all so he could finally have the peace he longed for. If it hadn't been for Eva, it would have been easier, but he knew he couldn't leave her.

He had raised her the best way he knew how, though he was admittedly lost and unsure of himself in every way. But he had made a difficult decision a long time ago to be there for her and he knew he had to do everything he could. He owed it to Eva and to Brynn. Adam knew he would've made a complete mess of it if it weren't for the help of Brynn's best friends, Jane and Kelly. *Thank God for them* was his daily mantra as they were always available at a moment's notice to help with any womanly crisis that Adam didn't know how to handle.

Jane had raised two daughters of her own, and ran the restaurant that had been Brynn's. She had done it so well, expanding it into a mini-chain, each restaurant unique, each one successful and bearing Brynn's signature passion for food and hospitality. Brynn had saved Jane when Jane was a single, young widow with two young girls and nowhere to go. And in turn, Jane had saved Brynn when Adam had left all those years ago and Brynn had nobody else to turn to. Jane was still saving Brynn, by helping to raise Eva while building a thriving business that continued to grow. Jane knew that Brynn would have been so proud of her and she missed her friend daily. As Eva grew, Jane saw more and more of her in the little girl, which pleased her. Jane loved Brynn like a sister, and had developed a soft spot for Eva, the girl who had fought her way out of the womb to live. She loved Eva nearly as much as she loved her own daughters.

Kelly had been the one Adam called when Eva started to become a woman and had questions about boys and her body. A nurse and caregiver, Kelly was gentle and nurturing, and was able to ease Eva's fears. Kelly was like family, agreeing to stay on in the huge Harper House to take care of Brynn, even long after sweet Noah, Brynn's half-brother, had passed away.

Ellie, Brynn's birth mother, had reappeared in Brynn's life and urged her to meet and care for Noah, but Brynn had been reluctant and untrusting. Ellie had abandoned both of her children on separate occasions, replacing her love for them with her incessant need for the drugs and alcohol that consumed her. Ellie finally succumbed to the drugs that ultimately destroyed her, leaving Brynn to care for Noah.

Noah had been slow to develop from birth, but had the heart of an angel and Brynn had instantly loved him. He had the sweetness of a child in a grown man's body and they formed an immediate connection. The adjustment to life in The Harper House had gone surprisingly well, brother and sister bonding as though they had known each other all their lives. Noah had not lived a long life, but Brynn had filled it with happiness until the accident. She filled the void in his life that Ellie never could.

With Ellie, the sole heir to the Harper fortune, gone, The Harper House was passed down to Brynn, as well as the majority of the fortune from Harper Enterprises. Run by a trusted family friend, John Palmer, Brynn was free to rebuild her relationship with Noah and her grandmother, Amy.

But after the F150 plowed into Brynn's car and Brynn was left in a coma, Amy and Noah's health deteriorated as well. Brynn had been their rock and their purpose and without her, neither was able to hold on for very long. Amy died first, followed a few years later by Noah. Adam felt guilty, knowing that Brynn would be disappointed in him for not being able to save them, just as he hadn't been able to save her.

Daily, Adam recalled the last time he had spoken to her. Brynn had been pregnant with Eva, and had refused to acknowledge that the baby she was carrying was Adam's. He had been angry as he stared into Brynn's dark eyes, more strange and distant from him than he had ever seen. He knew that he had betrayed her trust and love so many times that he no longer had any right to expect her to love him, though he desperately prayed for it every day.

Brynn had even gone so far as to try and convince him that she had slept with someone else, but Adam hadn't believed her at the time. He was convinced that Brynn had never been with anyone other than him. Adam had been her love since they were fifteen years old and there had never been another. Adam had done the math and knew that the timing worked with the last night they had been together. Their passion and pain had fueled their need for one another like nothing they had ever experienced together before, but when it was over, she had pushed him away, this time for good.

He knew the baby had to be his and he was excited and desperate for her to acknowledge it. He knew that he should've admitted to her that he'd never signed the divorce papers, but he was afraid. He had been the one to initiate the divorce. He'd been the one who left her, after he swore to her that he never would again. His drinking had changed him into a man he never imagined himself to be, but even after they sat at the lawyer's office and divided everything up, signing most of the papers, he hid the last paper that he was supposed to sign, refusing to make it real.

When he realized Brynn was pregnant, he knew it would be a good time for him to finally admit it, but he couldn't. Her big, beautiful eyes had always disarmed him. That time had been no different, even as she stared at him coldly and told him the child she carried wasn't his.

Adam couldn't blame her for her fear. After they lost their first child Sophie as a newborn, Brynn was never the same. She separated herself from him almost completely. He had gotten lost in his drinking until Brynn was completely out of reach. The drinking had been a deal-breaker in their marriage, the love between them dissipating because of it. Adam knew that no matter how much he drank, or what he did, he could never get Brynn out of his heart.

Adam had been walking down the stairs to Eva's reception when he heard Kelly shrieking from the hall. His heart froze and he wondered for the hundredth time if he was about to lose her forever. He raced back up the long staircase, nearly barreling Kelly over outside of Brynn's doorway. Kelly grabbed his hand and dragged him down the hall to Brynn's room where she suddenly froze.

"I-I-I'm sorry, Adam. I don't want to ruin the reception. If it's not true, don't tell me I'm crazy, but I swear … I saw it." Kelly stammered, her sweaty hands making Adam feel uncomfortable.

"Saw what?" Adam asked, his head spinning and his heart pounding wildly in his chest.

"Her eyes, Adam. Her eyes …" Kelly struggled to form a clear sentence.

"What about her eyes?" Adam was growing impatient, trying to walk into the room, but held in place by Kelly's strong nurse's hands.

"They were … open." Kelly's voice was nearly a whisper and Adam's blue eyes grew wide.

"W-w-hat do you mean?" Adam said, struggling to get the words out.

"Her eyes were open," Kelly said, trying to decide if she could believe it herself. "They were staring right at me … Brynn was staring right at me."

Adam froze, wanting to believe her, but also terrified that it might be true. He had dreamt for years that she would awaken, but he lived in fear that if she did, she wouldn't love him and would ultimately send him away. He was used to having her with him even if she was lying motionless in bed, unaware of the world around her. He always knew where he could find her and that was his comfort.

Adam knew that he hadn't always done right by her. The drinking had separated them and Adam knew that Brynn would never be at peace with it after what Thomas had done to her. Brynn hadn't told him *everything*, but he knew that her adoptive father had been cruel to her. The nightmares she suffered through for so many years hinted at some of the horror she had experienced as a young girl. Adam cringed with guilt at the memory of how he had almost hurt her in his own drunken stupor until ultimately, there was nothing else between them and they had agreed to divorce. But he always dreamt that he would win her back even though he knew he didn't deserve her.

He stepped cautiously into the room and walked to Brynn's bed. He looked down at her small, frail body, the feeding tube trailing from below her gown and the ventilator connected to her mouth. She had been nothing but an empty vessel for so many years and Adam felt the familiar weight crushing his heart every time he looked at her. The whooshing of the ventilator was the only noise in the room, and Adam found comfort in the familiar sound of the machine that breathed for the woman he had loved for nearly four decades.

His heart was pounding wildly in his chest as he tried to decide what to do next. He looked down at her face, at the scars left by the broken glass of the windshield that had faded with time. He thought she was just as beautiful as she had been so many years ago, and he tried to imagine that she was merely sleeping.

His heart stopped as he realized she was looking right at him, her big brown eyes beautiful, but blank.

"Brynn?" he said, his voice barely audible. "Brynn? Are you there?"

Brynn's eyes continued to stare at him, not blinking, not moving.

Adam was afraid to breathe, his mouth dry as he tried to say her name again. "Brynn … Brynn."

He thought that if he stared hard enough she might blink at him, but she didn't. Her eyes were fixated on him, yet empty, her body still tiny and motionless on the bed.

He was unnerved as he felt a shiver run down his back. Seeing her stare at him was eerie, and he hated himself for wanting her to close her eyes again.

"Kelly, call the doctor. We need her to be seen right away. This can't wait!"

Kelly nodded slowly and stepped out of the room to make the call.

As Kelly stepped out, she thought she heard Adam stifle a cry. She sighed in pity for her friend. It wasn't the first time she had ever heard him cry for Brynn and she knew in her heart that it would unlikely be the last.

CHAPTER SIX

Sandcastles

"You stupid bitch! You don't know anything. You're a complete idiot." I lie huddled on the floor, waiting for the boots to kick me in the side. He was never one to use a belt or a paddle. He liked to use his feet and his hands because he liked the feel of my flesh as he struck me. He liked to watch my face screw up in pain as his words tore deep inside of me, leaving a permanent mark. I tried not to show him how much his ugly words hurt me, but they always shredded me to the core. The pain cut as deeply as his blows would sting, even though I'd learned to just lie still until he was done, when he finally thought he had hurt me deeply enough.

"You stupid bitch, you stupid bitch." I don't know how many times he'd said that to me during my childhood, but it never seemed to be enough to satisfy him. He didn't ever seem to tire of tearing me down and I felt my insides begin to shrink until there was nothing.

I knew that is what he thought, that I was truly nothing. The look on his sour, ragged face told me so every day when he was alive.

Even now I try to move away from him, but I can't. And even though I know that he's been dead for decades, I can still see him in my mind as though it was yesterday. His watery, blue eyes full of venom and hatred toward me for stealing the love he thought that only he deserved are burned in my brain. He thought my adoptive mother, Rose, would somehow learn to love him, yet he didn't realize that beating and abusing her would never inspire love. I could still see his ragged fists going at her, punishing her for not loving him until he was finally too sick to even go near her at all.

I try and release myself from the memory, but my mind won't let go. I think desperately about the only person who can save me at a time like this and I invoke the vision of my little Eva with her long, dark hair and big, blue eyes. I know that Eva can save me from the misery of the past that I have tried to let go of without success. Even though I tried to hide from him, Thomas always seems to seek me out. It's as though he knows that I am helpless against him.

"You stupid bitch, you stupid bitch." Thomas haunts me, his words echoing cruelly in my head.

Like magic, Eva appears out of nowhere, almost as though she knows exactly when I need her, and in an instant, Thomas has disappeared and she is solid in my arms at just the right moment.

"Momma," she says hugging me close. I hold her tiny body in my arms and I feel my heart rate begin to return to normal. "Momma, why are you upset? Don't be upset. Let's go to the beach."

In what feels like an instant, we are on the beach and I look down to see my feet buried in the warm, soft sand. The sun is hot and bright and I wonder how many times we've been here together before. Eva is only about five, but she seems to be so much older, guiding me to a spot where our blanket, umbrella, and lounge chair are already set up and waiting for us. "Momma, sit."

I obey.

I always listen to Eva because somehow she seems to know exactly what I need and when I need it. I look down at her dark, shiny hair and lean over to kiss the top of her head, absorbing the warmth of it on my lips.

"I love you, Eva," I say, lingering close.

"I love you, too, Momma." Eva smiles up at me, her blue eyes bright. "Sandcastle?"

I follow her to a spot in the sand where an entire landscape waits for us to build something magnificent. We toil for hours in the hot sun, shoveling and shaping, careful to preserve our hard work with our meticulous fingers. We work in silence, and every once in a while, I catch her staring at me with a look that I can't quite read, so I smile at her and then she smiles back. She has my face nearly down to every detail, only slightly more delicate, with eyes as blue as the sea. She is beautiful and I can't believe that it's possible to love someone so much. Sophie, my first daughter, lived for only a few hours. I loved her, but my love for Eva is crushing and heartbreaking, and I can't even begin to explain the gravity of it.

We build for hours until the sun begins to fade and the sky begins to dim. The sandcastle is a masterpiece and she works with the patience of someone far beyond her short five years. I don't know how the day has passed so quickly without food or water, but somehow it has. The beach has been empty all day except for the two of us, but I can't complain. I've had Eva to myself all day and any day with her is so much more than I could've ever hoped for.

"Momma," she says, her voice musical and tiny as it always is. "Do you love me?"

"Of course!" I respond to her, shocked that she would even ask me something so obvious. I reach out and tuck a strand of her windswept hair carefully behind her ear, the smoothness of her sun-kissed cheeks mesmerizing me as my fingers sweep over them. "Of course I love you, Eva."

"Then why are you still here? Why can't you just let go of me and move on?"

I don't understand her question.

I look at her lovingly but something about her question creates a sudden emptiness in the pit of my stomach.

"I'm here for you, Love. I'm here because I've been spared so that I can live this life with you." She leans and puts her forehead against mine and closes her eyes.

I stare at our sandcastle and it's a masterpiece, intricate in every detail and far more beautiful than anything I'd ever built before. I am amazed that we are able to create something so massive and beautiful in one short afternoon.

Most of all, I marvel at her.

I don't know how she grew to become so beautiful and so incredible, but I know that it can't be all me.

"Momma, I want to go home now. I'm tired," Eva says, standing up and wiping the sand off her bathing suit.

"Yes, Love. We can go home." I'm tired, too. I look around once again for another living soul, but there is no one to be found. I should be used to this by now, but I always look anyway, hoping there will be someone else so that I will know that this isn't just a dream.

"Daddy must be waiting for me," Eva says, smiling at me sadly.

"Yes, I'm sure he is." I give her a quick squeeze. "We don't want to worry him."

"We did good, Momma," Eva says, surveying our castle, her eyes bright and full of pride.

"Yes, Love. We did very good."

I stand up and Eva grabs tight to my hand. We walk toward the sun and the bright light nearly blinds me. I'm not quite sure where we are going, but somehow, we always seem to be walking toward the light.

"Momma," I hear Eva's tiny voice. "I love you."

"Yes, Eva Love. I love you, too."

CHAPTER SEVEN

The Visit

September, Ten Years Earlier

For years, the memories became stronger and Nick realized that he could no longer live with himself and the day that he had driven away from Brynn after her accident.

Even though he had gone on to start a new life, Nick still drove to the scenic Harper House year after year and sat outside of the large gate, punishing himself for his cowardice. He sat for days simply waiting and watching out of morbid curiosity to see if he could catch a glimpse of Brynn. Something twisted within him looked forward to the annual pilgrimage toward the love that he had never claimed, yet mourned as though it had been his for a century. Something about his life had never felt as complete as the moments when he had held Brynn in his arms, inhaling her sweet smell and stroking her thick, soft hair, her beautiful brown eyes seeking his out.

Even though he told himself he would, Nick couldn't find the courage to walk up to the front door of the house and ring the doorbell, asking to see her.

It wasn't until during the tenth year of his pilgrimage and years of sleepless nights that he found it within him to walk up to the front door and finally attempt to see her. In all his visits, he had never seen a car leave the gates of the house and he often wondered throughout the years whether she ever left or was even able to. When he knew that he could no longer live without seeing her, he decided that he didn't have a choice — Adam or no Adam.

Even though the gates were usually closed on previous visits, it was almost miraculous that they were open on the day he decided that he would finally see her. He drove down the long driveway lined with trees and woods, marveling at the beauty that surrounded the large house. He took a deep breath and, for a moment, he wasn't sure that he could go through with it. The house was intimidating and beautiful and he thought about how much it reminded him of Brynn. He knew that he would never again be able to live with himself if he drove away now. After standing on the large, wraparound porch for fifteen minutes fighting the urge to run, Nick reached up and rang the doorbell. The door opened immediately, startling him, as though someone had been expecting him. He found himself staring down at a younger version of Brynn with the bluest eyes he had ever seen.

"Hello?" the girl said cautiously.

"Hi," Nick said, clearing his throat.

"Hi ..." The girl moved backward a step.

"I'm Nick ... I uh ... was a friend of Brynn's many years ago, and I was hoping I could visit with her."

The girl looked at him strangely and Nick suddenly realized he was staring at Brynn's daughter. His mind began to race. He'd imagined meeting her many times and couldn't help but stare, searching her out for any sign of himself.

"If Beth is here, she can confirm who I am." Nick
added, nervously.

"Beth died," the girl said simply, lingering with the door half-open, hesitant to let him in.

"Who is there?" a man's voice came from behind the girl, echoing throughout the house.

"A man ... Nick," the girl responded, never taking her eyes off him.

"Who?" the voice changed, sounded angry, and Nick instinctively took a step backward. Nick heard heavy footsteps pounding rapidly behind the door, then found himself suddenly face to face with Adam. The girl disappeared as she stepped back behind him.

"Who are you?" Adam demanded, his deep, blue eyes bloodshot and rimmed with red, his hair disheveled. Nick could smell the alcohol oozing from his pores and, for a quick moment, Nick felt overwhelming sympathy for him.

"I'm Nick," he replied, trying to keep the shakiness out of his voice. "I'm an old friend..."

Adam cut him off. "I know exactly who you are and you need to leave."

Nick knew that he should've been more prepared to face Adam and was immediately defensive. "No. I'm here to see Brynn and I'm not leaving until I do."

Adam took a forceful step outside, suddenly standing within two inches of Nick. Even though Nick was tall and lean, and used to towering over most people, he was surprised with how closely they stood eye to eye. Nick had never met Adam before and realized they could match each other physically. He could feel Adam's contempt and, without thinking about it, he realized that his fist had balled up, ready to defend himself. He hadn't been in a fight since high school, but Nick was confident, the adrenaline pumping through him.

"I said that you need to leave," Adam repeated. The only thing Nick could smell was bourbon, and Nick realized that Adam was drunk.

"I need to see Brynn," Nick said stubbornly. "Listen, I know this isn't what you want to hear, but we were going to be together. Brynn ... wanted to be with me, man. What we had was special and we were ..."

Suddenly Nick's jaw exploded with pain. He struggled to stay upright, stunned that he never saw the punch coming. Anger coursed through him and he tackled Adam to the ground, both of them rolling around on the porch until Nick realized that they were falling down the front stairs. They landed on the ground, Nick's back absorbing the brunt of their fall as he struggled to push Adam off him.

"This isn't helping anyone!" Nick yelled the best he could,

winded from the fall as he blocked Adam's punches. Despite being drunk, Adam's blows were coming at him surprisingly fast.

"It's helping me," Adam snarled angrily. "Brynn is my wife. You need to leave her alone."

"You divorced her," Nick said catching Adam off-guard with a right hook to the eye. Adam fell to the ground, howling.

"Daddeeeeeee!" Both men had completely forgotten about the little dark-haired girl who had been watching fearfully from behind the screen door. She ran out to Adam, hovering over him protectively as she stared up at Nick with anger and fear on her face. "Leave my daddy alone!"

"I'm okay, Eva. I'm okay," Adam said, slowly standing up. His hand covered his eye and a thick trail of blood trickled down the side of his face and on to his shirt.

"I'm sorry," Nick said seeing the blood and feeling guilty. He lifted his hand and fingered his jaw. It still radiated with pain. "I … man, I just…"

"I know," Adam said staring Nick directly in the eyes. "I know what you want. But you can't … you can't have her. She's *my* wife and she's everything to me. You can't … you can't …"

Both men stared at one another, nursing their wounds and wondering helplessly which man Brynn had loved more.

"Please, man. I just want to see her. I've come so far … so many times. I just … I just … want to see her." Nick heard himself begging but he didn't care.

Adam stared at him for a long time, his dirty, bloody face watching the other man with a mixture of anger and pity. They had never met, but Kelly had slipped one night and told Adam about Nick. For months, Adam had seethed in anger at the thought of Brynn with another man. Brynn had tried to tell Adam about Nick, but he didn't believe. her, guessing that she was making it up to make him angry. He couldn't imagine his girl ever loving anyone else but him.

As much as he hated to admit it to himself, he recognized the sadness and desperation on Nick's face because he saw it every day when he looked in the mirror. He could see in his eyes that Nick had truly loved Brynn and wondered hopelessly if she had felt the same for him.

Adam looked down at Eva and knew that he didn't want her to see the ugliness and possessiveness that he was feeling inside.

After glaring at Nick for a few more moments, he sighed in resignation. He gestured toward the house without saying a word and waited for Nick to follow him. Unable to believe his luck, Nick dusted the dirt from his clothes and slowly followed him through the foyer and up a long flight of stairs. They reached a wing of the house that felt like a mausoleum, quiet and cold, and Nick shivered without realizing it. Adam opened the door slowly and waited for Nick to step in.

Nick was in shock, first from Adam's attack, now because he hadn't expected Adam to let him see Brynn. As soon as he entered the room he realized why Adam was allowing it.

He knew immediately that Brynn would have no idea that he was there, and he felt a sharp pain in his chest as he looked around the room and surveyed his surroundings.

He took a deep breath, surprised at the quietness of the room, and shocked by the machines that Brynn was hooked up to. The whooshing sound of one machine and the occasional hiss of another was the only noise. He rolled up the crusty sleeves of his once soft gray sweater, now filthy and stained, and sat in the chair next to the bed, choking back a sob at what he was seeing.

The woman in the bed barely held any resemblance to the woman he had fallen in love with nearly a decade before. He was angry with himself for taking so long to knock on the door, but he had been avoiding the truth. He thought about his bad marriages and realized this was a trait he had been fighting his entire life. As he looked at the sparse shell of the woman who haunted his dreams, he knew that ten years had been too long as the pit in his stomach became larger and his chest became tighter.

"Dammit, Brynn," he cried as he took her hand and put it immediately to his lips. When he looked at her he remembered her only as she had been the morning he left her all those years before. He thought about the last time he had kissed her lips and promised her that he would return. He kissed her hand, cold and lifeless, putting each finger to his lips one by one, remembering what it was like to have them linger on his back and his face as she had kissed him deeply. He had replayed her kisses in his mind for many years, and touching her brought them back to reality, even in her slumber.

"I'm sorry … I'm so sorry that I ever left you and then never came back to you like I promised. I'm so sorry that I wasn't here to save you and be here for you. God, Brynn, I'm sorry for everything. Maybe if I hadn't left, this never would've happened, but I had to leave, I had to go home and take care of things and wrap up my life. I swear to you that I was planning to come back for you. I promise you." Nick held her hand, sobbing against it as he kissed her fingers over and over.

Nick waited and hoped for a miracle, his heart breaking in his chest as he stared at Brynn. She lie there, the only movement the rise and fall of her chest. He knew that if she opened her eyes at that moment, he would never go home again, even if that meant he had to figure out how to be a father to his daughter from a great distance. He knew that if he had a second chance, he would never walk away from Brynn ever again. He already knew the pain of living without her and without the promise of a life with her. Nick sat staring at her in silence, the image of her beautiful brown eyes staring deeply into him, locked in his mind.

He didn't see the small figure that had crept up behind him, staring at the tall man who had tears running down his face.

"How do you know my mommy?" Eva's small voice startled Nick who was lost in his own grief. He jumped as he wiped his face with the back of his hand and looked down at Eva who handed him a tissue without taking her blue eyes off him.

"We … uh … we were friends a long time ago," Nick said, shifting in his chair.

"How long ago?" Eva asked, unblinking.

"Um … before you were born," Nick cleared his throat uncomfortably.

"Did you like her?"

"Of course … of course I liked your mom." Nick was surprised by the question. "There's nothing not to like about your mom. Your mom was … is … a wonderful and amazing woman."

Eva looked at Nick, curious about the connection between

the mother she didn't know and the stranger who sat next to the bed. It was the first outsider she had met who knew her mom and she desperately wanted to know more about him. She searched his face for anything familiar, never breaking her stare as he pretended not to notice. He watched her out of the corner of his eye, fascinated and amused by her curiosity. *Is this my daughter? Does she bear any resemblance to me at all?*

Even though she had Brynn's beautifully shaped face, sweet button shaped nose and large eyes, the eyes were blue like the color of the ocean. Nick thought about Brynn's beautiful coffee colored eyes and his hazel ones that he found to be far less captivating. *Can brown eyes and hazel eyes even make blue eyes?* He searched for pieces of himself in the girl, but couldn't produce anything that reminded him of himself.

Just as he was about to give up, he saw it. His breath caught. *My birthmark!*

On her right wrist, just above the bone, he could make out the faintest freckle. He stared at it, amazed, his eyes then drawn immediately to the same freckle on his own wrist. He sighed, his hazel eyes filling with tears. He had a nearly uncontrollable urge to grab Eva and hug her as hard as he could, but he knew that such a gesture would be strange and alarming. *Keep it together, Nick. Keep it together until you can figure out what to do.*

He smiled at Eva, his lip quivering.

He looked at Brynn and silently cursed. *Did Brynn know that Eva was mine? Why didn't she tell me that we had a child? Why would she hide that from me?*

But Nick knew. He remembered with embarrassment that he hadn't told Brynn that he was married. Melanie had answered the phone once when Brynn had called. Even though he had tried to explain to her that his marriage had been over for years and that his wife was a hopeless alcoholic, Brynn had been furious. He had broken her trust and she hadn't forgiven him easily. It wasn't until she had finally agreed to meet with him did he see a spark of hope. She'd never made it. She'd been on her way to meet him when the accident occurred.

Tears flowed down Nick's face at the memories. He tried to

control himself, knowing that Eva was watching him closely. His tears were a mixture of regret and sadness for a life and a daughter that he had never known, and he wondered how he could ever be the same again knowing that Eva was his. Suddenly, he felt her small hand on his arm and he smiled at her effort to comfort him. She smiled back a sweet, innocent smile and Nick's heart ached because all he could see was Brynn.

There was a buzzing sound in the quiet room that hadn't been there before, breaking through the peacefulness like an unwelcome visitor. The sound was loud and insistent. Nick looked around as he searched the room for the source and realized that it was coming from him.

He fumbled with his phone as he tried to pull it out of his pocket. His heart dropped like a rock as he read the message.

Come home as soon as you can.
Mandy's in the ICU.
Accident. Please come, we need you, honey.

Nick stood up abruptly, startling Eva who had continued to watch him intently.

"I'm sorry, there's an … emergency. I have to go right now." He looked down at the bed, torn, his heart ripping into a thousand pieces.

He leaned over the bed and put his lips close to Brynn's ear, careful not to let his words be heard by anyone else.

"I don't know if you can hear me. I don't know if you're still in there, but I'll come back for you, as soon as I can. I'll come for you and Eva. I promise."

He kissed her gently, first on the forehead, then on the cheek. He knew in his heart what he needed to do and he tried to ignore the pounding of his heart and his head.

"Tell your … dad … that I have to leave … but I'll be back. I promise."

"Why are you leaving?" Eva asked, surprised by the suddenness of his departure.

"I just have to get home right away. There's been an accident." Nick turned the doorknob and gave Eva a long look, an expression on his face that Eva had never seen on another human being. "I'll come back as soon as I can."

Eva thought that it sounded like a promise and she wondered why this stranger was making such a promise to her.

As he turned and raced down the stairs, he hoped that he wouldn't run into Adam again. He made it out of the house unseen and sped toward his car, a heavy sense of dread falling over him as he picked up the phone and dialed.

"Honey!" Fiona's frantic voice on the other end made Nick's skin feel like there were a thousand pins ready to prick him. "Where are you? Come home, soon."

"What happened? Is Mandy okay? Why is she in the ICU?"

"There's been a terrible accident and I don't know if she's going to make it. She needs her daddy. You need to get home soon."

"What's wrong, Fiona? What happened to her?"

The silence on the other end of the line made him begin to panic.

"Just come home, Honey ... Mandy needs her daddy."

Nick hung up the phone, barely able to steady the wheel of the car. He drove away from The Harper House and headed toward the airport. A sinking feeling deep within his stomach told him that it would be the last pilgrimage he would ever take down this road.

CHAPTER EIGHT

A Miracle

July 15th, 2016

Kelly sat next to Adam in the waiting room, both of them silent, wrapped up in their own thoughts and memories. The reception had been ruined, and Eva and Chris had cancelled their honeymoon. The ambulance came and all the guests had filtered out quickly and respectfully. Eva had begged to come to the hospital, but Adam had refused. He didn't want his baby girl in the hospital on her wedding day.

"Daddy, please!" Eva's eyes were full of tears as she held on tight to his tuxedo shirt, makeup running down her beautiful face.

"Eva, no! This is your wedding day and your mom would not want you to spend it in the hospital. I promise you, I will call you or send for you as soon as I know anything. You've already cancelled your honeymoon. Please." Something in Adam's voice made Eva stop fighting. She adored her dad and knew everything he had sacrificed for her. She could never defy or hurt him, no matter how strongly she felt.

"Okay, Daddy." She said, her voice losing its fight. "I'll wait for you to call."

Adam was always surprised at how easily she gave in. In

that way, she was more like him than like Brynn. He always expected her to fight him tooth and nail, like her mother always had, but Eva had been raised in a safe and comfortable environment and didn't know what it meant to truly have to fight for what she wanted. As much as he admired her tenderness, he always found himself a little disappointed that she wasn't more like Brynn.

Adam had kissed her tenderly on the forehead, and then jumped into Kelly's waiting car.

As they sat in the hard chairs in the waiting room of the hospital, Adam pushed every bit of hope down as far as he could. He had been disappointed before and as he got older, he found that it became more difficult to get over. He gasped audibly as he wiped a single tear from the corner of his eye. *God, I wish I could have just one drink*, he thought, wishing desperately the day would come when he no longer had that thought.

He felt Kelly reach over and grasp his hand. Her long, cool fingers immediately comforted him. As he looked over at his friend, she smiled at him reassuringly and he remembered a time, many years ago when she had been more than a friend. There had been a time when he had found Kelly in his bed. He had allowed her to comfort him for a short time, with her smooth, soft skin and kind heart while Brynn lay down the hallway barely clinging to life. Kelly was a beautiful woman with crystal blue eyes. Her naturally blonde hair complimented her delicate features, and she had an ever-present smile. She had been a comfort to him, but eventually, the guilt had overtaken him, and they decided to end it amicably, both of them finding the comfort they needed in one another. As she sat next to him, their minds preoccupied with other things, he knew the connection from many years ago had died and he felt silly for even resurrecting it in his mind. He smiled at her, holding her gaze for a little longer than me meant to, hoping she couldn't read anything in his eyes.

Both of them jumped as a phone on the wall that neither had noticed before began to ring.

Kelly hesitated for a moment and when Adam didn't stand up to get it, she raced over to it, anxiously.

"Yes, we are Brynn Michaels' family. Yes. Yes. Okay."

She turned to Adam, her face serious. "They want us to come back to the room. They want to talk with us."

Adam took a deep breath. The doors buzzed and opened, allowing them access into the locked wing. He followed Kelly down the hallway to the ICU, their steps in sync. As they got closer, Kelly put her hand on Adam's back and tucked her hair back behind her ears, a gesture she often made when she was nervous. "It's going to be okay," she said, softly.

Adam nodded, unable to respond. His heart was beating wildly in his chest as they approached the room that Brynn was in. He imagined her sitting up and awake, waiting for him. "Where have you been? I've been waiting for you," he imagined her saying, her tone matter-of-fact and disconnected as she had often been during their marriage. Adam felt a pang of guilt. He knew that imagining her in a negative way was a coping mechanism. At least that's what the shrink had told him.

This is not what he found as they approached the room and walked in. He saw the ventilator first, and then saw that Brynn was in the same state she had been in for the last twenty-five years.

"Why isn't she awake?" Adam demanded to everyone but no one in particular.

Kelly put her hand on his arm to calm him. He looked at her angrily. "She's supposed to be awake! Where is she? Why isn't she awake?"

"Please! Stop yelling. Are you Mr. Michaels?" A young nurse that didn't even look old enough to be out of high school approached him and put a calming hand on his arm.

Adam jerked away from her, angrily. "She was awake when I brought her in here! Why isn't she awake now?"

"Please ... I mean, I don't know," the young nurse stuttered, taken aback.

"Get me your supervisor!" he said, spitting as he spoke. "Now!"

The young nurse scurried off, terrified.

As she ran out of the room, Eva ran into the room, nearly running the nurse over. Her long, thick, dark hair still tightly bound in her up-do, long wisps just beginning to escape.

"Eva ... Dammit! I told you not to come!" Adam looked at her, his mind racing and his words jumbled.

"What is going on with Mom?" Eva asked, ignoring him and grabbing Adam's arm. "What did you do to that nurse?"

Eva could tell by the expression on the nurse's face that Adam must've done something to upset her. She had seen that expression on many nurse's faces before when he wasn't being told what he wanted to hear.

"She ... just ... nevermind. Dammit! You know how it is!" Adam was frustrated. He pulled on his collar even though the top three buttons were open on his tuxedo shirt. "Why aren't you at the house with Chris like I told you?"

"Daddy, how could you try and make me stay away?" The determined look on Eva's face reminded Adam of Brynn and he was pleasantly surprised to see it.

Adam put his head in his hands and cried. "Your wedding day. Oh God. I'm so sorry, honey."

"Daddy, stop! You always over-react. Just calm down. You would think by now you would know how to act in the hospital!" Eva's tone surprised Adam and for a moment he caught a glimpse of Brynn, strong and commanding, taking control of the situation like she used to. He always admired that about his wife, running her own business and taking care of those around her all while hiding her own secret battle.

Adam sat down in the chair next to the hospital bed and grabbed Brynn's hand, stroking it gently, carefully. Eva stood next to Kelly, their arms around each other's waists as they all settled in, waiting.

Adam looked up suddenly as though he had a thought. "Where is Chris?" he asked, suddenly realizing that Eva's new husband wasn't here.

Eva hesitated.

"What is it, Sweetheart?" Kelly said, noting Eva's pause.

"I was going to wait to tell you, but ... we've decided to move into The Harper House. We want to be close to you. *All* of you." Eva's voice was low and barely audible.

Kelly smiled and paused, trying to hide behind her own blue

eyes. She always wondered if Eva knew what happened between her and Adam. She felt the old guilt resurfacing anytime Eva seemed to refer to them as a family. Kelly had once longed for a day when Adam could openly sweep her off her feet and declare his love for her, but she knew that it would never happen. His true devotion always belonged to Brynn. Kelly had long since given up on Adam. She'd stayed married to her husband, the time she spent with Adam a beautiful distraction from her young marriage. And when the children came, she spent the years raising them, splitting time between her family and Harper House. Still, she had never fully devoted her heart to her marriage. Finally, when the children went to college, her marriage became one of convenience only, and Kelly moved in almost full-time at The Harper House, telling herself that her marriage didn't matter to her any longer. She only went home when the children were in town on break.

Kelly knew deep down that it never would've worked between her and Adam. Her own love for Brynn would never have allowed her and Adam to be any more than the faint memory of two lovers who had once buried their pain in one another, hoping to forget.

Adam was speechless. "But ... I thought ..."

"We changed our minds, Daddy. We've decided that it's just time to move in. We knew we would end up in The Harper House eventually, so we thought we should do it now." Eva was careful with her words, not wanting to give anything away. She knew how sensitive and volatile Adam could be, and she didn't want to upset him anymore than he already was. Purposefully, she peered at him through her long lashes, unwilling to let him see directly into her eyes. She knew he could read her just as clearly as she could read him, and she wasn't ready to face him with the news quite yet. He looked beaten up and broken and her heart cracked for him. She wished for the day that he could be as young and carefree as he had been in the pictures taken of him and Brynn years earlier. Eva thought it strange that her mother never looked quite as carefree as Adam did, but Eva had heard bits and pieces of Brynn's life from eavesdropping as a child. She knew that from a young age, Brynn's life had been full of sadness and pain.

"I'm happy to hear that, Eva. I just want you to be happy. When I asked you before, you said Chris wanted the two of you to live on your own, so I didn't think you'd be moving into The Harper House so soon." Adam tried to hide his relief. He never wanted Eva to leave The Harper House, but knew that it would be wrong to pressure her. Eva needed to make her own choices, as difficult as it was to admit it. While he liked his new son-in-law, Eva had been his one constant and he wasn't sure he was ready to let her go yet. Adam was comforted knowing that Eva would remain under the same roof, and he suddenly realized how much he had relied on her throughout the years.

"Thanks, Daddy. I'm excited! Chris left to get a few of his things to move in. He thought he should do it while everyone was out so he wouldn't be in the way." Eva reached over and hugged Adam tight. The Harper House had been all she had ever known and she wasn't ready to leave. Chris understood that, and she adored him for it.

Eva's phone beeped and she jumped up, excitedly. "It's Chris," she said, bouncing out the door, forgetting for a moment where she was.

Kelly smiled at Adam. "Young love."

"Yes," Adam nodded. "Brynn and I were like that once. Or were we? I don't remember."

"I'm sure you were, Adam. She loved you very much," Kelly said, patting his hand. She wasn't sure she telling him the truth. She had only known Brynn, and then Adam, separately, never together. She had loved Brynn and they had become fast friends, but, like most people in Brynn's life, Kelly was never allowed completely in. After the accident, Kelly learned more about her friend than she had ever known when Brynn had been awake. Brynn was always guarded with the deep contents of her heart and her past and Kelly's heart had broken for her friend who had endured such painful solitude her entire life. Kelly never truly knew if Brynn still loved Adam at the time of her accident, though she knew from Jane there had been a time when she had loved him as completely as she knew how.

Just then, an older man with salt and pepper hair and a

matching moustache entered the room. His black-rimmed glasses were perched on the end of his nose, his thick hair jutting out wildly, almost as though he hadn't combed it. Despite his frazzled appearance, Kelly thought he looked respectable enough, though she doubted that Adam would think so.

Adam and Kelly stood up as the doctor entered the room and walked directly over to Brynn. Without looking at either of them, he picked up her hand and felt for her pulse, his eyes squinted tightly in concentration. He let her wrist fall gently onto the bed. He then opened her eyes, one at a time as he peered into them intently, searching as he flashed a little light into them that he pulled from an unseen pocket.

"Hmm," he uttered to himself. He shook his head and looked confused.

"What?" Adam said, his voice loud, unable to contain himself any longer.

"You said that she was staring at you?" the doctor asked, staring directly into Adam's eyes. His gaze was so intense that Adam immediately began to fidget uncomfortably.

"Y-y-y-es," Adam said, melting awkwardly under the doctor's gaze.

"I've seen her scans, sir," the doctor said, moving over to a mini computer station and logging in with a few clicks. He paused and cleared his throat as his eyes flicked back and forth, searching for something on the screen. "I've seen her scans …"

"Yes?" Kelly asked, frustrated with his fumbling.

"And for her to wake up at this point after her body and brain have been atrophying for as long as they have … well, it was more than likely just a …" the doctor paused, looking at Adam and Kelly who held onto his every word.

"For her to wake up, what?" Adam cut him off angrily, pulling on the collar of his shirt again.

"With the brain activity on the reports, for her to wake again … and I hate to be the bearer of bad news, but it would truly require nothing short of a miracle."

Adam stared at the doctor blankly.

"I don't think you have any idea what you are talking

about!" Adam's voice rose with each syllable.

"Adam!" Kelly grabbed his arm.

"No! He doesn't know her, Kelly! He doesn't know us! He has no idea about Brynn and what she's been through in life. She's a fighter and a survivor. You don't get it. She can get through this and she can wake up! She *will* wake up! She has to!"

Adam's body fell against hers and Kelly reached over to hold him up. She looked at the doctor apologetically.

The doctor had a small, sad smile on his face as he walked out of the room. Kelly thought she hear him mumble, "I'm sorry" on the way out.

She felt the weight of Adam's head on her shoulder as she tried to ease him back into his chair. "Adam ... maybe it's time you just come to terms with the fact that she's gone. Maybe you should just let her go. Would she want to live like this? Would she want *you* to live this way, waiting for something that's never going to happen?"

"But you saw her, Kelly. You saw her eyes open. You saw her! You know she's in there! I could tell when we were at the house that you thought she was there." Adam pleaded with her, desperate for any sign that she might believe him.

"We've been through this before, Adam. She's just ... she's gone. She's been gone for a long time. Don't you want to live ... truly live?" She raised her hand to his cheek and placed her palm against it, gently. She wanted so much to caress it, but she had been down that path before and knew that it would only bring her misery.

"I bet you're sick of me, aren't you?" Adam mumbled, his voice barely audible as he buried his face against her shoulder.

"No, of course not. I ..." Kelly stopped herself, trying to disguise the sadness in her voice. She pulled him close and felt his body fall against her as it had so many times before.

As she stared at Adam, weeping against her, she fought the emotion that welled up inside of her like an enormous rolling wave, tossing her heart back and forth. She had been adept at keeping her feelings in control for many years, but as time went on, she knew that it would take a miracle to keep her from walking away from him.

The same kind of miracle that would bring Brynn back to him.

CHAPTER NINE

Adam

Brynn

I can see Adam down on one knee with the ring in his hand and that hopeful smile on his face. I can still see his beautiful, youthful face and hear the tremble in his voice.

"Adam, we're only seventeen …" I protested, knowing that I was creating excuses because I was terrified.

"Well, will you?" he asked, his expression hovering between fear and hope, unsure of which it would land on. He wasn't sure if I would say 'yes', and neither was I. I loved him and he knew that, but I wasn't sure that I was ready to give the rest of my life to anyone yet.

I just didn't know.

"Do you believe in marriage?" he asked me early in our relationship when I thought we were way too young to even consider it.

"No … I mean … I don't know. I want to …" I thought about Thomas and Rose and how theirs had been the only marriage I'd truly ever seen from the inside out and it made my stomach turn. "You know, I didn't exactly have the best role models … like you did."

Adam flushed. He knew that his parents were the opposite of mine, who were the worst parents possible. He'd expressed guilt for having such great parents, which I always dismissed. It wasn't his fault he'd won the lottery with parents and I hadn't. All I had known of marriage was hatred and pain, abuse and anger, withdrawal and cruelty. That's all I'd ever experienced. I didn't know if I could imagine being married. I knew that I couldn't imagine having a baby, but that didn't seem to concern him in the least. He was convinced that I would change my mind. He thought that his love, our love, was enough to change everything.

Well ... are you going to leave me down here all night?" I realized that Adam was still on one knee.

"I ... I ... I'm sorry, I just don't ..."

Adam stood up, kissing me unexpectedly on the lips, his mouth soft and tender against mine.

"It's okay." He said, closing the box with a sharp click, the pretty little ring tucked away safely inside. "You will. You know that I'll ask again and again and again until you say *yes*."

Slowly, this vision of Adam fades away from me and I can see him again, only younger and cute, barely out of his awkward stage, passing me notes in class.

He'd been watching me, his eyes bright and mischievous. I pretended not to notice as I watched him out of the corner of my eye. I don't know why I can see it all so clearly, so well. Those moments seemed to have disappeared from my mind like long forgotten photographs, tattered and torn at the edges, the color faded with time. I remember seeing him, so young and beautiful and strong, but I don't remember what he would have seen in me. I don't understand why he chose me when he could've had his pick of any of the other girls. He surprised everybody when he chose me. Nobody understood why he would choose the quiet, bookish girl who kept to herself and had only one friend. Stacy. They never understood what Adam saw in me and neither did I.

My clothes were plain, my hair was long and un-styled, and I had never had a boyfriend, or even had a boy who liked me. Adam seemed too good to be true, and for a while, I thought he was making fun of me. Boys like him just didn't like girls like me. Boys like him liked girls like Tricia Ross who were blonde, blue eyed, and pretty. Tricia Ross was the head cheerleader, the class president, and one of the richest girls in town. Her father owned the mall in the town over, and being with Tricia meant the best of everything. Boys like Adam didn't like plain, lonely girls like me, who had an alcoholic, abusive father and a needy mother.

Boys like Adam Michaels liked girls like Tricia Ross, not broken, worthless girls like me.

But after some time passed, I could see that he did love me. He was kind and patient, and he saw the real me even though I tried desperately to hide it from him. He looked inside to see into my heart no matter how hard I pushed him away. The night that I finally decided to open up to him and give him all of me, he saw the scars on my body, left there by the blade I used to lose myself. I had tried so hard to hide the scars from him for so many years and I knew that showing him might mean losing him forever. It was then that I had no choice but to let him know me in my entirety. For the briefest moment, he knew me completely, and I was painfully vulnerable to him in every way, which terrified me more than anything in the world.

He asked me to marry him again after high school graduation and then again two years later.

When he asked two years later, lying in bed, his hands tracing the scars from the cuts inflicted years before, I finally said yes. When the cuts were no longer tender to the touch and I realized that I no longer flinched when his fingers found the scars, I knew that I no longer had an excuse to say 'No.' He pulled the ring out of his nightstand and held it in front of him, his blue eyes imploring, boring into mine. For once, I didn't want to look away and I kept my eyes on his. It was the first moment when I felt that saying *yes* was the right thing to do. When I said it, his eyes became wide and more beautiful as they turned bright with his tears. His fingers were tender as he wiped the tears from my own cheeks and we fell together in a moment of complete oneness.

The vision disappears and he reappears in front of me, and is replaced by an Adam that I never imagined, his eyes glazed over and barely recognizable, his speech slurred.

"You let our Sophie die ... You didn' wan' to be a mom and now sshhhee's gone because of you. It's all your fault. You've ruin-t us-s-s." His words sliced deep into my heart unlike any pain I'd ever felt before. Thomas had slapped and kicked me hundreds of times, but none of that compared to the pain of Adam's words as they echoed in my ears long after they left his lips. I knew it was the alcohol speaking but it was happening more often, his frequent apologies repeating hollowly in my ears until I could no longer hear them. His infrequent touch, empty and awkward, repulsive and apologetic became unwelcome. "You killed her, you let our baby die ..." His cruel drunken words echoed in my mind long after he had passed out, repeatedly cutting me deep down inside in the place I'd let only Adam see.

The moment is gone in my mind and suddenly replaced by Adam, his face worn and tired as he sat across from me in our lawyers' office surrounded by large, overly expensive furniture. His eyes are still as blue, but they are completely devoid of any promise or hope.

"You wanted this, Adam," I remind him. He looks at me, helpless and lost. "When Sophie died, you no longer had any hope. You chose this!"

He slumped in his chair, all the beauty drained completely from his face as he avoided my gaze and signed the papers, his hand moving slowly, his letters large and scrawling unlike his usual precise signature. I didn't want it to end this way and I didn't want to lose him like this after everything we had been through. He had been the one person I could count on, the only person I could truly call "family." He was everything to me, but then he chose his alcohol instead of me, and I knew that we no longer had any promise or possibility. He knew by taking that path that he was choosing the end of us. He was slapping me in the face because I allowed our baby girl to die, and nothing I could say or do would ever convince him that it wasn't my fault. I want to. Deep down, I knew that if I had wanted to be a mother more she might've lived, and I blamed myself, too. He had said it time and time again. He blamed me, and I blamed myself, for Sophie's death. Even though she was only hours from the womb I loved her deeply. The doctor told us that there was nothing that either of us could've done to keep her here with us. I wanted to believe her, but I couldn't, and neither could Adam.

Adam stared blankly, all expression erased from his face as he refused to look at me, his voice low and trembling every time he talked. He served me with paperwork at my restaurant because he wanted out, and he didn't want to do anything more to preserve it. He had moved out once and then back in, and had promised he would never leave again. But then he did.

Then I allowed him to come back for only one night and we allowed the familiarity of our bodies to attempt to heal one another. When he wanted to stay for good I refused. There had been a sense of finality to our last night in each other's arms, and I was ready for the door to close on what felt was a lifetime of pain. This man that I had finally allowed to love me had betrayed me, and I was gutted.

I didn't think that I would ever know love again until Nick unexpectedly came along. Nick's beautiful hazel eyes with gold flecks that changed in the light, and his chestnut hair were burned into my brain, and I loved that he was completely different from Adam. Nick made me feel like I was worthy of love for the first time in a long time.

Then my car was rammed head-on while my belly was full with Nick's child, though Adam was sure that the baby was his. Adam had wanted us to have a baby so badly after Sophie died, but having another baby would never heal our pain. He loved the idea of having a family, but he could never forgive me.

Then Eva came.

I know that it must have been torture for him to watch me love Eva and spend time with her but, I must. I need to be with her and nothing seems right unless I am.

Even though it doesn't feel like real life, I will take every moment I have with Eva, as long as she will let me.

CHAPTER TEN

Baby

June 1st, 2016

"I told you, I can't stay," he said, his voice getting that edge to it that Nora liked so much. Hearing his voice like that gave her the urge to pull him down against her naked body again and have her way with him, like she had so many other times. As she started to reach for him he jumped away quickly, out of her grasp. "No!"

"But, I want you. Now!" she purred, her green eyes beckoning, her long lashes fluttering at him the way he liked. Very few had ever been able to resist her when she had looked at them this way, and he was no exception.

"I said *No*. She'll be waiting for me and I don't have a lot of time." He buttoned up the shirt that had once been crisp and white, but was now hopelessly wrinkled from laying on the floor in a crinkled mess. He frowned to himself and wondered if anyone would notice.

"Why do you care? She's so stupid she'll never know where you've been. She's never suspected anything and she's not going to now, Baby." Nora was angry, her bottom lip pushed out, her green eyes flashing dangerously. She was used to getting her way and he wasn't cooperating. She tried to entice him by grabbing his body with her long muscular legs and pulling him toward her, but he resisted.

"What part of *No* do you not understand? You're being ridiculous!" He wrestled himself away from her, his hazel eyes turning dark and hard. "We're not messing this up. She is our *one* chance to have what we want for as long as we want it! You have to get a hold of yourself if we are going to make this work."

Nora sat up letting the thin sheet fall from her body, revealing her beautiful, pale breasts that she knew he loved and could barely resist suckling.

"Fine. Have it your way," she said, standing up slowly and deliberately, letting him get a good long glance at her complete perfection. She walked lazily over to the bathroom and slowly closed the door making sure that his eyes stayed on her. Even after all these years she could still mesmerize him by a simple move. She smiled as she thought of how uncomfortable he must be in his pants now.

"Baby, I'm sorry." Almost immediately his muffled voice came through the door as she waited on the other side. "Please, Baby, open up. I'm sorry. I can stay for a little while longer."

Nora smiled to herself as she waited to respond. Power. She had it and she liked to use it to tease him. It still gave her a tremendous amount of pleasure, making him squirm uncomfortably, both sexually and emotionally.

She had been teasing men all her life, for as long as she could remember, and by the time she met *him* she was already an expert. Nora's momma had taught her well, and Nora had paid attention to what she did until it was her turn. The moment she saw Chris at school, she knew that she would need him one day, though she was not sure exactly how or why. He was hot and confident and she wanted him badly. She had been drawn to him with his thick, unruly hair and beautiful hazel eyes that turned dark when he was angry or passionate. She had spent a lot of time observing how he dated and discarded girls, easily and without much care or concern. She watched how cruelly and carelessly he treated those who fell for him, and she found herself uncontrollably attracted to him even though she knew that she needed to be careful.

She watched him, knowing that he hadn't even noticed her—because she hadn't wanted him to notice her. Not yet. She had been patient, taking her time, studying him like a specimen until she decided what she wanted to do with him.

She toyed and played with *him* until he fell in love with her, and then she tested him. She always tested the boys to see how loyal they would be. Most failed, but she knew that *he* would be different. Unlike the other boys she had been with who were innocent and pliable, she knew *he* had a mean streak and would be a challenge. The thought of it excited her more than anything ever had and she found him irresistible.

Having someone to challenge her made her almost giddy, but she reminded herself that she was the one who always needed to end up in control. She pushed herself farther than ever before, even allowing herself to fall in love with him, though careful not give herself over completely.

Their first months together had been seamless as she satisfied him without asking for too much in return., Carefully and intentionally she left him wanting so much more. She had lured him in, making him want her over and over, and two years later she still knew how to entice him to do whatever she wanted.

She never admitted it, not even to herself, but she needed him. Somehow along the way, he had become the reason she woke up in the morning. She'd watched how love destroyed her momma, and there was no way she was ever going to let that happen to her. So, Nora kept her walking shoes on at all times, making sure to take many lovers on the side so she didn't become too attached. She vowed early and often that she would never let anyone ever destroy her because she knew there was always an end to everything, and she was going to be ready.

"Baby, let me in or you come out. I'm sorry." His voice came through the door and Nora waited, patiently, until she pictured him sitting on the floor, completely miserable. Slowly, she opened the door and he nearly fell, all his weight completely against it.

"Baby, get up, "she ordered, pulling him up, careful to push her nakedness against him so he could feel her flesh. She liked being pressed against him, and she could tell from the tightness of his pants that he liked it, too.

"I'm sorry, Baby," he said, pulling on her long auburn locks. "It's just ... I don't want to ruin this for us. It makes me nervous ... and I don't want to lose you. "

"I know, Baby, but if I tell you that I need you, then I *need* you. Now. And you can't make me wait!" Nora put out her bottom lip and looked up at him, enjoying their little game. "I can't stand the thought of you being with her ... and now there is no choice. You *have* to be with her. I hate it because you're mine."

"Yes, Baby. I'm yours. But this is what you wanted me to do. *This* is what we talked about me doing so you don't get to be mad about it. This is what *you* wanted me to do!" He held her body tight up against him as he struggled out of his clothes once again and buried his face in her long, thick hair.

"Do you like it? Do you like *being* with her? Do you like touching her?" Nora stroked his back with her long fingernails, sending chills up his spine.

"Baby, stop ... don't ask things like that." Chris squirmed at the thought of answering her.

"Do you? Do you like it as much as you like being with me?" Nora pulled him hard against her as she licked his neck.

"Stop! You know that could never happen!"

Nora stepped away from him, her tone changing abruptly.

"Good. Don't forget it. Don't forget that in the end you're *mine* and when I call you, you're going to have to make an excuse. You're going to need to figure out how to get away. But you're going to have to do it carefully because you can't ruin this. You can't ruin any of it. Do you understand?" She grasped his thick hair in her hands and pulled on it tightly, making him moan.

"Yes, I understand," Chris said, losing himself in her touch.

"Do you understand? Are you listening?" Nora's voice had risen in an alarming way. Suddenly she reached out and slapped Chris as hard as she could, leaving a red mark on his cheek, catching him off-guard.

"What the ..." Chris was angry and he resisted the urge to slap her back. "Don't slap me, Nora! You know that I don't like that."

"I'm sorry. Please, just don't leave yet. I want you to stay just a little bit longer. I'm so sorry I slapped you, Baby." Her voice was husky and her lips were red from biting down on them and trying to squelch the fire that was burning for him, deep down in her belly.

He bent over and covered her lips with his, unable to resist any longer.

"Of course, Baby. I'll stay, but then I have to go back and I have to work the plan like we agreed." He panted as he pulled away from her for a moment, his eyes wild with desire.

"Yes, Baby. You'll have to do whatever you need to do, but then you're coming back to me. Do you understand?" She pulled back and looked at him, her green eyes searching his. "You're mine, *Christopher*. You understand this, don't you?"

"Yes, Nora." Chris crushed his lips against her as she moaned against him, pressing his chest against her soft breasts, then finally filling her up as she surrendered to him. "Always."

CHAPTER ELEVEN

Home

July 20, 2016

After days of observation in the hospital, they moved Brynn back home and settled her into the beautiful, lavish room that had been hers since the accident. A comfortable, plush couch positioned by the large bay window was where Kelly often sat for countless hours as she read to Brynn or watched T.V with her.

The night nurse, Anne, was more formal, refusing to sit in a comfortable chair or sleep or eat while she was on duty. Even though Adam and Kelly tried to convince her to get settled in and relax, Anne refused. She was old-school and felt it was her duty to be more professional.

For the first few days, Kelly, Adam, and Eva took turns sitting by Brynn's side as they looked for any sign that she would wake up again. Chris came and went, bringing them food on their shifts, doting on and rubbing Eva's back, sore neck, and shoulders. Kelly watched them with a twinge of jealousy, wishing briefly that she hadn't alienated her husband so much. She had pushed him away so often that he would never consider rubbing her neck now. Her husband was rarely home anymore, always travelling for work, or taking little trips to who-knew-where by himself. Kelly slept alone at The Harper House most of the time, and she had convinced herself that it was what she wanted. Still, as she watched Chris and Eva with a sad smile on her face, she wished that her life had turned out differently.

The familiar sound of the breathing machine filled the room as they sat and waited for something to happen. As they settled into the mundane routine of the previous two decades, they nearly forgot that Brynn had opened her eyes and stared at them. Even Adam, who was beyond the point of exhaustion, gave up hope that Brynn would ever awaken.

"I'm tired. Really tired, Kel," he said, stumbling toward the door when Kelly walked in to care for Brynn on the fourth day. "I need sleep. A lot of sleep."

Kelly nodded, understandingly. "Get as much sleep as you want, Adam. I don't know that anything is ever going to happen here, as much as we would like it to." Kelly had been caught up in Adam's enthusiasm and the disappointment of knowing that Brynn wasn't really in there was depressing.

Kelly took a deep breath and ran her fingers through her thick, blonde hair. She didn't need to look in the mirror to know that she had bags under her bloodshot eyes. She had barely been sleeping herself, unable to get Brynn out of her mind. Even when she lay down to sleep, she couldn't escape from her thoughts. The doctor had given her tranquilizers for occasional use, to calm her nerves, but she was using them more often than she thought she ever would.

Kelly sat in the chair next to Brynn's bed. Her heart felt like the weight of the entire world sat on her chest, and she tried breathing as normally as possible. With Adam out of the room, she felt the intensity begin to dissipate as she settled into her well-worn chair next to Brynn's bed. She had been sitting with Brynn for so many years that she couldn't imagine doing anything else. She had read countless books, magazines and on-line articles, often reclassifying her recipes and keeping herself occupied as best as she could.

She looked over at Brynn and sighed.

"Brynn, I don't understand why you don't wake up. I know you're in there. I didn't believe Adam, at first. But now we sense it and feel you. We've seen you, for God's sake! Yet, you won't wake up which is so frustrating! It just doesn't make sense."

Brynn lie completely still; the only movement the rising and falling of her chest as the machine pushed air in and out of her lungs. Kelly's eyes filled with tears and she shamelessly allowed them to fall, the exhaustion flooding over her.

She sat next to Brynn's bed and grabbed her hand. Brynn's early life had been difficult. She never allowed anyone to see the pain she held close unless her guard was down and it accidentally spilled out. Kelly was amazed by the transformation that Brynn made when she was with her and Jane, seemingly more vulnerable and innocent when it was only the three of them together.

Since those early years, Jane had moved with her daughters and husband to the West Coast, closer to her ailing mother. Brynn's successful restaurants were sold and turned over several times since then, much to Kelly's dismay. She knew that Brynn would've been disappointed. Jane had been the backbone of the operation since Brynn had turned it over to her and it had broken Jane's heart to leave, but with her mother's failing health, she had no choice but to move.

Kelly stroked Brynn's hand, talking to her friend as she had so many times throughout the years.

"I want you to wake up, Brynn. You were my only friend, the only one who really understood me. I've been so lonely without you."

She paused, waiting for a response and was greeted with nothing but silence.

She continued. "When Philip started to take his trips, you understood. You urged me to divorce him, but you knew that I stayed for the kids because they loved their father so much. You told me that he would only continue hurting me, and you were right. Then I realized that when he was gone, it was a blessing more than it was a curse because I was able to stay here, with you. I rarely saw him and when I did I was indifferent because he didn't care about me either, and I realized that I was fine with that."

She looked at Brynn's face, waiting for a response or a reaction of any kind.

"You were the only person I was ever able to talk to about

that. You were the only person who understood and listened. You had been through so much more than I ever had and you comforted me. I loved you for it. You were my only true friend and that's why I've sat by your side year after year. But now, we're convinced that you're in there and you just won't come out. I've seen it … I've seen your eyes open and I need you to open them again. Please Brynn, open your eyes again. Please."

Kelly put her head down, holding onto Brynn's hand tightly, refusing to let go.

She placed Brynn's hand on her own forehead, relaxing against the coolness of Brynn's palm as she closed her eyes. She sighed and let herself melt against Brynn's flesh.

She felt the tears welling up in her eyes as she had so many times throughout the years during times like these.

"You always told me I could do better and that I deserved better and I never believed you. When I finally did, it was too late. It was too late."

She cried freely, the tears wetting the sheets, running down her hand that was intertwined with Brynn's.

She sobbed, her body heaving up and down, oblivious to the big brown eyes that had opened and were staring down at her.

CHAPTER TWELVE

Momma

Brynn

I watch as they bring Eva to me, tiny and pink, howling as they lay her on my chest.

It's as though my life swims around her without reason, or even a natural timeline, and while I know that it must be the damage in my brain, I am thankful for anything that reminds me that I'm alive.

When I get to hold her for the first time, I remember what it's truly like to be a mother. I let Sophie go. I promise that will never happen to Eva.

I was alone as a young child and all I yearned for in life was a mother. After my birth mother, Ellie, abandoned me on the side of the road, my leg mangled and broken, Rose adopted me. Though she thought she loved me, she simply used me as the balm for her own loneliness. She saw my abandonment as the perfect recipe for healing her own pain. As a child, I had been thankful for anything other than lying on the side of the road. That was until the beatings came.

I realized much later that Rose had done the best that she could, but I was still angry with her for not protecting me better from the physical and emotional scars that never go away. I wore the physical scars collected from years of cutting myself in an attempt to take away the pain. Those were hidden from everyone but Adam, and later, my lover, Nick. The emotional scars were disguised from the world, nobody every truly understanding my secret pain.

I watched Rose die and then found out later that she had poisoned her husband to defend me. Unfortunately, it had been too late. The horror was woven into the fabric of my being and into my dreams.

But holding Eva allows me to forget.

I look down at my beautiful baby and the world shrinks to every tiny part of her face and I am in love. I spend hours counting her long, beautiful eyelashes one by one and when I lose count, like I always do, I start all over again. I gently touch her tiny fingers and toes, marveling at their perfection, and giggling when she reflexively pulls one away. Every breath she takes makes me hold my own, and as she lays her head on my shoulder, her face only inches from mine, I am intoxicated by her beauty. In all my life I never imagined that love could be this simple and complex all at once.

I know that I could stay this way forever as I run my fingers gently over the top of her head and try and remember a time when I have ever touched anything so soft. I can't. With each sigh and gentle sleepy smile, I am drunk with love for this little person who has consumed every thought and every breath.

She is beautiful in every way and she never cries. She never requires anything more than to be held, and even when she is awake, all she does is stare at me with wonder and fascination at the very sound of my voice.

I know that nothing in my life will ever make sense more than the baby in my arms. She has given my existence a purpose.

CHAPTER THIRTEEN

Nora

June 1ˢᵗ, 2016

Nora showered slowly, reveling in the feel of the water on her naked skin.

She thought about Chris and how she loved having him wrapped around her little finger. She could make him do anything she wanted him to do, even when he didn't want to. She languished in the power she had, smiling as she thought about how easy he was to manipulate, though it hadn't always been that way. She had to fight to break him down and when she finally did, she wondered if she would get bored with him. It had been two years and he still kept her interest, even though she hadn't given up other men completely and had become an expert at hiding it from him.

She got out of the shower and towel-dried her long, wet hair. She decided she would let it air dry as she wrapped up in her favorite satin, pink robe and sauntered onto her bedroom patio. Lighting a cigarette, she selected the familiar contact on her phone and settled into the lounge chair for a good long talk.

"Hi Mother, it's me," she said, her voice low and sweet. She knew that starting conversations with her mother on a positive note were always best.

"Hi, 'me'," the voice on the other end sparkled with amusement. Her mother always enjoyed her daughter and her antics more than she enjoyed most. "How are you?"

"Things couldn't be better." Nora wanted to tell her everything, but she knew that she needed to take it slow. Her mother had always been unpredictable and if she wasn't in a good mood, then Nora knew the conversation wouldn't go the way she wanted it to.

"Do you still have that boy turned inside out, doing everything you want him to?" Nora could hear the tinkling of the ice in her mother's glass and wondered how many drinks she'd already had. From the sound of her voice, she hadn't had more than two.

"Yes, Mother. So far, he's still doing everything I want." Nora leaned back in her chair, waiting.

"I don't know what you're trying to do, but I've always told you that men can't be trusted. You know this." Mother's voice changed and Nora frowned. She knew the direction the conversation was going and it wasn't going to be the conversation she wanted.

"Really, Mother, everything is just fine."

"Be careful, Nugget. You don't want him to catch you playing with him. He's a good-looking one, but not too bright. I would be worried if I were you! The stupid ones usually like to hit because they're not smart enough to do much else."

"I'm *always* very careful so that he doesn't suspect anything. He has no idea that he's my puppet and that I'm pulling the strings."

"It's important that he doesn't suspect. I know you're careful, but just when you think you've done it right, double-check. Don't forget, I know *you*, and even though you don't mean it, you always mess things up. If you're playing with this boy, you better not screw it up. You know I love you, Peanut, but if I don't tell you these things then nobody will."

"I know," Nora was getting annoyed. She knew what she needed to do and didn't need to be reminded. She had been begging for approval from her mother for years and for the first time she felt like she might be earning it. She definitely wasn't going to mess that up!

They continued to chat for another hour, until Nora set the receiver down, finally exhausted. Phone conversations with her mother usually invigorated her and then drained her, but they always kept her on track. Her mother reminded Nora that Chris was just a distraction and that the real prize would be in the end. As she thought about his body and how he much he pleased her, she knew that eventually, she would be forced to let him go.

She walked slowly to the mini-bar in her room and poured two fingers of scotch. She let the peaty flavor wash over her tongue as she slowly felt the tension leaving her. She knew she had to limit herself to only one because anything after that would cause her to lose judgment and inhibitions. Alcoholism ran rampant in her family and she had experienced enough blackouts to know that losing control could be detrimental to her mission. She had awoken in many strange houses and beds over the years and had finally disciplined herself to only one drink at a time. She relished it. She took her time sipping and letting it slide down her throat, almost sensually, until her glass was empty.

As she stared into the bottom of the glass she felt a pit in the bottom of her stomach. In the end, Nora knew she was going to end up alone. She always had been, ever since she was a child, yearning for a mother that could be attentive and loving and for a father who never existed.

She fought the urge to pour another drink, though she desperately wanted to. She tipped the bottle toward her glass and at the last second, changed her mind. She stepped onto the balcony and lit the joint she had rolled earlier, enjoying its earthy smell. Pot always mellowed her out when she needed her mind to slow down and her body to give in to sleep. She had been so tightly wound ever since seeing Chris that nothing relaxed her. She knew that she had to play him tight and close, but not too close. She knew what the consequences of falling for him were and she wasn't going to let herself become a victim of love, no matter how much she was tempted to. She had seen first-hand the power that love had to obliterate, and she promised herself at a young age that she would never let herself fall in love with anyone.

She took a deep drag and allowed the smoke to fill her

lungs. She held her breath as long as she could and then blew the smoke out slowly. She took a few more drags until she began to feel numb and heady. She knew she was moving in slow motion as she picked up her phone and dialed the familiar number.

"Hey darling, what are you doing? Come over. I want you now." She hung up the phone, smiling to herself. She knew the doorbell would be ringing within the hour and she would be able to get lost in the distraction of one of her many men who made themselves available whenever she called. She was a skilled lover, and had perfected the art of pleasure by using her body in every way necessary.

She'd made a game of teasing and torturing her lovers until they were begging for more. She loved how she could make them do anything to and for her until she had her fill of them. Then she sent them home, always willing to come back to her soft, welcome bed. She especially loved the one she had just called with his hard body and affinity for hair pulling and slapping. He was just the distraction she needed from the emptiness that threatened to consume her.

She laid back and waited, anticipating the next few hours that would remind her that she was in control of her own life, and that she didn't need anyone to love her.

CHAPTER FOURTEEN

Firsts

Brynn

I try and think about all of Eva's firsts and I smile at the memories, happy to be there for all of them.

I can almost see her first birthday with the smash cake and how she cried when she realized that it was all over her, frosting everywhere; in her hair, her diaper, and all over me. I remember the first tooth that was loose. She wiggled it over and over, sticking her tongue through it until it finally came out, the blood making her throw up. I remember the triumph on her face when she held it up victoriously.

Everything that was a first for Eva was also a first for me.

This time she comes to me with another first.

"I'm pregnant, Momma," she says, her eyes downcast, avoiding mine.

She's afraid that I'll judge her and that I'll be angry with her for getting pregnant before she got married, but I'm not. I'm not angry with her in the very least. I just want her to be happy and when she tells me about the baby, I can tell that she is, even though she doesn't want to admit it right away.

"Are you happy, Love?" I ask her gently.

Eva hesitates and in an instant I can still see her as a tiny girl, venturing out into a world that seems far too big for her.

"Are you?" I prod, careful not to push too hard.

"I'm scared," Eva says, honestly. "I don't know how to do this."

I see her standing in the doorway of the classroom, frozen with fear on her first day of kindergarten. I see me kneeling down next to her and encouraging her to go in with the other children, and how she slowly walks into the room, looking behind her with terror in her soft, beautiful eyes. But then after a week, she couldn't wait to go to school. It was as though she had always been there.

"You do this like you do everything else. You do it with your entire heart and everything you have within you. You're going to be a wonderful mother."

I realized that I didn't know who the father was.

"You don't know him," Eva said as though reading my mind.

"How can I not know him?" I ask, alarmed that the gaps in my mind were growing larger and wider with every day. It seemed as though the medications could knock me out for days and it terrified me how much more frequently it felt that way. I feel as though I come and go so often that when I awaken I'm disoriented and it takes a long time to regain my footing.

"It's okay, Momma. He's a good man and I love him very much. I ... just ... need you for this because I can't do it without you. I need my mother."

My heart shatters into a thousand sharp pieces inside my chest as Eva's eyes shine with tears that refuse to fall. The look on her face is so desperate and sad and all I want to do is take her pain away.

"But I'm here, Love. I'm not going anywhere, and I'll be here for you and your baby. I promise." I hold her hand tightly, suddenly trying to convince her with my whole heart because I feel as though she doesn't believe me.

"I see you, Momma. But I need ... I need ..." Eva turns away, unable to speak, and the exhaustion hits me like a truck. I hate this medication and what it does to me! I hate that I can't be here for Eva like she needs me to be here. I struggle against it, my eyelids growing heavy, unable to hold my arms up any longer. I surrender against the cool pillows, no longer able to fight against the exhaustion any longer.

"I'm sorry, Love," I sigh as I close my eyes and allow the darkness to consume me. "I'm sorry."

As I fade into sleep I think I hear Eva say "It's okay, Momma. It's okay."

CHAPTER FIFTEEN

Husband

September 2ⁿᵈ, 2016

After weeks of settling back into normal life and realizing that Brynn was not going to wake up again, Chris convinced Eva to take a small honeymoon, though she refused to go too far from home.

Chris knew that she needed to get away to give Eva a break. As soon as they returned Eva began the task of getting the third floor of The Harper House renovated so that she and Chris could live there permanently.

They had already moved back in to her rooms after the wedding, but she knew that with the baby on the way, they would need a much larger space of their own. She hired an interior designer and had the many rooms, including the kitchen area, painted, updated, and restored.

Their space in The Harper House had once been her grandmother, Ellie's, where Ellie and Brynn had lived for the first two years of Brynn's life. The rooms were large and had been converted into a comfortable living space many years before. Adam had given Eva permission to make it hers and told her to spare no expense, even though she had never been comfortable with extravagance. She smiled at the beautiful simplicity of the rooms and how they reflected her classic taste. She thoughtfully chose comfortable items that she knew Chris would enjoy. She wanted him to be happy living in the house that had belonged to her family, even though that hadn't been the original plan.

She had convinced him to move in, especially when she found out that she was expecting. He had been resistant at first, worried about her and wondering if that was truly what she wanted.

"Eva, are you sure you want to do this?" he had asked, concerned. "I thought you wanted us to live on our own. I thought you wanted independence? I mean … I'll do whatever you want, but …"

"I *did* want us to be independent, but now, I just want our baby to grow up in the house that my mother should've grown up in," Eva said, pulling him close and breathing in his warm, masculine scent.

"Are you sure you won't feel too … stifled?" Chris asked, stroking her long, thick hair and trailing his fingers down her back.

"I don't think so," Eva paused, wondering if she was being honest. "I mean … I did want us to venture into the world on our own, but if our baby can grow up here, then I don't want to deprive it of that. I think Daddy understands and will give us our space. One day, I promise, we'll move out …"

"But you've felt so suffocated and lonely growing up in The Harper House," Chris reminded her. Eva appreciated that he always listened and realized that she had fallen in love with him because of it.

He knew the sadness that weighed on her and the massive loneliness of the house often made it difficult for her to breathe. She had told him about the many days and nights throughout her childhood when she wandered around the floors and rooms of the large house by herself, often not talking to a single soul for hours. Adam was busy grieving and trying not to drink while Kelly was taking care of Uncle Noah, and then Brynn. Everyone else who worked in The Harper House had a job to do, and while they doted on her, they were too busy to help fend off her loneliness for too long. For as long as she could remember, she had been left on her own to care for herself, finding her escape in the books that nobody read that lined the massive library walls once belonging to her grandfather.

Nearly three months after the start of the renovation, Eva looked around their new quarters, taking great care to put everything in its place. She thought about the first time she met Chris.

When Eva was finally old enough to drive, she often went into town. She would sit in a corner booth at the local coffee shop for hours, reading and drinking one cup of tea after another. The staff wasn't sure what to make of this rich girl who regularly left them fifty-dollar tips. They took her name from her credit card and did some research, learning who she was and from which family to belonged. She would return faithfully, day after day, week after week, and the employees were happy not only for the generous gratuity, but for her kind manner. They took pity on the beautiful girl who seemed so sad and alone. They were protective of her, though no one ever bothered her. That is until one day when Chris walked into the diner, sat down at her table without her permission, and wound up stealing her heart.

He came into her life on a day when she was especially lost in her misery, unable to wrestle her thoughts away from her father, who she was sure had been drinking first thing that morning, and the shell of her mother who lay in the bed unmoving. Reading distracted her, but on the more difficult days, she struggled to concentrate on the words on the page, no matter how hard she tried. The day she met Chris had been the worst and she'd been staring at her book, unable to turn the page for over an hour.

Chris was handsome and confident, instantly taking Eva's breath away. She was drawn to him immediately and realized right away that he was everything she wasn't.

She was suffering over her inability to focus on her book when he walked over to her table.

"Hi." The voice came unexpectedly from above her head and Eva looked up to find she was staring into the most beautiful hazel eyes she had ever seen. She looked around the near empty room, wondering if he had mistaken her for someone else.

"Hi," she said, her voice barely audible.

"Do you mind if I sit down?" Chris sat without waiting for her to say 'yes.'

They stared at one another for a moment and Eva could feel her cheeks getting warm.

"What are you reading?" Chris asked, trying to catch a peek at the cover of her book.

"Um ... Maya Angelou," Eva said, showing him the cover.

"Who's that? I've never heard of her," Chris said turning the empty cup in front of him over. The waitress materialized with a hot pot of coffee and glared at him suspiciously, which was lost on Eva but not on him. He gave her a charming smile, pulled a ten-dollar bill from his pocket and placed it gently in her hand. She took the bill and put it in her pocket without smiling, and looked over at Eva, protectively.

"Miss?" the waitress said, looking down at Eva's empty cup.

"No thank you," Eva said kindly. "I'll have some more tea in a little bit, but not quite yet."

The waitress smiled, walked away slowly, and Eva turned her attention back to Chris.

"So ... who is this Maya ... what's her last name?" Chris said, resuming their conversation.

"H-h-h-ow do you not know who she is? I mean ... she was amazing ... how ... do you live under a rock?" Eva asked, her voice going up an octave before she could stop herself.

Chris' eyes grew wide and then he laughed at her out-burst as Eva's cheeks grew even redder than they had already been. "I'm sorry, Angel, I just don't know who she is. Educate me then. Why don't you read it to me?"

"Angel? Why are you calling me Angel?" Eva was taken aback. Nobody had ever called her anything like that before.

"You look like an angel to me. Is it okay if I call you that?" Chris' eyes never left her face and Eva shifted uncomfortably in her seat.

"Um ... I guess ..." Eva stuttered.

"So, are you going to read to me?" His voice was seductive

and it made Eva's cheeks burn. Nobody had ever talked to her the way he did and she realized that she liked it.

Eva stared at him, hesitant. "You want me … to read it … to you?" Eva's eyes were wide.

"Please." Chris stared deep at her, not blinking, and suddenly Eva felt completely exposed. Nobody had ever taken such a deep interest in her before and she felt naked.

"Please. Read to me," Chris urged.

Eva paused and took a deep breath. She looked at him once more before she began to read in a low, quiet cadence as Chris listened intently and sipped his coffee.

From that moment on, they were inseparable, and after spending a few weeks together, Chris quickly became her refuge. She fell hard and fast, allowing him to sweep her away. He was handsome and funny, and he moved with the ease of someone who felt completely comfortable in his own skin something she did not. He always seemed to know the right thing to say, knowing her better than she seemed to know herself and she wondered how it was possible.

They had only been together for seven months, but Eva knew that Chris loved her. She hadn't hesitated to give him her heart and her body, the familiar emptiness disappearing with his touch.

She looked around the renovated space and was pleased with the choices she had made. She was confident that Chris would love it as much as she did. She made him stay in her old bedroom during the renovation, making him swear he wouldn't sneak a peek. She wanted so much to do something for him that he would love in order to give him a small taste of the happiness that he had given her. He told her that he hadn't grown up with much and she knew that the small extravagances, like the largest screen T.V. and all the updated technological touches she had added, were going to blow him away. The "Man Cave" she had created would make him so happy, and she glowed at the thought of what his face would look like when he saw it for the first time.

She couldn't believe how much she loved him. When he proposed to her, he gave her his mother's engagement ring. He had loved his mother so much and was careful to preserve his memories of her from his young childhood. Chris told her that she had passed away when he was ten, his face falling every time he mentioned it. They had that in common, the loss of their mothers, bonding them close. Eva was thankful to have someone that truly understood what it felt like to be alone. He was the first person she could open up to about how painful it was to be without her mom growing up. Even though her own mother was only a few rooms away at all times, the absence remained real and painful.

Eva walked slowly through the rooms one by one, running her fingers along the smooth wood of the doorways and pausing to make sure that every detail was in place. She paused in the doorway of the nursery, her favorite room. She had decorated it in bears and clouds, unsure if the life growing inside of her was a boy or a girl. She sighed happily as she imagined herself holding and rocking her baby with Chris by her side.

Suddenly she froze. The sound of a low wailing filled her ears. She looked around, frantically searching for the source of the sound. As suddenly as it began, it disappeared.

"Eva! Eva!" her dad's voice came shouting down the hall. "Eva! Come quickly!"

Eva ran from the nursery following the sound of Adam's voice.

"What is it?" Eva said nearly running into him, both of them breathless. She wrinkled her nose when she smelled the alcohol on his breath. Eva wondered why he still attempted to hide his drinking, and as time went on, he tried to hide it less and less.

"It's your mom … Eva. Your mom … she's awake! This time it's real, Eva! She's really awake."

CHAPTER SIXTEEN

Awake

Brynn

I open my eyes and everything is different.

I've opened my eyes a thousand times, but this time when I do it, I am struck immediately with a cacophony of light and sound, unlike anything I can ever remember experiencing. I feel as though I am choking from the inside out. I am starting to panic and I know without a doubt that I am suffocating.

Suddenly, there is a woman looking at me. She begins to yell for help, her blue eyes wide, her pretty face wearing an expression of shock and happiness. I know her, but I can't remember her name. It's the first time I've seen anyone but Eva in a very long time and something tells me that something … possibly everything … has changed.

"Brynn, just calm down and don't panic. There's a tube down your throat to help you breathe. Just relax, relax. We need to get you to the hospital."

I try desperately to calm down like she says, but my body doesn't want to cooperate. After a few long moments, I am able to calm myself down, but the feeling that I am choking sits on the edge, threatening to overtake me. I know that I am so close to losing control. I don't understand how I got here to this room and why things are suddenly so different. I look around, but I can barely move my head. I desperately search for any sign of Eva and I realize that she isn't there. Nothing about the room speaks to me of her. I've never been awake without her and I can't be without her now.

The room is alive and loud and I can't mute the sounds that are violating my senses, making me want to explode. I try and put my hands over my ears to quiet the sound, but something is wrong with my hands and arms and they feel as though they are weighted down. No effort can move them, not even a little.

The woman continues to tell me to breathe as tears run down her face. She lifts her fingers from where they'd been resting on my chest and speaks into something small she has cradled in her hands

"Adam! Come quickly! She's awake." She drops the small thing on the bed and stares into my eyes. Everything is so bright and I cringe. I hear footsteps rapidly approach the room and I flinch as the sound echoes painfully in my ears. All the commotion is hurting my head and I realize that this is far different than the peace and quiet that I'm used to. I don't know what has happened, but I want this woman to stop screaming so loudly.

"Oh Mom! Mom!" Eva's voice is a welcome sound and I strain toward it. I try and move my hands again, but nothing happens. It's in that instant I realize I have no command over any part my body. The only thing I can do is to blink, and even doing that takes a great deal of effort. "Mom!"

There is a beautiful girl's face suddenly inches from mine. I can feel that my cheeks are growing wet, but I can't tell if they are her tears or mine. I recognize her immediately, but she is not the Eva I know. She is not the delicate young girl I've made sandcastles with, or spent endless days at the park with. This girl is different. She is desperately beautiful, but fragile. I recognize the brokenness in her because it's the same brokenness that has consumed me my entire life. She reminds me of *me* as a young woman. Her eyes are deep, dark, blue, but the resemblance to me is uncanny and I see the connection between us immediately. While I had never thought of myself as beautiful, when I looked at the woman standing in front of me, it strikes me for the first time that maybe I had been pretty after all.

Eva's brows are perfect, just like the rest of her. Her face is oval-shaped and delicate. I can feel the soft strands tickling my face as she leans over me, her warm lips kissing my cheeks over and over. She buries her head in my chest, her small body heaving over mine, and I know she is trying hard not to crush or hurt me. Her voice is muffled as she cries into me with everything she has, though I don't understand a word she is saying.

I can hear the faint sound of sirens and for a moment, it becomes the only thing I can focus on. I fight hard to keep my eyes open, the sleep threatening to overtake me and steal me away once again. I'm afraid that if I go to sleep, I won't wake up. I'm terrified to lose this beautiful woman-child in front of me, afraid that if I go to sleep again, the Technicolor will disappear and Eva and I will be left with a gray landscape once again.

Without warning, Eva is gone and Adam's face is in front of me. I recognize him immediately though his face has aged tremendously. His eyes are still the beautiful blue that entranced me as a girl, but the lines around them are cut deep and they betray his youthfulness. His thick hair remains, but the darkness had been replaced by white and he is in desperate need of a haircut. The pungent smell of bourbon oozes from his breath as he speaks to me. I blink my eyes rapidly, wishing the smell away. He immediately backs away as though he knows what I'm doing.

"I'm sorry, Brynn," he whispers, his eyes sad and ashamed. "I-I-I've missed you so much. I just ... I've never been able to live without you. I've tried to stop, even after everything I've done to you ... but I can't. I've tried to ..." He buries his face in his hands, his body shaking uncontrollably.

There is a loud sound in the hallway as the paramedics and police walk into the room with their heavy boots.

I close my eyes and allow myself to drift off to sleep, unsure if I will wake back up, but too exhausted to stop. The noise disappears slowly in the thickness of my slumber. The last sound in my ears is the sound of Adam's sobs and a woman's voice saying, "It'll be okay, Adam. It'll be okay."

I awaken in what appears to be a hospital room, so much more quiet and sterile than the room that I woke up in before. I realize that I'm alone and am thankful for the blessed silence. There is no crying or sadness consuming the people around me. I am alone with only the blipping and whooshing sounds of machines.

I try wiggling my fingers.

Nothing.

I will them to move, but my fingers remain stubbornly still on the stiff sheet of the hospital bed. I struggle within, imagining that they are one-hundred pound weights, but no matter how hard I try, they defy me, and I find myself getting angry.

I want desperately to move my finger.

I want to move my damn finger.

I want to move my fucking finger.

I want to … suddenly my finger twitches ever so slightly and I am elated.

Nothing else on my body will move and I feel like I'm buried deep inside a cocoon, but the tip of my finger twitches just by sheer will.

My will.

I don't understand what is happening to me and why everything has suddenly changed. The world around me has become so much louder and more confusing than anything I've ever imagined or experienced.

A tired but upbeat nurse breezes into the room.

"Hi Brynn," she says smiling, cheerful. "Do you remember me? I've been taking care of you here in the hospital for a few weeks now. I'm Lil."

Weeks? I've been here for weeks? I just woke up … how has it been weeks? Time seems to move slowly but fly by at the same time and I feel dizzy.

She checks the machines that I'm hooked up to, then

carefully picks up my wrist to feel my pulse. I realize with horror that I can't feel her touching me. "Good." She taps on the keyboard and smiles at me, a beautiful toothy smile. "You're doing well, Brynn."

She says this in a way that makes me feel as though I should be proud of myself, but I'm not. I feel hopeless. Helpless.

I don't want her to think that I am ungrateful and try to blink at her.

Thanks.

My throat hurts and I swallow. There is nothing stopping me from doing so and I suddenly realize that I am breathing on my own. I feel a moment of panic as I wonder if I can do this. *Breathe in and out. In and Out. In and Out. In and Out.* I swallow hard again, my mouth feeling very dry and chapped.

"Is your mouth dry again?" Lil comes closer with a little sponge on a stick.

She opens my mouth and I feel some welcome relief as the liquid soothes me. I try to suck on the sponge, but there is nothing left. She dips it in the cup again and again until my mouth is less parched. "You're a miracle, you know that?" She shakes her pretty head at me and smiles. She seems genuinely happy that I'm awake. "The doctors are still trying to figure out what's happened to you and how you're awake like this. None of them have ever seen anything like it."

I listen carefully, still grateful that the horrible tube is out of my throat.

How long? How long has it been since I woke up?

"You're really doing so well. Even though it's only been a month, you're breathing on your own and staying awake longer. We're so happy for you! You even have your own Facebook page and there are a lot of people supporting you! The next step, young lady, is to be able to get rid of the feeding tube. Then home."

What is Facebook? Home. All I want to do is go home.

"You've been through so much. We all want you to get better so you can go back to your beautiful home and be with your family." Lil hadn't stopped smiling since she came into the room. As much as I want to dislike her because she's keeping me prisoner, I find that I can't

Where is my family? Where is Eva? Where is Adam?

I can hear Eva's voice from down the hall, beautiful and musical, mingling with a deeper voice, one I don't recognize. I'm sure that I would recognize Eva voice anywhere. It's the one voice aside from Adam's that is imbedded in my brain. Even as she's grown and the tone and timber of it has changed, I've always known it, feeling it in my heart first before it reaches my ears.

"Mom, you're awake," Eva floats into the room, her beautiful face glowing. She sounds excited.

I blink, still unable to move my head though I try with everything I can.

"Hi Mom," the handsome young man who is with her tells me as he leans over and kisses me, his lips harder than they look. I don't like the feel of them, quick and obligatory on my cheek.

I look at him, questioning.

"This is Chris, Mom. You've met Chris many times, both at our house and here. *He's my husband.*" Eva holds his arm tight, her face beaming.

He looks at me, his eyes warm, but something about him unsettles me. Eva repeats hopefully, "You've met Chris a lot of times."

Why can't I remember?

"It seems normal that she won't remember everything," Lil says, squeezing Eva's arm, reading the frustration in my eyes. I realized that Lil and Eva seem to be about the same age and there is an unspoken understanding between them. "She's getting better day by day, which is a very good thing. You have to take it one day at a time."

Eva smiles a small smile that doesn't reach her eyes completely, but when she turns her face toward me, it is bright and hopeful.

"Don't you remember, Mom? Chris read to you the last time we were here. He read Dickens to you, which is one of my favorites." Eva's voice is hopeful and she seems almost desperate for me to remember him.

I blink, hoping she will decipher that to mean that I

remember.

She smiles, seemingly relieved. *She does.*

The entire time Chris stands too close to my bed and I watch him out of the corner of my eye. I don't like the helplessness that I feel, and I realize that I haven't felt this way since I was a young child, cowering at the feet of my adopted father as he hit me. Something about Chris reminds me of Thomas, though I can't put my finger on it, When he is close to me I feel afraid.

At least when I was asleep, I didn't realize how vulnerable I was, but now that I am awake, it frightens me that I am unable to move, sit up, or stand on my own. Eva grabs Chris' arm and pulls him away from me as though she knows that I am uncomfortable. It's as though she can read me although I have yet been able to speak a single word. It occurs to me that she has never heard my voice and the thought makes my heart feel heavy.

Eva gasped, pointing to my hand, her eyes dancing happily. "Mom, you're moving your fingers! You're moving them on your own!"

I look down and am startled to see that my fingers are moving without me having to give much effort. I have been trying to move them for so long and had forgotten that I was still trying. Chris is looking at me, smiling a small smile.

I close my eyes, anxious for him to leave. My head has begun to pound slightly. I hope he will take this as a cue to leave, though I want Eva to stay. Almost immediately, I find myself sinking into a deep sleep, and the dreams still come even after all these years.

Thomas always haunts me at night. He always has throughout my entire adulthood; during my marriage to Adam, and even in my dreams now. For a long time, the dreams seemed to disappear, only resurfacing occasionally. They've come back again, this time more frequently. Lately, though, Thomas' face is replaced by Chris', and the fear I feel is no longer for me, but instead for my baby girl.

I realize with horror that I'm not afraid of Chris for my sake.

The fear I feel is for Eva.

CHAPTER SEVENTEEN

Eva's Momma

September 18ᵗʰ, 2016

Chris had gone out hiking for the day. Eva knew he would be out of cell-phone range for a while and come back a sweaty and disgusting mess, exhausted from his excursions but she didn't mind. She loved that he enjoyed nature and being so active. She was so proud of him and made sure to tell him so as much as she could.

With him being gone for the day, it gave her time to spend with Brynn in the hospital. It has been almost two months since Brynn had awoken, but she was still confused and slept most of the time, her body trying to regain its strength. Eva was fearful every time that Brynn went to sleep, watching her intently when she was there to make sure that she didn't stop breathing. She was terrified that she wouldn't wake up, although the doctors assured Eva that she was well out of the danger zone and was being monitored heavily.

Brynn was slowly getting stronger every day, still visited by doctors who were amazed at her progress, and that she had been able to wake up at all. They called her a medical miracle.

Eva continued to talk to Brynn during every visit just as she had been doing her entire life, but now she knew that Brynn heard her, and Eva was thankful to no longer wonder if she was listening.

Although Brynn couldn't speak yet, her dark expressive eyes told Eva that she was in there, taking in everything she said. For the first time in her life Eva no longer felt alone in the world, and her heart felt unusually light and happy.

Eva was excited to spend the day with Brynn. When she got to the hospital, even though Brynn was asleep, she took her place in the chair next to her bedside and settled in for a long visit.

"Momma, I know you're getting stronger, but you'll need to hurry because you're going to be a grandma very soon. I'm going to need you to help me with this little one!" Eva said, as she put her hand on her belly and smiled at Brynn, looking for her to make eye contact. "I've been waiting for you to wake up for so long, and now that you're finally here, there will never be a day that goes by that I won't see you or be with you. I just … I've … I've missed you so much." Eva spoke convinced Brynn could hear her. Eva held it in her heart that when she told her that she was pregnant it had helped Brynn wake up.

Eva had tried hard not to cry since the first night that Brynn woke up. She was filled with as much happiness as she could possibly imagine and she knew that she no longer had any reason to be so empty. But there were still times when her heart reminded her of all she had missed during her childhood and the sadness came over her like a sudden darkness, unexpectedly.

She watched Brynn as she slept, her chest heaving up and down, gently, her face slack with sleep. The scars on Brynn's face were still slightly visible though Kelly had diligently put cream on them, twice a day, as part of her daily care. Brynn had been very self-conscious about the scars on her arms and stomach from when she cut herself to forget the abuse from her adoptive father, and Kelly knew that she wouldn't like the scars on her face. Even though shards of glass from the accident had pierced her cheeks and forehead, Eva marveled that they didn't diminish her mother's beauty.

The only scar that still stood out was the one that ran down the right side of her face from her temple to the bottom of her cheek, deep and fairly straight. Eva ran her thumb down the scar, gently, as she had so many times when she was a child. Brynn amazed everyone by surviving the crash and now amazed everyone by waking up. Eva knew that it was nothing short of a miracle to have Brynn with her. But she often thought guiltily about the many times when she had prayed for closure and the opportunity to grieve the mother she never had. It had been difficult missing her mother, especially when she was right in front of her. She couldn't help wanting her, expecting her, to sit up at any moment, so she could ask her to braid her hair or read a story.

Eva shook her head, a single tear running down her face, angry with herself for even thinking about such things.

Suddenly she realized there was a hand lying gently on hers. As she looked down, she saw Brynn's hand on top her own. She gasped and looked at Brynn who still remained asleep but had somehow found Eva's hand during her slumber. Eva sat still, refusing to move and barely breathing. In Eva's entire life, Brynn had never reached for her, and Eva was both startled and thrilled, afraid that if anything in the room changed, that the moment would disappear.

She looked up just as Kelly entered the room, Eva's big eyes shining with tears. Kelly's eyes immediately went to Brynn's hand resting gently on top of Eva's, and she stared in stunned silence.

"Did she do that?" Kelly whispered pointing to Brynn's hands.

Eva nodded, unable to contain her happiness. Kelly pulled out her phone, took a picture, and sent it immediately to Adam.

Kelly smiled at Eva, happiness and relief flooding through her.

"That's so good, Eva! So good!" Kelly sat next to Eva and put her arm around her. "I told you not to lose hope. We have to take it one moment at a time!"

Eva leaned against her, careful not to disturb Brynn's hand.

"Thank you," Eva said, happy that Kelly was able to witness her beautiful moment.

"Why are you thanking me?" Kelly said, kissing the top of Eva's head.

"Because you've always been there for me. You've been ... like a mom to me ... and I don't know what I would've ever done without you. I just … I'm just so happy that you are in my life." Eva spoke softly but deliberately, as though she had rehearsed the words so many times before. "I never told you how much you mean to me because I was afraid it would betray the love I have for my mom, but now I know that she would be happy you were there for me. I don't know why I know, but I do."

She could feel Kelly nod above her. "Your mom was … is … a good woman. She would never want you to be alone."

Kelly thought about her own children, her youngest daughter at college, her middle son married and living across the country, and her oldest son overseas in the army. She wondered for the thousandth time if they would've stayed close if her marriage had been better, but she thought sadly that there was nothing she could do about that now. She had been openly more in love with The Harper House and the Michaels family than she had ever been with her husband, and he knew it even before she did. Now his absences were so long and so often that she knew the day would come when he wouldn't come home at all. She often wondered why he never divorced her, and no matter how hard she tried, she couldn't think of a good reason. Since she practically lived in The Harper House, she realized she wouldn't even know if he stopped coming home. Strangely, she knew that it wouldn't make a difference if he did.

"I wasn't alone." Eva looked up at Kelly, her eyes suddenly dark and serious. "I had you and your kids. I had both of my moms with me my entire life and I never realized how lucky I was until now."

Kelly's breath caught in her throat as she pulled Eva toward her and held her close. She had thought of Eva as her own daughter so often throughout the years, but never felt she could say so. She thought about the numerous shopping trips with her own children and Eva, the first time she took her to get her ears pierced, and the talk about the 'birds and the bees'. The first trip to the gynecologist and the daily ritual of brushing and braiding Eva's hair first thing in the morning when she would arrive at The Harper House, were all the moments that Kelly had spent mothering Eva. But Kelly never felt as though there had been a choice.

Jane, Brynn's closest friend would've helped, but when she

expanded the restaurant which had been Brynn's dream, and then had to move away to care for her own ailing mother, Kelly knew she couldn't let Eva down.

Kelly hugged Eva close. They sat in silence for a long time, both of them wrapped up in their own thoughts as they sat quietly with Brynn. All of a sudden Brynn's hand started to tremble and she began to moan as though she was in pain.

Before they could grab the call button for the nurse, Brynn turned her head toward Kelly and Eva, her coffee colored eyes opened wide.

She opened her mouth and Kelly and Eva held their breath.

"Save me," Brynn said, staring straight through them, her voice low and gravelly. "Don't let him get me ... please. I'm begging you."

"Who? Don't let who get you?" Eva cried, grabbing Brynn's hand and holding it tight.

"Him ... don't let him hurt me again." Brynn's fear was palpable and Kelly could feel her heart beating faster.

"Don't let who hurt you?" Eva asked, feeling helpless. "There is nobody here to hurt you. You're safe!"

"Adam. Keep him away. Where is Maxie? Please, just don't let Adam hurt me!" Brynn cried out desperately before she fell back onto the bed and into a deep sleep.

CHAPTER EIGHTEEN

Broken Plans

September 18th, 2016

"It's so strange, Baby. It's almost as though she *knows*." Chris was shaken up. Brynn had stared right through him during his last visit with Eva, her brown eyes dark and strange, and he felt as though she was looking deep into his soul. He shuddered at the memory as though a ghost had passed right through him and he couldn't get the feeling out of his mind.

"She couldn't possibly know," Nora scoffed, flicking a long ash from her cigarette and directly onto the balcony where they sat enjoying an after-dinner cocktail. "You're imagining things."

"No, Baby, you don't understand. She can barely fucking move, but she stares directly *through* me, as though she can see *inside* of me. It's so damned unnerving." Chris puffed hard on his cigarette.

"Relax, Baby. Just relax." Nora knew exactly what to do to help Chris relax as she straddled him and kissed him long and hard on the lips. She could feel Chris fight her at first, but then he gave into her like she knew he would. They weren't meeting as frequently as they had, careful not to arouse suspicion. She had missed him more than she realized she would and had been anxious and excited for him to arrive. She knew they had to be careful, especially now that Eva was pregnant. They couldn't get caught or it would ruin everything they had been working for.

"I've missed you," Chris moaned against her, their clothes coming off easily and naturally as though they had rehearsed it a thousand times. His hands grabbed her tight and positioned her firmly against him until there was no longer any space between them. Their bodies moved in complete sync with one another, each knowing exactly what to do to please the other.

"Me too, Baby. I've missed you, too," Nora was surprised at how much she had missed him. Ever since high school, they hadn't spent more than a few nights apart and she had convinced herself that she didn't need him to sleep next to her at all. But now that he was no longer in her bed, she had to find others to sleep next to her or she could barely sleep at all. Even when the others were there, she still lay awake staring at the ceiling, missing the feel of Chris beside her.

For the first time, Chris could tell that she missed him by the way she grabbed him so hungrily the moment he walked in the door. She had never held him before with such abandon. Until now, he hadn't been sure if she loved him as much as he loved her. Since they'd spent time apart, he could see the misery in her eyes when he had to leave and could feel the intensity of her touch when she was near him. Chris had always been the one to give into her completely, but now he felt the desire shifting between them, and it made him feel strangely euphoric.

He had missed her desperately, but he tried not to think about it when he was with Eva. He didn't want Eva to see through him, and he realized that he didn't hate his new life with Eva as much as he thought he would. He wasn't as anxious to get away from her and back to Nora as he had in the beginning. Eva was kind to him and he had grown accustomed to spending time in the "Man Cave" that she had made for him. He knew that his time with her could be much worse and he fought the pleasure that he felt when he was with her. She was hard not to love, and he knew that he could never let Nora see that side of him.

Still, Nora felt like coming home and, while he reveled in his love for her, every time he got to see her he understood why the separation was necessary. He realized that as Eva's pregnancy progressed that he would see less and less of Nora, and that it had to be that way or they risked exposure.

After they'd had their fill of one another, they sat in opposite chairs on the balcony, their fingers entwined, sweat still slick on their skin, and their clothes strewn on the balcony around them. They could feel the clock ticking as they pretended that their time together wasn't coming to an end.

"When am I going to see you again, Baby?" Chris asked as he stood to dress. He was reluctant to hear the answer.

"We should probably keep it to once a week," Nora said, her voice catching in her throat as she looked around for her discarded slip. "We don't want to get caught and ruin everything. It would've been easier if you weren't staying at that big goddamn house with all those people, but since you are, you can't be gone for too long or they'll wonder where you are. You know those rich people have a way of holding onto what's theirs ..." Nora's voice trailed off as though she had something else to say but didn't want to say it.

They sat in silence for a few moments, the air between them thick with dread.

"I don't know if I can go for an entire week without touching you. How am I going to survive without seeing my baby?" Chris asked, pulling her close to him again. "A week is just too long."

Nora pushed him away gently and settled back into her chair. "I know, but once this is all over, we'll be together again. And it'll all have been worth it! I promise you."

"I hope so ... it's just that ..." Chris paused, running his hands through his hair, unsure of how to continue.

"What?" Nora said, practically purring. "What is it, Baby?"

"It's just ... I want to change the plan a little. I mean ... I don't want to hurt ... I mean, I want Eva to be safe ... she hasn't done anything and ..."

Nora bolted up, practically exploding out of the chair. "What? What do you mean? What are you asking? We've talked it all out and planned this for a long time! We aren't going to change it now because you knocked her up and now you feel bad for her. You weren't even supposed to touch her, but then you convinced me that you needed to in order to gain her trust! I told you to fucking be careful, but obviously you weren't and … Jesus, are you in love with her? Are you changing your mind? You promised that you wouldn't go soft on me. Is that it? You're a fucking sissy now?" Nora was angrier than she had ever been with him.

"No … I mean … No … I just …"

"You just what? You love her? You want to actually stay married to her? Is that what you're saying to me? You don't love me?" Nora broke down in tears, falling to the floor. "I knew this would happen. I knew you couldn't handle it! If you think that I'm just going to be your bitch on the side while you play house, then you're out of your mind!"

"No! That's not what I want, Baby! I *can* handle it … it's fine. Stop it! I just … I don't know that we should go through with the entire plan. I just don't want to … hurt her. There are other alternatives …" Chris got down on his knees and tried to hold her but she shoved him away violently.

"I get it, Christopher. You don't love me anymore. You love her instead. I knew that would happen. I knew you would fall for her. God! I hate you!"

Chris took a deep breath and continued. "That's not true, Nora, and you know it. I don't love her! I love *you*. But you wanted me to seduce her and I did that! I didn't mean to get her pregnant, but now she's carrying my baby inside of her and that's a game-changer. I didn't expect that, but you should've known that it would change everything for me. Nora, please, she's a really good girl, and we should reconsider the original plan. That's all I'm saying!"

Nora stared at him, her green eyes icy. "I thought you were stronger than that, Christopher. I thought you were more focused and less emotional than that. I thought you would be able to stick to the plan, but clearly I was wrong."

"No … No … Listen, Baby, we can work this out. We can fix this and make it so that nobody gets … hurt. We can make it so that …"

"You should leave now."

"No … stop. I don't want to leave like this." Chris was desperate, alarmed by the look in Nora's eyes. He had never seen her so angry and never with him. As she stared at him, he felt himself shrinking in front of her.

"It doesn't matter *how* you leave. You just need to leave. Now." Nora was angry with herself for getting so upset in front of him. She knew when she devised the plan that she would have to allow herself to be okay with him sleeping with Eva. In her mind, she had envisioned it a hundred times, even when she was in her own bed naked with the others.

She pictured her momma sitting her down when she was eight. "Nora," she had said, the bright green eyes so much like her own, as serious as she had ever seen them. "Never, ever, ever, fall in love with one man, Peanut. All they do is break your heart when they don't love you back. And believe me, they'll never love you back the way you'll love them." Even as a young girl, Nora had nodded as her mother spoke, knowing her words to be true. She had watched her mother fawn over every man she had ever been with since Nora was a little girl, and they had all ended up leaving. None of them had loved her mother enough to stay, and Nora knew that had torn her up inside. "Never ever fall in love with one man, Peanut," her mother had said over and over.

Nora loved her mother with all her heart, and it pained her that she hadn't listened and had accidentally fallen for Chris. Nora had tried to protect herself by filling her life with others, both men and women, whichever she could sleep with or order around. But none of them stayed very long, often growing impatient with her demands and put off by her inability to commit to anything longer than one night at a time. While some of them understood they were just a pawn in her game, others fell hard for her and wanted much more. Nora refused to commit, even to Chris, though he was the closest that she ever came.

Nora never lied to Chris about her many lovers, but Chris had loved her so much and for so long, he allowed the assortment of people who filed in and out of Nora's bed believing she would change her mind one day. She never flaunted it and tried to be as discreet as she could, but Chris still knew.

"Never, ever fall in love with one man, Peanut," Nora's mother's voice rang in her ears as Nora looked at Chris with disgust.

"You need to leave. I don't even want to look at you right

now." Nora's voice was colder than he had ever heard it and he was stunned by her sudden hardness. He had seen her turn quickly before, but never like this.

"Baby, no. I don't want to leave like this," Chris said, his voice shaky. "We're not going to see each other for a long time, and we can't just walk away like this and not talk for a week. I won't be able to stand it."

"It may be longer than a week, *Christopher*," Nora said, emphasizing every syllable of his name as she said it. "In fact, we may not see each other ever again now that you've made it clear to me that you care so much about that little bitch."

She turned away from him, angrily.

"Leave. Now."

"No … please," Chris said, trying to sound strong and failing miserably. "You can't be serious, Baby."

"Don't beg. It's pathetic," Nora said, her voice flat and barely audible. "You're pathetic."

Chris slowly stood up and walked away, feeling as though he had just been run over by a truck. He knew there was no point in fighting with her any longer. Her mind was made up and he knew that he would need to give her space. He hadn't been without Nora for longer than a few days in many years. He wasn't sure if he could do it.

Eva flashed before his eyes and he pushed the image aside angrily. *If I lose Nora because of Eva, I don't know what I'll do.*

He waited for her to stop him, but when he finally closed the apartment door behind him and got onto the elevator, he realized that she was letting him go. He paced the elevator like a caged animal, wondering where he should go. He knew that he couldn't go back to Eva without cleaning himself up. He could still smell Nora's scent on him and he closed his eyes, breathing her in.

He stepped off the elevator, walked into the lobby and then onto the street. He looked around trying to remember which direction to go. When he figured it out, he took off anxiously. He knew there was nothing more that he wanted to do than drink until he could no longer feel the knife plunged deep into his heart, tearing it into a thousand pieces.

CHAPTER NINETEEN

The Stranger

September 19ᵗʰ, 2016

The loud banging woke him and he jumped up, disoriented.

He stood up clumsily, confused by the constant pounding in his head as he tried to figure out where he was and why he was on the floor. The surroundings were familiar, but no matter how hard he tried he couldn't place where he was. His eyes were fuzzy and his head hazy from too much alcohol. There was a sharp, stabbing pain directly behind his right eye that made it impossible for him to think.

It took him a few minutes to get his bearings as he stared at the red, sticky liquid that covered the floor and his clothes. It took him several long minutes to realize that the red liquid was blood. He couldn't believe how much there was, the smell of it nauseating him.

"Open up, right now! Police!"

Chris realized that the pounding wasn't just in his head, but was coming from the direction of the door. His heart began to thump faster in his chest. He stood unsteadily, willing his feet to move, but they felt cemented to the ground. The pounding continued until he heard the sound of wood splitting, then a loud explosion, and the sound of heavy feet entering the room.

"Get down now! get down!" A loud voice yelled at him and he obeyed.

As he slid back down to the floor, his hands instinctively went up in the air. He had done this before, but this time he knew it was different. As he lay down, trying to keep his face out of the blood, he felt a foot on the back of his neck. He didn't need to look up to know that he had several guns being pointed down at him. "Don't fucking move or I'll shoot you!"

He could tell from the intensity of the voices swirling above him that he dare not move even an inch. He barely allowed himself to breathe, the fear coursing through every cell in his body.

"Fuck, look at all this blood!" one of the officers noted, shock in his voice.

"Don't move, don't touch anything!" another voice shouted. Chris wasn't sure if he was shouting at him or at someone else, and he tried to stay as still as possible.

"Jesus, what did this asshole do? Look at 'em, he's completely covered in blood."

"Oh God, look at this shit!"

Chris lay still, trying not to breathe as more and more voices entered the room, shouting all at once. The voices kept yelling and he wondered what was going on and what they were seeing. He knew the room was a mess, but he'd barely had time to see anything, and was now keeping his eyes squeezed closed out of confusion and fear. The contents of his stomach kept threatening to come up as the smell of the blood continued to assault his nose.

"What are you doing down there?" The voice above him was agitated. "I told you not to fucking move, why are you moving?"

"I'm going to puke ... I can't help it." He was retching and trying not to vomit, but it was coming up in waves and there was nothing he could do about it.

The puke exploded out of his mouth and onto the floor, splashing up on his cheek. The smell hit him, and he opened his mouth again, unable to stop it from coming out. He had never felt more disgusted with himself in his entire life, and he hoped for a split second that the cop would just shoot him and put him out of his misery.

"Fuck! Stop it, dammit!"

It was the last thing he remembered before he passed out, and when he woke up, he was no longer covered in blood or his own puke, but was wearing a bright orange pair of overalls. His mouth felt as though it was full of cotton as he stared helplessly at the walls of the small cell. He sat on the cot, his head in his hands, and wondered what he was doing in jail. His memory was mostly blank. He knew he had fought … with Nora. It had been an ugly one and she had kicked him out. Instead of going back to The Harper House like he should have, where he felt like a prisoner, he went to a bar … multiple bars.

The flashes were hazy and he tried to lick his lips, but his tongue was dry and thick. He desperately wanted water, the taste of ashes and old whiskey coating his teeth and his tongue. He fought the urge to throw up again, but he knew there was probably nothing left in his stomach. He hated the thought of dry heaving and he pushed it down as deep as he could.

Chris tried to think about where he had been and what he had done to end up in a jail cell. *Oh God … Nora. Nora! I was in her apartment, but where the fuck was she? I didn't see her anywhere. I hope she's okay! Whose blood was that?*

He thought about her beautiful face and how angry she had been when he'd seen her last. She had been completely furious with him for wanting to change the plan, but Chris just didn't feel right about what Nora wanted to do to Eva. Chris shook his head at the memory, but he had seen her like that many times before and knew it would pass. But why was he in jail … *I haven't made my phone call! I need to make my phone call.*

Suddenly, a door opened and light flooded into the dim cell. Two officers and a man dressed in a button-down shirt, jeans, and a gun holstered against his ribs stood outside of his cell staring at him. The man with the button-down shirt looked pissed, and Chris felt himself tense up as the man stared at him with hard, steely eyes.

"Connor Michael Martin?" the man in the button down looked at him, his voice hard and raspy from smoking too many cigarettes. "I'm Detective Lyons, and we have some talking to do."

"No ... you have the wrong man. I'm Christopher Brian Garrett." Chris said, looking at him evenly.

"Who are you saying you are now?" the detective asked, his right eyebrow cocked slightly.

"I'm Christopher. Brian. Garrett." Chris said slowly, as though mocking the detective.

"No. You're Connor Michael Martin. There is nobody named 'Christopher Brian Garrett', even though your license says that's who are you are. We know it's a fake because we ran your prints. You're in the system quite a bit Mr. Martin, so cut the shit. You know exactly how this works."

Chris looked at the man, his eyes growing dark and angry, slowly transforming him into someone dark and sinister.

"You need to come with us. We have some questions to ask you."

"I need a lawyer and I need you to call my wife." Chris knew that Eva would help him, especially when he hadn't done anything wrong. He just needed to see her so that he could explain it to her.

"Of course you do," the detective said, sneering. "But your wife isn't going to want to come near you with a ten-foot pole after what you've done."

"I didn't do anything! I don't even know what happened. Is Nora ... the girl who lives in that apartment ... is she okay?" Chris asked, his voice angrier than he intended it to be.

"Are you kidding me?" the detective stared at him in disbelief. "Is that the angle you're going to play? Are you going to act like you don't know anything?"

"I don't, I swear!" Chris' eyes widened. "All I want to know is whether the girl is okay!"

"I'm not telling you anything," the detective said with contempt. "If you're going to pretend that you don't know what you did, then I'm not going to play your game."

The detective stood up abruptly and walked out of the room, slamming the door behind him.

The next hour felt like days as Chris waited for the detective to come back.

When he returned, Chris was panicked and agitated. "Did you call my wife? Did you call my lawyer?"

"You'll get to call both, when we say."

They led him to an interrogation room and he sat down on the uncomfortable chair, hating the shackles on his wrists.

"Okay, Mr. Martin ... do you want to tell me why you did it?" Detective Lyons asked, never breaking eye contact.

"You get right to the point, don't you Detective?" Chris asked sounding amused.

"Does that bother you?" the detective looked at Chris and fought the urge to break eye contact. He knew that he was being toyed with and he didn't like it.

Michael Lyons had been a detective for twenty-five years and had been in the interrogation room with psychopaths like this one hundreds of times. He had moved from Chicago to a smaller town five years ago, to get away from crimes like this because he no longer had the stomach for it. When he got word about the crime scene, he couldn't believe it, and sitting across from Connor Martin was more unnerving than he'd anticipated.

He tried to shake it off, trying to convince himself that it was just the pictures of the dead girl that were throwing him off. Whoever had stabbed the girl was pissed at her and wanted to see her suffer. The stab wounds all over her body had been deep and vicious and the detective had never seen anything like it.

"No, it doesn't bother me at all," Chris said, smirking. "But I'm wondering what you think I've done."

"That's what I'm waiting to hear from you, Connor. I can piece together what you did, but you'd make it so much easier on yourself, and on us, if you'd just tell us what happened and why you did it. You know we'll figure it out anyway."

Chris stared coldly through the detective, his hazel eyes dead and giving nothing away.

"I have no idea what you're talking about. I woke up and I was lying on the floor, but I didn't do anything to anybody. You're not going to get anything out of me, because there's nothing to tell," Chris said, his voice flat and low.

The detective flipped over a picture and Chris' voice caught in his throat. Long strands of red hair were mixed with blood, the face bruised beyond recognition.

Chris took a deep breath and looked the detective in the eye.

"I'm not saying anything to you unless I have a lawyer present," Chris said, his voice hard.

As Detective Lyons stood up, he flipped over another picture, and then left the room.

Chris looked at the picture and tried to stop the sob that erupted from his chest.

"Nora," he whispered, recognizing the delicate bracelet that he had given her for her birthday wrapped around the dead woman's blood-soaked wrist.

CHAPTER TWENTY

Sobering

September 20th, 2016

Adam sat in the cold, uncomfortable, folding chair in the old church hall two towns over from his own. He tried to shrink down in his seat as much as he could, tugging on his ball cap and hoping that nobody would recognize him. Married into the deeply affluent and public Harper family, he had been in the paper and on the news more than he ever wanted to be. He rarely went out in public, but when he did, he was always careful to disguise his identity. He had made a drunken spectacle of himself in the past, the sting of it difficult to forget.

That last thing he wanted was to be in the news going to an AA meeting, especially when it failed him, which it always did. Adam had attended meetings like this before, but had never gone to more than a few. He had tried rehab in the posh country club setting, and he had even been to jail and done court-ordered rehab, but nothing worked. He had finally learned over the years to stop driving after he had been drinking, but it had been a difficult lesson.

It took Adam many years to realize and finally face the reason that caused him to drink.

Nothing that Adam did, either sober or drunk, could make him numb or make him forget the moments he got to hold his daughter, Sophie, in his arms before she died. She hadn't even lived for an entire day, and letting her go was the most difficult thing he had ever done. What had made it even more difficult was that he had to convince Brynn to let her go. She had been paralyzed and completely unable to help make any of the difficult decisions. Instead, it was left up to Adam and the resentment he harbored grew like a slow dark poison, coursing through his veins. Even still, when he closed his eyes at night, he envisioned Sophie, soft and sweet, so innocent in his arms. She had been terribly fragile, her labored breathing torturing him with every shallow breath, and he couldn't stop thinking about those last moments when he'd been able to hold her just before she died. She had spent most of her short, painful life filled with tubes and electrodes. Letting her go had been the right thing to do, but he hated himself for it. He hated Brynn for not being there for him, and he was sure to punish her for it.

He had become a man that he no longer recognized, and he loathed looking at his face in the mirror, hating the weakness in his eyes that he couldn't hide from. They were so blue once, but now they reflected nothing more than failure, no matter how many times he tried to convince himself that he had done the best he could.

He had been a terrible husband and a horrible father to Eva. He knew that she'd deserved more from him, but he hadn't given it.

Adam was a broken man, unable and unwilling to stop drinking permanently, no matter how many meetings or therapy sessions he had been to. Nothing he had done since Sophie died could inspire him to stop drinking completely. Not even Eva's birth.

Adam hated himself, the pain so deep that he lay in bed for hours in the fetal position holding his legs close and tight so that he wouldn't cry out in the middle of the night. He was terrified of waking up the entire household and having them catch him this way. He had been struggling for years, and had recently given into the pain and the fear, sneaking sips of vodka until the sips no longer sustained him and he needed so much more. Adam knew that with Brynn waking up, he would need to get sober and clear-headed, but deep down, he was afraid that she wouldn't recognize him after all these years. He knew that he had changed, his handsome features dulled by the poisonous liquor. He was anxious about spending time with her, unsure if she would even remember him and afraid she wouldn't forgive him for divorcing her, though she didn't know they were technically still married.

He thought back to when their marriage had crumbled, the animosity still held cautiously at bay until the day he began drinking. It had been so long ago that the nearly twenty-year-old memories had been remembered and forgotten a thousand times, faded like a long-forgotten love letter.

Adam replayed one of the worst nights of his life over in his mind. They had been at their beloved Victorian house, the one that he bought for Brynn, and he had been drunk and in his usual state. He was so drunk that he could barely look at her, a mess of a man, and a poor reflection of the boy who had once loved her so much.

"What has become of you?" Brynn had whispered angrily, her brown eyes hard and rimmed with red. "I don't even recognize you anymore. I've tried so hard to forgive who you've become because you're not the Adam I fell in love with. You're not anything like him. What have you done with him? I want *him* back!"

Despite her anger, she spoke slowly and deliberately, her voice raw from crying. "Why have you done this to us?"

Adam's eyes were glazed over and when he finally looked up and tried to meet her gaze, he couldn't find her, his blue eyes wandering and unable to stay focused. "I-I-I-I don' know what happened to him … he's gone … dead … dead like Sophie … dead like our baby. Dead like you and our love."

"But I'm not dead, Adam. I'm right here."

"You're a liar," Adam slurred. "You weren' there when I needed you … you were selfish … only caring about yourself and your selfish bitch mottther … you didn' care about me more'n you cared about yourself … You didn' care about Sophie … It's your fault she's gone. Your damn selfishhhhness killed our baby."

Brynn sucked in her breath, her stomach suddenly hollow as though he had punched her. She stared at him, his face still handsome but unshaven, his hair longer than she had ever seen it before. His eyes, the beautiful blue she had fallen into as a teenager, belonged to a stranger, someone she had met but didn't want to know any longer.

She knelt down and hugged Maxie, her beautiful dog who stood close to her, protecting her like he always did.

"I want you to go," Brynn said, her voice low.

"Go? You wan' me to go? Go where? Where am I going?" Adam took a step toward her, swaying.

Brynn involuntarily flinched and took a step back. Her reaction automatic, unable to stop herself even after so many years had gone by and Thomas was dead in his grave.

"Dammit Brynn ... why do you always step back? Why are you always so afraid? I've never hit you ... never even touched you." Adam's eyes were suddenly wide, and he spit as he talked to her. "I never hurt you. I never wan' to hurt you."

He grabbed her arms and held them tight as Brynn let out a tiny squeal. Brynn felt herself beginning to panic as she looked up at him. Thomas' face flashed before her eyes and she could feel her heart beating wildly in her chest. Adam had never grabbed her so intensely, her arms beginning to hurt as he squeezed her.

"Stop looking so afraid! Stop it! Stop! You never trust me, you never ever trusted me be your husband." Adam was angry, his hands shaking as he stepped back and tried to regain control of himself. He had been frustrated with Brynn before, but he had always maintained his distance, always careful not to upset her, knowing that she would be fearful. Maxie stepped firmly in front of Brynn, his growl so low at first that neither Brynn nor Adam heard it. Adam's legs buckled, taking him off balance., He fell toward Brynn and suddenly Maxie jumped on him, toppling him over. Maxie latched on tight to Adam's arm, his teeth sinking into his skin refusing to let go. Adam cried out and Brynn screamed as she saw blood oozing from his arm. No matter what she did, Maxie refused to let go until Brynn gave up and fumbled helplessly for the phone.

Adam barely remembered it as she called 911 and he lay on the floor, blood oozing from his arm, Maxie still growling as he stood fiercely in front of Brynn, all loyalty to Adam gone.

Brynn approached Adam cautiously, trying to get past Maxie who was blocking her from getting to him and still looking at Adam threateningly. "How bad is it?" she asked, staring at the blood dripping all over the carpet on their bedroom floor.

"Bad, that stupid fucking dog." Maxie growled louder. Adam glared at him, angrily. "It's bad ... Brynn, it's bad. God ... Look what you made that damn dog do to me."

Brynn knelt down beside him and picked his arm up gently and carefully, tears running down her cheeks uncontrollably. The taste of salt burned her lips as she tried to lick the tears away.

She jumped up and grabbed a towel from the bathroom and held it tightly against the wound.

"I'm sorry Brynn, I didn' mean to yell at you. You know I would never hurt you ... ah Hell, what am I saying? I'm always hurting you, I just don' know why. I don' hate you, I mean, I don' think I hate you. I don' 'know ... I don' know." Adam cried out and Brynn wasn't sure if it was from the pain of his wound or the pain in his heart that he refused to let go of.

Brynn nodded, unable to speak. Brynn blamed herself for Sophie's death too, and Adam only reinforced that. She knew that nothing they did could get them past Sophie's death. Sophie was supposed to bring them together, but losing her was tearing them apart and any love between them had been buried with her.

He remembered how Brynn had held her hand on his forehead to comfort him as they waited for the ambulance while he faded in and out of consciousness. The only evidence remaining from that night was the long scar on his arm and the unsigned divorce papers that were still tucked in the bottom drawer of his desk. After all that had passed between them, the trust and love had disappeared and he thought guiltily about how he *had* wanted to shake her and hurt her, even though he told himself that he never would. Maxie knew that he wanted to hurt her, and he wasn't going to let him. Adam regretted that Maxie never let him get close again and never trusted him near Brynn. Adam's eyes began to burn at the memory.

He had loved that damn dog so much.

Then Adam had moved out and met Jessie. After that, Brynn had the accident that nearly killed both her and Eva, and Adam's heart ached at the memory.

He absently rubbed his scar as he thought about the past. After a while, he forced himself back to the present where he was no longer a young man. He sat in the folding chair and reminded himself that because of his drinking, he had hurt the ones he loved the most.

Adam knew in the end that divorcing Brynn had been the only way to protect her. The anger and rage he felt toward her was something he couldn't control when he was drinking. He'd never wanted to shake her or hurt her before that night. The fear in her eyes had been enough for him. He had tried to stop drinking intermittently throughout the years, but he always came back to it, needing it as much as the air that he breathed. Adam thought sadly that if it hadn't been for the accident, he would've lost Brynn forever, and was struck once again by the irony of it all.

Adam sat in the chair, his butt already hurting, his back uncomfortable, and listened as the "Welcome" began to start. He remembered that the meetings always started on time, and he was grateful for the entire hour that he would be around people like him, who struggled so much. He needed to hear from others who fought their demons much in the same way he did. Some fought and failed, while others were successful warriors, able to help others. Strangely, Adam found comfort in hearing from both.

Adam listened to the stories. After ten years of sobriety, Paul, had gotten drunk at work and lost his job after he found his wife cheating on him. Jamie had gotten so drunk she passed out for five hours, leaving her child at school without anyone to pick him up, and Sara had cheated on her husband and gotten pregnant by his best friend. As Adam listened, he was disgusted by them and with himself. Alcohol had turned him into a man he never imagined he'd be, full of anger and sadness that he couldn't control. He listened intently to each story, a painful reminder that he had his own terrible story to tell, and fought the urge to walk out of the meeting. But as he sat and contemplated the sadness of everyone's life in the room, a nagging feeling came over him. He felt that someone was watching him. He turned around and looked throughout the room, but wasn't able to see anyone staring at him. Still, the hairs on the back of his neck continued to stand on end.

The hour went by swiftly and when it was finished, Adam stood up quickly to leave. He never liked to talk to anyone, or about himself, at these meetings, and didn't want to mingle with any of the attendees. He had taken as much as he could from it, the urge to drink not diminished in any way.

"Excuse me," a light tap on the shoulder from behind startled him.

He turned around and looked into the most beautiful pair of emerald green eyes he had ever seen. They were almost glittering as they looked up at him, and he had the sudden and distinct feeling he had seen those eyes before.

"Yes?" he said, mesmerized.

"I know you," the woman said, tucking a long strand of red hair behind her ear.

Adam stared at her blankly for a moment until his eyes widened in recognition. It had been over two decades since he had seen her last and she had left without so much as a good-bye. While part of him had loved her, she had only been a temporary salve, a futile attempt to try and heal from his divorce.

"J-J-J-Jessie?" Adam was stunned. This was the last place he would've expected to see her. "What are you doing here?"

"So … you remember me? I thought you would've forgotten all about me by now." Jessie said, her voice soft and her eyes sparkling, just as he remembered her.

"Of course I remember you," Adam said warmly, feeling a familiar tug inside of him as he hugged her. He was surprised at how tightly she squeezed him after how she had left. For a small woman, she was stronger than she looked, and he remembered how strong she had been, often holding him through an entire night as he cried and sobbed. "Um … I guess we can't go for a drink like we used to. Would you like to get some coffee … I mean, would that be okay?"

Jessie looked up at him and smiled brightly. He suddenly remembered how her smile was the only thing able to get him through some of his darkest days. He was surprised at how much his heart suddenly ached for what might have been between them, if she hadn't disappeared so abruptly. "I would absolutely love to, Adam Michaels. I was hoping this moment would come one day."

CHAPTER TWENTY-ONE

The Guardian

September 20th, 2016

John "Jack" Palmer III was exactly like his grandfather in many ways.

He was diligent in his duties as CEO of Harper Enterprises and careful to honor the family name in everything he did. He was also committed to his care of the Michaels family, who his family owed everything to. James Harper, Brynn's grandfather, had been a good friend and mentor to John Palmer I. Jack knew that he could delegate the family's affairs to someone else while he attended to other important matters, but he knew that his grandfather would be disappointed in him. John made it his personal mission to take care of the family, like his grandfather before him, but he was forced to do so from afar. While he had initially tried to form a closer bond with the family, Adam had been resistant in allowing him to get too close. So, he did the best he could. He knew that he owed it to his grandfather.

Jack's grandfather had never forgiven himself for allowing Brynn's grandparents to be kidnapped, which resulted in the murder of James Harper and the kidnapping of his beloved wife, Amy. Even though John found Amy many years after her kidnapping and reunited her with her family, he felt personally responsible for allowing James to be murdered. The fact that there was nothing he could have done to prevent it didn't make it any easier on him.

Unlike his grandfather who had been a family man, Jack was a bachelor. He had watched his own father struggle to be there for his family. He refused to put any children through the long absences and indifference that his own father had shown him. John Palmer Jr. had been a disappointment to his father and to his own family. He wasn't kind or thoughtful like his father had been, and he was lazy. When given the opportunity to take the reins of Harper Enterprises, John Jr. had been quite a disappointment in every way. He frustrated his father who had put his heart and soul into the company in honor of his mentor and friend.

John became more of a father and mentor to young Jack than his father had ever been, recognizing his thoughtful brilliance at an early age. Jack and his grandfather bonded very early in his life, and he only cared about what his grandfather thought. He worked hard and excelled in everything he did; school, sports, and even in the arts, playing piano and guitar as a respite from the intensity in his life.

"Jack," his grandfather had said to him repeatedly throughout his young life, "Work hard and make me proud of you. I've put my heart and soul into Harper Enterprises, and I'm not going to watch it go down the drain. James would be so disappointed in me and I can't … I won't allow it. I want you to do well and take it over when you're old enough."

"I won't let you down, Grandpa, I promise," Jack had been earnest in everything he did and was more dynamic than anyone had ever expected. He was the only child and his mother adored him as much as his father ignored him.

Jack was true to his word. He took the company from his father very early in his career, which was a unanimous decision from the board. For the first time in many years, the company began to thrive and become the powerhouse it had once been under James Harper's direction.

Even though Jack could afford to live lavishly, he chose a modest house down the street from his mother. He knew that as she got older she would need him more often. Aside from his grandfather, she was the only other person he'd ever loved, his grandmother passing away when he was only four years old.

When he received the call that Brynn Michaels had, by some miracle, awakened from her coma, he was stunned. His grandfather had talked about Brynn often, admiring her strength and character. Jack managed the details of The Harper House from afar since his last encounter with Adam, but knew he must go there now in order to determine their needs. His grandfather would've expected it, and he knew that he couldn't possibly stay away.

He got into his car, refusing the request of his assistant to have a driver take him, and set his GPS for The Harper House. The drive from the city was pleasant, and forty-five minutes later, he pulled up to the massive gate of the house. The voice on the intercom was crisp as it asked him to identify himself. After a few moments, the gate opened slowly and he drove up the long, winding driveway to the massive house that James Harper had dubbed "The Harper House." The house had been designed and built to James' specifications. He had constructed it for his family envisioning an active, lively home, but was disappointed when his daughter, Ellie, had not embraced her life in it as he had hoped. With two massive wings, twenty-six rooms, an Olympic-sized pool, tennis courts, and a large gym, James had built The Harper House as a part of his legacy to pass down to this family, generation after generation.

Jack walked up to the front door, imagining his grandfather walking up the very same steps, and feeling more than a little nostalgic for him. He hesitated and rang the bell, wishing he had changed into jeans and a button-down shirt instead of still wearing the suit he had worn to the office that morning.

The door opened and a small woman with dark hair and the most amazing eyes he had ever seen came flying out, nearly toppling them both down the front steps.

"Oh, my gosh. I'm so sorry!" she breathed, as he reached out to catch her from falling. "I just ... I'm so sorry ... I wasn't looking where I was going."

"Oh, that's okay," Jack said feeling a little unsettled, which was unusual for him. He couldn't stop himself from staring into her eyes. They were large and blue, and as deep and glittering as sapphires. For a moment he forgot where he was and what he was supposed to be doing. The woman was about a decade younger than he was, and was so small that his 6'2" frame towered over her. Something about her made his stomach begin to churn unexpectedly. *What is wrong with me?*

"I'm sorry, I'm Eva ... Eva Harper Michaels," she held out a dainty hand for him to shake.

Jack's eyes opened wide in recognition.

"Of course! I thought you might be. I'm John Palmer III, but you can call me Jack." Jack shook her hand and felt a surge of electricity pass through his fingers. He pulled his hand back, alarmed. He had known many beautiful women in his life, many of whom viewed his bachelor status as a challenge and were determined to tie him down. Jack never stayed with one woman for more than a couple of months, easily bored by their lack of imagination, and always annoyed with their desperation. He didn't mind being alone, and he had never met anyone who he thought was worth committing to.

With Eva standing right in front of him, it crossed his mind that she was different. He didn't know why he felt that way, but something about the way her eyes sparkled made him curious about her. Her smile was unguarded, and when she aimed it toward him, his stomach fluttered though he tried to convince himself it was just hunger pangs.

"Hi ... Jack," Eva said, holding his deep brown eyes a moment longer than she meant to. His sandy hair had been ruffled when she ran into him and she thought about how handsome he was, almost boyish, even though he was clearly much older than she was. Jack was one of the best-looking men she had ever seen, and Eva looked away from him, feeling guilty for even letting the thought creep into her mind.

"I'm sorry I haven't been out. Until recently, it was always my grandfather who called on the family. He had a special bond with you all as I'm sure you know ... and after ... well, I tried to come and call on you but ... your father wanted ... privacy ..." his voice trailed off sadly.

"I know. I'm so sorry about your grandfather," Eva touched his arm instinctively. "We donated to the hospital in his name. He was truly such a wonderful man."

"Thank you," Jack said, gratefully. The service had been closed and private, his grandfather not wanting a huge fuss made over him. Jack knew that he deserved more. He had been a generous man who was well-loved, and many had honored his wishes by donating to the children's hospital. Enough so that they were able to renovate an entire wing, just like his grandfather had hoped.

Jack's father hadn't even bothered to show up for the service, which was half-expected. After Jack took over his position, his father had virtually disappeared, leaving his mother without a word.

"Where are you going in such a hurry?" Jack asked, curious.

"I'm going to the hospital to see my mom. Kelly texted and said that it's a good day and she's awake a lot, so I want to get there to see her."

"Would you like me to take you?" Jack gestured to his car that was right in front. "I've been meaning to go and visit and this would give us some time to catch up."

"Oh, no. I couldn't ask you to take me," Eva took a step back, shaking her head.

"I don't mind at all. I'd love to meet Brynn. My grandfather loved her and always spoke so well of her. He even told me that I'd met her before, though I was too young to remember." Eva enjoyed the sound of Jack's voice and how warm it sounded when he talked about his grandfather. Eva realized that she had never heard Chris' voice warm up quite like that when he talked about anything, and for a brief moment she wondered why.

"Um … well, if you really don't mind, then I would love a ride."

"Great!" Jack exclaimed guiding her to his car. He held the door open for her and closed it gently once she settled in. As he walked around to the other side, he realized that he was happier to be giving her a ride to the hospital than he should be.

As they drove, they talked non-stop and Jack was surprised

at how easy it was to converse with her. He wasn't used to speaking to women so easily and casually, and he realized that he was enjoying their conversation tremendously. She wasn't interested in impressing him and spoke freely. When she stared at him with her large, beautiful eyes, it was as though there was nothing in the world she would rather be doing than listening to him.

When she mentioned her husband, he bristled. He was surprised by how disappointed he was at the reminder that she was married, even though he already knew it. He didn't make it a habit to become interested in married women, and he told himself that his interest in her was strictly professional. The pounding of his heart told him something different.

When Jack had initially been told that Eva was dating, he had his people do a complete background check on Christopher Brian Garrett. Everything had come back clean. It was common practice to check out everybody who came in contact with the family, and Jack was glad that for once there would be some happiness at The Harper House. He had been unable to attend the wedding because he had been out of the country on business, but had his assistant send a beautiful and expensive gift.

"We've met before, you know," Jack said, smiling.

"Yes, I remember," Eva said, her face flushing a little.

"You do?" Jack seemed amused.

"Yes, it was one of the most embarrassing moments of my childhood." Eva turned and looked out of the window, her hand going directly to her lips.

"You kissed me," Jack smiled.

"I know! I know! That is so embarrassing! I was hoping you would forget that ... I was so young and so silly. I just had the biggest crush on you and I couldn't help it. I was eight, and you were ..."

"Much older," Jack grinned at the memory. "You asked if you could hug me and instead, you kissed me on the cheek."

"Yes, it was a very strange moment for me. I was a pretty quiet, shy child, but for some reason I took a chance ..." Eva's face was bright red with embarrassment.

It had been one of the few times when he had accompanied

his grandfather to The Harper House. Jack was always welcome to go with him to the office, but that time he had taken him to visit some of his favorite people. Noah had still been alive and Amy had barely been holding on at that time. It was Eva who caught Jack's attention, though. She had been a bright and beautiful child, but Jack had been surprised at how dismissive Adam had been of her, and he was saddened by how lonely she seemed. During their short visit she had followed Jack everywhere he went. Jack, who was much older than she was, had been flattered by the obvious crush she had on him.

He grinned at her, amused by her embarrassment.

"I can't believe you remembered that," Eva said, not meeting his gaze, "It was so long ago and so unlike me."

"It was a memorable kiss," Jack teased. It wasn't his nature to be so light-hearted, but Eva brought it out in him. He couldn't believe he was teasing her. He couldn't remember the last time he had teased anyone.

They drove in silence for a few moments, both of them smiling at the memory. As they got nearer to the hospital Eva's phone rang.

"Hello? This is Eva," Eva said, not recognizing the phone number. "Yes. Yes, of course I'll accept the charges."

Jack looked over at Eva, her voice immediately alarming him.

"Chris!" Eva said, her voice high and sharp. "Are you okay? Where are you? What's going on?"

Jack could barely hear the voice on the other end of the line, other than a few words.

Eva hung up the phone, her eyes wide and glistening, her breath coming in short, panicked gulps. "Please, turn around. Please. I have to go to the county jail."

"The county jail?" Jack asked, confused. "Why?"

"It's … m-m-my husband. He's been arrested. I need to go help him right away!" Eva was breathing hard, her chest heaving uncontrollably.

"Wait … what you do you mean he was arrested? What was he arrested for?" Jack asked, immediately alarmed.

"I don't know. I don't know. But ... Oh God ... he sounded like it might be really bad." Eva's eyes were wide with panic, her hand holding her stomach tightly. Jack was concerned for Eva as he looked for their new destination in his GPS and changed direction. Eva's face was gray and she looked as though she might throw up.

"Oh God," Eva repeated, her hands rubbing her stomach anxiously. "This is really bad, really bad."

Jack started to console her and at the last second, closed his mouth and didn't say anything. Instead he reached over and put his hand on top of hers, a gesture that seemed too intimate, but felt like the only thing to do.

He was startled as he felt her tiny stomach protrude. He looked down and saw the tiniest outline of what looked like a baby bump and wondered how he could have missed it as it suddenly sunk in. He kicked himself mentally as he realized for the first time that Eva was pregnant.

CHAPTER TWENTY-TWO

Going Home

September 20th, 2016

Kelly sat with Brynn and waited patiently for Eva.

She hadn't wanted to tell her the good news on the phone, but the doctors finally felt comfortable with letting Brynn go home, as long as she was under close observation and had constant care. After daily trips to physical therapy, she'd gained more movement and the strength in her limbs had progressively gotten better. She'd been reminded, though, that it would continue to be a long journey, and there was no way they could estimate what level of control or movement she would be able to get back, if any.

Brynn was frustrated when she couldn't walk as well as she wanted, and when her hands still knocked things over as she tried to grasp things. Kelly reassured her that she was doing far more than anyone had ever expected her to. She had never been expected to wake at all.

"We are still in uncharted territory with our little miracle," said Kelly's favorite doctor, a beautiful Indian woman whose soft spoken voice was both comforting and pleasant to listen to. "Mrs. Michaels is an unprecedented case at this hospital, and we will need to see her regularly in order to monitor her progress. We are pleased with how far she's come in the last two months, and feel she will possibly recover better at home."

Kelly had been pleased to hear the news and was anxious to see how Brynn would react

"Brynn, you're going home," she said, smoothing Brynn's dark hair across her forehead. She smiled at her friend and Brynn smiled back, but Kelly sensed there was something wrong.

"E-va?" Brynn said her voice hoarse and her words slow.

"She should be here soon," Kelly said, checking her phone for the time. "I called her two hours ago, and she said she was on the way. Did you hear me tell you that you're going home?"

"Ad-am?" Brynn asked almost cautiously.

"Adam isn't here, Brynn. I don't know where he is or when he'll show up. I don't know … I … wouldn't worry about him if I were you. The only thing you should think about right now is that you get to go home."

Adam's visits to the hospital hadn't been as regular as Kelly had expected. While he was happy that she was awake, his visits were intermittent and inconsistent, and nobody ever knew where he was. After years of waiting for Brynn to wake up, Kelly thought he would be there by her side every single day. Instead, Kelly sat at Brynn's side just as she had at The Harper House.

Brynn's shoulders relaxed when Kelly said she hadn't heard from him, almost as though she was relieved. The air between Adam and Brynn seemed to be thick with tension during his visits, which Kelly couldn't understand. She had watched her friend cry over Brynn's motionless body for nearly two decades, and wondered if the ugliness of the past was resurfacing to haunt them. When Adam visited, he was careful to do it only when Kelly or Eva were there, and he and Brynn never spoke too much. It was almost as though they had a mutual agreement.

Kelly wondered if Brynn remembered that she had been on her way to see Nick when the accident occurred. Actually, she was curious if Brynn remembered anything at all. Brynn still struggled with her speech, so Kelly was careful not to ask her too much. She decided she would wait to ask her about Nick until the time was right.

"Do you want me to try and get Adam for you so he can take you home? Do you need him?" Kelly asked, pulling out her phone.

Brynn shook her head back and forth a few times and Kelly wondered what she was thinking. Her friend's face was a dark, silent cloud.

"No? Okay, let me know what you need. Hopefully we can get you talking … I miss our talks." Kelly smiled at her, patting her hand.

Brynn attempted a small smile and, for a brief moment, Kelly could see a glimpse of her old friend, beautiful and unscarred, as she had been before the accident.

"If we don't hear from Eva soon, we'll just call Bill, the driver, and have him come get us and take us back to home," Kelly said trying to disguise her concern for Eva.

Brynn nodded. *Where is Eva? Wouldn't she want to take me home? I hope that she's okay and that nothing has happened to her. Nothing can happen to my baby girl. Now that I'm awake I don't know what I would do. We have so much to catch up on and I need her.*

Kelly texted Eva and got no answer. She stared at her phone, willing Eva to pick up. Eva usually answered immediately and Kelly was getting more anxious.

"E-va?" Brynn asked, her face showing worry.

Kelly tried not to appear afraid as she smiled at Brynn. "I'm sure she's just … busy, or maybe she fell asleep or something."

She called the house to confirm whether Eva was there and Rachel, the head housekeeper, told her that she was gone but her car was still there. This alarmed Kelly even more. She asked her to have Bill come and get them. She hung up and began to pace the hospital room, worry overcoming her.

Her phone beeped and Kelly jumped a mile as she stared down at her phone. The text had come from Eva.

"Sorry. I'm at the police station with Jack. I'll call in a bit."

"Jack? Who is Jack? Why are you at the police station? Are you

okay?" Kelly typed furiously, her mind racing as she tried to figure out who Jack was.

"Jack Palmer. Long story. Chris is in jail."

Kelly gasped as she read Eva's text.
Brynn looked at her questioningly and Kelly shook her head. She wasn't sure if Brynn could completely understand everything yet and she was hesitant to worry her needlessly until she knew more.

"Do you need your dad?" Kelly typed.

"Tried. He isn't answering. Probably passed out."

Kelly's heart ached and for a moment she flashed back to when Eva was a small child and couldn't understand why her daddy fell asleep so early all the time and couldn't play with her like she wanted him to.

"Let me know what you need me to do." Kelly typed.

"Jack will help me out here. I'm in good hands. XO"

Kelly sighed, grateful that Eva was safe. *Why would Chris be in jail? What could he have done?* Kelly was stunned but tried not to show it. She had never disliked Chris, but she had never completely trusted him, either. There was something about him that she couldn't and never tried to explain to Eva. She had dismissed it knowing how happy she was. She and Adam had discussed it privately, but neither one of them ever said anything out loud. Eva's happiness was all that mattered, but Kelly had her reservations until the background check came back clean. When the background check showed that he hadn't even had as much as a speeding ticket, she and Adam had sighed in relief and convinced themselves that they were just being overly protective.
"E-va …?" Brynn's large brown eyes were questioning as

she tried to control her arm well enough to reach out and grab Kelly's hand.

Kelly grabbed her friend and held it tight. "Yes, she'll be okay. She's with Jack Palmer, John Palmer's grandson."

Brynn's brows furrowed in concentration, her brown eyes lighting up after a few long moments, much to Kelly's delight. "John!"

"Yes! You remember John! You were very good friends. He was your grandfather's protégé and he took care of the family. Now his grandson, Jack, looks after everything for you." Kelly was thankful that Brynn remembered him. Her memory was still unpredictable, though it seemed to get better as the days passed.

After the nurse came to give them instructions, they wheeled Brynn down to the lobby. Brynn's eyes grew large when she saw the big, black car that was waiting for her. Bill had been with the family for many years and had never known Brynn before the accident, but he approached her with a warmth that surprised even Kelly.

"Hello, Miss Brynn. I've come to take you home," Bill said, tipping his hat to her and smiling with his eyes.

Brynn nodded and smiled back. "Thank ... you," she said, her voice husky and low.

He helped her get into the car and gave Kelly a quick hug. "She looks good, doesn't she?" Kelly said, wiping a tear away.

"Yes ma'am, she looks great!" Bill said, smiling at her. "You're a good friend, Miss Kelly."

"So are you, Bill." Kelly hugged him again, appreciative of the compliment.

They drove the forty-five minutes to The Harper House mostly in silence, Brynn staring out the window, her eyes big and full of excitement as though she were seeing things for the very first time.

"Does this look familiar?" Kelly asked as Brynn nodded, happily.

Brynn's eyes were full of wonder, and Kelly marveled at her childlike pleasure. Kelly realized that this was the first time Brynn had been awake on any of her rides back home. Kelly wondered how much Brynn remembered of the house that she had taken care of and renovated years before when she had first inherited it. The house remained exactly as Brynn had left it, with the exception of the floor Adam had given Eva for her new family.

Kelly stared at Brynn and wondered what she was thinking as she watched the expression on her face change from excitement to sadness and back to excitement again.

As they pulled up to the massive house, Brynn's eyes grew even wider and Kelly reminded herself that it had been years since Brynn had been awake in the home.

"Home?" Brynn asked, pointing awkwardly to the house, her mind desperate to grasp any memory that tied her to it.

"Yes," Kelly said smiling. "This is The Harper House, which was your grandparents house and they passed it down to you. This is your home. You lived here for a while. Do you remember it?"

Brynn closed her eyes as though trying to evoke a memory of any kind. When she opened them again, she smiled.

"Yes," Brynn said, her face warm and happy. "I do."

CHAPTER TWENTY-THREE

Old Friends

September 20ᵗʰ, 2016

As Adam slowly awoke, he realized how hot and cottony his mouth felt. It was an old familiar feeling, like putting on his favorite sweater or a comfortable pair of shoes. The moment he realized what it was, he felt an overwhelming sense of self-loathing that reminded him of how weak and pathetic he had become.

He was afraid to open his eyes, suddenly aware from the tightness of the sheets against his naked body and the weight in the bed next to him that he wasn't alone.

Jessie!

Flashes of her creamy-white, naked flesh and her bright, beautiful smile exploded in his mind and he fought the urge to groan out loud for fear he would awaken her. *Oh shit. What have I done? What time is it?*

The pit in the middle his stomach told him that he hadn't been in contact with Kelly or Eva for a long time. He had left the hospital to go to a meeting, but his internal clock told him that it had been much longer than it should've been since he had checked in. *Brynn ... why did I leave? I have to get out of here!*

Brynn had been awake but wouldn't speak, and the weight of her dark eyes staring at him had been unnerving. He had cried against her when she had awoken, but for months, no matter how hard he tried, he couldn't bring himself to get close to her or spend time alone with her. He had convinced himself that her eyes were warning him to *Stay Away*, and he had. He had no excuse to give when Eva and Kelly asked him why he visited the hospital less and less, knowing that he would sound like a coward. Deep down in his gut he told himself that Brynn didn't want him there, and it was ripping him apart from the inside out, shredding him slowly and painfully. After spending two decades begging her to wake up, his heart was shattered by the depth of her eyes, and he had no idea what to do next.

He decided that getting sober was his first step since he hadn't been able to do that in years.

Running into Jessie at the AA meeting had been sheer luck. He recognized her immediately, his heart leaping toward her before he could stop it. She had smiled at him with that amazingly toothy smile that had comforted him so long ago. The years that had separated them were gone in an instant.

"Why did you leave me without saying good-bye?" he vaguely remembered asking her after countless shots of tequila. Her answer had been deep and soulful as she grabbed at his unruly hair in the depths of their passion.

"I left because I loved you too much," she responded breathlessly, her long red hair silky and soft against his face. It had been so long since he had been close to a woman, and he realized for the first time just how much he missed it. "It hurt me too much to be with you."

"You shouldn't have left me," he said, trying his best not to slur.

"You didn't love me," she said, licking his ear.

"I would have … I could have," he said, grabbing her tight, pulling her as close against him as he possibly could. "I did."

"But you didn't love me like I loved you," Jessie said, sobbing against him.

"I'm sorry," Adam remembered saying, holding her tight and kissing her tears.

As he lie there next to her, he tried to ignore the pounding in his head and the panic growing in his chest.

He tried to pull his arm out from under Jessie, without waking her.

"Mmmmm," she moaned, and Adam froze until he realized she was still sleeping.

"Sorry," he whispered, as he successfully pulled free. He fumbled around for his pants, the cool air against his naked skin making him feel exposed.

Shit … where am I? He looked around the room trying to find a door, but it was too dark.

He heard a buzzing and desperately strained toward it, nearly knocking himself out on the doorknob. He followed the noise into the living room where he vaguely remembered tossing his pants. When he finally located them, he fumbled clumsily as he tried to pull his phone out of the pocket to see who was calling. He sucked in his breath when he saw that he had missed six phone calls.

Kelly had left him ten messages and Adam felt the pit in his stomach growing.

4:00 pm *"Adam, we are leaving the hospital today. Where have you been?"*

4:26 pm *"We are leaving in an hour."*

5:02 pm *"Are you coming to the hospital? Where are you? We can't find you or Eva."*

Eva? Fuck! Where is Eva?

5:17pm *"I called for a driver from the house. I'm taking Brynn home."*

6:07pm *"We are on the way to the house. I don't know where you are, but I'm worried and pissed. WTH?"*

6:39pm *"Eva's at the police station. Chris is in jail. It's bad. Where are you?"*

9:17pm *"Where in the hell are you? Brynn is home. She's sleeping. Things with Chris are bad. Call me!"*

10:45pm *"I hope you have a really good explanation for where you are."*

11:50pm *"Damn you, Adam. Call me as soon as you can."*

1:15am *"I'm calling the police in the morning if I don't have a text when I wake up."*

Adam looked at the time on his phone. *5:00 am. Shit!*

"Who is it?" The voice startled him, and Adam dropped his phone, swearing as it bounced off the floor, unharmed.

A light flicked on and Adam turned to see Jessie, covered in nothing but a sheet, her eyes narrowed.

"Oh … it's uh … Kelly. A friend," Adam stuttered, unsure if he wanted to tell Jessie what had been going on. His head was splitting from the impending hangover and he licked his lips, trying to find some relief from the dryness that had overtaken him from the inside out.

Without a word, Jessie walked over to the kitchen and poured a tall glass of water. She reached into the cabinet above the sink and grabbed a white plastic bottle out of it. As she did so, the sheet fell away, but Jessie didn't seem to notice as she walked toward Adam and handed him four little red pills and the glass of water.

Seeing her naked in the light, Adam's mind travelled back to the time when she had lived with him. They had spent days locked away in his apartment, naked and together, saving one other from their collective loneliness and filling each another's emptiness. He had loved her in his own way, but he knew it would never be enough.

"Do you love her?" Jessie asked, picking up her sheet and wrapping it around herself as she moved closer to Adam.

"Who? Kelly? Do I love Kelly?" Adam asked, confused.

"No. Brynn. Do you still love Brynn?" Jessie asked, her voice tinged with jealousy.

"Jessie … I don't know that we should talk about this right now. It's not the right time … I need to go …" Adam suddenly felt cornered.

"How can you just leave? We just found one another … I thought we could … spend some time together." Jessie's tried to keep her voice steady.

"It's just … It's not the right time, Jessie. I'm sorry … I just," Adam fumbled with his pants as he tried to pull them on, Jessie's eyes burning into him.

The silence between them was deafening as Adam searched for the rest of his clothes that were strewn all over the floor and the furniture.

"I know, Adam. One of us always has to go," Jessie's voice was low and sad, her green eyes filling with tears. "I didn't expect you to stay. I just hoped that you would want to."

"No … It's not that I don't *want* to stay. I just … I can't. Not tonight … I mean … I don't know what to say. I shouldn't have come here …" Adam dressed slowly, his clothes refusing to cooperate. He looked around blindly trying to find his sock, realizing that it was right on the floor next to him but only a few inches from Jessie. He reached over and grabbed it quickly, as though she might take it from him, his eyes avoiding hers at all costs.

"I don't know who you're trying to fool by going to AA, but I can tell. From one drunk to another, you always drink, and tonight wasn't anything special." Jessie's smile had a hard edge to it and Adam cringed, wondering how she could see through him so well.

"I loved seeing you tonight, I really did. But things are … complicated …" Adam stumbled, finally meeting Jessie's gaze.

"How?" she said, inching closer to him.

"They just are. I can't explain it to you right now because you won't like it, and I know that I shouldn't have come here. I'm sorry. I shouldn't have done this …" Adam stepped closer to the door.

"I don't understand why you can't talk to me or open your

heart up. After everything we were to each other and all that we meant, you can't even stay for a little while. I don't understand it. No matter what, you've never been able to love me," Jessie said, her voice rising.

"I'm sorry. This isn't going to work right now. There's too much going on … I'm sorry, Jessie. I … I can't do this right now, I have to go." Adam was sweating, the pounding in his head subsiding slightly, but not enough.

Fuck, I don't even know if I drove here. He fumbled around in his pockets and was relieved to feel the familiar jaggedness of the keys he had shoved in his pocket.

"But I don't want you to go. I don't want you to leave me, just yet." Jessie said, pleading desperately. "Please, stay with me until the morning."

"I can't, Jessie," Adam said, getting closer to the door. "Please, I'll call you."

Jessie stared at him wordlessly as Adam opened the door and walked out.

He didn't look behind him as he walked down the two flights of stairs as quickly as he could. As the door opened to the outside and the blast of cool air smacked him in the face, he looked around frantically for his car. As he spotted it and sunk down into the driver's seat, he leaned his head back for a moment onto the headrest and breathed a huge sigh of relief.

As he drove away, he realized for the first time that he had never taken Jessie's phone number.

CHAPTER TWENTY-FOUR

Connor Martin

September 20ᵗʰ, 2016

"Who?" Eva looked at the detective, her blue eyes as large as they had ever been, confusion etched all over her beautiful face as she strained to understand what he was saying.

"Connor Martin, Miss." Detective Lyons spoke slowly and tried to be as patient with the girl as he could. Connor had clearly done a number on her, and, after taking note of the ring on her finger and the baby that was growing in her tiny belly, the detective almost felt sorry for her.

"No sir, you've got it wrong. His name isn't Connor. It's Christopher. Christopher Brian Garrett." Eva looked at the detective with a mix of confusion and annoyance on her face. She stared at him stubbornly. She didn't want to be defiant and anger him. It was obvious by the look on his face that there was a lot at stake.

"I'm sorry, Miss, I don't know what he's told you about himself, but I've got fingerprints and numerous records to prove that he is Connor Martin. I can't go into detail, but he's in a lot of trouble." Against his better judgment, Detective Lyons' voice softened as he spoke to her. She reminded him of his own daughter, and he tried to keep his emotions in check as he thought about his little girl getting mixed up with someone as terrible as Connor Martin.

"Detective, I had my own people do a background check on him. I don't understand how this could've happened." Jack was angry with himself because he knew that his grandfather would never have allowed this to happen to Eva. His grandfather never would've been so careless, and Jack was ashamed of the position he had put Eva in.

"It happens all the time with career criminals like our friend, Mr. Martin. This is what they do," Detective Lyons said to Jack, trying to be patient. "I'm sorry, I didn't catch who you are or what your position is here."

"I'm Jack Palmer, the CEO of Harper Enterprises. I oversee the Harper Estate and take care of the family. I'm here to look out for Eva." Jack squared his shoulders and stood in front of the detective as he extended his hand. Detective Lyons shook his hand begrudgingly as he stared hard at him for a moment. The detective shook his head without saying anything as he turned his attention back to Eva.

"I don't know if you want to get a lawyer, Miss, but you might want to consider it. I'm going to need to question you and … well … my advice would be to have a lawyer present."

"Why would I need a lawyer? I haven't done anything wrong," Eva said, suddenly angry. "I don't need a lawyer for anything."

"I'm not saying you did anything wrong, Miss. I'm just looking out for you and your rights. I'm going to have to ask you some questions, and I want you to have the option of getting a lawyer in case you wanted one."

"I don't need one. You can ask me anything you'd like," Eva glared at him, suddenly transforming from a scared young girl into a strong woman, surprising the detective.

Detective Lyons paused, realizing that he had underestimated her.

"I'm married to this man, so if he's not who he says he is, I want to know and I want to know right now. I'm having his baby for

God's sake." Eva stared at the detective angrily.

"Okay ... then I have to ask you some questions," the detective said, eyeing Jack. "Alone."

Eva nodded, putting her hand on Jack's arm for a quick moment when she saw him flinch out of the corner of her eye. In the short time they had spent together, she had already seen his protective side and knew that he wouldn't like the officer talking to her alone. She also knew that he wouldn't have a choice.

The next few hours were brutal and Eva felt exhausted. The detective asked her question after question until the answers were all the same. Eva refused to cry, although she wanted to desperately.

"No, I didn't know his name is Connor."

"No, I had no idea that he was capable of any type of violence."

"No, he's never hurt me or hit me."

"I've never given him money."

"He's never stolen anything that I know of."

"I've never heard of anyone named Nora Symon."

"No, he's never pushed me. No, no ... he's never been anything but kind to me."

She hadn't known what to expect when she sat down in the stark room, but it had been so much worse than what she imagined. The detective hadn't treated her poorly, but she was frustrated and tired, and she still didn't know what Chris had done.

"Please, tell me what has happened. What has he done, please ..." Eva wanted desperately to know what Chris had done in the hope that the queasiness in her stomach could finally dissipate.

The detective had been waiting as he pulled a folder out, seemingly from nowhere. He held his hand on top of it as though he was stalling, debating with himself about whether he wanted to show her the contents. His gut told him that she didn't know anything, but he had to be sure. Eva stared down at the folder as though it were a vicious animal ready to attack her.

Two hours later, when she was finally escorted back to Jack who had been anxiously waiting, the detective looked at her evenly. "Don't leave town, Miss. We'll probably have more questions for you."

Eva nodded, the tears threatening to break free, her face white, and her eyes burning from the images that were now seared into her brain. She was in a daze, her eyes wide and glazed over.

When the detective walked away, she turned toward Jack and began sobbing. He instinctively reached for her and, without thinking, she fell into his arms. His shoulder was instantly soaked from her tears. He held her tight and was both surprised and happy to have her so close. He marveled at how natural it felt to hold her even though he had only just met her again. He pulled her closer and comforted her, feeling guilty about how much he enjoyed the feeling of her tiny body against his, her arms clasped tightly against his back. They stood together and time seemed to stand still until he heard her sniffling against him. She pulled slowly away, leaving him with a sudden and strange emptiness that he could hardly stand.

The look of shock on her face quickly registered with him, and he was alarmed as he searched her eyes for a sign that the interrogation hadn't broken her.

"Are you okay?" Jack asked wiping her tears away gently with his thumbs.

Eva nodded, her face red as she tried to hide the embarrassment she felt.

"Are you hungry? Do you want some coffee?" Jack steered her toward the exit, anxious to get her out of the police station that was suffocating both of them.

Eva shook her head, her dark hair framing her face. Jack couldn't help but marvel at her beauty, even in the midst of her pain. "No. I just want to go home," Eva said, her voice a whisper.

"I've got you," Jack said, keeping his arm around her protectively.

They rode for the first ten minutes in complete silence. Jack fought the urge to put his hand on hers, watching her out of the corner of her eye as silent tears continued to course down her cheeks. She held her hands clasped tightly in her lap.

He waited for her to speak first, wanting desperately to ask about the interrogation. Jack could see the fear in her eyes and could see her looking at him. She kept opening her mouth as if to speak, but closing it again. He waited patiently, knowing that she would speak when she was ready.

Finally, her voice came out raw and raspy, as though someone else was speaking for her. "They s-s-s-said that he's a really bad person. They asked if he ever hurt me or stole from me. They asked if he ever hit me ..." Eva's voice trailed off.

"Did he?" Jack asked, trying to hold his anger in at the thought of anyone ever hurting her. His pulse quickened as he thought about what he would do to the person who ever tried.

"No ... no ... he never hurt me. Chris ... I mean, Connor ... was kind to me ... he was always very nice to me." Eva flashed back to the many times he had brought her flowers and how he comforted her when she cried about her mother. She thought about the moments when he read to her and held her close anytime she needed it without her asking him to. He had been her first and only lover, never pushing her farther or faster than she was willing to go, his hands soft and gentle on her body. His perfectly muscled body warm against her own had enticed and excited her and she blushed at the memory.

He had only ever shown her kindness and love, and her mind was reeling as she tried to imagine the monster they made him out to be.

She shuddered as she suddenly envisioned his hands around her neck, and it made her cry even harder.

"It's okay, please, Eva ..." Jack suddenly pulled the car over and awkwardly gathered her in his arms. He held as close as he could without hurting her. "You're safe, Eva. Nobody will ever hurt you as long as I'm here. I should've looked into this guy myself, and I should've protected you. I'm so sorry that I failed you, but I promise that I won't let it happen again."

Eva cried against him, her entire world was crumbling. What she'd heard at the police station had destroyed the only true happiness she had ever known. She felt the familiar pain of emptiness as she realized that without Chris, she would be alone once again. She thought about the baby growing inside of her and how it would grow up with a father that didn't care about it. *I'm so sorry, baby. I'm already the worst mother in the world. How could I have let this happen to you? How could I have let this happen to me? Why didn't I know who he was? Why did I trust him so quickly without truly knowing him?*

"Did they tell you what was going on? Did they say anything about what he might have done?" Jack had asked the officers himself during the hours that Eva was in the interrogation room, but they refused to tell him anything.

Eva nodded, taking a deep breath when the images from the pictures in the folder resurfaced without her permission. When she closed her eyes all she could see was the blood because there had been a lot of it. There was thick red blood covering floors, walls, and skin. The detective had apologized repeatedly for showing her the pictures, but Eva was smart enough to know that it was all done by design. She could tell by the way he showed them to her, slowly and deliberately, pausing long enough to burn the image into her brain, that he was trying to lure her in. It was obvious that he thought she knew more than she did. The detective had been nice enough, but Eva knew that he was trying to trick her into telling him something she knew nothing about.

The pictures had made her sick to her stomach, almost as though she could smell the blood, or feel its stickiness on her own skin. She had never seen or imagined anything like it, and she knew that it would be difficult, if not impossible, for her to sleep for a very long time. The blood was intermingled with the victim's long, red hair and skin, and as hard as she tried, she repeatedly told the detective that she didn't recognize the victim. The crime scene was brutal, and she had been thankful when the detective finally felt she'd "had enough" of the photos. She never imagined that anyone would accuse Chris of doing something so heinous, the thought of it taking her breath away, and she had asked the detective several times to pause while he was showing her the pictures so she could catch her breath.

"Did they tell you what he did?" Jack repeated, alarmed by the way Eva froze when he asked her the question the first time.

Eva sat, staring straight ahead and Jack could see her flinch, almost imperceptibly. He watched her face carefully and patiently, not yet knowing her well enough to know if he was pushing her too hard. Eva was surprised to find that she wasn't ready to tell him about the pictures yet, and she decided to keep that part to herself until she could make more sense of everything. She could tell by his protective nature that if she told him, he would never leave her alone again, and she needed to be alone in order to think.

"Yes," she said carefully. "They said ... I was very lucky. They said ... he killed his lover ... and they said ... that ... I ...was probably next."

CHAPTER TWENTY-FIVE

Fear

Brynn, September 20th, 2016

As we pull up to the massive home, I'm overwhelmed by its size.

While my memory continues to come and go, I know that I should recognize this place, although there is still nothing specific yet. Now that I am awake, the world remains so loud and confusing, and I struggle to make sense of it. My body still moves slowly and refuses to move the way I want it to, my limbs incredibly heavy and awkward. While the world seems to be stunned and excited by this unexpected awakening, I am still not whole and probably never will be again.

As we walk up to the house, Bill and Kelly have to hold onto me, guiding my fragile, shaky legs as they slowly make their way up the ramp and into the house. Kelly wanted to take me in the wheelchair, but I shook my head and refused, my stubbornness the likely reason I'm still alive.

I have to admit that being at home makes me afraid of something I can't explain and I hate it. Fear is a familiar enemy that has crept slowly back into my heart and settled in my bones. As the years have passed, I had hoped that it might disappear, but it returns stronger and more intense than ever and paralyzes me when I least expect it. While my memories are hazy, by a cruel twist of fate, I can still see my adoptive father, Thomas, as clearly as I saw him decades ago chasing after me with hatred in his eyes and rage in his heart. The terrifying explosion of his anger often transitions into the explosion of twisted metal and wreckage from the accident that turned me comatose and stole my life and my daughter from me.

Fear plagues me every morning when I awake, almost paralyzing me until I find the strength to fight it. As difficult as it was to be asleep for all these years, it frightens me even more to be awake. Though I've somehow managed to become this *miracle* that everyone refers to me as, I'm terrified that one day I won't wake up at all, and that I'll never have the chance to love Eva the way I've always dreamed of. I realize that it makes me weak to be so fearful, after everything I've lived through, but the fear comes from the inside out, borne in me when I was just a small girl.

Still, I am thankful for those around me who help me fight.

Kelly has proven herself to be a true friend who is patient and compassionate. As she rides with me in the elevator up to my room, she steadies me against her so that I don't fall. I can feel the strength in her limbs as she holds tightly to me.

Though I know that my presence complicates her relationship with Adam, she still loves and looks out for me. I can feel that she cares deeply for him. Her confessions of love are somehow imbedded in my mind like a hazy dream, surely from a bedside conversation I overheard while lying in a deep sleep. And while she must wonder whether I remember, I'll never let her know that I do, happy to keep her secrets hidden in my heart until she asks me to show them to her.

Something about her love for him moves me. I don't know why Adam has held on so desperately to me. I want him to let go of his love and his guilt so that he can move on with his life and be the man he was never able to be.

Lying cocooned in my body has caused me to speculate how beautiful a life without sadness and guilt could have been. When I was so young, harshly abandoned by my mother in a puddle of mud, my life was wasted on cruelty and sadness, and I never wanted that for Eva. I just wanted her to be happy and free to live and love the way I was never able to.

But I realize as I've come home that there is still much sadness here and I wonder if this house will ever see the happiness that my grandfather intended.

Still, I remain hopeful.

CHAPTER TWENTY-SIX

Protected

September 21ᵗʰ, 2016

Jack had never met a female in his entire life that had ever piqued his interest as intensely as Eva Michaels Harper.

There was something about the frailty that she wore as a cloak to carefully disguise her inner strength that intrigued him. On the outside, she appeared to be a spoiled little rich girl, but the look in her eyes had told him from the very beginning that she was much more than that. He didn't know if she even realized how surprising she was.

After she told him that her husband "Chris" was accused of killing his lover, Jack decided that she and the family would need twenty-four-hour protection. It wasn't enough to have the surveillance cameras and security gate. He wanted armed bodyguards, even though Eva scoffed at the idea.

"Chris ... I mean, Connor, is in jail now. He's not a threat any longer, Jack. I don't want to talk about this. I can't believe we need to have this conversation," Eva said, trying to disguise the sadness in her voice. "I don't want a bunch of strangers with guns here twenty-four hours a day. I don't even know what's going on with my mom right now, and I don't want the house to be disrupted any more than what it already is."

Jack looked at her evenly, his brown eyes dark and serious, telling her that it wasn't up for discussion. "Eva, I'm not taking any chances. My grandfather would be very disappointed in me for allowing this to happen to you in the first place, so you're just going to have to indulge me and allow this for you and your family. We don't know if he was in this alone, or what his motive was. We have no idea why he changed his name and went through all of this to marry you. There is much more to this and I'm not going to sleep well unless I know that you're completely safe."

Eva stared out the window as they approached The Harper House. She sighed sadly and Jack fought the urge to reach for her hand. He tried to imagine what she must be going through, knowing that her husband wasn't who he said he was. Jack realized she had closed herself off and was keeping her thoughts close, careful not to reveal too much. Her vulnerability was appealing, and he was sure from the look on her face that she was completely devastated. It was her strength he was most drawn to. As the large gate closed behind them, Eva watched it in the side view mirror. For the first time in her entire life, she wondered if she had ever truly been safe at all. She had never questioned this before, but with the baby growing inside her belly and the bloody pictures burned into her brain, she felt very exposed as she tried to hide the fear that shook her to the core.

Jack stopped the car and jogged over to open her door before she could even grab the handle. As he reached out his hand to help her, Eva felt a surge of electricity flow through her fingers. His hands were strong and warm. She admired his strength and the way he carried himself, so self-assured and confident. Something about him made her feel safe, as though nothing could hurt her, and she admitted to herself that she needed that at the moment.

She blushed involuntarily as she allowed him to guide her gently to the house, his hand cradling her elbow.

As they approached the door, it flew open and Adam raced out, engulfing Eva in a hug.

"God, Eva, I'm so sorry that I wasn't there for you," Adam cried, tears streaming down his cheeks. "I'm a terrible father and I'm so sorry."

Eva looked awkward and embarrassed, her nose wrinkling

as she caught a strong whiff of him and his clothes. Jack looked away, trying not to notice the look of disgust and frustration on her face. "Okay, Dad," she said, pushing him away. "I'm fine, really."

"Eva, how can you be fine? Kelly told me a little about what is happening, but I don't understand ... how could you possibly be fine? How do you think that I would believe that after all you've been through?" Adam held her face in his hands and breathed directly in her face, causing her to gag.

"Dad! Please, you need to shower right now and brush your teeth. You smell like ... like ... you just smell. I've been at the police station all night and feel disgusting and I need to get cleaned up, too." Eva pushed him away and opened the door to go into the house. "Dad, go in, right now. Go and get cleaned up and I'll make you some coffee, I'm really fine. Jack has been looking after me and I'm fine."

Adam looked at Jack, as though seeing him standing there for the first time. "Oh ... Jack. I'm sorry. I was so upset that I didn't see you there. Thank you very much for looking out for my girl!"

Jack held out his hand reluctantly, remembering their last meeting when Adam had shunned him. He had told him that he didn't want him hovering like his grandfather had, which had stung Jack, knowing how much his grandfather had devoted of himself to the family. Jack knew it was the alcohol talking, but had followed Adam's wishes and allowed others to watch over the family's affairs from a distance. It was a decision he was beginning to regret. "You're welcome, Mr. Michaels. I'm adding security to the house, just so you know. I've already discussed it with Eva, but based on the current circumstances, I feel it would be best."

Adam looked at him, confused. After a long pause he said carefully, "You do what you feel is best to protect my family."

Jack nodded. "I plan to."

Adam and Jack stared at each other for a moment, then Adam looked at Eva and smiled weakly before turning to go into the house.

Eva lingered on the large porch for a moment, staring at the door long after he closed it.

"Is he okay?" Jack asked, nodding in the direction that

Adam disappeared.

"No," Eva said sadly. "He hasn't been okay my entire life. He's broken and sad, and there's nothing that can be done about it. He has always refused to come back to the land of the living, missing my mom and missing his life. I don't know what will happen to him now that Mom is home and awake."

"Love changes people, Eva." Jack thought about his own mother and father and how his father's hardness and meanness toward his mother had nearly ruined her. But when she met and married his stepfather, she seemed to be revived in a way that changed her completely. She had blossomed and was beautiful and happy for the first time since he had known her. "Love can either make someone better, or break them completely, and I've seen it happen both ways."

"Dad has been a mess forever, and just when I think it's not possible for him to fall any further, he manages to find a way," Eva said, tears welling up in her blue eyes. "I missed my entire childhood because of it. I think I jumped into this relationship and got married to Chr-Connor because I was so lonely and desperate to have someone love me. Foolishly, I thought that he did."

Eva eyes immediately looked toward the ground, tears falling continually.

"No! You can't blame yourself for this, Eva!" Jack grabbed her hand and held it tightly. "It happens to all of us. I had a pretty shitty childhood myself." Jack had never talked to anyone about his childhood and didn't even realize he was doing it until he heard his own words tumbling out of his mouth. "My dad was lazy and didn't love any of us more than he loved himself. He was an utter disappointment to everyone who loved him because he didn't care about any of us. At least your dad loved you even if he had a hard time showing it."

"Yes, well … I still fell for and married a psychopath … and now I'm going to have his baby. Oh, my God!"

Before he could stop himself, Jack pulled Eva close and held her, her tiny body trembling uncontrollably with grief. He was proud of her for even being able to stand upright, but thankful that he could be there when she needed to let go. He had grown unusually attached to her for reasons that excited and terrified him at the same time.

She cried for what felt like hours, and when she finally stepped back, exhausted, her blue eyes puffy and rimmed with red. "I'm so sorry," she said eyeing his soft, white, cotton shirt where her eye makeup had come off on both of his shoulders. "I've completely ruined your shirt."

"Oh," he said looking down and smiling back up at her. "This old thing? Don't worry about it!"

"I'm so sorry, Jack. I don't usually have meltdowns like that in front of someone I don't know that well ... I'm mortified that you've seen me this way. This isn't me ..."

"Eva," Jack said, grabbing her shoulders gently and tipping her chin up so that her eyes met his. "You've just had the worst day of your life. You can cry in front of me anytime. I hope you'll consider me a friend, so please don't worry about it. I just want to make sure that you're okay."

Eva nodded, gratefully.

"I do feel better now," Eva said, sniffling as she looked toward the door. "I should probably go in and check on my dad. Hopefully he's sobered up a little by now."

Jack nodded. "I just want you to know one thing. As long as I'm around, I'm going to make sure that you're well-protected like I should have from the very beginning."

"You can't possibly blame yourself for Connor! It wasn't your fault at all!" Eva's big blue eyes dazzled him as she spoke.

"I should've taken the time to have him checked out better. Of course it was my fault." Jack said, his handsome face full of guilt.

"The detective said that he targeted me for some reason and planned this all along," Eva said, matter-of-factly. "He was trying to get me, Jack, and he wasn't going to stop until he did. Please don't think there is anything you could have done."

"I should have been more careful," he said, his voice hard. "From now on, Eva, you'll be safe. I promise you that."

Eva nodded, suddenly conscious that the sound of his voice made her heart skip when he spoke. Her grief quickly crushed the thought as she smiled cautiously at him and made her way into the house to look for Adam.

As Jack watched her walk in, his phone buzzed and he looked down at it, irritated for being interrupted at such a moment. As he read the message from his private investigator, his jaw dropped and he turned back toward the house immediately.

"My source at the police station is telling me that Connor may not be the killer. It smells like he's being set up, but we won't know until the forensics evidence comes back. This could mean that Eva and the family are still in danger."

Jack dialed the phone immediately as he paced back and forth on the porch. For the next thirty-minutes he made arrangements for twenty-four-hour protection for the home and the family. He knew that Eva wouldn't like it, but he had no other choice. He knocked on the door and was let in by the housekeeper who graciously ushered him into the kitchen to wait, offering him coffee, which he politely declined. He sat and waited impatiently until a sleek gray SUV pulled into the driveway. He met and instructed the team to set up a plan for securing The Harper House, as well as replace the outdated security system that had been put in when his grandfather took care of the family's affairs.

Jack was exhausted and thankful he had a strong VP to relinquish his duties of the company to. As he prepared to leave The Harper House for the day, he looked around for Eva. Much to his dismay she was nowhere to be found. He walked out to his car, his shoulders aching and his head pounding. He suddenly understood the loyalty and commitment his grandfather had for the Harper family and Jack felt guilty, realizing that he had not done nearly enough to watch over them.

As he walked out to his car, he felt as though someone was watching him. He looked up to the house but could see no one. He shook his head, reminding himself that there were already a dozen men and the most updated surveillance system available watching over the home while he was not there. He got into his car cautiously and drove away.

As Brynn stared out the window at the tail lights pulling away she thought of how much the man reminded her of an old friend she used to have, her mind muddled with memories. She slowly wheeled her way back toward her bed and waited.

When will Adam come and finally talk to me? Is he going to avoid me forever?

It had been months, and aside from the first time she awoke, Adam had been careful to avoid being alone with her.

I'm ready to hear what you have to say. I'm ready to talk to you now if you would only find it in your heart to come and sit with me.

Brynn sat down carefully on her bed, happy to be alone for a short time. She knew that it wouldn't last long, but she hoped it would last long enough for her to collect her thoughts. She enjoyed the quiet as she looked around the room and did what she had been doing for two decades.

She waited.

CHAPTER TWENTY-SEVEN

Daddy Issues

September 23rd, 2016

Jessie lay on the floor where Adam's clothes had been, unmoving, as she imagined that she could still smell him. She missed him even though he had only been with her for a few hours. She realized that in all the years after she had run away from him that she had never felt truly whole. Now the emptiness within seemed even greater than it had before, and she wondered how she would move past it this time.

She had found herself on the floor so many times before, unable to breathe or move, her heart torn open wide over and over with the knowledge that Adam didn't love her.

She had never truly gotten over him, often seeking him out online and always trying to garner as much information as she could about him. He was a part of one of the wealthiest families in the area, so it hadn't been difficult to find what she wanted. His life overall was completely unexciting. Still, occasionally she was able to get small snippets of information that satisfied her curiosity. She had learned to stalk his social media sights where he was fairly inactive, but it was enough to make her believe she was still a part of him though she had spent many years without him. She'd tried her best to forget, but she knew that she never would.

The morning after she left him, so many years before, she called her sister who she hadn't talked to since high school. Then she hopped on a Greyhound bus to visit, thankful to have family to go to. She was desperate to find quiet, to still the chaos in her head and the misery in her heart. Jessie could still recall the two-day bus trip, fighting the morning sickness, her seatmate a crazed woman who snored incessantly. She remembered how she collapsed into her sister's arms when she finally saw her, exhausted and on the verge of a nervous breakdown. It had been a long journey from Adam's small apartment to her sister's rambling farmhouse, but when she arrived, she thought she might have finally found peace.

Jessie wrote letters to Adam every night in her journal, sharing with him the details of her pregnancy. For many long months she imagined that he was with her and was excited as she about the baby. When the baby finally came and she held him in her arms, she searched his face for any sign of Adam, convinced she would see it more as he grew older.

She had put off naming him for as long as she could until she was finally forced to put a name on his birth certificate. She wanted to name him "Adam", but at the last second changed her mind, deciding the baby needed to have his own identity. She named him after her brother who had died from an overdose, using Adam's last name for the child's middle name.

She wrote the baby's name out on the birth certificate form with a shaky hand, saying it over and over in her mind. *Connor Michael Martin, Connor Michael Martin, Connor Michael Martin.*

After Connor was born, things changed at her sister's house, and when her brother-in-law tried to shove his tongue down her throat, she knew she had no choice but to leave. For a split second, she thought about leaving Connor behind, knowing it would be easier for her to fend for herself alone. At the last minute she grabbed him. She knew that she would never forgive herself if she abandoned him. She took another bus back toward Adam, but settled a town over, unable to find the courage to return to him.

She was intent on raising her son to be the type of man she had never met but saw on TV and in the movies; the good kind who loved women and knew how to treat one. She was watching her son grow up, knowing that her boy was destined to be handsome and desirable. She taught him to listen to classical music and read poetry. She coached him incessantly on how to be a good listener and how to be affectionate, and she told him repeatedly, "You're going to be someone special."

She remedied the guilt she felt over almost abandoning him by showering him with love. It tore a hole in her stomach along with the alcohol she consumed to dull the pain of the memory. Jessie became obsessed with raising Connor to treat women the way she had never been treated. She wanted him to have everything she hadn't, and she convinced him that he deserved it.

As Connor grew up, Jessie did her best to make ends meet, bartending night after night, hoping to meet the man of her dreams who would rescue her from everything. She tried repeatedly, but could never quite pick the right one, and every man she ended up with was charmed by her beautiful smile, but disappointed by her booziness. It didn't help that she never remembered to tell them about the son she had right away, either.

Even with all the men who came and went in her life, she was never able to forget about Adam. When Jessie had read in the paper about Brynn's near-fatal accident, she thought about going back to him, but she could never find the courage. She knew from the news stories that he was staying at The Harper House, and she marveled at the massive estate and imagined that she might live there with him one day. But The Harper House was too intimidating and terrifying for her to approach, and she knew she could never force herself to go there, even for him.

Jessie always hated Brynn for ruining Adam. When she heard about the accident, she knew that some greater good was shining down upon her. Brynn had destroyed the promise of a life with Adam that Jessie felt she deserved. She had lain awake at night, her brain turning over with a thousand different ways to hurt Brynn, but when she heard about the accident on the news, Jessie was convinced that something or someone had heard her cries and had taken care of things for her.

As the years went on, Jessie's life consisted only of her fantasies of Adam. She found that more often than not, reality and fantasy would to converge into one, until she was barely able to tell the difference. She often referred to Adam as "her husband" when she was talking to others, and she imagined having a life with him. Jessie knew that she needed help and she tried, for her son's sake, to follow the doctor's orders so that the delusions would stop and reality could set in. But the medications were expensive, and they interfered with her drinking, so she often refused to take them or ran out without refilling them.

As her Connor grew older, he began to see how obsessed she was with a life that never belonged to her, and he began to resent the father who had completely abandoned the both of them. Jessie had told Connor about Adam's life before them, and how he had chosen Brynn over her. She told him that she was convinced that Adam loved her more, but hadn't the courage to leave his wife once and for all.

As the years went by, Connor became a strong, handsome young man. He watched Jessie nearly kill herself in an attempt to slit her wrists. She told Connor later that she thought it might bring Adam back, though they still hadn't seen each other since the night before she walked away.

"I'm sorry," Jessie apologized to him after every episode. "I just forgot to take my meds ... I forgot to pick them up ... please ... things will get better, Con. I promise. I swear I'll be good!"

Connor wanted nothing more than to believe his beautiful mother. She was the only thing he had in the world, and he adored her more than anything. When she was happy, their life was good, and laughter and contentment were abundant in their small apartment. Connor learned that the darkness always came without warning, and there was nothing and nobody to protect him either physically or emotionally from Jessie's cruelty and anger. He grew accustomed to the ups and the downs, and learned how to navigate the tumultuous waves of love and abuse that his mother could never control.

As soon as Connor was old enough, he began to question his own sanity and the genes that had been passed down to him from Jessie. He also became more curious about the man she claimed was his father. He watched her stability begin to deteriorate, and he wondered with pressing concern if this, too, would be his fate.

"If you know where my father is, I want to meet him," he insisted repeatedly.

"Yes, you are welcome to meet your father anytime," Jessie often told him during the times she was lucid and the world was full of excruciating reality. "But he doesn't know you exist. I never told him that I was pregnant with you."

"How do you know for sure who he is, then?" he had asked her, wanting desperately to believe her. "Are you sure it's Adam?"

Her face always fell and she looked embarrassed when Connor pushed her, and he could tell from the look on her face that she wasn't quite sure.

"I just ... I just know ... I knew your dad very well and I think you are just like him." Jessie was always so adamant. The thought of anyone being her son's father except for Adam seemed ridiculous to her. She had loved Adam with all her heart. He had been the only guy that she had ever been mostly faithful to, with the exception of those nights when she worked late at the bar and her friend Dean had arrived to close up with her. Dean, a lifelong friend, had often professed his drunken love for her, which Jessie found flattering. Even though he was extremely attractive and had a good job as a mechanic, she didn't love him, but he kept finding his way into her life much like she kept finding herself naked with him. Every time she'd swear it was the last. Jessie convinced herself that she only slept with Dean as a distraction to temporarily dull the pain of knowing how much Adam still loved Brynn. The memories of those long nights at the bar, her body entwined with Dean's, were fuzzy, and, after a while, she wasn't even sure if the details were real. She pushed them out of her mind and tried to forget that he even existed. She never mentioned his name to Connor, and when she talked about his father, she was talking about Adam. There were no other contenders as far as she was concerned.

Connor always pushed her for as many details about Adam as possible, knowing that her muddled mind didn't often share the most accurate information. It was then that she would tell him everything she knew, and Connor tucked it away in the recesses of his mind. He knew he would use it later, although he wasn't sure how. Without realizing it, Jessie had made her son afraid to love by hardening his heart against anything that could destroy him the way his mother had been destroyed. When he finally did fall in love with a beautiful little redhead named Nora, he shared with her what he knew about Adam and his mother.

"You don't look like him at all," Nora said, staring at a picture of Adam that she had found on the Internet. "You look a little like your mom, but you don't look like this Adam guy at all. Your nose is long and straight and his isn't. You don't resemble him in any way. Jesus, what is she thinking? This guy can't possibly be your father!"

Connor stared at the picture, amazed that Jessie could even pretend that Adam was his father. He agreed with Nora that there was nothing about Adam Michaels that even remotely resembled him. He and Nora dug through old letters and pictures, which were the remnants of Jessie's life, until they came across a single photo labeled simply "Dean". Connor knew at that moment that Adam wasn't his father. He immediately saw himself in Dean and realized that Adam being his father was a figment of his mother's imagination. It still hurt him to know that Adam had not loved her the way she needed to be loved, and an irrational hatred for Adam grew inside him until it was nearly uncontrollable.

Nora liked to feed his hatred by searching for Adam on the Internet.

"God, look how rich he is! Forget the petty stealing we've been doing to get by, this is where it's at, Baby. This could and should be all yours, and then you can take care of her and put her in one of those expensive hospitals that she needs to be in. If he hadn't hurt your mom the way he did, she would be normal and things could have been so much better for both of you." Nora's eyes had grown large as they stared at the picture of The Harper House on the Internet. "You deserve to live in a house like that with me."

Connor had stared at the house in awe and tried to imagine what it would be like to live in a place like that. He had never known more than a couple of rooms and a bathroom, and the thought of anyone living in a house so large made him angry.

"I want to hurt that selfish bastard for what he did to my

mom." Connor's hazel eyes flashed in that way that excited Nora, his voice gritty and angry.

"I think that the best way to hurt him is to hurt his daughter," Nora purred, staring menacingly at the picture of Eva and her father that was frozen on the screen in front of them. She was thrilled at the dangerous edge in Connor's voice and her mind turned over, searching for a way he could use this to get her out of the mundane life she was trapped in.

"How would I do that?" Connor asked, trying to imagine physically hurting Adam Michaels the way he truly wanted to.

"It's simple, Baby. You make his daughter fall in love with you, you marry her, and then you make her have an accident so you can take all their money. If you can make it look like the father did it, then double whammy," Nora said smoothly, as though the answer was obvious.

"That's crazy!" Connor said, realizing what Nora was suggesting. He had always loved her edginess and the way she loved to take risks, but he'd never imagined she could devise a scheme like that. She had already talked him into so many things, and he had already paid the price for it with a RAP sheet and a few short stints in jail. So far, everything she had ever convinced him do had been petty, until now.

They had talked it over for weeks until he had the courage to agree.

"Nobody says you have to sleep with that little rich bitch. Just … make her fall in love with you … and the rest will be easy. You should be able to do that, Baby." Nora pulled him close the way he liked, and Connor suddenly couldn't remember any reason not to do what she said.

Connor thought a lot about his mom as he moved forward with his plan to hurt the man she claimed was his father. He thought about her suffering and how Adam had caused her so much pain. It fueled his desire to take away everything Adam had ever loved. Then he met Eva, and something in him changed. He realized that he no longer wanted to hurt her as he fought his love for her, knowing how wrong it was for him to feel the way he did. Connor knew the connection was there, real or imagined, and he hid it away inside of him as best he could, afraid that Nora might discover it.

Jessie knew something inside of her son had changed, though she didn't know why. She had watched as the darkness that hovered around him lifted, and it gave her the courage to approach Adam after months of following his every move outside of The Harper House. She thought that if Connor could find happiness, she could, too, so she "accidentally" ran into Adam at the AA meeting.

Having him in her arms and in her bed once again was more than she had imagined. When he left her so abruptly, it was as though a bitter wind had blown in and the emptiness consumed her completely. While she waited for him to call like he promised, she slowly began to realize that he never would. The pain of his absence left her unable to get off her bedroom floor, the place where she last saw him. After a few days, she crawled painfully into the bathroom and ran a hot bath. She stood up only long enough to get into the tub wearing the thin slip she had been wearing when Adam left. She sank into it, ignoring the burning water on her skin. When the water stopped running, she picked up the razor blade she kept in the soap dish, testing its sharpness on her finger and happy for a moment to feel something other than emptiness. She watched as the blood pooled into the water, her green eyes mesmerized as it swirled around her slowly, until it finally disappeared.

She realized that this was what she had wanted for a long time. She had watched and waited for Adam to acknowledge her existence. She had hoped he could feel her near him just as she always felt him with her. When the moment had finally come, he had discarded her easily and thoughtlessly as though she meant nothing to him, just like she always knew he would. It happened again, just as it had all those years ago when he let her walk out the door without begging her to stay. She had forgotten that she had left him without any warning. Jessie's memories revised the past until she could no longer recognize the truth.

If he had truly cared for her, she told herself, she never would've left. In the deepest part of her, she knew that he didn't love her the way he loved Brynn, and he never would.

Now, after one final time in his arms, Jessie wanted nothing more than to disappear, because in Adam's eyes, she knew she didn't exist. She thought for a moment that she should leave a note, but realized it was too late. She didn't want to track water all over the floor, or slip and crack her head on the side of the tub. She thought that it was ironic that she would think about something so small at a time like this, but was thankful for the momentary distraction.

She held the razor blade to her right wrist and drew a long, deep line on the inside of her arm. The pain was intense, but then she no longer felt it as she put her wrist in the water and watched the blood quickly flow out. She laid her head back and closed her eyes. Briefly, she hoped that it wouldn't be Connor that found her, even though she knew he was the only one who would.

"I'm sorry for being such a shitty mother," she whispered into the steamy air. "I'm sorry. I thought I could be better, but I couldn't."

She inhaled slowly, feeling a little faint, and then marveled at how she no longer felt any pain. She wondered if Adam would ever find out what she had finally done for him and their love, preserving it in time with their last night together so that it could never be forgotten.

She held her breath as she waited for the moment she hoped would come, when she would finally and blissfully, disappear.

CHAPTER TWENTY-EIGHT

Pilgrimage

September 1st, 2016

Nick hadn't made the trip to The Harper House in over a decade. As he drove the familiar road to the house, he thought about the last trip he had made which was cut short by his daughter, Mandy's, suicide attempt.

When he had gotten home, he had joined his estranged ex-wife Fiona, at the hospital. The next few months had been nothing but a whirlwind as they reconciled so that they could work together to help Mandy manage her schizoaffective disorder. Thoughts of Brynn all but disappeared as his life became centered on his daughter, who needed constant care and monitoring. But as Mandy became older, with the mix of the right medication, she became more stable. As it became clear to Nick and Fiona that Mandy's condition would have its constant highs and lows, they finally came to terms with their failed marriage and decided to divorce. Any love between them was only found in remnants of the past and their daughter, who had decided to go to a nearby college in order to be close to home.

Nick no longer felt guilty about keeping Brynn close to his heart. He knew that his refusal to forget her never allowed him to love anyone else. He tried to open himself up to love, but he was unable to help himself no matter how much he wanted to. He had fallen hopelessly in love with Brynn from that first moment he met her in her own restaurant. She'd been reluctant to spend time with him at first. If it hadn't been for her friend, Jane, Brynn never would have met with him, and he wouldn't have fallen for her so hard. He knew that after that, nothing he could do would ever change his love for her.

As he packed his final bag for the pilgrimage back to The Harper House, his hands shook nervously. The thought had crossed his mind that Brynn was no longer alive, a sharp pain sparking in his heart every time he considered it. If she was alive, he knew he needed to see her again, and was prepared for anything, even Adam. Nick realized that it was time for him to start living his life, just as he should have when he met Brynn and knew immediately that he loved her. He was full of regret for leaving her the first time, knowing in his heart that he intended to return. Life, it turned out, had conspired against him, and he felt as though he was swimming upstream to get to back to her.

Nick was determined this time to claim the life he had walked away from all those years ago, and he knew that meant that he might have to fight Adam. Brynn had been coming for him when she had her accident, and now it would be up to him to finally go to her. He worried that she would've forgotten all about it, but he couldn't allow himself to believe that after everything he had been through that he would have been completely erased from her memory.

He called Mandy to let her know that he would be leaving, but she didn't return his call. He and Fiona no longer talked, an unspoken agreement between them. Though they had ended their marriage amicably, Fiona's bitterness at his inability to love her had grown over the years until she could no longer communicate with him civilly. When they parted ways, they realized they would only need one another for the sake of their daughter.

Nick drove anxiously to the airport. He thought about the conversations he'd had with Brynn, many of them muddled in his mind, some of the words lost forever. The memories he had of her, though, remained strong and intense. The vision of her huge brown eyes staring up at him with love was burned deeply in his mind. The subtle smell of vanilla always brought her back to him, if even just for a moment.

"I've never been able to talk to anyone the way I talk to you," he remembered Brynn confessing, her voice husky and low as she stroked the side of his face. "I've always been so closed, even with Adam, who I've known practically my entire life. With you ... it's different. I feel as though somehow ... maybe ... you and I were meant to be."

"I feel the same way about you." Nick remembered how he had kissed her lips over and over, enjoying their sweet saltiness. "I feel as though I've known you my entire life, almost as though I could never be whole without you."

When he closed his eyes, Nick could still feel her hands on his back and her lips on his. He could still hear her sweet, deep voice in his ear telling him to "go faster" or "go slower," her sighs setting him on fire with each one.

Their time together had been incredibly short, but it had felt like a lifetime, and Nick wanted so much more. Nick wanted what he knew was impossible because he wanted her to wake up so he could be with her. Every day. He knew that his life wouldn't be complete without her because he had already tried everything he could to forget about her, doubting that he could love someone so intensely and so completely after their time together. He had tried to find love, get married, and have a family. He had done all the things that he knew he should do in order to erase her memory from his mind. He had even been single for a short time between his two marriages, dating carefully and trying to find the woman who could heal him and make him forget Brynn. No matter what he did, whose bed he slept in, or what life he lived, nothing could make him forget. The more he tried, the more he loved her.

He sat back on the airplane and closed his eyes.

It would be a seven-hour flight and an hour to The Harper House. He sighed anxiously. In roughly eight hours, Nick would be with Brynn once again.

CHAPTER TWENTY-NINE

Daddy's Girl

September 23rd, 2016

Eva was having a hard time forgiving Adam for abandoning her once again. They hadn't spoken much since the night she had arrived home from the police station.

After leaving her alone when she needed him the most, he was making it difficult for her to find him so that he could properly apologize to her. She had been thankful for Jack who had taken care of her at the police station, but she had needed Adam. He had left her alone her entire life and she had never said anything about it, but after a day and a half, she couldn't wait any longer.

She searched the massive house and when she finally found him he was hiding on a soft leather couch in the library pretending to read. The library was a magnificent room with beautiful, large windows. It was adorned in rich wood with thousands of books lining the walls. It was a room that was seldom used anymore since the passing of her grandfather.

"Where have you been hiding?" she asked, her arms crossed as her blue eyes penetrated him.

"I'm sorry, Eva. I'm … ashamed." Adam refused to look into her eyes as he turned away from her.

"Turn around and look at me, Dad." Eva said, her voice low

and angry. Adam thought of how much she sounded like her mother. Brynn's voice had often reverberated in anger toward him, especially toward the end of their marriage. He would've given anything to hear her voice while she had been asleep, but now he thought that it was ironic that he was avoiding Brynn, too.

"You sound just like ..."

"I know. I sound like Mom. You've said it a thousand times throughout my life, yet you haven't been alone with her in a room since she's been awake. This is what you've wanted for twenty years! This is what you've begged for, dreamed about, yet you refuse to go to her! I don't understand it. I don't understand you." The words spilled out, quick and furious. Eva had watched him suffer her entire life and couldn't understand why he would behave this way now.

"Eva, please. Take it easy on your old dad." Adam looked beaten up and Eva thought he reminded her of a sad old hound dog.

"No! I'm not going to take it easy on you. I'm not going to let you off the hook. You're a coward and I'm angry with you. You've let me down my entire life and now when I've needed you the most ..." Eva's voice trailed off, her words stuck in her throat as she choked back a sob.

Adam stood up and started to take a step toward her but she stepped back. He sank down on the couch, dejected.

"God, I'm so sorry that I let you down. I don't even know what's happening with Chris ... please, tell me what is happening. Please, I'm sorry."

"No! I needed you more than ever. I've never ever needed you more, and you were nowhere to be found. And when you were finally found, you looked like hell and you smelled like a brewery. I just don't understand you." Eva tried not to cry as she looked at him. He looked small and pathetic. She thought about what he had looked like to her when she was a little girl and how he had seemed so big and strong. Despite his grief and many faults, he had at least always been there for her. The thought of him abandoning her was terrifying.

"Eva ..." Adam looked at her, desperate. He rubbed at the scruff on his face, his blue eyes, very much like her own, were bloodshot and tired. "I'm sorry ... I have no excuses. I'm sorry. I'm just ... I'm scared. I've wanted your mom to be awake, and now that she is, I'm terrified. I don't know what to do ... What if she hates me? What if she remembers how horrible I was to her when we were married and she kicks me out? Where will I go? Who will I have in my life if I no longer have her or you?"

Eva stared at him in disbelief.

"Do you truly think she would kick you out? You've taken care of her, you've looked out for her. Why would she hate you? Why would she not want you here?"

Adam sighed, knowing this day would come.

"There are a lot of things you don't know about your mom and I, Bitty." Adam used the nickname that she hadn't heard since she was a little girl. Eva immediately softened when said it, suddenly comforted against her will.

"I know, Dad. But you can tell me." Eva said, her voice more gentle than it had been. She sat down next to him on the couch, drawn in, her anger fading.

"You're going to hate me, too, once I tell you what I did." Adam's voice was so quiet she could barely hear him.

"No, Dad. I won't," Eva said, her heart pounding. "You can tell me anything."

Adam was silent for a long time, and when he spoke, his voice cracked. "Your mom and I ... divorced."

Eva sucked in her breath. The news was devastating, and even though she had known that her parent's life together had been tumultuous and difficult, nobody had ever mentioned that they had divorced.

"But ..." Adam continued. "I never signed the final papers that I was supposed to in order to finish everything. I hid them away. She had the accident before she was ever able to found out, but she thought it was a done deal." Adam said the words slowly, letting them sink in.

Eva was quiet for a few moments as she thought about what he had said.

"Is ... is that why you have been avoiding her?" Eva asked, finally.

"Yes." Adam admitted. "It's not that I don't want to see her. I love your mom more than anything in this world. God knows I haven't done anything that I set out to do where she was concerned. When we were young, I thought I would always take care for her and protect her, but … I failed miserably. I didn't want to get a divorce, but I drove her away. Your mom was …"

Adam paused, unsure if he should tell her about Thomas and her past.

"Please Daddy … tell me the rest." Eva could tell there was more to the story and she urged him to continue.

Adam looked at his daughter, so young and beautiful, and he was amazed at how much she reminded him of Brynn when she had been Eva's age. They were practically identical in every way. The only difference between them was the color of their eyes. But even as a young child, Brynn's eyes had been so much older and full of pain reflecting a horror that Adam protected Eva from in every way.

Until now.

For the next hour, Adam gave Eva a brief history of Brynn's childhood. He shared how she had been ruthlessly abandoned by her birth parents, and then abused by her adoptive father, Thomas. He hesitantly told her about Rose, Brynn's adoptive mother and her incessant neediness and selfishness, and how as a teenager, Brynn had resorted to cutting to free herself from the pain. Adam tried to be careful as he watched Eva's eyes well up over and over as she kept repeating, "I didn't know, I didn't know." Brynn's past became more colorful and more alive than she had ever imagined.

When Adam was done, Eva was completely numb, unsure if she could possibly take anymore. Adam continued to spill the truth about how he had ruined their marriage after baby Sophie died with his drinking, and how the guilt had eaten him alive every day since.

But he stopped, careful to leave out the part where the doctor told him that if he continued to drink, he would die. He knew that he didn't have it in him to quit, and he didn't want to burden his sweet daughter with that as well. Adam had been feeling the effects on his body for quite some time, even though he hated to admit it. The doctor had been warning him that this would happen and, as his body began to fail, he knew that the pain would eventually come. Adam had purposely ignored every warning that he had been given. He knew that it was already becoming more than he could handle, and that he would need to go to the hospital soon.

Eva stared at him as he paused, trying to decide what to say to him that could make a difference.

"You need to talk to her, Daddy," Eva said, keeping her voice steady. "She'll forgive you for whatever you feel that you've done wrong. You've taken such good care of her over the years, and there's no way she could be angry with you now."

"I don't know," Adam said, fearfully. "I don't know if she will forgive me. I don't know if *I* could forgive me. I haven't been an honest man or the kind of man that I thought I would be when I fell in love with your mom. Life has passed so quickly. I think that it's just too late for us now."

"Daddy, you've been there for her nearly her entire life. It would be impossible for her to not see how much you've loved her."

Adam grabbed Eva and held her close, wishing, not for the first time, that he had been a better father. He didn't remember much of her childhood, and when she had needed him as a child, he had turned to Kelly and Jane, unsure of what to do for her. When she had been the most devastated and needed him, he was completely absent. He knew that he would have to add that to the load of regrets that he carried with him every day.

"I'm sorry that I've been such a shitty dad to you," Adam said, his voice barely a whisper. "I wanted to be a dad so much and I thought I would be a better one ... but I wasn't. I tried to stop drinking so many times ... I tried to get help and I tried to do better, but I fucked it up every single time. I just couldn't ... I couldn't ..."

Eva looked at Adam and focused on his dark hair speckled with gray, the stubble on his face making him look so much older. She closed her eyes and tried to remember back when he had been a young father and what he had looked like. She remembered how she had always been so proud of her handsome daddy. She hadn't known that he was drunk when he held her, and didn't feel his absence in quite the same way he remembered it. She had convinced herself that her childhood was only filled with emptiness and loneliness, but as she tried hard to look back, she recalled the trips to the zoo and the nights reading on the couch. She remembered when he built forts with her in the massive living room, and how he had tried to teach her how to cook.

It was only as she grew older that she convinced herself she had always been alone, pushing him away, even when she needed him the most.

He had tried to be a good father, and even though she hadn't been as close to him as she would've liked for many years, she still loved him with everything inside of her. She didn't believe it could be any other way. She adored him even though the darkness had seemed to claim him more than anyone realized.

"I forgive you," Eva placed her hand on the side of his head and pulled it down on her shoulder. "You've been just enough, and you've been good to me."

She could feel him crying and she shushed him as though he were a small child. "We can get you the help you need, Dad. I'll help you and we'll get you through this darkness and through this pain."

Adam shook his head, against her. "No ... no," he said, his voice muffled.

"Why not?" Eva said, pulling his face up so that he could look at her.

"I just ... I can't ... I'm sorry, Eva," Adam said, wiping his face with the back of his hand, trying to compose himself.

"You need help, Dad. I can help you do this. We need you." Eva gripped his arm tightly, trying to keep the desperation out of her voice.

"It's too late, Eva. There's nothing else that you can do for me." Adam stopped suddenly as though he wanted to say more. Instead, he asked about Chris. "I need to know about Chris. I need you to tell me what's been happening."

Eva knew he was changing the subject, but she needed him, and for the first time he was truly listening to her. She slowly told him everything she knew about Connor Michael Martin. She marveled at how he listened so intently, and as she talked, she discovered that he was finally the father she had always wished he had been.

CHAPTER THIRTY

Redemption

September 23rd, 2016

The footsteps to my room are quiet and slow. I can hear them outside the door, waiting and pausing. I wait, wondering if anyone will come in. I can hear the clearing of a throat and know immediately that it is Adam.

The door opens slightly and I try to sit up as best I can in my chair.

I look up expectedly and see Adam slowly walking toward me, hesitant and shy, looking more like a little boy than the man he has matured into.

I wait for him to speak but instead he just stares, his beautiful blue eyes rimmed with red, his hair entirely too long and a tousled mess. The memory from long ago, of my fingers in his hair comes crashing back on me like an ocean wave, and I feel my lips respond to the memory with a smile.

He smiles back at me, his teeth still straight and white, his face even more handsome than when he was a younger man. When he smiles, his face transforms instantly and I can see the boy I fell in love with. Then the smile falls away and suddenly he becomes a tragic shadow. I can see the lines of age and heartache etched into his skin like a road map and my heart aches for him. As he comes closer, all the bitterness that was once between us slowly melts away.

As he sits down in the chair next to me, I can see that he is uncomfortable so I motion for him to move his chair closer. I want him to be nearer because I feel as though I haven't seen him in so long, and at that very moment I realize how much I have missed him. I can see by how his blue eyes widen, and by the somberness of his expression, that he is terrified to be too close to me.

"Hi," he says finally, his voice quiet and deep.

I smile at him again, trying to get the words to come out. Eventually, much to my relief, they come. "Hi."

The heaviness around us begins to dissipate until we fall into a more comfortable silence, though his shoulders and jawline remain tight and tense.

He finally speaks, breaking the silence. "I've missed you so much, Brynn. Nothing in my life has been the same since you've been gone." Before I know it, Adam is kneeling before me with his arms around my waist as he holds me close to him.

I circle my arms around him, holding him, though not as tightly as I would like, the strength gone from my arms and hands.

"I'm so sorry I haven't come to see you." His voice is muffled in my nightgown as his head is buried close to my chest. "I've been ... afraid. Completely terrified, if you must know the truth." He wipes his nose with the back of his hand, which makes him look even more vulnerable than he already appears to be.

I look down at him, questioning. *Why would you be afraid?*

"I've been afraid because I don't want you to hate me for what I've done, or rather, what I haven't done. I've been afraid because I've loved you all these years, but I've been a mess, and I knew that the moment you saw me you would know immediately. I've never been able to hide from you. I knew you would know everything about me because you're the only person who ever has."

I try to tell him that I do know, but instead I nod, afraid the words will sound silly, or not come out at all. Only this time, the fear is not unfounded as my body rebelliously refuses to cooperate with my brain.

He holds me tight and I hold him back, the time going slowly yet quickly at the same time. I begin to feel very tired, and, as though he can sense it, Adam stands up and lifts me onto the bed so I can rest. He moves his chair close, grabbing my hand and holding it tight.

"I have to tell you this because it's been eating me up inside. You may hate me, but you have a right to know. I didn't tell you when I should have and then … the accident happened." I watch him take a deep breath, summoning every ounce of courage from within. "I never signed the papers ... the divorce papers. I hid them like a coward and I … never divorced you. I know that's what you wanted and it's what I thought I wanted. The papers had already been drawn up when I realized I didn't want it, and then you had the accident and it was too damned late. I'm so sorry."

I grasp his hand tightly, his words a muddled mess in my head, and I look at him with confusion. *What?*

"I'm sorry," he says over and over.

I hear him and the anger wells up in me, bubbling slowly.

I know that he has been here and I know that he hasn't left me, but I wonder why he would do such a thing. He betrayed me and the anger floods through me, hot and slow. I know that he can feel it and he shrinks away from me, afraid.

"I couldn't let you go, Brynn. I loved you too much." Adam's voice is barely a whisper, but when he speaks, I think of Nick. I wonder why he isn't here and then I slowly realize that it must be because Adam is here instead. I imagine that Nick has moved on with his life, probably married with a lot of children, and I know that he must have forgotten all about me by now.

Adam looks so sorry. I can't help but soften and feel sad for him and all that he has been through over the years.

I know that I've always loved him, our love fading into a softer, hazier version of what it was so many years ago. I feel the fuzziness of our love in my heart and I realize that, as much as I want to be mad at him, I can't be. The anger that began to well up simply refuses to consume me. What's done is done, and, as beautiful and intense as it was, Nick and I were never meant to be. I don't have it within me to be angry and I can't fault Adam. He's suffered enough.

He looks into my eyes for a long time and I realize that he knows what is in my heart, like only Adam ever could. For the first time I watch him relax, his shoulders letting go of the weight that is crushing him.

It doesn't matter anymore. We can let it all go now.

He kisses me sweetly on the cheek, his lips lingering the way I always liked them to. He clears his throat and when he finally speaks, his voice is thick with emotion. "I'm so happy you are finally awake. Everyone told me that it was impossible, but I *knew* you were still here. I could tell, I could sense you just as I always could … like I always did. I couldn't give up, ever. I always knew you were in there." Adam's tears flow freely and easily down his face as I put my hand on his cheek.

The blue in his eyes is beautiful as he stares down at me, and for a moment I feel like the fifteen-year-old girl who loved him with all her heart. He rescued me, saved me, and has been loyal to me my entire life. He has stayed by my side and protected me, especially when I told him about Thomas and how he had abused me. He loved me with all of him even when I was unlovable and broken.

I squeeze his hand and he places his palm against my cheek. For a moment we slip back in time to a moment when there was nothing between us but the love that saved me. I smile at him and he smiles back and I can see that boy, buried deep down inside, fighting hard to resurface. I know that he isn't gone completely. Instead he is right here, begging me to remember how he was once so strong and loving, always protecting me.

I look at Adam and open my mouth, speaking slowly and praying that the words will come out the way I intend them to. "I. Remember. You."

Adam looks at me, his mouth open wide, stunned by my clarity.

"I remember you," I repeat, and he leans over and kisses me gently, his lips familiar and soft. I lean into him as though I had been waiting for this moment my entire life.

"I remember you, too." Adam smiles wide and I see nothing but joy in his eyes, the sadness and pain dissipating in an instant. I realize that I feel the same happiness.

As he leans over to kiss me once more, his body jerks and he falls to the floor. Pain floods over his features, and an agonizing scream comes out of his mouth. I struggle to reach out to him, but there is nothing I can do, my body fighting desperately against me.

He reaches out his hands to me as though begging me to save him. I try to hold onto him to no avail. I watch his eyes open and close, his face distorted in pain. He has been rendered helpless and cannot get up or move. He tries to speak but only gurgles and cries come through his lips. His body twitches uncontrollably.

"Help! Help us," I scream out, my voice lost in his cries. It feels like hours, but I know it is only moments until there are the sound of feet running down the hall and the door crashes open. Kelly's voice cries out, "Adam!" as I hear her scream for someone to call 911.

I watch as Adam falls to the floor, writhing in pain with Kelly holding tightly to him, tears running down her cheeks. Adam looks up at me and our eyes lock just as the paramedics rush in and start their work on him.

"Brynn, Brynn ..." Adam cries, his voice reflecting his agony.

"Adam," I call out, my voice thin as paper in the flurry of activity in the room.

"I love you." Adam's voice echoes down the hall and I realize that my chance to tell him that I love him, too, is gone.

All at once, the room becomes quiet and I am left completely alone.

I realize that the emptiness I feel is more than just the stillness of the room. The emptiness is separation, and, with slow realization, I know that Adam must be gone too, because for the first time in many years I can't feel him at all.

CHAPTER THIRTY-ONE

The Visitor

September 23rd, 2016

As the gates opened and the ambulance flew out of The Harper House, the small silver sedan smoothly drove in. Nick drove slowly down the long, familiar driveway, his mouth dry as he remembered the last time he had been to The Harper House; how he and Adam had fought, his visit with Brynn, and the twin freckles on Eva's arm.

Nick felt his heart pounding with fear at the sight of the flashing lights and wondered if he should turn around and follow the ambulance out of the gates. He took a deep breath and parked the car, leaping out of the driver's side and onto the front steps of the home as quickly as he could. His long legs covered the steps two by two until he found himself at the front door, his palms sweaty.

He rang the doorbell, his chest heavy with anxiety until a kind-looking woman of about sixty with soft blonde hair and a tiny frame answered the door.

"Can I help you?" she asked, cracking the door only wide enough for him to see one quarter of her face, her light blue eyes squinting suspiciously.

"Hi. I'm an old friend of Brynn Michael's and I was hoping I could see her," Nick said trying not to appear too anxious.

"What is your name?" she asked, stiffly.

"Nicholas Easton." Nick shuffled his feet.

"Please wait," she closed the door and Nick stood there wondering what she was doing. The door reopened and Nick jumped.

A somber looking man in a dark suit stood nearly toe-to-toe with Nick. At six feet five, Nick wasn't accustomed to being looked in the eye by many and was taken aback.

"Who are you?" the man said, staring Nick down.

"I'm Nicholas Easton. I'm an old friend of Brynn's and I want to see her," Nick repeated, trying not to sound intimidated.

"Let me see your ID." The look on the man's face let him know that it wasn't a request but a demand.

Nick pulled out his wallet and fumbled for his license which he gave to the man who disappeared with it back into the house. The door reopened a few moments later. He handed the license back to Nick without saying a word. He opened the door wide enough for Nick to enter. "Wait here," he said, his voice absent of expression.

The older woman who had answered the door stood just beyond the foyer and motioned to him. "I'm sorry for the security, but we just can't be too careful," she apologized.

"That's okay," Nick said trying to sound more gracious than he felt.

"We've just sent Mr. Michaels to the hospital, so Brynn is distraught," the woman said as she wrung her hands, nervously. "Please ... don't upset her."

"I can't say," the woman said motioning for Nick to follow. They walked into an elevator and she pushed the button for the second floor. "How do you know Brynn?"

"I ... uh ... we were old friends," Nick said, careful not to give his feelings away."

"I don't know how long ago you knew her, but you do know that she's been in a coma for a very long time? She doesn't get around very well yet, though she's doing better than anyone ever thought." The woman's voice was full of pride and Nick could tell that she cared about Brynn a great deal.

"Yes, I knew that," Nick said smiling at the woman.

"Good," she said, as they got off the elevator and walked down a long hallway. Nick was impressed with the beauty and simplicity of the house. It was just as he always imagined it would be, a reflection of Brynn, gorgeous but classic. He could see her in everything as though she had designed it herself, and though he couldn't understand why, it gave him hope.

He wondered for the thousandth time whether she would remember him. It had been so long since he had last seen her and he worried that she might've possibly forgotten about him completely. He had never been able to forget how she'd made him feel. When he was with her he imagined that anything in the world was possible, and the thought that she could forget him made his heart ache.

The woman slowed down as they approached a set of large double doors. She hesitated and knocked gently. Nick wondered impatiently if anyone on the other side could even hear her.

The woman knocked again, a little louder.

The door opened and a young, pretty, blonde nurse in pink scrubs opened the door with a big smile. She had taken over for Anne, the night nurse, who had finally retired. Becca had been a great addition to The Harper House and fit in well with the rest of the staff.

"Is it okay if Brynn has company?" the woman asked the nurse.

The nurse gave her a long look. "She's pretty upset right now about Mr. Michaels getting rushed to the hospital. We just gave her a mild tranquilizer to try and calm her so I don't think that company is the best thing right now. She really needs to rest."

Nick's heart sank to his toes and he prayed she would see the desperation on his face. *I'm so close. Please!*

"If you think that's best," the woman said, turning around.

The nurse looked at Nick's face and hesitated. "Who are you?" she asked staring directly at Nick.

"I'm Nick, I'm an old friend of Brynn's. Please, if you'll let me see her, I've come so far … I'm sure she would be happy to see me." Nick hesitated, shifting from one foot to the other anxiously.

The nurse looked at him for a long, intense moment with

scrutiny well beyond her years. She turned around and listened as though trying to decide. Nick held his breath until she finally opened the door and motioned for Nick to move closer. "You can come in, but only for a little while. If you upset her in any way, you'll need to leave immediately." The young woman stared at him evenly, not in the least bit intimidated by his height even though Nick knew he could pick her up and move her out of his way without much effort.

Nick nodded obediently, letting his breath out slowly.

"Whatever you say." Nick was grateful for the opportunity as he walked slowly into the room, nodding at the older woman on his way. She smiled encouragingly and closed the door behind him. As he walked toward the figure that lie still on the bed, he tried to prepare himself. He had dreamt of this day for almost two decades. Now, he was finally going to see the woman who had stolen his heart so many years before.

Brynn lie still, except for her breath, which came slow and even. Nick tried to mask his surprise as he took in her face, still scarred, yet beautiful. He could see that the years had stolen her youthful glow, but she had been transformed into a softer version of the woman he had once known. He reached out his hand, aching to touch her, but pulled back at the last moment. He didn't want to frighten her as he sat down carefully in the chair next to the bed and waited for her to wake up.

He fought the urge to awaken her and chuckled at himself, running his hands through his chestnut hair that had grayed over the years. He thought about when his daughter was a baby and he would watch her sleep, wanting to wake her up just so he could hear her giggle. He felt like that again as he watched Brynn sleep. His stomach churned as he wondered if she would know him if she were to open her eyes.

He thought about the last time they had been together. The details had grown fuzzy over the years, but he never forgot how his heart stopped when she looked at him with her large, dark eyes. Nobody in his life had ever looked at him like that, as though he was the only person in the world, and he longed to see her eyes once again. He stared at her intently, unable to believe that he was finally sitting in the same room with her. She stirred slightly and Nick felt his heart quicken in his chest. He wanted her to wake up but he had to admit that he was terrified. *What if I didn't mean as much to her as she meant to me? What if she doesn't remember me?* He had asked himself the same questions over and over, afraid that the connection he felt to her had only been in his own mind. He had never been a romantic man, but when the question arose about soul mates, Brynn's name always came to mind. Even though he had loved, nothing had ever come close to what he felt for her.

He cautiously reached his hand out once more and this time, didn't pull back. He gently traced her jawline with his thumb, careful not to wake her. He could feel the slight bumpiness of the scars and winced at the thought of how much pain she must have experienced. He wondered if she'd suffered, and his heart ached at the thought of it. It was the first time in many years he had been this close to her and even the smell of her skin intoxicated him. He marveled that he had been able to stay away so long. He cleared his throat without thinking, and Brynn jumped.

Nick held his breath, waiting for her to fall back to sleep, praying inside that she would. Instead, she turned her head toward him and Nick's heart fluttered as he watched her slowly open her eyes. She stared at him for a long moment and Nick was frozen, unable to breathe.

After what felt like an eternity, she began to blink rapidly as though trying to clear away a bad memory. He watched as her eyelids fluttered slowly, trying to bring him into focus. Suddenly, her eyes grew wide, and after what felt like an eternity, she opened her mouth to speak.

"You … how?" Brynn said as she struggled to sit up but finally fell back onto the pillows, groggy from the sedative they had given her.

"Y-Y-Yes," Nick said, letting go of all his breath at once, relieved that she recognized him. "I'm finally here."

"You … forgot?" Brynn said, her breathing labored and slow.

"No, never. I could never forget you," Nick said, his voice full of emotion.

Brynn laid her head on the pillow and closed her eyes. "Good," she said, her voice barely audible. "Good."

Nick leaned back in the chair and tried to control the tears that streamed down his face, afraid that his sobs would awaken her. He had been terrified that she wouldn't know him, but she knew exactly who he was.

"I'm so sorry I never came for you sooner. Please forgive me," Nick cried out, his heart emptying itself of all the guilt and pain he had wrestled with for so many years. Brynn's recognition of him healed him almost immediately.

"Don't ... cry." Brynn struggled as she whispered, slowly falling back to sleep. "Don't cry, Nick. Eva ... is ... o-o-okay."

CHAPTER THIRTY-TWO

Innocent

September 20th, 2016

"I'm telling you for the thousandth time, I didn't kill anyone!" There was a large vein popping out of Connor's forehead as he yelled angrily at the lawyer sitting across the table from him in the stark room. This lawyer was new and replaced the pathetic little man who looked like he was going to piss his pants every time Connor looked at him. This lawyer was much younger and looked expensive with his rich suits, manicured nails, and leather briefcase, but no matter how many times Connor asked who had hired him, he refused to tell. Connor knew that someone was looking out for him, but he didn't know anyone other than Eva with that kind of money, and he doubted that Eva would pay for someone to get him out of jail. "I swear, man. I didn't do anything so there is nothing for you to prove. I swear. I wouldn't have killed anyone."

The lawyer sat calmly, not at all affected by his client's outburst. According to them, they were all innocent, none of them committing the heinous crimes they were accused of. He knew when he looked in to the case that Connor Martin wouldn't be any different. The story read like a classic *little rich girl meets bad boy*, and before the lawyer even got started, he was already bored with the case.

The lawyer looked at him evenly.

"Listen, Mr. Martin, you're in here because they found you at the scene, covered in blood, with the murder weapon inches from your hands. Despite the fact that your fingerprints aren't on the weapon, there's been enough to hold you. If you add to that your violation of probation, the drugs they found in your system and the RAP sheet the police have on you that's a mile long, I wouldn't be very optimistic if I were you. If you don't tell me everything about that night, then I'm going to have a very difficult time proving your innocence. Now, somebody wants you to get out of here because they've paid me very handsomely, but I can't work with you if you don't at least tell me what happened and why Nora Symon is dead."

"But I didn't do anything, dammit. That's what I'm trying to tell you. We did get into a fight but I left and went to a bar and got shit-faced. The next thing I know, I woke up lying in a pool of blood in her apartment. I swear, I wouldn't have hurt her. Dammit, I ... l-l-loved her." Connor put his head in his hands and shook it back and forth in disbelief. *How could this have happened to Nora? How did I get myself into this mess?*

"You admit that you were in a relationship with Miss Symon, then, even though you were married to Eva Michaels under an assumed name?" the lawyer asked, leaning forward, repositioning the recorder in front of Connor.

"Yes ... I was." Connor's face turned red and he looked away from the lawyer, embarrassed.

"Did you love Eva Michaels?"

"Yes ... God help me... I did. She was ... kind ... to me." Connor admitted, his voice barely audible.

"Who were you involved with first?" The lawyer almost sounded bored as he asked the obligatory question.

"Nora. I was involved with Nora first. ... I've known her for a long time." Connor paused, as though there was more, but closed his mouth before he said anything else. "I met her in high school. When we met, I remember she said 'Finally' and we've been together ever since. She was a good person, she was just ... a little messed up. I loved her, man. I wouldn't have hurt her. We were going to be together forever, but then ..."

"'But then …'" the lawyer repeated as he leaned forward, his dark eyes suddenly glittering with interest.

"N-n-n-nothing," Connor stuttered, hesitant.

"It doesn't make sense why you would change your name, then date and marry Eva Michaels within a few short months while you were involved with Nora Symon the entire time. Then suddenly, Nora Symon ends up dead and you're lying in her apartment in a pool of blood with the murder weapon right next to you." The lawyer stared at Connor trying to read his face.

"I know! I know what this looks like. I know that it doesn't look good for me … and Nora and I did intend to … to … hurt Eva, but only in the beginning. Only to get back at Adam Michaels for how he hurt my mother, but then I couldn't do it. I didn't want to hurt her. She was so nice to me and cared about me and she was pregnant with my baby, and I just couldn't do it. I couldn't hurt her even if it was for the money. I swear."

"Your mother was Jessie Martin?" The lawyer flipped through some pages of notes and then fixed his eyes on Connor.

"My mother *is* Jessie Martin," Connor said, correcting him.

"According to these notes from your former lawyer, your mother took her own life a week ago," the lawyer said, his brows furrowed.

"What? No. No! That can't be true!" Connor buried his head in his hands, then ran his fingers through his hair, tugging at it in frustration, not wanting to believe it. "No! You're lying! You're fucking lying!"

"Oh … I would've thought your other lawyer would've told you. I'm sorry," the lawyer said, not sounding a bit apologetic.

"Oh, God no … no … how … why?" Connor already knew the answer. He had been rescuing her for years, and since he hadn't seen or talked to her for weeks, she had likely become unstable. Connor knew that he had himself to blame for her death and he suddenly felt nauseous.

The lawyer looked at him with a mixture of intrigue and disgust.

"I'm sorry about your loss, but I want to make sure that I'm clear with what we're looking at here. What you're saying then is that you tricked and impregnated Eva Michaels, even though you initially planned only to hurt her. Then you took pity on her and changed your mind, so you decided to kill your lover instead?"

Connor's face turned white, his hazel eyes bright red as his bottom lip trembled. Snot ran from his nose and he continually wiped it with his sleeve. After a long while he spoke, his voice broken and quiet, muted by the tears that ran down his face. "Yes ... I suppose that's what it looks like, but I swear to you, I didn't kill anyone! I didn't mean to care for Eva or get her pregnant, but she loved me and she thought I was a good person. Technically, I didn't do anything wrong because I decided not to hurt her. I loved her. I mean ... nobody has ever thought that I was a good person before."

The lawyer looked at Connor, trying hard to suppress his disgust for his client. "I'm going to do the best I can to figure out how to represent you, but nothing short of a miracle is going to get you out of here."

Connor closed his eyes and bowed his head quietly, Jessie, Nora and Eva's faces floating in the darkness of his mind, taunting him angrily. They all hated him and he deserved it for the despicable things he had done. He was a disgusting person. He saw himself reflected in the eyes of his new lawyer, repulsive and dirty, a man without character or worth, and he couldn't help but agree. He knew that nothing in his life mattered anymore as he silently surrendered himself to his fate.

CHAPTER THIRTY-THREE

The Truth

September 23rd, 2016

The hours passed like days and Eva was happier than she wanted to admit when she saw Jack walking down the hallway of the hospital corridor toward her. Relief seemed to flood over her and she was surprised that he had that effect on her after such a short time. Somehow, he made her feel safer in a world that she had never realized was so dangerous. That is until she discovered Connor Martin.

As they rode in the ambulance with Adam, the first person that Eva thought to call was Jack.

Eva was devastated as she held his hand and begged him not to leave her yet. After he was admitted, she waited patiently for Jack.

As Jack walked toward her she watched as his lean muscular body commanded the hallway. *Why couldn't I fall for a man like him and not someone like Connor Martin?* She felt guilty as the question popped into her mind, beyond her control. It felt inappropriate after all she had been through, and as Adam lie in a hospital bed, dying.

As Jack walked down the hallway of the ICU, Kelly came into the hall and motioned for them to follow her into Adam's room. The usual routine had already been done, and Adam was resting quietly, an IV firmly placed in his arm with oxygen lines and tubes weaving around his body. They were giving him medication for the pain and he was finally sleeping restfully.

Jack approached Eva and she hugged him, squeezing him harder than it looked like she could. He held onto her, enjoying their closeness and breathing in her sweet scent that he found so intoxicating. He took her in, silently assessing her, then quietly placed his hand on Eva's back and guided her into the room, unsure of what to expect. He tried to hide how nervous hospitals made him. After the death of his grandfather, he had made it a point to avoid them as much as possible. Eva looked at him and attempted a small smile as though to let him know she was okay. Concern was etched all over his handsome face and he stayed as close to her as he could, one hand remaining protectively on her back.

A young-looking, dark-haired nurse came in to check on Adam and asked impatiently if they had any questions. Eva wanted to ask her how long it would be and whether he would ever go home again, but she couldn't bring herself to say the words. Eva watched as the nurse took his vitals, quickly and efficiently, her dark eyes intent on her work. Eva thought briefly that the girl would be pretty if she smiled, but as she watched her work she knew there was no chance of that happening. The nurse quickly left the room and Eva followed her out, motioning for Jack to stay behind.

"I don't know … I want to help if I can. My blood type is AB … but I'm pregnant. If I'm allowed, if you need blood for him, I can give it. I don't know if you can do something to help him. A transplant … surgery, something, but I can at least do that." Eva stammered as the nurse busily typed on the keyboard of a small computer.

"Oh, thank you, but we don't advise that pregnant women give blood," the nurse said abruptly, without looking up. "Are you his adopted daughter or step-daughter?"

Eva looked at her, confused. "I'm neither," she said, her voice wavering. "I'm his biological daughter. Why would you ask me that question?"

"Oh!" The nurse stopped typing and looked up at her, her eyes large. "I'm sorry. That was completely inappropriate and I wasn't thinking. I shouldn't have asked you that. It's none of my business."

"No! I mean ... why would you ask a question like that? Why wouldn't you think that I'm his biological daughter?" Eva's voice was low but demanding.

"It's just that ... you can't be his biological daughter," the nurse said quickly.

"Of course I am! Who are you to tell me that he's not my father? How dare you even say something like that to me?" Eva was angry, her voice elevating slightly with each word. Jack heard Eva's voice and rushed into the hallway looking for her. When he found her he saw that all the color had drained completely from her face.

"It's just ... y-y-your blood type is AB, that's all." The nurse stammered, her face turning bright red as she looked from Eva to Jack and then back to Eva. "Please don't tell anyone I asked you that question or I could get fired. I'm already on thin ice around here. God, I'm so sorry. I can't keep my big mouth shut!"

Jack spoke up, his voice deep. "What does an AB blood type have to do with anything? What are you telling us?"

"It's just ... I should'nt even tell you this because I've already said entirely too much, but with his blood type ... it's scientifically impossible for Mr. Michaels to be your biological father. I'm so sorry."

Eva looked at Jack, and in an instant she realized that everything she thought she had ever known about her life had completely changed.

CHAPTER THIRTY-FOUR

Answers

September 23rd, 2016

The news the nurse had given them about Eva's blood type was devastating, and Eva knew she had to get to Brynn to find out what was going on. Her entire life had been spent knowing that Adam had been her father, but with her blood type it just wasn't possible.

Jack had held onto Eva in case she might collapse, but she stood strong, holding herself up. He wondered how much more she could possibly take. *First Chris, then Adam, and now this. How is she still standing?*

Jack watched her carefully, but Eva showed no sign of breaking down. She stayed strong, not mentioning the conversation with the nurse, even to Kelly. Eva wanted to talk with Brynn first. They sat silently in Adam's room watching him carefully, each wrapped up tightly in their own thoughts. After a few hours, the doctor came in and let them know that if they could stabilize him they would also treat his pain. There was nothing more they could do other than make him comfortable and call hospice to go to The Harper House.

Kelly sent Eva home, volunteering to stay at the hospital with Adam for as long as he was there. She was used to long nights.

"I don't want Adam to be alone and you need to take care of yourself," she said, hugging Eva tight. "Please, go. I'll let you know when he'll be coming home. It could be days until they've stabilized him, and I don't want you here in the hospital every day. It'll wear you out and it could hurt the baby."

Eva reluctantly agreed as she prepared herself to let Brynn know what was happening. She had a lot to talk to Brynn about and tried desperately to figure out how to do it. She looked at Kelly, her eyes large and fearful. "It's going to be okay," Kelly said, looking her in the eyes. Eva nodded, biting her lip to stop the tears from flowing.

"Please ... will you drive me home?" Eva asked as she grabbed Jack's arm gently, her eyes large and pleading.

"Of course, Eva," Jack said, smiling at her gently. Jack winced as he realized that Adam's coloring had gone from bad to worse, and he guessed that it might not be much longer. "Anything you need."

As they got closer to The Harper House, Jack could feel Eva tense up in the seat next to his. He reached for her hand and held it tight.

"What do you need me to do?" he asked, worried he would upset her.

Eva was quiet, the words caught in her throat. She opened her mouth to speak, but then closed it again, afraid to say the words out loud. Jack pulled over to the side of the road, the moonlight streaming in through the windows, making Eva even more beautiful.

"Please, tell me what I can do to help you," Jack implored, holding her hands together tightly in his. "I'm here for you Eva. I'm here to help you with whatever you need."

Jack marveled at his concern for her, and even as the words came out of his mouth, he felt as though they were coming from a complete stranger. He had never said anything like that to anyone in his entire life, or felt comfortable holding anyone's hands in his before. Something about Eva was changing him, and for the first time he felt his heart opening up to someone else. It was hard for him to admit that he hadn't stopped thinking about her and that his heart flipped when he was near her. She needed him and she brought out something in him that he never knew existed. He liked it.

Eva tried to speak again, Jack's eyes urging her on. "I-I-I'm just afraid, Jack. I don't want to be the one to tell my mom that he's going to die. I don't want to watch him die, and from the way things look, it won't be too much longer now. I don't want him to know that he's not my father. I thought I would ask my mom all of these questions about who my father really is, but now I don't think I can. I can't stand for him to die thinking that I'm not his little girl! I just can't!"

Eva was distraught, her mind racing back to her childhood and how Adam had been all she had. He had often held her close, reading to her, talking to her, and just happy to be near her. Eva knew that her childhood hadn't been perfect, but he had loved her, and every one of her memories was wrapped up in him. She knew with certainty that she couldn't bear to let him go knowing that she didn't belong to him.

As they pulled up to The Harper House, Eva threw her door open and burst out of it angrily.

"How could she do this to me? How?" she yelled, her voice rising, as she paced the length of the car.

Jack jumped out and kept pace with her. He was careful not to get in her way, to give her the space she needed to express her rage. He had never seen this side of her and, while it alarmed him, he understood it more than anything else. He had been full of rage toward his father for many years, and he recognized the same in her.

"My entire life, I grew up with this understanding that I was alone. Dad did the best he could to be a father to me, but he often failed, so I had nobody. Kelly loved me and so did Aunt Jane, but it wasn't the same, Jack! It wasn't the same at all, so I gave into my loneliness and embraced it, allowing it to become a part of who I was, until I met Chris. I gave him my heart because it was desperate and he knew that. He preyed on my loneliness and knew that I was vulnerable. All of this makes me feel stupid and angry and small! If my dad isn't truly my father, then who is? Why didn't he want me? Did he even know about me? Did she ever tell him about me?"

Jack let her rant, careful to listen and not respond. He hadn't known that Eva wasn't Adam's daughter, but he was sure that his father or grandfather had to have known. *Why wouldn't he have told me? Why would he have buried that information?* Jack knew the answer to his questions before he asked them because he knew that the number one priority was always to protect the family and this information could be devastating. This information was dangerous to both the family and their fortune.

Eva paced and yelled for an hour until her voice became hoarse. She knew there was nothing more she could do about any of it other than surrender to the inevitable. Jack watched as she began to slow down, exhausted by her outburst and tired of listening to the sound of her own voice. She leaned against the car, silent.

Jack leaned next to her, close enough to her that he could feel her body trembling from the cold as he pulled her closer to him.

Eva looked up at him, her embarrassment evident even in the moonlight. "I'm so sorry," she said, her expression quickly changing from angry to mortified. "I shouldn't have gone on like that in front of you. You don't even know me that well and you've seen me in every horrible situation you possibly could. I'm so sorry that you've had to experience all of this with me."

Jack looked down at her, a funny expression on his face. He had never understood the devotion his grandfather had to the family, though he always knew that his own father's interest was strictly monetary. Jack suddenly realized that his grandfather had *loved* the family, and he realized that taking care of Eva gave him a sense of purpose and pride that he never experienced before. In that brief moment, he understood the devotion that his grandfather had for Eva's great-grandfather, John Palmer, because he felt the same way about Eva.

Jack pulled her closer until she was in his arms. He knew she could feel his heartbeat because he could hear it beating wildly in his ears. He was pleasantly surprised when she didn't fight against him, and even happier when he felt her sink into his arms and lean against him with all of her.

"Don't be sorry, little one," Jack said stroking her long, dark hair. It was something he had been aching to do since the very moment he first met her. "I meant it when I said that I would be here for you. I'm not going anywhere. If you need anything, no matter when, I'll be here for you."

They held each other for a long time, both of them enjoying the stillness of the moment and neither of them ever remembering a time they had held anyone else so close. Eva closed her eyes and for the first time, her mind was blank, and she reveled in it for as long as she could. The anxiety rushed out her until she was empty of it all. Jack gave her a sense of calm that she desperately needed, and Eva knew the baby must somehow appreciate it too.

"Should we get going?" Jack asked, pulling away from her ever so slightly.

"Kiss me, Jack," Eva said, surprising herself as the words came tumbling out.

Jack looked at her cautiously.

"I-I-I don't know that is a good idea. I don't think that I should, Eva. You've been through so much." Jack looked at Eva, wanting to believe that he could kiss her, but not sure if he should.

"Please, kiss me. I've never wanted anything more than this right now." Eva looked up at him longingly, pulling him to her.

"Eva, you're confused. You don't know what you want right now. You've been through so much and I don't … don't … want to take … advantage of you." Jack ran his thumb down Eva's cheek and loved the silkiness of it. It took everything inside of him to hold himself back, but he didn't trust himself to kiss her when she was under so much duress.

"Jack, you are the one person that I know is right in my life right now. Everything else is crazy and wrong, but the only thing that I *do* know is you're here with me for a reason." Eva's blue eyes were large and glistening and Jack fought to stop himself from staring into them. He stepped back, distancing himself from her intentionally.

"Eva … I want to kiss you. Believe me, I want nothing more right now than to …" he paused, searching for the right words. "… to kiss you for hours. But I need to know that you want this for the right reasons. I need to know that this won't complicate things for you. You're going through too much, and I think you need some … time."

Eva pulled away from him, the silence falling like a thick,

dense fog between them. She felt herself falling into a cloud, and she suddenly wanted to cry. She knew that Jack was right and she kicked herself mentally for throwing herself at him.

When she finally spoke, her voice was so low that Jack had to lean in to hear her. "You're right. I ... I have a lot to deal with right now. I have a lot to face. I need to talk to my mom, and I need to see Chris and find out why he would do this to me. And I have to say 'good-bye' to my dad." Eva sobbed at the thought of saying good-bye to the only dad she had ever known, the thought of it tearing her apart from the inside.

"Yes." Jack said, relieved that she finally understood. "But I will be here for you. I'm not going anywhere. I don't think that seeing Chris is a good idea, Eva, but if you need to, then I'm not going to let you do it alone."

Eva smiled at him through the tears that refused to fall.

"I promise you, Jack Palmer, that when all of this is said and done, you will kiss me. I just hope you'll still want to," Eva said, her voice hopeful.

Jack smiled at her, pulling her close once again and happy to feel her body relax in his arms. "Believe me, Beautiful. I'll still want to."

From that moment on, Jack knew there would never be another woman for him. He held her for as long as he could until he was worried she would be too cold. Finally, he grabbed Eva's hand and led her to the warmth of The Harper House. Just as she was about to walk in the door, Eva looked up and gave him the brightest smile he had ever seen. For the briefest moment, he knew she was no longer thinking about telling Brynn that Adam was about to die.

CHAPTER THIRTY-FIVE

Confessions

September 23rd, 2016

Nick watched Brynn as she slept peacefully. He hadn't been sure what to expect, but just being in the same room with her, being able to touch her again, was enough for him. He didn't even mind that her beautiful, brown eyes were hazy with the sedatives she had been given to keep her calm. He was thankful for the opportunity to sit quietly and study her for a while.

Her beauty remained, the scars on her face visible, but many of them faded over the years. There were still long scars and burns on her arms, but what alarmed him most was the frailness of her body. She had always been slim, but now Nick felt that if he touched her the wrong way he would snap her in half. He cringed at the thought of hurting her and he stroked the back of her hand lightly with his index finger.

"If only I could tell you everything I've done to come back here to you," Nick whispered, staring at her face for any sign that she might be listening. "I divorced Melanie because after I got home, she had become quite unstable, which I know you experienced some of. I can't tell you how much it broke my heart to have her lash out at you the way she did, but it was one of the reasons I was trying to get away from her. After we divorced I lost track of her. Even though I tried to convince her to get help, she refused. She was a lost soul who had sunk into alcoholism and addiction. I had heard rumors that she had a child and a string of broken relationships after we divorced, but I never heard from her again. She made my life hell and if it hadn't been for her, I never would've left you to begin with. I never should've left you, Brynn. Never.

"Over the years, I tried to stay away from you, Brynn, but I just couldn't. I've come back here nearly every year with the hope that I might be able to see you, but I cowered, knowing that Adam was here. I know that I shouldn't have. I know that you wanted to be with me and that I shouldn't have let him stand in my way, but I was weak and afraid. I regret that I didn't try and that I missed every chance that I ever had to be here for you. I hated looking at myself in the mirror all those years, knowing that I was living without you and wondering if you had woken up yet. Every morning I woke up and thought of you immediately until I finally realized that I would never be able to live with myself if I didn't come back here for you. Now ... I just hope that it's not too late."

Nick placed his hand gently on her face and continued confessing, realizing that he was doing it more for himself than he was for her. He had ached to talk to her for so long that he couldn't stop himself once he started.

"I don't know why I did it, maybe I was lonely and trying to move on, but I got married to a woman named Fiona. We have a little girl. Her name is Mandy. I didn't love Fiona, though I swear, I did try. She's a good woman, really, and she was good to me even though she knew that I couldn't love her the way I loved you. She knew that I came back here every fall. She never knew exactly why. I told her one night when I was drunk and stupid that I came here hoping that you had woken up, but the next year she let me come as though I had never told her. When I finally found the nerve to come in and see you, Fiona called me to come home because Mandy had been in a car accident with the babysitter, and nearly died. I ran out of here so fast, but I don't think Fiona ever forgave me for not being there. Eventually, she divorced me. She deserved better and should've done it years before, but for some crazy reason, she truly loved me. I didn't deserve her. I was a terrible husband, Brynn."

Nick paused to see if there were any signs that Brynn could hear him, but she remained still, her breath even.

"I fought for years to find the courage to walk back up to those steps again. I don't know what I was afraid of. I don't know if it was of you, or Adam, or ... I don't know. And now that I'm here I don't know what I'm supposed to do next."

Nick could feel the softness of her cheek against his hand, and he closed his eyes, trying to think of what he should do next. He had never been able to get the twin freckle on the girl, the same one he had on his own wrist, out of his mind. He knew in his heart that she had to be his, but Nick wasn't sure that he was ready to claim her yet. Even though he had thought about it for ten years, he wasn't sure he knew how.

Nick stroked her cheek gently. He still couldn't believe that he could have such a strong connection with this woman after having spent such a short time with her, but even looking at her now, lying there so peacefully, he knew the connection remained. If he tried to explain it to anyone, he knew that it wouldn't make sense, but he was sure that he couldn't walk away from her again. Looking back, his life had seemed so short, but it felt as though it had taken him so long to get to this point, to get back to her.

"God, Brynn, I missed out on having this entire life with you and I feel as though I've been robbed of having you with me my entire life. But I'm here now, and I'm not going anywhere. I 'm never leaving you again. Ever. I swear."

Nick laid his head down on her bed, exhausted. He knew that he would have to tell her everything all over again once she had awakened. He knew that he might have to tell her many more times. But he was prepared. He had sold his home and moved his life, just to be near her. Nick closed his eyes as he held Brynn's still hand. He fell asleep in an instant, drained.

Nick hadn't heard the door open, nor did he see the small woman standing in the shadows behind him. He didn't know that she had been listening to him the entire time he laid his soul bare.

And he didn't see the angry tears coursing down her cheeks as she realized that he was the father she'd yearned for her entire life.

CHAPTER THIRTY-SIX

Bitter

April, Twenty-Five Years Earlier

The little blonde girl with the long lashes and bright green eyes sat on the steps of the beat up front porch, clutching Sadie, her favorite doll. She did her best to fight back the tears as she remembered how Momma had yelled at her to get out of the house as soon as the man had gotten there. Momma had started kissing him as though she forgot that the girl was there, and when Momma realized she was staring at them, she screamed angrily. "You stupid girl, what are you doing? Get out of here!" The girl knew that it shouldn't hurt her feelings because Momma always said she was sorry after she was mean, but it still made her heart hurt anyway.

The girl sat on the porch with Sadie for what felt like hours until the man left. The sun was beginning to go down and she shivered as the air started to get a little colder. She hoped that she would be allowed to go inside soon. She thought about the man and wanted him to leave. She had only seen him a couple of times, but she knew that he wouldn't be around forever. They never were. She didn't even bother to remember their names anymore until they had been to their house at least five times. Her rule was always five. One.

Two. Three. Four. Five. The man inside was only on three.

Finally, she heard the door to the house open, and the man walked out on the porch and lit a cigarette. His clothes were wrinkled and his face was slick with sweat, and she thought that he wasn't handsome at all. He paused briefly, taking a deep drag of his cigarette, not realizing that she was on the top step watching him. He startled as he looked down and saw her, but didn't say a word as he continued to stare at her and smoke. After a few moments, he jogged down the stairs and walked away without saying a word. That was fine with her. She didn't mind. She didn't like it when they talked to her. Sometimes they tried to be nice, bringing her candy or toys as a bribe, and sometimes they were mean. There were a few of them that made her feel funny and afraid inside, especially when they wanted to hold her too close or too tight, or tried to kiss her on the cheek with stinky breath. But Nora knew that no matter what they did, or who they were, they never stayed.

She sat on the porch for a while after the man left, trying to remember all the ones who had been through that door. There had been the tall one with the brown hair, the bald one with the glasses, the plump one who smelled like cotton candy, the ugly one who smelled like cigarettes and stared at her in a way that made her want to crawl out of her skin. There had been the cute one who Momma said was as dumb as a box of rocks, and then there had been the one with the muscles who had tried to get Momma to stop drinking and smoking. Only two of them came around for as long as a couple of months. Most of them didn't last more than a few weeks. The girl hadn't cared much about any of them. She was always happiest when they were gone and it was just her and Momma, because Momma seemed to be happier when the men didn't come and go.

"Nora!!" Nora could hear Momma's voice through the tattered screen door. "Nora, get in here right now!"

Nora could tell from the thickness and high tone of Momma's voice that Momma had already been drinking a lot. It was earlier than usual, but this time of the day always came no matter what time it was. Nora was accustomed to the tone in Momma's voice that always signaled the change in her mood after she'd been drinking.

Nora walked slowly up the stairs and into the front hallway, her stomach tight. She dreaded talking to Momma at this time of the day and hoped that Momma might get sleepy soon and fall asleep like she often did.

"Nora!" Momma was nearly screeching. "Where are you, girl?"

"I'm here, Momma. I'm here," Nora said, breathlessly as she ran up the stairs and into Momma's bedroom.

"Aren't you a little old for that stupid doll?" Momma eyed Sadie dangerously.

Nora gripped Sadie and held her close to her chest. "Y-Y-Y-You gave her to me when I was little. I always have here with me."

"I s'pose I did," Momma said, lighting a cigarette and blowing the smoke in Nora's face. "You need to put that ratty thing away and not carry it around with you. You're too old to carry around a doll like a baby."

"Yes, Momma," Nora said, putting her head down. "I'll keep Sadie in my room."

"Good girl," Momma said opening her pill bottle and taking out two pills. She placed them carefully on her tongue and then took a big swig of the clear liquid in her glass. Nora knew enough to know that she wasn't drinking water and that the pills would make Momma even more drunk and sleepy.

"So ... tell me, little Nugget, what did you think of my new friend?" Momma asked Nora, taking another big sip of her drink and smiling at her expectantly.

"Um ... he was ... nice. He seemed like he would be ... okay," Nora said, careful with her words. She didn't want to make Momma angry.

"Okay?" Momma said, her voice taking a dangerous edge. "Just okay?"

"I mean, I-I-I didn't really talk to him," Nora said slowly, her voice faltering.

"Oh, well, you should, Nugget. I have a good feeling about this one. The rest have been ... well, you know, but this one ... there's something special about him. I can tell." Momma's eyes got a dreamy look in them as she smiled a little crooked smile.

"Oh ... that's ... good," Nora said, unsure of what to say She didn't like to talk to Momma about the men because she never knew what she should say and was always afraid to say the wrong thing. The edge in Momma's voice told Nora to tread lightly.

"Just good? That's all you have to say? Do you know how long I've been alone and how hard it is for me to take care of you? You know that I've been trying to find you a daddy, but you're too selfish to pay attention to how much I do for you and all you have to say is 'that's good?'" Nora cringed as Momma's voice grew thin and strained. Nora hated when Momma became this angry because it usually ended up with a few smacks to the face or a hard whack to the back of the head that made it hard for Nora to remember that Momma loved her.

"No, Momma. I mean ... I thought he was nice. I did! I swear!" Nora tried to make her voice sound happy because she knew that Momma would like that.

Momma smiled. "Good girl, Nugget. Thank you."

Momma's eyes glazed over even more than usual as she talked and Nora watched with dread as Momma talked about her new love with words that didn't make sense to Nora's eight-year-old brain. "This one may be the one." Nora had heard her say that before.

"The one for what?" Nora asked, her voice low, almost hoping that Momma wouldn't hear her.

"The one who will be your new daddy," Momma said yawning, her eyes growing heavy. "Come closer to me, Nugget."

Nora stepped closer to Momma the way she would get close to a snake. She thought Momma was happy enough not hit her, but Nora could never be too sure.

"Oh, stop being such a baby!" Momma said, grabbing Nora and pulling her close. "Why do you make that face? You act like I'm going to hurt you or something."

Nora tried to smile.

"Listen, Nugget ... You know that I love you, but taking care of you on my own is so damned difficult. You don't understand it because all you have to do is wake up and expect that everything is going to be done for you. It's hard for me and I'm alone. Your daddy didn't want anything to do with me ... or you. And you're going to have to do so much better than I did!"

Nora nodded, obediently.

"I'm trying to find a daddy for you. I'm trying to find someone to take care of us ... and take care of you. And when you're old enough, you'll need to find someone to take care of you, too. Someone who has money, someone you can make do what you want him to. Do you understand? You're going to need help because you'll never be able to get by on your own."

"I can take care of myself, Momma," Nora whispered, hoping Momma wouldn't hear her.

Momma grabbed her arm so tight that it hurt.

"Nora, you're such a stupid little girl! You would *be* nothing without me and you would *have* nothing without me. Your father didn't want you and he didn't want me, and now all you have is me." Momma pulled her so close that their noses were almost touching. "If you're lucky ... very lucky, you'll find a man with a lot of money. And then if you're smart, very smart, you'll take his money and get rid of him. But only if you get smarter and don't end up being the stupid little girl that you are right now."

Nora pulled her arm away and rubbed it trying to stop the pain. She wasn't surprised to see that a bruise was already starting to form. Nora knew that it usually didn't take very long.

Nora looked at the peeling paint on the walls and the smelly, worn-out second-hand furniture and promised herself that she would never be like her Momma. She knew that she would need money in order to escape this life, and decided that she would do everything in her power to make sure that she had it so she would never need anyone to take care of again.

CHAPTER THIRTY-SEVEN

Home Sweet Home

October 1st, 2016

Adam lie restlessly against the pillows of his hospital bed, blankly staring out of the window. The eight days in the hospital had been brutal. He'd been poked and prodded with needles, put through test after test, but everything came back with the same result.

There was nothing more that could be done and he knew it.

Adam had felt his body was dying for a long time. It was close to being over and the excruciating pain told him this every day.

"Please. I want to go home now," Adam said, grasping Kelly's hand tightly. "They've done what they can and you and I both know that there's nothing else that anyone can do here."

Kelly had been there, only leaving to go back to The Harper House to change her clothes. She refused to let Eva stay there overnight, protecting her from the pain of watching her father die. Instead, she carried the pain herself, unable to choose anything else.

Kelly looked at the nurse who had been checking his vitals.

"Will you please let the doctor know that we've decided to go home?" Kelly said, her voice low.

The nurse nodded and smiled a comforting smile. She had worked on the floor for quite some time and knew that these decisions were never easy.

Kelly held onto Adam's fingers tightly, fighting back the tears that threatened to erupt. She knew that she had to be strong and that she couldn't let him see that his end would also be her undoing. She had been hiding her love for him for so long, she didn't know what she would do without it.

The doctor had been in earlier and given Adam the news that his counts were poor. It was only a matter of time. This was something that Adam thought he had been prepared to hear, but the words still knocked the wind out of him. He thought he would be relieved, but when faced with the end, he was filled with an uncontrollable dread and a futile desire to live. He tried to force those feelings down as much as he could, but they were beginning to overcome him. He felt as though he might lose control if he stayed in the hospital any longer. Dying in such a stale and stagnant place horrified him.

Adam wanted to be at home for the end, with Brynn and in the comfort of the home she had given him for the past twenty years, even if she hadn't done it consciously.

Kelly looked down at Adam, his skin sallow and his cheeks beginning to sink in. She thought about how handsome he had been and how much she had loved looking at him, especially when he didn't know that she was watching. She had made it a habit to stare at him out of the corner of her eye, and her stomach dropped at the prospect of losing him completely.

"I'll take you home," Kelly said, kissing his hand softly.

Adam looked at her, tears glistening in his blue eyes.

"I'm sorry for what I've done to you, Kel. I meant to be a much better man than the one I ended up as. I thought ..." Adam's voice cracked, betraying his emotions. He took a deep breath and did his best to continue. "You deserved so much better than loving someone like me. You should've had more happiness. I wish ... I wish ..."

Kelly nodded as the tears flowed freely down her cheeks. Adam tried to wipe them away, his arm falling to his side weakly. "I wish you had loved me, too, but it just wasn't meant to be." Kelly attempted a smile. "You loved me as much as you could, and it was more than I ever should have hoped for. I was a big girl, Adam. I knew that I was in love with a man who couldn't love me back. But you've been my family, and for that I'm so grateful."

Adam buried his head in his hands, his body racked with pain and sadness.

"I ... just wish that things had been different. That we could've all been happy and gotten the life that we deserved. You deserved so much more than me. I don't know why this has happened to me ... to us. I'm sorry ..."

Kelly swallowed, trying to rid herself of the lump in her throat so that she could talk. "I-I-I wish that I could've chosen who I loved, but I couldn't. For some reason, my heart chose you, and nothing I could ever do was able to change that. I knew that you loved Brynn, yet my heart couldn't let go. But please, know that I don't regret that even for a moment."

She leaned in close to him as she spoke, placing her forehead against his and closing her eyes as she spoke. "My life has been centered around taking care of you and Eva and Brynn, and I love all of you so much. I would never want you to feel bad for loving Brynn the way that you have."

Adam smiled, gratefully, and Kelly noticed for the first time that the whites of his eyes were yellowing. "Please ... take me home."

Kelly arranged for a car to pick them up from the hospital as she sat quietly with Adam and held his hand. The doctors hadn't been very specific about Adam's prognosis, and said that it could take weeks or months. Judging by the way Adam looked, Kelly feared that it would be weeks, but she prayed for much longer. The thought of never seeing him again gripped her heart so tightly she felt as though she would never breathe again.

"Have you talked to Eva today?" Adam asked, lying his head on the pillow. He was becoming more tired as the morning went on and he hoped that he would be able to leave soon.

"I'm going to text her and let her know that we'll be bringing you home," Kelly said, reaching for her phone. She knew that the timing wasn't going to be good, but there was nothing she could do about it.

Today was the day that Eva was planning to go to the prison to see Chris. Kelly had tried to talk her out of it but Eva insisted, saying that she needed to do it.

When Eva told her about it, Kelly had been upset.

"Eva, you never have to see him again," Kelly said to her on the phone as Adam dozed restlessly in the bed. "Please don't do this. You don't need to torture yourself by seeing him."

"I have to, Kelly. I have to face him or I'll never know why he did what he did to me. I'll never know why he did this to me and I'll never be able to move on." Eva had sounded as determined as she ever had about anything her entire life.

Kelly understood, but she still didn't agree.

"You can't go alone." Kelly said, finally.

"I won't be alone. I'll have Jack," Eva said. Something in her voice caught Kelly's attention, but she chose to leave it alone. She knew that Eva didn't have any experience with men other than Chris, but something about her and Jack together made sense to Kelly and she didn't want to jinx it.

Now the day for Adam to go home and Eva to face her fear had arrived, and Kelly prepared herself for what was to come.

Eva had told her that telling Brynn that Adam would die hadn't been easy, but that she wasn't sure if Brynn fully understood what was happening. Kelly was shocked to hear about the arrival of Nick, and Eva begged Kelly to tell Adam about Nick before he came home. Nick was refusing to leave the house, and Brynn seemed to find comfort in having him there. Kelly had always anticipated that he would return, but hadn't heard anything about him since his confrontation with Adam ten years earlier. She had always known that there was a chance that Eva was Nick's daughter, but it had never been discussed with anyone aloud. Kelly had tucked it away in her heart until now. Kelly noticed that Eva's voice had grown tight when she mentioned Nick, but they had been interrupted before Kelly could ask her about it.

Telling Adam about Nick had been surprisingly easier than she thought it would be.

"I remember him," Adam said at the mention of Nick's name. For a moment, there was a fire in Adam's eyes, but the flame went out just as quickly as it had come. "He was there to see Brynn and I kicked his ass. But then I let him see her and afterward, he disappeared without a trace. I don't think he'd ever hurt her, and it was obvious that he really cared about her."

"Are you going to be okay if he is in the house?" Kelly asked, taken aback by Adam's strange acceptance of the situation.

"What can I do?" Adam asked, his voice strangely calm. "I always knew this day would come."

Kelly stared at him, filled with curiosity. "How?"

"When you love her, it's impossible to forget about her." Adam said, apologetically. "I could tell from the moment that I met him that he loved her, and when I let him see her, I knew that he would come back. It just took a lot longer than I thought it would. His timing really sucks."

Kelly marveled at how peaceful he seemed to be and it made her admire him even more.

"I don't like this. I don't like it at all ... but I've been selfish with Brynn her entire life, and I realize that now. I ... I ... don't want Brynn to be without love in her life when I'm gone," Adam said finally, and Kelly realized that Adam's love for Brynn ran far deeper than most people ever loved in their entire lifetime.

The house had been readied for Adam's arrival, and the plan was to make him as comfortable as possible for as long as he was alive.

When the private van arrived to take Adam back to The Harper House, Kelly left the hospital, grateful for the fresh air that filled her lungs. She took a deep breath in as they settled Adam into the van.

The ride home was somber and silent.

As Adam stared out of the window he thought with sadness that it would be the last time that he would ever get to be on this journey ever again. He had made so many trips to the hospital over the years with Brynn and for himself, that he knew the route by heart. He was thankful that it was scenic and that he had a good view to look out at. As they drew nearer to home, Adam sighed heavily.

He was nervous about seeing Brynn. He wasn't sure how

much she would understand and wondered if she would even care that he was going to be gone soon. As they pulled into the long driveway, he was astonished to see that she was outside waiting for them with the new, pretty, young nurse, Becca, that Adam had only met a couple of times before he left for the hospital. Brynn waved as they drew nearer and Adam could see that she was smiling as well. He was relieved to see her, and his heart swelled as he realized how much he had missed seeing her. When he looked at her he still saw the girl he had fallen in love with, and he hoped that she would remember him, too.

As they helped him out of the van and into the wheelchair, Brynn approached him slowly with the nurse's help. Adam looked around for Nick, but was relieved to see that he wasn't there.

"I-I-I've m-m-m-issed you," she said, taking a long time to get the words out.

Adam's eyes filled with tears as he pulled her onto his lap as gently as he could and held her close to him. She was nothing but skin and bones and he was careful not to hug her too tight for fear that he would break her. Having her in his arms felt right.

"I've missed you, too," Adam said, kissing her softly on the cheek. Kelly stood by and watched them, a smile on her face, the sadness evident as she wiped the tears away. She convinced them to allow her to wheel them onto the large, spacious porch, where she left them alone to sit for a while wrapped up in one another.

As Adam held Brynn, he stroked her long hair and enjoyed the closeness of her.

After a long time, Brynn spoke.

"Is … it … t-t-true?" Brynn asked, her large brown eyes boring into his, searching. "Are you d-d-ying? Is this it?"

"Yes, it's true." Adam said, hating the effect that his words had on her. He watched as she seemed to crumble in his arms, her face full of devastation. "Please, don't … don't …"

Her sobs came heavy and long as he held onto her as tight as he could, willing her to stop. "Please, Brynn … don't … it's okay, it's okay."

She cried in his arms until she could cry no more, and when she was done, she collapsed against him exhausted. Adam's legs were beginning to fall asleep, but he dared not move her or ask her to move. He knew that having her close to him like this was something he wouldn't get to experience for much longer.

"Don't cry, Brynn. My life ... has been worth every moment because of this, because of you." Adam kissed her softly on her cheeks, trying to kiss the tears away. The saltiness from her tears burned his dry lips and he searched for the right words to comfort her. "I've loved you every day of my life. There was never a choice about loving you. If I had never met you, I don't know what would've become of me, but I do know that nothing in my life mattered until you loved me. Nothing else matters now. Nothing."

Brynn nodded in agreement. "H-h-how long?"

"I don't know. It could be days, it could be weeks, it could even be months," Adam said, lost in the silkiness of her long, dark hair. "However long it is, all I wanted was to be home ... to be with you. I hope that ... that is okay."

Brynn nodded, placing her hand on his chest. "Y-y-y-yes ... it's okay."

As the evening got cooler, Kelly and Becca came out, brought them in and got them settled for the evening. As Kelly wheeled Adam into the guest room that they had set up, he was pleased to see that the hospital bed was very large.

"I thought that we might want to give Brynn the option of staying in here with you, if you'd like," Kelly said, as though reading his mind. Adam was struck with how well Kelly knew him as he gave her an appreciative smile.

Adam paused, overwhelmed by Kelly's kindness. He knew that if he had never found Brynn he would've been fortunate to have someone like Kelly to love him.

The nurse settled Brynn into the bed and then Kelly got Adam ready. As Adam got comfortable he tried to remember the last time he had slept in the same bed with Brynn and found that he couldn't. Adam was embarrassed as Kelly helped him undress and get his nightclothes on, but she talked pleasantly the entire time, trying to distract him from the awkwardness of it.

When Kelly and the nurse had left the room, Brynn and Adam lie in bed, the silence falling over them like a soft warm blanket. Adam was exhausted, but tried to find the strength to move his body over so that he was side-by-side with Brynn until he couldn't get any closer. He loved the warmth of her body and the way she instantly reached for his hand, like she used to so very long ago. He focused on the way her fingers entwined with his and tried to ignore the excruciating pain that shot through his shoulder. It was becoming more and more constant. His stomach was beginning to swell more and more, and he knew that it wasn't going to be too long.

"What about Nick?" Adam asked, unsure if he should.

"Nick is my ... friend," Brynn said gently. "He understands ... and he respects that I need this time with you."

She could feel Adam nodding above her.

"Adam," Brynn's voice was sleepy.

"Yes?" Adam said, thinking how much he loved her voice.

"I-I-I'm sorry," she said, her voice barely audible.

"Sorry? Why would you ever be sorry?" Adam said, surprised.

"I-I-I lost you," she said slowly. "I should've h-have n-e-ever l-l-et you go. My fault ... my fault."

"No, no, no," Adam said, rolling to his side so that he could look at her. "You didn't do anything wrong. I left you ... I lost you. I never should've let you go. If anyone is to blame, it's me. I'm the one to blame!"

"No. I ... l-ove you. I al-ways h-have." Brynn said.

"I've always loved you too," Adam said, tears filling his eyes as he leaned over and kissed her forehead. "Always."

Brynn's eyes were closed and Adam realized that she was asleep. He silently promised himself that no matter how many minutes or hours or days he had left, he would never again, leave her side.

CHAPTER THIRTY-EIGHT

Closure

October 10th¹, 2016

Eva took a deep breath as she stood outside of the prison.

"Are you sure that you want to do this?" Jack asked, his face full of concern.

"Yes … I mean … no. I don't *want* to do this, but I *need* to do this. I need to face him because I need to ask him why he would do this to me. Why he would have chosen me. I need to face him or I'll never be able to move past this and …" she put her hand on her growing belly and rubbed it slowly. "I just need to do this for me and … for the baby."

Jack nodded.

They walked slowly and checked in. Eva still thought it was strange that she had to check in for Connor Martin, but she reminded herself that her Christopher never existed. She had worked herself up to the visit and tried to remember that she needed closure and that the person she had fallen in love with wasn't real.

They sat in the visiting area, waiting.

Eva's palms were sweaty and her chest felt heavy.

How do I do this? How?

"Visitor for Connor Martin."

Eva stood up and saw Chris staring at her. His hair was longer and shaggy and his beard was long and unkempt. He looked like a completely different person and she was grateful for that. It made doing what she came here to do so much easier. She was astonished at the weight he had lost and alarmed at how empty his eyes looked. There was a part of her that enjoyed seeing him miserable, but even though he looked like a complete stranger, she felt her heart aching for him beyond her control.

He sat down at the table, heavily.

They stared at one another for a few long moments until Eva finally spoke.

"How are you?" Eva asked, trying to ignore the large bruise under his eye while a tiny voice inside of her begged to know how he got it.

"How do you think I am?" Connor said, his voice flat as he refused to look at her.

Eva looked at him apologetically, even though she had nothing to be sorry for.

"Who is he?" he asked, gesturing to Jack, his voice turning hard. "Why did you bring a stranger here?"

"He's a friend of the family," Eva said, nervously.

"Oh," Connor said, staring at Jack in disgust. The two of them sized one another up, until Connor's attention shifted back to Eva. "What do you want? Why are you here?"

"I just want to know ... why ... Why ... Chr... Connor. Why did you ... lie ... to me?" Eva asked, her voice low but determined.

"Does it matter now?" Connor asked, angrily.

"Yes! Yes, it matters." Eva said, surprised at his anger and matching it with her own. "You lied to me and you took advantage of me! You used me and now I'm going to have our child. Why would you do something like this? What did I ever do to you to deserve having you treat me so horribly? Answer me, dammit!"

Connor finally looked at her, staring for a long moment, clearly stunned by her strength.

"Please ... I need to know." Eva said changing her

approach, her voice pleading.

"I wish I knew. I knew it was wrong ... I knew that I shouldn't have done it, but I just got in too deep." Connor said, his head buried in his hands.

"Why did you pick me?" Eva asked. "Why would you want to hurt me?"

"It wasn't about you, Eva. It was never about you," Connor said, his voice tortured and full of conflict. "It was about my mom, Jessie Martin, and getting back at your dad ... Adam. I wanted to hurt him for what he did to her ... for what he did to us."

"Us? Who is Jessie Martin?" Eva asked, a feeling of dread growing deep in her belly.

"Jessie was my mom. She was Adam's girlfriend after he and his wife split." Connor said Adam's name with disdain.

"But ... why ... what ..." Eva was confused. "Wait ... are you saying ... did you think that you're my... brother?"

Eva thought she would faint, the room spinning around her uncontrollably. The realization of what he was saying slapped her hard as the bile rose in her throat. She looked around the room desperately, knowing that she was going to throw up at any moment.

"God, no! No ..." Connor said, his voice loud. He looked around the room uncomfortably and lowered his voice. "She always told me that he was my father, but I never believed her. One night when she was especially smoked, she admitted that Adam wasn't my father even though she didn't remember it the next morning when I asked her. She refused to acknowledge that she ever said anything at all, but I knew that she had told me the truth for the one and only time in her life. She had fooled around on him, getting pregnant with someone else, but she refused to admit it."

Connor looked at Eva, a look of disgust on his face as he thought about how indiscriminate his mother had been. "I never would've agreed to doing this if I thought you were my sister. Never for one second."

Eva breathed slowly until she began to feel as though she was no longer going to throw up. "Oh, thank God," she said, finally.

Despite the circumstances, Connor found himself amused

with her, and he couldn't help but wish that things had been different between them. He resisted the urge to touch her, even though he wanted to. He still remembered how it felt to hold her hand and he desperately wanted to reach out and feel the soft silkiness of her hand in his. He knew that he would never have the opportunity to do that again.

Eva looked up at him, suddenly registering what he said. "What do you mean, you never would have agreed to this? Who made you agree, and what exactly did you agree to?"

Connor looked at her, realizing his error.

"Nothing ... I ..."

Eva felt that familiar tug on her heart as he spoke, even though she hated herself for responding to the sound of his voice the way she did. It was easier for her to forget about him when she didn't have to see him. She shifted awkwardly in her chair, feeling Jack's eyes on her and hoping he couldn't read her thoughts as she struggled desperately to forget what made her fall in love with Connor in the first place.

"You owe it to her to tell her what you were planning to do and why you hurt her the way you did." Jack's voice was sharp as he stared at Connor menacingly.

Eva held her breath, expecting Connor to react angrily. Instead he folded his head in his hands, his body shaking as he tried hard not to cry.

She looked up at Jack. She was at a loss.

"I never thought I would do something like this. I always thought I was a better person than ... I ended up being, and now ... I'm getting what I deserve by trying to hurt you. I'm sorry, Eva. Please believe that I did care about you very much. I did try to protect you, which is probably why I'm in here. I ..." Connor sighed, wiping the tears away, feeling the eyes of the other inmates on him and knowing that he had just made a dangerous mistake by showing his weakness.

"What did you do?" Eva said, staring at him evenly.

"I was in love, with a woman named Nora, the woman they are saying that I killed. And we agreed ... I agreed to ... I was going to ..." Connor struggled with the words, unable to believe that they were coming out of his mouth," ... kill you."

Eva gasped and stared at him, her blue eyes large as she imagined how she had planned to spend her entire life with him, his child growing large in her belly. She reached down and touched her stomach instinctively, the words stinging and unexpected.

"Oh, God. But why?" Eva said when she could find her voice.

"Money." Connor whispered carefully. "You had it and I didn't, and neither did Nora."

"So, you were going to marry me, get me pregnant, and then kill me so that you could have my money?" Eva's voice rose angrily as the reality grabbed her and gripped her so tightly she could barely breathe.

"Shhhh ..." Connor said looking around, his eyes meeting briefly with the inmate known as Scorpion, who was feared more than anyone else. Connor's face turned bright red, his voice suddenly fearful. "Jesus! Please, don't talk so loud, Eva. Are you trying to get me killed? You can't talk about money like that!"

"Should I care?" Eva said, her voice rising even more. Jack watched her carefully, impressed with how well she was standing her ground.

"No, you shouldn't," Connor said, desperation etched on his face as sweat began to bead on his forehead. "But I know you and you're better than this, better than me. Please... don't ..."

Eva could see the fear in his eyes and she realized that he was terrified. As much as she hated him, she couldn't bring herself to hurt him, and she tried to rein in her anger.

"What happened to ... Nora? Why did you kill her?" Eva said, trying to control her voice as she whispered in loud, hushed tones.

Connor's face turned white. "I swear, I didn't kill her. I know you won't believe me but I promise you," Connor said, his voice pleading.

"Why would I believe you or anything you say ever again?" Eva asked, her voice dripping with doubt.

"You shouldn't, but I swear, I didn't kill her. I would never hurt anyone, just like I could never hurt you. Think about it, Eva, have I ever harmed you? Have I ever even come close to hurting you?" Connor asked, reaching out to grab Eva's hand. "I don't know how to explain it, but I don't think she's dead."

Jack stepped forward as Eva pulled her hand back from Connor.

"I'm sorry, Eva. I'm so sorry," Connor said, his voice catching in his throat as he struggled to meet her gaze. "I ... I'm sorry for hurting you this way."

Eva stared at him, her blue eyes dark like an angry storm. "Is that what you want me to tell your unborn child? That you're sorry?"

Connor's face suddenly became blank.

"No. I don't want you to tell my unborn child anything," Connor said, his voice empty. "I'm never getting out of here, and I don't want my child to know anything about me. I don't deserve that child to know who I am or anything about me."

"If you didn't kill Nora, then who was that woman in her apartment? Who exactly is it that ended up dead? Wouldn't they have found that out during the investigation?" Jack's voice startled Connor and he lifted his head to look at the older man, his eyes narrowing.

"I don't know anything, but I know that I'm still in here so they still think that the dead woman is Nora." Connor said, never taking his eyes from Jack's. "Nora and I got into a fight after I told her that I had changed my mind and wasn't going to ... hurt you ... and then I got plastered and woke up in a pool of blood. That's what I know."

Eva stared hard at Connor, the part of her that thought she once knew him wanted to believe, even though her head warned her not to. She looked around the room and saw that a vicious looking inmate wearing a patch over his right eye was staring directly at them. When he saw Eva staring, he smiled, displaying a mouth full of gold teeth that sent a shiver down her spine.

"I just ... I had to know why you did this to me." Eva said trying to tear her eyes away from the man she had once promised her heart to. She stood up slowly. "I had to look at your face and know that you are no longer a threat to me and to my family. Mostly,

I needed you to know that I'm not afraid of you."

"No," Connor shook his head, sadly. "I'm not a threat to you, Eva. And even if by some miracle I ever get out of here and see the light of day, I promise that you'll never see me again. But it's unlikely that will ever happen."

Eva's heart ached as she stared at the stranger in front of her. Less and less he resembled the man she had fallen so much in love with and so quickly. As hard as she tried not to cry, she felt a tear slip down her cheek. She knew that it was the last time she would ever see him. As the reality sat heavily inside of her chest she felt as though she would be sick.

Jack stepped forward and put his hand gently on her back. He saw her expression change. The gesture was not lost on Connor, either, and the two men caught one another's eyes briefly.

"Good-bye, *Connor*," Eva said, her blue eyes glistening with the rest of the tears that she refused to let fall.

"Good-bye, Eva," Connor said, his chin trembling as he tried hard not to show any weakness. "Please, know that in the end I did do what I could to protect you, even though I have a horrible fucking way of showing it."

Eva turned around and walked away, her hand on her belly. She suddenly felt naked as she realized that the eyes of the other inmates were on her, a palpable danger suddenly in the air. She felt certain that they must have heard her comment about the money and she thought about how careless she had been to talk about it with Connor.

"Don't worry. They can't hurt you," Jack whispered, noticing the goose bumps on Eva's neck. She had done so well up until this point, and Jack steered her quickly and carefully out of the prison and back to his car.

"Why wouldn't that one inmate with the patch stop staring at me?" Eva asked once they got in the car. She was visibly shaken.

"He probably heard you … about the money. Any talk of money is unsafe, but you didn't know. I should've warned you about it, but it'll be all right. Connor will be fine." Jack said, giving her a small smile.

Eva wasn't convinced as she envisioned the inmate with the

eye patch staring at her, and she knew that she wouldn't be able to get him out of her mind for a long time.

Connor felt danger everywhere he walked throughout the prison, and no matter where he was he knew that he would never feel safe again.

He was a prime target and he had no way of defending himself. He had only been in a few bar fights, but nothing prepared him for what happened to guys like him where he was, locked in maximum security with violent offenders, murderers, and rapists. He knew the moment Scorpion saw Eva that his fate was sealed, and there was nothing he could do about it. He had already made the mistake of looking into Scorpion's good eye, the other one covered with a black patch, and knew that it was only a matter of time until he came for him.

He waited for days, sweating it out in his cell, huddled against the wall and barely sleeping. He knew what was coming because he'd seen it happen to too many inmates since he'd been put inside. Connor had kept his head down and tried to stay out of the way as much as possible, but he was marked now. Now that they thought he had access to big money he would be an even bigger target, and they wouldn't believe him when he told them that he didn't. Court was coming soon, but not soon enough for Connor. His lawyer told him that they had enough to keep him locked away for a long time, but Connor knew that the outcome in court wouldn't matter. He knew that he was never going to walk outside of the prison walls ever again. Deep down, Connor knew that if he called Eva, she might help him. He knew that she was kind and generous and that she wouldn't want to see him get hurt, but he had already tortured her enough.

As he walked in the yard, keeping to himself, his head down as usual, he saw a large shadow on the ground as it approached him. He looked up to find himself face to face with Scorpion, his good eye cloudy and horrifying to look at. Connor's eyes rested on the large, faded Scorpion tattoo on his massive forearm and shuddered. The stories about him that circulated throughout the prison had sent chills through Connor, and he knew that his time was up.

"I saw your pretty little girlfriend. She looked like a rich, sweet, little thing," Scorpion said, making an obscene gesture at Connor while standing way too close to him. "How come you didn't tell us about her?"

Connor tried to back away from him, but he was flanked by two of Scorpion's companions.

"Are you ignoring me, you little bitch?" Scorpion stepped up until his nose was touching Connor's, his one eye glaring at him. Connor shivered in fear, sweat popping up on his forehead.

"No," Connor mumbled.

"I think you're ignoring me," Scorpion said his voice angry and dangerous and he ran his hands over his own naked scalp in frustration. "I don't like to be ignored!"

Connor found himself struggling to breathe.

"I'll forgive you if you can get your little girlfriend to send me some money. Or maybe you could call her and she could come and give me one of those conjugal visits," Scorpion said, smacking his lips, the vibration of them tickling Connor's ear.

"No! She can't help you. Leave her out of this," Connor said, his voice louder than he intended it to be as he tried to step back once more.

"Ain't nobody says 'no' to me!" Scorpion said, his face twisted up angrily. "What's a little bitch like you going to do about it?"

Connor didn't realize he'd been punched until he felt the blood flooding from his nose. He put his hands up, but the blows came fast and furious, the pain catching up in slow motion.

"Nobody tells Scorpion 'No'!"

The dirt began to sting Connor's eyes before he registered the fact that he'd fallen on the ground in a heap. He could barely see a crowd forming around them chanting, but he couldn't hear what they were saying as the pain became even more intense, his belly exploding as he felt the heavy blows from Scorpion's feet.

He tried to open his eyes, but could tell that they were swelling shut, grateful that the tears were washing away the stinging from the dirt.

Connor felt himself fading in and out of consciousness, and wished desperately that the pain would stop. He didn't think that it was possible to feel this much pain at once, but his entire body hurt and he couldn't tell if it was just Scorpion beating him or if there were others. He groaned and tried to keep from crying out, but there was nothing he could do about the sobs that escaped.

He thought about Eva and what he had done to her and he knew that he deserved everything he was getting. If he had never gotten involved with Nora, none of this would have happened and Connor couldn't help but feel sorry for himself. He silently cursed Nora for letting this happen to him, and he regretted the day he ever laid eyes on her, even though he had loved her so much. He knew that it was too late for regret and that nothing could be done about what was about to happen.

The faint sound of a whistle and more shouting assaulted his ears, but he tried to give into the darkness that consumed him. Everything had nearly gone black and Connor remembered thinking how relieved he was to let the pain go.

He didn't feel the blade plunge into his side the first time, but when it went in the fourth time it went in deep. That's when Connor knew he was going to die. He lay on the ground and thought about Eva's beautiful blue eyes and nothing else. He began to pray as he felt the blood gurgling up into his throat, nobody coming to help him as he lay on the dirt, drowning in his own blood. He couldn't remember the last time he prayed and he wondered for a brief moment if there was even a God to hear him.

As he fought for consciousness, he thought he heard his mother calling his name. He closed his eyes and listened for her again and knew that there had never truly been another voice that had ever sounded so sweet.

Soon, he could no longer hear anything at all.

CHAPTER THIRTY-NINE

Settling In

December 1ˢᵗ, 2016

As Adam grew weaker, Brynn grew stronger, walking and talking as though her life depended on it. She spent every waking moment with Adam, and they cared for one another as though they were the only two people on earth. All of Brynn's sadness and torment seemed to lift from her.

Nick was a frequent visitor to The Harper House and was relieved to see that Brynn continued to get better and become stronger. She often met him on the large wrap-a-round porch, each visit feeling like the first time.

"I miss you so much," he said, caressing her cheek with the back of his fingers.

She smiled as she leaned into his hand, but then pulled away.

"I've … missed … you," she said her speech still slow, but getting better.

They sat on the porch in silence, his arm around her as he waited for her to speak. He knew she had something to tell him by the way she looked at him anxiously. Finally, he turned and looked at her.

"You can tell me, Brynn. I know you have something you

want to tell me and you can say it. You can tell me anything." Nick's heart was beating in his chest as he watched her struggle with the words. He prayed that she wasn't going to tell him that she never wanted to see him again. That had been his biggest fear since he'd moved to be near her.

"Adam ... is dying." Brynn said simply, as she looked at Nick with large brown eyes the size of saucers. Nick could see that it was tearing her apart inside as he began to realize what she was telling him.

"I know, Honey. You need to be with him," Nick said, saving her from having to say the words. He always knew that despite his love for her, Adam would always be first in her heart and that he could never replace him. While he wanted to be angry with her, he knew that he couldn't. He felt the same about her, having walked away from his life just so that he could be near her. He understood what her heart was saying even though he hated that she still loved Adam as much as she did.

"Yes," Brynn said, leaning her head against his chest. "I'm sorry to put you through this."

Nick was silent for a long time trying to find the right words.

"Brynn ... don't be sorry. I'm here for you and I'm not going anywhere. I'll still be here when you're ready."

Brynn looked up at him gratefully. Nick had imprinted himself on her heart and she was astounded by his love for her.

Adam had grown weaker, but was holding on to meet his new grandson. Eva's stomach had grown rounder with each passing day as she waddled around The Harper House, getting ready for the baby to come. Jack had become a permanent fixture in the home, claiming that he was there as a monitor, but the entire household knew that he was completely in love with Eva.

The house was full of life for the first time in many years. Becca and Kelly were there night and day, and Kelly added more help to ensure that Adam stayed as comfortable as possible. Kelly knew that the end was rapidly approaching. As the days went on, she tried to ignore the break in her own heart.

Even though she knew that she wouldn't have Adam for

much longer, Brynn felt at peace for the first time since she could remember. Her family was together, and her body was healing.

But Eva was distracted as Adam faded away and the baby began to grow larger inside of her.

Ever since her visit to the prison, things between her and Jack had been different. Eva had been different. She was afraid and Jack could sense it, even though he stayed near hoping she wouldn't be so fearful. The banter and the closeness between them had all but disappeared, and he missed it. The only thing he could do was to stay close to her, close to the family. No matter how much she pushed him away, he stayed near, knowing that she would need him again one day and ready to be there when she did. He had never met anyone like her, and he wasn't going to let her go easily. Jack was a patient man. He was willing to wait it out. Wait for her.

As Eva's due date approached, Adam, Brynn, and Eva spent as much time as they could together, and Eva marveled at the love between her parents. For the first time, she saw what had bonded Adam to her mother so completely, and why he never let her go. The love between them was palpable and strong. Eva wanted desperately to live in it for the rest of her life.

"Dad, feel! The baby is kicking!" Eva grabbed Adam's hand and placed it on her belly just as the baby moved inside of her, her stomach rippling as he touched her.

His smile was weak but his eyes shone as he felt his grandson moving against his hand.

"Wonderful," he said, simply.

Eva smiled, fighting the tears, praying once more that Adam would live long enough to see his grandson. She knew it wouldn't be much longer until he arrived, her belly protruding so much that her skin felt as though it was stretched as far as it could go. She was glad to have the pregnancy nearly over, as well as her marriage to Connor Martin annulled. That last part Jack had gotten started as soon as Connor had been sent to prison. She no longer had any ties to Connor, and after her visit to the prison, she no longer worried that he could hurt her or their son. Jack had taken care to ensure that she would never hear from him or the prison again, and she knew that she had nothing to fear now that Jack was protecting the home. Jack was intercepting the mail and had security fielding phone calls to the home, but thankfully, Connor hadn't tried to contact her.

The prospect of motherhood excited her and she did her best to let go and be happy. She found it difficult to ignore the tiny, nagging feeling that refused to let her be completely at peace.

I'm losing the only father I've ever known, the little voice in her head reminded her every waking moment as she struggled to smile and breathe through the pain that she knew would come when Adam drew his last breath. Eva loved Adam with all her heart, and even though he hadn't been the perfect father, he was paying for it with his life, and Eva could no longer be angry with him.

As Adam lie in bed with Brynn and Eva at his side, he looked as though he was finally at peace. Eva loved how much stronger her mother looked, and Eva finally began to see how much she resembled her. She was happy that her baby boy would know her, and thankful for the chance she had been given to know her as well.

"Noah Adam, will be his name," she had told her parents happily.

She planned to name him after her uncle and father, and Eva smiled as she rubbed her belly and thought of holding him. She couldn't wait to meet her baby. Her entire life she'd wanted nothing more than a family of her own, and now she would have what she had always wanted, and the excitement bubbled up inside of her.

Jack stayed close, afraid to leave the family for fear that he would miss some unknown threat, even though Brynn and Eva both tried to get him to relax.

"We are safe," Brynn said, patting Jack's arm as he sat in the kitchen, sipping coffee and enjoying the promise of spring from his view in front of the large bay windows.

"I know," Jack said, smiling at Brynn. He had come to like her so much over the past few months, and could see why his grandfather had been so fond of her. She was much stronger than she appeared, and his grandfather had always admired strong women. "I just want to make sure it remains that way. How is Adam doing?"

Brynn shook her head as she got herself a cup of coffee, moving slowly, but purposefully. "Adam is ... surviving but when the baby comes, he will go."

Jack was silent, no words coming to mind, unsure of what he should say.

"It's okay," Brynn said, sitting down at the kitchen island across from Jack. "He's ready. He's just waiting. For Noah."

Jack smiled. They were all waiting for Noah.

"How are you?" Jack asked Brynn, worry creeping into his voice as he saw how tired she was.

"I'm good," Brynn said, smiling a weak smile. "Tired, but good."

They sat in silence sipping their coffee.

"Eva is good, too," Brynn volunteered, her brown eyes staring into Jack's.

Jack flushed, taking too large a sip and choking on it, coffee spilling all over the granite countertop.

"Good," he said, when he had finally recovered. "Can I talk to you about something?"

"Yes," Brynn said, leaning forward.

"Why ... I mean ... do you know why ... why she has pushed me away? We were getting close and then ... she ... it's almost as though she is afraid of me. I thought she felt the same way about me as I do about her, but then ..." Jack threw his hands up in the air in exasperation.

"She's been through a lot," Brynn said, understanding his frustration. For a moment, she felt as though she was looking at Adam years ago, frustrated that she refused to return the love he tried to give her. Brynn understood her daughter more than Eva realized because she was just like her. "Give her time. She'll come around."

Jack looked at her, embarrassed. "I know. I'm sorry. It's just that ... I ..."

"You love her." Brynn said, smiling. "I know. I can see it."

"Is it that obvious?" Jack flushed.

"Yes," Brynn said covering his hand with hers. "I was very much like Eva when I was younger. I had been ... abandoned and hurt by everyone who was supposed to love me the most, and I was terribly afraid. Just give her some time, but don't give up. Never give up."

Jack smiled as he stood up and enveloped Brynn in a hug. "I won't. I can't. I don't know that I can ever feel about anyone the way I do about her."

Brynn stood up just as Eva walked into the kitchen, holding onto her belly, her face white.

"I think we need to go to the hospital ... now," she said, her voice strained.

Jack and Brynn stared at her in shock as the red seeped down her pants and onto the floor.

"Oh, my God," Brynn yelled, moving as fast as she could. "Kelly! Becca! Somebody, help!"

Jack moved quickly, picking Eva up as carefully as he could, yelling for Brynn to open the door. Just as he cradled her in his arms, Eva lost consciousness, her head rolling back and finally resting against Jack's chest.

Becca arrived first and when she saw the blood, she startled, but regained her composure quickly. "Go," she said to Jack as she followed him to the car, grabbing towels from the kitchen as she did so. "I'll go with you."

Brynn stood in the kitchen, helpless as she watched Jack's car speed away.

She fell into a chair as tears streamed down her cheeks. The memories came flooding back to her as she thought about how so many years ago she had lost her first daughter, Sophie. She prayed with all her heart that Eva wouldn't have to go through what she had, and that she would be able to bring Noah home to them.

Home to Adam.

CHAPTER FORTY

Coming Home

March 15th, 2017

Becca sat in the back seat with Eva, holding her tight, trying to keep the blood from flowing all over Jack's car with the hand towel she had grabbed on the way out.

"How is she?" Jack yelled back, driving as fast as he could toward the hospital.

"She's hanging in there, but you need to hurry," Becca yelled as she held Eva's wrist. Her pulse was getting weaker, and Becca could tell that she was barely holding on.

Jack had memorized the route to the hospital and got there in record time. As they wheeled her in, Jack tried to follow, but the nurses refused to let him go in with them. "You'll have to wait outside until we know what we're dealing with, Daddy," the nurse said giving him an apologetic smile.

"Dammit!" Jack swore, as he paced the length of the waiting room.

Becca sat silently in one of the chairs. "She's going to be okay," she said.

Something about her voice grabbed Jack's attention. He looked at her with irritation and wondered for a second if he had heard her tone correctly. Her voice sounded flat, unconcerned, but when he looked at her he saw a look of worry on her face.

She met his eyes briefly, and he relaxed a bit seeing the same concern on her face that he often saw when she was caring for Adam. I'm just going out of my mind, he thought, shaking his head.

The minutes passed like hours, and the hours felt like days. He texted Brynn and Kelly, but there was no news to tell them and he knew they were just as anxious as he was.

Finally, a nurse came out and looked around the waiting room. "Family for Eva Michaels?"

Jack jumped up, the nurse approaching them with a kind smile.

"She's okay. We had to do an emergency C-section, but the baby is healthy and she's resting. She lost a lot of blood, but she's going to be alright."

Jack blew out a sigh of relief as he grabbed Becca and hugged her.

"What happened to her?" Jack asked the nurse, trying to get the sight of her blood out of his mind.

The nurse hesitated, "That's not for me to say. The doctor will come in and talk to you, but she is doing well now and is resting. She should be just fine."

"Thank God!" he said, his entire body finally relaxing.

"Would you like to see your baby?" the nurse asked, smiling.

"Oh ... he's not ... I mean, I'm not ..."

"Come on," the nurse said, grabbing his arm gently. "Miss Michaels wanted you to see him."

Jack followed up, happily, as though in a dream.

Becca shook her head and refused to follow as Jack left her behind in the waiting room.

As he walked up to the large glass in front of the nursery, he knew immediately which baby was Eva's.

"That's him," he whispered, as he stared in awe at the tiny person with the head of dark hair like his mother's. "That's Noah."

Until Eva, Jack had never imagined that he could love another human being so much, but the moment he saw Noah, he knew that nothing about his life would ever be the same again.

When Eva awoke in her hospital room, she looked up to find Jack asleep in the hard, plastic chair next to the bed, his body contorted in a way that was not possibly comfortable.

"Jack," she said, her voice weak.

Jack jumped, his neck snapping. He grimaced as he opened his eyes, confused. The moment he saw Eva he was awake and alert.

"Eva! What do you need? Are you okay?"

"Yes. I'm fine," she said hoarsely.

"Have you been here this entire time? Go home," Eva marveled at Jack's commitment to her. She didn't know what she'd ever done to deserve his dedication.

"No way. You should know by now that I'm not leaving you in here like this," Jack said, smiling at her and making her heart flutter.

"You don't have to be here. You don't have to do this for me," Eva said, knowing that she was pushing him away but not sure why.

"Eva, please. Stop doing this. You and I had ... have a connection, a strong connection. You and I both know it. Please stop." Jack's deep voice was pleading as he watched her carefully to see if he had any effect on her. He saw the tears fill her eyes as she refused to look at him.

"Yes, we do," she said, sniffling. "But, you deserve so much more than me, so much more than raising a child that isn't your own, the baby of an idiot and a ... a murderer. Do you really want to be here for that?"

"Yes! I do! I want to be here for that," Jack said, picking her chin up so that she was looking at him. Even in the hospital he was in awe of her beauty, and he knew that he was completely in love with her. "Yes, I want to be there for you and Noah, for all of it!"

"How can you say that? You barely even know me," Eva said in disbelief. "I'm a sheltered little girl who married a murderer and has no idea how to navigate through life. How can you want someone like that? You can have your choice of any woman you want. Why me?"

Jack looked at her long and hard, unsure where her doubt

came from.

"How can you think so poorly of yourself, Eva? You made one mistake by falling in love with the wrong man, but that's not your fault. You can't punish yourself for that for the rest of your life." Jack placed his hand on her cheek and felt her resolve begin to loosen as she listened to him. "When I look at you, I see a beautiful, strong, and amazing woman. You've kept your family together. You've been your father's purpose your entire life. You are ... the most ... unbelievable woman ..." Jack's voice caught as his emotions got the better of him.

Without thinking, he leaned over and kissed her, losing himself immediately. The moment he felt his lips on hers, he felt her respond to him and his eyes grew wet with happiness and relief, the tears flowing freely down his face.

"God, I just love you so much," he said, holding her face with both of her hands.

Her large blue eyes glistened as she stared up at him. Relief and happiness flooded out of her. "I love you, too. I've been trying not to love you, but it's not working. I don't know what I ever did to deserve you, but I am so thankful for you," she said, kissing him over and over again. "Please don't ever leave me."

"I don't intend to," Jack said holding her close, finally able to breathe normally. "It'll always be you and me and Noah, and I'm never going to leave your side. Ever."

As the week went by, Jack was amazed at how easy it was for him to hold Noah in his arms. Noah responded to the sound of his voice and Jack realized that soothing came naturally to him. He had never been able to picture himself as a father until he met Eva, and now that is all he wanted to be. She made him want more than he had ever imagined in life, and he promised himself that he would always keep her and Noah safe, even if she wasn't completely ready to let him yet.

Eva was anxious to get home. Adam had been declining and Brynn and Kelly refused to leave his side. Once they were finally cleared, the ride home seemed long and unsettling as Jack drove below the speed limit. He had never driven with a baby in the car and the thought of it terrified him. Jack was never as grateful to pull into The Harper House as he was with baby Noah for the first time.

Brynn and Adam met them in the driveway, both anxious to meet their grandson. Adam had suffered through a difficult week, and Brynn knew that it was only a matter of time until he decided to let go for good. She watched him like a hawk every second of the day, not wanting to miss one moment with him while he was awake. As Jack's sleek, black car pulled into the driveway, Brynn smiled with amusement. His car was not very child-friendly, which she figured he would soon realize.

Adam was nervous. He hadn't held a baby since Eva was one, but he was eager to. He didn't want to leave, but he knew the time was coming. His body was growing weaker and he was asleep far more than he was awake. He fought to hold on for as long as he could.

As Eva got out of the car, Adam marveled at how beautiful and strong his daughter was, and how much she resembled Brynn in every way. He admired her strength and goodness, and he reminded himself to tell her before it was too late.

"Daddy!" she said, walking quickly toward him with the baby, her blue eyes sparkling at the sight of him. Adam gazed at her and the baby taking a mental snapshot in his mind, vowing to always remember how she looked at this very moment. She approached his wheelchair and carefully laid the tiny bundle in his arms.

The baby awoke just as Eva laid him down, looking Adam directly in the eyes as he did so. Adam's eyes filled with tears as the emotion overcame him. He found as the days went on he cried easily. "Meet your grandson, Noah Adam," Eva said proudly, kissing Adam on the cheek.

Adam stared down at the baby lost in eyes that were bright and alert, realizing that he had never felt so much love for another human being in all his life. Noah stared up at him with quiet curiosity as Adam cried helplessly. At that moment, he understood that he would miss every important moment in Noah's life, and he hoped with everything that was inside of him that Eva and Brynn would make sure the baby knew who he was.

"Hi Noah, I'm your grandpa. I'm so happy that I got to

meet you and that you're as healthy and beautiful as everyone hoped you would be. I ... wish you so much happiness and love. I only wish that I could be here to see it, but... I'm leaving you in good hands."

Adam looked up to see Brynn and Eva holding one another, the sight of Adam and Noah tearing them apart as they gripped one another tightly, unable to let go. Adam sighed, wiping the tears from his eyes and surrendering himself to a reality that was far beyond his control.

He gestured for Eva to take the baby.

"I love you," he said to Noah, planting a kiss on his forehead as Eva carefully took him from his arms.

"Please take me inside," he said quietly to Becca, putting his head down. "I need to lie down."

Becca pushed his wheelchair up the ramp easily. Adam was barely skin and bones and wheeling him around had become much easier.

Brynn looked at Eva and Jack, her bottom lip quivering.

"I'm so glad you've come home. Your dad can go home now, as well."

CHAPTER FORTY-ONE

Jealous

March 20th, 2017

Nora watched Eva and the baby for days, her skin tingling with jealousy and anger.

She hated that little rich bitch for everything she had taken from her, first Connor, and now his child. She blamed Eva for everything and knew that the time was coming when she would take everything that was important to her. First, Nora planned to take her child and then her life, although she didn't care which order she did it in. If she could take her child first and make her suffer, she knew that would be much sweeter, but she was willing to accept whatever she could get. Nora smiled as she gazed at Jack under her long lashes, imagining what she could do to him if she ever got her hands on him for even just a moment. She let her mind wander to thoughts of him naked, sweaty, with her on top of him, until she was interrupted by the sound of Adam's voice.

"Becca, can you help me get to my room? I need to rest." Adam's voice was beginning to grate on her and she was starting to regret that she hadn't found another way to infiltrate the house. He constantly called her name and she hated how hard it was to put him in bed, even though he couldn't weight more than one-hundred pounds now. Taking care of him had to be the most unglamorous job she had ever imagined, and she thought that even housekeeping would have been better than being Adam's personal nurse day and night. She wondered why that lazy bitch, Kelly, had relinquished most of his care to her, instead of just doing it herself. Nora hated Kelly's weakness, crying anytime she was anywhere near Adam or the rest of the family, and she wondered how she had managed to stay employed for as long as she had.

I wish he would just fucking die already!

"Of course," Nora said, smiling her sweetest smile at Adam "I'd be happy to help you."

Nora always knew that she was a good actress. Her entire life, everyone had always believed her lies.

No, Momma, I didn't take the last cookie.

No, Mrs. Stephens, I would never pinch anyone! He pinched me!

No, Momma, I would never undress in front of your boyfriend!

Momma, he forced me do that to him, I would never do anything like that with someone you liked that much, ever!

Connor, you are my one and only love, I promise.

Detective, I'm terrified of my boyfriend, Connor Martin. He's extremely violent toward me and I don't know what he'll do next so please, I need a restraining order.

Nora wondered why she had wasted all that time killing herself in nursing school when she should've gone into movies or television and made it with her acting skills. But Momma had insisted that she do something more than work in a bar like she had, and with her grades in school, it had been easy for her to get a full ride scholarship.

"You've got a brilliant mind, Nora. You've never even tried and you get perfect grades, so going to school will be free and you can get out of living in a shithole like this one. Get a good job because God knows that you'll never find a man to put up with you for too long."

Even Connor believed every word she had ever told him, following her every instruction. She had stumbled upon him accidentally, and when he had told her the story about his mom and the rich guy, Nora knew that he was her ticket to an easy life. Getting him to seduce and marry that pathetic weakling had been easy. Nora had even anticipated that he would end up feeling sorry for the spoiled brat, but hadn't imagined that he would love her or end up getting her pregnant.

Nora thought about Connor as she prepared Adam for a nap. Her chest tightened slightly as she thought about the lengths she had to go through in order to frame Connor for her murder. It had taken a great deal of time and planning, and seducing her look-alike had been fun, although shorter than she wished it had been. She thought about Hannah Leigh, and her heart quickened as she remembered how easy and incredibly sweet and innocent she had been. The first time Nora had kissed her, she knew that Hannah was something special, and the first time Nora touched her naked flesh and pressed it against her own, she realized she would regret what she had to do to her. In the end, it had been much easier to bash her skull in than Nora thought it would be. Nora found that she had actually enjoyed it. She had anticipated that he would return to the apartment after their fight, like he always did. He was predictable in every way. When he returned, she drugged him. Her only regret was that she hadn't gotten to have sex with him before he passed out.

Nora hated having to punish him so brutally, but she didn't have a choice. He had betrayed her and she couldn't allow him to treat her that way after everything she had planned to do for him. She was going to make him very happy, but he ruined everything. She was looking forward to seeing the look on his face when she went to the prison to tell him what she had done, but was shocked to find out that he had been killed by an inmate. There had been nobody listed as next-of-kin, and he hadn't even had a proper funeral.

Nora grieved as much as she could for Connor, but she knew that it would have to wait. She had infiltrated the house months before Connor had been sent to prison. She'd played the role of her lifetime as Becca, and nobody suspected her of a single thing. It was the only way she could get close to Eva and pay her back for ruining everything she had worked so hard for.

Eva had gotten everything that Nora ever wanted, and she waited patiently for the moment that she could look Eva in the eyes and punish her for what she had done. Nora knew the opportunity would present itself soon, and she was going to ready when it did.

CHAPTER FORTY-TWO

Good-Bye My Love

March 25ᵗʰ, 2017

Adam knew that the end was almost near.

He had been waiting for Eva and the baby to come home, unable to leave the house any longer to visit them at the hospital. He knew that he had to see Noah Adam just one time. The moment he laid his eyes on baby Noah, he was finally at peace. He thought it would be so much harder to let go once he saw him, but instead the baby had given him hope. He knew that life would go on, even without him there, and he decided that he was no longer afraid.

The doctor had been in to visit him and told him that the end was near. It had already been three weeks since Eva had come home with the baby, and he knew that he was living on borrowed time. His organs were failing and the family had been vigilant, staying by his side. Even Jack, who Adam had grown fond of, stayed close, clearly taking care of Eva and anything she needed. Adam could tell that he loved her deeply, and he hoped that Eva would someday reciprocate the love he had for her.

"I hope you will let yourself love him one day, Bitty" he said to her when she came home from the hospital, holding her hand as he spoke to her.

"Dad, don't worry about that," Eva said, her voice

quivering. She was having a difficult time as his skin became more sallow and his strength all but disappeared. "I ... please don't worry about me."

"Of course ... I worry for you," Adam said, his voice barely above a whisper. "I ... worry ... for all of you. But ... you are in ... good hands."

"Yes, Daddy. I know that I am, and I do love Jack, but right now, I want to concentrate on making sure you know that I love you. So much." Eva hugged him as gently as she could, hoping his heart could feel the love that poured out of her.

Adam nodded and sighed. "Yes. Now ... please ... send Jack to me."

Eva looked at him, pausing. She hated leaving him, never knowing when the last time would be that she would see him. "Daddy, I can stay."

"No, Bitty I need to ... rest, but first ... Jack." Adam said grabbing her and pulling her toward him.

Eva rested in his arms, hesitant to leave the room.

"Please," Adam said, staring into the blue eyes that were so much like his own. "I love you, Bitty"

"I love you too, Dad," Eva said kissing him on the cheek. As she closed the door carefully behind her, a sense of finality overcame her and she couldn't hold the tears back any longer. She hated feeling this way and sought Jack out, knowing that she would find him with Noah.

When Adam's door opened and Jack peered in, Adam was sleeping soundly. Jack turned around to leave but then he heard Adam's voice call out to him.

Jack sat next to the bed reluctantly.

"I'm sorry if I woke you, sir." Jack said, clearing his throat. He liked Adam but was intimidated by Eva's love for him. He knew that it wouldn't be long before Adam was gone, and he desperately wanted Adam's approval, a feeling that was completely foreign to him.

"Do ... you have ... something to say to me?" Adam said, making Jack immediately uncomfortable.

"Um ... I don't know," Jack said, suddenly feeling like a

ten-year-old boy who had thrown a baseball through the window. "Do I?"

"Yes … you do," Adam said as Jack felt himself begin to squirm even more.

Jack sat and thought for a moment, hundreds of thoughts racing through his head. He didn't want to patronize Adam, but knew that Adam was looking for something specific from him.

"Yes!" Jack thought after a few moments. "Yes … I do."

Adam's expression was serious as he waited for Jack to find the words.

"You know that I … l-l-l-ove Eva," Jack said, awkwardly, his words finding a strange voice on his own lips. He sounded like a stranger, even to himself, but he pressed on anyway.

"Yes," Adam said, smiling.

"I would like …" Jack cleared his throat nervously. "I would like to ask your permission to marry her when the time comes, and to take care of her and your family."

Adam looked Jack over for a few long moments until Jack felt as though he would faint. He had never imagined himself in this situation, and hadn't even realized it was happening until Adam searched his soul and pulled it out of him.

"Yes", Adam said finally as Jack let his breath out loudly, relieved. Being a bachelor his entire life, he had never imagined ever facing anyone in this moment and was relieved when it was over.

"Yes, you can … marry Eva. But promise me … you'll take care of … all of them. Brynn … my love … please, don't abandon her. Don't leave her behind," Adam said, his voice imploring.

"Of course, of course," Jack said, the thought of leaving Brynn to fend for herself never even crossing his mind. He had fallen in love with the entire family and could never imagine walking away from any of them, ever.

Adam started to snore within minutes as Jack silently left the room, knowing that Eva would want to know what they had talked about. Jack decided that he would keep it to himself until the time came, even though he knew that Eva wouldn't be happy about it. Eva was everything Jack had never imagined wanting, and she had changed him for the better. She challenged him, excited him and mesmerized him in every way and he knew that loving her wouldn't always be easy, but he was ready for it. He just needed her to give into him completely.

I will wait for her for as long as I need to, until she realizes that I will never leave her or let her go.

Brynn lay on the bed next to Adam watching him snore gently.

She loved watching him sleep and had never told him how often she had done so during their lifetime together. As a younger woman, it was the only time she had felt completely safe with him, even though he promised her that he would never hurt her or harm her. Even after Sophie died, she watched him while he slept, but then it had become different. Brynn thought sadly that after Sophie died, everything between them had changed for the worse, and as she let her mind wander back, she wondered how much different their lives would have been if Sophie had lived. She sighed knowing that there was no way she would ever know as she once again tried to accept that this was the way their lives had been meant to go.

Brynn was thankful that most of her mobility and speech had finally returned. After countless months of therapy and hard work, she was finally close to being 100%, although the therapist had told her that she needed to be happy with anything she got back. Brynn fought hard and worked herself as much as she could, even on her own, and her doctors and therapists were amazed by her progress. Even though she knew that she would never be completely healed, she was thankful for what she had been able to do.

As she stared at Adam she thought of how unfair it was that she was about to lose him again. She knew that this time there would be no turning back. Once he was gone, she would never see him again. She shifted her body slowly, careful not to wake him as she fought back a sob that threatened to escape her. The emptiness she felt within threatened to consume her, even though she tried not to show it in front of Adam. He had been the only man to know her completely, and while he had rejected her after Sophie died, she knew that part of him had always loved her. If he hadn't, he never would've cared for her the way he did for twenty years, waiting for her to return to him.

Brynn realized that Adam's eyes were on her as she roused herself from the memories that had overtaken her.

"Hi, Love," Adam whispered, smiling.

Brynn smiled back, seeing him still as the fifteen-year-old boy who had stolen her heart.

"Hi, Love," Brynn said, touching his cheek gently. "Are you in pain?"

Adam lied. "No. I'm fine."

"Good," Brynn said, kissing him gently on the forehead. "You look good, today."

"You look ... beautiful." Adam said, his voice tender. He thought Brynn was the most beautiful woman he had ever seen in his entire life, and his heart warmed at the sight of her.

"Stop," Brynn blushed. She touched the faded scar on her cheek and frowned without realizing it.

"Don't ... don't do that," Adam said pulling her hand away. "I mean it, Brynn. You ... are beautiful."

Brynn could tell by Adam's breathing that talking exhausted him. She snuggled against him, loving the warmth of his body against hers.

She heard his voice above the top of her head as she closed her eyes, vowing to remember every moment they had left.

"You ... have been the best thing to ... ever happen ... to me. I'll never ... regret passing you... that note ... when we were fifteen. It was ... the smartest thing ... I ever ... did," Adam's voice reverberated in his chest as Brynn fought back the tears. She hated when he spoke like it was the last time he would talk to her, even though she knew that it might be.

"I'll never forget reading that note and giggling," Brynn said, trying to control her voice so that he wouldn't hear her heart breaking.

"You have been ... my greatest ... love," Adam said, squeezing her for a brief moment. His arms relaxed and the sound his breathing became slower and shallower as he fell quickly asleep.

"And you have been mine," Brynn said, hoping that his subconscious would hear her. She lay against him sleepily.

As she felt herself drift off to sleep in his arms, she thought she heard his voice in her dreams say, "Good-bye my Love. Good-bye."

CHAPTER FORTY-THREE

The Final Farewell

April 2nd^h, 2017

Eva sat in front of her vanity, brushing her long dark hair, and staring at her red puffy eyes. She knew that no amount of makeup in the world would be able to conceal what she was looking at, and she didn't care. The dark dress fit her perfectly, her body almost back to where it was before she had Noah. She was thankful for good genes and thought that it was an odd thing to be thankful for on the day of her father's funeral.

She'd dreaded this day her entire life, knowing she would have to say good-bye to one of her parents. She had always been prepared to say good-bye to Brynn first, but not to Adam. Adam had been her rock, albeit, a spongy one. Still, he had been the only parent she had ever truly known. She looked at her watch, counting down the hours until she would have to stand in front of his casket. Four hours. Her heart thumped anxiously.

The thought of never seeing him again gutted her inside in a way that she couldn't prepare herself for.

Jack had been the only person keeping her sane. Even though he admittedly hadn't been close to his own father, he still experienced a lot of the same emotions when he lost him. Jack understood her and Eva realized that he always seemed to understand her. As she brushed her hair and thought of him, she briefly allowed a smile to touch her lips.

She went to Noah's nursery to prepare him and his bag for the long day ahead. Brynn had given everyone the day off as they prepared for the funeral. She and Kelly had gone out to make a few last minute preparations, and Eva was thankful for the near empty house. She worried about her mom who had fallen asleep next to Adam and then awoke next to him to find that he had died with her in his arms. Brynn had been by his side non-stop in the last weeks, returning the love that he had given her. He had spent so many years making sure she was given the best care in The Harper House, and she knew that she could never abandon him. Brynn had been heartbroken when she awoke to find that he had passed on, but didn't give herself the time to grieve.

She'd insisted on helping with the funeral arrangements, taking care of as much as she could on her own. She knew that nobody knew him like she did and she wanted the services to honor him.

Eva wondered what would happen to her mother when everything had finally calmed down. She desperately hoped that Brynn wouldn't break.

As she walked into Noah's nursery she was surprised to find Becca standing in the middle of the room, almost as though she was waiting for her.

"Oh ... hi," Eva said, stunned to see her there. "What are you doing in here?"

"I come here a lot." Becca said. The unexpected hardness in her voice made Eva's hair stand up on the back of her neck.

"Why? W-w-w-hy would you ever come in here?" Eva said confused. She noticed for the first time how close Becca was to Noah's crib.

"I come in here to visit Noah," Becca said taking a small step closer to the crib. Eva felt herself beginning to sweat, her nerve endings tingling as she looked around the room for something she could throw.

"But ... w-w-why would you come in here to visit my

baby? When … when would you come here?" Eva stepped closer to Becca, focusing her eyes on the dark piece of metal that Becca suddenly had in her hands. It was pointed directly at Eva.

"I come here because I want to see my baby, because I want to feel close to Connor. I come here because I can and because you've been too stupid to realize it and stop me." Becca's green eyes bore into Eva, enjoying the look of fear and confusion she saw on her face.

"*Your* baby? … Connor … what does this have to do with Connor? You knew him?" Eva's voice rose sharply as she felt terror replacing the fear that had been in her heart only a few seconds before at the mere sound of Connor's name.

"Yes, of course I knew him! He was my lover. He was the only love of my life. I was the reason that he was here. With you," Becca said waving her gun at Eva, carelessly.

The room began to spin as Eva fought to steady herself.

"Oh, God…" Eva's right hand rose to her lips in horror. "Are you … Nora?" Eva asked, reality setting in slowly, her blood turning to ice.

"Yes," Becca said, her eyes bright and full of hatred. "You're finally getting it! You're not nearly as stupid as I thought you were."

"B-b-b-ut … your dead. Connor killed you." Eva tried to step a little closer to the crib, but Becca motioned with the gun for her to back up. "Please … please, don't hurt Noah!"

"I would never hurt Noah! Noah is going to be my son since you stole Connor from me! Connor was never supposed to get you pregnant! He was supposed to kill you, take your money, and then marry me. We were going to have a family together with all your money because we knew you would be too trusting for a prenup. But then you had to go and fuck it all up by making him fall for you. You ruined everything, you selfish bitch!" Becca's eyes glittered at Eva dangerously.

"No … God, no. Connor didn't love me, he never loved me or he wouldn't have hurt me the way that he did. Please … if it's money you want, I can give you money. Please, just get away from my baby," Eva begged, tears falling helplessly down her face as she struggled to think of a way to get Becca to move away from the crib.

She could hear Noah begin to stir from his nap and she desperately wanted Becca and her gun to be as far away from him as possible.

"It *was* about the money, at first. But then he didn't want to go through with hurting you because he *cared about you too much,* and said that you were a good person. You wove some magic, rich girl spell over him, and then he shot our plan all to hell. So, I had to punish him and send him to jail. I was going to go in and tell him everything, but then I found out that he's dead and it's all because of you." Becca's voice was full of hatred as she waited for her words to sink in.

Eva's face turned white.

"Connor is dead?" Eva felt her knees go weak as she struggled not to collapse. "I'm sorry, I-I-I didn't know."

Becca snorted. "Of course you didn't know because you didn't really love him like I did. So, this is how it's going to go. I'm going to pick up my baby and then I'm going to shoot you and you're going to let me. Because if you don't, then I may accidentally shoot Noah, and neither of us wants that, do we?" Becca held the gun directly toward Eva's heart, enjoying every moment as she absorbed her fear and reveled in it.

"No. No. Please, don't touch my baby! Don't!" Eva screamed, anger welling up deep from inside of her.

A noise behind her made her turn, and for a split second all she could see was a blur as someone ran past her at full speed. Nora's eyes became huge as she shifted the gun toward her attacker, a loud crack exploding through the air. The attacker rushed toward Nora, knocking her over hard, flat on her back and onto the ground. As they struggling violently, another crack exploded from the gun and Eva realized that she could smell the sulfur assaulting her nose. She ran to the crib and scooped Noah up as quickly as she could, his sudden crying from the sound of the gun instantly breaking her heart. She inhaled his sweet baby scent, stunned, as she struggled to make sense of the pile of limbs in front of her. A thick pool of blood began to mingle onto the carpet, both bodies lying still. She felt as though the world was moving in slow motion as she held Noah as close to her body as she could, kissing the top of his head and over and over, trying to soothe his crying. She looked at his beautiful face, the thought of anything happening to him crushing her.

Eva could hear her name being called from a distance as she stood frozen to the floor, Noah miraculously asleep in her arms. She tried to replay what happened right in front of her, but all she could smell was the sulfur as her ears rang slightly from the sound of the gun.

"Eva!" Brynn's voice got closer as she and Kelly ran into the room, Kelly's phone in her hands.

"Eva!" Brynn grabbed Eva and pulled her close to her, holding her and sleeping Noah as tightly as she could. She stepped back and examined her for injuries, anxiously combing over every inch of her. "Are you okay? Are you hurt? What happened?"

Eva could hear Kelly's voice in the background calling 911 and she realized that she was barely able to breathe or move, the seconds moving like hours. She stared at the bodies on the ground, both unmoving, the sound of her own heart thumping in her ears. Brynn held her tight, waiting for her to speak.

"I think … I think … that Jack is dead," Eva said, her eyes refusing to leave the bodies.

"Oh, God," Brynn said, her eyes large. "Are you sure? What happened?"

Without saying a word, Eva handed Noah to Brynn as she walked cautiously over to where the two bodies lay, one on top of the other. She knew she shouldn't touch them, but she grabbed the top body and pulled it over, surprised by its heaviness. She cried out as she recognized Jack right away, his suit covered in blood from the large hole in his shoulder, his eyes closed. She kicked Becca's body cautiously with her foot, a large hole directly in her chest with blood flowing from it.

As the sound of sirens approached, Eva knelt next to Jack and cradled his head in her lap. "Please Jack, I need you to wake up. You can't leave me like this. You can't save me and then leave me. Please, I love you. Wake up." She wept above him, her tears falling onto his cheeks, unsure if she would ever be able to survive the heartbreak if Jack were to die.

As the sirens grew louder she felt Jack slightly stir.

"Are you alive? Please, Jack, are you there?" Eva leaned

over his face, her hands on his cheeks willing him to be alive with everything she had.

His pallor was slightly gray as he struggled to open his eyes, his lids fluttering open and closed.

"I'm here." His words were gentle like a warm mist and she leaned in closely to hear them.

Eva sobbed in relief. "Please, don't leave me. Don't ever leave me."

Jack's lips turned up ever so slightly.

"Did I save you?" he asked, grimacing in pain and closing his eyes once more.

"Oh yes!" Eva said, kissing him over and over on his forehead and cheeks. "Yes, Love. You did. You saved me."

"Good. That's all I've ever wanted," Jack said, relief washing over him as he struggled through the pain.

"I love you, Jack Palmer," Eva said, cradling his head gently. "I love you and I'll never ever let you go. I promise."

A single tear squeezed out from the corner of Jack's eye as Eva finally did what he wanted her to do from the moment he first met her.

She finally gave her heart over to him, fully and completely.

CHAPTER FORTY-FOUR

The End

October 20th, Three and a Half Years Later

The bride stood in front of her mirror, brushing her long hair. It used to be darker and less gray, but she didn't mind. She liked the long white streak that was growing down the front of it, making her feel more glamorous. She admired her body that had grown stronger over the years with countless hours of exercise and hard of work. She had been determined to get back to where she had been before the accident. She was finally there.

She touched her face, the scars more faded than ever before. Now they were barely even visible and she reminded herself how fortunate she was. She smiled at herself and thought about Adam and wondered whether he would be happy for her. She decided that he would be.

It had been over three years since Adam had gone. The first year had been a blur. Brynn could barely remember it, lost in her sadness and grief. Nick had given her all the time that she needed to grieve, knowing that she needed it to become whole again. He had been as patient as he could until he could be no longer.

Brynn remembered the night he came for her, vividly. Nick stormed up to the porch of The Harper House, flowers in hand and fire in his eyes. She met him at the door on her way out and before she could say anything, he had swept her in to his arms.

"I've loved you from the moment I met you and I haven't been able to forget you since. It's our time now, Brynn. Please." Nick gazed into her eyes and she was immediately swept back to the night they had spent together so many years ago, their hearts and bodies completely entangled together with an intensity that neither of them could ever forget. She was thankful that Nick had given her the time and space to love and grieve Adam. He'd shown his love for her by understanding what she needed to do. Brynn could never have imagined that he would be so kind and understanding, and when he finally came for her, she knew that it was time, and they found themselves inseparable.

As they sat on the front porch on that warm, fall night remembering their love, Nick had finally found the courage to ask her the question that had been burning within him for many years. "What about Eva, Brynn. Is she my daughter?"

Brynn hesitated. She had a difficult time imagining anyone other than Adam as Eva's father, but Eva already knew the truth. Brynn had told Eva the story about Nick shortly after Adam's death and Eva had been more accepting than she imagined she would be. Eva always suspected that Nick was her father, but wasn't ready to claim him yet. She was still grieving for Adam.

"Yes, Eva is your daughter."

Nick bowed his head and cried, the tears overcoming him unexpectedly. He had long since suspected that she was his, but never had any proof until now. His only daughter, Mandy, had succumbed to her mental illness the year prior, and Nick had lost her to suicide. There had been a deep emptiness within him ever since. The thought that Eva was his daughter both excited and unnerved him and he longed for a relationship with her, but he had been more afraid of her than he had of anything else his entire life.

After Adam's funeral, Nick asked Brynn if he and Eva could talk. Brynn agreed that it would be a good idea for the two of them to finally discover one another. She knew that, with Adam gone, Eva would need a father, though she was unsure if Eva would accept him.

"I have something to tell you," Brynn said as they sat in the library where Eva sought comfort from the ghosts of the past. "I hope you don't mind that I have Nick here as we talk."

"I already know," Eva said, staring at Nick's right wrist, her eyes resting on the freckle that was identical to her own. She stared Nick directly in the eyes and said, "I remember you. You were here for her, and then you left. But I remember you."

Nick embraced her and she held him tight, the connection between them immediate and palpable. She had always remembered her heart always waiting for him to come back for her.

Both Nick and Eva accepted their father-daughter relationship almost immediately. Eva had always remembered him from that night so many years before when he had sat at Brynn's bedside and cried. Something about his tenderness touched her even then at such a young age. Even then, she had known that there was something special about him, though she had been too young to put her finger on it.

Noah had taken immediately to his new grandfather, calling him Pa-Pa. Although he didn't take immediately to strangers, he allowed Nick to hold him within moments of meeting him. Nick and Eva spent a great deal of time together, getting to know one another. They found that they had many of the same preferences and dislikes, and the bond between them grew strong.

"I can't imagine ever living my life without you in it," Nick said, holding her close months later. He was proud to call this beautiful, strong daughter his own.

Eva had beamed at him, wondering how she had been so lucky to have two such wonderful men in her life that she had been able to call "Dad."

Over the course of the next year, with Brynn and Nick finally together, he was overjoyed to find that he was immediately accepted into the fold of The Harper House. Everyone was desperate to see Brynn finally happy. As Nick spent time with Brynn, Noah, Eva, and Jack, he finally began to feel as though he were a part of a true family, and he knew that this was what he had been missing his entire life.

Three years after Adam's death, as Brynn readied herself for her wedding, Eva entered the room, remembering when she had life, I know why I was allowed to survive through all of the horror and loss of my childhood, and the accident that nearly took my life, but did not destroy me.

It was for this very moment and all the moments that are to come. It was for Adam, Eva, Noah, and Nick. It was for the chance to finally have hope.

Most of all, it was for love.

The End

www.ingramcontent.com/pod-product-compliance
Lightning Source LLC
Chambersburg PA
CBHW060208030726
47499CB00004B/958